Praise for Cynthia Ozick

"A distinctive and utterly original voice . . . The result is fiction that has the power to delight us — and to make us think."
—**Michiko Kakutani,** *New York Times*

"Ozick is a gorgeous writer." — *Vogue*

"An important voice in American fiction, a woman whose intellect . . . is so impressive that it pervades the words she chooses, the stories she elects to tell, and every careful phrase and clause in which they are conveyed . . . We can look upon Ozick as a part of the royal priesthood of the art of fiction, a writer of uncommon magical gifts." —**Doris Grumbach,** *Washington Post Book World*

"Cynthia Ozick is a carver, a stylist in the best and most complete sense: in language, in wit, in her apprehension of reality and her curious, crooked flights of imagination."
—*New York Review of Books*

"Ozick is one of the most inventive and mind-expanding story-tellers writing in this country now." — *Village Voice*

"[Ozick is] obsessed with the words she puts on paper, with what it means to imagine a story and to tell it, with what fiction is. The re-sult is a body of work at once as rich as Grace Paley's stories, as deeply rooted in Jewish folklore as Isaac Bashevis Singer's tales, [and] as comically ironic as Franz Kafka's nightmares."
—*Saturday Review*

"If making ideas incarnate is Paradise, then as a writer Cynthia Ozick may well already have arrived." —*Atlantic Monthly*

"One of the finest and most imaginative writers of our time."
Post-Dispatch

TRUST

Books by Cynthia Ozick

TRUST

CYNTHIA OZICK

A Mariner Book

Houghton Mifflin Company

Boston · New York

First Mariner Books edition 2004

Copyright © 1966 by Cynthia Ozick
Afterword copyright © 2004 by Cynthia Ozick

Visit our Web site: www.houghtonmifflinbooks.com.

Library of Congress Cataloging-in-Publication Data is available.

ISBN 0-618-47051-4 (pbk.)

Printed in the United States of America

QUM 10 9 8 7 6 5 4 3 2 1

For My Mother and Father

"Everything is mine," said gold.
"Everything is mine," said iron.
"I'll buy everything," said gold.
"I'll take everything," said iron.

— *Aleksandr Pushkin*

Offer the resourceful man one of two legacies:
a mammoth trust fund by inheritance of wealth,
or a minuscule fund of trust by inheritance of
nature; and he will choose the one which least
inhibits venturesomeness.

— *from the unpublished aphorisms*
of Enoch Vand

PART ONE

AMERICA

1

After the exercises I stood in the muddy field (it had rained at dawn) and felt the dark wool of my gown lap up the heat and din of noon, and at that instant, while the graduates ran with cries toward asterisks of waiting parents and the sun hung like an animal's tongue from a sickened blue maw, I heard the last stray call of a bugle—single, lost, unconnected—and in one moment I grew suddenly old. All around, the purple-plumed band had broken ranks, making a bright dash for the cool of sugared grapes and lemonade on long tables under trees, and the members of the procession, doffing their hoods as they dispersed, raised in the air veils of blue, mauve, crimson, and jade, like the wings of geese. The bugle's voice unfurled, shivered, fell. Although I did not move and stopped my breath and hoped the wail would lift again—why? as a signal perhaps, the witness we spend our lives waiting for—it would not. Only the year before Enoch had told me that the sign of understanding would be the absence of any sign, that revelation came unproclaimed, that messiahship was secret; but Enoch was himself so abundant in signs, revelations, and messianism that, on the basis of his own doctrine, I did not believe him. Enoch would have said that because the bugle did not speak again its first utterance was also in doubt; after an hour of discussion he might even have convinced me that I had not heard a bugle at all, just as, in my childhood, he had once demonstrated that, since God had made the world, and since there was no God, the world in all logic could not exist. It was true; the world did not exist; Enoch was middle-aged, and knew.

After a while, because the bugle would not rise again, no

longer expecting the sound of redemption I ceased even to hope for it and took off my white shoes to save them from the mud and began to cross the field. The goal posts were hooks for garlands: flowers woven through wires had turned them into awnings, and gardenias clambered down the poles like breeding moths. It was late, the field was half-deserted, the gatemen had let the porters through; they came swarming after the camp chairs, shutting them with loud snaps and piling them, dozens high, in barrows. I passed under one of the goal posts and a pink flower, loosed from its plaiting, tumbled onto the sleeve of my gown. If another had fallen, and a third, or a rain of those fleshy petals, I might have been cheered, and willing to believe myself saved after all. But it was only a single one; already browning at the edges, the stem twisted dry, a tiny pale worm feasting in its eye; so I brushed it sadly away. A little girl ran to snatch it up, but when she saw how uglily it was blighted, she tossed it to the ground and challenged me with her contempt. "My sister's getting married tomorrow," she told me spitefully, and rubbed the bridge of her nose with an admirable gesture. Under the trees all the weddings of the world had coalesced, vapor into vapor. A straw pierced my stocking and stuck up through my toes while all the brides in their black cloaks embraced one another with green grapes between their teeth, and all the visitors applauded decorously, like Roman senators. There was a shimmer of mass marriages. To whom would they be wed, these nuns and sisters, these blooming abbesses? I knew at once, without speculation: to the world. From my sudden agedness, I looked out at them with envy in the marrow, because I was deprived of that seductive bridegroom, I alone was deprived of his shining hair and the luster of his promised mouth. Envy—Invidia, they named it in a Latinist and sacramental age—ought not to be accounted sinful, for sinning is what we do by intent, and envy, like the plague-fly, desires us against our will. I did not wish to envy them, I felt disgust for myself, but greed for the world had bitten me. I longed to believe, like these black-gowned brides, in pleasure, in splendor, in luck; in genius, in the future, most of all in some impermeable lacquer to enamel an endless youth.

The rows of chairs had all vanished by now; their sharp little feet had left pock-holes in the turf, and the grass, again revealed, looked less green than before, trampled and sparse everywhere. Already a crowd of servingmaids was removing the striped cloths from the refreshment tables, shaking off crumbs as deftly as mariners hoisting sails. The ceremony had long since ended, and now the celebrants were scattering at last, uncurling their make-believe diplomas and dropping them to the ground. The rolled paper sheets, blank as snow, covered the grass like wet laundry—our real diplomas would come weeks later, routinely, anticlimactically, in the mail. Was there nothing that was not a fraud? Under the highest branches a gracile Puerto Rican, incarnation of some sacred cat, went from shade to shade spearing the blowy papers into a sack with the keen point of his gardener's pick, tilting at them as though they represented something more noble than merely garbage. He stabbed and stabbed with considerable rhythm, so I gave him my own document, still whorled and ribboned and like all the others utterly empty, to pierce. With the art of an islander, a born fisherman, he lunged—a leg in the air—and harpooned it for his crackling canvas bag; and from his fleshless smile, his broken golden teeth, his ruined and crooked Spanish, I took evidence of sham and imposture, deceit and hoax: he was not what he pretended, no brown joyful boy with paper-pick, but rather some principle of Time marking out his choices with a honeyed wand. When first Time makes himself known to us, it is not as that ancient progenitor who comes to announce that we are mortal, but inadvertently, accidentally, in a moment unforetold especially by himself; and we see him then in his everyday disguise, that of a young bridegroom, and he brings us then not death but recognition, and not the end of knowledge but its beginning; and he whispers, in a ruined and crooked Spanish, "fraud!"

No aunt, cousin, mother, sister, father had come to see the commencement of this strange diaspora. I surrendered the hired costume and went into exile alone. And when, approaching the graveled road, I put my shoes on and ventured through the gate of that place and from an open window heard the buglers in their locker-room blaring jazz, I could think only of the peril, falseness, and allure of the world. And I reflected mournfully how bitter it was to wear the face of youth, to be rooted among jubilants, to feign delights, and all the while to keep close that clandestine disenchantment, that private corrosion of illusion, which belong to the very old.

2

A few weeks after graduation my mother returned from Paris, bringing with her, as usual, a great many boxes of dresses. She kept me with her in her room as she displayed them to herself in front of her long mirror; and while I buttoned, hooked, and zipped, or was made to appraise hemlines and bodices, she gossiped persistently. Enoch had been delayed in Geneva by the arrival of a Bulgarian, she explained. "We were about to take off, so I saw him only for a second, through the plane-window," my mother said. "He had a long brown beard, like a spy. It must have been fake. And he gave Enoch one of those polite continental kisses."

My mother regarded herself as a woman of comedy. She was anything but witty—she did not love language enough—but, because her generation valued solemnity and responsibility and believed very much in banks and political parties, she had taught herself to think everything amusing. She laughed at the League of Women Voters and at the President of the United States (F.D.R., Harry, and Ike in turn); she was exultant when anyone seemed anxious over the High Cost of Living or the Threat of Another Depression; she tittered at phrases like Iron Curtain and Asian Bloc and Free World. She was determined to be taken in by nothing and to respect no one, and to ridicule whatever presented itself as awesome, fearful, or holy. Unfortunately she was incapable of satire and too intent for burlesque. Her intelligence failed her at the point just beyond laughter, and she could not make a weapon of scoffing, or turn amusement into scorn. Hence no one imagined her as dangerous.

Although my mother did not approve of me (she thought me too serious) I found her altogether attractive and fantastic. She was, I believe, a kind of entertainer, in the cheap public sense: she liked simply to be looked at, and, if possible, to be talked about. She rarely told the truth, not because she was an avid liar, but because the truth was too commonplace. Consequently she had no friends and while other women of her age endured one another's society tediously and without irony, my mother turned over the pages of all the morning newspapers, hoping to come upon her name, or, lacking that, one of her scandals: and occasionally her vanity was satisfied.

The scandals were minor, of course. Once, having hidden her few unimportant jewels (she always wore the important ones) in an old evening purse, my mother telephoned the police to declare them stolen. The next day the papers carried photographs of the confessed burglar, a poor fellow on narcotics whom the detectives had selected for a likely culprit. I was away at school at the time (this happened years ago) so I don't know how the affair was untwisted—though I do remember that the raffish innocent (my mother's clipping shows him as cross-eyed and surly-looking) was jailed anyhow, for illegal possession of heroin: they found it in a little bag tied around his waist under his clothes, and they thought surely it was the jewels. My mother, it seems, was good-naturedly forgiven: the headlines identified her, with a certain affection, as "Foiled Society Prankster." "He was a thief anyway," my mother liked to justify it long afterward, whenever the story was recalled; "all I did was help catch him." I think she was proud of herself: it was the only time she had ever come out squarely against criminality.

Plainly, none of my mother's devices was original. She gleaned them all from the tabloids—her memory was good —and to the tabloids they were in the end returned. Another time, during a bad first act—but this, too, happened a long while ago and I tell it as a legend—my mother left a big old-fashioned vest-watch wrapped in tin foil under her seat, and complained to the ushers of a queer bothersome ticking noise. The whole theatre had to be emptied while a bomb squad, attired gingerly in blastproof masks, crawled on all fours like comical musketeers between the rows. The audience was first alarmed, then unnerved; nobody stayed for the rest of the play and it closed the next day. But my mother, in spite of these episodes, was not really a practical joker: she abhorred that sort of mediocrity. Beneath all her travesties there remained some residue of her native and primary temperament, which was humorless and ambitious, so that she was able to laugh at everything except herself. Like many deeply moral people who have betrayed themselves, she needed the gorgeous gesture, the sign of recklessness; she had to declare that she was not responsible. And she was able to act as shè pleased because she was very rich.

"How rich?" she echoed me. "Oh, I don't know, it's not in dollars, you can't count it. It's the kind of rich only lawyers understand. Ask William."

"It isn't money then?"

"Of course it's money. You'll get some of it if there's any left when I'm through. Though I don't expect to die very soon. It's all in securities and mortgages and bonds and trusts and things. I don't know what any of that means, I just know it turns into money and then I get it. Here," she said, and browsed among her boxes, "I brought you a ball dress."

It was all of silk, of an unbelievable golden color, like leaf-metal: there was a great silver sash which, untied, became a dazzling train.

"A graduation present," my mother said. "I suppose there's a round of parties?"

I tried to explain that the parties—there had been only a few—were all over.

"Then give some."

"There's no one to ask any more. All the girls have gone to find jobs."

"And the boys?"

I shrugged at her stupidity. "Mostly they've left for the Army."

"Oh, the Army!" She looked at me half-startled, as though I had suddenly reminded her that there *was* an Army after all. "Well, if they want to make idiots of themselves . . . there's no culture in all that, you know! If we keep this up, sending off our young men like that, we'll end like Sparta"— my mother specialized in historical abominations—"with naked girls and drowning the weak babies and iron money and everything!"

"Really," I began hastily, "I don't need a ball dress. It's a very old-fashioned idea."

"Well, you have to dance in *something*," my mother insisted.

"I don't want to dance."

"It's a very nice dress. You see how it's made? The trick is in the facing in the bosom—stiff, so it stands away. They're very clever about that in Paris. I can't understand why you don't have a bosom of your own—heredity is so mysterious,"

my mother observed, showing off her high classical front.
"My corset-woman over there thinks my figure is amazing for
my age!" She examined me contemplatively. "She's a Baron-
ess, you know. White Russian. They shot her whole family.
She's married to the man who runs the elevator in the Eiffel
Tower."

These remarks failed to astonish me.

"It's true," my mother protested. "You mean she might not
be the real thing? So many of these Russian nobles aren't.
This one is, though, I can tell by her manners—they're so
coarse. When she's draping you she always says 'backside'
straight out, never 'derrière'—an impostor wouldn't have the
nerve! Do you know what her business motto is? The Baroness wrote it down for me; it's a proverb or something." My
mother immediately produced a scrap of tissue paper scribbled over in a foreign hand. "Here it is: 'Ogni medaglia ha il
suo rovescio.' It's very apropos."

"Is that Russian?"

"Don't be foolish—it's Italian, of course. Etymology explains everything. 'Ogni' comes from our 'ogee,' I'm perfectly
sure: an ogee's an architectural term, I looked it up once. It
means a sort of curved arch. 'Ogni medaglia ha il suo
rovescio,' " she repeated in her haughty literary-voice. " 'A
nicely arched posterior deserves a medal,' you could translate
it. It's one of those down-to-earth sayings they have over
there."

"But you said she's Russian."

"Yes, but then exiles are very cultivated, you see. She
speaks nothing but Italian and a little bad English. She visits
the Louvre every day." She hesitated. "I suppose we ought to
begin making arrangements in that direction."

"Arrangements?" I said.

"It's time you saw Europe, after all."

"I've been to Europe."

"Nonsense, you were only ten. I kept *telling* everyone you
were too young to appreciate travel. Oh, how I suffered! Till
my last breath I shall never forget how you vomited all over
the South of France," my mother finished gloriously. "You
had one of those nervous stomachs, just like your father."

My mother rarely mentioned my father; she never thought
of him, since she was concerned only with the present. Occasionally—perhaps every three years, but with great irregularity—she would receive a letter from my father, and then she
would be reluctantly reminded of him. "Well, it's starting

again," I would hear her tell Enoch. "Go ahead and do it and get it over with," Enoch would advise her, and from their tone—although nothing was ever said to me—I suspected that my father had written to ask for money. I was faintly ashamed of him, as of an invisible and somehow disreputable intruder. At the same time I had very little curiosity about him; quite early in my life my mother had dismissed him as a figure of no importance and less reality. "To be perfectly objective about it," she remarked once, "all that is terribly remote. After all, I was *with* him for less than two years over twenty years ago! You can't reasonably expect anything but the vaguest impression by now. It's hardly left a trace," she said, and looked out at me from her wedge of curls with an uncharacteristic bewilderment—"except for you." This was not the case with her first husband, who had preceded my father—not only was her impression of him still lambent, but she did not appear to have any desire to extinguish it. Of the three lawyers she retained, this man, my mother's first husband, was the one she most often consulted; now and then he would dine with us, and my mother would call him "dear William," and ask after his wife. He was married to a woman so different from herself—so clearly diligent and domestic, so innocently self-aware and eager to be courted—that it was obvious, even to my mother, what had been the trouble. William was too august and substantial a personage to be diagnosed as happy or unhappy; it was plain, however, that my mother thoroughly respected him, since in his presence she chose dull and meagre endings for stories which, in other company, she used to conclude in the liveliest manner imaginable. And William, while he was rather stiffly cordial to my mother, and very gentlemanly toward Enoch, seemed less than charmed by the dinner chatter. He would quietly talk trusts and investments, and finish by handing my mother a check in the gilt-edged envelope of his firm, a bi-monthly mission which he only very rarely allowed the mails to perform Once he brought with him to dinner his oldest boy, a correct, wan-lidded adolescent with an artificial stammer, who was so submissively attentive to the rite of passing the croutons that I was horrified lest Enoch's imprecations, muttered bearishly into his soup, be overheard. To tell the truth, William's son fascinated me. He looked remarkably like a dog of a choice and venerable breed. His dark glazed head was too small for the padding in his shoulders, but otherwise I considered him formidably handsome, even elegant. He was known to be precocious: he already had an interest in juris-prudence and he carried under his arm a copy of Holmes' *The Common Law*. This reputation for intelligence, and the trick he had of faltering in the middle of a syllable, ravished me from the first moment. William's son seemed to me the image of brilliant commitment, of a confident yet enchant-ing dedication to dark philosophies—in short, of all that I might have been had my mother's marriage to her first hus-band endured. It was not that I wanted William for my fa-ther: I wished merely to have had him, in that preconscious time, for my sire. Since we are born at random, as an after-thought, or as an enigmatic consequence in a game of Truth, and are not willed into being by our begetters, they accord-ingly fall under the obligation of surrendering much of them-selves to us, in the manner of forfeits; hence we are burdened not merely with their bone and blood, but with their folly and their folly's disguises. Nonetheless William's son had somehow been exempted from this fraudulent heirship, this pretense that we are auspicious inheritors when we are in reality only collectors grimly fetching what is due us:—those evils (dressed as gifts) which we are compelled to exact al-though we do not desire them. William's son was sound, he was fortunate, he had providentially escaped his birthright. I saw him as the brother I had lost through my mother's absur-dity. The more so, since we shared the same surname.

As is the custom with divorced women, in order to display her proper status my mother had retained the latter part of her marriage title against the time when she might acquire a new husband, and, with him, a new name. But after her sepa-ration from my father, she explained, she had reverted to the name she had carried as William's wife; she did not care to style herself, or me, after my father. As a result, while my mother through her third alliance had long ago become Mrs. Vand, I continued to be called after her first husband. I was generally believed to be William's child. My father was by this means virtually obliterated from our lives, since I was not permitted even to bear his name. For many years it was not revealed to me: I discovered it by chance myself one af-ternoon, when, rummaging in Enoch's desk for a stamp, I came upon an empty envelope, the address run over in a wa-tered and rusted ink. Some notion about the handwriting, which was educated but wild, as though scratched on by fin-gers used to grosser movements, made me search after the sender. He appeared to have been reluctant to record himself plainly; not only was he absent from the face of the envelope, but from the back, and when I found him at last, it was in a hidden place, on the inside of the flap, a little furtive and blurred by the glue:

> Gustave Nicholas Tilbeck
> Duneacres
> Town Island
> New York

That this was my father I was convinced at once, although I was fleetingly put off by the starkness of his lodging, for I had imagined him as living under a congestion of tenement flats in a far and uncongenial, perhaps sinister, city. It had always been my idea that my father was some sort of artist —or perhaps a kind of sailor, a voyager or adventurer—although no one had ever told me this. I supposed him to be improvident, impoverished, and discreditable; I was given to understand, subtly and by prudent indirection, that he was a great embarrassment to us all. My school applications had always cautiously evaded mention of him, and I can recall awkward conversations when, looking away, I did not dare to deny my interlocutor's convenient assumption of William's paternity. It was a substantial relief to pretend to a relation with William, who was red-faced, jut-chinned, and white-haired, like an elderly and reliable monument toward which one has patriotic feelings. I thought of my father, on the other hand, as dun and dank and indecent and somewhat yellowish; I thought he had yellow-tarred teeth, and a porous nose, and bad eyes. At the same time it seemed perfectly plausible that such a man might be a genius. The nature of his talent my imagination did not explore, it being quite enough that I saw the man himself as moist and dirty, quartered in a moist and dirty cellar, in the manner of geniuses. It was not inconceivable that he might be an inventor, and I even believed it likely that he was a foreigner, since the only thing certain I knew of him was that he had marched with my mother in Moscow. That she, with all her gaiety, her fabrications, her enthusiasms, her adorations, could have been attracted to the repugnant wretch I had fashioned did not, to be sure, seem altogether reasonable. And yet it was not impossible: she was stupid enough to talk romantically of "indeterminate taints" and "vital sparks" and she was quick to spot, in queer people whom everyone else avoided, "un homme de génie." Still, I had no real reason for my judgment that my father was in some way singular, or at the least unorthodox. I had only my guilty instinct for his character. Sometimes, when my mother would stare at me in a certain apprehensive way—her painted eyebrows pulled together in a cosmetic frown—it would seem to me that I was wrong, or crooked, or even bizarre; and that some source of error in me, so perverse and elusive that I was not myself sensible of it, had reminded her of my father. But immediately afterward she would be laughing again. "It's not like the fairy tale, you know, where you can tell the king by the mark on his breast!" she took up mockingly. "I'm sure *I* don't speak of that person from one year to the next—though that's not the point." In spite of her hilarity—acrid and nervous and somehow shackled—I could not see what she insisted *was* the point. Nevertheless she did not deny the truth of my surmise. She only demanded that I explain it. "Oh, well, if you want me to believe some formula about blood will tell, that sort of thing," she accused when I could not oblige her; "you saw your father's name and you simply *knew*. Not," she finished without pleasure, "that we ever kept it from you!"

In this way, and alone, I learned who my father was. But, lest my mother feel the shame of my shame, I was discreet; I did not disclose all that I knew. There was nothing extraordinary in my recognition. Toward the end of a dark March, while an endless snow lay swarming on the sills, going by my mother's door I heard the rattle of bracelets on her furious arms; she clanked them like shields and cried out; and then, while I stopped wretchedly aware, Enoch's voice came maundering from the fastness of her room: "It's all right; come, there's nothing else to do; besides, it doesn't matter. Let's go ahead and get it over with." It was all hidden, and all familiar; it meant a letter from my father—a summer's beetle swaddled in the cold storm, prodded and found miraculously preserved, and more, atwitch with ugly life. My father's letters, infrequent as they were, always brought their own oppressive season into our house, suggestive of a too-suddenly fruitful thicket, lush, damp, growing too fast, dappled with the tremolo of a million licking hairs—deep, sick, tropical. And then my mother's eyes, which delighted her because of their extravagant decorative roundness, like roulette wheels, would shrink to hard brown nuts. We came to live with heat, barely breathing; we came to live with the foul redolence of heat, like fish rotting in a hull. Outside my mother's windows the snow continued to mass, but in the

house we sickened, enisled, hung round with my father's
rough nets. "What does he want?" my mother cried out behind her door in that frozen March; "how much now?" And
Gustave Nicholas Tilbeck like some indolent mariner lay on
the beach of his island, nude to the waist; I saw him—my
father; he lay there cruelly, like refuse; he had the patient
lids of a lizard, and a yellow mouth, and he was young but
half-blind; and he lay alone on his beach, in the seaweed-lit-
tered sand, among shells with their open cups waiting; and he
waited. And with confidence: the day came, it would always
come, when my mother could withstand the siege no longer.
Then gradually my father's presence, humid and proliferous,
thick and invisible, less an untutored mist than some toxic
war-gas pumped by armored machines into the flatulent air,
or a stubborn plague-wind slow to cool away, would recede
and die. Unseen, unknown, proclaiming himself with doubtful omens, like a terrible Nile-god Gustave Nicholas Tilbeck
invaded, vanished, and reappeared. Nothing would secure his
eclipse but propitiation of the most direct and vulgar nature,
and my mother, as enraged as any pagan by a vindictive
devil, had to succumb. Money was what he wanted. Money
came to him at last where he lay, and he blinked his torpid
jaundiced lids and was content. My mother had her peace
then, which she would celebrate at once by a journey abroad,
to some cold and rain-washed country, perhaps in Scandina-
via: a far and bitter place where my father had never
touched. And yet the money was an act of allegiance, it appeared; she reviled the Nile-god but she rewarded him. It was
not for charity, and not for pity, and not for the sake of a
righteous heart: for charity, pity, and a righteous heart would
not have seized her with fury or churned those wrathful cries.
And afterward she had to travel, as for relief after excess.
Was it love then that he sent her—my father, the man of talent—in his jagged inkings? And year after year was it love
turned to money that reverberated from her hand? As I have
said, my mother had no concern with the past, which she
considered eccentric, because it differed from the present. Everything old struck her as grotesque, like costumes in photographs of dead aunts. She did not believe in old obligations
or old loves; she was wholly without sentimentality. Every
autumn I saw her give away capes and hats and purses which
she had cherished effusively only a few months before. She
had no regard for an article on the simple ground that, because she had loved it once, it must for that reason alone

merit her warmth. She considered that everything wore out
extrinsically, by virtue of her own advancement, no matter if
it were as good as new. I began to see that her indifference
was not for the thing itself, but rather for her former judgment of it: it was her old self she discarded.

Gustave Nicholas Tilbeck alone endured and transcended
—if not corporeally, then in the actuality of his nature. It
was an extraordinary victory—he could not be ousted. He
took her money, I imagined, as a man takes a trophy—with a
modest smile, yet smelling conquest. But if she did not yield
it up for alms' sake, still less could it have been in tribute to
used-up desire. Between them lay waste and silt and the endless shards of my father's yellow beach, and the long barren
shoal. They had left that old time depleted. It was not love or
the memory of love—and yet something active, present, and
of the moment festered there: some issue turned mysteriously
in the sand. My mother felt its sting under her hand that
March, as our private sirocco blew woe into all the rooms,
upstairs and downstairs; and not long afterward the empty
envelope in Enoch's desk acquainted me with Gustave Nicholas Tilbeck, and not only with that unknown name, but with
how much they had paid him, and in what sequence, and
how much was promised for later, all rapidly registered in
Enoch's hook-like unmistakable pencilled digits—and what
gave it away was March. I saw that they had last sent money
to this person in March. It was all obscure; it was all pene-
trating; and what gave it away, as I say, was March. To
whom else would those sums (in amounts not impossible, not
unreasonable, remarkable rather for their disjointed recur-
rences) have gone in the very month when my father's per-
spiring ghost breathed the money-sickness into the secret fis-
sures of our lives?

But I did not tell my mother any of this. It comforted her
to think that I was unaware; I pretended that some oddity of
intuition, or else an accidental and unremembered word, had
brought me to my father's identity. I did not say that I knew
him to be a mendicant and a leech. Nevertheless, she was
careful to turn the key to Enoch's desk, and during the tranquil period that followed I heard nothing of that languid
merchant of the past, that inventor or sailor, that homme de
génie, Gustave Nicholas Tilbeck.

3

My mother decided that the "arrangements" which were to send me to Europe should begin the moment Enoch returned from Geneva.

"They'll have to clear you for a passport," she explained. "And that means they'll have to clear *me*."

"But you already have a passport. You've been cleared."

"They'll have to clear me again, watch and see. The Government is very simple-minded when it comes to these matters. After all, I *was* a Party member. I *am* the author of *Marianna Harlow*.'

"Well, I'm not the author of anything."

"Only because you have no talent. At your age I had already published in the *Worker*. It was a letter to the editor. I think it was about strikes. Not that I knew anything about strikes," she added accommodatingly, "but I thought I ought to have them on my conscience."

"It's a free country," I pursued. "I don't see what my passport has to do with *you*."

"Guilt by association," my mother said glibly. "You could tell them you went away to college and didn't associate with me for the whole four years. It's practically the truth. Anyway, Enoch will take care of it. He'll see some people who can simplify things. God knows how, with my record."

My mother, with typical perversity, was very proud of her "record," which she exaggerated in order to shock. As I understood it, she had joined the Party the very season she was to have come out: it was the first, possibly the most flamboyant, of her scandals. She showed me clippings of the event—it was her habit to save everything that had ever been printed about her—and crowed over them as though they had been fresh that morning. "Debutante Puts Solvent Daddy in the Red," one said. There was even a picture of her holding up a

banner—"The World in One Peace." It all looked stale—the
slogans, and my mother as a young girl, and the date on the
newspaper. "I wasn't the only one to get interested in the
working class," she defended herself, "of people of our *background*, I mean," and she began to name several sons and
daughters of wealthy families, some of them famous, who
had taken jobs in factories. In my mother's factory—she was
fired after two weeks, not for inciting the workers, but for
inefficiency—they made chocolates. "It wasn't a *bad* place,"
she reflected; "the washrooms were very clean. But I couldn't
tell the cherry creams from the plain cherries—they were the
same shape only the creams had a different sort of curlicue
on top—and I packed them into all the wrong boxes, and
three whole shipments were sent out mixed up like that, and
then they let me go. And after that we all came and picketed.
Then it began to rain and we tried to go inside to get dry,
and they sent for the police."

"Then what happened?"

"Naturally they arrested us. I think it was for trespass.
Anyway, your grandfather was so angry he wouldn't put up
the bail. The other parents did, but they really *were* working-class, so it made sense for them—and that left me there
overnight all alone. It was rather nice, though. It's where I
learned to play bridge."

"In jail?" I marveled.

"Oh, it wasn't a *cell* or anything. We just sat up all night
and drank hot cocoa—three policemen and me, and one of
them said, 'If she plays, we've got a fourth,' and they taught
me how."

I thought I recognized this scene. "Isn't that in *Marianna
Harlow?*"

"Oh, God." My mother scowled. "Those gangsters. Those
thieves. Do you know that in the Soviet Union I'm still a
best-seller? Among American writers second only to Jack
London! I'm even ahead of Howard Fast." These remarks
were familiar: this was my mother's favorite complaint, for
she had not received any Russian royalties since 1936. "Oh, I
know what I'm talking about when I say they're capable of
anything," she offered indignantly whenever the question of
the purges came up. "After all, twenty-one years of open robbery!"

I had never read *Marianna Harlow;* try as I would, I could
manage only a part here, a part there, but never the whole
from beginning to end. It was an astonishing novel. It had no

style, its unhinged dialogue was indistinguishable from my mother's own prattling, and its chief influence seemed to have been *The Bobbsey Twins* (in fact, it was about twins); and yet it had had a great success. "They said it sold so well on account of my *social* position; they said it was the absurdity that appealed, but really it was because of the plot," my mother contended, and she undertook to recount it to me. "You see, the good sister, that's Marianna, sides with the foreman when he's accused of the murder of her father, and the jealous capitalist sister, that's Deirdre, goes prowling around the factory one night in order to plant evidence against Marianna, and there's a terrible fire, and she's cremated—well, it's all in the synopsis on the jacket," and she pulled one copy from a row of identical volumes. " 'The glorification of man and labor,' " she read diligently, " 'as shown through the conflict of a pair of beautiful twins, children of an unscrupulous manufacturer, over their father's dismissal of a progressive-minded foreman whom both girls love.' —Of course," said my mother humbly, "the proletarian novel is out of fashion now, and I make no claim to immortality . . ."

Although my mother's subjects were passion and death, Enoch regarded *Marianna Harlow* as a piece of comic art. He repeatedly told me that I should read it, that in spite of its bad prose I would not regret it, that it was a prize example of the lampoon, and that he had often thought of recommending it to the State Department as a work of counter-propaganda. My mother was pleased. "It's the difference between William and Enoch!" she cried. "William hated *Marianna* It's no coincidence that the divorce came right in the middle of Chapter Twelve—you know—where Marianna organizes the workers' council? William won't talk of it now, but at the time he called it anarchism—it just petrified him, you know, but Enoch says that if the government had had it translated it would have saved China." The notion of *Marianna Harlow*'s saving China threw my mother into her chair, laughing.

"Then it seems to me there's very little danger of my not getting a passport," I said practically.

"Oh my dear! You don't understand," my mother assured me, very much in earnest, "it's *me* that's the obstacle. I'm afraid I shall always stand in your way in regard to official matters. They know who I am, after all. They know what I have been. What do you think the F.B.I. is for? Poor Enoch!

He could have been Ambassador by now, you know, if not
for me."

"Oh really," I said, "it has nothing to do with you."

"Doesn't it?" she answered haughtily. "I was a member of
five subversive organizations. I belonged to Women for Peace
and Equality, The Common Man Club, The League for Enlightened Socialism . . ."

"You've repudiated all that."

"Do you suppose for one *minute* that makes any difference
to the F.B.I.? They think I *still* care about Peace and Equality. Every time I go out of the country they send *spies*. The
last time I was at the Baroness' place there was a woman getting fitted for a corset, and I could have sworn she was a government agent. She kept writing things down on a little pad."

"Maybe she was only recording her measurements."

"Oh well, if you want to joke about it!" my mother
brought out, turning her back on me, offended. "But it's the
jesting of an innocent. You young people today confuse patriotism with adulation. You're all practising Shintoists, if you
ask me—you think the government exists to be worshipped.
I'll tell you what it exists for," she declaimed, appraising me
bitterly—"to be laughed at! If it can't be laughed at it had
better not pretend to be worth anything. Do you think I'm
afraid of their spies? I spit in their faces!"

She was obsessed with the idea of spies. It was her theory
that Enoch's superiors in Washington required him to go
about Europe interviewing people who might be persuaded to
inform for them. She thought of him as a roving personnel
department looking for malcontents to dress in false beards.
And some time later when a cable came from Enoch stating
that his business in Geneva would detain him for several
weeks more, she did not hesitate to blame it on the Bulgarian
whom she had seen from the plane-window. "It's the East
European temperament. As a group they're very unstable,
you know; you can see it on every page in Dostoïevsky. It's
such a shame—it just spoils July for me, and for no good
reason. I can guess what the trouble is. That Bulgarian agent
probably wants to start a revolution. They all do out there.
After they get their underground movements put together
they're always on tenterhooks to blow things up. It's very un-
wise. They're very impatient people," she observed, looking
astute; "I suppose Enoch will talk him out of it." Actually,
my mother knew nothing of her husband's official life beyond
the indisputable circumstance that he toted a weighty attaché

case which was fortified by a combination lock and which he always kept at his side—even at dinner parties it materialized under his place at table, leaning familiarly against his shoe. His peregrinations she regarded as less than convenient, although she was an energetic traveler on her own account. The difficulty was that when *she* was ready for London, *he* had pressing reasons for going to Berlin; and once, having accompanied her as far as Madrid, he discovered he was needed immediately on Cyprus. This was a great trial to my mother, who believed in unpacking thoroughly. Wherever she was she stuffed the bureaus and wardrobes, and could not be expected to vacate them without two days' notice. Hence she frequently found herself abandoned among strangers in foreign hotels, and understandably the urge for notoriety would overwhelm her in these places. She would go out on the streets and hire anyone who looked like a musician and bring back a troop of improbable cellists for an incredible concert in the lobby. Or she would purchase canvas and an easel and go to museums, which bored her for their own sakes, and make outrageous copies of celebrated paintings, disrobing all the chief figures, except of course those already nude, which she would chastely clothe. Sometimes, out of desperation, she would try to make friends, consulting for this purpose a list of local ladies whom Enoch had entreated her to call on. These occasionally turned out to be less fashionable, but invariably more intellectual, than my mother; they would chatter scornfully of "the American language," and they were uncommonly inquisitive about American writers. None of them, to be sure, had ever heard of *Marianna Harlow*. In one city —perhaps it was The Hague—a purple-coifed dowager, a court confidante and patroness of belles lettres, disclosed that one of her pensioners was at that moment engaged in a majestic translation into the Dutch of the poetry of Karlen Dustworth, the Minnesota laureate. My mother was overcome, not by the poet's reputation, or even the translator's, for she had been aware of the existence of neither, but by the idea of patronage, which seemed to her both novel and elegant. When she returned home she went immediately to William and arranged for the establishment of a fund for a poetry pamphlet, to be issued quarterly. She commissioned as editor a young assistant professor of English, with a Belgian accent, who came from the University of Nebraska expressly to sort verses in the narrow office my mother had rented down-

town. This project kept her at home for some months, until
at last a dispute with the editor over policy concerning asso-
nance rhyme (the editor was for it, my mother was opposed)
grew into a hideous quarrel, and he was dismissed, only to be
replaced by another young man, from New York University,
who looked and talked exactly like the first, but hated asso-
nance. She was so delighted with this second literate that she
permitted him to have a staff, an extravagance which alarmed
William. "It's better than paying *taxes,* isn't it?" she demanded of him shrewdly, although she was altogether ignorant of the rule for charitable trusts and had never seen an
income-tax form; at which William, who was a Republican
and admired Thoreau, subsided. And my mother went abroad
again. She had ceased to travel regularly in the company of
Enoch; she maintained it was no use: on the plane he read
books instead of talking to her, he was too unpredictable anyhow, he concealed his Washington cables from her, he would
leave her, without a moment's remorse, for any spy. He had
actually bounded down the entry-ramp at first sight of the
Bulgarian, and bounded up again, to snatch his valise and
shout farewell; and then he had allowed the Bulgarian, fake
beard and all, to kiss him, and in public, an act which was
severely prohibited to his wife.

"Do Bulgarians kiss?" I wondered. "I thought only French-
men did that."

"Ah," my mother threatened sadly, "Europe is a strange
continent. Of course you'll go with letters of introduction; it
will be different for you. Still, we should plan an itinerary.
First you must go to England and see the Bridge of Sighs at
Cambridge, and then directly to Florence: it's the most aristocratic city. Then you must all the time avoid refugees, who
are everywhere, even these days; cultivate the indigenous
only. It's a rule I never fail to practise, except in the case of
noble families."

It almost seemed she no longer believed in a classless society.

Three weeks after this conversation my passport came in
the mail, without incident.

"They gave it to you!" My mother was incredulous. "And
without settling things! Not a soul came to question me," she
continued to marvel. "But it isn't logical. After all, I *was* a
member of the Society for Revolutionary Ideals! I belonged
to the Marxist Book Club! And besides," she wailed, "I'm the

author of *Marianna Harlow!*" She blew through her nose in astonishment or vexation: "Do you suppose that Enoch—"

But Enoch was still in Geneva.

4

The summer wheeled on sluggishly, until in the brilliant heart of July it teetered, hung poised, and suddenly stopped dead. On the terrace the aspidistra in their ceramic pots withered. Night never came. It did not rain. The days were as pointless as childhood afternoons.

In the mornings my mother took me shopping with her. We moved slowly down the long row of air-conditioned department stores, through endless revolving doors; there were high flags on lances over the street, and not a pucker in them. Through the perfume mist that meandered in the cooled currents inside the stores we could smell the cars in the street, glistening, yet quiescent, trapped like beaten doves in front of traffic lights, their exhausts rising and mingling with the odors of gasoline, molten tar, the fiery circles of breathing manhole-covers. The city burned. We went from counter to counter, touching everything—kerchiefs, gloves, buckles, mothbags, jewel-boxes, nooses of pearls, the rigid wrists of manikins, bits of leather, candlesticks, tea sets and trays from Japan, Denmark, Italy. In one place, murmuring saws about the English weather, we bought a khaki raincoat for me, but the rest of the time we eschewed escalators and silently circled the lower floors, fanned into a kind of trance by the confusion of scents, the flash of glass cases, the idle shudder of the feet of little dogs.

After lunch my mother would leave me and go to her room and sleep until dinner.

I began to read newspapers feverishly and irrepressibly. I read every edition of every paper. I read the funnies, the beauty columns, the editorials, the lovelorn advice, the politi-

cal analysts, the women's pages, the advertisements down to
the dreariest minim of color, price, and branch-store location,
the lost-and-found boxes, the captions of pictures, the classified sections, the letters to the editor.

I also read the news.

It was a brutal and curious time. Old ladies were dying of
heat prostration; in Montana cows swooned. A New England
farmer became heir to a dukedom. Everywhere children were
falling down wells, down drains, down ten-inch pipes. In the
cities the young girls were already jumping. They jumped
from bridges; from penthouse windows; from the railings of
national monuments. They left behind passionate notes
pinned to their dresser-scarves. In Indonesia an American
philologist was arrested for paddling a rubber boat from isle
to isle at three o'clock in the morning.

Toward the end of July the heat broke with a roar of rain
and roots of lightning. My mother came out of her room into
the sudden night of the terrace, and stood under the awning
amid the dead plants.

"Seriously," my mother said in her somnolent summer
voice, "that dress I brought. You ought to wear it. You ought
to have a going-away party."

I tore off the theatre page and made a boat out of it and
sent it on to capsize in the torrent that poured off the awning;
dried white sleep-particles cracked in the corners of my
mother's eyes as she watched.

"Is there anything in the papers about a disturbance?" she
inquired after a moment.

"No. Everything is very quiet and ordinary."

"I mean in Bulgaria. In Sofia perhaps. That sort of disturbance."

"Nothing has happened anywhere."

"Poor Enoch. He must still be talking. I'd feel better if
they'd have their revolution and get it over with—then he'd
have nothing to do. As it is, there's no telling when he'll
come home. We'll have your party anyhow."

"It isn't necessary, you know."

"Necessary?" My mother observed me with deliberation.
"On the contrary, it's urgent. How else do you expect to become acquainted with decent society? That college of yours
did nothing for you."

"I expect it civilized me a bit."

"Civilization contributes nothing toward marriageability,"

my mother remarked crisply: she had come brightly awake. "If anything, it detracts from it."

"You know a great deal about marriage," I said. "You've had so much experience with it."

"Don't be impudent—it sounds so labored, coming from you. Men have always wanted to marry me. It's not an original idea, but I don't hesitate to believe that I show a certain *écart*."

I was sure she meant *éclat* (her flights into foreignisms were usually unfortunate), but I let it pass.

"An absence of civilization," I suggested.

"Don't be too shrewd," advised my mother. "I may lack culture, but that's one of the privileges of wealth. I have an abundance of talents to make up for it. Moreover, my talents aren't clichés, like so many people's. It's not what I *can* do, but what I can't."

"What you can't?" I repeated without expression, recovering the soaked paper boat; it dissolved into paste and grime under my fingers.

"Certainly. I can't be ordinary. I can't bear that. I can't take anything seriously, and I can't be bored. I would rather go to sleep. And I can't understand myself—that's a talent too."

"Or anyone else," I supplied.

"What makes you say that? It would distress me to be somebody else even for a minute. But that doesn't mean I have no sympathies. I consider myself very sympathetic. If I weren't sympathetic I wouldn't be fretting about Enoch."

"*Are* you fretting about him?"

"Isn't it obvious? These impromptu conferences always worry me. I'm convinced they're dangerous. You read so much about assassinations these days."

"No one," I offered with authority, "has been assassinated during the whole month of July."

"Is July finished?" my mother said vaguely, beginning reluctantly to calculate. "But you'll be embarking in September! In that case I suppose we should plan to have the party the second or third week of August." It appeared she had already forgotten her anxiety, although it was so obvious, about Enoch's safety. "We'll have a saxophone and some strings," she concluded confidently. "And the piano, of course."

I reiterated—looking through the screen of rain—that I had no one to invite.

"No one to invite!" my mother scoffed. "Don't worry

about the guests. I shall ask them for you." And with unexpected vitality she threw off her dressing-gown and leaped into the downpour. In a moment her arms and hair were streaming; an eddy spun in the bow of her lip. "In the future I'll have cactus," she said, ripping the desiccated leaves from their stalks, "and cactus only! And if I take in a pet, it's to be a camel! I feel like a Bedouin come to an oasis!" she shouted, and gargled the rain that rushed from the awning. Barefoot, she stood with her long thighs apart, wetly skeined, and her face welcoming the deluge, like a nereid in a pre-Raphaelite painting, or one of those fountain-nymphs from whose mouths a pillar of water, full of the mystery of flow and return, ascends.

In a few days the terrace had become a lake, with carpenters sloshing through it, carrying try squares—my mother had decided that a small dais should be built at the end of one room to accommodate the musicians. "Otherwise they'll be under*foot*," she insisted, snuffling: she had caught cold. She trotted about wrapped in a woolen shawl smelling of camphor. At length her sneezes gave way to coughs, and her coughs undertook to resemble the sound of a ragged bellows emerging from some remote area in her interior. But she would not go to bed. She looked out at the rain resentfully, as though it had purposefully done her an injustice, and went on wheezing instructions. Maids, florists, saxophonists, and pastry-bakers paraded through the lake to be interviewed and waded out rejected. My mother was fastidious: she shivered, and no one could satisfy her visions. Plainly, it was all to be a spectacle—she planned embankments of flowers, a whole heaven of colored lanterns, bowers of ice cream, antiquated syncopations. It was to be very like the coming-out party of her own girlhood, which had miscarried—the invitations withdrawn in anger and shame (the former hers, the latter her parents'). "They said I had to choose between capital-P Party and small-p party," she reminisced hoarsely, while the rain and the carpenters' hammers continued to drum, sometimes in one voice, sometimes fugue-like, through the house. Half-sick and hallucinated, she was about to succumb to what had never taken place. She blew her nose and coughed, and wandered about with streamers of tears escaping her round lids; and her special little snort, preceding her down a hallway, made the hammers beat faster, and the rug-men roll, and the polishing-machines race in circles, and the doors fly from their hinges. Only the rain could not be frightened into a display of conscience: it came down wearily, systematically, reservedly, meticulously, and ladled whirlpools into the lake on the terrace.

I tried on the gold and silver gown. My mother held her handkerchief to her chin and struggled with what promised to be a violent exhalation: instead it was only a gasp. "Everything looks better in Paris," she scraped out, surveying my figure. "I suppose it's their light."

"You don't think I'll do?"

"Perhaps under the lanterns," she equivocated. Her meditative glower alarmed me: it was indirect; it was queer.

"What's the matter?"

"I'm afraid I made a mistake. I don't like you in those metallic colors."

"They don't become me then?" I said, appealing to the mirror.

"Oh, they become you. It isn't that. And the fit is very nice, you know. It's only—" she hesitated scrupulously— "you look as though you're dressed up in money."

"You mean I advertise you."

"No," she said pensively, "not me."

"I can't help it," I murmured, "if I look like cold cash."

My mother rasped privately into her cloth. "You look like your father," she ventured at last.

It was the first time in months she had spoken of him; she cast her head regretfully aside, as though the gesture could erase the smudge of sound from the air. But I continued to hear it; her words hovered tangibly near, like wingèd insects, prowling and skimming; and the dress she had brought for me singed my skin with a blaze of gold and silver, the hot gold of my father's beach and the burning silver of his sea.

5

I wore it. I wore it while the little orchestra assembled, and the violins, tuning up, quarreled with one another; I wore it while the guests and their umbrellas came jollying through the door in bunches, like complicated domes of cabbage, dropping shining puddles on the glazed ball-floor; I wore it all that while. And then the dancing began, and at once and pleasurably and plausibly the moon bloomed behind a trellis of corpse-thin clouds, like an old skull working itself out of a grave, and a certain smell steamed up from the river, and at that moment the long flood ended. And still I wore that gown, silver and gold, lust-bringing, redolent not of wealth (which I knew to be capacious, freeing, salubrious, like air or water) but merely of money—small money, cheap and bad money, beggar's money. And he, brought on by my mother's look, which could conjure but never exorcise, he wore it with me, Gustave Nicholas Tilbeck: when I glittered it was with his greed, and when, on the other hand, standing quite still that I might subdue the flash and clink, I tried to dissemble dullness, it was with his cunning and his guile. But he was with me, and all around me; he clung; he was the terrorist guest at my mother's party.

For it *was* her party, although ostensibly it was mine; it was plainly hers despite the swaying of the Bon Voyage banner among those Oriental lanterns. Everything had taken place exactly as she had foreseen. All the rooms had become one room, and butlers slid here and there dumbly offering canapés; the bar was very discreet. It was a gallant scene, albeit a little soiled with romantic overuse, and I felt that the dancers, who composed themselves too decorously, as for a pointillist picture in a suburban dinette, knew it: even the musicians were uneasy with their worn dogmatic tunes evoking nothing, and their jittery short chords and dated trios, and a kind of dissatisfaction, or perhaps merely impatience, sighed through their playing.

I went upstairs to my mother. She was in bed with fever; she lay kneading the bedclothes and sweating angrily.

"What are you doing up here?"

"I came to see how you are."

"Go down, I hear a waltz."

"Are you all right?"

"I can't sleep, I'm sick. I'm fighting ghosts." She menaced me feebly. "Damn it, go down."

"I'll stay awhile if you want."

"No, your perfume is agonizing. I can't bear sweetness, I have ghosts in my head. Your rustling is killing me. Go down, damn it, go down."

The party was failing. There was laughter, but it belonged to arguments and mockery. The strangers ate, danced, drank. They did not know me, they did not care about my voyage, they did not believe in it: they sat on gilt-legged chairs wiggling their long black shoes and cursing the music.

I appealed to the saxophonist.

"Can't you get them to play something else?"

"Mrs. Vand gave us our program, miss."

"I don't like it. Do something else."

"We promised Mrs. Vand we'd follow her list exactly."

"You sound terrible. They just woke you up after thirty years."

The saxophonist blushed. "We do our best. You know Mrs. Vand instructed us exactly."

"Look, it's my party—"

"Sorry, miss. Mrs. Vand is paying us."

One of the butlers came by with a tray of crystal goblets.

"Stuff tastes like watered punch," someone remarked. "Is she a teetotaler?"

"Who?" his friend wanted to know.

"Mrs. Vand."

"Not on your life! Though maybe the daughter is. It's the daughter's party, after all—"

"Do you know her?"

"The daughter? No. Do you?"

"No. No one does."

I went upstairs again.

"Are you back?" said my mother.

"Who did you ask here anyway?"

"Is something the matter?"

"It's a rotten idea, the whole thing."

"I'm sick," said my mother. "I'm sick, go down."

"They can't tell they're drinking champagne," I accused her.

My mother plucked the sheet upward to her face and coughed into it guiltily, warding me off with it. "It must be the poets," she scratched out finally. "You know —My staff."

"Your what?"

"It isn't easy to find people in summer," she broke out in her odd fever-voice. "Practically everyone's out of town. I asked whom I could," she acknowledged finally. She took a harsh breath. "Why won't you go away?"

I waited. "I thought you said something about decent society."

"I'm sick, I have ghosts in my brain. Go away."

"The ghosts are all downstairs," I murmured, getting up and going to the door.

Behind me I heard my mother bore fitfully into her pillow. "So is William's boy," she uttered faintly; her huddled back divulged not how far she had gone for me, but how far she had given me up.

I found them after a while, my mother's "staff," eight pale poets, small light-eyed supercilious lads; two of them were the critical young men I had overheard earlier. I observed that their goblets, which the ingrates were still clutching, had been freshly filled. They had camped down all together, in a cluster, surrounded by idle dancers still vaguely bobbing on the margins of the talk, and ferocious-looking girls with violently curly hair, and girls as plaintive and unaware as butterflies, and earnest angry minuscule-nosed balding young men with slipping eyeglasses. The latter, I soon discovered, were a contingent obligingly sent down from Cambridge at the request of my mother. They were all law students, classmates of William's son. I felt ashamed: my mother, scraping for guests and disquieted by the scarcity of a certain kind of young person, had appealed to William, who had in turn consulted with his son; and to this unimpeachable youth had been entrusted the delicate and infamous affair of collecting dancing partners for me (although I had so far attempted the floor only once, and then with the fat doctor who lived in the duplex below ours, and who had been called up to attend my mother: on his way out, jogging me toward the terrace in his minuet-like foxtrot, he confided his disapproval of all such festivities on the ground that they abused the health; also he warned me against contracting in my travels the Asiatic influenza which had recently spread to•Genoa). For this hive of squires, lovers, boy friends, suitors—whatever my mother in her expectant fancies believed them to be—I was, it appeared, clearly indebted to the Harvard Law School. And the neophyte attorneys were easily distinguishable from the parasite poets. The attorneys were glabrous, ambitious, social, and grave, the poets mendacious, flagrantly seedy, thinly optimistic, and (worst of all) poetic. The two factions slyly prospected one another, leering face to face in a nook formed by the newly-built dais—in the lists, as it were—while the musicians, vying nearby but ignored, inexorably pursued their own dread list (they had just arrived at my mother's favorite military tunes). They were all of them yelling—the poets wildly and poetically, the musicians out of resentment for their buried grace notes, the girls in animal gratitude for the fray, the attorneys perforce.

"What's it all about?" I asked one of the poets.

"Oh, it's a fight," said one of the dancers.

"There are idiots present," offered one of the law students in a politic tone.

"Quite," said the poet, glaring. "And I wish they'd go back to Cambridge."

"Don't be so charitable," interjected one of the frizzy-headed girls, who had taken the side of the poets, "Cambridge isn't hot enough."

The embryonic lawyers were losing, outwitted by the nimble poets, who were becoming a little coarse in their style of speech: the poets were aggressively circular, intuitive, and periphrastic, whereas their opponents were logical and spoke in syllogisms—hence it was transparent that they would go down. It was less transparent what it was they would go down *for*—I could make out their cause only in part: in the indirect language of Constitutional Law (a second-year course, it developed) they sedately expressed a hope that the First Amendment might be re-amended in order to prevent the free and unhampered publication of verse pamphlets. I half agreed, for my mother's choice of poets was lamentable —she might better have determined to support a covey of vegetarians, whose dependency would be to a higher purpose and who would have eaten more cheaply in any case. The law students, on the other hand, were as wearisome a crew as ever entered Langdell Hall—one of their Cambridge buildings, apparently a temple of some sort, to which they never ceased referring, on account of the phantom presence in that place of their local divinity, Justice Holmes, whom they seemed to honor by having forgotten his decisions. Like my mother's versifiers, they showed no innocence of spirit. It was not merely that they were as worldly as profligates, but rather that they insisted on their own version of the world, exactly like the poets. I decided to abandon both camps—neither side had any originality. I thought them rank phonies. And so, because I was still in the dark about the meaning of their assaults, and to get away from the noise, I wandered into the kitchen.

The refrigerator was disconnected—someone had removed the plug from the socket, and had inserted instead the attachment belonging to my mother's portable phonograph. The turntable, set at a low speed, was doggedly going round and round, tended by a pretty girl in blue shoes.

"When the icebox needs defrosting," I said evenly, "the maid does it."

The girl tossed out an unperturbed smile. "Hey, I found these cute records—they're French lessons. You want to hear? I'm already up to Lesson Four."

"Where did you get the phonograph?" I asked.

"It was sitting right in the broom closet. So were the records."

"That's right," I concurred. "Now tell me what you were doing in the broom closet."

"Looking for a broom."

We stared at one another.

"My date is out there bringing back something to eat," my informant took up. "The food around here is out of this world."

"Thank you," I said.

"How d'you like that?" my friend stated in surprise. "Is this your party?"

I observed that I supposed it was.

"Well then, you see, about the broom. It's what started the fight out there. You know those boys who work on Mrs. Vand's magazine?"

"Pamphlet," I corrected.

"Oh—well, I've never seen it, that was part of the trouble. One of 'em said it's called *Bushelbasket*—can you believe it?" (I did: the title had been invented by my mother as a piece of paradoxical sophistry—"You see," she had maintained, "they've been hiding their light under a bushel all this time

—and now here I am, about to help expose it. Also," she had added worriedly, "it suggests abundance . . . do you think *Cornucopia* is better?" But William had favored the former for its humble and homespun sound. "Call it *Cornucopia*," he admonished, "and those fellows will get the idea that's just what your pocketbook is.")

"And then," the girl was going dutifully on, "the editor said—Ed McGovern, that's his name—that he'd had the damnedest time with Allegra over the last issue—I guess Allegra is Mrs. Vand."

"I know."

"She your stepmother?"

"No."

"I heard you had a stepmother."

"I have a stepfather," I said. "Enoch Vand."

My friend cocked her head; she was very pretty. "*Enoch* Vand. Haven't I heard of him?"

"Maybe," I assented, glum with jealousy. "He works for the Administration. He gets to see a lot of Cabinet members, and once in a while his name's in the paper."

"Oh, I never read about politics, it's such a bother. The news changes all the time, who can keep up with it?" She crossed her little blue shoes with their little blue straps and gave me her quick suspenseful glance. "Has he seen the President?"

"Enoch? I guess so."

"No, I mean really *seen* him. Up close!"

"I guess he's seen him up close," I said, "every so often."

"Are you lucky!" she marveled eagerly. "You know I always feel so *out* of things on account of my parents are Democrats. And they're so *adamant* about it!—I heard Mrs. Vand used to be a pinko," she said suddenly.

I blinked. "What?"

"A radical. All that out-of-date political stuff. Ed McGovern says she's *still* trying to be radical, only she's so old hat it beats him. Like with the capital letters.—You know the story, don't you?"

I hesitantly confessed I did not.

"Well, Allegra took it into her head that she didn't want capitals in *Bushelbasket* any more, and Ed said he'd be damned if he'd print any poem of *his* in lower case, like some old fogey. *I* couldn't see why not, until he told me he was afraid of being taken for a relic, like that antique, Eeyee Cummings." My informant carefully lifted a phonograph rec-

ord out of its folder and brushed it with a chamois-cloth.
"Eeyee Cummings is some kind of old-fashioned author
who got famous long ago on account of never using capital
letters," she explained politely.

"How long have you known Ed McGovern?" I inquired.

"Oh, I just met him maybe half an hour ago, out there.
That's what started things off. I'm telling you," she chided.

"All right," I said, and got out of the way of the barman,
who had come for more ice cubes.

The trays were full of water.

"I put them in to freeze over twenty minutes ago," he
wailed; "I can't understand this refrigerator, miss."

"Serve the drinks without ice," I suggested.

"Mrs. Vand wouldn't like it. She told me expressly to watch
the ice supply," he mourned.

"The electric plug is out."

"Oh my God."

The refrigerator began to buzz and the turntable stopped.

"What a pig," remarked my guest to the barman's receding
back; she plugged in the record-player and anticipatorily
watched it resume its lazy revolutions. The refrigerator died
out into silence. "I'm putting Lesson Five on now," she announced. "The man on the record grunts something in
French and then he waits a minute, and you repeat it after
him. That's how it works. It's crazy."

"Look," I said, "what happened to the capital letters?"

"Oh, Allegra got her way. Naturally. Ed said he couldn't
risk being thrown *out*, like the fellow before him. Then someone else said maybe she wanted the little wee letters all over
because she was too stingy to pay for capitals—and Ed said
no, she was too well-heeled to bother being stingy." The girl
thrust her frank gaze at me. "Is she *that* rich?"

At that moment the record began to speak out of the void
—mellifluous, consoling and caressing, incorporeal, like the
voice of Jesus Christ in the movies.

Et ceci, c'est moins cher ou plus cher? said the voice, and
paused hollowly. *Y a-t-il l'eau courante, chaude et froide?*
Another pause, slightly longer, and then, slowly, lingeringly,
unctuously, with the assurance of heaven's abiding love, *Cer-
tainement*, it whispered; *Les salles de bain ont été refaites
récemment.*

"You know why I ask," the girl persisted.

I shrugged.

"Because they said she has gilt monograms on *everything*. Then one of them yelled he'd take bets."

I repeated dully: "Bets?"

"That she'd even got her broomstick monogrammed!" My companion gleamed joyously. "They sent me after it then."

"You had very little trouble finding your way," I commended her.

"To the kitchen, you mean? Well, my date was here before, you know."

This seemed improbable; I looked at her coolly.

"One of the fellows down from Harvard Law. His father brought him here to dinner once, years ago. His father is Mrs. Vand's attorney." She swooped into a laugh. "You know it didn't have a thing on it! It was just an ordinary broom."

"That must have disappointed everybody," I observed.

"Oh no, just the ones who'd lost. And the ones who'd won said she was a snob anyway, and then they began to argue about whether she was or wasn't a snob."

"Which side did McGovern take?" I quietly wondered.

"He said he knew she was a snob, because she supports him. I mean she actually feeds him and clothes him, and all he does is write poems for *Bushelbasket*. It's weird."

"It's weird," I agreed.

"He said patronage is the business of snobs. It gives them somebody to look down on. Then one of the law-school fellows asked him how he could stand being looked down on all the time, and Ed said, 'Oh, it's a job like any other.' And all the law-school boys started to laugh. They just *howled*."

"It doesn't sound like much of a fight."

"Well, so then I was going to take the broom back to the kitchen—and Ed said, 'Give me that thing, will you?' and he grabbed it and cracked the other fellow with it—right across the shoulder, you know, and said, 'I dub thee damnfool,' or something, and then they all piled up on each other. —Didn't you *see?*" she exclaimed. "It was right out of a Western."

"I was upstairs. All I heard was a lot of yelling."

"You missed the best part! After that it deteriorated to just a discussion, I don't know on what—I hate discussions, they're such a bother. Then after a while Ed McGovern got up and started to dance with the broom—he kept screaming how it was the effigy of Mary Shelley—so I came on in here."

The tale was ended, and all at once we had nothing more
to say to one another.

We listened to the record.

Vous n'avez qu'une heure, cooed the voice, and permitted
itself a starchy well-bred silence.

"Christ, what a creamy tone," remarked my companion.

Je n'ai pas beaucoup de temps, the voice warned.

"I can't understand a word."

Quel dommage! simpered the voice. *Voyez-vous la maison
du coin? Celle avec une lanterne rouge?*

"What the hell," said the girl, and stood up impatiently.

Donnez-m'en un peu, the voice pleaded with mannerly
piety. *Encore un peu,* it repeated prayerfully, *encore un peu,*
it intoned, *encore un peu* . . .

There was a noise, half rubbing, half knocking, on the
other side of the door.

"Stefanie! Come on—open up, my hands are full."

"Oh, give it a kick," advised Stefanie; "the needle's stuck."

I swung the door wide and came face to face with William's son.

He set down the two plates of sandwiches he had been carrying and Stefanie introduced us. After the first confusion she
discovered our surnames were the same.

"Say!" she ejaculated. "Are you cousins?"

"Us two?" I said. "No."

"You could be, you know," she pointed out, "several times
removed."

"It's a long story," began William's son.

"It's a short story," I interrupted. "We're almost the same
age, you see, and when we were four years old we were be-
trothed. It was agreed upon between our parents—the dowry
was settled and everything. At five we were married. Now all
we have to do before we can live together permanently is
wait."

Encore un peu, the electronic voice of Jesus Christ kept insisting.

"I don't get it," said Stefanie, putting her knuckle against
her incisors. "Wait for what?"

Somehow I no longer envied her comely little feet or her
quick eyes the color of tea. "For puberty," I told her.

6

It was, I suppose, a kind of reunion, although we did not meet as old friends, and scarcely as comrades-in-arms whom an occasion has brought together. We had nothing between us, William's son and I, except the one cramped and tedious social meal, dominated by my mother's inconsequential monologue, of at least half a dozen years before. And whereas William's son at seventeen had resembled nothing so much as a young dog of honorable pedigree, he now had all the characteristics of a larger and somehow more humorous, more democratic animal—a horse, perhaps, or the buffalo as it used to appear on the nickel, neither grazing nor butting: nonetheless a figure of action. I immediately noted the loss of two of his former distinctions. He had given up his odd little calculated stutter and he had dropped the habit of clutching an important book for ballast. For both he now substituted a more profane and impressive mannerism: he smoked cigars, not ordinary cigars, but a narrow, tubular, tightly-rolled dark-leafed variety, which imparted to his fingers a bronze stain of incomparable elegance. He was still very polite, to be sure, but a little cynically, I thought, although it might merely have been the shock—it was a shock—of his maturity. He had, as they say, developed. I had seen him briefly at the end of his boyhood; now he was at the high moment of young manhood. He was, as they say, riding the crest. The curious thing about this zealousness was that it could not have been predicted—at least not in the boy who had spooned up his soup with such ponderous forethought, like a pharmacist meting out a potion or a priest overseeing some libational rite, that day at my mother's table. He had developed, but not in a straight line. It was as though he had begun to form himself, and he had left himself unfinished— long ago he had abandoned himself for another idea. It occurred to me that I had been outwitted. I felt not so much deceived as maliciously but comically hoaxed. He had not even turned out handsome: his head, which then had seemed a bit undersized, but splendidly polished and poised and potent, now looked to be altogether too large for the rest of him, which was encased in black rough cloth. Even his haircut had a vaguely shaggy air, so that he emerged, withal, a wonderful bison. That intellectuality which I had so much admired in my adolescence he had nevertheless retained (as if in spite of himself), but in a submerged and transmogrified fashion: he was still engrossed, still excepted from common fortune and common folly, and he still aroused in anyone who might be glimpsing him an unfamiliar Faustian recognition (in more intense shape, greed or envy) of his possibilities. Only—and this was crucial—his possibilities had changed. What they had become it was too soon to say, but watching him nudge the needle into sailing properly and restore the refrigerator plug to its socket and descry another outlet within easy reach of the phonograph wire and ply his hungry partner with sandwiches—observing all this astonishing setting-to-rights, I began to perceive which of those beautiful possibilities of his beautiful boyhood he had foregone. It seemed to me very clear and very brutal and (above all) very commonplace. He had given up, as they say, his ideals.

I was able to take all this in bit by bit, as we moved from the picnic in the kitchen out across the ballroom to the damp terrace. The strides of the butlers, the groans of the debaters, the hesitations of the dancers, the martial obedience of the musicians had all grown desultory. Aimlessly the girls leaned their chairs back against the wall and examined the wrinkles in their dresses. One of the poets had gone down to buy beer for his colleagues and now they were all wearily tilting the cans up to their mouths. There was a pile of broken champagne glasses, fallen from a tray, at the foot of the buffet table; a bewildered maid, whose orders came directly from the head-butler—a former waiter well-known for his Germanic tyranny—stood weeping because the broom had disappeared. And meanwhile William's son was leading us in and out of these melancholy tableaux with the detachment of a guide ushering visitors through an Egyptological gallery, gripping his thin cigar between his excellent lips as though he were well used to walking in the midst of things that did not matter and which did not at any rate affect him. I paced behind him, queerly charmed, and saw that halfway through the room he dropped his partner's arm, tusk-white and tusk-arched, on the pretext of having to re-light his smoke; but after that he did not reach out for her again and let her follow alone. As if to make it plain it was *she* who had asked for release, Stefanie stepped back reluctantly to my side; and the two of us trailed after him as deliberately and intently as rival valets or polygamous wives making the best of things.

The awning was dry enough by now so that the canvas Chinese birds with their upturned wings had begun, gradually and effectively, to show their dark breasts; but the aluminum rods which parasoled them into flight were still dripping, spout-like, with Oriental patience.

"Encore un peu," Stefanie murmured, coaxing the plummeting drops into the core of her palm—"encore un peu." Her ridiculous accent suddenly seemed plausible, there on the terrace: she tucked her little heels, sharp as sermons, into the new cactus, and when some of the nested leaves snapped in two and spoiled her footing, she scolded them—"Little pigs!" —vexedly and chopped at them with a delicate but forcible movement of her admirable instep.

"Watch it," I said, not really caring any more; "they're not footstools."

"Maybe they're toadstools," offered William's son, far away.

"Plants are such a bother," Stefanie lazily held out, "they die so quickly if you forget to water them." With the thoroughness of a radar-antenna she slowly pivoted her neck in search of William's son, who stood with his elbows over the railing, looking down at the river. "Your dress is fabulous," she told me, fixed on his back.

"It's from Paris," I said, embarrassed; she had not asked me where it was from; she was hardly listening anyway. "My mother got it on her last trip there."

But this roused William's son; he came and tested the wetness of the chair next to Stefanie's and settled instead for the one at my right. "I hear Mrs. Vand is ill," he said gravely, but idly.

"She's in bed with a cold." I wondered what he thought of me. If I did not know him, at least I had always known *of* him, for William on his gilt-envelope visits had endlessly supplied me: I could name all his son's schools, and the collections he had kept at different periods, and how he had spent his holidays every year since he was seventeen. All this had to be circumspectly sorted out from William's accounts, for

there were two younger sons and a daughter, and lately even
a baby, and William's conversation (rather mechanically and
dismally dispensed while he waited in Enoch's study for my
mother to come down) included all his children. William was
a little afraid of me: I believe the circumstance that I bore
his name, old issue that it was, made him uncomfortable with
me, as though I might somehow construe this isolated fact fil-
ially, or at least emotionally; hence he always sat with his
great pink hands on his flannel knees, talking slowly but con-
tinuously—as if he thought I might at any moment spit up a
"scene." Perhaps he more than half expected me to throw
myself into his formidable lap, crying real tears. The barrier
his egotistical family-talk put between us was defensive: he
knew as well as I that I did not care what rôle Nanette was
to take in her school play, but if we did not speak of Nanette
we might have had to speak of my mother, which would
have been dreadful, or, worse yet, of me, which would have
been intolerable. Staunch as a mountain, poor William grew
nervous when confronted with me—I was one of my
mother's doings which he not only could not approve, but
which he in fact entirely deplored and silently bewailed, like
Chapter Twelve of the reprehensible *Marianna Harlow*. He
regarded me as a serious and damaging mistake, and he
feared I would ask him for rectification. He was always apprehensive lest I somehow exploit his obsolete relation with
my mother, and this made me speculate whether it was really
so obsolete, on his own part, as he imagined it: and so I was
sorry for him and really liked him. All in all, it was hardly
credible that he should have carried home to his boy information about his first wife's daughter—he never once asked
for an anecdote, or even so much as inquired how I did at
school—even if his boy had declared himself interested, an
impossible notion; and I concluded that William's son was in
a state of ignorance—half imposed, half preferential—concerning my mother and me. Half a minute later, however, I
was doubtful:—from our eyrie on the terrace we could catch,
now and again, the furtive exceptional seaweedish fragrance,
almost a taste, of the river, which usually smelled of electricity and dirty oil; and when, licking up a wisp of it, I began to
tell how at certain seasons a ladder of scents mounted as high
as the seventeenth story (enmeshed—I did not say this—with
the spoils of briny triremes, and irrigated valleys, and the
proconsular image of William's son, helmeted) he cut me off
with a cluck and asked about my mother's trust fund.

"My father is its trustee, isn't he?"

I said I believed this to be true, although I did not understand its meaning exactly.

"He controls the amount your mother gets, for one thing."

"Oh, no—she can have as much as she wants."

"Not if my father doesn't approve," he pursued mildly. "It's in the terms of the trust. If she does something foolish with it he can withhold it."

"No one superintends my mother," I protested. "Not even William. She runs her own affairs."

"It's in the terms of the trust," he said positively.

"Nevertheless she does as she pleases."

"I'm afraid she's not permitted to—except as an indulgence. It's all in the trustee's discretion. But you see my father is very indulgent," he countered, and smiled, withdrawing his cigar, with half his face.

"I'm certain she gets as much as she wants," I maintained once again. "Nothing has ever been withheld. She spends her money just as she pleases," I repeated haughtily. "William has no right to discuss these matters with you."

"I haven't said he ever did," he asserted. "You know I'm clerking in my father's firm this summer."

"What does that mean?"

"I've a job in his office—for the experience. It's rather nice. We have a coffee hour every afternoon at four. I expect I'll be taken into the firm when I graduate," he explained. "Right now I'm getting to handle documents and things. It's very instructive."

I had to look away. "You've been snooping through my mother's papers."

"Oh, don't accuse—it's too stupid," he objected without heat. "Your mother's been giving away batches of dollars."

"How do you know that?" I cried.

"Not all at once, you see. I mean it adds up—over the years. That's why I say batches. It's really a tremendous sum all together. I suppose you think it's odd," he finished.

"It's not at all odd. My mother is always nurturing one project or another. And sometimes when she's abroad she'll buy a picture."

"I can't tolerate Old Masters, especially on slides," Stefanie put in boldly, trying not to acknowledge how the talk was fatiguing her; "it's such a bother to keep gaping at the same old Madonnas. Anyway, abstract art is so much more expressive, don't you think?"

"My mother's interests are very wide," I said, with severity. "She has many charities."

"I'm not speaking of *Bushelbasket*," observed William's son.

"Is it eleven o'clock?" asked Stefanie, jumping up with pique. "I'm supposed to dance with Ed McGovern at eleven sharp." She turned hopefully to William's son. "You know why eleven? Because it's T.S. Eliot's bedtime."

"It's nearly twelve," I told her, and regretted it at once, for she pulled her chair closer to William's son and sat down again. "Perhaps it's *your* bedtime," I added conspicuously.

"Hoot," said Stefanie. "Hoot, I'm an owl."

"There's this fellow Connelly in the firm," continued William's son with an assurance of conspiracy that suggested lights going off everywhere; "he's the accountant—very sharp, they don't come any sharper—not a thing gets by him. He's done Mrs. Vand's income tax for twenty years or more; I guess he knows her checkbook like the back of his own right hand."

"Why not like the canals of Mars?" Stefanie inquired delicately.

"Oh, better than that—much better," said William's son.

" 'The canals of Mars' sounds more poetic"; and I recognized in this a tribute to the tutoring of Ed McGovern.

"But no one can account for them: they're only a theory. Connelly is far too sharp for theories—he has to account for everything. He's analyzed Mrs. Vand's expenditures and he knows them precisely."

"And then I suppose he confides them to you." I rose and took several turns among the cacti; the music, suffocated by the scarves of sweet wind which slapped against the terrace railing, came out to us funereally. We might have been in the vestibule of a chapel, wondering how much to press on the widow for the sake of her orphans. There was the sick breath of money all upon us; it rushed out dirtily, as from a beggar's foul mouth (that beggar who always waits in the vestibule), full of waste, clogged with sores and boils; and suddenly the chapel shivered with tiny sounds, obscure meek little noises, the cries of small coins—chink, chink—trivial and tedious.

The bow of my sash had come untied (pulled loose, I thought, by a finger of cactus) and a long silken train dragged ignobly behind me, rustling its silver voice.

Chink, chink, it slyly chimed.

"Listen to your dress," said Stefanie; and listened; and William's son listened; and at last I too was compelled to listen; and I heard the smothered call of greed.

William's son was not indifferent to it. "And Connelly is so meticulous," he went on, in his tone of thieves a-plotting in the dark night, "meticulous, you know how accountants are, and now and again this check would turn up, a certain check made out to no one—no cause, mind you, no charge, no invoice, no broker's statement, no charity, no bill of any kind, no reason on earth for it—money for no one in the world. And Connelly went to my father to find out who it was for, to name a category for it at least. He had to account for it, you see—he hates theories, and he has none of his own. But my father wouldn't reply. I was there, you see—I saw it all. 'Never mind,' my father said, and a terrible look came over his face. 'Go ahead and post it anywhere,' I heard him say, 'and never mind.'"

"What sort of terrible look?" Stefanie demanded, leaning close.

"Angry, but more ashamed than angry. My father is never ashamed. He was angry because he was ashamed."

"Ah," our companion murmured, "he's ashamed of Mrs. Vand."

"He's fond of Mrs. Vand," William's son amended, staring over her head at me. "He's engrossed in her affairs."

"I should expect so," I retorted. "Her attorney ought to be."

"But he doesn't think her responsible. I suppose he never thought so—not even long ago. Nevertheless he's fond of Mrs. Vand," he asserted. "I imagine he's forgiven her."

"There was nothing to forgive."

"True: it was all unforgivable," he said.

"They did each other no harm," I declared.

"I'm in the dark!" cried Stefanie. "Were they in love?" she marveled, searching out my reply, "your mother and his father?"

"No," I gave out. "They were married."

"How absolutely crazy!"

"We," William's son supplied rapidly, "were born after the divorce—both of us. Don't get the idea that we're related."

"But in a way—" she began doubtfully.

"Not at all," he vouchsafed her.

"Not at all," I conceded, and reflected how I had once claimed him for a brother.

We sat for a while in the ambiguous air—after rain a

mid-August night breaks the heart—and no one cared or dared to speak. The little orchestra, worn down by the clamor (or my mother's program worn out beyond its last Valse Militaire), was playing a samba too quickly, in somewhat clandestine style, as though trying to get through each bar as unobtrusively (although contrariwise as loudly) as possible. The saxophonist had rid himself of his instrument and was now plying a shining brass horn. Perhaps it was our distance from the dancers that charged them uncannily, like charmed snakes emerging from baskets: from afar they seemed miniature but dangerous: if too clever for snakes, then clever enough for leaping swords. They thrust toward one another and away, dueling, while the horn, choked off by the wind in our ears, rose and rose. It towered finally, and I thought of the bugle that did not sound again while I waited for it in the washed grass; but it was not the same. The horn was no more holy than the workaday lips, pressed to the tongue of the brass, of its shallow-jowled master—it did its duty merely, and screamed as well as it could, and promised nothing. The stiff high note broke off eventually, and the ballroom sent out applause like ululations of the leaves of countless paper forests; it was, as celebration, counterfeit and sad. Nothing in the world can be sustained, neither bugles nor hope nor woe nor desire nor common well-being nor horns, and even redemption, that suspect covenant, can be revised by the bitter and loveless Christ to whom alone nothing, not even life, is irretrievable. Relief is our reward for recognizing this truth, that the note cannot be sustained forever and the irretrievable can never be returned to us; and there is no alternative but to go on with the facts exactly as they are.

I came away from the cactus plants and stood against the railing, as in a ship on the high seas, and because William's son had done so before, I looked down into the meditative river. But there was little to see, only a moon-shaped excursion boat with its hundred lights and its hidden cargo of contraband lovers, and I moved instead to the other side of the terrace to watch the city churn inaccessibly below. The wind was strong in that corner; I turned my back against it and clasped my arms and felt the little hairs spring up on balls of flesh; and the wind blew through my dress, and caught up the silver of its loosened train and flew it like a ship's standard, freely, over the city. It was a banner of presence and identity, a sign to Gustave Nicholas Tilbeck that I knew him to be not far; it was a money-flag, and the chink of money went rattling through it.

It made me reckless as a pirate. "William needn't wear his terrible look," I burst out. "It's impertinent of him to be ashamed for my mother."

"No; no," he murmured, smiling and smiling, "you don't follow. It's simply a question of where the money goes. It's simply a question," he repeated steadily, "of the terms of the trust." He bent forward, vivid with interest. "He's got to know everything."

"I suppose it isn't the function of a trustee to trust anyone."

"It's his job to protect the fund. And Mrs. Vand."

"Mrs. Vand protects herself," I countered, growing tired of it all.

"By giving away her money?"

"There must be some left over, isn't there?" Stefanie consoled.

"Connelly had to post the check under Miscellaneous Expenses," William's son informed me ominously.

"Poor chap," I said. "What a blow."

"Who d'you suppose it's for?" Stefanie wondered. "I mean the check."

"I don't know," I said.

"Don't you want to find out?"

"I'm not a spy."

"But you must think about it sometimes," she pressed. "Don't you have any ideas? You know—theories."

"I'm like Connelly," I revealed. "I'm too meticulous for theories."

"She doesn't need any," William's son confidently perceived. "She knows."

"She knows and won't tell," Stefanie improved. She stretched appealingly; she yawned. "Maybe the money's for something wicked."

"Or something good," William's son suggested. "A poor but respectable family, hoping someday to repay the bountiful lady, wishes to receive its disbursements anonymously."

"But then your father would approve," she promptly recollected. "No, it's for something wicked. What can you think of that's bad?"

They went on teasing and speculating in this fashion for some minutes. It soon became plain that it had nothing to do with me. All along it had had nothing to do with me. It was a

flirtation, and I their plaything; and now, at its climax, I was
in fact quickly excluded, and occupied myself with retrieving
my sash and tying it behind me. It was difficult to do; it rus-
tled and slipped away and tinkled and whispered; and for a
time my hands were entangled in silver and gold. At last I
contrived to finish the knot, and drew the ends before me in
two full loops; and through the circle of silk I held in the air
just then—it might have been the gesture of a panhandler
who puts out his hat with both hands—I saw the two of them
leaning across the little space between their chairs, susurrant,
kissing.

They laughed because I had glimpsed them.

"Encore un peu," William's son demanded flawlessly, and
grasped her small bare complaisant wrists.

She admonished him remotely: "Is that *all* you can think of
that's bad?"—kissing him.

But they did not mind my standing there; perhaps they
thought me benevolent. They entwined, at any rate, their two
bright shadows, with a fuss of shoe-soles on flagstones and
much scraping, before they settled into immobility, of sleeves
and voices and thighs thickly swathed. But still I did not go.
The illusion of their pleasure captivated me: they had the de-
sirable grace of seeming not to plunder the moment but to
charm it, as though it were really the moment itself which
took the spoils of their long, long kiss.

But the prize of pleasure is only an imagining, for there
was nothing there to be ensnared but myself—an attendant
more bereft than curious—, the air swift as money and the
horn's howl.

7

Crossing the ballroom I was confronted by my mother's editor. I recognized him as the young man who had observed to
his friends that Mrs. Vand's daughter was known to no one. It

was at once evident, despite his smile (he smelled a great deal of beer), that I was, to be sure, not known to *him*.

"Stefanie!" he greeted me. "What a disgrace—where have you been?"

"Stefanie is out on the terrace."

He bowed low at his error, and inadvertently struck his ear with the broomstick. "Should you like to replace her?" he invited, indicating the broom. "The next piece will be a gavotte, and after that, watch and see, a saltarello. Allegra has the latest notions of music. At midnight we'll dance the two-step—twelve o'clock sharp, you see, because it's E.E. Cummings' bedtime."

"Let him sleep," I advised. "Don't wake him."

His colorless eyes disliked me. "You have extremely negative views."

"Your ear is red," I noticed. "Did you hurt it?"

"You're very rude," he remarked, "to look so expensive."

"I'm no more expensive than you."

"Nonsense, I'm as shabby as can be."

"I wasn't speaking of your morals. I was speaking of your keep."

"I am one of the advantages of Mrs. Vand's wealth," he declaimed, turning his implement upside down and articulating into its straw face. "I am an instance of private enterprise. The Edward McGoverns of the world are luxuries which only the very rich can afford."

"You are less a luxury," I said, "than a defect of character."

"Your views," he repeated firmly, "are socialist. I was not bought for my usefulness. I am an objet d'art. I am rare and fragile"—he pointed—"like that little porcelain over there, the one with the lady and the fan. Try to understand that this broom and I are in different categories. My whole purpose," he finished, "is to give pleasure."

"How do you do that?"

"By providing an atmosphere," he said shallowly, "through the exploitation of my talents."

"Aha," I began, "when it comes to exploitation, your talents are considerable. —But I rather prefer the broom."

"You are the worst example of your class," he resumed. "You know nothing of the great. You know nothing of Maecenas, the Medicis, or the Guggenheims. Ford was a crank until he became a Foundation. I have a friend in Salerno, a sculptor and a pederast, who does nothing but the busts of

young men—a Roman family of ancient lineage supports
him. He lives with his boy lover in a house under a wheat
field . . ." He went on naming the patrons he recalled, from
history and from life, and their wards and dependents,
all of them in some way freakish, mad, or criminal. His talk
was no more than that of a hired man defending his pride by
flattering the gentlefolk who give him his bread.

My mother, it seemed, had, directly or indirectly, many
such hired men—not only her staff of poets, but William and
even William's son, men whose relation to her rested not
upon love or duty, but squarely and simply upon the compli-
cations of wealth. It was in the nature of things that her servants should be chiefly lawyers and intellectuals of one sort
or another, persons with smeared lenses and sleepless eyes beneath them, and apparently no private lives; and it was also
entirely natural that these menials, superior to their mistress
in taste and brains and conduct, should feel contempt for her.
They were all bought, after all, as Ed McGovern had not
been afraid to express it (the humiliation inherent in this was
hers, not his)—even the incorruptible William, who had put
her away as a wife, could take her back again as a client.
And the hired rôle, that of family adviser, was not dissimilar
from the earlier one—except, of course, that now he was
bought and paid for.

The curious element in this commerce was that nobody
pitied her. It is not usual, admittedly, for the rich to be pitied,
except in crude jokes and bathetic tales, and Allegra Vand, to
be sure, enjoyed her status excessively. She enjoyed it, moreover, with confidence enough to believe that she scorned it,
and pointed to her fellow-traveling as proof—but the most
stupid reader could perceive at once that Marianna Harlow's
passion for the workers was not unlike a former generation's
devotion to tatting or playing the piano: it was an "accomplishment." Still, I thought it odd that no one ever saw my
mother, in her maturity, flying about the world in aluminum
airplanes without her husband, boring into one city after another in search of an ideal Vatican or Jerusalem of cities, as
a kind of victim. She was like one of those god-kings chosen
by lot among certain tribes, raised from infancy in fantastic
luxury, emblazoned gorgeously in feathers and jewels, magnificently feasted and fattened at innumerable jubilations and
sacred festivals, worshipped and called holy, all his whims
elaborately encouraged, looked-after, desired and fulfilled, his
person made strangely autocratic, empowered to command

every happiness but one, that of being left to live and to die in his own time—and led at last to the greatest celebration of all, his brutal and unbeautiful death by pounding of sacrificial clubs at the hands of those kind uncles, the priests who had fed him splendor. My mother was as innocent as this, and as ambitious and arrogant; and in the same way she did not suspect that she was hated for her glories. It is true that money attracts; but much money repels. My mother was pillaged, looted, ravished and ravaged: men crept at her pockets like so many mice; she was cynically robbed by her superior servants, footmen, and beggars a hundred times over, and was cursed with every burglary. Hence her wildness and her pranks—like everyone else, she longed for the sensation of robbing Allegra Vand.

I felt like one of those plunderers, going up the stairs in my jingling dress, noisy with my father's avarice, and sickened by McGovern's hackneyed exchanges. I could scarcely tell the two of them apart—McGovern and Gustave Nicholas Tilbeck; they were two birds of the same species perched upon my mother's shoulders talon-deep, one a fledgling of thirty years, no longer an amateur but not yet dangerous, the other invisible but shockingly present, a great sleek cruelly churlish falcon notched into her flesh for eternity: two terrible hawks. And William's son fluttering also, with his knowledgeable questions and his knowledgeable answers, pecking and probing into the money's secrets, as covetous as the rest —for a trust fund is labyrinthine as a cave, and as difficult to comprehend, and has room for the beatings of many bats. And the little blue-shod beauty too, kisses springing from her mouth high above the black dead river; and the dancers and musicians and maids laying waste the ballroom below—all of them chattering rapaciously on their little hanging chains in my mother's aviary, smelling up her money.

In my room I tore off my dress—tore it off literally—and did not care that twenty tiny buttons glittered like scattered coins everywhere, or that the floorboards ran with silver and gold.

I sat in the dark and tried to remember Europe. I remembered the freckled thumbs of my Dutch governess, and her little pink birdlike nostrils, and how she had fed me a queer shellfish they called *oursin*, which made me sick. To be sick at my stomach was to take after my father . . . And I thought of Geneva, an unknown city, and Enoch negotiating with the Bulgarian whose cheek he had kissed above a false brown beard.

Enoch, my mother's darling, buyer of spies, up to that moment had not been bought.

And then it seemed I heard him, as always before I had heard him—"There's nothing else to do," he said, "it can't be helped," he said, "we'll go ahead and do it." It was all a murmuring, low and dim, from my mother's room; but the violins were rising like smoke up the stairwell, and now and then the horn shrieked with the mad vacuity of a parrot: it was impossible to listen. I was sorry for her, stung with fever, moaning in her bed alone, while her party raged against her: she knew her guests, she had herself asked them one by one, she knew the terror of them all. And she lay talking to her ghosts, saying her piece, and saying Enoch's piece, and pouring a burden of gold and silver upon my back, and gold and silver into the hands of Gustave Nicholas Tilbeck, and softly gnashing her lamentations in Enoch's voice, a voice so very like his that I went down the hall, the better to hear it— "There's nothing else to do," I heard, "we'll go ahead and do it," I heard, "is there anything left for us to do but this?"

My mother was sitting up in bed, rigid, her hair like needles or rays or cobras' tongues slowly stabbing toward the ceiling. She moved vaguely but jaggedly, in a stirring too stiff to be called rocking, too brief for swaying—it was almost infantile. The lamp was lit—it stood on her dresser, on the far side of the room near the bathroom door, and I wondered whether she had left her bed to turn it on. But she was still tightly wound in the coverlet, and when I came near to touch it I felt the fever-heat in every fold.

She heaved—I followed the crest and trough of her wide back—and her head came over, unpropelled, and she saw me. "You're in your slip!" she croaked, with the quick awareness of the sick; "why do you come in here like that? Go down, do you think I give parties for nothing? Go down," she raved, and I thought at first she was much worse, for her skin had the slipperiness of certain deep illnesses which drive out personality.

I told her that my dress had torn in the dancing, and I had come upstairs to don another.

"It was the train," she concluded hoarsely. "Somebody stepped on that damn train. I knew the moment you tried it on it was no good. It was a cheat, in spite of that built-in brassiere, a cheat absolutely, I don't care! I could shoot that

old woman, Baroness only maybe, I wish they had shot her
with her whole family together, even supposing she's not real
—those gangsters, those thieves! Twenty-one years of open
robbery! What does she know about dressing a young girl, I
told her I had always protected you from politics and sinning
—they're the same, don't you think I know that by now? It's
not as though I left out telling her—my young girl, I said, in
America they are younger . . . how old are you?" she broke
off suddenly, and I said my age in the interval she offered
me, and then again she called out across the room, "She's old
enough to take care of herself, you see? It's all right then,
she'll take care of herself"—nevertheless it was nothing like
delirium. Manifestly it was a calculated recitation for an
audience: it had the ring of the concert hall. "Eight hundred
dollars, and torn—to shreds, did you say?" she descended
finally, mumbling, "I knew from the first moment, believe
me, a run of sheet metal, pieces of eight, the U.S. Mint, In
God We Trust . . ."

Underneath it all there were irony and the distortions of
some unimaginable and overwhelming anger. Her eyes were
at the same time receded and protuberant, like out-of-the-way
buttons or switches purposely removed from the anterior on
account of their terrible potential; they controlled a machine
at once subtle and fearful. And it was as though someone had
indeed come and charged those awful round swellings, her
unhappy eyes, and set off the perilous machine: my mother's
pale arms emerged from the windings of her sheets and
flailed the air; her mouth chattered like a motor. It soon
came to me that her ragings, which shook her still, were not
those of sickness or fever. She was claimed by something
else. A wilderness of tears complicated her already laborious
face; her thin nose narrowed. It was a weeping that assaulted
her, no access of mere fever and sickness. She ailed with an
extraordinary bitterness. It was strange to see. I had been witness, all my life, to my mother's good humor: her laughter
was both captivating and abashing—it sometimes shamed me
But now I heard those shrill and abstract bawlings, wordless
as a child's, and I felt deceived to have fallen upon this questionable anguish—questionable because there was no way of
telling on what it was founded; it might have been some
small moroseness urged upon her by the solitude of her bed
and the reminiscent music in her ears all that summer's night
And yet it was not: clearly she was diseased with sorrow
"Get away," she muttered, and resumed her wail, and next

took up her innumerable complaints, alternating between inarticulate sobs and a rush of verbose invective—against her corsetiere the dubious Baroness, myself, the musicians who were now launched into the newest song of the season, the pervasive sanctimonious smell of beer; and none of it seemed relevant to the figure of my mother in her violent bed, greenish in the lamplight, none of it was connected, the words and moans ran everywhere and did not meet: she railed not against these designated offenses and offenders, but against some hard impassable wall behind and around them. "There's nothing for you in Europe," she cried, "and there won't be any Europe, it's all quite clear, no Europe any more. The thing to do is go down—go down, I'll tell you what to do, you know that banner hanging there, the one for bon voyage? tear it down, that's the thing to do, rip it right off if you please; your gown is ripped, then rip again! since there's no more bon voyage," she scowled, "it makes no difference," now whispering and now breaking into a harsh sore scream, glaring at me as though I had intruded at an ungainly hour, like some ill-trained maid, and had caught her in the act of love.

And then, abruptly and noticeably, the sound of steadily running water stopped—a faucet turned with a tiny squeak behind the bathroom door, and I was all at once conscious of having heard, without really hearing it, the bounce of water all that while.

Out stepped Enoch, gravely rubbing his face with a towel.

We stood and took each other in—I in my long petticoat, Enoch in his undershirt, patting the back of his neck.

"I had no idea you were having a party," he said.

"It's for going abroad."

My mother sent out a wrenched sob—half sigh, half whine.

"I had no idea," he said again, aimlessly.

I moved to switch on a second lamp, and there, on my mother's dresser, lay Enoch's attaché case, shut up, dangling its round combination lock thick with numbers. "Did you come straight from the airport?" I asked, reaching up to pull the chain—my elbow tapped the lock; it was open.

"It's all right—it's absolutely empty," he assured me quickly. "There's nothing in it. —No, I've come from Washington."

"It changes everything," my mother said briefly. She lowered herself to the pillow, blew her nose, and breathed as if to prevent another spasm.

"Washington?" I said, puzzled by my mother's quick control.

"Nothing will be the same," Enoch affirmed. "Did that doctor leave you any pills, Allegra?"

"They're a sedative. I don't want a sedative. Go ahead and tell her."

"Perhaps after the party," Enoch said. "When they all go home. How did you catch this cold?"

"Tell her now," my mother said.

"She stood out in the rain," I announced.

"I think we had better get rid of the musicians," said Enoch.

"They're contracted till one o'clock," I recalled. "Does it have anything to do with Geneva?"

"Geneva," my mother echoed senselessly.

"No, no, not with Geneva," he said, "Geneva was the last of that sort of thing. I've emptied my briefcase once and for all. I'm to have another job."

My mother was now soundlessly crying; her hands held her throat. "It wasn't a Bulgarian," she murmured.

"No," said Enoch, "it wasn't."

"What kind of job?" I pressed.

"Well, a bit better. Less exciting, but more standing to it."

"You had better hurry up," my mother warned, snapping off the switches of her eyes—her lids fell to, her arms halted on the coverlet, her tears dripped as languidly as oil—"Tell her."

"In a couple of weeks the committee hearings begin. There'll be plenty of opposition, you know," Enoch commented.

"There usually is."

"And then it has still to be weighed by the Senate."

"Not weighed," my mother interrupted—her voice scratched like chalk—"confirmed."

"It all depends," said Enoch.

"Tell her," my mother commanded bitterly.

But Enoch went back to the bathroom to hang his towel. "It's about Europe," he called out to me; "it won't be possible for you to go. It won't work," he said behind the door—"at least not now."

I stared down at my white pumps, the ones I had saved

from the June mud. "Is there something the matter with my
passport? It came without any trouble."

"It's not the passport. The passport's all right, you know."

"I've had a smallpox vaccination and two polio shots. Dr.
Leverheim told me tonight he'd give me a flu shot before I
leave. And the ticket's already paid for," I argued. "Nothing
could be safer."

He came back wearing his shirt and buttoning the cuffs.
He looked older than middle-aged; he looked like a reasonable man, that fictive "reasonable man" of whom William
spoke perpetually and whose judgment was a legal touch-
stone; I thought he must face his spies with just this impeccable omniscient gesture of his tidy chin, daubed with tiny ra-
zor-cuts and the hazy smell of after-shave. "Oh, it's not *your*
safety that's in question," he informed me. "Still, it won't do,
not right now. We can't contemplate your going."

"Why not?" I pursued.

"It won't work," he said again. "Your mother and I have
decided."

"It's out of the question," my mother dolefully assented.

"In that case there's no point in all that noise down there,"
I said, "if I'm staying home. I'll go down and send them
away."

"Keep your presents," my mother briskly advised. "It
would be rude to give them back."

"No one brought any," I told her.

"Not for bon voyage? My God," she exclaimed, "they
don't know the mores! They have no manners! Not even William's boy?" she rasped, incredulous. "Not even a hamper of
fruit? William's boy must have come with *some*thing."

"He came with a girl."

"Ah," she acknowledged softly, "I didn't know that." And
she turned her head into the pillow. "Tell her, Enoch, tell
her."

He appraised me shrewdly. "It's still a voyage, but shorter
than the other—" he sounded positively political—"in brief
you're wanted somewhere else. There's a person," he went on
steadily, "who wants you."

"Tell her the other thing first," said my mother, muffled.
"It isn't fair."

"It's fair." He put his undistinguished peremptory hands on
my shoulders and consulted with my look; it was a motion as
authoritarian as it was unpaternal. He might have been sentencing me to a long term of imprisonment, exactly as though

he were convinced it was a measure for the protection of society. Certainly he believed he was protecting something, perhaps my mother, who lay as if wounded, droning her long torpid whimper into the bedsheets. "If it isn't fair it can't be helped. This person," he told me, "has written me a letter. He has a great interest in you—you can't imagine how great."

My mother's sorrow pierced the air—a shriek exactly like a curse, "Hurry, hurry," I heard her cry.

"He wants you to come to him."

"Yes," I said, "tell me who."

"You don't know him—"

"Do you want me to go?"

"Perhaps you should," Enoch said, "for your own sake."

"Ah, don't lie to her," my mother groaned. "It's not for *her* sake."

"Then for his," Enoch amended.

"How you lie," she spit out, "when it's only for ours."

He shrugged inexpressively, viewing her in her tangled bed. It was impossible to know what he thought just then. "It's your father," he resumed at last. "He has asked to see you and we intend to agree to it."

For the first time in my life I said the name aloud; I said it as though it were a riddle which I had myself invented: "Gustave Nicholas Tilbeck"—but I had not known how sad that sound would be.

"Hurry, hurry," wept my mother; Enoch had turned away, and stood posted at the dresser, keeping vigil over the mirror's version of himself—a big, reasonable, assaulted man confronted by his balding head.

"How much does he want?" I asked in my mother's old and grievous tone.

And Enoch: "How much does she know?" in the same voice.

"Her," my mother motioned coarsely, "that one, who can know what she knows? She's like him, why hide it any more, they're alike—"

I felt bare and cold and lone; I shivered in my thin slip. "Isn't it money he wants," I stated with no modulation at all, "Gustave Nicholas Tilbeck."

The name was as desolate as some uninhabited strand.

"Not money," Enoch rapidly opposed, "it's you he wants. He doesn't talk at all of money."

"Hurry, hurry," cried my mother from the bed.

"Why does he want me?"

"I *told* you to hurry!"

"He's never wanted me before," I said.

Enoch, weaving his head like a schoolmaster, mused. "He heard about your graduation—he read it in a column. It hadn't occurred to him that you were grown—"

"Never mind," I said. "He couldn't have written that."

"All right," my stepfather capitulated. "We don't know his reasons. Will you go?"

"I thought I was going to London and Paris and Copenhagen and Rome."

"Will you go?" he repeated; and because I saw how his tongue, quick with resolution, glimmered cynically on his lips, I consented to surrender those shimmering capitals, London and Paris and Copenhagen and Rome; and I said I would go.

At this my mother raised her eyes: "Now we have it."

"Perhaps," answered my stepfather, and scrutinized the person in the looking-glass without mercy.

It seemed they were absorbed in one another, although they were not near and did not exchange their two heavy gazes; yet their colloquy was plain; in avoiding the response of gesture and look, they met again and again, as if in mid-air, conferring and devising, and taking a stand at last. It was a conspiracy: they stood, the two of them, Enoch and his wife, against me.

"And will it make a difference," I defended myself, "if I go?"

"I hoped," said my mother, griefworn, "you would always live freely."

"A difference to whom?" Enoch took up. "To your father?"

"Nothing can make a difference to Nick," my mother remarked faintly to herself.

"No," I specified, and felt them draw invisibly together. "To Mr. and Mrs. Vand."

"Oh," said my stepfather. "—as for that!"

But my mother was too intent to go on weeping. "You haven't told her, Enoch."

He clicked shut the lock belonging to his abandoned briefcase and twirled the knob. "The principal religious tenet," he observed, "is that one does not dare to manipulate circumstance." Meanwhile his fingers deftly stalked number after number—he had not rid himself of the habit of the combination. " 'I am the Lord thy God' means nothing else. —I believe the orchestra's finished," he noted finally.

It was true; the music had vanished. A babel of calls spiralled up the steps, wavering like flags or candles. "One o'clock," a voice swept up, "it's one o'clock." "But they haven't petitioned for a writ of certiorari," said another. "You'd better not," said a third, very far, "Mrs. Vand wouldn't like it." "Stephen Spender's bedtime," yowled the stentor from the bottom of the stair, "at one o'clock," and my mother's head, wild with heat or rage, fell back subdued upon the pillow.

"Enoch has been appointed Ambassador," she burst out after a moment; and, although this was her great hour, the ambition of her years, she suddenly moaned—as if she had just been informed of his assassination.

8

It was, as I have said, her ambition, for my mother was ambitious: a thing not usual among the rich, who have no aspirations. True, some few of them fly after fame of one sort or another, and some fewer still after good works and love of men, which is what philanthropy, despite its granite art museums and bequests to second-rate universities, means. But for most, there is no use going out to seek one's fortune when one has been born with it, already made, under one's nose. And so most scions of acquisitive parents are mutants who cannot close the fist to grasp—their fingers are perpetually splayed, and their fathers' fortunes slip through. There are legal dams and dikes, to be sure, like my mother's trust fund, and lads with decimals as well as digits in the dikes, like William, whom my grandfather had early seen to be a youth of uncommon good sense, with the lucky exception that he was likely to marry my mother:—my grandfather saw them wed, then died of the relief. And some will spend a

lifetime spending; which will in fact satisfy many. But there
are those who are too imaginative to be shut up quietly in
country mansions and counting-houses, raising heirs or horses
or interest-rates; if an evil star has prevented them from seeking their fortunes, they nevertheless insist on seeking *something*. My mother was one of these.

She scoffed at solemnity and pageantry and men in high
office (the election of a woman Senator shocked her beyond
amusement, and she remarked that if we were to have
women in government we should begin in the post office with
femailmen); and the puns she made about what went on in
the Cabinet were frequently obscene. But all this signified
nothing; it was actually the obverse of her true feeling, and
allowed her to dwell shamelessly on what she pretended to
abhor. Like many Americans, she followed the schedules and
tours and ceremonials of the British Queen minutely, and had
come to know by heart the royal figure's public modes and
private habits (tabloid-borne), ardently burlesquing and
sneering at every hat, trip, speech, and birthday at Balmoral
—but the satire was an excuse for passionate study, and the
passion was the end. "All that money," my mother said
stalely, "to pay for a useless institution! They could build
twenty schools a year with it, but the English are so sentimental they'd starve themselves to death to feed the gullet of
a parasitic survival"—her asperity hid her delight in every
new account of the Queen's duties and her keep. And one
year when a movie star married the reigning prince of a
duchy the size of a chickenyard, my mother pored over radio-
photos of the wedding rites and hooted joyfully at the immense vulgárity of everyone's curiosity: "It's only an Irish
girl married to an Italian in a Catholic ceremony—it's as
common as peas in any immigrant neighborhood!" she snob-
bishly dismissed it—but she knew how many pearls were sewn
into the bodice of the bridal dress.

I will not say that my mother wished to be Queen: but she
wished for something that America could not give her. The
trouble was the middle-classness of her home country—she
had tried to be proletarian and had failed, and not even good
family (my mother's mother was third cousin to Theodore
Roosevelt) and much money can produce an aristocracy in
America—we do not have the style, our palaces are dated
nineteen-twenty, and our castles are imported piecemeal. The
egalitarian temperament is content with Presidents and Secretaries of Commerce or the Interior, and glad enough to see

law courts run in a businesslike manner, wigless: the egalitarian temperament has its own notions of nobility, which it confuses with efficiency, so that in America the élite (whether generals, corporation executives, or Secretaries of State) are merely those who have more work to do, and more decisions to make, than anyone else. But an Ambassador is not like any of these. A President must represent the Common Man, but an Ambassador may not. He is expected to cultivate the influential and the aristocratic; he is accredited not to other men in their offices, but to monarchs in their trappings. Hence the early republic, scorning kings and courts, sent abroad only envoys and ministers of medium rank, and it was not until the final decade of the last century that Congress authorized the making of Ambassadors. It gave us a borrowed taste of oligarchy. And it sufficed as an ambition for the rich. All this I had long known from my mother.

She was fulfilled. What lay ahead of her now was the prospect of becoming a great lady. Perhaps she intended to grow more haughty and more sedate and end as one of those queer expunged Americans whom European living fossilizes. Or perhaps she merely believed her traveling days were over, and she had at last attained that Europe of power and beauty which she for years had vainly pursued in the courtyards of its fatigued cities. Or, further, she might have thought of the ambassadorship as a kind of ideal mission, in the Roman style (she lately preferred the straightforward Romans to the squabbling overintellectual Greeks), with all the world a province in need of enlightenment from a central culture. Nevertheless she had arrived, whatever her conception. Enoch had been to see the President; Enoch had been appointed Ambassador. They agreed that it changed everything.

And yet she wept. She was like those piteous beasts of legend, humans whom a bad sprite has transformed into pigs or dogs or swans—but for their memories they are all animal, and yet they weep for the glory of what they have been. I suppose it is the same when we are old, and learn that some spell has trapped us—our fair strong able selves!—in an aged and hideous body which cannot possibly belong to us—which has likely been stolen for this unspeakable purpose from some crone or dotard; and this is why the blessed die before they are thirty. For my mother, then, it was a moment of incredible transmutation and conversion—nothing would ever again be what it was before.

Nor would Enoch. Enoch, as I have said, was messianic.

He came out of the heaven under the compulsion of circumstance. His nature was metamorphic, which is another way of
saying that he was adaptable, and took his resurrections
lightly. He had something in him of the refugee, which was
absurd, because he had been born in Chicago. But he was
both visionary and resourceful, one of those "interior" refugees of the kind which America throws off from time to time,
adventurers who seem always to be fleeing some impractica-
ble environment and the persecutions of ordinary life, who
turn up all over the world practising the cult of a single idea.
If they do not swim the Hellespont, like Byron or Leander,
they will attach themselves to some craving or pretension
equally mystic and rigorous—a hero, a book, a theory, a
woman. Enoch professed himself a skeptic, and yet he believed in mysteries of all sorts, and reverberations from every
direction, and had his own pantheon of saints, gods, angels
and demons, all of them intensely political. He had Alexan-
der and Napoleon, but he also had Lycurgus and Gandhi.
What he had them *for* no one exactly knew, least of all my
mother, who now began to joke a little in her bed, gradually
getting better. She called him Disraeli in the mornings and in
the evenings Moses.

They spent many hours shut up in the sickroom, dining
from trays and mumbling together inaudibly. Not another
word was said. to me about Europe. And yet it was always
Europe *they* were talking of; their room and the sounds that
occasionally came from it vibrated with schemes for foreign
excitements. But often there were long periods when they did
not speak at all. My mother slept, and Enoch read. A young
man came every day with a carton full of books—once he
passed me where I lay in a chair on the terrace, and I saw
one of the titles. It was a history of the Empire of Charle-
magne. I thought of him as a messenger or delivery boy
merely, but he appeared to be a secretary also, for one morning Enoch led him out into the sunshine and, pulling at the
tassels of his bathrobe, began to dictate; it was a survey of
agriculture, full of statistics and data on crop rotation and the
erosion of soil, and how many heads of cattle, and how many
inches of rainfall. The young man propped his notebook on
his skinny knee and put everything down in a legible long-
hand with astonishing agility—his pen streamed. Now and
then Enoch stopped him—"Now read back that last"—and
the young man fled down a column of numbers in a voice as
weak as a reed until Enoch said, praising, "That's right, that's

right," blowing on a bit of paper he kept in his hand, as if to make it perfectly clear that this was no ordinary secretary, and that he himself was to be congratulated for a lucky man.

I did not see my mother very much during these days. She had settled down to the business of recovering from what Dr. Leverheim, alarmed at the unexpected severity of her illness, had left off calling a cold: he now termed it a "virus," and increased his fee accordingly. Once when I heard her stir after her long morning nap I knocked on her door and asked to visit; but she would not admit me. She did not want me there. She plaited her fingers through her ruined hair, distraught, and sent me away. I felt she did not like to look at me.

On that same afternoon William's son telephoned. "I hear Mrs. Vand is worse."

"No," I said, "she was, but now she's better."

"I'm glad to hear it," he said without interest. "The papers are full of your stepfather's appointment."

"Yes," I acknowledged.

"Do you think he'll get it?"

"Certainly," I said. "The committee hearings are purely routine."

"I suppose you'll attend them."

"No," I said, "I'll be away."

"But you don't embark until September. You can still make Washington."

"The trip is off," I told him. "I'm not going to Europe. I'm going to the country instead."

"What a shame. I meant to send you a seeing-off present."

"A basket of fruit?"

"My father's suggestion exactly. But no, I hadn't given it any thought yet."

"Now you needn't at all."

He laughed slightly. "I want to apologize, you know. For that business about the check. I expect I made Mrs. Vand out for a criminal."

"Or yourself for a prosecutor," I suggested. "Forget it."

"Look," he began, "my father told me about that money."

My mouth went suddenly dry. I let the silence gather; I had nothing to say.

"Hello?" said William's son.

"I'm here. Yes," I said.

"The money," he persisted. "I found out where it's going."

"Your father's too discreet," I demurred, "to have told."

"He didn't want to. In fact he refused to."

"But in the end he did."

"He was awfully reluctant."

"He did though."

"I'm afraid I badgered him into it. He broke down finally."

"He's not like that," I said apprehensively. "He doesn't give in."

"I never thought so myself. But that's neither here nor there." His thick cautious breathing crackled like static in the wire. "It's strange. You know she's been sending it for years to a place on Town Island. It's for the upkeep of an old estate."

I echoed him without understanding. "An estate?"

But he disbelieved in my ignorance. He said suspiciously, "Your mother's property. Your grandfather's place. Where she was brought up."

"My mother has no such property," I objected.

"My father told me," he said, settling it. "It's a sort of museum now."

"A museum?" I said in the same tone.

"Oh, it's not in actual operation. It never really was. Part of your mother's trust money was earmarked for it. The trustee was supposed to set it up. Look," he interrupted himself impatiently, "you know all this, don't you?"

"I never heard of it," I said truthfully.

But the guilty static which continued to measure out his hesitation was an accusation. "You know it all," he declared, and carried on. "It was supposed to be a museum, but the thing got managed badly. The money's for a caretaker they have now and again. He goes out there every once in a while to clear away the brush and start up the plumbing. The chimney's fallen. There are weeds growing up through the kitchen floor. The place is a ruin."

I pondered and was still; between us the wire soughed.

"And it used to be worth a hundred thousand dollars," said William's son.

"William told you that?"

"I tell you he told me all of it."

"All of it," I repeated doubtfully, docilely ("all" was Til-beck, Tilbeck was all), and in an instant, by a clairvoyant inspiration, in a vision of sympathetic comprehension, I was certain that William had told none of it.

Nevertheless I went along with it. I rounded it out. "Did he say what sort of a museum it was going to be?"

"He said a museum, that's all. According to the terms of the trust."

The terms of the trust: this already familiar phrase, humming with threats, now hung before me brilliantly, as though freighted with imagination. At that moment I thought William wonderful. William as fabricator and fabulist, William as author of a ruse! "They show the skeletons of whales," I triumphantly supplied. "And species of shrimp, in green bottles. A marine museum," I exclaimed, elated by perception, elated by invention.

"I knew you knew!" said William's son.

Privately I regarded it as fantastic that my imbrication upon William's construction, conceived in irony (it was my father I saw as a marine creature), should touch on the actual with all the delicate tenacity of a bivalve rooted in the shallows. A museum: and then, behold, I had made of it a marine museum—a thing not unlikely, for I had heard how my grandfather Huntingdon had furrowed through all the world's waters, a seafarer upon the luxury decks of ocean liners, and how, moreover, he had steamed eastward as far as the Indies to buy my mother's and William's wedding-present. Well then, a marine museum! And why not?—and "I knew you knew," William's son said again. "It's how I got him to tell. I said I'd get it out of *you* if he wouldn't. He didn't want *that!*"

William would hardly want that, thought I, since the tale William had given his son was no tale I knew. "I'm not easy to get things out of," was all I said—though fleetingly I speculated on just such a scene: William's son persuading, myself unyielding but secret in the chance joy of watching him persuade: the stern but remarkable bone of his nose and the imaginary helmet being all his means while all my admiration. I should not have objected to such persuasion, and I deviated sadly into a fresh summoning of his "encore un peu," murmured on the terrace into a yielding ear that had no French, but had the round beauty of a wreath instead.

"Neither is my father," he pursued, and, while I wondered —"easy to get things out of, I mean. Because he's *in* them."

"In what?"

"In things." He gave a little cough that came through the filter like a far queer birdcall. "He told me. Oh, he's *in* things, all right. I suppose you know it. He's *involved* is what I mean. I couldn't believe it. You know"—again the cry of the bird, cough or perhaps scanty laugh—"I always thought my father's nose was absolutely clean. Imagine, it's what I always thought. You always think that about your own father," he concluded hoarsely.

"Yes," I said, "you always do."

"It's funny how you find things out."

His smitten gravity called for a spectacularly original utterance. I changed ears nimbly. "Eventually," I observed, "everything comes out into the open."

He sounded positively chastened—the grand great buffalo with his head down, not for butting but for bathetic shame. "It was awfully fine of you not to say anything the other night," he burst out.

This puzzled me. "When do you mean?"

"In front of Stefanie. I don't say she's derived from a band of angels herself, but it's nothing I'd want her father to know. Not right now, at any rate. It really mattered to me," he wrung out gratefully. "You were really fine."

"Don't mention it," I said in a parody of neutrality, and we talked a little more, until it became quite plain that he was not going to ask me to go to the movies with him, or anything in that line: so I hung up soon enough.

Meanwhile I smiled to myself. In what fabrication or tale of shady dealings the guileless William had implicated himself it was beyond me to guess. It was enough to know that, for the sake of my mother, he had put off his son: and he had put him off with a lie. And yet not really, if what he had said were to be taken as metaphor and not invention. For the museum on Town Island, looked after so assiduously by my mother's checks, was Gustave Nicholas Tilbeck: and a man can be said to be a museum. Surely my father, constituting present evidence of a buried time, was a sort of museum—he housed matters which had to be dug after, collected bit by bit, and reconstructed. And William, as curator, had determined that the museum was to remain closed to the public, closed even to his son and prospective law partner. Whatever it was he guarded he must have considered either very horrible or very fragile—perhaps both, as, for instance, a shrunken head. He would do anything to prevent its exposure; he would even declare (if it might in some fashion appear helpful) that he was a headhunter himself.

But it made me hesitate. William as headhunter or trafficker in imprudence, William as liar, was unimaginable: here was a man who shunned novels on the ground that they are always fictitious. And yet he had defrauded his son of knowledge; what difference if it were the knowledge of evil? It was perhaps the first falsehood poor William had ever discharged in all his life. I could no longer regard him as incorruptible. The touch of greed carried far, it seemed; my father's touch carried far. It was not possible to conceal or elude it without defilement. I thought how money-lust spawns deceit even among mere watchers or bystanders, and saw my father as owning some iron god or demon nourished by the taste of purity and panting after innocents with his long iron tongue, licking them to rust and corrosion at last. This was one of the creatures, neither legendary nor extinct nor caged, who roamed about the halls of that museum which William had fearfully closed to the public, Gustave Nicholas Tilbeck's museum: the cost of the exhibit was too high, and the admission price was ferocious. What you paid was yourself. In order to get in you had to join the bad and dirty things on display: you had to change and be one of them. And William, who had entered and seen and learned how the rust of iron decays on the hands, and the rust of truth in the mouth, would not permit his son to enter, see, or learn.

Though I pitied William, I continued to smile: in trying to preserve his son's illusions (that man was not depraved, that no Gustave Nicholas Tilbeck existed), he had passed himself off for a cheat and a crook—and broke thereby the last illusion his son had retained in the world.

9

Early in the morning all the next week Enoch came out on the terrace to dictate to his secretary. He put his feet up on the railing and talked into the sky while I lay nearby, listening. It sounded like a military history or plan—there was mention of trenches, border-points, atomic warheads—but since the rivers were called X and Y, the towns Redplace, Whiteplace, and Greyplace, and the generals Tweedle and

Twaddle, it was impossible to know what part of the globe he was describing.

By Thursday Tweedle had advanced within three miles of Twaddle's encampment behind Whiteplace, and Twaddle was beginning to think of retreating.

On Friday, however, the young man reverted to delivery boy and carried away, one by one, four great boxes full of books. "That's as much boning up as I intend to do right now," Enoch said.

"Is it for the hearings?" I inquired. "All that reading?"

"One doesn't read for a purpose. One simply reads," he told me, affecting amusement.

"And the report?"

"There was no report."

"But you've been dictating for days."

"I never dictate. It's contrary to my temperament. I merely recommend." And he went in, smiling, to join my mother.

I did not accompany him; my mother's single wish was to avoid me. She had said she had hoped I would always live freely, and without perceiving her meaning I caught the guilty regret in her voice. Left alone on the terrace, I amused myself with guessing at her visions. I supposed, first of all, that she had schemed for me to become a cosmopolitan. "Always remember that you were born in Europe," she would remind me on the backs of picture postcards mailed at whim from the vortex of those falsely outrageous and half-secret parleys, congresses, and merely meetings that sprang like self-propagating plants in the path of her travels—"it is your lost continent," she would write, "enlarge character by recoupment of Europe" (the latter was rather like the operatic journalese of parts of *Marianna*), and occasionally I would recognize upon those rumpled three-color reproductions of aged citadels, photographed from helicopters and machine-painted with machine-vivid unreality, not simply the dry sheddings of her acquired and too-conscious myth—the romance that America cannot be "experienced" except through its sources—but also the vaguer significations of my mother's desire.

Her aim, I conjectured, was to re-father me. She had tried it with William, and I had acquiesced, impressed with William's substantiality. Her acknowledgment of her first husband's practical authority was the nearest my mother had ever brought me to any kind of religion, but she was not altogether mistaken in it, for William, with his sober inherited scruples, his cautious hook of jowl, and his pious distaste for all the things of this world except notes and bonds, which he somehow regarded as divine albeit negotiable instruments for good in the same way that he imagined capitalism to be the ordained church of the economic elect—this same deliberate William was one of that diminishing honor-guard of armored and ceremonial knights whose Presbyterianism is stitched into the orthodox width of their hat-bands, coat-lapels, and shoe-toes, and who preserve by its rites a creed which no longer exacts or enacts tenets. William was all my Protestantism; and if my mother, in atonement for my bad education and her own bad taste (I had once actually confused the Holy Ghost with a new kind of candy bar), had sent me to him for the sake of a patriarchal, as well as a paternal, judicature, poor William could hardly be blamed if in the name of that same Protestantism he had had to turn me away. Not William's own presumably more charitable bent, but rather the higher connivance of Christianity, prevented him from accepting that filial homage which my mother promoted in me: for she had always chosen to say "ask William," and "tell William," and "show William," while he withdrew in a sort of noble terror from the confidences and questionings of a child not his own—but his denial and his recoil were not wilful: they burgeoned out of the spirit of the integrity of the family (an abstraction which I quickly identified as a Protestant virtue), although it was clearly the integrity of his own family he meant (his preoccupation with ownership being a further example of a Calvinist probity). He believed unashamedly in the influence of private institutions. And if he was willing, as I have observed, to have Gustave Nicholas Tilbeck pass for an evil museum or palace of crime, a kind of still-alive Madame Tussaud's, then surely he would not have been reluctant to think of himself as a temple, or, at the very least, a minor but equally sacred outer chapel. Besides, William's wife hid behind kindness her plain dislike of me. Although she had no fear or envy of her husband's earlier bride (arguing logically enough that it was William, after all, who had wished for the divorce in the first instance and in the second for a woman like herself, devoted, spiritual even, who put candles on her dinner table every evening and garden-flowers in her vases every morning), it did not please her that William on his visits should encounter me so often in corridors and corners or the dark parts of stairways, where she imagined I must lurk like a process server with a summons or a creditor with a claim. Out of the most upright reservations, then, William had refused to become my custodian or my confessor. His Lares and Penates were against it; so was his whole morality; so was his wife.

After some time my mother ceased to summon William, and at last erased in me any look of claim. She gave up her hope of Puritanism with the shrewdness of a seer; she saw, in her politic way, that a temple can never supplant a museum: history has it the other way around—the friezes of the Parthenon turning up in Bloomsbury, bits of Scottish-Norman churches with ice-cream carts at the door. But no barbarian relic-gallery (even supposing there were such a thing, collected by some rich odd old Visigothic Rome-lover) has ever been replaced, within its own walls, by ecclesiastical paraphernalia, altars and elders and the rest—how then, in that singular time of Protestant rebuff, when William's costive integrities were shutting me out, how could my mother have dreamed that spires might sprout from the iron museum roof? or that Tilbeck's halberds might change into bishops' crosiers? She dreamed it mistakenly and therefore only briefly, and gave me Enoch instead. What Holiness might not undertake, said Enoch, Worldliness would.

PART TWO

EUROPE

1

And upon what Holiness cannot build, Worldliness is founded. Now when Holiness essays introspection and ends with self-deception, it gives birth to Worldliness. That moment when Holiness, with whatsoever good will, enters the museum hall—in the guise, oh, of the quaint artifact, grail shown under glass, for instance, or miracle-working saint's toe-bone displayed as remarkable (for new reasons, in a newer sense)—in that moment exactly Holiness dies, and in that moment exactly Worldliness inhales its expirations and lives.

—These aphorisms (for all their windiness I don't hesitate to call them that, for they were less than parables and more than mere turns of phrase) were Enoch's long ago, when my mother attempted to compensate me for the inaccessibility of Puritanism with its opposite, cosmopolitanism, which (I have already mentioned it) she liked to term the recoupment of Europe. And she equated Enoch with Europe, and carried me to France the very year the war ended, together with the refugee from Holland whom she had taken on as my governess, and stood with us at the border of Germany, a place where too many roads met, each infested with a line of abandoned tanks like enormous vermin—and there, while I writhed and vomited close by one of those great dusty tractor-wheels, full in the sight of a handful of unamazed Cockney infantrymen (afterward my mother learned that the country cow whose milk I had been given to drink had a disease), the Dutchwoman said, "I shall not go across there." And my mother complained, "But I'm married to a Jew, and I don't mind going across." We did not go across, but wan-

dered southward instead, pleasure-seekers among the displaced, hence more displaced than anyone—"I feel like a survivor," my mother said now and again, "I don't mean from
the war of course," while the Dutchwoman reached out for
me with strong freckled arms and, fiercely and privately,
trusting I would not betray her, whispered, "a survivor from
the age of governesses!"—before Hitler she had been a medical student at the University of Leyden. ("Yet she didn't even
ask whether the milk was pasteurized!" my mother fumed.
"She could have asked to have them boil it at least! I don't
approve of refugees, they have no sense of responsibility.")
So I was sick against a tank, and in the pit of that sickness,
while the pad of dust on the tank's steel belt swam spasmodi-
cally under my rain of filth, I heard my mother rail against
the unsanitary survivors of a war not yet three months dissolved into history.

For some reason—perhaps it was the laughter of the soldiers, guiding and advising me: "Puke on, darlin', lots of
muck on the Jerry barstid, 'ere naow 'aven't yuh missed a bit
of its bluddy foot?"—my mother felt compelled to explain
herself: *she* was a survivor, she made out, not of bomb and
blaze—one could always get over a *war,* and if one didn't
one was dead anyway and it didn't matter—in short she had
survived not mere catastrophe but a whole set of wrong
ideas. She had outlasted her moment and outlived her time.
All the ideals of her girlhood had betrayed her by unpredict-
ably diminishing; "see," she said, and pointed down one of
those many roads at a one-legged giant who had hobbled out
of the horizon, "that is what has become of the social consciousness of my generation." The Dutchwoman frowned so
horribly at this that I had another fit of retching. "I don't pay
you thirty-five dollars a week to poison my child," my mother
promptly admonished her, but she did not have her mind on
it: the maimed fellow had come into view and all of us—my
mother, the Dutch governess, the three Cockney infantrymen,
and I—looked on in fearful admiration as he swung himself
forward on a staff the thickness of a young tree. He was
burly and dark, and, for that place and season, not at all hag-
gard; he thrust a paper at the soldiers and propelled himself
over the border. " 'E'd got a pass from up back," said one of
the Cockneys. "Big for an I-talian," replied the second.
"They'd ought to get back where they cyme from, them
blowkes," observed the third, and then turned back to me

with a whistle: " 'Aven't yuh myde a job of't, girlie! It's all
the shype of the Mediterr-y-nian Owshin yuh've give up!"

And it was a kind of map I had spewed over the hem of
the German tank—a map made of vomit, with viscous seas
and amorphous continents, a Mediterranean of bad milk in
the heart of this known and yellowish world—not simply
known but precisely known, exactly and profoundly known
(although land and lake were joined and parted indistin-
guishably by a lava of wakened dust), known, memorized,
and understood, unmistakably and perilously known by its
terrific stink. My mother covered her face in disgust—"God
knows what was wrong with that damned cow," she mumbled, half stifled, into her glove, "it's like her to be sick and
make a stench," and pulled me back to the car. Although she
was not fond of me, the Dutchwoman, who during the final
eruption had been obliged to support my head, took my hand
almost kindly. The map had begun to drip off the tread, hung
with nuggets of mud. And then Africa succumbed, and then
the shadow of Asia, and then the vague Americas, and lastly
Europe gave way, split open by sudden rivers; the yellow
Mediterranean of milk overran them all, sucking up mass
after mass and sending out those reeking fetid familiar airs,
so that even the hardy Cockneys swore and moved away. "It
is not her fault," my governess quietly snarled; she had her
foot on the clutch. "It is the stink of Europe." One of the
soldiers pressed his nose in a music-hall gesture: the button
on his sleeve caught the sunlight and danced it up and down:
—his arm snapped up with a start. The bit of wire that
marked the border was all at once murmuring with tremor.
"What is it?" my mother cried hoarsely—"Did you hear?"
"The bluddy devil!" screeched the soldier, letting go his nose.
It came at us again just then—a sting of noise grave and
quick. The Dutchwoman had started the motor and was
slowly turning us, creeping off the gravel into the edges of a
blighted field, silent; our wheels grew muffled in grass. The
echo of the discharge lay embedded in the morning light as
punctiliously as a surgeon's gash. "Is it backfire?" said my
mother. "What *is* it?" She fretted at her fingernail as the car
righted itself in the road, and looked out behind her through
a small side window: "There it is again!" she exclaimed; the
precise little roar stuttered in the sky; the knobs on the dash-
board chattered. "Ah, they've gone over," she said, "look." I
looked, and in a queer detachment of motion seemed to see
the three Cockneys dangling like marionettes or hanged men

over Germany; beneath the three arcs of their simultaneous leaps the border-wire dimly strummed. They struck the ground a second afterward like felled game, all in a crouch; we watched them spring erect. "I think," said my mother in surprise, "it was a shot. It must have been a shot," she repeated, craning backward. The Dutchwoman did not stir. My mother swung open the door of the car and jumped decisively out. I followed her—suddenly I felt immensely better, not sick at all. The three infantrymen were running down one of those roads that fingered out like a candelabrum on the other side of the border. "They're chasing someone," my mother shouted excitedly. "Can you see him? It's that man without the leg." "No," said my governess from inside the car —resolutely her eyes shunned Germany; she kept her speckled hands on the wheel and would not move—"they are not chasing him. He has shot himself." But we saw him then, and the soldiers flying toward him, whipping dust but never coming nearer, as in a dream; he had gone far, that giant, farther than it appeared, for it took half a mile to diminish him, and when the soldiers had run themselves into midgets, still racing and yet no nearer, his big shadowy head continued to loom, and his staff seemed no less a leafless tree—it was as though they pursued the irreducible moon, or a god. He was fixed in the middle of the road, and the legless thigh rocked fitfully, kicking. "She's crazy," my mother sneered, "I see him now, I can see his stick in the air"—it swept the sky and seemed to writhe from his grasp and slipped like a straw to the ground, and the giant, with the shudder of cut-down tower or sail of ship, sank after it.

The three soldiers carried him back, each one bearing a single member. From the border-wire where we waited it was a strange triangle—first they took the head and the two arms, then they tried one of the arms, the good leg and the head, and after that the leg, the head, and the stump. But is was no use, the fellow was too heavy and big, they could not divide his weight properly in this fashion; the man who had the head was always at a disadvantage. At last they each took one of the three good limbs, and let the two shorter appendages, the stump and the head, hang down out of the way, with equal freedom and equal unimportance; and in this manner they struggled back to their station at the border.

"Ah," my mother muttered resentfully, "I didn't come to Europe for *this*." The body lay where the soldiers had heaped it; one was shouting into a walkie-talkie, and the two others

stood sweating and sighing, fumbling with their trousers,
rubbing their damp palms on their damp shirts. "On the far
side of the line," the shouter shouted, "in the groin, the cryzy
blowke. In the groin, darlin', I said groin," he went on yelling, "not spine, *groin*." We got back into the car and the
Dutchwoman drove as though whipping a horse; we cantered
into the white sun of noon. "You've dirtied your blouse," said
my mother, picking at my collar—"that putrid smell." She
opened her nostrils over the yellow stain, but her nose in meditation was as alien to me as the look of my own vomit. I
did not feel responsible. "Leave her be," said my governess in
her brutal accent, "when you are so near Germany there are
worse things to smell." My mother frowned warily—"What?"
"Corpses," said the Dutchwoman, kicking the flanks of the
gas pedal. "Well, well," said my mother, "you people like to
turn every stink into a moral issue. Can't you go any faster,
Anneke?" she demanded, unlocking her brows, although the
landscape flew. "The way you step on that pedal you'd think
you were a corpse yourself."

But it was, in a way, corpses which had brought us to that
place at that unlikely time, it was on account of corpses that
we were there at all: corpses and Enoch, who had been appointed an adviser to corpses, an amicus curiae with respect
to corpses, a judge, jury, witness, committeeman, representative, and confidant of corpses. He had no office, but went
wandering from boundary to boundary sorting out corpses,
collecting new sources of more corpses, overseeing and ad-
ministering armies of corpses. Some he yielded to their claim-
ants for burial, and some he had dug up and re-buried for no
plain reason, and some he let lie where they had been
thrown: he was a liaison between the dead and the living,
and between the dead and the dead, and between the soon-
dead and the too-soon dead. And he was a liaison among the
dead of all the nations. "In Europe" (in one hotel-room after
another his ironic growl would wake me between nightmares)
"there is only one united country, only one with unanimous
voters, a single party, an uncontradicted ideology, an egalitarian unhierarchical church, an awesome police-power . . ."
"Go to sleep, Enoch," I would hear my mother's whine, reprimanding out of the dark. "The country of the dead," he
gave out at last, and gave in, and fell asleep and snored,
gravely, like a hawk over carrion—until, in the morning (for
he hated to get up), "Wake up, Enoch"—this from my
mother—and then, "Wormy, wormy, wormy, early in the

mourning our curse shall rise to Thee"—this from Enoch, hymn-singing.

For at that time my mother still went everywhere with her husband. Sometimes we would all travel in a body—Enoch, my mother, the Dutchwoman, and I in the lead-car, and two cars full of Enoch's assistants following after—but more often I would be left behind with my governess to play on some littered and sorrowful beach, where I would amuse myself by searching for shells—not seashells: for the Dutchwoman had taught me how to dig after empty cartridges nesting just below the wet sand, like clams, at the margin of the water.

"Can't they explode?" my mother objected, handling my collection of shells at the end of a day's harvest. "If she happened to drop one? She shouldn't be allowed to keep them."

"They are empty and harmless," remarked my governess without interest.

"But there might be a good one mixed in with the others," my mother said, tying a veil over her hat; she was preparing to take a night train with Enoch to a city in the north, where a fresh shipment of corpses waited.

"They are all of them already exploded," repeated the Dutchwoman. "They have been used," she observed almost angrily.

"Oh, but you really can't be sure!" my mother reproved. It seemed she was angry too, and not at the cartridges. She sheathed her forefinger with one of them, tapping it like a thimble. "How can you be sure?"

"Because there has been a war, madam; there has been shooting," said the Dutchwoman.

"As though she owned the war!" my mother announced to the ceiling. "What a nuisance you are, Anneke—you aren't the only one who has had to take hardships, you know."

"Yes," said the Dutchwoman tonelessly, "we were told that in America the sugar was rationed. How bitter your tea must have tasted."

My mother pretended to laugh; her mouth drew wrathfully back. "You don't like Americans, Anneke."

"I don't like *you*, madam."

"I pay you for your duties, not for your approval." But my mother's mirth had turned inexplicably genuine: she was amused, up to a point, by aggressiveness in servants.—"After all," she used to say, "if they go *too* far one can always fire them."

The Dutchwoman was careful not to go too far; she valued
her position, since she had so little to do. While I ran about
in the foam, she would doze on the mossy rocks, and did not
care what I did, or whom I found for a playmate. A little
country boy, whose hair had been shaved off altogether and
whose red scalp shook out scales, gave me the ringworm;
patches round as pennies emerged on my hands and on my
chin, and my armpits itched intolerably. But the Dutchwoman declared that I had touched poison-ivy leaves against her
warning, and I never contradicted her to my mother. Often
she took me to eat in dim restaurants black with flies where
there were no tablecloths or menus, and the food was so unfamiliar that I felt ill at the sight of it—brown and green
sauces under which chunks of white fat lay folded in a bath
of grease. All the while my mother believed that we dined on
the boulevard, and made alarmed noises over the restaurant
bills my governess used mysteriously to produce. But still the
Dutchwoman was careful, very careful. "If you say one
word," she would threaten me, "Mrs. Vand will send me
away, and you will be left alone. Soon you will lose your way
in the roads, and they will mistake you for a refugee child,
they will put you in a camp for refugee children. Then you
will contract a disease among all the sick little Jewesses. Afterward they will send you far away to Palestine where you
will die in the desert of thirst."

"But I'm not Jewish," I protested. "And I'm not afraid of
being thirsty, Anneke; I hate milk anyhow since it made me
sick."

"Milk! You'll beg for water the way you begged for fake
Coca-Cola on the boulevard today. Or else," she went on
menacingly, "you will be shot before the Wailing Wall by a
firing-squad from Arabia. Why not, since your father is Jewish?"

"Enoch isn't my father!" I cried, exuberant with relief.
"He hasn't even been married to my mother very long—that
makes him only my stepfather, you see, Anneke?"

The Dutchwoman chortled scornfully. "Did you think I'm
so stupid not to understand that? But still you do not know
who your real father is. What makes you sure *he* isn't a Jew?
Do you think they will spare you when they find out that?
No, I warn you, confide to your mother how you rubbed
Jean François' contagion and off you go to Palestine."

Thereafter I could be relied on absolutely.

"She's loyal to you," my mother stated firmly, in frequent

recognition of my governess' success with me. "The child is devoted, although she seems so cold. But she's cold even to me, without showing half so much loyalty, so what am I to expect? If not for that, I should have dismissed you long ago. I'll be frank with you, I can't bear a surly temperament. Of course you're not paid to like me, I don't say that. But at least you ought to conceal your bigotry."

"Bigotry?" the Dutchwoman sneered innocently. "I do not know that word."

"Don't you? It comes of being so conceited. It's a good thing you didn't finish at that medical school. You would have made a very bad doctor. You would have cared more for your own prestige than for anything," my mother noted with the acuteness of complacency.

"I had already chosen my field," the Dutchwoman said abruptly. "It was chemical research—I should not have liked to practise. But then haven't I told you how the German soldiers were billeted in our laboratories? They closed the school, and it did not matter what I liked." She shrugged and eyed my mother's pocketbook. "When is madam coming back?"

"Not for a week at least. It depends on the size of the job my husband finds up there. We're going to Normandy for some sort of ceremony afterward. It's to commemorate the invasion. You know it will all be as boring as the grave, full of speeches in atrocious English by foreign generals, but *c'est la guerre,* it can't be helped."

"The war has made many new positions," the Dutchwoman remarked quietly.

"You mean in relief work? Enoch is not in relief work. Unless you count burial as relief. I suppose it is, for the dead."

"No, I was thinking of my own position," said the Dutchwoman, looking first at me and then again at the pocketbook.

"My husband regards his corpses as displaced persons. He's very sympathetic toward them. His aim, you know, is to have the murderer lie down with the murdered. It's a kind of prophetic view. But in almost every case it can't be done. All the murderers are still alive, it seems."

"Mr. Vand is full of sayings," the Dutchwoman said slyly.

"He's a clever man," my mother agreed. "I just wish he'd exert himself a little with the child. I brought her out here expressly for that, but he won't take the trouble."

"Perhaps he is too busy," said the Dutchwoman accommodatingly.

"He holds a very high post," my mother persisted. "He is devoted to his work."

"Yes," the Dutchwoman affirmed in a very soft voice, smiling fixedly, "grave-digging nowadays leaves time for nothing else."

"That doesn't sit right with me, Anneke, you are too arrogant," my mother warned.

"But it is all meant in good faith, madam. The Americans have bureaucratized even grave-digging. It will be done much faster by the Americans. Your husband will see to it."

"My husband has great administrative capacity," my mother petulantly defended herself. "He has a kind of political genius. In fact," she concluded proudly, "he's often mistaken for a European on that account."

"What a shame," observed the Dutchwoman, slyer now than before, "that his present job is not political."

"There is no job today that is not political," my mother said. "It's only the dead who can afford to have no politics."

"That is another of Mr. Vand's sayings, isn't it? He is so clever it is a shame really," my governess repeated, "that he has no political influence. Perhaps that is why he is thought to be a European."

My mother blazed. "He has influence enough."

"He would do nothing for my brother. My brother was deported for underground activities. He has three children and speaks seven languages. Now he is an orderly in a hospital in Amsterdam. Mr. Vand would do nothing for him."

"There are already too many interpreters."

"Last month there was a position open. I heard Mr. Vand speak of it to you. But it came to nothing."

"Perhaps your brother did not qualify."

"No," said the Dutchwoman, "he did not qualify. They would take only an American. So many of the refugees are Polish, and the American did not know Polish. In spite of it they chose him."

"You don't understand, Anneke," my mother protested. "My husband's organization is merely an arm of the Government. It isn't in his hands to make policy."

"Of course," the Dutchwoman concurred, still steadily smiling. "That is precisely what I said. He has no political importance whatever."

"You cannot belittle Enoch Vand," my mother retorted.

"Perhaps you should measure his importance by the number of people he has it in his power to dismiss. I have some importance myself in that respect. Be careful, Anneke, or I'll decide to show my importance in a way you would not like."

I looked up from my shells in alarm, but my mother's speech did not appear to have frightened my governess. "Certainly," she resumed amicably, "nowadays you Americans decide everything. But the child would not like you to send me away. It would not be good for the child."

"Nevertheless," said my mother, but there was no real menace in her voice any more. She opened her pocketbook and took out a wallet. "Do you want your wages now or when I come back?"

"Now," said Anneke without hesitation.

"You had better get rid of those shells."

"Yes, madam."

"See that you obey your governess," my mother admonished me.—Outdoors the chauffeur's horn called.—"Goodbye."

I did not answer. "Goodbye," said the Dutchwoman generously, pushing me forward to be kissed.

My mother bent to me quickly; I saw her tense stretched nostrils. She steamed with toilet-water. "My husband will be Ambassador some day," she stated, and went out without rancor to her car.

The Dutchwoman was counting bills and folding them one by one into a little purse. "That will be a great jump from the burial committee. Here," she said, and threw me a five-franc piece.

"Anneke, I want to keep my shells."

She was at once serious. "I'll show you where to find more," she offered promptly, "if you promise to stay in the room by yourself tonight."

"You know I'm not supposed to be left alone," I reminded her.

"If I swear not to tell Mrs. Vand?"

She gave me another coin, light and smooth as a wafer, and we shook hands on the bargain.

In the evening she went away wearing a blue dress and a yellow band in her hair, and did not come back until morning.

"Were you afraid?"

"No," I said bravely, "but there were noises."

"When you sleep there are no noises. Tonight you must be sure to sleep."

"Are you going away again?"

"I have to spend the night with a friend. Come," she urged, "I know a new place near the sea wall where there are cartridges."

But I had a dream, and saw a thing with ochre eyes and a brass tail which ended in a dagger; monster-like it leaped through the window and rattled its metal forelock on the metal bedpost: and I screamed in my sleep and woke the concierge's husband, although he was somewhat deaf.

All the keys trembled on his great steel ring, and his teeth were ridged with gold, and his tongue churned the spittle in the forest of his lip-hairs. But I understood nothing. And so the concierge came down the corridor in her coffee-smelling robe, rubbing her glasses with the vigor of suspicion; and very slowly and loudly, as though I were the one who was deaf, she questioned me. "Où est Madame Vand?" "Elle est partie pour le nord," I said in the French I had learned from the children on the beach. "Et ta soeur?" "Je n'ai pas de soeur." "Ah! Une gouvernante!" "Oui," I replied. "Où est-ce qu'elle est?" "Je ne sais pas." "Est-ce que ta gouvernante est sortie de la maison?" "Oui." At this information the concierge assessed her husband's considerable mustache with a look of disgust. "Ah, nous y violà!" she shrieked. "Quand est-ce qu'elle va venir?" "Je ne sais pas," I said again; "la nuit passée elle est venue à . . . à six heures du matin." "C'est ca!" mumbled the husband, "pas de chance," as though it were all up to his wife, and while the key-ring dangled and jangled from the crook of his knuckle they went on conferring sibilantly. Finally the concierge prodded my pillow with her fat squat fingers; it was the motion of a judge with his gavel. "Qu'est-ce que ton père fait?" she demanded with a terrifying solemnity; and because I did not know the word for stepfather, I answered as though Enoch were really what she thought him: "Mon père est fonctionnaire," I said in the phrase I had often heard Anneke use on the boulevard. "Américain," the concierge conceded in triumph, and waggled the tassel of her belt at her husband: "Le grand malheur! Alors, de quoi te plains-tu?" And I saw from the swagger of their departing backs that they were satisfied: Monsieur Vand was good for the rent-money; an abandoned child had not been left on their hands after all.

The Dutchwoman returned with the daylight; I had not slept the whole night. She went to the window and stood

veiled by the early glimmer, pulling at the ribbon which had
raveled in her hair; and while she leaned, her elbows on the
sill and her fingers working invisible as submarines in the
short tough snarls, it seemed she listened, as for footsteps; but
only the faint knocking of a chain, and then the rocking of a
quick bicycle on cobblestones came up to us from the street.
I lay amazed: there were long creases in her dress, and long
creases in her cheek carved by the wrinkles of some alien
bedsheet: the side of her face was grooved like the belly of a
beach against which the tide has repeatedly shouldered, and
the red dawn lit into bright shallow scars the fluted skin. She
was, for the moment, qualified by some private act or notion—
an ugliness new in the world had mounted her and reigned
in the ruts in her flesh and in the swift sly receding clangor
of the bicycle and in the secret morning.

She began to hum, rolling down her stockings.—"Anneke?" I ventured.

"Are you awake?" She looked over crossly. "Go back to
sleep. It's too early."

"The concierge was here, Anneke."

"What?"

"The concierge—"

"In the middle of the night? What did you tell her?"

"I said you would come back in the morning."

"Now you have done it! Listen, if your mother should find
out—"

"Oh, I won't tell her, I promise!"

"The concierge will tell her. Now I am finished."

"Ah, no, Anneke," I moaned under her fierce palms loosened from their lair; they hung against my face, broad and
retributive and racy with an oiled nighttime odor and the distinguishable smells, like fog and ash, of her hair; and in the
warm pale hearts, sentencing and consigning me, of the
palms of her hands I seemed to see those deserts of Palestine,
warm and pale, hot and white, laden with drifted sand like
salt.

In the afternoon, although the sun poured honey, we did
not go down to the sea. It was my penalty. The Dutchwoman
took up my box of shells and flung it into an iron barrel,
filled half with kitchen refuse and half with rain-water, that
loomed in the yard behind the concierge's rooms, busy with
flies; innumerable foul splashes of rust leaped up and scattered their thousand wings into the dread colonial airs ("irretrievable, irretrievable," roared the gypped black carousing

flies)—"If you had cherished each one like the separate gems
of a treasure I should do the same," she announced with the
bitter strength of justice: "I do only what your mother
wishes." And now everything must be explained to the concierge (how mild my punishment compared to that!), who
was snooper, intruder, prevaricator, twister, telltale—everything must be set out straight. "The foolish child," the Dutchwoman took up, "she had a bad dream. What a pity, the very
hour I was called away."

The concierge made a noncommittal sound against her
upper palate. From the porch of the house the far waves
flickered.

"On such short notice it was impossible to get a nurse . . .
the doctor had to ask me for the night—"

"Exactly what is the matter with your friend?" inquired the
concierge with dry civility.

"A serious disease, poor thing."

"*Quel dommage!*" The concierge neatly bit off a hangnail.
"Will she live?"

"With God's help," the Dutchwoman said piously.

"Let us pray the disease is not of a contagious nature," remarked the concierge, outdoing my governess in solicitous re-
ligiosity by crossing herself briefly; but her voice seemed
oddly cool.

I thought I would placate them both by a show of concern
equal to their own. "Anneke," I gave out penitently, "does
your friend have the ringworm?"—remembering the torments
of poor Jean François.

"No, it is something else."

"Does her head itch?" I pursued nevertheless.

The concierge howled. "*Voilà!*" She slapped her shinbone
as though in the presence of a stupendous joke. "You have
the right idea, but the wrong end," she went on boisterously
cackling, and took her hilarity into the house.

"Sssstupid alleycat!" hissed the Dutchwoman after her.
"Rotting eye of a fisssh!" And when she turned to glare at
me, her mouth was wild and wishful as though it had tasted
quarry.

Some days afterward Enoch and two of his assistants arrived quietly in a mild brown car. "Your mother stopped in
Paris on the way down," he told me. "Her car's smashed up
—she had an accident. The chauffeur was injured, and she's
gone to see about the insurance."

"And Mrs. Vand?" said my governess with a disapproval faintly discernible. "Madam is all right?"

My stepfather looked surprised. "Of course she's all right. She's coming the rest of the way by train.—Meanwhile I have some paperwork to take care of. I may as well do it here as anywhere, since it's on the way."

"On the way where?" I wondered.

"Zürich. We're due there day after tomorrow."

"Is my mother going too?"

"It's up to her," he said, and threw me one of his rare amused visionary smiles: "Do I ever know what she'll do? Not until it's too late, you can bet on that."

The men retired to my mother's room, where the concierge had set up half a dozen card tables; and all afternoon the two assistants, light-haired bashful earnest young men, drew meticulous marks on yellow form-sheets, while Enoch, reclining elbow-deep in mimeographed documents as thick as Russian novels, disputed with them in a clatter of alien syllables.

"What language is that?" I asked the Dutchwoman.

"Don't eavesdrop," she chided me, although she was plainly listening herself: the windows were open and the dark and serious voices of the men fell to the garden. We lay in the shade of the eaves on a strip of blue canvas. The Dutchwoman took off her sunglasses—she had been peering into an old stained American picture-weekly in which my sandals had been wrapped. "It is Czech and Rumanian and Polish and Hungarian and German."

"Do they know all those languages?" I marveled.

"They are reading lists of names.—Where are you going?" she broke off. "You are not to bother Mr. Vand!" She snatched after me, but I left her pinching air and faintly calling, and when I gained the threshold of my mother's chamber her cries had grown too dim to matter, or too indifferent.

"Well, come in," said Enoch, absorbed and aloof.

"We heard you in the garden," I began.

The two young men lifted their fountain pens curiously, watching Enoch.

"What are those names?"

Enoch did not reply.

I tried again. "Whose names are you looking at?"

"Everybody's," said the first assistant.

"Europe's," said the second assistant.

"Nobody's," said Enoch. "They are all dead."

"I saw a man shoot himself," I readily offered, "once when I was throwing up. He had only one leg."

Enoch tamely viewed me. "That's better than none."

"But he died," I countered, as though that were some sort of argument. "In the road. Anneke saw it too."

"Well, it's what your mother brought you for," he broke out in his businesslike way, folding and unfolding a leaf spotted with black numbers; under the little table his impatient feet turned caustically outward. "In America everybody has two legs. She wanted you to be enriched," he said, clinging to the last word disconsolately; I wondered if it were a bit of mimicry.

In any case it reminded me of my pocket. Smugly I felt in there. "Anneke gave me ten francs," I boasted. "I still have three. I bought Coca-Cola."

"As a state of being childhood has nothing to recommend it," Enoch murmured, and lifted, without assurance of comfort, one of those great volumes crowded with death.

"Well, it's temporary," one of his assistants gave out just then.

The air seemed discommoded. Enoch seized the moment. "That depends." His big brown head fell forward on his page like a statue tumbling down. His hair had already begun to grow sparsely: it made him look like a Julius Caesar bare of laurel. He creaked around to face his young men as though discovering a pair of intruders—"Go on," he ordered, and set them to work again by the elevation of a single finger.

"Lev Ben-zion Preiserowicz," intoned the first assistant.

"Auschwitz," answered the other.

"Wladzia Bazanowska."

"Belsen."

"Schmul Noach Pincus."

"Buchenwald," came the echo, slow as a thorn.

"Velvel Kupperschmid."

"Dachau," the voice fell like an axe.

"Wolfgang Edmund Landau-Weber."

"Buchenwald," the reader yawned.

"Roza Itte Gottfried."

"Belsen," said Enoch's young assistant, picking at his teeth with an ivory thumbnail.

They went on in this manner unremittingly; I was soon bored. It was like what I imagined prayer to be, full of attack and ebb, flow and useless drain, foolish because clearly nobody heard, neither deaf heaven nor the dry-lipped deafer communicants; it was in short a sad redundant madrigal, droned out for its own sad sake, and all those queer repugnant foreign names, cluttering the air without mercy, seemed pointless, pushy, offensive, aggressive, thrusting themselves unreasonably up for notice: I thought of the flies spraying out from their barrel of filth, whipping wing-noises as savage as the noises of these wingless graceless names. "Itsaak Lazar Chemsky," said the first young man, smoothing his creamy mustard hair, tugging now and then at his constricting too-hot tasteful tie: and "Rivka Czainer," he said, and "Mottel Yarmolinski, Chaya Tscherniknow, Dvora-gittel Langbeiner," he said, "Pesha Teitelbaum, Janek Kedlacki, Sholem Shlomo Pinsky, Yoneh Hillel Yarmuk," he said, and the sun slunk lower into the room while the concierge came and went with coffee cups; and he said "Maishe Lipsky, Dovid Ginsberg, Kalman Dubnitz," and still the list was not exhausted; and the other had his list, but it was even more soporific, the same sounds again and again and again, Dachau, Belsen, Auschwitz, Buchenwald, the order varying, Auschwitz, Buchenwald, Belsen, Dachau, now and then an alteration in the tick and swing, Belsen, Maidenek, Auschwitz, Chelmo, Dachau, Treblinka, Buchenwald, Mauthausen, Sovibar—tollings like the chorus of some unidentifiable opera of which I could remember the music but not the import—and all the while Enoch sat spitting on his thumb and crackling the hides of those book-thick blotty documents, heaped like masonry, through which he drove his indefatigable pen.

After a time I broke through their chant and counterpoint. "If they are all dead why do you keep their names?"

"To have a record," said the first assistant.

"To arrange for the funerals," said the second assistant.

"For no reason in the world," said Enoch, and peeled from his shoulders a finely-rolled shrug. He blinked at me portentously. "Smoke leaves no records and cinders don't have funerals." It was one of those futuristic or apocalyptic statements which were his habit; his tone diagrammed a moon-surface, pitted and piteous, burning incomprehensibly into eternity. It was a reminder of his perpetual dialogue, of his idolatry even: he was always addressing some image or apparition or muse, perhaps Clio, perhaps some crazed Goddess of the Twentieth Century whom he had given up appeasing, and could only malign.

The others detected his calumny, and, without recognizing it as a sort of worship, supposed it to be the ill-temper of an ad-

mirable eccentricity. It made them shy of him, yet imitative.
They were grave and diffident youths, yet not without the
sing-song of fancy: they gazed at me full of secret teasing.
And they wrinkled their papers with an obliging and casual
horror, plainly believing that Enoch apostrophized, if not
themselves, then merely Death: and all in the manner of a
man possessed of scorn. But Enoch was forty then, immured
in careerism and beyond romanticizing death. He did not
think (as they did): Lethe. For him it was instead (a thing
for them impossible), briskly, brutally: slaughter. He was
well past Lethe, and well past Nepenthe, and far past the
Styx or Paradise. He took it all as simple butchery, and a demeaning waste of time to poetize. What he put down in those
immense ledgers was, I suppose, notations on his creed: perhaps he thought of himself as a scholar-saint, Duns Scotus or
maybe Maimonides, feeding data to his goddess as others
swing censers or take ashen thumbprints on their brows—he
gave her what he could. She might have been, as I have said,
History; or, what is more probable, the grim-faced nymph
Geopolitica, wearing a girdle of human skin and sandals sin-
ewed and thonged by the sighs of dead philosophers. She
might even have been Charity, although that is less plausible.
Still, whoever she was, he vilified her roundly; his imprecations were sly but to the point. He cursed her for the smoke
and the cinders and the corpses, and pleaded for the Evil In-
clination and the Angel of Death jointly to carry her off; but
she remained. I wonder how he saw her, whether all gold and
Greek and comely, or hideously whorled and coiled with intellect. Howsoever it was, he was himself her cultist, he had
succumbed, she owned him absolutely. She had achieved terror, power, majesty, the throne and crown and sceptre and
sway and seat of his mind—seizures, above all, of genius.
Perhaps he conceived of it all as the old wearisome affair
called getting ahead, or making a career, or driving on, or
reaching for the topmost rung—whichever phrase the moment favored—and did not meditate on those fabled pursuits,
Argonauts after golden fleece, Israelites after Zion, which
were like his own. He pursued: the others knew that he pursued, and imagined (as surely my mother imagined) it was
promotion, a better classification, more men under him,
something reckonable and recognized, that made him pant—
in short, the future. And he could not confess for the sake of
whom or what he dug down deep in those awesome volumes,
sifting their name-burdened and number-laden leaves as soil

is spaded and weighted in search of sunken graves and bones
time-turned to stone—he could not say or tell. That apparition (image? vision?), succubus barnacled to his brain, was
a cunning mist there in my mother's room where Enoch
leaned brooding among the paper remnants of the damned:
the lists and questionnaires, the numbers and their nemeses;
every table spread with the worms' feast; the room a registry
and bursary for smoke and cinders. Over it all his goddess
hung. If she wore a pair of bucklers for her breasts, they
gleamed for him and shimmered sound like struck cymbals;
if slow vein-blood drooped like pendants from her gored ears,
they seemed to him jewels more gradual than pearls—she
formed herself out of the slaughter; the scarves and winds of
smoke met to make her hair, the cinders clustered to make
her thighs; she was war, death, blood, and spilled the severed
limbs of infants from her giant channel in perpetual mis-
births; she came up enlightened from that slaughter like a
swimmer from the towering water-wall with his glorified face;
she came up an angel from that slaughter and the fire-whi-
tened cinders of those names. She came up Europa.

Europa: so my mother was right. She had desired for me
the recoupment of Europe, by which she plainly meant conversion; and she had borne me purposefully and hopefully to
the scorched plain, all the while swearing to castles and
cathedrals, and seizing like a missionary on those improbable
doctrines of hers, those feudal sentimentalities of tapestry and
cloister, rubric and falcon, shrine and knight's tomb, as
though she imagined spells lay inchoate in that old stained
soil. She had brought me to see the spires of those places,
quick as scimitars, and minarets like overturned goblets, and
the domes, windows, and pillars of those exhausted groves;
also icons rubbed beyond belief; and moats flushed with
mold; and long vaporous seacoasts; and portraits of shallow-
necked ancient ladies with small ringed hands; and, by the
hundreds, mild madonnas suckling. We were bare and blank,
by comparison, at home; we were all steel. So she brought
me to those points of germination, in fact to her idea of civilization, as savage as anyone's: and she promised from this
fountain of the world (she called it life, she called it Europe)
all spectacle, dominion, energy, and honor. And all the while
she never smelled death there.

Enoch and Europe: she saw them as one, and in Enoch
saw plainly a capacity for spectacle, dominion, energy and
honor—and more, a kind of command without speculation,

an unbrooding place-oblivion that breathed Europe as though
Europe were a gas more natural to him than any air. And all
the while she never thought what that gas might be; she saw
him dizzied by it, driven by it, claimed and owned by it; and
all the while she never thought what that gas might be,
dreamed it as some sort of nimbus to praise him, or film to
gild or tissue to adorn him, or lens (cloth-of-gold, wing of
butterfly) through which he glimpsed rare and secret refrac-
tions of the Europe she desired, secret and brilliant incarna-
tions of her illusions. And all the while she never smelled
death there, or thought what that gas might be.

But it was deathcamp gas, no nimbus, that plagued his
head and drifted round his outstretched arm and nuzzled in
the folds of his trouser-cuffs and swarmed from his nostrils to
touch those unshrouded tattooed carcasses of his, moving in
freight cars over the gassed and blighted continent.

So my mother was both right and wrong: right because,
through a romantic but useful perspicacity, she had penetrated the cloud of power that brightly ringed her husband,
and guessed how Europe had mastered him; and wrong, at
the same time deeply wrong in thinking it was *her* Europe to
which he was committed and had given himself over, her Europe of spectacle, dominion, energy and honor, a Europe
misted by fame and awe. And all that while my mother did
not smell the deathcamp gas. She wondered that Enoch was
not a stranger in those places and among those deeds; but she
could not smell the deathcamp gas welling from his eyes. She
saw him overwhelmed, and thought it was by ambition; she
saw him dedicated, and thought it was to his advancement;
she saw him absorbed, and thought it was in his career in
government. But she did not see the goddess: that Europa
who had engulfed him with her pity and her treasons and her
murderous griefs, and her thighs of cinders and her hair of
smoke, and her long, long fraud of age on age, and her
death-choked womb.

It was not merely that the goddess in her dark shapes was
invisible, for my mother was used to the invisible; she entertained ariels of her own, and could readily exchange one
magic for another, and would have celebrated distress and
decay and eery hopelessness (even trading in spectacle, dominion, energy, and honor) if only someone had taken the
trouble to point out their withered elegances: she was not
blunt to beauty's divers opportunities. It was not, then, that
my mother, with all her cunning and all her inspiration, was

incapable of seeing or imagining who or what had him in thrall—what violent figure, what vast preoccupation, what preying *belle dame sansi merci* (she was bold enough for these and anything). It was precisely his thralldom that escaped her. No goddess eluded Allegra Vand; she failed rather to catch hold of Enoch himself. She did not suspect the priest and cultist in him: how then could she picture icons round his halls? She did not guess that he worshipped because she did not think him accessible to the devotional impulse. About Enoch she was quite stupid; she was quite mistaken; she blundered into ironies. To amuse himself, he compounded them. She could not take him in, as she had taken in William entire, turning exact assessment into a devouring. Did she wish to re-father me? (Ah, that stark and persistent notion of hers.) Very well; he made bad-mannered noises and hoped the while I would always emulate his example. And did she wish him to strike in me Europe's lovely note? He clangored his lists of the murdered. Did she wish him to be for me what William was not? He obliged her by being profane.—It was clear that she had carried me from the disaffected William to fling me at a misconceived Enoch: from Homo Puritanus, as she supposed it, to Secular Man. And, mocking her error, he went at his secularity with the fanaticism of a preacher bursting into homilies. Then began the grand burlesque of those burgeoning aphorisms: "What Holiness would not undertake," he avowed, damning and deriding William for his finicky lawyerish hesitations concerning my moral education, "Worldliness shall"—and my mother watched in pleased innocence as he thumbed his breast with gusto. And then, rapidly following, he would bellow all those other maxims on the subject which I have already recorded: Upon what Holiness cannot build, When Holiness essays introspection, That moment when Holiness with whatsoever good will . . . and further confessions of Homo Profanus, Worldliness Incarnate, Cosmopolitanism Idealized, the Adam of Europe fallen into Paradise. But still my mother did not hear the brittle mirth in those saws and convolutions. And all the while freight-trains scratching on bomb-twisted tracks howled out of the east with a cargo of tatooed corpses for Enoch the Secular Man; and racing from border to border he said aloud to his wife (who thought it very clever of him), "The house of death hath many mansions"; and in the privacy of his intellect he lit centuries and burned history to hallow his intemperate goddess. My mother was deaf to his iro-

nies and did not dream she traveled with a man anointed. In
short, she missed the whole sense of his character.

It was the reason they got on.

2

All the next day the Dutchwoman continued to keep to the
garden. She had moved away from the cooler shadow of the
eaves, where hour after hour Enoch's cruel syllables dropped
with the sadness of rain, stifled sometimes by little jokes—we
could not always hear them—and now and again by the distinct quick din of the young men's laughter.

"He had his mother cremated," one of them said. "He
thought it was rather a nice idea."

"Come off it, will you? Go blow."

"No, it's a fact. I read it. It's in a letter to Mrs. Patrick
Campbell."

"What do you expect? Shaw, that nut. He didn't eat meat."

"All the more reason not to cook his own mother."

They tittered and sneered: but the Dutchwoman sat on a
wooden kitchen chair under a roseless rosebush and ground
her feet vengefully in the fallen petals.

"Ah, those." She waved contemptuously up at the napes of
their pale heads in the window. "If your stepfather had room
for those, certainly there was a place for my brother. My
brother speaks seven languages, he carries bedpans in a hospital, they pay him nothing . . ." She stared at me severely
and held up a triumvirate of fingers like flags. "My brother
has one, two, three babies. Mr. Vand has no care for that."
One by one, counting, she lowered her angry masts, and
strained after the clatter of a bicycle invisible beyond the garden gate. "He has no care for *you*," she spat out finally.

The concierge's husband stood on a ladder clipping the overgrown stalks of a tall hedge. He worked very slowly, calling
down to us bits of his biography: his old man's veins swelled

in his wrist each time the shears snapped. He twitched his mustache and talked about his wife. She was a fine woman, he said, industrious and strong; she was not even bad-looking. When they were married he had been a bachelor of sixty-three—the property, of course, was his, and although his wife was nearly twenty years younger than he, she had not a thing to complain of. Meanwhile the hedge took on the shape of an eagle or an angel: the wings hunted up the sunlight, and he went on snipping away at the head. He was a plain soul, he said, his tastes were very plain, he didn't ask for much out of life (and sure enough, it turned out to be only a duck), he had always lived in the country, he did not like running a pension, there were too many worries, the boarders seemed to think clean towels grew on trees—this was not to deny that his wife was very capable, always on the watch for the benefit of all—still, the town had decayed, it wasn't what it used to be before the war. There were too many bad characters.

The Dutchwoman took out a pair of little scissors from her pocket and began to peck at her nails with it. She spread out her mole-dappled hands and methodically manicured each one, stopping to watch the arch of each brittle sliver of nail as it clicked off into the air. Nearby on his ladder the concierge's husband copied her: first he cut and then he meditated on the uncertain descent of each severed stalk.

"Bad characters," he repeated, scowling as though he knew a secret; he scattered green tail-feathers and pared the leafy bill of his fowl, wielding his slow shining blades until the garden hissed with their iterated bite.

"Old ox!" muttered my governess. "Close your teeth, dotard!" For a moment she winked up at the sun-crowded figure of the duck, which was now riding a freshly-scalloped crest, and was reassured by the sculptor's delighted nod that at this distance he really was deaf enough.

"They ruin the town and empty the pensions," said the concierge's husband in an excessively loud voice.

"May the birds leave dung in your white hairs," replied the Dutchwoman, going at her thumb with fervor.

"No one will come where there is a bad reputation," shouted the concierge's husband.

"May your nights be as sweet as what you make in your pants!" the Dutchwoman shrieked back. "May your parts shrivel seven times in every week!"

And they went on clipping companionably away, the two of them, my governess and the old man, so intently that neither heard my mother's high heels on the cobblestones behind the hedge.

"The arrogance of that station driver!" she cried, thrusting open the gate. "He left me at the bottom of the hill, bag and all. The road wasn't good enough for him because they ration his tires! Lord knows I paid him enough, and the worst of it is he's right, there isn't a decent road from here to . . . The Garden of Atropos!" she broke off, wheeling round to confront me. "Put that thing down. She shouldn't be allowed to play with that, Anneke, she'll slice herself in two."

I had found a sickle under the rosebush and was swiping at the grass with it.

"Put it down," said the Dutchwoman obediently, "you will behead someone. Was the accident very bad, madam?"

"Well, the chauffeur had a concussion, but the trip back on the train was worse. I don't know which was thicker, the soot or the mob. There must have been a dozen people in the one compartment—half of them were Algerians. It was like riding in the coal car. I'm dirty as an Arab myself. How I hate these French trains! They're worse now—if you can imagine it—than before the war."

"And Armand?" inquired my governess.

"I went with him in the ambulance. They had me filling out forms all the way to the hospital. I didn't have a scratch on me, but it didn't matter—they have a form for everything, you know—and all the witnesses had to sign too. But they might almost have questioned Armand as me—believe it or not, he was conscious all the way!"

The Dutchwoman slipped the little scissors back into the pocket of her smock. "How strange," she murmured.

"Oh, but a brain concussion doesn't necessarily knock you *out*, you know," my mother declared with the authority of one who knew no more of medicine than to daub iodine on a skin-scrape.

"No: I meant about Armand. He is always so cautious."

"I know, and it's a nuisance when you're in a hurry. The roads south were full of military traffic, and he *wouldn't* pass—"

"They will keep him in the hospital for long?"

"I didn't have time to inquire—I had to find out about the insurance, it's all so complicated over here. It kept me dashing from one end of Paris to the other, and I couldn't make head or tail of it anyway, so I wired William—my lawyer, you see, in New York. He'll work it out somehow. As it is,

I'm two days late getting back, and all on that chauffeur's account. I didn't want to miss driving to Zürich with Enoch. He hasn't left yet?" she finished anxiously.

"No." My governess shook her head gravely. "Mr. Vand is here. He is in the house."

"I can't say how glad I am. I need to talk to someone sensible. I've been harassed—actually harassed. That man lay there on that stretcher and just kept glaring and glaring up at me from out of those bandages they'd wound him in. It was terrible. He couldn't get out a word of course, but it was an accusation all the same. And afterward he blamed me right to the doctor's face."

"I have never seen a better driver," said Anneke, affecting deep interest. It appeared she very much wished to please my mother; she had put away all her insolence. "He sits behind the wheel with great confidence. I had often noticed it."

"He had no confidence to speak of just before we crashed, let me tell you! He was jittery, and that made *me* jittery—"

The Dutchwoman wondered. "You?"

"Well, at the rate we were going it was plain we'd never get back in time"—my mother seemed to hesitate—"so I made him shove over and I took the wheel myself."

"But madam has not a license!" the Dutchwoman exclaimed.

"That doesn't mean I can't *drive*, does it?" my mother retorted. "The fact is, that chauffeur did everything he could to get me in trouble."

"But if it was *you* who was driving," began my governess.

"Exactly. If it was I who was driving it was all my own affair. Especially since it was I who had hired him, and since he was hired to do what I told him. It was my own affair entirely. That's precisely what I told the police."

"The police!" screeched Anneke.

My mother indulged in a sly silent smile of triumph. "They insisted on arresting me," she continued proudly, cleaning the smudge on her chin with her glove, "although I carefully explained that I supposed I had plenty of insurance. They weren't interested in any of *that*, you can imagine. The issues didn't concern them."

"The issues?" my governess echoed. She stood up, genuinely agitated. "But Armand with his head cracked, and you without a license, and the auto in what condition—"

"Disintegrated," said my mother promptly. "You talk just

like them, Anneke, I believe all you people over here suffer from the authoritarian personality. It's because you've tolerated kings for so many centuries. You don't have the revolutionary spirit. You're colonials in your own back yard. The American and Soviet Revolutions changed everything for everybody at the two ends of the world, but I can't see that the French Revolution made any difference at all for Europe—the police still act just as though they're secret agents for Louis the Sixteenth. Which is exactly how I treated them."

"The American interpretation of history," the Dutchwoman noted stiffly.

"The American interpretation of the European character," responded my mother. "When they got me to the police station I gave three thousand francs to every uniform in sight, including the sweeper—they certainly believe in *égalité* and *fraternité* when it comes to distributing francs!"

"Ah, madam has the true revolutionary spirit. Madam buys her *liberté,*" said Anneke, turning her caustic eyes on the concierge's husband, who was climbing down his ladder.

My mother laughed resentfully. "I certainly didn't intend to get stuck in a foreign jail. I doubt whether Enoch *or* William could have done anything to get me out, once I was in, and poor William hates his clients to become involved in scandals, even overseas, it's so bad for his office." Her mouth grew tangled with intrigue and pleasure. "Even so," she pursued, "there were stories in all the Paris papers yesterday morning. French reporters are very gay, I'll say that for them. They have the virtue of exaggerating the worst—it *is* a virtue, you see, because then the truth is always such a relief afterward. Half of them said Armand had a broken neck and was already more than dead, and the other half described me as a big American social criminal, whatever that means. It's an awfully good joke, I think, especially if they meant *socialist* criminal—I'm never sure about French adjectives. You know," she said, looking round for a chair and finding me in it, "there was a French edition of *Marianna Harlow*—it sold rather well. Anyhow it's true socialism is still popular over here, although it's poison at home. —Get up, dear, and let me have that seat, I'm exhausted. Here, I'll show you my picture in the paper . . ."

There were two photographs, one the familiar portrait with its wavy points of hair fringing her brow, which occasionally appeared on the third page of the New York tabloids—her favorite likeness, taken soon after her marriage to Enoch, dis-

playing what she liked to call her "autobiographical eyes,"
the lids very thin, the pupils round and wild as thrown din-
ner-plates, belladonna-big and brimming with notoriety, the
lower cheeks with their sweep of hollow too general to pass
any more for mere girlish dimples—my mother the in-her-
thirties debutante, adventure-broker, scandal-seeker. "That's
the one I *gave* them, because I was practically invisible in the
other," she maintained, "and it was only fair." She measured
out her image complacently between two forefingers. "Look,
you'd hardly know there was anyone sitting inside the cab, it's
so shadowy. And here, all around, are their motorcycles." It
appeared to be a photograph of her arrest: Anneke and I
vied to see the dot of my mother's face at the rolled-up window, blurred and light-blinded through the glass, peaked at
the chin under a blunt excited snout, and four gendarmes,
two severe, the third grinning, the last sucking his lips like
the ideaman for a prairie posse, the thicknesses of their
thighs slammed against the mass and maze of their trembling
motors.

I asked if there had been sirens.

"Ah, no, they don't have any," my mother told me sadly.
"But there was plenty of other noise to make up for it. A
crowd of adolescents kept yelling 'meurtrière' at me all the
way."

The Dutchwoman, bewildered, was still studying the photograph. "They took you to the commissariat like this, in a taxi-
cab?—"

"Oh, no, this wasn't when they arrested me, it was when
they let me go. I had to catch the train at Saint-Lazare, you
see, and so they gave me a motorcycle escort from the commissariat."

"For only three thousand francs each!"

"That's not why," my mother protested. "It was all their
own idea. I believe they think it's the custom in America, for
celebrities."

"Celebrities," my governess repeated blankly.

"People of reputation. Oh, not me," said my mother, gratified, "after all they don't know me here. It must have been
on my husband's account. And you supposed he had no importance!" she brightly charged. "The truth is his recent work
has made him moderately famous—at least in Paris, where
they read the papers. You see they managed to get Enoch's
name into it too"—she pointed to two long columns, grim

with italics—"it's very amusing. They call him the American Saviour who raises the dead without reviving them."

My mother lengthened her neck with a quick little twist and released, upon the margins of her smile, one of those high plumed cries of hers that occasionally passed for an extreme of mirth or token of a private journey into some unbelievably comic and raucous netherworld: it was not laughter, certainly, but rather a Dante of laughter, a guide to ghosts and goblins too funny to contemplate with ease. Out of sorts, the Dutchwoman nevertheless imitated her—it was quite outside of her intention, for her pink face coarsened with displeasure. She stood fawning in the grass, a little bent with the habit of covering scorn, rigid as mahogany and as redly brown, like a newly-set telephone pole bristling with invisible electrical signals. But my mother continued remote—"What a lovely smell," she said, "like fire, or the smell of the sides of horses": it was the pile of hedge cuttings, not sweet but joined by the sweetness of the roses rotted underfoot, and still green-thick and glistening with syrup. My mother's wide and sybaritic Chinese sleeve, hung from the chairback, at last disclosed her arm, gliding out cautiously as a white eel slipping downward; she lowered it until the fingertips barely discoursed in the grass. A crest of little hairs lay beaded with pellets of grey soot. She sat resting and immobile, an exile from the palace of event: she looked all terra cotta, the knuckles and creases grainy; this vaguely-haired pale dirt-fleeced limb dangling languid and long, almost like another neck, upside down, for the face secreted in her palm and the medusa-scalp of her wavering fingers; the hidings of her gape-mouthed sleeve bundled and tumbled with loose-flung folds and skews; every part captive and quiescent, stunned by unknown charms, dipped and spilled, leaning, invaded anyhow by vitality, a liquefaction above all fixed. She sat and was shape: an abstraction, theory, and ideation of shape. And the Dutchwoman also, duplicating her through duplicity—so that side by side, the standing figure ankleted by grass, the seated figure with fingers dabbling in grass, the two of them grew like old vases out of the ground. Their lips were stained; my mother's with illusion, Anneke's (I fancy now) with the opposite—she was intent on getting on my mother's good side, and traded smile for smile and look for look with comfortable cynicism. "There's Enoch," began my mother, listening, but she made no move to rise. "That's Joe and Hank too," she said; "have they gone on like that all day?" "Yes, since morning," my governess replied. And they wove their glances through conflicting breezes toward the house. My mother's rings blazed. "They called me 'meurtrière'—that's jumping to conclusions!" she exclaimed, and reached out to tap me with a jewel-freighted hand—"it means murderess, you know. As if I'd managed to kill the fellow!" she told me in her clearest voice. Still it was not so clear as those other voices, if one chose to hear them, gnawing in the garden—like flocks of pigeons they raised a rustling and could be noticed, or could not. It was by now a matter of will. I could not tell if my mother heard. The laughter was still bright in her remembering face, and the thick breathing of the cut boughs below the hedge seemed to cage her. "I'll go and tell Enoch you're here," I said, starting to run—but no, she stretched and caught me and swept me with her rapt eyes: "No, no, I'll simply sit and wait awhile. It's a smell like horses, or like fire. Someone's trampled the petals, they're brown as grease."

The Dutchwoman circled her. "The concierge," I heard her begin, but she went not a word farther.

"Like horses, I mean when the sun is hot on them, like fire," my mother said, brilliant with imagining. "The concierge spoiled the roses?"

"No, no, something else . . ."

"No one *spoiled* them. They fell by themselves. It's too late for roses on bushes," said my mother, restless although she did not stir, only let the shadows re-arrange themselves in her spacious sleeves and draperies: then it was the sun, not she, who moved.

She was struck and cracked by dazzlement. She smelled joy like gunpowder or rich ether—each deadens with its spiralling and ringing, yet no one can resist them: we are blasted and sung by one or the other in our lives. Therefore she arched her arm and withdrew it, aware just then how she startled and adorned that place; she gave out zealous energies and ornaments. "How I shook up that crowd," she asserted, but softly: she was as exhilarated after scandal as an arsonist after some great gloom and conflagration; she had had her burning. Yet a thread of greed hung in her eye. It was not enough. I could feel the world shudder in the garden then, and shimmer in the roseless bush, like a great quick wing; it seemed to rush against our beaten eyes, and my mother, helpless, closed her lids in agony for its passing. She could not keep it long; soon its sense and odor vanished, nothing lured it any more. Then she would invent new diversions to pierce

its sudden tail and trap its silken feet. For my mother really
thought the world was a bird to be pursued with audacity and
pleasure, and she deemed herself a huntress, and tipped her
arrows with fabulous coins. And she fashioned immense and
brilliant scenes over which she ruled poignantly and without
justice, a picaro or lady-rogue all fantastic, among crowds,
fabricating event, dining on the heart and bowels of this wild
splendid bird which was the world. My mother believed that
the world existed to be consumed by the rich and leisure-
gifted. She chose travel and scandal and worse, for snares;
but everything failed her, no enchantment or blow of recognition astonished her for long, experience evaded her, and
that which she contrived, through bribes and police and
whatever accidents or whims overtook her, through whatever
scheme or outcry, through pretenses and declarations of
changed philosophies, turned dry in an hour. Ah, my poor
mother, she was prompt to dare, but her dares withered as
promptly. Not then or afterward did she dream that the bird
of the world never lights, while we cast for it, on human
shoulder. If it comes to rest at all, it is when the hounds are
silent, and silently it roots in flesh its golden claws, so that
afterward we have only those ecstatic scars, in place of incredulous memory, to show. But even as she sat, the Paris
papers growing stale in her hand minute by minute, yesterday's climax old and already out of date, the very photographs fickled into period-pieces, I saw joy die away in her.
She had no work in the world. Desire stung her face, and she
jumped up and would have run toward Enoch's voice, but all
at once was altered and stood instead and listened. I listened
too, and my governess, and the concierge's husband lumber-
ing toward us from the sculptured hedge. He dropped his
shears on the grass where I had dropped the sickle and the
two blades briefly fenced. "Ah, those lists," my mother murmured, "he'll get nowhere with those lists. No one sees how
hard he works, shut up in there. He's better off, you know, in
the field," she said, using the last words expertly to show she
by no means meant a meadow, but rather some closed busy
place where conscientious toil could be witnessed and rewarded. "Sometimes I think he doesn't know how to push
himself. He gets so wrapped up. He gets involved," she concluded. "Listen to their droning. As though all that meant
anything any more, except to the relatives," she said, sighing
into the continued sigh of Maidenek, Treblinka, Chelmo, and
the sobs and soughs of those others, Sovibar and Mauthau-

sen, Dachau and Belsen, Auschwitz and Buchenwald—the
bitter sounds twisted slowly like fumes—"of course the things
that went *on* in those camps, they've no place to *ship* them to
—Oh look! A duck actually!" she broke off chastely. "That
foolish old man's carved a duck out of the top of . . ."

We all turned and squinted into the glare of late afternoon.
Already a wanly realized moon, ghostly in a sky still luminous with day, peered out, although the sun was barely below
the nearest roofs. Over the tall hedge the duck rode, large-
billed, verdant, eyeless. It seemed not an insect breathed just
then, and nothing cared to move, only the concierge's husband, who vacantly caressed his mustache—the voices had
taken everything prisoner, and had strangled the wind, and
with the deliberation of an evil bellows sucked and blew,
until Buchenwald, Belsen, Auschwitz and Dachau, Maidenek,
Mauthausen, Treblinka and Chelmo (over and over and over
again) at last lost reason and meaning, and grew more and
more unintelligible and inane; and the garden was choked
with nonsense.

"My bird cannot fly."

But my mother did not hear, and the concierge's husband
said again in his cryptic country dialect, "She must stay always
there in the bush. I have her better than a cage."

My mother vaguely echoed, "A cage?"

"I clip her wings!" he yelled with an obscure laugh, and
bent to take up the shears. Instead he snatched the sickle
lying nearby and spun it in the light until its cresent flamed;
he stood and brandished it like an idiot Crusader. "She cannot fly to her lover. Neither by night nor day," he said, grimacing at my governess. "A duck without a mate"—it was a
village jingle—"will not propagate."

The Dutchwoman glowed with fury. "Sterile guts yourself!" she burst out in her ready French. "Brain of a fowl!
Pantaloon!"

"What is it?" asked my mother, dazed.

"The old man is crazy," Anneke said.

"I didn't get a word."

"Oh, he has made a portrait of his wife."

"What?"

"In the hedge," said my governess irritably, "the duck in
the hedge. He did it to punish the concierge. *Vraiment,*" she
shrieked into his ear, "the resemblance is very close. It is the
picture of your wife exactly!"

"I thought it was just an ordinary duck," I said.

"What would he want to do that for?" my mother wondered.

"To cure her of lying. His wife has a crooked tongue. It is a punishment for telling stories, you see," said the Dutchwoman dangerously.

My mother shrugged but did not comprehend.

"She will come to you with a bad story."

"The concierge?"

"You will hear how she lies with her dirty mouth. It is a shame, madam, it is a shame for the child."

"Oh, the child," said my mother abstractedly; she looked toward the house. The windowpanes blazed with sunset. "Listen—I think they've stopped!" It was true: a barren voicelessness roared in the garden. "Do you suppose that's the end?" my mother cried. "If it is we're off to Zürich tomorrow—you had better pack," she advised my governess. "Take her to supper and then get the suitcases ready. I'm going in to Enoch," she called, and fled across the darkened grass.

It was very quiet now. Nevertheless the rhythm of the voices still faintly beat, as though lodged over our heads in a specific piece of sky, eternally. Until the moon brightened dusk delayed, then hurtled greyly down. The concierge's husband leaned like a pillar of ash.

"Well, come," said my governess, and the look she wore that moment, and the cadenced psalmings of the deathcamps which did not leave our ears, were for me then a hieroglyph of Europe, and have since so remained.

3

It happened that after that I never saw Anneke again.

The next morning my mother called me to her and announced the plan of my banishment. "There's no use your staying. Not any more—there's no sense in it," she gave out hoarsely. "Enoch was perfectly right. He told me when I brought you this wasn't the place for you." Sleeplessness had skeined her eyes with complexities. "It was a terrible mistake!" she charged me, as though I were somehow guilty. "You're going to go away, that's all that's left to do."

Her voice was heavy with accusation—I could not tell whether of herself or me. Yet there was nothing I had done. "Away?" I said weakly.

"It's the only possibility. We talked it out all last night, and it's decided."

Cautiously I considered her words. "I thought I was going with you and Enoch. To Zürich, you said."

"Zürich? Certainly not! It would be the worst thing imaginable."

"Then where?"

She sighed and resumed her excavations in her bureau. "Everything's changed," she said, as though this were an explanation: she went raging through her drawers to hide from me the fever of her breathing. "I can't expect Enoch to have you in his tracks after *this*. It isn't logical. The responsibility is too much." She raised her head to answer me; it was weary and beleaguered, and badly-groomed for that hour. "Where? Oh, out of Europe, that's the thing. Out of Europe altogether."

She dipped her hands back into the bureau drawers as into waterbasins, and churned up a rumpled mound of shirts and socks. "Your suitcases are already downstairs. I locked them up myself this morning. Well?" she waited, turning her spoiled swollen face to me.

"Is it because I made Enoch cross?" I asked meekly.

"No, no, Enoch's not cross," she said, hardly paying attention.

"Well, I *did* make him cross the other day," I confessed timidly. "Anneke said I had to play in the garden, but I ran in to see what he was doing. He didn't want me there."

"No, he wouldn't want you there," she agreed.

"Then is that why I have to go away?"

"It has nothing to do with it. Now go and get some air," she admonished, "and don't ask questions beyond your years."

I went out into an absence of sunlight, only half-amazed at my predicament. The concierge was spreading newly-washed laundry on the grass to dry, flapping the loose heels of her ugly worn slippers; she laid a pattern of sleeves and trouser-legs, and set a sheet to sail, and looked up contemplatively at the unpromising sky, and then recomposed her white geometrics. The bare rosebush sagged gloomily and had no shadow; someone had raked away the petals. I roamed about and poked after worms in a seeded patch with a stick, until the concierge saw me and called wrathful threats—but at that distance I could not disentangle her cries: they might have been the quibbling of a sea-gull. Red-faced she started toward me, swiveling her fleshy neck, slapping air, screaming. It was as though she were a puppeteer, with strings leading from her rapid fingers to marionettes of raindrops, large and warm, obedient to her flying arms as she pulled them down out of the sky. Midway in pursuit of me she fled again, her brow all splattered, her nose bathed and streaming; she snatched up the wash of triangles and rectangles, shouting at me as if it were I and not she who had willed them drenched.

It rained for only a moment. A pang of sweetness quickened the air. In another part of the sky the sun made a slit and shot through like a spear. Then it rained again, but more lightly and generally, less violently. The strained droplets were blown about like powder, falling through the thinly purple beam of sun as through a slung net. Nevertheless the hedge quivered and swayed in a palsy of rain, and pendants of water hung from the duck's broad side, until it was no longer a duck, but only a cluster of twinkling wreaths. I roamed again and roared in the fresh fragrance, prevented by nobody—the concierge had vanished, her imprecations and doomed laundry with her. The color of the grass altered, grew more blue than green. There were influences: "Everything's changed" was my mother's view of it, but clearly there were influences. I felt purified and simplified, and transmuted, like the grass, less by a force than by an illusion. It was not chemistry but atmosphere. I stood in the awesome light, exciting a puddle with my shining stick: meanwhile aware of a sort of peril; meanwhile abandoned by all plausible caretakers. My governess was nowhere—not asleep in bed, and not for a walk in the road, not anywhere. I thought I saw the flap of her smock-tail behind the gate, but it was only the concierge's towel thieved by the wind. I thought I heard her call my name from the house, but it was the rubbed moan of a twig caught in the door-hinge. I began to be afraid, because I despised her and was pledged to her and would perish without her. She had trussed up my destiny, and I sought her all around, in every wet path. It did not matter that they were sending me off, if it were in the ordinary way, leashed to the

Dutchwoman's melancholy and shipped abruptly to some new spot of ground with a difficult name—I hardly cared, I was indifferent, for when we arrived it was always a disappointment: there was nothing to do there. Never mind that my mother spoke to me, at the journey's start, of high and tremendous deeds which had once shaken that very piece of soil, this very scoop of hallowed granite—by the time *we* set foot there, it had all been long over. And never mind, that sometimes a bemused and persuaded Enoch, sunk in scorn, told of lootings and pillage, massacre and lust, which the place, by its nature, gave rise to—for when we came, it was always too late: the looters, robbers, assassins and sinners were gone; I never saw anything of them or their works; and usually they had departed years ago. Tumult never touched these crannies where we lighted. So what difference to me if it were Zürich or some other part? Zürich too was old, everything had happened long ago, nothing would happen now. And for me what would there be but the ragings of my bitter governess?

But she, like the looters and the sinners, was strangely gone.

I threw away my stick and went in again to learn more of this decree.

My mother fingered my dress at once. "Oh, for pity's sake, you're all damp!"

"I can't find Anneke," I said. "I looked and looked."

"And when all your clothes were sent to the station not two minutes ago," she exclaimed. "Now what shall we do, I ask you!"

"Won't I dry? I suppose I'll dry."

"You'll dry into pneumonia. Here, take off everything, and get into bed. Not in mine. Go into your own room. Enoch is having a conference in a little while";—she pushed a swatch of hair from her forehead, distraught—"with a visitor. He'll need to be private, really private, do you hear?"

"But I haven't had anything to eat."

"At eleven o'clock?"

"Anneke always takes me out to breakfast."

"Very well, I'll have the concierge bring you something."

"Anneke isn't anywhere," I persisted, "not in the garden and not in the house."

My mother threw down the blouse she had been folding and confronted me. "All right, you may as well know now as later—there's no use your looking for her. She's gone. She's been dismissed."

I grew cold with disbelief.

"Enoch sent her off late last night, bag and baggage. Well, don't look so stricken. I knew you'd be affected, but there was nothing else to do. I paid her for a whole extra month, if that makes you feel any better—God knows she didn't deserve it! With the situation as it stands—"

I stumbled fearfully, "You sent Anneke away?"

"We had to, don't you see? Now whatever you do *don't* cry," my mother rasped. Her scorched eyes slid from me. "I can't imagine what made you so attached in the first place. She's a callous type, aside from everything else—didn't the concierge tell me how you screamed to send a chill through the devil himself? She's not responsible."

"But she'll come back?" I said in horror.

"Not on your life! I told you, she's been *dismissed*. And after she left you that way, alone—"

"Oh, I didn't mind, I didn't mind!" I wildly assured her.

"She had no conscience," said my mother; she was implacable. She pointed her foot this way and that, restlessly, almost like a horse at the barrier; her nostrils widened nervously, her tongue flashed at the edge of her mouth and flicked away. She had determined to withstand all possible remonstrance. "You'll simply have to adjust to the idea," she told me, shifting her hands jaggedly from hair to breast, as though finding her body unfamiliar—"At your age these things are forgotten soon enough."

Still I held my ground. "I have to have Anneke," I maintained, but I was frightened at my mother's exploring instep, so like a hoof, and at the neighing of her harsh breath.

"Eventually you'll stop thinking of her. It's only reasonable," she continued, very well controlled despite these excessive movements: she was a tree assailed by storm, with confidence in nothing—yet her roots clung. "The thing is to get you out of here as fast as we can."

"I won't go."

"You can't possibly stay. It's been decided," my mother answered firmly.

"I don't care if it's been decided."

"Stubborn!" cried my mother. "You'll go and that's the end of it."

I suppressed a wail. "I'm not a refugee."

"What? What's that? What do you think you're saying?" she burst out.

Her voice was terrifying, strung and beaded with black threats. I flung myself on the floor and sobbed without interruption until a dozen of those howls and gasps summoned Enoch; he had run up the stairs and stood panting, clutching the underside of one of his list-crammed ledgers, on the threshold.

"Berserk," announced my mother angrily. "It's not a child, it's a mad-goat."

"Ah, be fair," Enoch said, surveying me.

"Fair!" She gave a fierce laugh. "All right, you predicted it! Say that you predicted exactly this!"

"I predicted exactly this," he repeated obligingly. "What's the matter?"

"She won't go. She's carrying on."

"What on earth for?"

"I'm telling you. She doesn't want to leave. It's pure defiance."

"Oh, defiance," Enoch said, as though he had never before encountered the notion. He came into the room and walked all around me, slowly and with an investigatory air. I felt like a dog there on the bit of rug; Enoch's shoes, thickly creased above the toes, sent out an agile whine close by my ear, and I smelled leather and mud. "My God, aren't you packed yet, Allegra?" he suddenly asked, catching sight of the disheveled bureau.

"I'm putting things together. As if there weren't enough tension—"

"There's no need for any of it. We'll see him and talk to him and then leave."

"And if he follows you?"

Enoch emitted what seemed to be a snort, disdainful and positive. "How's he going to manage that? I drove by his place. From the looks of it he hasn't got a sou."

"But suppose—" My mother's fingers leaped to her lips; a little twitch ticked in her cheek. "Suppose he tries," she finished.

"What, on a bicycle, with a rucksack?"

My mother looked unexpectedly alert. "Does he really have a rucksack?"

"Good God, how should I know? I'm only saying by all appearances he can't have any money."

"That's just what I'm afraid of," my mother said, and wandered off a little. "What that can lead to." She sank down on the edge of the bed—the mattress whushed air like a pneumatic valve—and worriedly jumped her ankle, narrow as a mare's, up and down. "He used to have a rucksack," she vaguely added.

"If you don't want to see him—" Enoch began, and put his ledger beside her on the bed. But he himself did not come near her. "I'll handle it alone if you prefer."

"Then you think it needs 'handling'?" my mother wondered, throwing him her fullest gaze.

"You want to see him," said her husband. He waited, but my mother did not speak; he felt in the pocket of his shirt. "Here's a cable for you from New York. They gave it to me at the station. The car's practically loaded—I had the boys do it this morning," he went on briskly; mechanically he brought up his watch. "I'm putting in the last stack now. You'd better get on with sorting your things."

"All right." She rubbed her rings and hesitated, as though anticipating a djinn. None came—no apparition of any sort. She asked, "How did you happen to be at the station?"

"I sent Hank and Joe on ahead, to get started with the work."

"You put them on the train? They're not driving?"

"I thought the fewer ears in this place this afternoon"—his wave had only a pretense of generality; it swept over me directly—"the better."

"Ah." Gravely my mother took the cablegram from him. "I'm not the only one who's afraid. You think he's too disreputable to deal with safely."

"It's the disruption, not the disreputability, I mind. I'm used to the other. There's nothing so disreputable as a corpse."

"Or so safe. I wish *he* were a corpse," my mother muttered savagely.

"It would simplify," Enoch admitted. Unaccountably their two glances converged on me, difficult and incomprehensibly unspontaneous, as by some exterior agreement of which they were hardly aware. But they did not divulge their queer collusion, even to themselves. "Up till now he's been as good as a corpse," Enoch mildly pointed out.

"That damned Dutchwoman," my mother grumbled. "Obscene troublemaker."

"There's no sense in putting the blame *there*," advised my stepfather in his practical tone.

"Then whose fault *is* it? I hope you don't think it's mine; *I* never intended to set foot out of Paris—I assure you I wouldn't have come to this ragged place on my own," my mother protested, contorting her mouth. "And in Paris he would never have found us. He would never have known we were there."

"Never?" Enoch repeated. "With the illustrated papers full of the peccadilloes of Allegra Vand? No," he agreed mockingly, "he would never have known you were in Paris."

"Well, he wouldn't have found us so easily," my mother resumed weakly.

"It was an accident that he found you at all. The fact is, he didn't find *you;* he found *her.*"

"Her?" murmured my mother irresolutely, although it was plain she understood him exactly. "You don't seriously mean Anneke?"

"Anneke," Enoch reiterated. "Precisely Anneke."

"It wasn't Anneke he was interested in." Apprehensively my mother watched her husband indulge in one of his leisurely dictatorial shrugs. "Well, you don't think he would bother with her for her own sake? His taste used to be better than that!" she asserted after a moment. "He knew she was the child's governess—he took up with her only to get near us," my mother said with a soft and wavering emphasis.

"Just as you please then." Enoch's tumid cheeks drew his under-eyes down as though by concealed weights; it made his face look sharper than it was, and older. "But it isn't in character for him to have schemes, you know."

"You're not excusing him!" my mother exclaimed.

"I only say that he's too unstable to be relied on."

"No, I wouldn't rely on him," my mother said coldly.

"He never *was* one of the schemers," Enoch declared. "It was the feel of it he cared for, not the dialectics, do you remember? I used to think it awfully ignoble of him. He would always go off on his own hook—he had that sort of flair. When everyone else was bankrupt he could always think of things to do on the spur of the moment. He knew how to make them turn around in those days!" he reflected serenely.

"I don't remember," my mother replied, without the note of truth.

But Enoch seemed not to expect truth just then. "He wasn't consistent. He had the imagination of disaster."

"That's just a phrase," my mother said scornfully.

"But you see the schemers have it to their credit that

they're consistent. They can be trusted, in their own terms. I mean the stages in their campaigns can be anticipated—at least one can rely on there *being* stages. It's possible to comprehend and distinguish their aims. The point is they have motives," he concluded.

My mother almost sneered. "And *he* doesn't have motives? I'd like to believe that! If he didn't have motives he wouldn't be coming here today," she stated, springing up from the bed.

"All right, but there's a difference."

"I don't see any difference. He's coming for a purpose."

"Oh, I'm certain of it."

"Then how can you say he's not a schemer?" said my mother, exasperated.

"Because a schemer begins with motives, and his motives produce a situation. But with him, it's the situation that produces the motive—"

"How I hate when you talk abstractions!" my mother wailed. "I don't know what you're saying, not a single word."

Enoch smiled slightly. "If you like I'll put it . . . nakedly. Take that as a pun if you want—he saw this girl and he made up to her. Nothing more. It was a question of one night's need."

My mother flushed, but not with delicacy. Her nose turned dangerously rosy, pinched by anger. "He's not so cheap as all that!"

"Then say he's not. Say it's she who is. But it wasn't an intrigue, I'll swear to that. He had no more idea, to begin with, of her being in your employ than the man in the moon. It wasn't a case of machination—does that distress you?" he asked, but it was rhetoric merely; he went straight on, still with his small, hinting, ironic smile. "He didn't invite her to his room simply in order to pick up news, that's clear!"

"Nevertheless he picked up quite a bit."

"I don't deny it. He's an opportunist. More than that, he's an improviser—that's the main thing. He plays by ear, according to whom he finds next to him in bed on any given morning."

"Ah, don't." It was unmistakably a moan. She came slowly round, sick with distaste, visibly detaching herself from his words. Her glance fell on me and automatically stiffened— "How can you, with the child listening," she developed it, but she was not thinking of me and had seized on my presence there as she would that moment have grasped for any convention or piece of etiquette. Nothing tempers suffering so

much as ritual, and it was altogether according to some ceremonial of purity that she rubbed her knuckles along her lip-
line, frowning at her husband.

"That's only by way of illustration," Enoch pursued, unwilling to admit to any transgression: he gave me a long,
elaborate look, as though I were a set of sums. Sprawled
there on the square of carpet I felt transparent, easily susceptible of solution. "All I mean to say is that he doesn't dream
things up—not out of the air, anyway. He wakes up into a
situation, and the situation dictates the motive: it's what I've
already described. He could have, right now, any number of
possible intentions toward you."

She echoed, unconvinced, "Any number?"

"He's not singleminded, if you follow me."

"He's a crook," my mother said flatly.

"Oh, well. For that matter—" Enoch renewed his clinical,
almost scholarly posture; his head strained forward after
some dangling omniscient lens, telescopic: his manner
brought all far moons near. "None of us is singleminded," he
stated, peering for confirmation through his invisible hanging
glass as though he had my mother's agitation quite in perspective.

She succumbed to a startled diminutive shudder, quick as a
blink. "You're not thinking of giving in!" she cried.

"How can we talk of giving in till we know what he
wants?" he said reasonably.

"Whatever he wants he won't get it."

"He may want one thing now, and another thing later,"
Enoch observed.

"I don't see," said my mother, going to her bureau. "He
can't want anything but money."

"It's what he wants it *for* that counts. That's the danger.
It's what I say, he's not consistent."

"It doesn't matter—he won't get it in any case."

"Not in any case," Enoch experimentally repeated. "And if
he tells you he's starving?"

My mother's arms, thrust in the drawers, whipped deri-
sively through a foam of silk. "Let him starve!"

"Ah, the Christian temperament," he noted.

"I don't care. He won't get a penny out of me."

"Not as mere largess, no."

"Not as mere anything," she retorted. "It's my habit to
sympathize with organized charities only. On that principle
you don't get taken in."

"Oh, I agree the fellow's disorganized." He gave a mournful little laugh. "I suppose it's his nature."

"Never mind his nature," my mother bit off.

"Still, it's not a question of sympathy."

She swooped up a pile of underwear and tossed it into an open valise waiting in the corner. "If I don't give alms out of sympathy I don't give it at all."

"Then out of the eleventh commandment," he suggested.

She raised her wrists suspiciously. "What's that?"

"Exigency."

Carefully she shut out contempt. "There's no such thing. Not for me. I do what I please," she summed it up.

More than ever he seemed to sight her through his conceptual telescope. But he had turned it around; he reduced her altogether. "You had better be prepared for another course, Allegra," he told her. "One that favors your interests instead of your wishes,"

"My wishes are identical with my interests."

"Save me from a renegade Marxist!" he vividly came back. They stood, the husband and wife, humorless and embattled, quarreling and speculating over the visitor, the private visitor, who had not yet arrived. Yet obscurely they were allied, and had old pacts and treaties to consider, and bickered behind their common walls on strategy only, on whether longbows were suitable, or simple spears, for subtlety of defense: each feared the other's plan, but both feared the visitor more. "I don't predict," Enoch began again, "I only warn. We'll have to wait and see. The chief thing is to remove the child." He hesitated. "What time is he coming, do you know?"

"I sent word with the old man—he took some bags to the station a while ago. —I wrote down noon."

"So early? He never used to wake before two," Enoch offered skeptically.

My mother appeared displeased by this allusion. "But the train doesn't go until three. That's plenty of time, isn't it?"

"Meanwhile I'll finish loading the car." He took up his ledger and was, on that note, ready to leave; but he came to me instead and bent somewhat and smoothed my head with a showmanlike hand that seemed, for the moment, to put me on exhibit. His touch was cool and brief, message-bearing—a signal, in fact, to show the enemy's arsenal. It was the touch of espionage. I did not like it, and sat up straight to confront my stepfather's suddenly ominous intricate eyes, unexpectedly of the most characterless blue under tawny lids. There was something of connivance in the room; the rain mumbled on the windowpanes; my mother breathed plaintively. Somehow I was included, and more and worse than that, involved. They had ringed me round with secret links and implications, those two, Enoch and my mother, and had drawn me in and made of me, despite my passive witnessing, a deep participant. It was as though (but once more with polished fingertips, casual and swift, Enoch stroked my hair: a hangnail momentarily enmeshed him, and I felt the pull of a tiny brutal twinge) they blamed me and held me accountable for their tense mysteries and ignoble conversations. They did not think me free of their condition; and although I ventured not an inch beyond the fringes of the mat—this to prove that if my fate was circumscribed I was at least its captain—and conceived of their conjoined lives as a thicket too unintelligible even to wonder at, and could not comprehend their voyages and explorations and doubted their objects, deeds, dealings, precious things (in the same way they could not believe in what I chose for toys), still they supposed me bound to their condition: and severely viewed me as locked in the world with their visitor and foe. "My God, Allegra, she's soaked through," Enoch said, pulling away his dampened hand. He dropped it limply in disgust, but in the very instant of his gesture my mother had her own, and lifted high her arms, guaranteeing everything.

"She won't be here when *he* is, I promise you," she vouchsafed him. "I'll put her to bed next door until her clothes are dry—they're all she's got at the moment. If they ever *do* dry in this weather."

"All right, but keep her out of sight," Enoch warned. "Don't let him see her."

My mother reflected. "I'll say she's gone. I'll tell him we've already sent her off," she calculated softly, and picked up the yellow cablegram which had fluttered to the floor.

"I won't go," I broke in: it was the first time I had spoken: their two startled looks leaped out at me in tandem. "I won't go, whatever you say."

"You see?" my mother pounced. "That's what I've had to listen to all morning!"

"You should be glad to get out of Europe," my stepfather said sternly.

"It's no use lecturing," admonished my mother. "That sort of talk won't work. She's too obstinate. —You'll do as you're told," she finished.

"I'll die," I whined. "If you make me go I'll die of thirst."

"Good heavens, there's plenty to drink on the boat. What's the matter with you?" my mother inquired testily. She groaned and fixed on Enoch. "If she's getting sick again——"

He expelled an awkward sigh; it might have passed for a type of snore.

"You know how her stomach is," my mother persisted. "Well? Does your stomach feel all right?"

"They'll shoot me," I said. "They'll shoot me in the desert."

"What?" they jointly cried.

"The sheikhs from the Wailing Wall. They'll take me out into the desert and kill me. It's what they do in Palestine."

"What has Palestine to do with you?" my mother demanded, stunned and growling with bewilderment.

I thought her more stupid than ever. "It's on account of my father. Because he's a Jew."

"Enoch's not your father. You know that surely," she burst out. "I tell you, the child hasn't got a mind, really!"

"No," I plunged on in a passion of opposition. "Not Enoch. My *father*. Anneke told me. And if she doesn't come back they'll put me in a camp. I won't go to Palestine no matter what. I won't," I sobbed, "you can't send me. It's not my fault—not if I'm not a refugee, is it?"

"No," Enoch said, "you're not a refugee."

"Nor a Jew," my mother put in quickly. "Tell her she's not a Jew either."

"She couldn't be trusted," Enoch said, grown fervid with a kind of rage-chastened pity I had never before seen in him. He was plainly sorry for me, and did not hear his wife. "Where did you find that girl?"

"Her qualifications were very good," my mother said. "The University of Leyden and all. She used to be a medical student."

"She couldn't be trusted," he said again.

"She's a refugee, that Dutchwoman," my mother said. "They're all no good. I mean they've been corrupted. The victims of oppression are always corrupt," she added with a grave philosophical frown that stood like a mockery in her ravaged face.

I went on solemnly weeping. "*I'm* not a refugee," I gave out, stifled.

But Enoch had drawn up the heavy ledger with its black cardboard covers vaguely glimmering, bordered with the black tape of an obituary-rectangle. It tipped slightly, and to save it from sliding out of his grasp he supported it against his chest, flattening it close to him as though it contained life. It shone on his breast like plates of armor and he clung to it in the fancy that it had powers still untried, and might, if he lowered his head in just such a way and showed himself preoccupied and possessed and willing to dare, then and there call out the Shechina in a blazing presence too terrible to remember afterward, as the excruciations of giving birth yield their own forgettings; and he wore on his body that book of woe as he might have worn Urim and Thummim, to deliver up manifestations and to court the unmanifestable and dazzle it into disclosing its faceless face, the way a woman dumb with grief will cradle in her bosom her dead baby, pretending it is alive and cuddling it in the ordinary way, hoping to woo it back to life by the subterfuge of the familiar—but the familiar has changed irrevocably into the extraordinary, and her arms hold carrion.

My stepfather said deliberately, "You're an idiot to talk that way, Allegra, you have no right," while she trailed after him with a stare so literal and wondering it almost moved him.

"I only meant there must be something wrong with a person in the first place," she began, shoveling after excuses, "to make him end up a refugee. There's logic in that, isn't there? And morality too," she dug deeper yet, "because there's no such thing as gratuitous harm. I mean who would chase or murder someone for no reason at all?" She was all worry and concern, and congratulated herself on that account. "You believe in progress, don't you? The human race *has* advanced since Cain and Abel, I should hope."

She missed him entirely; was blind to his furious erupted breastplates (saw instead only his thick foolish ledger, one of many, all the same, each stuffed uselessly with the incinerated, each heavy as a brick or cinderblock, product of that impractical drudgery—not art or work-of-mind: unless brick-kilns are inspirational ateliers—which shut him away from the favor and influence of his superiors: saw that dismal ledger, in fact, in the shape of a blotched black wall—it had the size and harsh squareness and bulk of a wall—cruelly built, brick by brick, between herself and the ornate celestially-radiant embassy-house in the shrine-city of some historic, preferably anciently ·monarchic, land, a house whirling with footmen-attended balls at which innumerable high personages

beg to waltz with Allegra Vand—whom'd you say? ah! lucky
fellow!—the Ambassador's Lady); and, for all she felt him
out in the minute that he stood, zealously assessing her and
me, for all she descried his ardor in that long and violent
minute, she might have been emptying bureau drawers in another room on another continent. She stuck to her position,
anticipated discourse (which did not come), and was oblivious—while she looked for signs and symbols—of the palpable. And there it was, the palpable, right-angled and hard, as
articulate and unanswerable as a coffin-box, pressed against
(what could satisfy the literal-nosed more?) his actual and
living heart—the black covers of the ledger held on that
priestly spot like a tablet of the Law: not God's but Europe's.

He was engrossed; did penance; kissed the arch-cup of the
splendid feet of his baal, the Lady Moloch, nude as ice but
for her diadem of human teeth and her ankle-ring of human
hair; until it was at last enough.

My mother did not brush against this piety, and saw nothing and knew nothing.

So it was enough. "We're all refugees from something or
other," he surrendered. This was weak and irrelevant. My
mother shared his sadness without exactly sensing why (her
nostrils partook of the smell of fire and of horses, and were
clogged with the spittle of fleet hot horses, sweating and
slowly salivating, on whose sleek brown backs in ebony sad-
dles, with razor-spurs, stinging with thumb-thick whips,
murderers rode) and turned to me and quite competently explained how my governess had gulled me: they did not send
American children to the Jewish desert, or to any camp, or
anywhere. So I understood it was a made-up story invented
by the Dutchwoman to induce me to keep her horrid secrets.
Had she often directed me not to tell this or that? (my
mother asked, all naïveté, all unaffected casualness); did she
sometimes converse with men and stroll away? Did anyone
come to see us on the beach in the middle of the day? And
did we ever take walks into the bad quarter, where all the
houses sprouted in out-of-breath bunches, with colored tiled
roofs, the sounds of water leaking, grey flash of rat and gruesome cognizance of public fart? She named other malodors,
and suggested to my memory types of insects—flies, too—
and of men.

"But that's where we used to eat every day," I supplied.

"But the bills!" she uttered in astonishment. "At the end of
every week the *bills* that woman presented me with—from

the Restaurant Palatin, on the boulevard." (I had never heard of the place; we had dined on the boulevard only once, in a café.) "She kept the money for herself, and fed the child on nothing," my mother gruffly established. "What a cheat! — How did she ever get hold of so many bills?"

"Pilfered," Enoch stated without hesitation. "He got them for her."

"I don't see—"

"Don't you remember?—she let it slip last night that he had a little job there occasionally."

"I thought he had no job at all."

"It seems he plays the piano in these places now and then."

"I didn't believe it, it sounded so unlikely—when he used to drill through Chopin like a robot! —He can't live on it though."

Enoch muttered steadily, "It couldn't have been much of a trick to pick up a fistful of blank *additions.*"

"Blank?" she bleated, catching his tone. "Then Anneke filled them in very nicely!"

"A swindle," Enoch agreed. He paused on the threshold and seemed to meditate. "Well, at least tell the child where you're sending her!"

"The whole world is a fraud," my mother said tragically.

Once more, very cautiously, he carpentered his sarcastic smile. He saw her face to face, and as she was in relative truth, with no alien lens disfiguring her for him now, only that eternal double-mirror which hangs between husbands and wives when they undertake to judge one another: that they may in fact judge the image of themselves. "The human race advances," he reminded her, but did not stop: "Golgotha with it." He viewed me from the doorway without interest or immediacy. "The best thing is for you to go away," he announced, continuing to look at me in a detached mood of pity and anger.

It seemed altogether settled between them. They were prepared to manipulate all—Anneke whose brother hungered in seven tongues, the imminent private visitor rich with betrayals, myself chained to their condition and without a fate, for the time, except for theirs. Yet Anneke was a liar; no Wailing Wall existed (what vasty rock so brute and serpentine it could wind round the valley of swindles and bones or shut up all wailings?) and there was nothing to depend on but contrivance. But there was no one on the planet who did not depend on contrivance, and if not on contrivance on fraud, and

if not on fraud on deceit, and if not on deceit on hoax, bluff,
or manipulation, whichever came easiest to hand. —Between
them, my mother and her husband devised and contrived.

"I'm taking you back to America," my mother said.

So she had failed, it seemed—or instead perhaps reneged a
little. In any event she had not succeeded in recouping for me
either Europe or a father. Enoch would not be enlisted in one
game or the other. I did not care for earth or sky of those
old places she had too much praised, but concerning Enoch I
was more sorry than bitter, for I suspected even then how
hard it is to re-father the fatherless, and how much harder
yet to re-father the wrongly fathered—the badly, mistakenly,
regrettably fathered. What was there then for us to do (my
mother asked) but the clean, the brave, thing—plainly to declare ourselves victims and ride the sea for home again? She
considered, anyhow, that Europe was a ruin. It smelled of
machinery and strained like a winch. It ran on gears. The
motors in the belfries snarled; the bells spit lubricating oil.
Meanwhile Enoch burrowed; scarcely offered an ear to her or
me; kept his eyes for those dense and obscene ledgers. But
my mother thought them the blemish and bad guests of her
journeyings, and shunned them as though they would defile
her: they did Enoch no good and spited her hopes. It was the
fault of those ledgers, she insisted, that Europe was a ruin—
and not the noble ruin of a burned-into-rust-and-filigree abbey,
the sort of ruin that time has brought to its knees not cruelly,
but in the manner of a sacerdotal genuflection, and graces,
and eventually condones—but a twisted machine-ruin instead: those giant slabs and piles of scoriae, stumps, butts,
smut, slag and scum thrown off by a derailed and raggedy-
holed, gear-gone, slime-seeping, steel-pounded wreck of wild-
flung fuses, grotesque and braided pulleys and generators,
pipes like dead-end tunnels, all those mutilated heaps of
scratched bits still luridly shining among multiple deformities.
My mother simpered with shock and defilement, and wiped
her tight mouth. She had come for an elegy and found,
where the country churchyard used to be, a mechanized and
howling abattoir. It was on account of the ledgers . . . what
else was to blame, if not those silent black-taped books, for
the burial of spectacle, dominion, energy and honor in a hill
of skulls?

And so, because there was nothing else she could do, my
mother sentenced herself and me to America.

And Enoch? It might have been that he, on his part, felt

himself a victim. Perhaps he believed he was a failed Ezekiel. Thigh-deep in all those names and designations—crumbled, a million times over, into ash, and the ash of ash—he could not recall them into flesh and sinew (what would renewal bring but smoke?); and even if he had been able, who would summon in them the wind of life?

I started to ask him how long we would live on the ship— but when I stood up to speak the door had closed and he was gone.

4

In half a minute it opened again, and the head and neck of my stepfather reappeared in the crevice. "Allegra—"

My mother jumped urgently out of contemplation. "What, is he here already? What is it?" she said in alarm.

"No, I was only wondering—" Enoch's head came a little farther into the room. "What does William say?"

They had, all that while, forgotten the cablegram.

My mother slit the envelope and began to read quickly. " 'Heard accident report on radio'—didn't he get my cable?" she interrupted herself. "Oh!—yes he did—'before receiving wire; glad no injury to you.' That means he's furious," she noted crisply, "I mean about the publicity and fuss and all!" She crackled the paper and went vigorously on with it. "Well, thank goodness, he's getting someone who's over here anyhow to take care of it, the insurance and everything—and oh God, if Armand should really sue—*that* would be nerve!— but isn't it lucky! it's a man who happens to be on a commission in Paris right now!—His name's Pettigrew, do you know him?"

"You might have killed that chauffeur," Enoch said.

"But I didn't, so it's all right, isn't it?" she countered. "Are you sure you don't know a Pettigrew? He's in your area, sort of, I mean he's in Europe to see what the war did—" she consulted the cablegram—"he's a Special Assistant to the State Department: doesn't that sound like a wonderful appointment? —Only he's a Democrat," she added. "How I wish you'd get a job like that, practically a stepping-stone—"

"If you don't finish packing before he gets here you'll have to do it afterward," Enoch said, "and you'll miss your train."

"Well, the Democrats can't *always* be in power . . ." My mother grew thoughtful. "There was a Pettigrew who went to Miss Lamb's with William and me when we were little, and afterward married a girl from the West, if it's the same Pettigrew—only I didn't think he'd grow up to be a Democrat.— Miss Lamb's?" she repeated, picking up Enoch's look. "Oh, that's a dancing school."

"Then I don't know him," Enoch observed shortly, and drew his head behind the door and bitingly shut it.

5

In the room which had lately been Anneke's and mine I took off all my clothes down to my underwear and put them on a hanger to dry, and let the hanger dangle on its hook from the light-chain in the center of the ceiling. And then, because I was damp to the skin, I stripped off my underwear too, and spread it out on one of the two empty beds.

After a while the concierge brought a pair of flat buns, a lick of jelly, and a cup of pale tea, in which the narrowly rolled leaves quivered like bits of hair. "Beurre?" I inquired feebly, but she seemed offended at this and pointed to the jelly as though even that were a luxury beyond reasonable expectation. "Madame Vand asks me to oblige her, so I oblige her; it's a great concession," she said in the deafening French she reserved for simpletons, foreigners, and the dull ears of her husband (but *he* was in the first category anyhow); she stared and stared at the madness of my mid-afternoon nakedness. "I don't run around every day carrying trays—I have plenty to do without it! I hope she knows I expect her to pay for it—she's rich enough, she'd better not think she can fool me. I sleep with one eye open! I'm not so gullible as my old rooster, you may tell her, who's so played out he can't see the difference between a pauper and a millionaire . . . What! One would suppose she could afford another dress for you," she broke off. "You don't expect anything to dry in such weather?" I maneuvered my cold buttocks onto a chair and carefully aproned the tray across my knees to hide myself from her inflexible scrutiny; but she did not leave off her looking. "What age do you have, ha? You don't even begin to show your little bumps? Not a shred of hair between the legs yet, ha? In the armpits?" She grabbed my arm, lifted it, and let it fall in triumph. "Nothing! I've always heard they come late to these things in America," she confided. "A cousin of my old rooster, on the mother's side, gave birth at eleven years—she started having her courses at seven! But that was an unusual case," she admitted loudly. "One would think that at least in matters of this kind the nations would all be alike, but by no means. I've heard that in England the women don't take lovers! And in Holland it's only the women who *do*—the lowland vapors make them especially fit for it. If you don't believe me just consider your own governess!"

She went on zealously babbling, and, since I understood not half of that gossip and roily patter, and could only sit shivering in my prickled hide, dumb and with scarcely a glimmer of her meaning, it seemed clear it was not for my sake that she whirred her nasal rhetoric through those gaps and bits of yellow bone (her teeth were shocking) where her in-and-out tongue tumbled: for now and then she waited, and appeared to listen, and plainly intended her monologue, which was more than audible and altogether public, to be received next door.

But it was already one o'clock; the private visitor had not yet arrived; and my mother had been out of her room for some time.

"I know those Hollanders, believe me—they're always in need of a finger in the dike!" the concierge bellowed hopefully at the wall. "Didn't I say I sleep with one eye open? There's little that goes by *me!* Madame Vand would have known nothing of it if not for me—she owes me something besides a thank-you, I may tell you, for putting her wise. Oh, I don't say much, only a small tip . . ." But the wall neither affirmed nor protested. "Who do you think gave the alarm?

And who do you think sniffed out the fellow's identity? —
There's not a single occupant of any room in town I can't
catch news of—especially the paupers and foreigners! I don't
believe in competition. I'm with all the landladies like *this"*
—she interlocked the fingers of both hands and gripped them
suspiciously. "Well? Where is she? Your mother's not in her
chamber?" she demanded finally.

"I think she went to sit on the porch," I murmured.

"If it's to watch for the rain to finish she'll be sitting a long
time," the concierge said resentfully, and stamped over to the
beds and began pulling off the sheets. "Here—take your
bloomers, they're in the way. You think I have time to waste?
I have to prepare for the next occupant—Madame Vand paid
only until noon, all the rest is unofficial. But I'm good-
hearted, I allow it. In the busy season, on the other hand, I
wouldn't be so good-hearted." She charged toward me under
a snowbank of linens and offered me her crinkled frown.
"Listen, it's nothing I can say to her face: so be sure you tell
your mother afterward how you thought I could use a little
tip for my trouble—little, I don't say cheap. She's well rid of
that girl, you know, it wasn't such a cheap favor I did her.
It's one thing to deceive a husband—I've done it myself in
my time and prime, and without discovery—but it's going too
far to deceive an employer!" She clucked and cackled close
to my ear, feeding me her breath of boiled farina, until my
defensive wince assured her she had delivered her point.
"Aha, you're an intelligent child after all, although if one
were to go only on looks one wouldn't think so. The brain
isn't as backward as the glands, that's lucky. —Be sure to tell
your mother what I said!" she reminded me at the door. —
"But it always rains on laundry day," I heard her sigh into
her bundle as she lumbered into the corridor: *"tant pis!"*

6

At two o'clock the private visitor still had not come.

I finished my little meal very slowly, to make it last, for my mother had warned me we should not eat again until we were safely on the train. .

But at half-past two she suddenly reappeared. "No, your things aren't still wet!" she marveled hoarsely.

Suspended from the ceiling and vaguely sweating, my dress turned and turned in the humid air.

"Well, never mind, we'll have to wait anyhow," my mother said. "It's too much to hope for that he's had a change of heart and won't turn up! But he will, he will," she miserably intoned. She went rubbing and scratching at her neck. "Enoch won't let me near him any more, I'm that nervous— he shooed me off the porch actually. I wish I could hang myself!" She ripped away the collar of her traveling-dress to clutch the peevish spot—and sure enough, her uneasy relentless nails had marked out a sort of rope-burn there.

"The concierge wants some money," I informed her.

"I'm sure that doesn't concern *me*," my mother said haughtily. "She charged us as much for her rat-trap as the best Paris hotel, that shrew."

"But I think she wants a tip."

"Enoch tipped her plenty. The old man, too. And the kitchen maid. —They think Americans are to squeeze white," she snapped. "My blood doesn't run dollars, you know—I like to get something in return!" She sounded positive enough; and I considered that I had done as much as could be expected in behalf of the concierge (toward whom I felt an obligation on account of what had seemed a real solicitude on the night the brass demon invaded my sleep—how disturbed she had been to find a deserted child!); and I would have said nothing further: but my mother was watching me slyly. "What made her tell you that?"

"Because of Anneke. You would never have known about Anneke without her," I repeated faithfully, although I was still uncertain of my governess' crime.

My mother resumed her fretful scraping. "She takes a lot of credit for herself, the old bat!"

"She sleeps with one eye open," I acknowledged in awe.

"One eye isn't worth rewarding. I give prizes for two eyes only," my mother said with a quick rough laugh. "Do you need to go down the hall?" It was her habit (an Americanism, Enoch observed) to refer obliquely to the toilets; she waited scrupulously until I assured her I had already called on them. "Because I'm going to lock your door. Enoch's afraid you may forget and run out. We don't want anyone to know you're here," she suggested suspensefully.

"The concierge knows I'm here."

"The concierge knows too much," my mother admitted. "I was thinking of the visitor."

"Maybe he isn't coming."

"He's two hours late already," she remarked, but more to herself than to me, and dipped after a large key in her pocket; a worn bit of paper was caught on the teeth. She unfurled it and gave it a surly squint. "But I was the one who set the time, after all, and that by itself's enough to persuade him to ignore it. He'll come when it suits him," she said decisively, holding the little square sheet stiffly before her.

"Is that the cablegram?" I asked, peering after a portent of William in her melancholy evasive hand—but clearly it was commerce of a different sort she just then crumpled from my glance. "No, it's not, and never mind," she charged me severely, but a moment too late: I had seen one word, ambiguous to my eyes, and a signature plain as a primer. My mother withdrew the whole with a rapid sense of error, and signified by her gasp of denial that she had permitted something to happen which ought not to have happened. She attempted to deflect me: "Are you certain you don't have to go down the hall right now?" she insisted.

But I pursued, with my finger arrowed at her fist, "What's in that?"

"Nothing," she said shortly.

"Is it a letter?"

"I told you never mind"—but consternation marred her authority.

"I know what it says anyhow," I ventured.

"Don't be too tricky with me!" she advised; her expression tacked from disbelief to fear. "It has nothing to do with you." Nevertheless she continued to hide it from me.

"Doesn't it say 'confer'?" She did not answer. "Then it says 'career'," I hastily tried again.

"*Must* you badger!" she blew out at me. "I've said it's nothing to do with you, isn't that enough? —It's a business letter," she went ahead with a deliberateness almost too convincing, "it's someone asking for an appointment with Enoch. I *hope* you don't disapprove," she finished heavily.

"I don't like that name," I observed.

"What name?"

"The name in the letter—Nick."

"You saw that!"

The long shock of her breath lingered.

"Is Nick the man who's coming to see Enoch?"

"Haven't I just explained—" She scowled and struggled palely. "Now look, a person has simply written to ask for a business appointment, is that so complicated? Really, I should slap you for this!"

"But is it the same man? The one who's coming right now?" I persisted. "The one the concierge said—"

But she would not allow herself to hear, and instead quickly gave in. "Yes," she said, "all right, yes."

"Then the concierge *ought* to get a tip."

"That gloating old bat gets nothing. Madame Pandarus, the go-between! I hope I'm not obliged to her for telling me what I already knew," she muttered, stuffing the ball of paper into her pocket as though it were an invidious apple from the Tree of Knowledge. "I'd like to wring her neck! Well, go sit on the bed," she commanded, "I'm going to lock your door."

"I don't like that name: Nick," I said again. "Nick. Nick." I kept trying it out, rattling the sound. "It goes too quick. Nick."

My mother blinked with each needle-prick of repetition, as with a sting. "Quit that, for heaven's sake—as though it had anything to do with you! I've told you that, how many times do I have to say the same thing? No wonder Enoch decided to turn the key on you"—she brandished it—"he's absolutely right. You can't be trusted."

"That's what he said about Anneke too," I reminded her.

My mother maintained uncomfortably, "That was quite another matter."

"It must have been," I said. "You didn't lock *her* in."

"Well, don't think we wouldn't be better off if we had. — It's only for a little while though," she told me guiltily. "Until he's gone. Just so he doesn't see you're around."

"If he doesn't have anything to do with me," I said, "I mean Nick—"

"He doesn't," she jumped in.

"—Then why can't he know I'm here?"

"Really, you're disgusting!" My mother turned on me in a sickened rigorous wrathful spasm; a blotch like a berry burst out on the side of her chin. "What's the matter with you? You don't think I care about your stupid notions, do you?" She spat and howled and rang her big key on the bedpost in a wild clatter and gong. "Why can't you keep your eyes where they belong? —And then you get insulted if it's said you can't be trusted!" She unleashed herself at me and struck my arm, but the awkward unexpected pitch of her half-closed palm flattened with surprise midway in its arc, and it was no blow at all—nothing happened: only a harmless shrill zing of skin on skin. "There, you see? It's just what you deserve! A child like you is the worst sort of danger yet!" She put a long angry space between us, scratching at her throat where the collar lay back unbuttoned, and rooting in that raw patch of neck with the very hand (how stiff and plain the fingers now) that had leaped out to punish; meanwhile yelling sorrowfully, bleating at my badness, until on the verge of clarity the word I had spied in the scrap of letter, the picture of the word, renewed itself—was it "cross"? was it "church"?—and almost came to mind and life: only just rose and rose to the brim—

("Listen!" said my mother.)

—and fell short.

A chug came out of the sky: and then the blurred din of whistle and strident cough and blare of bell and blast of steam; and then a kind of crash, also of steam, in resonance with the windowpanes, which vibrated delicately; and then at last across the town, far and clear, out of the station and up from the trembling platform where the alighted passengers felt the engine's lungs shiver in their feet-soles, the eye of the sound rushed down. The eye of the sound just then rushed piercing shrieking down; and my mother said, "It's three o'clock, we've missed the train"—falling out of violence as into a furred and noiseless pit, where the pelts of commonplace animals muffled her calls and curses.

—I wondered whether the word were "curse," but knew in a second it was not.

"There won't be another one out of here until midnight—I checked the schedule. We're stuck," my mother said, "we're stuck until twelve o'clock, and I don't intend to go dragging off like a thief in the middle of the night! All right," she said, "I suppose we're stuck until tomorrow."

The prospect did not content her.

"And now will we be late?" I asked.

"Late for what?"

"Getting to America."

"No," said my mother. She had ceased to founder and was in possession of herself and of me. "There are always plenty of ships in that direction. —It's never too late for America."

She looked desolately down into the bed of her open hand, where the key with all its cold big limbs and juts was laid out like a figurine: and in the moment when with small commotion she locked the door, unaccountably the lost word returned, the picture of the word, and where it had lain, neither at the beginning nor the end, but in the very center, of the letter, like the inking of a figurine primitive and jagged in the letter to my mother (for I did not believe that Enoch claimed it), the letter from the private visitor who had not yet arrived, that Nick whose name was quicker than himself, for whose sake the train even now could be heard barking into the distant wounded hills without us: the lost word unimportantly returned and prophesied, to my disappointed curiosity, nothing. "Confer" might have promised some enlivening; and "career" surely (my mother cared for nothing of Enoch's so much as this); and "cross" and "church" some bright procession; and "curse" might signify imaginings and rich complexities. But this!—the real word was simpler and duller than any; it was not worth having been teased and tormented for; it shut off all hope for the spectacular, and failed to tantalize.

Nick had written "child" merely.

So it no longer mattered how my mother had come by that pointless paper which inexplicably she treated as dangerous and secret. It did not attract me now; no seed of event or fable could grow from that name or word. It was as she had avowed: "business," and I was all at once convinced of the justice of her slap—administered to a meddler—and forgave her. But on the same ground I could not forgive the locked door: for their business was always the same; it was barbarous; and I wanted nothing more than to avoid their dealings, and keep cleanly away, and go sailing home to America.

Meanwhile I thought, for pleasure's sake, of all the days on board, and of certain birds that nip fish out of the ship's fat wake: but very soon the locked door (wood painted white, and set in the wall like a nose) and the slow turnings of my dress in a faint moist draft took my musings from me. I felt the void of my nakedness, and the void of the rain, light and continuing, barely ticking like a wristwatch held in concentration against the ear, a rain without voice, and sitting on the bed nearest the window (through which the garden gate and the duck in the hedge and beyond these a bit of cobblestoned road all mingled with the sway, farther still, of mist-blackened waves) I said into the empty room: "Nick Nick Nick" and then, a moment later, "Nick Nick Nick Nick Nick"—as though that could somehow rouse the stillness and the lurking void.

7

He came finally. It might have been in an hour, or less, or more—I had no clock to tell me how long. Worn out by idleness, I had fallen, without seeming really to sleep, into a sort of density, where a long row of torches went round and round a black stone; and the stone itself was a vast nostril from whose edge a great stabbing jewel menaced, clinging by means of a clip: and the fires, which kept going out, were brought in darkness to be rekindled in its phosphorescent heart. Behind all, in all, a knocking and a rattling, as though the torches (but there were no bearers) jostled one against the other, clanking their wide hollow flanks in a sound so gnawingly familiar that without delay I awoke and ran to the window and saw, leaning against the hedge, an old blue bicycle. It stood tilted and twisted, with its front wheel doubled back on itself, like a stork preening its tail, and the handle-

bars thrust almost into the rear spokes: and tied to the back
fender, under a newspaper tent which the wind shortly ripped
away, was a sharp-cornered bundle very much in the shape
of three or four books. It looked harmless enough, this vehicle, and inconsequential, quite as though it belonged to some
student lad or (except for the books) to a younger laborer, to
anyone but the private visitor whom my mother feared. For
plainly my mother feared the private visitor, and suspected in
him influences and powers, and regarded him as an enemy,
and supposed him to be formidable and dire and sly: hardly
the sort to come jangling up on an old blue bicycle, with a
missing front fender, and a searchlight clamped to the tubing,
and a pile of books strapped and wrapped against the rain in
thin green paper, and every metal part, frame and chain and
hidden rusted screw, bouncing like a rope of bells. Nevertheless I heard behind the wall the sudden peopling of my
mother's room, and steps both confident and leisurely (not
my mother's walk, for she unhesitantly hopped and sped, nor
Enoch's, uncertain, slow, rhythmically unpredictable), and
the brief shriek of a chair pulled across wood, and the closing
of a door—and then, at that moment after the settling and
confrontation when voices always rise to frequent a first
meeting: nothing, no noise or sound of any kind. I leaped to
the other bed, and listened close to the wall, and still nothing,
not a whisper. And I wondered whether the three of them
were somehow stunned and could only sit and gape, or
whether no one had come after all, and the bicycle, like the
torches, were part of some dread viscosity of imagination.
But there it was; I saw it in the garden, embedded now by
the force of its own weight deep in the hedge; and just next
to its rear reflector, from the protruding point of a little stick,
hung a fragment of cloth. It fluttered wetly, then sagged, then
once more was blown full, and I thought it was perhaps a
handkerchief the wind had mistakenly impaled there, or else
a bit of wayward rag, until I looked again, and recognized it
for what it was meant to be: an adornment, a declaration, a
trimming, a boast even. A tiny American flag stuck up, waving fitfully—the kind seen at carnivals, and growing out of
houseplants, and in the clutch of celebrants—a mean, wild,
alien, homeless and comical little flag, heralding not so much
nationality as temperament. And I fancied how on downward
grades it unfurled and showed all its petulant shabbiness—but
workingmen and serious scholars pedaled unbedecked; and
gay students went in for squirrel-tail plumes or colored rib-

bon-streamers rippling from the hub-nut, and then only if
they followed the United States trends—and so I took it (not
just then, but afterward, when I learned about the categories
into which certain persons willy-nilly throw their lives) for a
badge of Bohemia. It gave notice, at least, of an irregular
identity, not energetic, not enterprising (American virtues
which these particular stars and stripes, faded but dripping-
dark, half-folded, limply dangling from a casual stick, denied
—no, scorned), but rather calmly wistful, even hopeful, even
optimistic. It put a favorable construction on things (with
reservations), anticipated a favorable outcome, flapped in the
most favorable of all possible breezes. And again turning
from it to listen (face down in the bare crotch-and-armpit-
smelling mattress) to the doubtful silence in the next room, I
tried to see Nick astride that loosely-jointed self-spanking
metal ganglion, all spinning teeth and rim and wheel, fife-
and-drumming down some narrow street with sparrow-rump
of flag upright behind him, part-gypsy, part-scout, his shoulders bundled into the very rucksack my mother claimed to
remember from some undisclosed long-ago; but it did not
work; the picture had too much of the jolly vagabond, in
spite of all I had overheard, and sputtered and failed. My vision persisted in producing a sombre dark stark fear-figure,
one who would more likely deliver himself out of the black
maw of a government-sleek Rolls-Royce—but no, he was
poor, they had said he was poor, Nick was poor, and nothing
I dreamed would do, nothing would account for the perverse
uncanny absurdity, the stupidity, the sinister out-of-placeness,
of an American flag sticking straight out of a soaked French
hedge.

So it would not come right; the look of the invaded garden
would not come right; even the silence, humming out of my
mother's room, did not seem a proper silence, and breathed
with mysterious interior exchanges. Whatever their business
was, it kept them mute, it seemed; it kept them dumb. But in
a moment, while I lay on the bed close to the damply flowered wall, the hush on the other side gave out a motion of
expanding, opening; it revealed latent murmurs, loudening
distinctly into troughs of conversation, like a distant iron ship
ploughing nearer: the strain and creak and hollow rumble
come groaning through the sea, and bobbing like a bell afloat
it dongs and calls; yet until it is upon us we think it soundless
and do not perceive those light circumspect signs of its ap-
proach (a rush of cawing fowl, a running hump among the

foremost waves, and certain busy warnings in the ocean-quiet) which expectation might have detected—while all the time, for miles of audibility, in creak and strain and rumble the iron ship has been crying out its coming; and we would have heard had we believed in its existence. In the same way I listened for the vigorous wrestle of a bargain made, or a blatant quarrel, and could conjecture no other relation behind the wall; and expecting this (as who, in a day of steel, would guess at an iron ship?) I did not know how my mother might ceremonially change, face to face with the private visitor, and how her voice might grow thin and high and stiff, like telephone speech accidentally filtered over a crossed wire. It rose and narrowly hung, a thread of something spectral, difficult. to recognize as hers or anyone's; wordless yet glutted with words; a line of sound glimmering with unintelligibility, like the line of sound that the oscilloscope converts to a cruel fence of notched and palpitating light. It was strung, quivering, over the bed: a voice made of wires: and I thought of the tremor in the border-wire when the killing shot sprang out of Germany, and the one-legged giant broke; and how at his huge fall the pulse ran halfway round a country in that slender girdling fence, strummed like a guitar-string by the feet of leaping soldiers: and how I had stained the dust with bilious contours, surfaces, realms.

Realms and a map: it was another map beneath me now, in the shallow place where so many transient bodies had warmed themselves. I found that groove easily; it rolled me down, and took my bare belly comfortably and naturally, as an old bed will, and when I stirred on the mattress a private odor crept from it—a public sort of privacy, intruded on by a public change of sheets, and a public pair of hands smoothing out the marks of night. Shapes and configurations gleamed there, though not of nations and still less of continents—it was not that sort of map: rather, it resembled strewn human features, and now and then an anatomical drawing—the curved sac of a human stomach, a section of a leg with tracing of the circulatory tree, the channel of a nostril all finely haired, a large, bold, wide-open eye—and all of it cleverly and indelibly delineated in old blotches, streaks, soiled islands. Water, wine, urine and blood (the essential liquids) had made that map. The water left only outlines, flat airy pancreases; the urine flamed and faded; the wine bit deep, and ate the fabric (it was the wine, wild and sour, that sent out that secret visceral scent); but the blood had dried to clean black spots. All shone like crenulated scars and entrails.

Meanwhile the negotiations continued—led mainly by my mother's slender unusual wail, and often cut off, still trembling, by a laugh. It was a laugh of confidence (unlike my mother's familiar laughs of self-delusion) and I thought for a moment it was Enoch's, but when it flew out to claim the room, the window, the yard, I caught the assault hidden in it and knew it was not. And immediately after its intrusion my mother began to speak again, so the laugh had no victory. Her tone was new and perplexing—it was a kind of plea that streamed from her. She was alone against the laughter. Enoch did not support her, although he was not far—a series of small noises revealed how he moved in halting circles, a habit of his when he went punching his pockets for the feel of cigarettes: his step approached and diminished regularly. And still the laughter hung and wafted, while my mother demurred, waiting for it to pass (how remorseful that little gap in the rhythm of her voice!), and then again took up her tireless whirr, yielding it like the yawn of a wind through the wall. Now and then it was almost provoked into meaning— the semblance of a word rose and faintly beat, then shrank back as though whipped—and even at the window, where I went to pull a finger through the drops accumulated on the wide dusty sill, they were still phantom notes she sent murmuring out. I drew a calligraphic "Nick" in the dirt, and extended an arm far over to measure the sill—it was wider than my whole arm from the shoulder, so with considerable care (for the garden looked strangely miniature below) I lifted out first one knee and then the other; and found myself on a long stone block, edged with a spiked railing, which ran like an abbreviated balcony beneath a row of shining windows. I turned myself around, clumsy with caution, and crept a little way out; my kneecaps were pitted with granules of lime, and the rain licked gauzily down my back—until suddenly it was lifted away: I looked up and saw the upper eave overhead, cozy as an umbrella, and the gutter spilling beyond reach of me, and all unexpectedly I had a view of my mother's room.

It was stung with light; the panes gleamed with double reflections; the ceiling was a lake of light. A brown curtain came winging out of the window, and behind it lapped a vague seepage of voices. The curtain stirred, and blew back into the bright room: its film of shadow swam across the ceiling like a cloud or wash of fog. My mother was remonstrating—"No," I heard her bleat into the wool of the other's derision, muffled by his fresh and stupendous roar—"Oh, no."

I could see the corner of the high bureau, and the worn nape of an armchair, and the bulbs blinking with uneven current, and I dared myself to crawl out a foot farther along the ledge, and then another longer space, until the flat grey sky swung obliquely into sight in the big oval mirror on the bureau.

"Don't talk to me about *terms*," my mother moaned. I was astonished: her words had leaped into clarity. "What do terms have to do—"

"With you and me?" the visitor asked pleasantly.

My mother rasped. I heard the coarse congregation of spittle in her throat—she might have been breathing in my ear, so close and wounding was her cry. "You said you were coming to talk at arm's length."

"All right, then say I have a short arm." The visitor sent out one of his rattling laughs, and the sound of cold rain running from the gutter went gurgling through it. It seemed to chill his mirth. He resumed, a trifle spitefully, "Still, I only reach for what I can get. The world won't blame me for that, will it?"

"I'm not the world."

"But you run it—it comes to the same thing. It's all in the literature of social protest—anyone who can pay off the gendarmes runs the world."

"Then you saw in the papers we were here!" my mother exclaimed. "You saw all about it!" she said with the thickening note of satisfaction.

"In the papers? I'm afraid I gave up the papers months ago. They're no good without a war."

"But how—"

"They're getting stupidly political, haven't you noticed? Or else they're full of blown-up International Society news—it's part of the trend toward world Americanization. All the editors are becoming surly as a result. Every time you read a column you feel someone's picking an argument with you. I'm a man of peace, I hate to be disturbed. A regular war's more sensible—the news worries you, and when you're worried about a thing of that scale you feel important, and when you think you're important you feel flattered. —And I really like flattery, you know."

"I gave you credit," my mother began weakly.

"Oh, look, that's not flattery!" He waited a moment before

flushing the room with his laughter. "Not when it's cash I've come for!"

Inadvertently she abandoned the tone of entreaty. "I *did* give you credit. I really thought you might have some vestige left of—"

"Vestige!" crowed the visitor. "Vestige! If I've got anything, it's got to be a vestige!"

"Self-perception," my mother finished.

"Oh, good, that's much better. I thought you were going to say decency. Human decency, in fact—that usually runs in vestiges."

"I didn't believe it was an ordinary liaison. A simple ordinary liaison," my mother went on with unexpected scorn.

"Annie, you mean? You want to call it a liaison, you go ahead and call it that. They call it something else in Dutch." He gave an artificial half-sneeze, a sardonic noise just between humor and malice, which seemed to emerge from the flooring; he might have been squatting or bending in some imitative or satiric motion. Whatever the gesture, it could not, according to his satisfied snort, have been obeisant. "The poor girl really *did* get in Dutch with you, didn't she? I suppose you've already fired her?"

"Of course. She went last night."

"Expeditious! I congratulate you, Mrs. Vand."

"The child can do without that sort of influence."

"At all costs?"

"At no cost," my mother spit out.

"Oh, you're very determined, I can see that. But it's all to the good—it shows you administer a good bringing-up. According to all the rules of pedigree—the horse code. No vestiges."

"None," my mother agreed sharply.

"Then I'm glad I came. I really had misgivings—I didn't think we'd be on the same side! I'm very, very glad. That's from the heart, you know."

"I wish you'd state your business and keep your heart out of it."

"It bothers you, my speaking from the heart? You don't like me to be sincere?"

"*You* talk about sincerity!" My mother gave an automatic cough, for poise; I heard it very clearly. "Don't be obscene."

"If I can't be sincere I've got to be *some*thing. It isn't enough to be vestigial, after all. You think it's pleasant to come here and find I'm looked on as a sort of refurbished fossil—"

"Oh, you don't have to worry about that—you can't be a fossil if you were never alive to begin with," she assured him.

"That's the tone to take!"

"I'm not taking any 'tone'."

"I beg your pardon, wasn't that Mrs. Vand's tone? The high and mighty tone of the high and mighty Mrs. Vand? —I've heard about it."

"You've heard a great deal—your friend didn't keep back a thing. Apparently there was nothing she denied you."

"Very few people deny me what I ask for, Mrs. Vand."

But my mother had for the moment marvelously recovered. She might have been addressing Anneke, so purely sovereign was her sally. "Then your requests must be generally worthless," she superbly brought out.

He seemed not to mind this a bit. "In that case there must be something in the *way* I ask!"

But she was no less sly. "Is it your tone?"

"Don't compare my tone with yours!" he rallied. "Mine's perfectly charming. You don't see me intimidating anybody, do you? The nicest thing about me is—you know what?—I'm amenable."

"Yes," my mother said. "I'm aware of your amenability."

He permitted himself a practised hesitation. "Oh, when it comes to that, I can recall *yours*. It doesn't take much digging up, if you're interested in the archaeology of it. You remember that night after the parade—"

"There were lots of parades," Enoch said suddenly; his voice came between them with the brusqueness of a guardian or keeper. I had nearly forgotten the third person in the room, and all at once I thought it odd that the private visitor, Enoch's visitor who had come on Enoch's business, should direct everything all deftly at my mother: and odder yet that Enoch should pace and pace (his footfalls continued to shudder and tramp and weave a ring) and let them sniff up their cage unhindered. "Dozens of parades," he said, "nothing *but* parades"—still, it was impossible to tell from this whether he spoke in defense of my mother, inside the bars; it might as easily have been an accusation.

"*She* knows which one I mean."

"No," my mother protested. "I don't."

"It was January."

"I don't remember any January."

There was a brief disparaging silence.

Then: "She doesn't remember any January," Enoch said.

"There!" confirmed my mother.

"I see it does you good," the visitor said softly, "to think of me as a fossil."

"I never think of you at all."

"A real moral good. It's what makes you Mrs. Vand." He stopped and loosed a self-amused sound, not really laughter any more. "You don't mind my saying Mrs. Vand? I'm rusty on Allegra, and I think I *ought* to say Mrs. Vand, under the circumstances, I mean—"

"Under the circumstances that's who I am."

"What?"

"I *am* Mrs. Vand." my mother responded stoutly.

"I don't argue it. It couldn't be plainer. I admit to it," said the visitor, "gladly, gleefully. I even applaud it. Look, I admit to it with all my heart—"

"I told you to keep your heart out of it."

"—only I'm somebody too. Look at it that way, Mrs. Vand."

"You're Nick."

"All right—"

"And Nick doesn't exist. That proves it."

"Proves *what?*"

"That I never think of you."

"Never?"

"You're the man in the moon." She was all confidence again. "You're not there, that's all. You don't exist," she repeated.

"Not for you, then maybe for someone else."

But she was practical and patient. "You don't exist for anyone."

"No one?"

"Isn't that what I'm saying? No one. Not a soul."

He seemed to suck on the moment that mildly intervened. "You prefer it that way?" he pretended to wonder after a while. "You really prefer it?"

"I more than prefer it. I intend it."

"You intend it. See!" he said. "Didn't I tell you we were on the same side? We peep through the same pair of eyes, Mrs. Vand!"

"You might just as well keep your eyes out of it too," she came briskly back.

"Eyes too? Eyes and heart—you don't leave me much to

negotiate with. There's nothing left but arms and legs! You
didn't think I came for a wrestling match?"

"You're rough enough, even for that."

"Rough? Oh, like a diamond in fact! But I know what you
mean. I haven't any facets. I come all in one lump—not a
solitary shiny part. Still," he reasoned, "it doesn't change
what I'm worth."

"*I* can tell him what he's worth, can't I?" But it must have
been the window and the walls as much as Enoch my mother
sneeringly addressed; and there was no reply from any of
them. Meanwhile the visitor appeared to be mopping away a
long meandering trickle of fresh amusement: from all that
foam his intimate skeptical tones came up horny and hard,
like the dogged dependable back of a turtle. "I'd like to hear
it, Mrs. Vand," he pursued—"it's just for that I'm here. Perhaps"—and surely the hearty din of his "perhaps," with its
far convivial reverberations, was struck for Enoch too—"perhaps we can all agree on a price," he gave out, and let the
notion stand.

It stood. "Price," said Enoch solidly. "There you are, Allegra."

"It isn't as though I didn't expect it," she complained. "It's
exactly what I expected, didn't I say so?"

But Enoch once more only answered "Price," and went on
dropping muffled steps around the room.

"If you expected it," resumed the visitor, "that's better yet.
We accommodate one another—that's even more than *I* expected! Although I'm not surprised at your point of view.
Mine is just the same. That's the crux of it all—we hold a
single intention, Mrs. Vand: you and I! It's remarkable, isn't
it?—when you think of it?"

"I have better things to think of," countered my mother.

"Of course. You're thinking of a price."

A syllable of outrage fell from her.

"Ah, but when I bring you exactly what you want," he
comfortably reproved. "I'm perfectly willing not to exist, you
see, for someone else"—somehow she obliterated the flare of
her little cry—"as long as I can manage to exist for *you*.
That's the thing, after all. One wants one's due."

Her spite was light and fine. "Oh, if you were to get
that!—"

"Well, put it that one wants a little acknowledgment," he
conceded.

Enoch darkly emerged: "It depends of what."

"Of who one is; of what one is. Oh, I don't say as a regular thing—only now and then: I want to be fair. I don't ask for anything contrary to temperament."

"*Your* temperament, you mean," said my mother.

"My temperament—of course. I like to think of the long run."

"You've never noticed the long run," Enoch said with the precision of recitation, quite as though he had come to the end of one of his lists, "in all your life." But my mother overwhelmed the bareness of his declaration with a dozen sudden hoarse condemnations, which passed without purpose through the bright panes and into the oddly coarsened air—the rain had begun to multiply, and changed its pitch to avoid the eave, and came against my nape and cheeks in little blows. I did not mind the rain; it was endurable; for meanwhile I was preoccupied with the arrangement of my limbs. My left leg, which had been twisted under me for a sort of bolster, was stiff with cramp. It was partly numb and partly thick with black pain; I had to drag it after me across those eroded concrete inches, turning halfway on the ledge and reassembling myself as best I could. My mother's wails had quickly grown familiar. They left me no curiosity; I was bored by all that vivacity without intelligibility, and thought to retrace my cold brief trail. So I crept on with the solemnity of disappointment, and looking down saw the garden, through interstices, grey and drenched, and the blue bicycle sunk almost out of view behind a grating of bobbing twigs. The concierge's husband's silly bush bounced: and under an assault of big drops the little stubborn flag beat like a fierce rag-bird to escape the tether of its stick—it tore away and would have flown off, but each time the wind struck it back and furled its striped plume. The private visitor, returning, would find his things in ruin. Already his bundle had slipped off the fender and was dangling like an out-of-rhythm pendulum, square-edged, from a wet string. I watched it queerly hang and rock, and wondered whether he would be angry and would blame my mother for keeping him long, while all the while his flag and books (I thought I knew what sort of books) were getting spoiled. She did keep him; she kept him and talked, and sent out her unaccountable faint whine, and would not buy. For I did not doubt that he had come to sell. What else could he have come for? I supposed he was a salesman, one of those curious entrepreneurs and pursuers who made secret appointments and uncommon offerings, dogging my mother: sometimes it was gems they sold her, and frequently cars, and often paintings, owned previously by duchesses; and if the man chattered of gems, cars, or paintings, my mother would not buy, but if he spoke of something else (of the duchess, say) she would. Usually, therefore, the man would wisely speak of something else, for though he may have looked a fool (uniformly they looked to be fools, breathless, hairless, flat-thumbed), he had come a long way and grown clever on the journey—he might throw down his traveling-box, certainly he would hurl aside his window-frame portfolio stuffed with touched-up photographs, as though these were impediments to the style he knew my mother's brilliance required, and smiling and fawning and whirling his elbows he seemed obliged to sell, before anything else, himself. And regularly afterward my mother would glitter in a new place (a long-unused finger would suddenly spawn a fantastic ring; or a shining stone looped from temple to temple by the dark deft hands of a Parsee salesman would sit astride her brow) or she would be driven off gaily in a snail of white enamel, or she would confront with comfortable purrings a preposterous picture full of rosy gnats, and carry it under her arm all day. But she never minded when I attended, as once or twice the occasion had it, one of these odd private entertainments, rich with flattery and implausible pleasurable gossip; she never pretended the man had come on Enoch's business. And I no longer believed that he had come on Enoch's business, this Nick who avoided speaking of nothing, and who was careless of my mother's feelings, and seemed unaware of the expectations of her brilliance. It could not have been Enoch's business he had come on, whatever my mother might say: and he had arrived with no merchandise but his bicycle, his bundle of books, his bit of spangled rag. Did he mean to bribe their favor by waving the flag of compatriotism? And having won it, did he mean to sell his old bike? (How I would have fancied just such a vehicle for my own, miraculously blue, clanging and ringing!) Or did he mean merely to hawk his books? —But Enoch's visitors came discreetly, presenting their accounts and inventories with the deep attention of the very bored; they drove dusty little French cars; they complained of their territory; they complained that their merchandise was slow to move: that it was too fresh, being redolent still of factory-handling; that it was too stale, being old as violated Eden. They complained that the market was reluctant; that there were no reputable outlets; that facilities for distribution were a tangle of contradictions; that the supply of the product exceeded by ten thousand percent the demand for it; that it was consequently impossible to dump even whatever portion was already released from the wholesalers and the chains. This was their language, although I knew it was corpses they meant, and mass graves, and exhumations, and freight cars lurching westward, and names lost forever, and the blind tongues of the dead, and cinders and smoke. It was their language, practical, purposive, and without whimsy: it was the jargon of trade. The gem-men and the auto-men and the picture-men had the same difficulties with turnover: in trade it is all the same, whatever the merchandise. But this Nick was something new. If he had not come to haggle over late acquisitions with Enoch, if he had not come to fatten my mother's velvet jewel-sack, why did I hear his calculated tradesman's laughter just now beading the wind?

He was a secret from me. And in his letter he had written "child."

So I supposed he had come for me—for a surprise; I really supposed he was a salesman of children's books, and that my mother (who could be indulgent when it suited her) believed my behavior on the homeward ship would be tolerable only if I were soundly beguiled. And the private visitor, a confident salesman, laughed, because despite his assertion the bargain was all on his side—what, in that part of the world, at that instant of history, could be rarer than a child's book in English? But they had known him before; that much, from the quality of their unfathomable talk, was plain. Perhaps they had even turned him away once or twice—I hadn't needed books when Anneke had let me have my shells—and now his price, out of malice, was even higher. His price, it seemed, was too high.

"God damn you," my mother flung out suddenly.

His price was sinister. And I did not care for books just then; I coveted his bicycle, and thought, if only they would let the books go and bargain fearlessly for the bicycle, how I would mount it and ride it home to America, round and round the ship's deck, spinning more clamorously than the gulls, and bluer than the sea. But while I was musing into the far-down garden, the little offending muscle once more twinged; and to relieve it I stopped short and arched back to stretch away the cramp, with the rain's slant salting my eyelashes: and, sloth-like, upside down, the big wide curtain-winged square of my mother's window, and inside it her

room reversed—the ceiling was the floor, and the ceiling-
lights a pool flashing in the middle of the floor, and the armchair all gone. But the black frame of the bureau-mirror
seemed suspended all by itself, without a top or a bottom,
like the oval mouth of one of those magic mirrors which can
speak out who is the fairest of us all. The answer, just then,
appeared in the form of a face, which marvelously emerged,
just as you would expect of a magic mirror, out of a packet
of clouds showing exactly the configuration of the clouds
over the garden. The fact that the mouth in this face was sit-
uated a nice distance above the nose hardly made the sight
less wonderful. I rose to my haunches to persuade it to come
right, and recognized in the reassortment of these features the
reflected portrait of my stepfather. It was a serious and
deeply realistic study, not in the least astonishing: the mirror
with justice had conjured the fairest of them all. It was not
that his long sallow chin, already growing jowly, the blade-
high nose-bridge, that triangular forehead veering back in a
style my mother called Canaanitic, and all the other particu-
larities of margins and pockets which, in spite of so many angles, suggested (for the future) bulk, even portliness—not
that these marked him out for such a compliment. This
wasn't the sort of fairness the mirror, taking the wizard's
privilege of ambiguity, meant. If it had been merely Enoch's
face that had swum up out of chaos, it would hardly have
mattered, to the mirror or the moment. But it was not simply
Enoch's face: it was Enoch's look. It was the dispassionate
and judicious look of a man intimate with passion and injudi-
ciousness, and all the more prepared against them. He was
fair. Nothing could be clearer in his look than his unshak-
able, unbreakable fairness. It almost made me pity whoever
might have been the object of it. "Allegra," I watched him
say—for an instant his head ducked away, then reappeared;
he had taken a short turn and come back to the spot where
the mirror unerringly transmitted him, down to the shoulders,
like a library-bust—"Never mind that, Allegra," he commanded her fury. But the words were derived from the air,
and although I saw his mouth flicker, I might have been
watching a crude early piece of sound-film, not quite syn-
chronized, in which the actor has not yet discarded the rule
of the broad and trustworthy gesture. Whoever it was he
stared at—he *was* staring—could not have escaped the full
fanatical sense of that determined unfanaticism. Oh, he
would be fair!—even I could read that, in spite of the light-

splinters that now and then spoiled the portrait in the mirror. "Didn't I say what he was after? Didn't I know it?" my mother went on, sending out her quick beratements: but Enoch's eye did not waver.

"Allegra," he said again, and stopped, as though that were enough.

But for the private visitor it was not enough. The private visitor plainly valued expansion and reiteration. "I'm not 'after' anything, Mrs. Vand—except what you're after yourself. You can't call *that* villainous!"

"The soul of the noble motive," my mother murmured.

"Well, why not? Only nowadays," the private visitor amiably developed, "you can't get somebody to vanish by mere intention. I mean you can't simply yell abracadabra and have it happen. Try it and see." The face in the looking-glass only very slightly frowned at this—the frown of an efficient administrator who discovers his underlings in the act of folding paper airplanes. But it was without effect. "Listen," began the private visitor experimentally—"Abracadabra. I've said it. You see? Nothing. I'm still here. It isn't as easy as all that, Mrs. Vand! It isn't in accord with modern business practise. In today's market you have to secure your intention."

"Oh, get on with it," Enoch said. "Let's finish it up."

"Yes, let's finish it up," my mother joined in. "There's no point in dragging on this way, when the fact is I have all the security I need."

"I know, Mrs. Vand, I know! But it's not a finish I have in mind, it's really only a beginning, don't you see? Because I understand you exactly, Mrs. Vand—oh, trust me to understand you! You take care of your interests, isn't that right? You watch out for them."

"If I didn't they wouldn't have stayed so unsoiled."

"*Are* they"—he gave a doubtful little crooning chuckle at the word—"unsoiled?"

"Perfectly. It's how I intend to keep them."

"I was confident you would. It's the reason I came. —Only you make them sound terribly psychological!"

"I make them sound what they are. My interests," affirmed my mother, "are identical with my wishes." But this gaudy bloom of a notion, left over from her argument, with my stepfather, of hours before, fell from her stale and shrivelled; it would not yield twice in a day, and had all the juicelessness of a quip forced to make do as a credo, decked out above its station and beyond its powers. The stare the mirror gravely emanated must have met and deflected her bravado: as quickly as possible she amended it. "Oh, more than that even!" she put out—"you'll find my wishes identical with my intention," she explained, as though this would set the matter straight, "and as far as *that's* concerned—well! My intention is—absolutely—my security."

But the matter, encouraged by her pushing hopeful tone, had turned crookeder than ever. It was too ludicrous— Enoch's view, almost fiercely detached, showed just how ludicrous it was. His left eyelid drooped—it was an old weakness, the consequence of the barest touch of strabismus—and in contrast to it the other eye seemed more than humanly open, a whole wide observing sky only briefly and accidentally limited by an aperture. It gave him—it was not inoffensive—the disinterest of an ideal judge taking in horrendous testimony. Meanwhile the other's laughter rammed like a shock wave— "Put 'security' in the plural and you have it!" The private visitor opportunely whooped. "Maybe I'd care about psychological interest if it *accrued*—which is where stocks and bonds have all the advantage!" He submitted to being wrung out by his joke and even allowed it to suck his breath away; he did not appear to mind that Enoch's half-shut scanning marked it all out, down to the last whimsical tremor, as evidence.

"Have we come to it then?" said Enoch.

"Come to what?"

"The point of your being here. I can't wait all day."

"Oh, you mean my proposal," the private visitor swallowed it up, in a voice faintly cracked from rubbing his joke in his throat.

"Do you *have* a proposal? I thought you didn't bother with 'em," my mother offered.

"All right, call it a proposition then—if you're thinking of poor Annie! But don't let's hurry, I have all the time in the world. If I didn't have the time I wouldn't be here. Blame yourself for it—it's only because you sent her packing that I've *got* the time. A liaison, after all—that's your word y'know, not mine—but anyway they're terribly occupying, did you ever happen to notice that?"

"No," my mother said shortly.

"And with your good memory!"

Her cry fell softly, softly against him. It had something of his laughter in it, not so much an echo as the laughter itself turned inside out and showing its hasty ugly seams. She was all at once subdued. "God damn," she gave out, but it was

too vague to intend efficacy; it was the merest wisp of a sigh,
an exhalation voiced for want of something less striking than
silence. She was, anyway, no good at conventional imprecation—it might well have been the legacy of William's stiff
proprieties. Still, looking into herself for a glimmer of savagery, she tried hard: "Damn you, Nick, God *damn* you"
sprang from her once more, and whether the malediction required the usual three chantings to set it going, or whether
she had at last, by an utterance of perfect hatred, unwittingly
charged and unleashed its magic, her quiet deep curse nevertheless brought forth a marvel. I started at her achievement
—she had blotted out the mirror. It hung empty, filling up
slowly with the impalpable images of clouds—the glass
turned grey, breathed-over. Enoch was gone. It was as
though, by an unspeakable error of the spoken, she had mis-
directed her damnation and eradicated her husband, when it
was the other man who had challenged her to make him dis-
appear.

But the other man was still there.

He said: "I'm interested in that, the idea of damnation"—
it was easy to suppose that here he smiled—"*my* damnation,
not no-one-in-particular's," and out of the smooth dim murmur of his pleasure I just then lucidly took the truth. It was
brilliantly clear to me, all at once, whom he had come for.
Why did not matter, for some reason: I could not divine
what he wanted; I did not comprehend it until years afterward, when William told it to me one strange evening on
Wall Street; but I knew whom he had come for, for whose
sake he spread his legs invisible to me on the bed in my
mother's room, booming out his subtle commands, weaving
mockeries, inventing new notes for laughter, supplanting
Enoch with a big untamed authority. He was not, at any rate,
the peddler my ingenuity had churned up out of the garden
—not a peddler of books or bicycles or anything. My
mother's first "God damn" had done away with whatever
might be made of the observed facts; her second had obliterated even theories. I was wrong, wrong—gently and with a
dismayed fist I beat my concrete floor. He had not come for
me. He had not come for Enoch. He had not come for my
mother. He had not come for corpses. He had not even come
for Anneke, although now and then it almost seemed he was
there to fetch her back to nurse him through perhaps another
night's perplexing illness. —Oh, he had not come for any of

us. The advantage, whatever it was, was all his. He had simply come for himself.

He said: "In case I *am* damned I'll let you know what the road to hell is really paved with—it won't be with intentions, believe me! —I seem to see a long highway surfaced with checks"—now it was merely a snicker, quick and short, that waited on his vision—"miles and *miles* of pink checks—"

"Then we've come to it," said Enoch. Now only the clouds were the fairest of them all—dirty bags of wetwash wringing out their corners: the mirror had given up its witness, and since seeing was no help I embraced my head between my knees in a circle of self-wondering and listened. It was quite as though the trial were over, and the moment for sentencing had come. Enoch could be as vindictive as he felt like being now, as long as he kept to the law; and the law, from his changed voice, harsh, partisan, strict, was a bitter one. "If that's what you've been thinking of why didn't you come before?"

"Before? When before? You mean before Annie?"

"Years before."

"It's a pity I didn't. Blame it on the war."

"Yes, blame it on the war," my mother mocked him.

"But actually it wasn't the war," he said, almost apologetic. "I really have no complaints about the war. In my position it doesn't matter, war or peace—"

And Enoch: "In your position? What is your position?"

"Well, I don't see the point in taking sides, you know. I don't care about countries," he told them, and thinking of the colored shred that badged his wheel I marveled at his lie—who but the profoundest patriot would travel always with a flag?

But my mother insisted, "What is your position?"

"I am a piano-player, Mrs. Vand," he said in a dark voice. "I mean by that I'm more of an international person. It's in the nature of playing the piano not to care about countries."

"Chopin didn't mind being a Pole," my mother retorted.

"You remember about that, hah? But I don't play him any more. Nowadays it's only the American things that go over. I always have to do 'Rhapsody in Blue'—they don't hire you if you can't do 'Rhapsody in Blue,' they won't even audition you. But I told you you had a good memory, Mrs. Vand! — You remember that hall off Trafalgar Square, somebody'd let in the goons, and I got to the black keys—they'd ripped out half the white ones—just when the constabulary popped in,

and instead of a riot they found the Chopin Freed Poland Society? They couldn't take in a single man, not with the Polo-
naise going—it had all the signs of Polish respectability—
what a noise! My God, you couldn't do a thing like that with
'Rhapsody in Blue'; it just isn't possible!" He spoke like a
man hinting at a delightful reminiscence common to all the
company: he does not need to give the whole story, even a
small grimace is enough, for they have all been there together, and together have lived the anecdote through in all its
hilarious rococo (the past is always rococo) rich little quaint
little details, bumps, and crevices; and together they are now
all expected to roar at each suggestively funny word. But no
happily remembering sound came from my mother, although
it was, certainly, just the sort of adventure she liked best,
with its incitements, eludings, dupings of the police (of whatever country), and its titillating threats of arrest; so I could
easily believe she had been a part of such an imbroglio, and
waited to hear her remark on it.

Instead she kept an avid silence, and surprisingly not she
but Enoch remonstrated, "It wasn't Trafalgar Square"—quar-
relsomely. "It wasn't even near Trafalgar Square."

"Well, I said *off* it—"

"It was a hall on New Oxford Street. And they *did* take
someone in. It was Sparrs."

"Sparrs! I forgot about Sparrs, you're absolutely right.
He'd cut jigsaw puzzles out of a gross and a half of cardboard portraits on the Royal Children and hawked them in
the lobby. He had them in cotton string-bags, all in pieces."

"It wasn't for that they arrested him. It was for stealing.
He made off with one of the chairs."

"It wasn't a chair," my mother said finally, nettled into
speech by the plain error of it. "It was a stool, the one he
was using to yell from. He stood on top of this high stool, it
was a kind of ladder, and bawled 'The Little Princesses Dis-
membered! Elizabeth Quartered Limb from Limb! Margaret's
Torso Sawed in Two!" —And when the police came he simply ran off with the stool. I don't think he *meant* to take it."

The private visitor praised indulgently, "I've always admired that sort of retention. With a memory like that you
can't lose the past no matter how hard you try, can you?
Poor Sparrs, *I'd* forgotten all about him. —God, how we
used to hate royalty in those days! But he was Old Philadelphia; his mother made him come home. I bet he hasn't been
out of Philadelphia since."

"They won't let him out of the country," Enoch said. "He's an Esperantist, one of their big men by now, but he isn't allowed to go to their overseas meetings. They won't give him a passport."

"On account of his hating royalty?" my mother said. "What could please the State Department more? It's how they got started!—hating royalty."

"If you'll change R to L," Enoch said. "—All those old memberships . . ."

"Not the Chopin Freed Poland Society!"

"Conceivably even that."

The private visitor whistled. "Loyalty, that's very interesting; you can see I'm out of touch." He went on shrewdly, "You know all that sort of thing, don't you? I suppose it's your business to know. —In *your* position."

"Oh! my position," Enoch vaguely answered. "I don't get near politics."

"Well, if they won't let you out . . . But they can't keep you from coming *in* again, can they?"

"No," Enoch said, "they can't."

"In that case I might go back."

"To America? You wouldn't!" my mother gasped.

"To keep in touch, why not? I like to go where I'm comfortable—"

"You were comfortable in Germany," Enoch remarked.

"Ah, you've heard about that! But I had to get out—that was '38 or so. They said I was spying for the Communists. So I went to Prague."

"Where somehow they got the notion you were spying for the Germans?"

"You *are* remarkably political."

"They were none of them mistaken, I suppose."

"A man has to make a living," the visitor said mildly. "You make yours; I make mine."

"Certainly," Enoch agreed. "There's not a spot in Europe that couldn't use a piano-player during the war."

"Clever mind, cold nature, that's an old story. Annie told me how unsympathetic you were."

"Enoch had no room on his staff for her brother, and even if he'd had, they're centralized appointments," my mother began to protest, "Enoch doesn't have any say in them. These people ought to stay in their home countries anyway. Wherever you go you find all the wrong people in the wrong places. Europe's become a scramble."

"True enough. From that point of view alone you owe me something," the visitor pointed out. "I'm a Displaced Person, after all, just like all the others. I wouldn't be surprised if your husband's got me somewhere in his books. I'm registered everywhere, they catalogue everything; just let him look in his lists—"

"You are not in my lists," Enoch said.

(And faintly, from my mother: "If only he were!")

"You've got bad lists then."

"Yes. Very bad."

But the visitor did not see, did not shudder, did not know; and only said, "When it's your business to have all that sort of information? When you've kept your finger on where *I've* been—"

"I've kept my finger on nothing," Enoch said.

"Haven't you?"

Enoch tightened: "I don't see that it's reasonable to go on. If it's all talk, and no conclusion . . . It's too late for talk."

"It's too late *not* to talk. Look at it that way," the other said, seeming to cajole. "I can't say you're very hospitable."

"You're not exactly in the situation of a guest. At any rate our tenure here was over at noon—hospitality isn't ours to give."

"Oh, let's not have a dismissal! Not quite like that; don't think of it. Throwing me out's not the thing. It's against conscience, especially against an Oriental conscience—a tooth for a tooth! I'm speaking of, well, you remember, that time after the parade—you know which parade: I mean the one in Brighton, you had that whole side of the face swollen, big as a balloon, it was a Sunday and no dentists—*we* didn't throw you out, did we? And we had only the one little room, cramped enough for two, all full of that greasy bed, and only a hotplate, and that nasty puking—"

"Oh, shut him up, Enoch, can't you!" my mother shrieked.

"—and still we put you in the bed and got you through it —how we figured out about that icebag!—and finally snow from the window-sill wrapped in my only pair of sound socks—"

"God Almighty, shut him up! He's got no right to bring up Brighton, has he?" The raindrops tottered against the high sob of her lamentation; she groaned helplessly. "You don't have to bring up Brighton!"

"My dear Mrs. Vand"—he barely hesitated—"I expect I have to bring up everything."

No one answered him, so I thought it was all over then, the meeting, my mother's pleas and growls, all. A thread of rage, already too much used, dangled briefly in her throat without effect, until a sudden click of quiet cut it off. Were they afraid to answer him? Or were they even now surrendering with who knows what terrible mute sign? Someone walked across the room, walked pickingly and windingly: I recognized the croquet-tapping twitter of my mother's steep Parisian heels. Would she for an answer leave him planted there, the private visitor, abandoned where he sat among probable mounds of discarded stockings, and not a word to cry him down? "The wind," I heard her say, all quickly meek, "how strong the wind's become, it's blowing half my things"; she was coming to the window. In the dusk of rain I felt safe enough, and wondered whether to retreat: but when her lustrous reaching arm slid out to pluck the curtain from the air, like a coward I slumped back and struggled to fold myself away at every inconvenient hinge. The curtain went on flapping dizzily, long yards of peacocks and vines, while up and up she leaned after it, so that once, for a moment only, I saw the side of her cheek: it was raw and pressed with markings, as though she had squeezed her fingers brutally against it (meanwhile I remembered Anneke's cheek, furrowed at dawn); and then the peacocks descended like a brown mask and covered her. She had caught hold at last, and began to pull the folds of cloth in to the sill almost too impatiently, her hands grasping at plumage while the wind worked and my mother worked, tugging with a Rapunzelian eagerness, as if a live reward would clamber in at the end, clinging to the curtain's tail; but at the end, when she had gathered it all into the room, there was only a fringe of cheap thick tassels. I heard a sound of rings drawn on a bar, and then the peacocks fell against the panes as noiselessly as some gross dark membrane dropping downward. The mirror was all at once shut off; and the ceiling, and the ticking bulbs. I could see nothing now; my bit of ledge grew black; my mother had fastened the fabric across the window. It was a seal; it was distinctly a seal. Or perhaps, more simply, it was merely time she wanted, a delay, knowing what would follow. But the lid was drawn down and hooked, and the clouds driven from the room and made to swim in their own night, and every snooping stir of air defied. She was out for privacy. It was not time she wanted then, time being of no possible use. On my blackened ledge, in the stinging slant of rain, I felt the uselessness

of time. Time was tedium, time was talk. They talked like
dancers in a figure seen too close: the pattern was obscured
by approaches and digressions, by chase and retreat: by plain
dead repetitious goalless tedium. And so once more my
mother's step went drumming over the floorboards: windingly
and pickingly. She had drawn the curtain and sealed in time,
although, knowing what would follow, it could do her no
good. Nevertheless she delivered herself of the gesture, and
immediately afterward delivered herself up to Enoch.

To Enoch; to Enoch only; for who but my stepfather
might understand that language of her pantomime, the drawing of the curtain? She drew it not against spies or witnesses
—who could she sensibly suppose might crouch watching on
the ledge beneath her, what sinister fool would ride the sky to
hear? But she drew it anyhow, simultaneously leashing the
peacocks printed on the fabric and her bewildered image of
the bird of the world; she leashed them both. The curtain
strained from hook to hook, an inviolable tissue. It was quite
as though she had pulled her crescent eyelids down, standing
in the middle of that ambushed room with ruthless fingers
daggering her cheek; the stigma of her rings stood in her
flesh. Her husband was there; and the stranger who was no
stranger; and at their feet the bird of the world, slaughtered.

And at last: "Give him what he wants," my mother said.

But the other man demurred, "You don't have to be
ashamed."

"The wind," she said, "blowing all my things—"

"You don't need to hide," he comforted without pity.

"It was the wind," she said again, "and the curtain went
wild."

And Enoch then: "There's nothing else to do, don't you
see, Allegra, there's nothing else to do; let's go ahead," he
said, but it was not the voice that spoke his lists, "we'll go
ahead and get it over with," he said, "there's nothing else to
do."

I did not like his voice. It was full of judgment, thick with
formal disposition, embroidered with the breathings of unsus-
pected cruelties. "Give him what he wants," my mother
yielded once more; and I plainly knew it was not the private
visitor he was sentencing without mercy, but Allegra Vand.
"How much does he want?" she murmured, "he talks and
talks of price, but he doesn't say how much—"

"We'll give him what he wants," Enoch said.

So my mother was condemned. It seemed it was not the

private visitor who had crushed her, but Enoch himself, with his ease of anger and his clarity and his practical wary judicial voice. "Oh well then, what he wants," she trailed off, and long afterward, when I had buried that day and all its tokens, there remained the broken sigh of her acquiescence like a primitive hut built upon an old, lost, artful, and infinitely aristocratic city of gold.

I crept back then, clinging to the wall beneath the eave, while Enoch briskly settled and administered—"No, no, nothing now, you spoke of being businesslike. Checks; checks only, that's fair enough; well all right, there's got to be a record; think of our side! There's the trustee to consider, if *he* won't allow it—" ("Oh, William, I can handle William," my mother sadly interjected.) "Checks then," Enoch repeated, "but you'll have to write, how will we know—" ("It isn't as if we could help it," my mother said.) And then, jumping out of meditation, "Don't let him write!" she cried, "there's nothing worse than letters with that one! Invisible ink's no good with that one! Burning's no good! What's the point, if you let him write? You don't know that one, such a pair of eyes!" "They won't be *letters*, Allegra; don't be stupid. He'll send a figure and an address, how else are we to know where he is?" —but all the while they were mumbling out their quarrel I was scraping and scrambling to get away. For the first time I saw the untrustworthy deep rust in the railing; the ledge looked shockingly narrow. My absorption had split in two—I was all at once terrified of falling. But "Sssh," my mother said in the middle of my fright, "there's something, don't you hear? Out there, a funny sort of noise." "It's the rain." "No, no," she persisted, "besides that, listen." "A cat," clucked Enoch, "the concierge must have a cat." "A cat? I never saw a cat." "Look, you'd better pay attention," he said impatiently, "it's your money, isn't it?" and by the time I heard her answering moan of "money, there's no way out, give him what he wants and get it over with," I had climbed down to the floor of my own safe room. "How I hate money," I thought I heard her say, but the words came muffled through the wall; she might have said something altogether different, after all.

8

I began to dress myself. I put on first my socks and shoes and then, mildly shivering, my underwear. The hanger had become entangled in the light-cord; I twisted and twisted but could not dislodge it, so I pulled at my dress until the collar and sleeves slipped free and the dress flew down like a wing. Unexpectedly the light jumped on. This was pleasant: until then I had not noticed that the ceiling had grown darker than the sky.

From the next rōom came no hint or scratch.

I went to sit on the bed and for some reason—hunger, perhaps—decided to cry. Seriously and neatly I willed the tears. I was able to bring them up without resorting to contortions of eyes or mouth, for my mother had often maintained that for each pair of tears an ineradicable wrinkle sprang up; at that time I occasionally still believed her. The proof, moreover, was that she herself never wept. She had only two small lines, shallow but strictly parallel, across her forehead, and these were usually obscured by the dark fringing crownpoints of her hair. I calculated that in all her life she had dropped only four tears. It seemed to me very few; I had already, in a single minute, sent down many more than that. Nevertheless I knew that the scarcity of her tears did not signify my mother was happy, just as the descending parade of my own did not testify to any abundant sadness. I was not sad. It was my theory—I was unaware that I held it—that sadness is a deliberate sentiment, similar to my mother's exclamations over, say, art. The pictures she continually bought did not overwhelm her; she overwhelmed them. Sometimes, after carrying a painting under her arm for part of an afternoon, she would all at once become unusually melancholy and would set it up on a chair and stand away from it to survey it with discontent eyes. And then I would know that the picture had

not induced this dissatisfaction; she herself had imposed it on
the picture by her terrible reflections. Once a salesman
brought her a woodcut. It showed a hill speckled with flowers
and in the distance a house with a smokeless chimney. It was
indisputably cheerful and pretty and commonplace, but the
salesman—a small, thin, very blond young Austrian with no
teeth at all—insisted there were only seven such inkings in
the world: the Duchess of Windsor had purchased one and
the other five were owned by the Hartford, Connecticut Mu-
nicipal Library. My mother hesitated—Hartford cancelled
the Duchess—and insisted that she could see no value in such
a subject: it was too ordinary, it offered nothing, it represented itself entirely in a single glance, it belonged on a calendar, it failed to challenge, and so forth. But the salesman
put out his fine slight fingers audaciously to pluck her sleeve,
and led her to the mirror and made her look into it: and
there, astonishingly, while he held the vulgar little scene up
before it, the hundred tiny flower-dots turned into Gothic letters, and the house was transformed into an axe, and the hill
into the line of a burly shoulder over which the axe was
slung: and the petal-letters read, "Kein Gott ist." "It's a
trick," my mother said, "it's only one of those optical tricks,"
but she paid for it immediately. And shrewdly, knowledgeably, she asked, "And the original woodblock? What's become
of that?" The salesman rubbed his knuckles and smiled.
"Burned, madam, burned. The whole house burned down."
"And the artist? Where is the artist?" "He was in the house,
madam." "How awful!" she exclaimed. "Where could such a
thing have happened?" "On a hill," said the young man,
showing the healthy orange-pink of his gums, "near a meadow full of flowers. It was a great tragedy for that time of
year: not a spark in the chimney. Thank God for flowers—
that is the best philosophy, nicht wahr?" And he went away.
Forever afterward my mother, as an act of will, hated the
picture, although it was so mild and so commonplace. She
never again looked at it in reverse. And finally she left it behind in the wardrobe of a hotel in Westminster; but I knew,
anyhow, that she had not really been horrified. She had only
chosen to seem to be, for the sake of accommodating mysterious circumstance. In the same way my own evidence of
sadness opened out to me with bland artificiality: it did not
come persuasively, it had to be persuaded; it could not be
evoked, it had to be provoked; it was not on the face of
things, but rather stitched on the underside in some back-

wards occult style. I believed, with that inchoate mysticism which characterizes the stark tenets of the very young, in spells. No feeling was real which did not cast one into the pit of the extraordinary; and even as the tears fell, I was conscious of my equanimity.

The tears fell. One by one they pounced upon my dress. Clearly I was unbewitched by woe, and even strangeness could not move me; yet they came falling, round dark blots teasing the blue cross-stitch along my hem. My dress felt cold and smelled of an unclean, unprivate moisture, oddly like the concierge's breath. The tears left frayed circlets in my lap: wreath after wreath sprang down, and anticipating my mother's orderly inspection I turned aside to save my skirt and watched while the naked mattress drank up the stains. All around the mattress-buttons those timeless marks gleamed in a frieze; and meanwhile new arteries seeped out of old organs, luminous anatomies proliferated, cleverly the map adjusted its topography. Under my tears the essential stains swelled—I continued to suppose they had been grooved in that place by so many accumulations of urine, so many cardinal smears of blood, so many night-thirsts for water, so many bloated spillings of wine, of those so many sleeping travelers: belonging to travelers, they were the essential blotches, blights, and streams of humanity: the wanderer does not carry what is superfluous, what passes for luxury at home shows for spurious in an inn. —This last maxim belonged, of course, to Enoch, chiding my mother for her elaborate packing of a dozen pairs of shoes. Their door opened, they came out talking in ordinary voices. "Well, I can't go down to a ship's dinner *barefoot*," my mother was protesting without a sign of her ordeal; her tone was usual, she was not overtly chastened. Enoch had forced her to recover. "Here, give me that key," he said imperiously, and then, "control yourself, Allegra, don't act like a fool." The key's big teeth clamored furiously this way and that, and took hold with a ringing bite. At the same moment up from the garden came another jangling, as irregular as though someone danced in a cap of bells; it was irresistibly familiar, a roily clacketing sound, like the clinking and rolling of a giant coin over the cobblestones. and I ran to the window to see what Anneke had looked out upon in the early morning light and beheld, while behind me the lock obeyed and the two of them, Enoch and my mother. stopped short of the threshold like conspirators—beheld nothing. Nothing, nothing, only the grassy place below the hedge where the blue bicycle had leaned. It was gone. The scar of a wheel lay pressed in the ground. I listened and wondered at that jubilant rattling—was it the chain swinging like a now-and-then carillon, was it the tongue of the book-strap sweeping a zither of spokes?—It lasted for a space and mingled with the rain, until it was impossible to know whether I pursued the distant spin of the bicycle or a nearer splash on the sill.

"I can see you had the sense to put your clothes on," my mother began; she had stepped into the room as through an invisible noxious element thicker than air. "Well, look, don't hang out the window with the rain slapping at you that way! You'll only get wet all over again." She took the key from Enoch and tossed it on the dresser—it landed with an angry bounce—and stood for an instant looking back to see if he would follow. But he had no intention of coming after, and only arranged his shoulders against the doorjamb with a movement not so much of impatience as of simple weariness. "You and I are going out to dinner. Enoch's got to start out right away—I told you he has a very important conference with some Government people"—she had not told me; on the contrary this was her usual way of imparting to me my step-father's business: by hinting that it was no use going into what I already knew—"people from Washington, and he's dead tired and has to drive all the way to Zürich by himself! It's not going to make a very good impression," she turned to him, "coming in that way without a chauffeur. They won't think you're *any*body. No one's ever going to know how valuable you are as long as you go on dealing with, with—"

But she did not wish to say the word, and winced when Enoch offered her one of his perplexing and infrequent little grins. "A silent client is less of a handicap sometimes than a talking one. Ask William," he said slyly.

"Ah, you're gruesome!"

He quietly rubbed his back on a protruding hinge. "You've never complained of that before."

"After today I'll complain of everything. It was horrible, horrible."

"It was no more," he reminded her, "than what you expected."

"I didn't expect he'd *look* like that!" she burst out.

"He looked harmless enough."

"Harmless, yes. Like a python.—I don't care if it *is* a Freudian image," she yelled.

"Well, don't abuse *me* for it," he said mildly. His face was all at once full of ironic compassionate affection. "He was perfectly all right. He did what he came to do and he went away.—Oh, he drew it out, I admit, just for the pleasure of the thing, but the point is it's done; there's no use thinking about it any more."

"But the way he looked—"

"As ordinary as possible. I noticed nothing in particular."

"There *wasn't* anything in particular. That's just what I mean. He looks the same, just the same." She clasped her hands in quick anxious awe. "He looks like a boy."

"A boy. I suppose you're right."

"But it's ten years at least. And the war!"

"The war didn't bother him. He told you that plainly. For some people," Enoch said, "war is a fountain to drink from."

"The Fountain of Youth," she answered wryly.

"Call it that, if you want."

"There isn't any other sort of fountain that matters."

He said tiredly, "I sometimes forget how sophisticated you can be, Allegra."

But she did not catch his satire. "Sophisticated. That means old. When people start calling you sophisticated there's nothing left but death and decay."

"For a decaying woman you have a great deal of ambition," he observed.

"Well, why not? I don't see why you can't get promoted into a nice clean job."

"I *have* a nice clean job."

This was beneath her scorn. "I mean something higher up. All you do is—I don't know, coördinate the sectors. I mean something diplomatic. You won't get anywhere just supervising channels."

"Bravo." Once again his smile flickered. "You've mastered a foreign tongue."

"You should make them give you something dignified."

"There's nothing more dignified than death," he said, smiling still.

"No, I'm serious. You should make them give you what Pettigrew does," she insisted.

"Pettigrew's a Democrat."

"Then you be one too!" said my mother, trotting out her funny clown's voice in order to toy with the inconceivable. The idea of anyone's becoming a Democrat, even for political advantage, always convulsed her; except for the time she had been a Communist, my mother was a hereditary Republican.

She considered Enoch with a swift intimate glance and suddenly, for the first time that day, together they fell into laughter. Brief as it was, it brought my stepfather from the doorpost and pulled them side by side. "Well," my mother said into his ear, "there must be something you can do short of that."

"Oh, I'd hang myself short of that," he obliged her.

"There's no rope short enough to be short of that," she giggled. They were enclosed, it seemed, behind a scaffolding which the disclosure of their alliance abruptly threw up around them: I peered in at them easily enough, but saw the adumbrations of a wall, and knew, as surely as though the bricks were there, that trespassing was forbidden. This was their obscure goodbye: my stepfather put a finger below my mother's chin to lift it and withdrew his touch in an instant. It was their goodbye. What came afterward would be form only. It had been settled long ago that they would not correspond. My mother's letters skipped in pursuit from place to place, accumulating new forwarding addresses with each increasingly blackened postal mark; besides, they were interminable, fattened by trivia; when at last they overtook him he found them an insufferable affliction; he called them the single Egyptian plague unimaginable even by God and begged her to send no more. They communicated by cables: this restricted my mother to the necessary.

Yet somehow I had intruded. Enoch's eye discovered me and turned indifferent; whatever he had kindled there died out at sight of me. They separated reluctantly. I felt my mother's anger; she opened her nostrils and accused me in silence. It was on my account she could not join the race to Zürich; instead she had to buy me my supper. "Enoch's going to drive us to the restaurant," she stated sourly. "He's just got time, if you don't hold us up. Though you'd better go down the hall first.—Good God, what's the matter with her hair?"

She took up my wrist like a handle and pinched me toward her.

"Where's your comb? I put a comb in there." She was nimbly investigating my pocket. "Can't you for once not lose what I give you? I told you," she threw out at Enoch—but immediately I spied the little white comb on the floor where it had fallen and snatched it up—"I told you she'd be the one to hold us up!"

Without mercy she tore through my hair.

"He's gone," I said, my head down, my mouth hidden.

"What a mess! What's made you frizz up like this? A little dampness in the air, and she turns into a sort of Zulu."

"He went away," I tried again. "Nick."

"Yes, yes, he's gone," she acknowledged.

"I saw the bicycle he came on."

"He didn't come on a bicycle!"

"Yes. he did."

"Well, suppose he did," Enoch said.

The comb hesitated.

"It was all blue, even the handlebars," I said.

"Out here everyone gets around that way," she capitulated.

"But even the handlebars," I persisted.

"That only means it's second-hand and painted over," my mother murmured, stifling what might have been wonder or disgust; it was, in any case, fascination. Furiously she resumed combing and tweaked my scalp until I squealed. "You weren't supposed to be looking out the window! I told you to stay in bed. It's no concern of yours, you don't want to have anything to do with people like that.—Stand still! How do you expect me to get through the snarls?"

"The concierge took the sheets off," I said.

"Too bad, she'll just have to put new ones on for tonight. It should teach them a little cleanliness. They think dirt and thrift are the same thing. I never heard of a Paris hotel that didn't change the sheets every day! Let them learn, they're too greedy. You have to fight greed in this world," she went on authoritatively, "even if it makes you a little less comfortable. Never give in to greed. There's no telling what can come of giving in to greed."

Enoch coolly kept his gaze on my mother's lips; she had made a little tunnel of them and was blowing the uprooted tangles out of the teeth of the comb. "I thought you were going to show some sense, Allegra," he said.

"Sense! All right, I'll show some sense. Pick your head up, why are you so difficult?" she muttered at me. "You don't mean sense, you mean resignation."

"I mean keeping your mind on the highest good," he began.

"Oh, what's the use," she interrupted.

"—for the greatest number," he finished diligently.

"Philosophy!" she spat out. "As though a whole crowd were involved. As though the whole *world* were involved.

You're always making things sound as if the universe depended on, oh I don't know, on every single private act."

"Maybe it does."

"I hate that sort of talk, you know I do. I always have and I always will. It doesn't *mean* anything. What's private is private and what's public is public; that's all there is to it."

"Do you know of anything more public than the universe? And yet all the private things happen inside it. In the end," he said softly, "everything private turns out to be public, if you don't take care." He pulled from his breast pocket the handkerchief my mother had folded for him earlier. It was in the shape of a triangle. With a rapid wag of its points he flashed it open and lapped corner over corner meticulously, until he had made it into a rectangle.

"Poor Enoch," said my mother, pausing to watch these maneuvers, "you have no notion of dress."

"But I have distinct ideas of design." Amiably he restored the cloth to his pocket. "That compensates, doesn't it? It was a question," he took up finally, "of choosing the most intelligent tactics"—almost as though he were referring to his adroitness with the handkerchief.

"It was a question of getting rid of him," my mother bluntly denied. She tugged at the last strand curled at my nape and put me off at arm's length. "There, you're finished. Let me see you. You know, I think she looks a little like my great-aunt Huntingdon. That was my father's aunt on the paternal side. She had very close-set eyes, not at all like mine. It's really remarkable about genes—they have such a definite idea of where they're going, only nobody can find out where until it's too late.—She doesn't look anything like *me*."

"No," Enoch agreed, "nothing like you."

"She looks like someone else."

"I suppose so," he said without interest.

"The chin. And the temples, diamond-shaped in that funny way, can't you tell? Even the nose. The nose very much."

He scarcely deigned to shrug. "I'm not competent to judge."

"What?"

"—Not having been acquainted with great-aunt Huntingdon," he explained, but he had no smile.

"All right, if you want to take that attitude," she said reproachfully. "You *know* whom I mean." She brooded down over me. "Maybe she'll change. Although it doesn't matter to you. You don't care anything about her."

"You expect too much, Allegra."

"No, no, you never even try. You leave it all to me."

"You expect the impossible."

"I don't, it's not true. I just wish you wouldn't be so *detached*, that's all."

He permitted a moment to go heavily by. "I'm not the child's father," he said at length; his weak eyelid stood up suspended in the aftermath of a blink. "You seem to keep forgetting that, Allegra."

"Oh no," she said at once. "You're wrong. I never forget it." Her hand flew defensively to her bosom; she searched him out, wondering after consequences, but the expression he quite readily delivered had nothing for her. She came from him empty. It appeared he had chosen to punish her—not severely; it was only that he had deprived her of his comfort. She turned her head here and there like a parakeet in a frenzy of escape, not knowing where to light: she lit on me. "Look at her—look at her eyes. She's been crying," my mother charged. "You can't leave her alone for an hour without her making *some* sort of mess. I suppose we're in luck, it could have been the stomach-thing. You can go to the ends of the earth, there's no getting away from *that*. It's genes," she pronounced, shoving the comb into the laced slit of my dress. "Oh my God, give me your handkerchief, will you?" —she snatched it out of his coat and blew her nose into it urgently—"I'm allergic to something, it must be those damn hedge-clippings, I can't stand cut greens in the rain—"

She exploded with a tremendous sneeze.

"There goes my last clean handkerchief," said Enoch. "Oh no, please!" as she meekly offered it to him, "do me the favor of keeping it."

"I spoiled your design," she said penitently; it was crushed in her fist.

"It doesn't matter. I can buy more."

"You won't have time. Anyhow I think there's some unopened laundry in your grip. In the tan one, I think."

"No, there are shirts in there. You mean that bundle with the blue wrapping paper? Just shirts, no handkerchiefs. I should think you'd know, you put it there."

They dallied back and forth in this manner, domestically, troubling themselves about handkerchiefs. My mother sneezed again, almost on prescription; and afterward she apologized and Enoch blessed, both in the same breath. They were all at once restored to laughing: "I really wasn't going

to give it back to you. I mean I have *some* sense of hygiene."
"You expected me to fold it up again and put it in my
pocket," he accused. My mother rushed in, struck with an
invention: "You know what? I've just had a thought—it's
about Iago. I've never been able to understand his motive. I
mean it's always seemed so *wanton*. But now you know what
I think it was? When he picked up Desdemona's handkerchief"—she wiped her eyes and tested her nose more out of
celebration than utility—"when he picked it up, well, it was
just so full of *snot,* and his fingers—" Enoch snorted in disgust, but she played it out to the end. "It was such an unpleasant experience he *had* to get even. So he got Othello to
do her in." "Oh, oh," my stepfather said admiringly, "she has
a child's faculty. Alarming Allegra." "I wish it could be Al-
pine Allegra. I wish I could go to Switzerland with you."
"You will another time," he promised her. The vagaries of
her talk for some reason failed to repel him; he would not
have endured it for a moment from his assistants.

Yet it was plain that their hilarity—half secret, half capri-
cious—had nothing at all to do with a handkerchief.—They
had forgiven one another.

"I don't see why you had to cry," my mother said, dropping down to me; she was softened. "I'm taking you home,
isn't that just what you want? What in the world is there for
you to cry about?"

I could think of no reason. She was just then so pleasant
and jolly that I felt ashamed.

"Then what's the matter?"

I had stiffened for her scent, but somehow it did not come,
although she stooped so near: either it had worn off or she
had forgotten to apply it. The fading welts of a pattern of
hives stippled the long curve of her chin and ran down along
her throat like spilled paint. Her face was close to mine and a
pretty little dent in her lip, the remnant of her better mood,
encouraged my reply; and because I could not think what to
tell her I pointed to the bed.

"It's all dirty."

"What? What's all dirty?"

"The mattress."

"Oh, my God," she sighed, but she went to look down at
it. "There's blood on it." She was examining the stains with
revulsion; she had turned severe. "Enoch, come and see."

He leisurely crossed to her. He was pretending it was a

joke—the same joke she had made up for him. "If it's Desdemona's bed—"

"No, look. Really there's blood."

He laughed outright, as though she were still recounting
witticisms. "What do you expect, in Europe?—Is it fresh?"

"Fresh? Of course not, it's old, it's all dried up."

"Then there's no point in contemplating it. Stale murders
don't interest me."

"Oh, if it were only as decent as a murder—more likely it's
shaving blood."

"Or virgin's blood."

"Ah, don't," she objected, "what a way to talk, she's only
ten"—snapping up a mouthful of air: it was difficult for her
to simulate shock. "I don't care what it is, they don't have the
simplest idea of cleanliness. They have no standards. It
doesn't matter to them *what* they let you sleep on." She
scratched a fingernail across one of the black spots, and
jumped away with a little cry as though she had struck a
spark. "Ugh, the slime of it. Something's wet."

She had come upon my tears.

"Rain," said Enoch promptly. "All the windows are stuck
open. I don't doubt it's rained in on this bed the whole summer."

"You blame everything on the rain."

"Only wetness," he teased, "is that so bad? I like to con-
tend with facts."

"And don't I?" asked my mother, smarting at this, "I always think of facts. I give a lot of thought to facts."

"If you did you wouldn't have brought her here in the first
place."

"But I'm taking her back. It's not as though I weren't taking her back."

They began to bicker over me, but without intensity. I left
them and went to the toilet and came back and found them
sitting on the bed, separated by the glistering stains, looking at
one another in a silence so piteous that I briefly mistook it
for fastidiousness. But then I saw that my mother's hand lay
directly in the golden urinous outline of a tear-furred stom-
ach-sac. "We're going now," she told me, scowling. "You had
better say goodbye to Enoch."

"Goodbye."

He put his forefinger below my chin and raised my face; it
was a parody of what he had done with my mother. The arc
of his wrist, lifting, was ironically exact: he required me to

understand that his intention was sardonic—that I must not expect anything from him, that he was incapable of any gesture not a husband's, that not in the slightest would he crook a knuckle to fatherhood. He had a wife, no more; and deliberately affecting an archaism—a trick of his when he wished to make plain, by indirection, his aloofness—he patted his chest after a cigarette and sedately uttered "Farewell."

My mother was altogether fooled. "How pretty that was," she said as we sped down the hill in the car; we were squeezed all three in the front seat. Behind us, riding the floor, a pile of boxes rose to the middle of the windows, bristling with hairy rope: it was as though my stepfather had feared some sorcerous violence lay lurking in his ledgers, ready, if he did not noose them, to leap out and away. "How pretty to say farewell! There," my mother told me, "that means he wishes you luck."

He deposited us on the boulevard, in front of a canopied restaurant I had sometimes passed while walking with my governess. But it was not the Palatin, although, while my mother zealously cut into her steak and I gnawed lamb chop bones, a piano-player sidled brown machinist's fingers languidly across the surface of a shining claw-footed instrument. He was dressed as an Arab in a long striped skirt, but he had the pressed nose and extraordinarily opened nostrils of a Negro, and somnolent pale eyes. "P'teechka, maya p'teechka," he sang in what my mother readily observed (on the strength of having once been in Moscow, which, for the effect, she just then called Moskvá), was a seriously bad American accent. He performed thinly, in an impure, very high woman's voice, and when he finished a group of travelers not far from us put down their knives and forks and applauded. My mother went on eating—"I don't like countertenors," she muttered at her potato, "they're too eery," but I supposed she was thinking still of the piano-player at the Palatin: she looked remarkably cross. The seeming Arab, without stopping to acknowledge his audience, began another song, again in his inscrutable Russian: "Volga, Volga, mat rodnaya," he piped, "Volga, russki reka," but the travelers were dissatisfied. "P'teechka, p'teechka!" they yelled, giggling (the men behind their napkins, the women openly across their dinners), but he did not blink at them and would not play it again. A man in a white waistcoat, short and brisk, flew across the floor, in and out of the tables, with his toes pointed out and his full buttocks vaguely jellying, to whisper in the pianist's ear; after which he struck a petulant chord and undertook to execute, with more vigor in his angry mouth (his lips drawn flat became purple petals) than in his hands, the "Rhapsody in Blue." The travelers at once turned reverent, chewing with the solemnity of superannuated conductors: every bite a baton. But my mother said without patience, "You're finished, aren't you?"—although I had barely started my pudding.

9

We lay that night on fresh sheets, which the concierge angrily spread. "I could easily have given both these rooms out," she complained, her little nose wriggling like a caterpillar, in one place, without getting anywhere, "to two very nice honeymoon pairs, a double wedding only last week, on their way home from a visit to the capital. Such charming children, such good friends! They would not be separated, they asked for two rooms side by side, they had to be next door to one another, as at the nuptial moment! *Bien entendu*, I mean the priestly nuptial moment, nothing more, I don't poke into people's bedroom affairs. But then Madame Vand insists she will stay another night in this very room, no matter that I've already prepared it for newcomers, and gone to the trouble of laundering every scrap of linen, not excepting the dresserscarf, which, I assure you, was abused like a desk-blotter in a post office, but I don't say a word, I let it all go without a word, I'm famous for my good nature, although I assure you there's not a landlady in this vicinity who wouldn't charge for it, that hawk Berthe especially; and on top of that didn't I give her the privilege of conducting a conference without extra charge, and haven't I myself seen to every courtesy that in those so-called marble palaces she is used to in Paris they are too cold-hearted to think of? Well, thanks to her I've lost not two but four for tonight, and it's well known that newlyweds tip like kings—it's the wives' influence in my opinion, it has to do with their easing themselves after twenty years of continence: still, I've lost a room, they couldn't be satisfied, both chambers had to be free, you don't imagine I would give two couples one room? I keep up standards here, after all I keep up my own moral feelings, I didn't dare to suggest it. *Cependant*, they looked capable of it, those four, they might have made a riot, they smelled a little bit of something stronger than water. Still your mother might have told me earlier she was staying, at least before I took off the sheets. I suppose they went across to Berthe, in fact I know it, didn't my spying old man tell me so? I don't doubt she'll accommodate them, but don't worry, she's not a competition, she's always empty, may the Lord bless her vermin. To tell the truth she grows her cockroaches as big as dogs and they eat her out of customers and kitchen. Nevertheless won't she rake the francs out of those poor foolish honeymooners!—much good may it do them to be bitten in the act of love, that's a consoling thought. Not that the little wives looked without experience, I don't mean one week's worth, and neither one an hour older than seventeen. And rings bigger than their heads: the rich pamper their sons nowadays to let them give like that. What do you think, if a bunch of this sort ever dared to lodge in *my* house I assure you I wouldn't fail in my duty to stand in the passage the whole night, if necessary I would give up my dear rest of which I never get enough, if only to make certain the bashful brides didn't skip from one husband to another! Berthe may not, but in this house I have my moral feelings to keep up. And why else would it have to be two rooms side by side if it weren't for the purpose of sampling one another's goods—you think I don't know what these sentimental friendships are? It's not for nothing that I sleep with one eye open!—Here! *J'ai tant de travail à faire!* Tell Madame Vand I don't spread counterpanes this late in the day," she departed in a fury of self-satisfaction, "not when I know there's no appreciation for everything I have done for her, and I assure you I don't mind the sort of appreciation that feels the same as air when you try to get it in your hand!"

"What? What did she say?" demanded my mother, coming into the room a second afterward. She had gone downstairs to the parlor to telephone for a taxi to take us to the train the following morning. "I suspect it's a racket," she declared, not caring for my reply, which I soon abandoned, "they want two hundred francs more to come up the hill! I called four driv-

ers, and every one of the four talked about broken cobblestones and insisted he's afraid of blow-outs—well, it's not logical all *four* should have the same story, unless the old bat gets
to keep half of it. I'd swear she does. She probably sent that
deaf old man out with a pickaxe to ruin the road in the first
place, if I know her type. They prey on genteel people, you
know, but I won't have it. I walked *up* that hill and I'd just
as soon walk down it as get taken advantage of because I'm a
genteel American." "Genteel" was her sneering substitution
for "rich," left over half-consciously from her proletarian period. But, not so secretly, she really did think of herself as
possessing instinctively distinguishing airs. She did not fail to
exhibit them now. "Well, answer me! I asked you a question
at least three minutes ago. What was the concierge saying to
you behind my back?"

"She still wants some money, I guess," I doubtfully
summed up, for this time the woman had not spoken directly
of a tip.

"Oh, is that all!" my mother breathed out, but hesitated,
and would not permit herself relief. "She didn't speak of this
afternoon? Did she say anything about the man who was
here?"

I reflected. "I think something about its not costing you
anything to see him."

"Oh, just because she let us use the room, the pig. If she
knew how much it really cost she'd probably make a deal to
get half of it," she mumbled to herself, and sniffed for comfort into Enoch's handkerchief. "All right, I'll give her a few
francs then. She didn't interfere, I suppose that's something
to be grateful for with such a snooper." Thoughtfully she
twisted the handkerchief like a bracelet around her forearm.
"I wish Enoch were here to tell me how much. He always
knows just what to do in these situations, I mean when it's a
choice between practicality and spite. He *senses* European
people, you know. It's something that's inborn, it's part of
having a political mentality," she said; clearly she was not addressing me, or even herself, but rather some imaginary ad-
versary before whom she saw herself as her husband's advocate: perhaps the "people from Washington" whom he had
gone to meet in Zürich. "Born diplomats shouldn't be
wasted in obscurity," she concluded, and ordered me to bed
sighing.

We slept until midnight, my mother deeply but irregularly;
now and then she released an exhausted snore, so shrill that

she frightened herself awake. Meanwhile I was propped watchfully on an elbow. "Look, it's clearing," I said one of these times when I saw her eyes snap open, "maybe the sun will come out tomorrow." I was thinking how the roofs of farmhouses and the handles of wheelbarrows would throw their quick glints into the train-windows. "This isn't an hour to gape at the sky. Go to sleep, we have to get an early start, sun or no sun," she grumbled, and stumbled into her backless slippers and her hall-coat, groping for the doorknob. I heard her steps in the corridor, slapping towards the toilets, and then an interval, and then, far off, shouts, thumps, laughter, spinning nearer every moment, and the night-time slide of my mother's slippers seeming to draw it all behind her, a chariot of noise reined to her hurrying heels. The parrot-clicking voice of the concierge's husband whistled in the passage: "It will come to no good, it will come to no good, it will come to no good." "Shut up, you feckless rooster," his wife consoled, "no one else would take them, not even Berthe, that sloven, that paragon, who is so cautious she would investigate the good-conduct references of her own grandmother before selling her a pillow. Would you let them spend the night out under the moon? They won't leave any francs with the moon, believe me." "They have left them all with the bottle, you idiot. You don't imagine that just because I'm a tiny bit deaf my nose has stopped working? I tell you you are too liberal, it will come to no good." "You don't need to boast to me of the keenness of your nose, pantaloon, don't I know it already to my sorrow? Scarecrow! That banana of yours doesn't have to go far to sniff the stuff, no farther than its own end, which is often enough left to soak in alcohol overnight. I'm not easily fooled, you crackbrain, watch out whom you call idiot!" "Ha? Ha? What do you say?" "You hear when you want to well enough. Here, take the keys, let them into the corner room where the American international fonctionnaire compared techniques all afternoon with the Hollander's lover. As if he hadn't had a sample of her himself along the journey!"

And still clutching her wrapper, my mother threw herself on the bed. Her slitted eyes signalled anger. She dangled her ankles and the slippers fell off. "Thank the Lord we're getting out of here! They've actually let in a horde of drunken hooligans, two by two. I saw Mr. and Mrs. Noah in the hall, collecting in advance. This isn't a place for decent people. If you ask me I think they're running a bro— oh never mind, go to sleep!"

But the shouts and the thumps and the laughter rattled the house till morning. They called to one another all night in the wild sharp syllables of an aviary, exhausting the hours: "Irène!" "Paul!" "Thérèse!" "Guy!"—each call unaturally sibilant and gross and not unlike its neighbor. Eventually it was possible to recognize which name matched which shriek. My mother turned wretchedly in her bed; her backward-reaching arms encircled the pillow, the silhouette of her chin stabbed upward. "Ah, that pig, what a piece of spite-work, because I wouldn't tip her"—but she was listening conscientiously. Her lids beat alertly in the dark. "Paul!" "Alors, Thérèse!" "Guy! Guy! Guy! Guy!" "Irène, ça va?"—as though each screamed-at-the-ceiling name were some wondrous, drunken, wholly obscene joke. The names flew out of the big central double-bed where the four were clustered and pecked exuberantly at everything, like tethered birds—escaping so far and no farther. Sometimes only two were let loose at once: as when Paul exhorted Thérèse, and she did not answer; as when Irène stuttered "Guy Guy Guy Guy Guy Guy" to no avail. And then all four would rise up again with a clamorous swish of wing-tips and falsetto laughing astonished chirps: "Paul!" called Thérèse; Irène!" honked Guy; and Paul hissed back "Thérèse!"; but Irène, bird-of-paradise or merely pigeon, notched the night with "Guy Guy Guy Guy Guy Guy" a hundred times over, until I found myself wondering whether the barcarolle of all the names sung into that room, Enoch's ledgered names and these, and the names of those wanderers sans identity or talisman who left behind their tracings of blood and waste and wine, and the names of my governess and the private visitor and the boy with the ringwormed scalp and the Negro in his Oriental skirts, and my own name and my mother's, would climb the wind at last to some great collection-place, some chief bank or storage-house of names, a nursery-bursary spot designed to nurture and preserve all the names of the world, the living and the dead together: so that immortality might consist merely in one's name having been uttered even a single time, by anyone at all. It would not matter if a king addressed you, or a garbage-man. Up, up your name would flutter, to be gathered in and pinned to the roster of all who had ever breathed; up, up it would fly, an assurance of one's doubtful existence. (Hadn't I heard my stepfather protest "I am called Enoch, therefore I am," on those stubborn days when my mother scolded him for "blanking out," as she put it, because he would not hear her shout him awake—"Get up, Enoch; Enoch; *Enoch!"*—and because he willed his return into the self-extinguishing nirvanic deeps of his morning sleep? For there is no proof of being, outside of one's own mind, Enoch claimed—roused by then—except for the solidly indisputable fact that one's friends call one by name. How can you be said to exist if you have no name? Who could prove a fly was there, if he could not call it a fly?)

The sky began to whiten. One by one the cries and hoots next door died out, the squawks dropped down, the names came in to roost.

Paul, Guy, Thérèse, Irène. They slept.

I said: "Are you awake?"

"No," said my mother.

"I was wondering—"

"Don't wonder, it's bad for your digestion, you'll start throwing up. Am I awake! What else could I be?"

"I was wondering if there's a God."

"Oh my God," she groaned with unexpected relevance, "not that again. I thought Enoch settled all that with you."

"But is there?"

"I don't know, how should I know?"

"But if there *is* a God, is it the same God for everywhere? I mean, the same in America as here?"

"Well, I don't see why not," she evaded me.

"All the same, I wish there were a different one for America."

"How could that possibly matter to *you?"* she argued, yawning enormously, her shoulders straining and her arms thrust stiffly out. "You're getting everything that's good for you anyhow, here, there, anywhere." She slumped down into her pillow and watched her feet change color in the awakening light. "Besides," she gave out—it was an educative afterthought—"there's only supposed to be one God. It's the whole idea of religion. They call it monotheism," she encouraged, vaguely stretching her knees; "I've just *got* to doze off for a minute"—rewarding herself: she had, with this piece of theology, done her duty by me.

After which she did not move until half-past eleven.

In the middle of the morning a prolonged hiss, misty with regret, crept up from a far part of the world, and swept away again: it was the ten o'clock train silkenly departing, repining, swishing its complicated petticoats over a shimmer of track.

I escaped into the garden. The air tasted green and ready. Amulets of rain lay scattered in the grass—bright puddles and patches of glistening mud drying with a delicacy in the fresh warmth. The sun burned like a ship; it burned in the sides of the iron barrel, pursued by the growls of a confraternity of flies; it burned in the bush. A long feather-fan of light waggled in the hedge-duck's bill.

In the groove where the blue bicycle had leaned I found a limp little book, the pages all soaked and fused. It was so small, no wider than three inches, that I supposed it had slipped out of the string that had bound it with the others to the fender. Bits of wrapping paper still clung to it, but the violet dye of the covers had run off into the ground; the title was almost watered out of legibility. I labored to decipher it; this would have been difficult for me even if the letters had not been blurred, for when I had made them out at last I did not know the word I had constructed. ENCHIRIDION, it was, and underneath: OF WOODLAND FLOWERS. I tried to force the leaves apart, but they broke off in my fingers like bunches of dough. Then suddenly while I turned it over, looking for an opening, the little book seemed to melt in two; each surprised hand came away holding the exposed part of a dampened page, with half the volume stuck behind it. On the top part of each was reproduced a colored illustration of a plant, in minute and literal detail. Every hair on every petal of the two drawings shone with the artist's struggle for exactitude, and since the book had split open at its core, in spite of that outer drenching the pictures had been kept from ruin; even the print remained clear.

In my left hand I read: "False Hellebore; American White Hellebore. *Veratrum viride.* (Lily family.) The False Hellebore, a baneful but noble plant of splendid and vigorous aspect, may be seen blooming in wet woods from May to July. Its extremely poisonous thick rootstalks are used in the preparation of emetics, and its seeds can kill small creatures. The stems are stout and notably erect. Although adult beasts cleverly avoid eating its abundant foliage, young ones are sometimes fatally lured."

Above this was a drawing of some unfortunate spinach-leaves with greenish caterpillars growing out of them.

My right hand's prize was more attractive—little dangling bells of orange. The artist had not compromised with truth: the stalks stood rigid in a cardboard woodland where   ind ever blew. "Jewelweed; Wild Touch-Me-Not," said the caption. *"Impatiens biflora*. Blooming season, July to October, near water. How like rare gems are these delightful flowers when dew dances in their little tender cups shaped like horns-of-plenty and culminating in short spurs the hue of a kitten's tongue!" Only momentarily did the legend give up science for rhapsody; briskly it recalled itself to botanical sobriety. "The name Touch-Me-Not almost certainly derives from the quick, spasmodic action of its ripe seed-pods which instantly erupt at a touch and spurt their seeds in every direction."

I thought this a very curious thing; it was nothing but a silly guidebook to put in one's pocket while walking in the woods, if one could, after all, find a wood to walk in; and being urban, I did not believe one could. It was so innocent I thought it sinister. It could not have been left behind, even by the wind, without some inner consistency of chance; for (according to the dogma of my stepfather) what appears to be chance is in reality the last confirmation, for the pious and the ignorant, of a superior intention. Just as—Enoch liked to say, with how much atheistic irony I do not know—when Titus' monument to the sacking of Jerusalem, that great arch made for eternity, crashed among the plunderers of Rome, nothing remained to speak glory but those raised representations of the Scroll and the Seven-armed Candelabrum; as though not chance but the Temple had ruled, even for mere sculpture, what was to survive the boot of history. And I did not suppose it extravagant to think of the private visitor as a sort of Titus who had come to arouse my mother's vengeance and to despoil her sanctuary, remembering how piteously she had beseeched her husband to shut him up, the legionless tyrannical but mild-voiced and laughing adventurer, to bring him down, while all the while he went on probing her sanctuary, a place and time forbidden and improbable to me: a bed in a room in Brighton, an alien unsung city, for all I knew as desolate as barbarian Rome, unimaginable Brighton, where snow had once grown beyond the door like a toothache-herb. Therefore I looked on that ENCHIRIDION as on the scratching upon some tablet or reliquary or arc de triomphe set up to outlast man—a trophy which, if properly scanned, might disclose the victor's ominous damning flaw, his singular lust or proclivity, his doomed miscalculation or weakness, in short the whole secret of his nature's dark rot —precisely as the Arch of Titus still reveals the fateful broken sneer of the god-emperor who believed that in diminishing the Temple he diminished the Law. But these ozymandian ideas, as I say, are not so much mine as Enoch's, who in those days used to take satisfaction in emphasizing his purported descent from Solomon the King—if only for the pleasure of teasing my mother into a fever of exasperation. And although I was influenced by him more than he or his wife guessed (it was true, for instance, that he taught me by example: the homely opposite of which I would faithfully resolve to follow), I never succeeded in copying that swiftly acrobatical turn of his intelligence which could all at once outrageously associate cabbages and kings, and could even call the symbiosis, no matter how peculiar or antipathetical, by the name of common-sense. To an ordinary mind (and the child-mind is the most ordinary of all, the least capable of convincing juxtaposition), there is a difference between a conqueror's monument and a picture-book; and if I could see a profligate general in my mother's tormentor I could not, on the other hand, descry thick theories-of-character in those two moist remnants of his appearance, those painfully decent bugless pictures so perfect that they seemed to bowdlerize nature. What I saw was, as I have said, innocence, or, at worst, whimsy—the mildest sort of domesticated caprice. It exactly matched the fact of the blue bicycle; it exactly matched the little flag at its tail; it declared nothing but merriment hindered ever so charmingly by impertinence (quite like the "Rhapsody in Blue," after all, insolently performed. It was all innocent, and at the same time all admittedly queer; all admittedly baleful. It was innocence out-of-place and therefore suspect; yet innocence all the same. My mother had awaited evil in a conviction of harm, a certainty of terror, and it had come riding in upon the wrong vehicle, wearing (undoubtedly) the wrong clothes, full of old wrong anecdotes, gushing freshets of wrong laughter; and instead of leaving behind the correct imprint of its class—an unmistakable cloven hoof eloquently delineated in slime—it had stamped in the mud, wrong again, the comfortably innocent mark of a bicycle tire. And as if this were not wonderful enough, the protocols of Beelzebub had turned out to be nothing more pernicious than the jewelweed's habits and the hellebore's way.

Jewelweed and hellebore! The private visitor—in spite of everything—was fond of hunting for commonplace flowers in non-existent woods: a poacher of gardens. I thought how relieved my mother would be, and scarcely able to wait for her to waken I set the little book out to dry in the sun; then lay in placid ambush.

At noon the honeymooners arose with a clamor, and began throwing their shoes out of the window. "Thérèse!" "Paul!" "Irène!" "Guy!" they cried as the shoes came flying down; but a bit of rusty scrollwork in the railing caught the tall red heel of one of them and held it fast. "Guy!" shouted the girls; "Paul!" shouted Guy, and after a minute a furtive young man crawled out upon the ledge in a loincloth made out of a towel, with a scared face nearly as red as the shoe (which he saved), and big intricate ears that somehow seemed far more naked than the rest of him. "Paul!" they applauded as he climbed back in; and immediately the shoe, wrapped in the towel, went soaring away. In midair the bundle separated: the towel fell here, the shoe there. After the shoes they tossed out a pair of blankets; next someone's eyeglasses, which landed safely; and finally the girls' underwear. Garters and brassieres gracefully descended, ballooning, pants were briefly inhabited by the breeze of flight—but there were not enough of these to content the throwers, so they cut open a pillow and beat it on the frame of the window and sent out ten thousand eddying feathers. A white storm stirred in the sky, until little by little its center floated away, dispersed, and wandered downward to nest in the grass. A feather fluttered over the drawing of the hellebore, then settled. I blew it away. "Guy, Guy, Guy," they endlessly praised. The whole yard looked full of snow.

I called out, "Come and see," for my mother just then appeared on the porch with the concierge, arguing bitterly. Meanwhile the concierge wrung her apron, clutched at her hair, put a finger up her nose, another in her ear, wiggled a loose back tooth, and finally as a last vain resort, crossed herself. "I do not understand," she was saying over and over again, although it was in a version of French that my mother scolded: "please to proceed more slowly, I have the difficulty . . ." But my mother went on complaining hoarsely: she had not been allowed to sleep, she had been forced to oversleep, she had missed the ten o'clock train, the taxis would not come up the hill. "Madame Vand," the concierge began, and from the half-conciliatory, even obsequious style of her rapid peasant's hands I concluded that my mother had been intimidated into giving her a tip after all— which made her contempt so much the bolder, since she had in effect paid for the felicity of exercising it. "Madame," the concierge once more attempted, but my mother, incensed, broke into violent English: "*Ma*dam! Look here, don't you call *me* such a name! *I* know who's the Madam around here! *I* know what sort of a place you're running!" and to display her vehemence she almost waved her arms, but luckily at the last instant happened to remember that this was one of those disgusting practises, typical of Mediterranean peoples, which she was always deploring, since she regarded it as a habit nourished only in the blood of inferior races—and just in time she pulled her uplifted hands to her head and pinned her hat down tight, quite as if this had been her intention from the beginning.

"Come and see," I said impatiently. "Look what I've found."

"Found where," she answered, continuing to glare at the concierge, although she knew perfectly well that scarcely a word was comprehensible to her. Neither was French, however; her French was almost never comprehensible to a Frenchman; and as long as they weren't going to understand her anyhow, she had long ago decided not to be understood in the world's only truly easy language—through sheer good fortune her own. "Found what," she said carelessly, returning to the attack. "The taxis won't come up the hill, there's a racket going on all night—and look here, when it comes to rackets I'm not *that* naïve, don't tell me you're not in cahoots with every driver in town!" ("Ca-hoot, Ca-hoot," said the concierge, who was apparently eager not to miss an opportunity for adding a new word to her foreign vocubulary. Perhaps she thought it useful for tourists. "Ca-hoot," she repeated willingly.) "A brothel!" my mother was saying, "and outright, and with a child next door!"

Since she plainly meant me, I hoped I could now get her attention. "Look," I called again, "look what I found near the hedge."

"What, what, what," she acknowledged, and stepped off the porch, the concierge pursuing, all the while imploring "Ca-hoot," as though this were some singularly efficacious American term denoting great courtesy; she must have supposed from my mother's emphatic tone (had not my mother politely—albeit excitedly—addressed her as "Madame" again and again?) that it was a very important word indeed, suitably all-serving, a possible sesame to good will (it had chronologically followed the really good tip my mother had certainly produced—the poor woman could not count in francs, and always overestimated—far larger than the concierge had dreamed). "In cahoots with each and every one of them," my mother was still insisting, dipping an unsuspecting foot into a carpet of feathers. The word sounded unusually businesslike, firm, yet not unfriendly. "Ca-hoots," the concierge mouthed it, adding a highly audible "s" to give the syllables a native sophistication; it seemed she intended to memorize them then and there. But "Oooowah!" she suddenly wound up; and "Ooooh!" my mother joined her; for a moment they spoke an identical language of animal surprise. Overhead a second and a third pillow were being emptied—it snowed convulsively in their faces. The two of them stood howling. "Ah, the little beasts!" screamed the concierge. *"C'est se moquer du monde!* I'll get them! Nothing is surprising nowadays! I'll show them! I'm not a moralist, even Our Blessed Lord forgave the woman . . . Little beasts! No wonder Berthe wouldn't have them, this is her revenge on me—stop! Stop! You are destroying property, what do you think, *par le temps qui court rien n'est surprenant!* Murder! Murder!" A cloud of feathers—this was the fourth pillow—drowned her arms, whitened her hair, coated her lips. She spat and caught a feather on her tongue and spat again, while the honeymooners deliriously celebrated their hero—"Guy! Guy! Guy!" "Guy is it! I'll show you Guy!" yelled the concierge. She stooped quickly to grab a shoe and aimed straight for the open window; my mother picked up another and did the same. The girls, retreating, squealed and swelled with the pleasure of warfare, but the young men hung over the ledge, feigning gallantry with a diffidence that seemed to plead for fig-leaves, and posed like sheepish shortstops, elbows out against the missiles; and the shoes sailed past their heads. *"That's* not the way," said my mother, who sometimes liked to boast of how good she had been at volleyball (under the auspices of Miss Jewett's Classes, *circa* 1928, in the basement gymnasium of Saints-Cecilia-and-Elisheva-of-Haworth's); she reached for another shoe, a man's big brogan, but it only struck the side of the house and chipped a shingle and came swiftly down again. "Bad shot," my mother called out with a teamcaptain's groan of dismay. "Now they will show themselves naked, will they?" screamed the concierge. "It does not matter that I slave night and day for the sake of honor and a good name, they will come and stand on the roofs with all the machinery of their sin open for the world! In, go in, hide yourselves! Like cats on a fence! Since the war the fathers

don't whip the sons, and the sins of the fathers set the teeth
of the sons on edge—believe me, if they had *me* in the Government—cats, go back in, what do you imagine God made
trousers for?—shame is worse than poverty, and better than
gold is a golden reputation, don't think I don't know the
words of our Holy Saints," she went on wildly, running back
and forth in the mud and punching air. In response Paul and
Guy merely grew braver and whistled through their teeth to
demonstrate exactly how divine doctrine had set them on
edge, and behind them Thérèse and Irène tinkled and
sneered. "Now watch *this*," my mother promised, weighing in
her hand the red pump with the long sharp heel: shrewdly
and expertly she balanced it behind her ear and heaved it.
The concierge watched its trajectory with a loosened jaw,
spewing alarm; the boys ducked, the girls shrieked, there was
a distant indoors crash. "The window!" said my mother looking up; but the window was intact. "Oh oh! Then it's the mirror!" she gave out. She was enjoying it all. "The mirror over
the dresser. There's seven years bad luck for you! *Sept ans—*"
she tried it, but abandoned it in a suffocation of laughter.
The concierge fled in the direction of the destroyers of
property, encountering her husband on the way, his mouth full
of complaints and bread. Half a narrow loaf stuck up from his
pocket. "Eat the profits, you!" she stormed. "Go upstairs and
throw them out! But for you I would never have consented to
admit them, rooster! Grandson of an ass! Wastrel! Old monkey, see that they scat before I send you with them!"

They vanished, the two of them, angrily breaking the long
loaf between them and brandishing the pieces at one another
like a pair of caveman's clubs, while my mother in her toga
of feathers crossed the white-strewn grass. "Here, help me get
this stuff off," she commanded cheerfully—"how it *sticks!*"
With rounded cheeks like a caricature of Aeolus she peered
down her bosom and blew and blew. The feathers clung to
her as poignantly as blossoms; one by one I flicked them
away. "Don't pick at me," she objected, "just brush me off,
can't you? If Enoch were here I bet he'd die laughing—my
God, look how I'm shedding, what a nuisance! But I don't
mind, it was worth it, I feel absolutely avenged." She lowered
her head so I could sweep the feathers from her nape. Her
shoulders and neck were pink with exhilaration. "The fact is
she deserves it all, that woman—I wish I'd smashed the window too. What a cheat! She pretends she's the concierge in
order to get tips, and she's really the landlady, she owns ev-

erything"—this seemed a plausible revelation—"don't think I didn't see through her from the first"—this was certainly false—"but listen, they're all cheats, they've gall enough for anything, it wouldn't surprise me a bit if that chauffeur goes ahead and sues.—Enoch thinks he will, you know. It'll just be spite if he does. Are they all out of my hair, those damn feathers?" She shook herself delightedly and looked around her. I almost thought she was in search of another shoe to throw, but instead her quickly darkening eye lit on the EN-CHIRIDION. "What's that filthy little book you're fooling with?"

"I'm not fooling with it, I'm drying it."

"You're always fooling with something filthy," she said, staring.

"It's what I found. See, the pages are all stuck."

"Oh for goodness' sake! Found *where?* I've already asked you half a dozen times, haven't I?" she complained, picking up both pieces between two fingers and dangling the bunched leaves.

"In the grass. Where the bicycle was. It fell off."

"What?"

"It fell off his *bike.* There were a whole lot of books strapped on. Nick's bike, I mean."

"Don't say that!" she cried.

"Say what?" I wondered, undistressed.

"That name, Nick."

"Isn't that his name? I thought you *said* it was his name."

"It doesn't matter. As far as you're concerned he has no name."

"But what can I call him?"

"He's nothing to you," she said fiercely. "You don't have to call him anything."

"He isn't coming back?"

"You can bet he isn't!" Spitefully she let the halves of the little book drop to the ground.

"Not even to get his book? I mean after he sees it's missing."

"To get his book!" she sneered; all her good humor was gone. Angrily she slapped away a feather caught in her sleeve. "That's how you catch germs, haven't I told you often enough?—grabbing at every dirty thing you see. First those bullet-things, now this."

"It's not a dirty thing," I objected. "It's a real book—it's got pictures of flowers. Look, it's full of flowers." I handed it up to her, insisting. "What's that word mean?"

She absorbed it for the first time. "Enchiridion? I don't know, a manual, I think. I think that's what it means. Like a handbook. I had something called Enchiridion once—" But she trailed off purposelessly. "Let me see it." She took the limp pages and began to read out words here and there, elliptically: "Touch-Me-Not. False American—What a sneak. Oh, what a sneak."

"One of those you read is poisonous," I said enthusiastically. "You chew it and it kills you."

But my mother's look was rooted in print. "False American Hellebore," she repeated. "Touch-Me-Not. Ah, that sneak! That petty sneak! He'd try anything!"

"Is he a gardener?" I asked.

"Who?"—She lifted her head suddenly.

I blew out a recklessly defiant, but soft, sigh. "Nick," I pronounced it.

"A gardener? Who said he's a gardener?"

"Because of the flowers," I said, "a whole book full of flowers."

"Well, what of it?"

I turned briefly silent at the uncalculating oddity of her reprimand: hadn't I expected her to be pleased by the private visitor's artless droppings? But she did not think them artless. She rubbed her foot in the feathered lawn and speculated; now and then her blouse grew vast with agitation, although she tried to shield her big bold breathing with an arm flung across her chest—but I was not so much curious as disappointed.

"Can I take it with me, to look at on the ship?"

"No," said my mother.

In reaction I began to negotiate. "But when it dries the pages will come all unstuck, won't they? And there'll be more flowers."

"You can do without flowers," said my mother.

"I only want to look at the pictures."

"No. You'll be sick anyway. You've never once *not* been sick on a boat."

"I won't be if I have something to do. I mean something to look at."

"Not this." She glared. "What do you want *this* for?"

"I don't know. I just want it." I really did not know, so I

said what sounded to me the most reasonable. "I want it for a souvenir."

She broke out wrathfully, "A souvenir! A souvenir actually! If I thought you knew what you were talking about I'd slap you—I did it before and I can do it again, *I* don't mind. If Enoch hadn't had to leave, he'd know what to do with you!" she exclaimed in her illusion of her husband's assured competence with me—if only he had been willing to extend himself. She spun out a little thread of suspicion. "Just what do you imagine it's a souvenir *of?*"

I was afraid, assessing her predictable ire, to say the truth —that I had coveted the blue bicycle, and would have liked to think of hellebore and jewelweed riding it—and said instead, "Of—him" because I did not dare just then to brave his name.

A fever blossomed in her face. "I told you he's nothing to do with you! It's that Dutchwoman," she informed herself, "she filled you with things. How I'd like to get my hands on her!"

"I can feed her poison flowers," I politely offered, "if you want," disposing on my mother's palely clenched knuckles a smile of peace grown out of imagined vengeance: here was the villainous Anneke on the beach, she who had threatened to send me among the fearsome Arabs, sucking on a stem of hellebore; she sucked, and sucked again, and fell delightfully dead.

"Where did you get this?" persisted my mother.

"I *told* you. In the grass."

"When?"

"Before. While you were still asleep."

But she was not satisfied. "*She* didn't give it to you? Anneke?"

"It fell off his bike and I found it," I said again. "If he doesn't come back for it it's mine, isn't it?"

"He won't come back," my mother said grimly.

"Then it's mine," I said. "Losers weepers."

"It's nobody's," she said, and marched across the lawn of feathers to where the iron rain-barrel stood under a black halo of flies; with an arced and lifted arm long-sleeved as a judge's she let fall the little ENCHIRIDION. Hellebore and jewelweed splashed down; up charged the flies in broken battalions. "There," said my mother, returning, stirring up around her heels as she walked a white downy dust: "I know what to do with his little props—he came with the tools of his trade, all right! It just surprises me he didn't bring along a black silk hat to pull them out of. You didn't happen to find a black silk hat too?"

"You threw it in the barrel," I said bitterly.

"Well, where else? It's as good a place as any to toss a dead rat."

"It wasn't a dead rat. It was flowers."

"Literal mind! All right, withered leaves then. I got rid of a few withered leaves."

"But it's mine, I wanted to take it with me." I regarded her with dull shock. "You threw it away."

"Why not? I can't think of a better fate for the rose of yesteryear.—Never mind, what's the matter? Don't stand there pop-eyed! What did you expect me to do?" she demanded; her scowl was creased with guilt. "It's a dead rat, believe me. Dead rats have to be disposed of, otherwise they bring the plague."

"It was mine," I accused.

"You're mistaken. Anyhow we're going now. Come on."

"But I wanted it for the ship, it belonged to me."

"To you!" But though she exclaimed, her face was stolid. "Don't tell *me* who it belonged to!"

"I found it."

She strained between not-speaking and speech.

"I bought it," she sent out at last. "Or a copy just like it, it doesn't matter. The point is it's mine, and it's nothing I'd forget easily. I don't forget things! I bought it from one of those stalls in the Southampton station, passing through, and used it the whole winter afterward. You don't think I'd forget a thing like that, do you?"

Just that moment it was almost as though she were talking to Enoch.

"In the winter?" I wondered, interested at once. "In the woods?"

"Don't be a fool—woods, what do you mean woods?" Immediately she was restored and cónscious only of addressing me, and not another. "I had to have realism, I had to have everything right, I couldn't make botanical errors, I didn't dare. I'm not that sort of person, slipshod. I had to have it for the picnic," she emphasized.

But I only asked again, "In the middle of the winter?"

She hissed at my stupidity. "For *Marianna Harlow*," she clarified with scorn.

Then I remembered about the flower-eating scene. My

mother had once or twice recounted this to me: she regarded it as her legacy from Poe. "It's the horror part," she reminded me, this being the reason she would never again attempt another novel. On account of this scene alone, she maintained, she had used herself up. It had taken her three months to write, and had exhausted her gift. "When it comes to invention, I'm an empty mine. I show evidences of former deposits, and once in a while I cough up a few crystals, but there's not enough ore left for commercial exploitation." This, Enoch liked to interpret, meant merely that she was lazy; he was always suggesting subjects, usually historical. "I can just imagine your mother's treatment of Genghis Khan! Ivan the Terrible! Bloody Mary! Oedipus Rex with dripping eyesockets! God giving the tablets to Moses with the mountain suddenly blowing up underfoot!" For he knew that she had a weakness for volcanoes.

"What chapter was that?" I inquired.

"The picnic? Thirteen," she said ominously.

"Then you weren't married to William any more?"

"I was working on Thirteen just before you were born." She stood with her head drooping, thickened by melancholy. From the windows of the house came the savage noises of a freshly-declared war. The bridal pairs were being driven out. The voice of the concierge's deaf husband cawed like an iron hinge. "It snowed all the time," my mother reminisced, but it was not clear whose birth this sign had marked—the difficult and remarkable chapter's, or mine. "It may have been trite, but I had to have the thunder and lightning," she admitted, "for the effect."

"In the *snow?*"—although, recalling her plot, I knew better.

"Don't be silly. In the chapter. Marianna invites all the factory folk"—"factory folk" was a phrase which appeared often in my mother's egalitarian fiction—"for an outing in her father's gardens—she's naturally against privately-owned pleasure domes. Of course the foreman comes too, and then an electric storm breaks out—"

My mother slung her long hands around the back of her neck, tilting her head upward to catch the sunlight in her uncertain nostrils; she put one foot behind another, and rooted her toes for story-telling. Recollecting, she transmuted sadness to vanity there and then, despite the absurdity, despite the disparity of tale and auditor. Enough that she had an auditor, even if it were only I; nothing seemed unlikely, not the hour, not that hostile spot, not even myself listening, and since she did not think herself strange, I did not question my own impression; I only flinched at having to hear her tiresomely recite. She charmed herself; she plumbed her plot; she paled at her own ingenuity.

"—and Marianna and Deirdre and the foreman all run for shelter into the factory-owner's greenhouse, where he grows thousands of flowers, exotic and poisonous types, because he always wanted to be a doctor and develop a new drug—" She interrupted herself pleasurably, glad to sustain the telling. "His father wouldn't hear of it—his father insisted on his becoming vice-president of the factory. And Enoch said"—she laughed aloud—"Enoch said that's what made him anti-labor, an autocratic temperament derived from a lifelong frustration. It was a rebellion against the father-figure, with the pattern repeating itself in his own attitude toward labor, which he regarded as a type of rebellious offspring . . ." I had no idea of her meaning; did she intend to go on standing there the whole afternoon, marooning me on an island of boredom? "Enoch thinks *Marianna*'s psychoanalytical! So maybe I owe more to Freud than to anybody. —Well, come on, let's get out of here," she finished suddenly.

She caressed her lips with her tongue in imitation of a movie-star's slowly burgeoning emotion, lowered her hands, and looked at me almost hopefully, as though I might unexpectedly blink out encouragement.

But I only clung to my resentment all the harder. "Anyway I don't see what you needed that flower book for."

"For the drug!" she cried. "What do you think? I couldn't have done without it."

I pursued logically, "If you couldn't do without it then why did you throw it away?"

"What a brat you are, a born little vulture. You'd eat your own mother." But she said this abstractedly, depressed. She was still musing over the triumph of her scene, and I was all at once petrified at the notion that—in spite of her palm reaching out to tap me toward the cobbled road—she would plunge into a review of all the rest of it. Her conscientious but self-absorbed unfolding of it, slangy, quick, always gave me a sense of unease, almost of guilt, as though, beneath the story, some buried and repugnant symbol mouldered. The story itself was foolishness, and was, I learned long afterward, pretentiously based on some Korean myth or other which my mother had gotten, not from a book, but from a

guide in one of the upstairs galleries of the British Museum.
Two sisters, alike as two rice flowers in beauty but one
pledged to evil and the other to good (on different sides in
the class struggle, in my mother's version), are rivaling for
the love of a single hero: they take him captive to their glass
house and tease him into eating strange plants, each to lure
him from the other; but alas, the wicked girl, by means of
mysteriously sweet and brilliant petals, instead of converting
his heart, succeeds only in sending him straight asleep in her
sister's arms. "It was a sedative instead of an aphrodisiac,"
my mother smirked. "I had to know the details of that, didn't
I? I couldn't make up a drug out of the thin air without research, could I? I mean it was a question of the chemistry of
flowers. Don't think I didn't study all winter about aphrodis-
iacs in all sorts of queer books!" She pretended, however, to
have inadvertently erred: "Don't ask me to explain that
word, it's not for you."

But I had already been given a definition, long ago, by my
stepfather. "Enoch said they're things to make somebody love
you who doesn't. Like the apple Eve picked for Adam."

"Well, if you think you know absolutely everything!" said
my mother, exasperated, and at the same time pleased. She
was pleased whenever I quoted Enoch, as though it were a
particular merit in me to choose to do so, even if it revealed
to her that her husband thought Genesis almost as psychoanalytical a book as *Marianna Harlow*. "Besides, you can't
make somebody love you who doesn't. If you try, they only
love you less. Afterward they hate you and want revenge for
your having loved them. Don't drag behind, let's go," she
said, tugging at my elbow with a listlessness appropriate to
her philosophizings. But I did not follow after. Screeches and
bellows enflamed the porch, and turning toward the house I
saw the turbulent wedding party dance out barefoot—Guy,
Irène, Paul, Thérèse. They swarmed across the lawn, searching for their shoes in the feathers, lit by midsummer midday,
honeyed over by jubilance. They were all of them uncompro-
misingly, lavishly blond, like a covey of cousins, the bridegrooms long-haired with straight formless columns fluting
downward over their brows, the brides shorn short, the divi-
sion in the nape like a dark ravine as they bent. Their naked
heels were black. They raced across the dewy grass like
Greek runners, chasing one another in an impromptu game
that half resembled tag, and half something Biblical: the honeymooners cast out from Paradise by two croaking angels,

more or less toothless, beating staffs of broken bread upon the lintel of Eden. My mother rounded the hedge; but the girls between them took hold of the rain-barrel by its rusty rings, and displaying exaggerated winces, groaning at its weight, they raised themselves on their strong toes and tipped it. Out ran Niagara—rain, and rags, and fats, and innumerable chicken bones, and fish-heads, and all my shells one behind the other in a clanging cascade, and the private visitor's EN-CHIRIDION like a frigate in that horrendous sea; the laden water sped and spread, tumbling out a crazy river down toward the road, cutting through the coverlet of feathers, now and then lifting one in its current, where it might have been mistaken for a white fern swirling. And "Hurry up!" called my mother from the other side of the hedge; and "What a stench!" I came slowly, reluctant, watchful: the iron barrel fell to the ground dumping thunder, and rocked twice, and lay like a toppled urn. On its side it had a certain mythological beauty—an idol thrown down. The spew trickled off innocently. Meanwhile the bridegrooms had snatched up twigs and were playing at catching the hoops of my shells over the points, dabbling them in the sluice. The brides took turns aiming their shoes at the hedge-duck's tail. Guy, Thérèse, Paul, Irène. The sun lived in the flanks of all their sheeny heads; and on the porch, not minding the stink, the concierge's husband stopped up his plaints with a big bite of bread.

But the concierge stamped on the floorboards and howled.

"Barbarians," muttered my mother behind the bush, "they're just what this place deserves"—and her high heels wavered with great delicacy between the cobblestones.

I went dismally down the hill behind her, and halfway along spied the flag. It was not a true flag. It was only an old handkerchief printed over with Stars and Stripes, not even the right number of each, and a long rip in the middle where the stick had pierced it. A car had run it over; it was ragged and soggy, and I left it where I found it. Ahead of me, my mother's back was sentry-straight—only her ankles were unsure. She picked her way down the hill and never noticed this patriot's handkerchief, although she had been talking of loyalty and Othello only yesterday. "Why are you hanging back like that?" she shouted, vexed at the honeymooners and at me for having interrupted *Marianna*. With admirable exactitude she resumed. "The fact is"—she balanced just then on the crown of a stone—"I mean, what with the three of them locked in the greenhouse, and the lightning stabbing through the glass walls and flooding all the flowers and the erotic *scent* of the flowers, and both sisters in love with the same man, and him not only of another class but, well, actually out cold and lying limp, no wonder they said it was spine-tingling!" she praised herself. We had come to the bottom of the road. Without warning two taxis jumped into being, begging at the curb. Their rear doors gaped. My mother waved off the first as a sign of vengeance, and leaned down to rub her shin until she was satisfied the walk down had left her without a crack; then we drove off to the station with the favored man. The seats were threadbare plush and alive with heat. Asthma choked the driver. "To think that I could write of eating flowers, just flowers, and scare myself, and call it horror! When it was all just flowers, and I never saw them really, just colored pictures in a book . . ." My mother's forefinger ticked against her cheek. "I didn't know what horror was!" Inside the cab, for an act of mercy and as though it were a flower, she took my hand. But sweat ran from the underside of my knuckles and she surrendered me to myself with a grunt. "Ah, you're clammy. You don't feel clean." She sat in silence, listening to the driver cough for his lungful of air, while the wheel wobbled and a vein at his wrist bulged. I suppose we were in danger of dying of his disease (we had joggled over to the wrong side of the narrow road and were struggling to joggle back again) and wondered whether my mother would construe this as a punishment for having snubbed the other taxi, but the windows did not draw her eyes; she kept them for herself, and let her anger loiter where it pleased, and was all at once stung by the worse danger of enlightenment—she seemed to see: "He brought it in case I didn't remember! As though I couldn't remember without his little showpieces! The tools of his trade!" And she spat out the window, although we were within two yards of the station.

So I could not decide whether Nick's lost flag were a tool of his trade too. But on account of it—because, although it was abused and torn, a painted rag, I felt somehow its optimism and lighthearted power, and imagined that it had been flung off its stick for my feet to find as a sort of glorious and healthful omen of America, of everything that was not Europe—on account of this despised swatch and remnant, I could not hate his trade, whatever it might be, and however threatening.

10

Although my mother had predicted worse, on the ship going home I was sick for only a day. After that my stomach made its peace with the horizon: both were unstable, but both were eager not to be noticed. The sky over the ship was tall and narrow, like a vertical tunnel or chute through which the horizon seemed to be perpetually escaping. Every twilight we heard the birds, not seeing them. Their cries were smoky, as though upon some far pyre live human babies wailed.

My mother passed the time making lists. Most of them were insipid, but some were brilliant. The longer they were, however, the more ordinary they were. She wrote down, for instance, the names of all the places outside of the United States she had ever visited, divided into three parts: 1. Capitals. 2. Cities and Towns 3. Villages, and this list was very long. So was the one cataloguing Favorite Dishes and Beverages. The smallest list of all was headed Books I Have Written. Another one, showing three items, was called Books I Intend to Write. Below this appeared the following: 1. *Moods and Memoirs of the Embassy*, by Allegra Vand, Well-Known Connoisseur. 2. *Capitalism and Communism, A World Struggle as Witnessed by a Participant*, by Allegra Vand, LL.D. ("Well," she justified this piece of imagination, "my *father* had one, a Doctor of Laws degree; it was honorary. He got it because he gave them the money to build the new Alumni House, and if I'm his heir, I suppose I'm just as entitled to call myself LL.D. as he was!") And finally, 3. *Forward the Bold Haven: A Historical Novel of Old New York*, by Allegra Vand, author of the Best-Seller *Marianna Harlow*, listed in Drilling's Famous Compilation, "Best Literature of the Masses, 1937."

"What's it going to be about?" I said.

"The novel? Oh, I'll never write another novel. It's just to round out the list. Biography, politics, fiction."

"No, I mean this," I said, pointing to Number One.

"Oh, that. That'll be about my life."

"But it's got something about an Embassy."

"Well, where do you think I expect to *spend* my life?" she retorted.

The most inspired list of all was called Celebrities I Should Like to Have Known, and Why. Among the "celebrities" were Napoleon, Catherine the Great, and Booth Tarkington, and from each she drew an admonition for herself.

> Gandhi [she wrote]. Type of pure
> national saint. Because would not
> eat meat or drink goats' milk.
> (Give up goats' milk.)

> Mme. Curie. Because dedicated
> scientist. (Devote more time to
> Dedication.)

> St. Joan. Ditto Dedication.

> The Buddha. Enlightenment and
> Union. (Think more of non-Matter.)

> Wright Brothers. Daedalus' dream.
> [This was crossed out.] Courage? [So
> was this.] Poetry of the machine.
> (Develop for separate list.)

"Are the Wright Brothers priests?" I inquired, putting down the paper.

"They invented the airplane, stupid. Besides, I don't think brothers are priests in the Catholic religion anyway. Fathers are. Here, give me that, I'm going to add one more."

"Was the Buddha a Catholic?" I pursued.

"Naturally not, he was a Buddhist. Now be quiet and let me think. Ssh, I need a composer—for God's sake go away. Why don't you take your game and find somebody on deck to play with—" for in an access of last-minute remorse over her arbitrary dissolution of the ENCHIRIDION, she had bought me a box of checkers and a board.

When I left her she was wavering between Stephen Foster and Wagner.

On the first-class deck I dutifully set up the checkerboard

in my lap and waited for a partner. A few passengers, mostly
in military uniform, strolled by, intent on the water or their
cigarettes. Nearby a foreign-looking baby just learning to
walk came hobbling between its mother's legs, holding her
thumbs with its fists and dribbling onto its shoes; it might
have been either male or female—its haircut and the shirt
over its little pants gave no clue, the one being too short for a
girl and the other too long for a boy. "Volódya. Volódya,"
crooned the mother, urging it on with gentle kicks of her
knees. "Okean," she said, pointing beyond the rail, "vodá."

In an unoccupied chair next to mine someone had forgotten his sunglasses. I picked them up and looked through the
wrong side of the lenses, with the ear-pieces standing out before my face, while the deck-boards turned dark green and
the big jellying waves changed to grass. The black grass fled
my gaze like a long, long field, shimmering and trackless. It
was the middle of the night behind those glasses; I did not
like it there, and leaned out to drop them down again upon
their seat, but a bristly-knuckled hand reached out to intercept them, and upset the board. The checkers spilled out on
my skirt and rolled away. One skittered across the deck and
under the railing and into the sea, and one the baby caught
on the way and put into its mouth. I had to go after them all,
avoiding the legs of the walkers, who were glad enough of
the diversion. There was nothing to do on the decks of that
homeward-heaving ship but think where it was taking us: so
the walkers walked, in the landlubber's illusion that the more
they walked the sooner they would arrive. Only my mother,
sticking to her cabin and missing Enoch, did not walk. It was
as though she rode against the tide.

The baby cried when I opened its jaws to force out the
checker; and to win it over I smiled at its mother and said,
"Is it a boy or girl?" The baby bawled louder and wider at
the sound of my voice so close to its face, and inadvertently
spit out the checker. "Yes," said its mother, grinning silver
teeth-fillings back at me, "that is you know true." So I put
the last checker, wet with the baby's spittle, into my box, and
was about to close the lid: but the brindled fingers slipped a
coin under the cover. "That's half a dollar for you."

"What for?"

"To use instead of the piece that went overboard. It was
my fault it went in but I can't tell you how to fetch it out
again. This isn't an admiral's suit, you see."

I observed his buttons with modified scorn; I knew perfectly well and at first glance what sort of uniform he wore. He was a colonel. On account of Enoch I had seen many colonels, and they all dressed alike.

"Don't you have to stay in Europe?" I wondered.

"Not when there's not a war," he said, and hid behind his sunglasses the froggy skin-scallops that circled his frog-eyes. Over his speckled scalp limp rows of white thread lay stretched, trained upward from where they grew at the side of his ear; they covered his skull like a very bad wig. He hinged the knees that were concealed somewhere in the long tubes of his military trousers and sat down in the deck-chair beside me.

"Are you being retired?" I asked, imagining the greyish pits in his skin to be the accumulation of very old age.

"Nope. Just going home to get some lawyers. Then I have to come right back to Nuremberg. Do you know any riddles?"

I said I did not.

"Okay, then why does a chicken cross the road?"

I said I knew that one.

"Never mind, I've got another. What didn't come into Noah's ark in pairs?"

I gave up.

"Worms," said the colonel. "They came in apples."

"What do you need the lawyers for?" I said.

"To present the evidence. What has no legs and runs?"

"A train," I ventured.

"Nope."

"A ball."

"Nope."

"A watch?"

"Nope. Ice-cream cone on a hot day. Like that one?"

"It's all right," I said politely. "My stepfather had to go to Zürich. Is that near the place you said?"

"Different country. Your stepfather Army?"

"Nope," I said, catching on. "He sort of works for the Government."

The colonel laughed. "Don't you think the Army does too?"

"I don't know much about the Army," I admitted, remembering the three English soldiers at the border, how they had carried back the cut-down giant, the big head dangling loose.

"Neither do I. You'd make a good colonel," said the colo-

nel. "How about the five copycats sitting on a fence? One
went away, so how many were left?"

"Four," I said promptly.

"Nope. None. They all copied the first one, and that's all the
riddles I ever heard of. Except the Riddle of Life. Your stepfather in refugee work?"

"He keeps lists," I answered, thinking how curious it was
that my mother was also impelled, at that very moment, to
keep lists. But then, while the colonel scratched the hair on
the back of one hand with the straight clean nails of the
other, quite as though the inadequacy of my reply had set
him itching, I tentatively offered him one of Enoch's sardonic
phrases: "He reclaims relatives, I think."

"Oh," said the colonel, "he brings 'em back alive?"

"I don't think alive."

"Dead?"

"I guess dead," I acknowledged, gnawing my lip with
shame. I knew from my mother how ignominious Enoch's
obligations were; she feared the corpses had made him taboo.

And now it seemed she was right. The colonel took off his
green glasses and examined me through the mole-splattered
creases ringing his light-stung eyes, damp with distaste. "Well,
well," he said, "I see what you mean, the Riddle of Death. So
you're Vand's daughter probably?"

"Stepdaughter," I corrected, but my head stayed down.

"Rotten job, could turn the stomach of the best of 'em.
Well, it's made his name, that's the point—I suppose that's
why he does it. I run into him now and again, you know."
His heavy clench gripped my shoulder and then abruptly
opened—I felt on me the seal of his contempt. "Can't see
why they brought *you* over."

I said humbly, "I came with my mother."

"Made the Paris papers, didn't she? Crashed up her
chauffeur?"

"He only had a concussion."

"Only?"

"He didn't get *killed,*" I said defensively.

"That's a riddle too," the colonel remarked without a
blink. "Half a mind to take back my fifty cents."

"I bet you've killed a hundred people," I accused him, "on
account of being in the Army."

"A hundred thousand's more like it. But it wasn't the
Army's fault. It was the war's." I could think of nothing to
say to this, so he explained, "The Army doesn't make the

war, the Government does. The Army only does what the Government tells it to," and looked at me as though he thought I should understand. "That's what they're saying in Nuremberg; that's the defense, and I can't say I don't think they have a point. You take that Russian kid over there—" I turned to follow his nod: the baby was drooling. "Some sort of U.N. connection," the colonel went on, "but I'll tell you something: I'm more scared of that kid over there than I am of all the generals in the Nuremberg dock put together, you know why?"

I could not imagine why. The baby, reaching up for an almost-empty spool of yellow thread its mother was swinging just beyond its grasp, seemed harmless enough, if not especially intelligent; for when it captured the spool it only put it into its mouth. But I did not see why the colonel should be afraid of it.

"I heard an Arab sing a Russian song last week," I told him, thinking how my mother, with equal inexplicability, had been afraid of the singer's voice. "It was in a restaurant, but he wasn't really from Arabia."

Unimpressed, the colonel returned his big dark spectacles to his face, shutting me out of the green world there; but I could see my reflection, distorted against a background of sea, on their curved surfaces. "It's that kid we've got to watch out for, that's the generation of the real enemy. The lawyers are wasting their time. So's Vand and all the other post-war bureaucrats. What's done is done. We can't waste time going back, we've got to prepare for that kid over there." It was plain to me that he was no longer addressing me; he had grown unforeseeably formidable, and seemed incapable of riddle-making.

To placate him I recited, "They haven't paid my mother royalties since 1939."

"Who?" he sternly asked.

"The Russians."

"Royalties on what?"

I bit my fingertip doubtfully.

"I see what you mean," he conceded, although I had not spoken. "You know what royalties are?"

"No," I said.

"You're a nice little girl," the colonel said. "I like you."

"Do you want to play checkers?" I inquired at once, to take advantage of his sudden amiability.

His strong public laugh blared. "I always win against civil-

ians, that's fair warning. It's part of my battle-plan." Between
us we dared the tilt of his chair-arm, balancing the board.
His furred tidy fingers lined up the checkers until he had his
black squadron at attention. Methodically he charged my
troops, piling the losses in a neat round red tower at his side,
and shortly won. "A field situation," he described it, "it's over
your head, it's not for you. You haven't learned how to calculate your advance." The pieces fell in at his command for
the next game; democratically, we exchanged colors. "I've got
the Red Army now, have I?" he muttered, and without conscience decimated my forces once more. "You've got to be
able to see the other side's advantages, you've got to be able
to anticipate them. No, I don't like the way you play—you
take foolish chances, you're a wild patriot: now look, don't
love your side so much you won't let yourself think about
mine! Too much patriotism always loses," he concluded, and
gave me a sharp smile that was not really humorous. "They
shouldn't have brought you over there. Not now, not in the
middle of everything."

"The middle of everything," I repeated, wondering where
that was and watching, as he rose, the flash of the half dollar
representing the sea-swallowed piece: it came and went in his
left lens like a frantic semaphore.

"Europe," he said firmly, and by the consciously severe
rasp he entrusted to his tone I was immediately reminded of
Enoch. "It's no place to bring a kid any more. You tell 'em I
said so." He waited until he drew from me what he imagined
was consent. Then: "Europe's for the scavengers now, and
for the lawyers," he told me, going off.

I did not know what he meant by scavengers—he seemed
to dip in and out of conversation with himself, generally in
my mother's fashion—but when, after a yard's hesitation, he
stopped to call to me to be grateful for America and to listen
to my teachers (he did not again mention Enoch or my
mother), I thought he must be right about the lawyers. Europe made work for lawyers: for my mother's lawyer Europe
made work. In the middle of violence, in the middle in fact
of everything (the colonel's phrase came clear), had she not
had to send after William's strange tools of peace? Insurance
would heal the chauffeur's wound, checks would surfeit the
private visitor's greed; and, for both, William's techniques
were as ample as my mother's trust fund. Lawyers were a
cult, the colonel implied, his voice not liking them.

His walk across the deck dispelled the moment's similarity

to Enoch which that vocal scorn of his had conjured—unlike my stepfather he had the military gait, the chin low, the belly inconspicuous, the flat ears subtly on guard, the utilitarian shoulders jutting at either side as sparely as rifle-racks, and soldier's legs stiff half from habit, half from some perhaps secret ailment. His whole movement signified departure—not the casual leavetaking of ordinary men who might soon come together again (as we might, and did, meet in the dining room half an hour afterward), but the hailed, paraded, pitied, and applauded embarkation, at the dock's mobbed edge, of the sacrificial armored few. He proceeded, in brief, like a man who of all things knew least whether he would return. And with just such a swerve to the side of his clipped and visored head as one would expect of a man of fate, he bent to nuzzle out the alien baby's dalliance. There against the brown rail, while the white-stitched ocean bounced beyond, he squatted face to face with his enemy. And while he talked at it, sending out curling sounds between the varied jackets, foils, and crowns of his crapulent teeth, his enemy warily reconnoitred—sucked its fingers, then swiftly, a blitzkrieg, with small fierce fists snatched the sunshades from his nose. "Volódya!" cried its mother; and "Nyet, nyet," chided the colonel, struggling to open his enemy's moist positive grip. But too late and in vain—in and out of the baby's mouth went the ear-pieces; it licked with relish, and tried its tongue up and down the smooth green lenses, and bit hard little gums, red as strawberries, joyously on the colonel's intervening hairy forefinger. "Nyet," said the colonel, and "nope," said the colonel, persuading, entreating. The woman lowered her bright braided and ribboned head into the skirmish, slapping the baby's hands to free its prize-of-war. Cautiously she squeezed its cheeks until its small tongue-tip pushed out and relinquished the colonel's nibbled finger. Then she handed him his glasses, ruefully framing signs, inserting her own fingers into her mouth and pressing her gums. "Teething," the colonel translated. "You should give him something to work on." The woman grimaced to show how well she had understood —"You see yes quite," she stated in a voice pitched too low for English, and displayed tiny mysterious notches on the wooden spool. At once the baby grabbed it away and took it to its mouth. The colonel smiled at the mother of his enemy. "Nice little boy, nice fellow," he said, wiping his smeared sunglasses across his breast with a sweep of complicity. Meanwhile the baby gnawed on the spool, then suddenly

laughed aloud. It was a shriek of open satisfaction. Its
mother patted her thickly banded circle of braid, embarrassed
by pleasure and pride. "Female," said the mother of the colonel's enemy.

I was astonished into bravery and out of politeness. "You
played with the baby," I burst out when, not merely with the
air of a man who has had an afterthought, but as something
of a hero chewing the cud of his self-esteem, the colonel restored himself to the march and came to stand by the chair
where I was dropping the checkers one by one into their
black box. I assumed he was one of those people, easily recognized by children and almost certainly childless, who congratulate themselves on being especially attuned to the men-
talities of all the inferior races. I sensed by now that it was
his custom to speak to children as though he were accosting a
tribe of amicable bushmen, and (supposing he had ever encountered a bushman) vice-versa: in either case he could
leap from the simple to what he hoped was the profound
without expecting to offend. In this, as I had already observed, he somewhat resembled my mother; but she, at least,
had the virtue of not concealing, from herself or her subjects,
her plain dislike. "You said you were afraid of it," I pointed
out, "and then you played with it."

"It's the future I'm afraid of." But this was too cryptic. "I
don't like to think of the future," he finished.

"I do," I said quickly, and thought of the future then and
there—I saw a great white ring of light, and myself in the
heart of it, elevating a snow-encrusted violin. For in one of
her lists marked Things After Getting Home: Winter Preparation, my mother, under the banality of "school clothes,"
had written "music lessons."

"Well, you," the colonel said, "you *are* the future." This
sounded so much like another riddle that he had to scratch
his small upper lip. "Which reminds me, let's see: some boy
scouts are out on a hike," he plunged on so earnestly I almost
forgave him, "and after a while come to a forest. Now—how
far into it can they go?"

I considered. "Are there trees?"

"Of course. I *said* it's a forest."

"And wolves?"

"Plenty of wolves, but it doesn't matter."

"Then I give up," I said.

"Knew you would," said the colonel, pleased by his
triumph. "Answer's halfway in."

"Halfway?" I wondered.

"Well, because after that they're not going *into* the forest, they're coming out. It's the same as now," he commented, lifting a vague salute to the sea. "We're halfway to America."

But though it might have been the truth, I did not think this a witticism. If we were halfway to America, then we were halfway to Europe too: it was only a question of reversing the engines; it was only a question of point of view. "I don't see how anybody can be afraid of a *baby*," I told him with more uneasiness than spite; and looked toward that part of the sky, littered with shards of clouds like broken white teacups turned upside down, under which Europe invisibly lay.

11

When we came home a cable from Enoch was waiting. My mother read it jubilantly. "They've given him a promotion! I can hardly believe it!" Her tongue moved skilfully past the exact governmental phrase. "They told him about it right after he finished outlining his report at Zürich!" She threw herself onto a hassock beside the foyer table and began to laugh. Her eyes were brilliant. "I never expected it so soon! But it's astonishing!"

"Does it mean he'll come and stay with us now?" I inquired.

"Oh no, he'll only get home now and then to see all these new Washington people. He's got to go all over Europe," she crowed, sniffing the cablegram as though it were somehow perfumed with her desire.

"Then how is it different from the job he's got now?"

But she was exultant. "Different! Oh, it's marvelously different; it's *clean*. In the first place it's with the State Department—look, don't bother me now," she broke off, "I've got to send an answer right away." She pulled off her gloves and tossed them at the maid, who had only just returned from the family-visit to Toronto which my mother's absence had enforced. "Paper, paper! Get me some paper, Janet. You should have managed to get back yesterday, I wrote you the ship was due today—look at the dust on that bannister! Oh, I knew they'd give it to him, they couldn't let him rot in that horror forever"—she sipped a breath of innocence, of detachment, of turning-from-evil—"I could *feel* how morbid it was making me . . ."

She wrote, under the heading of DARLING, as though this too were a sort of list: THE AIR IS CLEAR AT LAST CONGRATULATIONS GLORIOUS FUTURE AHEAD NO MORE CORPSES

And when I said, "I don't want to study piano, I want the violin," she pressed with zeal upon her pencil point and added: SAFE

Nor did she again question my safety in the world until a dozen years later, when Enoch stood at the doorway of his ambassadorship and when, as its price, I was sent to my father's unknown doorway, the yellow, dank, and unknown doorway of Gustave Nicholas Tilbeck.

PART THREE

BRIGHTON

1

I was sent, but not immediately. They delayed, my stepfather and his wife, they reposed, they hoarded quiet days. The crisis had secured my consent: I had said I would go: and this seemed enough for them. They settled into old-fashioned domestic scenes and sounds; rather too purposefully they "relaxed," and the long conspiratorial drone behind the closed door of my mother's room one morning turned out to contain nothing more of intrigue or cabal than Enoch reading aloud the haying chapter from *Anna Karenina.* "How wonderful!" my mother exclaimed now and then. "I'd like to do something like that, something oh, you know, just thoroughly *physical.*"

"Why not start with getting out of bed?" Enoch said.

"Oh you," she mildly scolded. "I don't feel like it yet. It's too soon."

"Leverheim told you to get out of there last week."

"Leverheim. What a fool. If he has any license at all it's a plumber's. Him and his pills, they'd choke a whale. They made my hair fall out. Look, it's coming out in chunks."

"He told you not to worry."

"It may take months to grow back thick again! Even *he* admits that. You don't expect me to walk *around* this way, do you?"

"I don't expect you to stay in bed either."

"Why not? I like it here."

"It's neurotic."

"Good. I'm glad. It's a compliment to be called neurotic, especially by you. You never say anything psychoanalytical."

"But I'm always listening psychoanalytically, and that's even better."

"Well, it may be better for you, but it's not better for me. I can't stand not knowing what you think of me."

"All right, I think you're neurotic. Now get out of bed."

"Not until I look human."

"It's not important to look it, it's important to *be* it."

"Don't start talking that funny way again. You're starting again."

"I only said—"

"An epigram. It's disgusting. I hate it. You said I'm not human. You think I'm a dog in the manger or something. You have an Aesop complex, you know that, Enoch?"

"Look," he said, "I thought you wanted to be read to."

"I do, I'm listening. Go *on*. I love this scene, don't you? It makes me want to jump right out of bed and mow alongside some peasants."

He sighed, but he went on. His voice briefly lifted before descending into murmur again, and soon my mother was regularly interrupting with little moans of joy and protest. They were full of play, she and he; they were full of peace and gossip and mutual disobedience and delight. Neither one of them had a thought beyond the other.

Nevertheless I was sometimes allowed to visit with them, since my mother no longer had the excuse of sedation to keep me away. Her head was turbaned grotesquely in a gold-and-white shawl patterned with the Taj Mahal. She was lively and restored. Though her cough was rare, her talk was not, and its familiar disconnected patter continued for long periods (but plainly not meant for me), and reached and roused even Enoch's stingy smile. He shone with uncomplicated good humor almost all the while: my mother was exaggeratedly querulous, therefore unconsciously witty—but not so clever as Enoch's response measured her. Perhaps he laughed —he, committed at least superficially to the utilitarian—because there was, for the moment, nothing more useful for him to do. The fact was that we were waiting.

For what? Tilbeck had specified that I was to come alone. This was the paternal command. I was not to be chauffeured or chaperoned into my father's mysteriously tardy jurisdiction: quite the opposite, he meant me to deliver myself up to him unaccompanied and free of home-snares, in the manner of Beauty returning, unguided and unguarded, to the terrible Beast. That is to say, I supposed this to be the manner he had in mind; what he had actually written, and more especially his way of writing it, was promptly made inaccessible. The

letter had been briskly hidden: Enoch had locked it up in his
desk almost at once, as though it were a sort of dangerous
animal he was afraid to have roam within sight of its prey.
And strangely, it was his wife, not me, whom he regarded as
its prey.

So I loafed in my mother's room and, against their jokes
and teasings, waited. After several days it somehow came
clear that a dispute had thickened about the time they were to
surrender me to Tilbeck. Our side appeared to want to put it
off another month—until nearly October—until, I surmised,
the Senate hearings had safely ended. "It doesn't matter to
me," I told them once, although they had not asked me
whether it did. "After twenty-two years," Enoch answered,
"he can afford another few weeks' delay. It doesn't matter
that it doesn't matter," he obscurely finished, "to *you*." And
my mother, who had wept because she had meant me to be
always free, listened to the joyous haying scene, thought jealously of the Embassy, and was quickly reconciled. But the
final date was so nearly a compromise-in-the-middle that it
was difficult to tell who had won—that is, who had had to
give way. For no reason at all—or perhaps because at that
time he was growing fatter every day—I assumed that Enoch
had not troubled to resist the other's proposals: had not troubled over anything at all, in fact, and was simply ready to
hand me over and be done with it. Now and again the book
smacked shut in his lap and he fell back into his chair with
his palms slapped down upon his two spread-apart thick
thighs, absorbed in adoration of my mother's foolishness,
looking like a sultan or grand vizier; and my mother's wildly-
wrapped turban with its print of queer Indian scribbles over
her suddenly balding head, leaking hank and scraggle, side by
side with his neat damp ruddy crown, threw over the room an
Oriental comic chaotic cast that startled them both into self-
satisfaction. They had settled me; they had smoothed me away
like a snag; they had negotiated me, for a time, out of their
existence. Who had done the real negotiating, however, was
soon apparent: twice in one week the letterhead of William's
firm had passed across my mother's knee-humped sheet, after
which she spoke: "Is the tenth of September all right with
you?"—and did not stop for my reply. She fingered her forehead indifferently; she saved her passion for herself. "Now
how am *I* supposed to know?" she counter-questioned when I
wondered how long my banishment would be: "Ask Enoch."

But Enoch, who had no idea, mumbled: "A week maybe?"

"A day or so," my mother amended.

"A month or so?" I interpreted.

"Well, take a full suitcase, you never can tell," she acknowledged ominously.

In short they would reveal nothing. They kept to themselves, and pitied one another for their predicament, whatever it might be: with nothing left over, neither wonder nor regard, for the fact of my exile: only, I suspected, relief. They were saved; I had saved them. They had put me between themselves and Tilbeck; this time money was not enough, money would not do, money was not what he wanted; he wanted me.

I decided to speak to William.

But first this happened: Ed McGovern telephoned and asked to see my mother.

"Good," she said. "Tell him to come. I want his opinion on Vronsky." For two days she had been arguing with my stepfather about the characters in *Anna Karenina:* she was angry that Tolstoy had made Anna's lover feel ennui. "It isn't sensible," she said, all vague and pouting, "it's rude. It's insolent."

"You mean it's real," Enoch said.

"*I* wouldn't have done it. First those silly asterisks"—my mother believed in literary "frankness"; she owned an unexpurgated copy of *Lady Chatterley's Lover,* of course, a smuggler's copy, and had modeled her foreman's love scenes with Marianna after the gamekeeper's—"and then, practically right after the consummation, he's bored to death with her!"

"*You* wouldn't have done it," Enoch repeated.

"No, I wouldn't."

"You wouldn't have had her throw herself under the train either?"

"What a way to end a book!"

"Nobody denies it's a tragedy, dear. Then I suppose you would have had her go back to her husband?"

"Not *that* husband. What a prig, exactly like William. What *I'd* have done," she said meditatively, "if I were Tolstoy, is"—she really did not know, and had to suck her lip for inspiration.

"Remember," Enoch said, "divorce wasn't available—"

"Well I know that! Ssh, I'm thinking." But just then the maid knocked to announce the arrival of Ed McGovern. "I'd simply have found a new lover for her!" she burst out.

"—who wouldn't get bored?"

"Well look, for goodness' sake, it's not Anna who was boring. She's not a *boring* woman, after all. That's why I can't see Tolstoy's conception, I just can't see it. There's something wrong with a man who'd tire of a bright woman like that. I mean, I sort of see a bit of myself in Anna—"

"So do I," said Ed McGovern.

"There! You see, Enoch? Now don't look me all over please, I have to stay in bed."

"If it's too much for you—"

"No, no, stay, I'm perfectly all right. I'm not sick any more, but my hair's all coming out. I don't see *how* I can remind anyone of that beautiful Anna when I know how awful I look. It's just lucky for me that a turban's becoming to me. In the thirties I used to wear them all the time, it was the style, even though it *was* a little old for me—did you bring the proofs?" she broke off.

"Well, no," said Ed McGovern, and stopped.

"Didn't they come yet? Really, that printer—"

"Oh, they've come, they've come."

"Then what's the matter? You don't have to be nasty about it!"

"They look lousy, if you want to know the truth."

"You're not going to start about the capital letters again, are you, because I warn you if you do—"

My mother's editor very slowly sat himself down on her bed and began moodily searching for an ashtray. "It's not the capitals, it's the commas. You just can't print sonnets without commas, Mrs. Vand, they don't make sense."

"Then *don't* print sonnets. I never gave you permission to have sonnets anyway, did I? We've discussed it a thousand times—*Bushelbasket*'s got to be really revolutionary or nothing at all."

"Then it's nothing at all."

I brought him the cap of a cold-cream jar from the dresser and received in it the long grey snout of his cigarette, just in time.

"Maybe you're having a sterile period," Enoch suggested from his chair. "Artists usually do."

"Artists yes, but editors aren't allowed to," my mother said severely. "Don't joke, Enoch. I pay this young man perfectly good unfunny money, and he's got to do what he's told."

"There's a Rat in my room," the young man morosely observed.

"Don't try and tell me I'm responsible for that!" said my mother. "I didn't advise you to live in that sort of neighborhood."

"You said it was a romantic part of New York, didn't you? Full of writers, ha, ha. How should *I* know New York? I took your word for it, didn't I?"

Enoch asked, "Where are you from?"

"Boston."

"*South* Boston," said my mother maliciously. "That's pretty far from lace-curtain."

"Don't cast aspersions, Allegra."

"Anyhow he went to N.Y.U., he knows all about New York."

"I did not go to N.Y.U.," said McGovern haughtily. "I merely registered, I did not *go*."

"You also registered at Columbia, the New School, St. John's University in Brooklyn, and the Henry George School. I know. I paid all the fees."

"You did not. The Henry George School is free."

"Free hot air," said my mother, who even in her radical days had been against the single tax. "The point is, Enoch, he's lived in this city for six years. Where do you think he got that fake Flemish accent? He can't blame his rats on me —it's a subterfuge."

"I did not say rats. I said Rat. One Rat."

"How do you get a Flemish accent from living in New York?" Enoch innocently inquired, but both my mother and her editor snubbed this foolish question with a simultaneous shrug. I suspected that my mother had copied hers—a rather steep lift of the left shoulder—from her protégé.

"It's really hard to understand the poems without the commas," I offered meekly.

My mother yielded up all her scorn: "Who asked you? You don't understand the first thing about modern poetry. I know what they taught you in that college, they taught you *Wordsworth*," she sneered.

"Wordsworth's not so bad," Ed McGovern said.

My mother stared. "Dear boy, are you undergoing a conversion?"

"All I said was Wordsworth's not so bad. You'd probably like him if he'd left out the commas."

"If that's sarcasm, you might just as well forget you've ever been an editor."

"All right. I'm going to San Francisco."

"What!"

"I mean I'm going if you'll give me the carfare."

"What about *Bushelbasket?* You just can't pick up and leave without—"

"You fired me, just now, in the presence of two witnesses."

"Oh stop, I didn't fire you."

"You said if that was sarcasm I might just as well forget I've ever been an editor. O.K., it was sarcasm. Honest it was."

"Listen, don't you dare resign just before mailing-time! Not when circulation's just *about* to boom. I've got fifteen new people who've promised to subscribe—"

"I know, I just got their fifteen contributions."

"Money?" said Enoch.

"Poems," said McGovern.

"One of them is from Euphoria Karp," my mother said admiringly.

"Who's that?" —Enoch.

"She publishes practically every other month in *Harpers! You* know. William suggested that she submit to us as a sort of, well, charity, wasn't that nice of him?"

"William?" I could not help wondering at this; for if William thought novels imprudent, then he must have found poetry positively immoral.

"Light verse," McGovern explained. "Light *medical* verse."

"Ah, an invalid spinster," Enoch ventured.

"Don't be silly, her husband's Professor of Copyright Law; but he was dropped from *Who's Who,* don't ask me why. He's one of William's closest friends—I mean William's cultivating him nowadays," said my mother, "for a particular reason. What's this about San Francisco?"

"The Golden West," said McGovern.

"Yes, but what's *there?*"

"Fresh Horizons."

"Look here," she said, blowing out a long breath, "do you want a raise?"

"I've got a Rat," he persisted. "What more could anyone want?"

"I'm perfectly sure they have rats in San Francisco too," said my mother. "Be reasonable. I'll give you five dollars more."

"Per what?"

"What do you mean per what? Per month."

"Per week."

"Oh, all right," she capitulated. "Bring the proofs tomorrow. I want to look them over and take out all the sonnets."

"Not tomorrow. Tomorrow I'm leaving for San Francisco. I need an advance on my salary, please. I need an advance on my *new* salary, please."

"I told you there was a subterfuge! He simply came for money, Enoch. Hand me my pocketbook, will you?" she commanded me; and to McGovern said in a loud monotone —as though she were addressing an opposing volley-ball player across an immense gymnasium—"How do I know you'll come back?"

"Because you're the least boring woman I've ever known, Mme. Karenina; and because it's a tremendous opportunity to be editor of *Bushelbasket* and in charge of a staff of three part-time graduate students; and because I don't take my duties lightly."

It was his longest speech so far. "And because you're bound to run out of money," I said stiffly, but my mother pretended not to hear me; or perhaps she did not really, for she was busy grimacing after what she must have supposed was a shrewdly leonine eye, lit with an elegant mistrust, to turn upon her editor.

But she succeeded only in looking teased and pleased. "You see! He's impossible! Now I can't find my checkbook —oh, here it is. All right: get back here in one week, no longer, you hear? And don't spend it all on beer. William would be furious if he knew I was giving in like this."

"No doubt it's intelligent editorial policy," Enoch remarked. "Besides, beer is art."

"Well, sir, you can ridicule me if you like . . ."

"An Ambassador can ridicule anybody, you're perfectly right," my mother said hastily. "I suppose you saw in the papers about Mr. Vand's being appointed Ambassador?"

"It so happens that this Rat I have eats newsprint; but I heard about it on the radio."

"Don't be difficult. I'm letting you go, and that should satisfy you. Anyhow you're mistaken."

"But he does eat print, honest he does. He ate right through my paperback Schopenhauer, if you want to know the truth."

"It's a pessimistic beast, isn't it?" Enoch said.

"Have you tried poison?" said my mother.

"Or Kant? Perhaps a change in its diet—"

"Enoch, don't badger the boy."

"You just said yourself he's mistaken."

"I meant about going West. The point is there's no one who really *counts* in California."

"Not past seventeen, anyway," Enoch said mildly.

"Now what's that supposed to mean?"

"It means I'm as alert to Trends as the next man—they're all writing imitation Japanese poetry out there, aren't they? The kind that has exactly seventeen syllables."

"Oh, haiku," said my mother abruptly; but Ed McGovern glanced at my stepfather with a slight increase in respect. "I don't care for that sort of formalism. It's like a straightjacket. As far as I'm concerned it might as well be a sonnet. Look here," she said severely, "don't go bringing back any haiku. I won't have that sort of thing in *Bushelbasket*. I don't care if it *is* the wave of the future."

"The wave of the future," said McGovern, solemnly killing his butt in the bit of cold cream that lined the cover of the jar, "is philistinism."

"In that case," Enoch said, "if we're going to have a discussion about Literature, I'd better get poor old Tolstoy out of earshot."

"Don't!" squealed my mother, but it was too late—he had aimed the thick green weight of *Anna Karenina* straight for her pillow, where it landed neatly beside her shining shoulder. "Ouch, you nearly knocked my head off."

"That dear old hairless thing. Quick, hide it under the covers."

"My *head?* Enoch, you're mean."

"Tolstoy. So as not to offend him. He knows nothing about Literature—most great writers don't: all they know is life. Now ssh, what's this about philistinism?"

"Enoch, you're *mean*. Leave the boy alone."

"He ought to be able to defend his opinions, Allegra."

"Well, if you'd let him get a word in."

"It's a mark of diplomacy not to. I thereby save him from himself. Watch and see, he'll tell us the East is effete."

"It is," said McGovern.

"And decadent."

"Right," said McGovern.

"And tied to outmoded forms."

"I don't deny it."

"And under the thumb of the academic critics?"

"Absolutely."

By this time McGovern was viewing my stepfather with positive enthusiasm.

"Well, don't let Mrs. Vand hear you say all that, or she'll cut you out of her will."

"Enoch!" protested my mother. "I'm the one who's the real revolutionary—you can see it just on the *face* of things. I never print anything that doesn't have symbols, or an objective correlative at least, or tension between images, and things like that! I just *said* I can't stand formalism—"

"Exactly," said Enoch. "That proves it. You're effete, decadent, outmoded, and academic."

"I am not!" She appealed to her editor: "Am I, Eddie?"

"Is she, Eddie? There's a moral choice for you! Before answering, consider carefully the benefits of literary philanthropy."

"I already have," McGovern responded promptly, entrusting to my stepfather a tone both of solidarity and admiration.

"Well, am I?" she whimpered.

"Mrs. Vand," said McGovern, "you are the most avantgarde person I have ever encountered."

My mother giggled.

"An art pioneer," Enoch recommended.

"Certainly an art pioneer," McGovern conceded.

"Then why are you always arguing about the capital letters?" she demanded.

"I won't any more," he modestly promised. "Ora et labora."

"What?"

"Pray and work," McGovern said, folding the check in tres partes, like conquered Gaul. It slid with the expertness of familiar surrender into the side pocket of his jeans, which publicized a ritual poverty as fastidiously and formally as a friar's rope-belt. "It's a motto to remember me by."

"You'd better come back or you'll have it for an epitaph. No later than next week, I'm warning you."

"On the stroke of thirteen minutes after three P.M. — That's when Albert Schweitzer takes his afternoon nap, you know."

"One of the philistines?" Enoch inquired.

"The greatest of them all," McGovern answered.

"Sound chap," said Enoch, when the door had closed. "Think how lucky you are."

"He has a very original temperament," my mother remarked, gratified.

"I agree, and if it works to your advantage I doubt whether you'll ever see him again."

"I just gave him a big advance!" she exclaimed, but with plenty of confidence. "I just gave him, let me see . . ."

"Don't tell me. Please don't. I can't bear to hear money getting counted."

"That's because you've never had any to count," my mother said aloofly; her rapid look of scorn fell unexpectedly and brutally upon me. "Don't you have anything better to do than hover?"

"I'm not hovering," I objected.

"Then what do you call what you've been doing for the last half-hour?"

So she dismissed me; and because I did not know where she expected me to go, or what—aside from my concealing an attentive curiosity behind a false patience—she expected me to do, I went quietly out to the terrace, on the theory that it was the only part of the house that was at the same time outside of the house. It gave me the sense of hanging over the city (despite the cactus and the affectation of garden furniture and the anti-suicidal design of the railing) on the thinnest of wafers. Out there I might with justification be accused of hovering; but a fog of guilt hovered with me, and I wondered why. Then I knew, or almost knew: it was a ledge like that other ledge of my unredeemed childhood, a natural platform for one who is part of the scene and is at the same time outside of the scene—the habitat, in short, of an eavesdropper. And my mother and her husband devised scenes; they invested every conversation with a Doppelgänger; they seemed to speak of an absent being even when they spoke only of themselves. In their most innocent discussions I felt myself an intruder whom they wished away as smoke is wished away with the wave of an ineffectual and wandless hand; but smoke distends itself and vanishes, or else has a chimney to go up into. I had not even that. Hence they thought me less substantial than smoke or imagination, and only noticed me when I got in the way of their other, their constant, listener, the ghost of their joint aspiration (or to be still more accurate, Enoch's aspiration which my mother, convinced she knew its nature, shared), to whom they addressed everything, even when they appeared to be addressing only themselves, even when they might have been supposed merely to be attending to the claims of subordinates and servants. This romance—whatever wraith-of-the-future it was

that had won Enoch's concentration and my mother's allegiance—crowned whoever stood between them: for its sake
my mother had to cause even her editor to acknowledge my
stepfather's elevation; for its sake she had, long ago, to wreak
upon my governess the news of Enoch's grace; and to succor,
for the sake of its nameless name, the private visitor's dangerous laugh of avarice. On account of this secret romance—how
foolish that phrase is, yet it correctly describes their betrothal
to my stepfather's destiny, another foolish yet relentless and
exact phrase—they sold everything and everyone for smoke.
Not myself but smoke they were sending to that homme de
génie, my evil-genius father, that Tilbeck who rose from
murk like a half-forgotten creature of the strait to claim his
tribute (I was educated enough in myth to know that in
every tale of this sort it is a daughter who is taken to feed the
slime); and anyhow what harm could come to smoke? They
trusted in my unimportance, and meant me to trust in the
same. Not that I had fear: I only had surprise. Without a
concrete shock, it never occurs to us that we really do not
matter. And we do not.

The terrace was like that long-ago ledge: a wafer in the air
on which one accumulates reality.

I had not had much more than a moment to consider these
echoes and matters new and rehearsed before Enoch arrived
and put *Anna Karenina* in my lap. "I think we've had enough
of this. Keep it, if you like."

"All right," I said.

"You might take it with you."

"I've read it twice. Anyhow I suppose he'll have something
to read there, won't he? It's not a *desert* island."

"Ah, then don't expect treasure!"

"I suppose he's literate, after all."

He peered evasively over the rooftops facing us and the
crowded river, showing himself to be too diverted by the
bright day to reply. "Your mother won't get out of bed," he
said finally. "She's being self-conscious about her hair, actually. It's a bit of a vanity, but I imagine it *is* a hardship for
her."

"She didn't send you out here to apologize for that hovering business?"

"No."

"Then don't take it on yourself. I forgive her outright."

He paced for a little and then sat down. "This is an inter-
lude for her, you know."

"You mean *Bushelbasket* and all of that?"

"They sustain her, these literary interests, between events."

"She isn't capable of literary interests," I said bluntly.

"She's capable of events, however."

"They're not *her* events. They're yours."

"But she enjoys them, so it comes to the same thing. She lives for them."

"I'd like to see that letter," I said. "Tilbeck's letter."

"I've told you what's in it."

"All the same I'd like to see it."

"I gave my word to your mother—"

"Not to let me see it?"

"Not to produce it in any case."

"That's what I said. You always state concrete things in the abstract," I complained. "Like saying 'art pioneer' for dilettante."

"Which in turn avoids something so much worse. But that's not half so bad as the young man's saying 'philistinism' and meaning hooliganism wrapped in mysticism. Though where he fits Schweitzer I can't tell. Still, I imagine your mother thought he was talking about People's Art; but she won't stand for that any more—she's given up the whole idea of it. The one certain thing about verbal obscurity and that seven-types-of-ambiguity school of hers is that they're at least unambiguously and unobscurely anti-socialist."

"You're awfully tolerant," I said, "when it comes to my mother."

"I like her."

"So do I," I admitted.

He shot out a restless little smile. "I notice she persecutes you somewhat."

"You too. She's always sending you after me—like now. She keeps trying for a Relationship. The only thing to do is ignore it. That's how it was solved before."

"Before?"

"By William. When she was pushing *him* at me."

"Aha," he said with a crispness I had long ago recognized as both concealing and conciliatory. "She has her notions," he defended her after a minute; but he did not again deny that my mother was responsible for his uncomfortable attendance on me now: halfheartedly he rocked his big square knees; zestlessly he dug for a toothpick and played it between two lower incisors.

"And you have yours," I said, hunting for some part of his mind. "Only nobody knows what they are."

"Why? Am I missing capitals and commas? In that case I'll acquire them immediately. Without punctuation no one can claim to be a gentleman. The obscurity of omission is unquestionably as insulting to the perpetrator as to the perpetratee."

The last word made me laugh: the funny official sound of it conjured up an image of his traveling bag; and anyhow his sentences seemed to have emerged, unrevised, from the sort of documents suitable to such a traveling bag. "With you it's just the opposite," I exclaimed. "It's not the obscurity of something missing—it's the obscurity of abundance."

"A good phrase," he said, staring at the point of his toothpick, "if you can explain it."

"Like your briefcase—all those numbers on the combination lock. Too many numbers and too much significance," I continued. "Who'd know where to begin?"

"You'd prefer a lock with a single key? Like your mother; one easy pattern throws open the whole woman. Well," he said, "the fact is after plenty of years I'm done with that Pandora's box. I only mean my briefcase; don't construe that as a metaphor for your mother. Though I don't deny she's capable of letting loose mischief of her own on the world." Once more, and before I had quite caught up with what he weakly meant to be taken for wit, he suddenly unfolded the diffident fan of his smile. behind which he hid himself as shyly as a stage geisha. "You can have the lock as a souvenir if you want. It's a pretty good one—it was given to me by J. Edgar Hoover Himself, so it ought to be reliable. You might need it some day, for old love letters. —Unless, of course, the Senate doesn't confirm."

"You're not worried about that?" I said in surprise.

"No one likes to be raked over publicly." He drew his look from the sun-gauzed haze over the river to my unexpectedly conscious hands. "Or privately either, for that matter."

I supposed this to be a reproof: so I subsided, and let him be. "You don't *want* me to find the combination," I ended, with the sort of joke that always means what it says.

"Next thing I know you'll be taking up criminal psychology. Or lock-picking. Your mother's right," he pronounced. "You've been educated into ordinary inquisitiveness. It's a sort of intellectual burglary."

"I want to know things," I confessed.

"But I'm not the one to tell things. Especially when they're not entirely my affair."

"I only want to know why he wants me all of a sudden—it doesn't make sense. He never wanted me before, did he?"

"That again. You'd better ask your mother about that."

"I *know* he never wanted me before. He always wanted money."

"Everyone wants money."

"You don't," I pointed out.

"Only because I want something else that doesn't happen to have anything to do with money."

"What?" I challenged. "Doesn't everything have to do with money?"

He gave out a curious little whistle that drilled the air: the hole it left, empty of light and dark, clean of happiness and unhappiness, neutral as another planet's moon, took our common stare. What my stepfather saw or felt lay unspeaking, although enlarged, behind the trap and fence of his face, which he wore like wickets—through them watching perpetually for the luminous, final, and victorious toss and advent of a ball. But I, unaccountably, in the aftermath of the solemnity of that high sound (for which he at once apologized by putting a finger in his ear, in order to show a couple of his bad habits one after the other, and the second offense even worse than the first, both derived from boyhood in Chicago, where he had been, presumably, indifferently bred—all of this he meant me to note), I scraped a foot across the flag-stoned floor and thought how I had paced just here alongside the parapet not long ago in the vigil-light twinging from the point of the narrow cigar William's son now and then brought up to wreathe the air; and how against the bored flat-soled tap of the girl's blue shoe (now always afterward blue seems the bare color of impatience, the color of the thing deferred), he tapped out those imperious questions freighted with money and suspicion; and there was nothing then that did not have to do with money—myself, the waiting girl, the tight cylinder of cigar glinting. And it was the same now, though daylight: the river muddled with brightness like a woman's scarf thrown shining down, the railing three horizontal spears of gold: all of it a place and means for talking money.

And Enoch, whom my mother had not (so far) bought, talking money too: "Perhaps it's that I'm cold-hearted—I've been accused of that, you know—but money is an emotion that I lack," he said, willing enough now to settle himself into conversation. "I can't *feel* through it; that's the test, since everything has to do with money only if you're equipped for it from birth—by having it or wanting it, either one. The same with religion. If you have the capacity for God you see him everywhere; if you don't, you never miss him."

"I don't know about God," I said with mild experimental spite, "but at least it's true you don't get much chance to miss money."

"Only because of my circumstance as a man who in the traditional way has married an heiress with a very large trust fund. I don't go unaccused on that account either," he conceded. "In fact, by an uncomplicated analogy, it might be taken as a proof for the existence of God."

"What, the heiress' trust fund?"

"Don't look surprised. It's what pervades, after all—it's your mother's most obvious perfume, attar of cash. It's there, it can't be denied, it's all very nice and fragrant, there's nothing wrong with it, it's interesting enough—only it fails to move me. Which however doesn't mean it's not all around us, do you see?—in spite of its being ineffectual. The commonest argument," he concluded, "for the Divine Presence."

"Don't tell me you've given up atheism," I marveled.

"Oh, I've never been an atheist, you misunderstand. I've always been aware of God. My complaint has been that he hasn't returned the favor—not that I ask much, only an equal effort. It's God who's the real atheist," he protested. "He keeps denying himself by lack of action; he's turned his back on being God."

"I guess you want a mountain to smoke," I said.

"Or a bush to burn, I'm not particular. Mortals require signs; that's an axiom. And the truth of the matter is I've given God and your mother's money all the chance in the world to make a difference in me, and neither one has had any success at it. They don't speak to me. They can't influence. The void's in me maybe, but I blame them. They overestimate themselves. They think they dazzle simply by being, when what they ought to do is demonstrate."

"It seems to me money never *stops* demonstrating," I said, intending to leave God out of it and bring McGovern in. "Like just a little while ago, if you want an immediate example."

"You mean the easy way your mother sends her philistine on a tour of the bars of San Francisco? Oh, admittedly a

demonstration, but only of power. Power is what we expect
of God and money—but it's too ordinary, considering the
source. And I'm not willing to give my devotion to a commonplace; of God and money I have a right to expect something extraordinary. Especially since power is really nothing
more than a reward for this or that." He hesitated; he closed
his eyes, the weaker lid minutely tremulous, like a clairvoyant anticipating a signal from the beyond. But it was only
his way of deliberating before a climax. "Faith in God rewards with the power of complacency, which is exactly why
I find most piety obnoxious. And money rewards with the
power of permitting or compelling, depending on one's
temperament—though I ought to say that your mother's
money, being permissive, manages to escape my entire disgust. All well and good, but the world as it stands needs
something holier than a reward for mere survival."

"You're talking politically now?" I wondered. "You're talking about the cold war?"

"I'm talking about the world," he reiterated. "It needs what
neither God nor money can give it. It needs something extraordinary."

He appeared to insist on my understanding him. "You're
waiting for the Messiah then," was all I ventured.

He strangely did not deny it. "Oh, I've been witness to
crimes!" he said with a fierceness so quiet and even so civil
that I was altogether startled.

"But that was years ago," I said. "You've had a clean job
ever since."

"Clean," he echoed coolly, "that's your mother's language,
not yours."

"Well, even if it is."

"Your mother thinks the State Department is a sort of san-
itation squad marching with big brooms and led by an Ambassador in a homburg," he said. "All singing Yale fraternity
songs."

"Well, even if she does."

Perspiration sat in gilded globules on his melancholy lip.
"The trouble is the brooms don't work. Nothing works," he
said. "The brooms are cursed, the dustpans are full of spells.
There's no possibility of cleaning up."

I was suddenly impatient, and could not bear his talk. It
was too abstract; it was too withdrawn; it was too esoteric; it
was too hiddenly prophetic. It was Enoch's talk as Enoch always talked, but I did not like it: he was willing to give an

hour to the problem of evil in the universe, but he would not surrender a single moment to speak to me of Tilbeck. And it was my father I wanted to hear about, and not the world.

"The world," he said; he would talk only of the world. "It's the whole world that's been dipped in muck, the whole world in the aftermath of crime. You can't clean murder away," he said; he cared for generalities of evil only: he would not talk to me of my father. "How do you clean murder away?" he brought out, rubbing away the sweat.

"By forgetting it," I promptly offered.

"I've heard that before," Enoch said. So had I; it was obscurely reminiscent but as yet had no place. "What's done is done," my stepfather recited in the singsong of disgust, and at once I recalled checkers and riddles, and the advocate of never going back.

"Time makes you forget," I added without sympathy, "anyhow," for I could now scarcely remember that shipboard face, and in spite of imagination's effort could see nothing more than the colonel's green sunglasses filled with a meadow of ocean. "It was long ago, all that."

Nevertheless Enoch held back. "There are crimes which time chooses to memorialize instead of mitigate," he said stiffly.

"It seems like a hundred years already."

"There are crimes which can't be forgotten."

"Then," I sighed, not knowing what better to do, "for the sake of peace they ought to be forgiven."

"Ah, for the sake of peace," he said.

"Isn't peace what everything's about?" I caught him up, thinking to match him generality for generality, vacuity for vacuity.

But he only smiled. "A while ago you said it was money," he truthfully reminded me. And into the whip of my chagrin muttered: "Murder fouls the peace-dove's nest forever. Or at least while people blather of money and peace and power and God, and that's as good as forever. The world will stay dirty until it gets what it needs."

"Don't keep saying the world," I objected. "It's the same as saying nothing at all."

"What the world needs," he said again, growing soft, "is vengeance. Is that nothing at all?"

"I don't know about the world," I began.

"Then that's the second thing so far you don't know about. You said earlier you didn't know about God."

"The third thing, if you want to count. I said first of all I didn't know about my father."

"I don't know about him either."

"But you know about the world."

"Yes."

"And what it needs."

"Yes."

"I suppose my father's not in the world?"

"Your father's in a house on Town Island, I've told you. Locate that wherever you please." But having said this much, he made a sardonic retreat into the usual bramble of word-manipulation, a thicket he frequently inhabited. "As for any-one's being *in* the world, it's not the same as being *of* the world. One is a matter of existence simply, but the other has to do with attitude—so to begin with it's too worldly a ques-tion." He paused to acknowledge his skill; I heard a weary exhalation or throat-tick. "Anyhow I'm not the one to answer, though I know it's meant to elicit all sorts of possible attitudes. I have no attitudes. I won't engage in personal things. In that sense I'm as unworldly as a nun."

On account of swift resentment I had not followed him all the way into these intricacies, and despised the lightness with which he juggled worldly and unworldly, in-the-world and of-the-world, like so many word-nettled wreaths; and moodily I was pricked by his final glibness as by a thorn. I said in the thick opposite of haste, "If you were really unworldly you wouldn't talk of vengeance. You'd talk of mercy."

"Mercy!" he scoffed. "Mercy doesn't raise the dead; and that's the sign one waits for."

"Neither does vengeance."

"Oh, you're gullible," he took up immediately. "What else do you think will bring on a sign? —I mean something to show that Creation was a covenant and not a betrayal. You're very gullible," he said again, blinking down at the scratched dull globes of his shoe-fronts as though they were sudden oracles, "if you think vengeance belongs to men. Mercy belongs to men, but vengeance doesn't. We aren't al-lowed such a terrible capacity. It's not only that we wouldn't know how to apply it if we had it—it wouldn't work for us. We're allowed mercy, after all—we're more than allowed it, we're commanded to it—and yet we haven't applied it even when the faggots have wept for it with human blood. Mercy is human duty, but vengeance is too pure for our foul use— it's not something we're able to perform. It's too extraordinary for us even to conceive of properly: our notion would be to leave a corpse for a corpse, an obliteration for an obliteration." Slowly and vividly he displayed his square palms with their red wet centers, like puppets; he made them evenly meet and nod. "It would come to the same thing as Christendom's idea of mercy, a tit for a tat—mercy granted in exchange for guilt confessed. Guilt is what feeds mercy—it's mercy's primary requirement," he said harshly, "that's the trick and pulse of it. And if there is no guilt to be given over as a unit of barter, then no mercy at all, then the stake and the oven instead. That's the way it would be with vengeance, can't you see it?—though it's not prohibited only on the ground that we'd abuse it. We abuse all our powers anyhow, we mutilate ourselves. Human crime is a bloated craw, there's no waiting for it to finish because no matter how full it seems to be it only stretches for more, it's tremendous, both in itself and cumulatively, it's turned into an enormity of enormities—it's left the human dimension, it's vanished out of politics and gone to fertilize history, that's the thing!" And now my stepfather slapped the air, as though to erase what he read among the scribbles of gnats herding around our knees. I was astonished to see a tremor, all by itself, in his middle finger. At the same moment he noticed it himself. "You're watching that? It's the digit of dogma, that one—it gets bulls issued, it accuses and anathematizes, it beatifies. Only in my case the crucial nerve is weak. I can't dogmatize without trembling, because from a certain point of view all the world is on fire; the sky is on fire, having caught it from the sun—" He hesitated, assessing my bewilderment. "I mean," he said, "no matter what, it's already too late, even for right action. A merely human vengeance would be as out of proportion to evil action as a hoe is to a tank—no, that's too finite an image—as a wheel is to the sun then. A sun of fire in a sky of fire, remember! To exercise human vengeance would be indecent, that's what I'm getting at!—it would be obscene. Nobody has a right to look at the ash and the bones and say: I am merciful, therefore I forgive this crime. So how much more perverted to look at the spared criminal nation and say: I am righteous, therefore vengeance on this seed is mine. No holy tit for tat permitted, nothing liturgical, no ministerial exemptions, no hope, no expiation! You want to know why? Because the crime is too big for us, in our human littleness, to presume to forgive it or avenge it. The crime is the crime of crimes! It's too huge! too heinous! too foul! too

fiendish and monstrous!—Too big! We don't dare spit on it
with the presumption of human forgiveness or human vengeance—we're not big enough for that, we're too little, we're
not God! It would be ourselves we would have to forgive or
avenge, and who can avenge himself? who can forgive himself?"

Poor Enoch! He halted; he sat blasted, stopped, blighted;
his head was delivered into his open hands like a mourning
bell or chained cannon ball; he was heavy and terrifying, a
black burden to himself, with oil making sleek crescents in
the sides of his nose and his mouth knitted up.

In the shock of this long turbulence I had nothing to con-
cede. "The dead are dead," I said merely, but he hardly
heard.

"Listen," he told me finally, hoarsely, reluctantly. "I know
what I know. It's because I don't have the gullibility of
worldliness. When I can seize the seizable I admit to it. The
point is there's nothing in politics. I don't believe in politics. I
believe in history."

"You believe in vengeance," I said, but it was only in order
to stop him short.

He moved on all the same. "Exactly," he said. "I believe in
vengeance and history. Vengeance belongs to history and not
to men. Vengeance is a high historical act."

"And history?" I wondered.

But he thought my tone too thick and too raw and he
swelled against it. "History? What about history? You want
to know what it is? It isn't what you think. It isn't simply
what has happened. It's a judgment on what has happened!"

He uncovered his eyes to the saddening rim of sunset. The
tugs were eating away at the river like larvae in a braid of
old wool. It was half-dark below us, but the brows of buildings were notched with golden scars; their long windows
flared. The last light yearned behind a far high gas tank,
which took the horizon like a silver lung set poignantly
afloat. In the house a sound ceased; the air-conditioning had
been switched off; it had grown cool; too early it smelled of
evening and of September. Suddenly a single cough of my
mother's needled the dusk, as audible and sharp as an insect-
sting. Enoch sat refusing, denying, maneuvering his rutted
neck like a sultan or king awaiting in unbelief the nightin-
gale's note.

"I think she's coming out here," I said.

He appeared for a moment to crane toward the possibility

of my mother's step, attentive: but no, it was his own voice he was all at once singularly open to, and only that. He listened to it briefly without speaking.

"You don't know what I mean," he said at last. "A pity, a pity. You ought to know."

"I ought to know," I doubtfully admitted.

"You think history is a sort of bundle one generation hauls off its back to launch onto the next. Every twenty-five years or so the bundle gets heavier and heavier. Nobody dares to throw it off and walk away and leave it behind. Even the heroes are afraid to stand naked without it; even the cowards think it somehow or other contains civilization. But those are not the facts. Those are not the facts." He raised the tremulous middle finger and stared it down until it steadied. "That isn't what history is. It doesn't keep on accumulating without conscience forever and forever—don't think the universe wouldn't choke on the glut of it all! It stops to clear away and begin again."

"Like Noah," I said. "Noah and the Flood."

His cautious eye took me in curiously: to see if I were on his side or not.

"*That* was vengeance," I said appreciatively. "But what about all those poor giraffes and donkeys and pigeons who hadn't done anything wrong and couldn't get on the ark and had to die all the same, just because it was a historical necessity for man to be wiped out?"

"A wicked generation," he observed. "Still, not so wicked as ours."

But I ignored his emendation and pressed for more. "The giraffes too? At least admit the giraffes were innocent."

"All right, the giraffes were innocent. So were the donkeys and pigeons, if that's what you want."

"Then it was a mistake," I said complacently. "The whole Flood was a mistake."

"A mistake," he assented.

"God's mistake," I noted. "A historical error."

"But an acknowledged one. God acknowledged it," my stepfather insisted, "when he swore there would never be another Flood in all the rest of history."

"There!" I exclaimed. "And he's stuck to his word. That proves you're wrong."

Enoch said, "I'm not wrong."

I had another try at dialectic. "But if there hasn't been another Flood since, it means that God has taken vengeance out of history, doesn't it?"

"No. It means he's put it in. He took vengeance away from man when he punished Cain; and he took it away from himself when he covenanted against making more Floods. And instead he gave it to history. Believe me, God doesn't have that power any more! It used to be 'Vengeance is mine, saith the Lord,' meaning man had no right to it, but now it isn't even God's. God has abdicated—it's what I said, God's become an atheist. It's history that's the force! It's history that avenges and repays! It's history that raises the dead! And when we talk of redemption it's history we mean!"

He stopped; my mother stood on the threshold.

"Then you *are* waiting for the Messiah," I murmured once more.

He looked at his wife and answered without consciousness of any irony. "The Messiah and I wait together. The Messiah waits too."

"Waits for what?" I had to say; plainly it was what he wanted.

His reply was quick. "Revenge," said my stepfather. "Revenge on Europe. We wait for that."

"And if it doesn't happen soon?"

He nearly smiled. "We'll wait anyhow."

"Then you'll wait till the conversion of the Jews!" my mother threw in with unprovoked perturbation, shaking the loosened tail of her shawl: two or three of the Taj Mahals curled round her neck. "You'll wait till the dead come running out of their graves!"

"Why not?" he said, calmly enough. "Haven't you come running out of your bed?"

"I had to hear," she confessed. "I had to hear what you were saying."

"We were talking about Noah's ark," I volunteered, and since this was the precise but incredible fact, suddenly laughed. "There's a riddle about that," I finished obscurely, not sure I remembered it: but even if I had, my mother would have interrupted the telling of it. And then I felt foolish at having wanted, childishly, to tell it.

"My eye you were!" she said. "You were talking about the Messiah. I distinctly heard Enoch say the Messiah. I suppose it was some sort of blasphemy." Her teasing was half merry and half grim. "When it comes to the Messiah you won't find

Enoch any different from all the other Jews. They won't admit the Messiah's already *come*."

"Evangelist Allegra," Enoch said.

"Jews are a very stiff-necked people.—That's a Bible phrase, you know," said my mother. "They always want religion *their* way." She swung round the cactus pots and stationed herself behind Enoch's chair, encircling his head. Her fingers scratched along his jowl. "Ouch, you haven't shaved. You never shave when you don't work. You're simply too lazy. Grow a beard and you'll be a patriarch, you know that, Enoch? I mean you would if you had any descendants."

"It's quite enough for me to have had ancestors," he said.

"You see!" she cried. "Racial pride! You're all alike!" She turned to me to pursue her odd comedy more emphatically. "Next thing he'll remind me how my ancestors were running around in the forest primeval with their bodies painted blue when his were—were I don't know what."

"Writing the Commentaries on the Commentaries," he mildly supplied.

"Well, what did it get you anyhow?" she sniffed. "The ghetto, that's all."

"The ghetto," he said in a voice familiar with its lines.

"That's why you talk of revenge on Europe. All those beautiful cathedrals! All those saints! And for the sake of a single little misplaced tribe, you'd throw the whole thing over!"

"A pogrom against the gentiles," he summed it up. "Try to live till that day; it's as good as immortality."

But her good humor was inexplicably thick with danger. "Now you're talking like a Jew. Don't talk like a Jew, Enoch."

"How shall I talk?"

"I don't know. Not that way."

"Was I muttering from the Zohar all unawares?"

"Not that way," she said again. "You sound—" She gave a great calloused sigh. "You sound *separate*."

He pulled her round to him. "Well, not from you, Allegra."

"What I mean is, don't talk religion."

"I never talk religion. I only talk metaphor."

"That's what I mean. I heard you, you were talking about raising the dead."

"But that's talking like a Christian, isn't it?"

"Oh come, Enoch, stop it."

"You don't want me to talk like a Jew and you don't want

me to talk like a Christian. That leaves the recitation of the
Upanishads, I suppose."

"Don't, Enoch," she implored.

"Oh, it's not simply a question of don't. Believe me, it's
more a question of can't. Not a single chapter. My Sanskrit's
rusty, what a pity—"

Vaguely she resisted his tug. "I knew it, you always end up
with ridicule. You make a joke out of everything."

"A Jewish joke?" he inquired with a twist of his tone.

"You don't think the way an Ambassador ought to think,"
she accused.

"Well, I'm not the Ambassador yet. There's time."

"You haven't recovered, that's the trouble. I'm not *stupid*,
I can see how you've been contaminated—"

"By your not being stupid?"

"Enoch, you're not listening to me seriously."

"Yes I am. With high seriousness. It's like listening to an
epic. As though you were a troubadour."

"Damn it!" she said.

"All right, if it's only an access of boredom and you don't
mean it theologically. Damn what?"

"You! That old job you had *ruined* you. Those ledgers!
Those numbers!"

"Ruined," he said with amiable melancholy.

"Your mind's ruined, your whole sensibility, I can *see* it.
You haven't recovered. As though all of it had to be *your*
fault to satisfy you! That's masochism, you know it is. It's
perfectly obvious—you *know* masochism is a Jewish trait,
otherwise the Jews would have disappeared long ago. It's simple ordinary psychology. They're always looking to suffer,
and then they turn right around and complain when they
do."

"Simple ordinary psychology," he repeated.

"Well, I'm a realist!" She thrust her chin up with so lively
a movement that her turban slipped free; the little feathers of
her sickened hair roamed like animate cilia in the air. "I've
got my name on all those Zionist charity letterheads, haven't
I? You know perfectly well how I feel. After all, I'm not an
anti-Semite! I've read everything there is on the Dreyfus case!
—All I'm saying is it's all over."

He looked at her dully. "What's all over?"

"Is that the Socratic method? What do you mean what's all
over? The concentration camps are all over!" she almost
shouted.

"Your daughter says the same," he noted languidly.

My mother was scornful. "Just as though she ever had a single political idea in her head! Well, she's right, for once."

"I wasn't thinking of politics," I said humbly.

"I told you she wasn't," my mother gave out with a click of satisfaction.

"I was only wondering about what you said," I pursued, "about how the demonstration would come about. What you were saying before, the extraordinary sign—"

But my mother scowled with annoyance. "Leave Enoch and his metaphors be, can't you?"

For an answer my stepfather merely groaned. It was an unexpected noise. "Oh my God," he finished it off.

Nevertheless I would not let go, no matter what. He had opened himself to me and he had no right, in my mother's presence, to shut the lid: not, at any rate, after having revealed the combination. "I was wondering in what sense you thought the dead could be raised," I patiently probed, ready for anything.

"In what sense! Oh Lord! What a provocation!" my mother complained. "I'm telling you, leave Enoch alone. He's not going to be Ambassador to the dead, after all! It's all over and he hasn't had anything to do with it for ten years and he still isn't recovered from it, isn't that plain enough?" And she tore the vagrant Taj Mahals from her throat, where they lay fallen and bunched; furiously she shook the silk all around her.

"Put your shawl back on," Enoch reprimanded. "You'll cough again. You'll get your disease back."

"There, that's just the thing I'm driving at. It wasn't a disease *you* had," she argued sternly. "I mean it wasn't gangrene! It was only a job."

He appeared to be rewarding her with successive satiric nods—a nurse with a recalcitrant patient. "That's a very practical view of it. —Put your shawl *on,* will you?"

"It's not just practical, it's the sacred truth," she continued, but she obeyed him. "It was only a job and it got you where you are now. That's how you ought to regard it. That's how *I* regard it," she resumed.

"Where I am now," he echoed.

"At the brink of everything!"

"I'm to have what's known as 'a brilliant career,'" he interposed.

"Call it what you want. I know what *I* call it!"

"You call it Everything."

"I'm a grabber," she admitted.

"There's candor for you," he acknowledged. I almost thought it a pilgrimage of violence that trailed across his eye just then. But in a moment he had diverted it to an ambush somewhat milder. He began, as though they had been speaking of nothing else all the while (though it seemed my mother, at least, had not), "Do you think the Senate will confirm?"—which made her watchfully bristle.

"We've done what we could," she said.

"I don't deny it."

"We've done it all," she said.

"Down to the last," he agreed. He fixed on me meditatively, rubbing his blunt nose. His fingers were stiff, square-edged, short, his elbow was looped up high for defense, his mouth was incomprehensible, even invisible. Without our noticing it, night had happened. Already we were sitting in the rush of blueness before the final dark, surveying one another's heads like foreign silhouettes. "I don't deny it," Enoch said, feebly, once more: he looked, then—what I could see of him, what I could hear of him, his face and voice disguised by bleakness, and masked, and bound, and put away—he looked altogether what my mother had said of him: separate.

"It's not as though anything stood in your way," she encouraged him. "There's no risk now, after all, is there? We've taken care of the risk!"

"We've disposed of the risk," he corrected her.

"All right then! You're safe. You're absolutely safe."

Safe: it was the word she had used long ago, in flight from Europe, in flight from Nick; only then she had used it for me.

Enoch, behold, was safe. The word had been transferred to him like a quality. Did it mean that I was robbed of it?—that "safe," like some gold-plated school award, some little shiny molded Rome-muscled statuette, the only one of its honorable kind, had to pass from winner to winner, to be conferred only at the expense of someone else's having to give it up? However it was, Enoch, at least, had the coveted thing—he was safe. My mother had dubbed him safe; but also she had dubbed him separate. For if he were not altogether and actually separate he could not be altogether and actually safe: I saw him as one of those whose natures forbid them to partake of the profane, whom no persuasion and no temptation can absolve from their strict flagellations. Yet my mother made him partake and even indulge (the bird of the world lay steaming, stuffed with hierarchical dumplings, on the exquisite table of her imagination—dead but not in vain; dead but savory; she meant to have a good meal of it yet), she insisted on it, he was to be Ambassador, and not to the country of the murdered. So he was neither safe nor separate, I observed, from his wife, who took his apocalyptic captivity no more seriously than she would have taken a report of his indigestion—having no trouble with the feast herself, she failed to be roiled; and being in a manner Christian, she could do what Enoch-the-Jew had no notion of: she could eat her god. Poor Enoch! He was an apostate. His god ate him.

For what could it have been other than a dybbuk which had entered him and had taken hold of his escaped Babylonian intellect and his infidel compassion?—the dybbuk of all the lost dead, the dybbuk of the martyrs, the dybbuk of the slaughtered millions, the dybbuk of cinder and smoke, the succubus Europa who lay crouched at his organ with her teeth in his bludgeoned tissue? Rapt Enoch! I comprehended him at last. I saw what he waited for, the extraordinary sign, the consecrated demonstration, which he did not dare to name Messiah. He was waiting for the deliverance of history. I saw him: he had been formed at Creation, he had been witness at Sinai, and he went on raptly waiting as those obsessed by timelessness always wait. He kept his bare secret vigil as devotedly as the high priest of the Temple in the moment of the utterance of the Name of Names with the Holy of Holies. He awaited justice for the wicked and mercy for the destroyed. He awaited the oblivion of devouring Europe. He awaited the just estimate of the yet-to-be-born. —How else am I to put it? In the long, long, long, long memory of history (put it this way) the dead are at last resurrected: even at the price of sublime civilization. It is the exactly balanced irony of vengeance that only the wronged survive. Where now is Assyria? Who sleeps under the pyramids? Where has sleekbooted Caesar gone? Who afterward will recall the cathedrals of the Rhine? History (put it this way) is the Paradise of the lost. When we remember the martyrs we bring on the Messiah.

Well, how else *am* I to put it? What ate Enoch was no metaphor, in spite of what he claimed for it. And he did not believe in his own aphorisms. Why? Because he took them for mere prayer.

It was, as I have said, night. My stepfather stood up and stretched and opened *Anna Karenina* and read out the first sentence: "All happy families are alike," he said, crashing it into triviality. It was trivial, trivial. He took his wife firmly by the arm and went into the house.

And she, my mother, freshly fed on the bird of the world?

My mother was waiting for the Messiah too—only she thought he would come dressed as an Ambassador named Enoch Vand.

2

The next day I determined to see William.

This was not easy to arrange. I could not telephone him, in the regular way, for an appointment at his office; it was my mother who was his client and not, by any stretch, myself; and anyhow it was not on a matter of law that I had need of him. Whether I had need of him at all was itself a question, but, like my mother, I suddenly found myself valuing his sanity. Enoch, who was on all things reasonable, was at the same time not precisely "sane," since it was his habit to avoid a discussion by having a vision. If a part of his mind, exposed too long to the curious, began after a while to feel the chill of too much airing, he merely shut it off and opened another part; he was as full of valves of this sort as a trumpet—as, in fact, the Last Trump, of which it may without offense to anyone be assumed that the notes are many and odd.

By William's sanity I meant, I suppose, his detachment, his aloof and cautious respectability, and even, in a way, his ordinariness. It was William's auspicious lacks, his being without any of the gildings of a seer, that gave him his solidity. He had an excellent intelligence; his son, who had inherited it, was, if nothing else, its genetic proof. But his sensibility was more thorough than imaginative, and this of course was what made him useful and kept him intact. Without ever intending it, William had gained a certain limited fame, even beyond that which the coveted obscurity of his caste unavoidably brought on him. This fame was something more and something less than the simple "fame" of old family: it was reputation, and it threw over him a celebrity radiating not from who he was but from what he had done, though plainly he could not have done what he had done had he not been what he was. It was often enough made patent to me that I could not be expected to understand this hushed machinery of William's "clubs" and William's "classmates," who were usually not law classmates at all, but ex-boys from Dr. Peabody's school, or simply men of a particular breed, accent, and cut of nose, immediately acceptable and "right." I could not be expected to understand this because my grandfather was dead and because I had no uncles and because, as my mother pointed out, I had not grown up in sight of it—she meant to say, but did not, that I had no "instincts" (which the clubs and the classmates in reality were) because I had no father, or at least not the father my grandfather had arranged for me. But even without such instincts and near examples for these great but silent workings, I felt their vast motions, and knew that what William had done, without spectacle or outcry, was mountainous, thick, purposeful, immense, and had nothing to do with courts. For William, it appeared, never went to court: his whole power was struck just in that distance from trials and judges and newspapers, which he left to the lesser firms, the three-partner sort, energetic and aspiring, composed of an Irishman and a pair of Russian Jews. Without spectacle and without courts—but I knew what he had done: he had saved a railroad from the common wolves, he had effected the merger of two gigantic banks, he had consolidated and cleft and amalgamated and dispersed fabled monoliths—and all of it durably, quietly, without spectacle, without courts, without clamor, all of it murmurous, and in aspect somehow luxurious and even benign.

William had, then, on this account, accumulated a moderate renown—accumulated, because it came to him bit by bit; he would turn up in a footnote in, say, the *Vanderbilt Law Review*, or his name would emerge, in passing, in a long article entitled "The Secret Royalty Behind American Capital" in *Business Week*, and now and then he would actually be mentioned in an undergraduate class in journalism as one too fastidious to allow *Fortune*'s interviewers to exploit him. Very

gradually his reputation had penetrated the academies of law:
they did not exactly call him a lawyer's lawyer, a term they
jealously reserved for one another, but they showed their awe
by inviting him, spring and fall, to this Forum and that Assembly. I had seen for myself in the *Times* how he had declared Harold Laski to be a marxist scoundrel and a national-
izing thief (this was at a Books for the Bar meeting at the
Law Center), which, however, expecting no better, he hardly
minded—the real affront being that the fellow had *exaggerated* in his letters, and pulled the wool even over shrewd old
Holmes' eyes by telling funny anecdotes that could never have
happened at all. —For all these reasons William was transmuted for me into a Personage, unlike Enoch, whom my
mother liked sometimes to call Nobody's Boy, although his
name had already carried farther than her first husband's. The
difference was that William *acted* like a Personage; he could
not help it, he was hardly aware of it—it was only that rectitude sat on his shoulders all darkly visible, like a lidless bird
on a bust. It was for the sake not of his reputation but of his
rectitude that I had need of him, though here again he might
not have had the former had he not been known for the latter.
If asked, he would answer. His answer would be unambig-
uous, non-allegorical, serviceable—not a philosopher's but a
lawyer's view, open to an admittedly faceted but solvable actuality. If he invoked at all, it would be merely a precedent,
and not the gods. I had this confidence in William: he would
not lie to me about Gustave Nicholas Tilbeck.

He would not lie to me, William, my not-father, though he
had lied to his son, presumably on the principle that it is by
their ignorance of the devil we can be certain of the elect.
That William himself might be barred from salvation as a
consequence of this knightly act—was it not to conceal from
his son the folly of my mother's unseemly obligations that he
had denied the existence, the very possibility, of a Tilbeck?
—he had no doubt considered worthy of the risk. But there
was no necessity to close the door of heaven on my account;
I was the devil's own seed and, alien and odd as it might
sound, Tilbeck's very daughter. No lack of devil-knowledge
could turn away that predestined bleakness; no answer William withheld could erase that unpromising daughtership. If
asked, William would reply.

So I resolved to ask: and went to see him the next afternoon. I went, in fact, to his office, without telephoning beforehand—I was afraid, I suppose, that he might dodge any ap-

pointment that looked like an appeal. I descended (it *was* a
descent, somehow, under a bronze September sun that stood
between the angles of those greyish towers like a weighty funeral urn, menacingly brilliant, too acutely polished for the
eye to endure, in which the scorched limbs of antique great
undreamed-of lizards lay)—I descended into Wall Street in
an orange taxi, hired—bribed—on Main Street in New Rochelle earlier that day. For my first thought had been northward to Westchester and the lawn-quickened lands where
pretense-Tudor houses had their seats, among them William's
house in swan-girt Scarsdale. For my mother and even for
me that dale was scarred indeed: it was the house my grandfather and my would-be grandfather, the two heads-together,
rejoicing fathers of the newlyweds, William and my mother,
had built in joint celebration of the pairing of their prosperous lines, and in which the young attorney and his bride had
officially lived, without the comfort of quarrels, until their divorce. It was the house my mother, who had already begun
her novel and her travels, had had to persuade William to
keep, though it embarrassed him by making the settlement
look ungentlemanly. He kept it: my mother, scorning the
green-treed lanes of Scarsdale, declared herself urban, and
worse, cosmopolitan, and promptly went off to Moscow for a
youth rally against the cosmopolitan bourgeoisie. So he kept
it, poor practical William, and let his new wife redesign the
interior, and replace her predecessor's triangular hassocks and
Ugandan salad-implements and black sofas and (especially)
her light-violet bedstead with soft gold, and soft blue, and incorruptible ochre, and vases, vases, vases everywhere all radiant with flowers. (My mother had hated gardening.) This
was the house I had never seen and knew everything about:
how my grandfather had insisted on a ball-room, how my
would-be grandfather (William's father, the editor of the
civic documents of an obscure ancestral Hudson Valley alderman, the author of "Autumn Gleanings," a book of spiritual
verses, who three times had gone tiger-hunting and had sold
his little railroad-spur out of boredom with trains) had insisted on an elevator, and how prudent William had vetoed
both. In this somehow familiar house, this hearsay house, I
had cautiously placed the plan of my unfamiliar scene—William apprehended in the act of presiding over his breakfast
egg, and his wife, whom in vain I tried to banish from my
construction, impersonally beside him, taking my measure
with the rule of her thoughtfully-apportioned, slow, penetrat-

ing, hostile smile below a slim fair nose as tight-pored and youthful as a college-girl's. Upon this astonished and unprepared William I meant to force the indecent whole of what was being done to me—how in two days' time the "arrangements" (whatever they were—*he* knew, having himself brought them into being) would fructify, and the long-suppressed daughtership begin in all its legendary horror. What he would be obliged to answer me my diffident imagination had so far failed to supply: I merely saw myself in a tall-backed chair at the round breakfast-table, a cloth-covered boulder made of inlaid teak with four carved Sphinx-like paws opened in sinister fashion upon the carpet, and little hinged gates which at a touch could snap into verticality to make a fence all around the edge. It had been ordered for the captain's cabin of an immense and palatial steamship (hence the barrier, the captain's own invention, to keep the dinner plates from sliding off when the Pacific frowned), but the captain had suddenly died before it could come aboard, and my grandfather on his mourning-tour (undertaken to console him for the loss of his wife, my grandmother Huntingdon, who, older than himself, had fevered and withered), just then passing through Jakarta, where he came upon the table standing in a woodyard, about to be crated, bought it and sent it on to Scarsdale for his daughter's house. So particular a gift was it that it was in fact the only furniture which had gone unreplaced: my mother had broken the sole of her shoe with the kick of disgust she gave it when it came, all foreignly labeled and stamped and smelling of the freighter's dank hold, and, she assured me, the mark of her disapproval was there yet, a gash on one of the hideous stretched paws; but afterward it altogether ravished William's new wife, who took it to her heart as her own, and joked that with its sides up it would do nicely for a crib. How my mother had scowled when William told her this, William who was still so innocent in his contentment that he confided it to his newly-become client! Not out of any pique of jealousy did she scowl, but rather because this was the very joke the giver, her father, had made, and she had thought it a poor joke the first time —a table for a crib! (and she not married three weeks, and anyhow a believer in Margaret Sanger)—when, tossing a man-to-man wink at his son-in-law, my grandfather had explained "To keep the babe from slipping down," and then, "though what's to keep it from slipping *out* in nine months' time I don't know"—a statement which had reddened William's two cheeks so thoroughly that it seemed they never again reversed their color. Still, my would-be grandfather had laughed at it—whether out of charity for my mother's chagrin or perhaps simply to affirm his shy son's virility was not apparent: the tiger-hunter in him clashed with the Christian poetaster.

At this breakfast-table, then, which was my birthright though lightfingered from me before my birth and given instead to the children of William's second wife so that at it daily they all might eat their mess of breakfast-pottage, I expected to confront William with my grievances, though what I was after I hardly knew myself. Perhaps it was only the opportunity to put the horrendous question: why? and why now? But when I thought how the thing would be—the children ranged all around, Cletis in her pinafore, and Jack, and Willy Cornelius, and Nanette who as Sir Toby Belch had won the school prize, and on the far side, behind the rose-vase, William's wife with her round clear forehead tilted upward to observe the descent upon the stair of the eldest son of the house, languid but sharp, tying his tie with immaculate fingers and parrying his mother's unspoken disapproval with the unspoken dicta of the law school dormitories; when I imagined them all there together in this way, and myself a stranger in that place where I was to have been born but was not, and William as paterfamilias and administrator of all their fates but not of mine, and his wife with the delta-crease of suspicion now vivid in her tall brow turning from her eldest son to accuse the blue-bells and pansies at her plate, and, worse, the son himself trying on the shut-up smile of an omniscient satirist, avoiding any probable tangency of our eyes by a gaze driven straight across the legendary table into the strawberry-spot on Cletis' bib—oh, when I day-dreamed them all, how inviolable they seemed! how like a guilty dauphin I felt, leaping out of exile to usurp!—and the train-wheels rattled with a private confusion in my teeth, and I dared not go.

I dared not go, and in the heat of a rush of cowardice came out dazed upon an empty platform. There was no sign to tell the name of the place. The train left me behind without caring, though angry somehow. Momentarily it stamped like a wrathful fist on a lectern, then swept away. I watched it for a time, charging northward along a rusted track, as though out to civilize some remote and savage village with the example of its faintly-swaying silver sides, carrying its cars of pews filled with penitents, its conductors walking up and down and waving their punches like Sunday-school directors, ministering to each little orange ticket with the sobriety of missionaries attending to certificates of baptism. But in all the fury of my stupid dash I had forgotten to take my ticket: it was still in the crack of the seat in front, where the conductor had tucked it, and where I had conscientiously been reading and re-reading it, all along its margins: New York to Scarsdale, Scarsdale to New York, One Round Trip. It was a kind of liturgy, and a minute afterward, standing on that unpeopled platform at eight o'clock in the morning at some nameless spot of which I knew nothing except that the divine order had laid it between New York and Scarsdale, between, that is to say, major and minor, torrent and rivulet, William-as-lawyer and William-as-father, I suddenly saw myself for what the train thought me, a sort of heretic, a kind of outcast, too paganly frail of spirit to be worthy of a Christian breakfast. It made me sigh and count the money in my purse and the people on the other side. There—on the other side—they were bunched together under the plank of roof as though it rained; but the sun already blazed. It came up between us, that impartial orb, motionless above the central tracks, dividing northbound from southbound with a leaded glare, resting and panting. Under their eave the nomad crowd stared back at me with what insolent righteousness I could conjecture—they were a tribe sure of their destination, while just then the New York train slid in like a long adroit tongue to vindicate their certainty and lick the platform dry. It was empty there, and empty here, and I climbed the steps to read a street-sign printed Huguenot. So I supposed it was New Rochelle, and, glad enough not to find myself in Larchmont or White Plains or other place of that sort, I walked out to see the town.

The town. I wished just then to be touched by the town—to see it burnished, tender, as accessible as anything imaginary. It ought to have made me weep, since it was (that morning) Camelot I was after; an odd remorse, half-consolatory, half-accusing, teased me down the street. I felt clogged with mean failures, quite as though I had fallen short of some expectation not my own, yet was, on that account, not altogether to blame. A new town, or square, or even bit of unknown wall, should tell us what we were meant to be: when where-we-are is strange, the self is all at once familiar. Then—according to this redoubtable traveler's notion (an ancient remark of my stepfather's set upside down: in his more

metaphysical version, the self first feels the alien singularity
of its identity among old scenes and long-apprehended
things)—every new place is Camelot, cold, far, polished, secretive and shut-up, full of the happiness of others. The happiness of others!—the possible, the probable, the likely, and
then at length, since there is no test for it but belief, the certain. If in my progress through Main Street I fell short of
happiness, it was just the measure of that distance between
New and Old Rochelle the French pilgrims, in christening
their town, had upheld in sad celebration: a necessary distance separating the haven which is fact from the coveted impossible. And we in the same way feel toward the happiness
of others as though already a dozen dozen times we had sent
out a lamentation, Oh, here is my old home, and I am ban-
ished from it; and even though we may never have been
there before, we long to return. All facts are aloof; still Camelot lures: the happiness of others, behind a wall. And when
we suppose that what we were meant to be is at last revealed
to us—look! it is so ingenuous as to be pitiable: only to be
happy. Who believes he was ever fated for anything else?
Who does not invoke justice to save him from the haven
where reluctantly he counts his despondent comforts? Who
does not curse the single unreachable moment in his past
when an ogreish craft wizened and despoiled his proper destiny? And who does not remember the untried exaltation at
the crest of life, when he knew himself to be extraordinary,
when he believed in the power of purity and thought beauty
a commonplace? Happiness always has the texture of memory, even when it is the happiness of others. What never was
is irrevocable. Well, and if on that early walk past shops as
still as windless flags, where no one stood in doorways, I
seemed to quote Enoch to myself too much, the fault was not
all mine. Perhaps if he had been willing to be, as my mother
wished, the father-surrogate and deputy of my course, I
might have thrown him over, as one *does* throw over fathers
and regents, saws and sceptres and all. And William too:
would I have cared to fly to his consultive closet if he had
not shut the door? But this was all theory—and, to make it
appear even more suspect, my mother's theory withal. It had
a touch of Freud.

As for myself, I ran clear of theories, and merely wandered this way and that, thinking where I might go. I went
out like an explorer—not to find a destination, but a route.
The difference is sly but imperative. So I voyaged past the

silly little City Hall, a squat adobe like a whitewashed toy
with a cupola and window-frames painted a whimsically brilliant blue, and submitted at length to the big blank stores.
They took me in as though I were no more than a lozenge
for their raw taste—first the yellow-paneled Grant's and then
the red-and-gold Woolworth's and finally the wide bright tunnel of Bloomingdale's basement, full of foreign crockery.
These places rocked and sucked me; I swam round and
round the counters, touring housewares, now and then darting
in and out of the road after vanishing taxis. The slothful advance of morning, moving encumbered by heat and an ungainly heaviness of atmosphere toward noon, pushed me in
the way of my intention. I meant to have my confrontation
after all, but in isolation, behind a partition, in a box, in the
dark, in an eyeless place untrafficked by any witness: William
trapped, in short, by the insularity of my demand. Insularity:
it was an island I was headed for; they would have me be
Robinson Crusoe without any of the skills or imaginings of
civilization, and worse, without a memory of how I came to
be swept to that shore. But I was bent on learning that mariner's tale, and purposed to have it from William, and spa-
ciously—and not from the protected domestic grateful William, rescued and relieved by his wife's commanding dip-of-
head telegraphing confidence and support and, so refined her
sense of the appropriate, abhorrence of whatever vulgar intimations intrusion might trick itself out in, but instead from
the severe and noble William, the grand monarch of those
Wall Street treasure-houses connecting partner with partner:
from that William who came discreetly to my mother's table,
rubbing his mouth with an embossed napkin as though wine-
sauce were an evil ointment, and waiting with all the simplicity of a privately taciturn spirit for the moment that justified
his dinner—the yielding up of the gilt-edged envelope. And
once my mother had spoiled the ceremonious transmittal with
a disconsolate joke—"guilt-edged," said she, spelling it softly
and with mock earnestness. "Oh, I don't see why you feel
that, Allegra," he responded; he drew his gloves up over his
fine wrists; she had, by that, reflected on his dignity, perhaps
even on his charitableness. He had in her presence always the
bearing of a wounded man. Long ago she had wounded him.
He was still afraid of her jokes. He continued to think of her
as a radical, and never heard her laugh without listening to
the high sound of ridicule. "It's not that I mind being a capitalist," she amended it, to please him with a kinder fancy,

and took from him the thickness of the prodigious envelope: "Only it's almost obscene, the way the thing reproduces itself." She always spoke of her trust fund as "the thing," as though it were somehow too unreal to deserve classification or a name. "I mean I never *do* anything about it; nobody does. It's like a virgin birth," she gave out, in spite of herself, and was so struck by her image that she failed to look regretful at having brought it off. "Parthenogenesis! It happens only with bees and money." William—exemplary even when disconcerted—regarded his clothed palms with a secret distress. "Ah," said he, "but you can't *rely* on the bees," and hurried into his overcoat like a man of daring. William the man of daring! Exemplary William! William the abashed crypto-adorer of my mother! And—this chiefly—dragon William, guardian of the moat, keeper of the riddle of the castle, warder of the lightly-laden envelopes with their dazzling seals and golden margins, castellan of their ark, governor of the place where the money bred, invisibly, overnight, like bacteria in a jar, at dusk, at closing-time, at three o'clock, in the hour of the market's hush, in the holy moment of the maturation of a bond: this inflexible, serious and sincere, altogether upright and responsible man of business, *this* William, William as trustee, William as inmost bursar of the treasure-house where the treasure was unseen and intangible though rigidly codified, William at the source: this William I meant to see.

At ten I drank a chocolate ice-cream soda; it seemed meal enough. At two I bought, for no reason at all, a small square aluminum dipper with a long handle. The lip said Detroit. It would not fit in my coat pocket, so I threw away the paper bag it was wrapped in and swung it. I told myself its use would be to remind myself of the heavens—of the North Star, which the Dipper admonishes. But all day long the taxi-drivers could not be persuaded to venture out. They came to the curb, listened, and ground away with shakes of their dwarfish, dull, droll heads. "Wall Street? Wall Street?" they echoed, and slammed their doors against my pleas. "Sooner kick myself alla way downa Canarsie," they reproved me. And they said, "No than' *kew!*" And they said, "That's where they send you Judgment Day, put you up 'gainst it and shoot you"—gesturing with dirty cuffs and denying me, though I wheedled repeatedly. "Well, look, I'll pay the empty fare *back,*" I urged, holding up the sidereal token like a wand of hope. But afterward I put it to better purpose, and reached out with the handle and tapped insistently on the cab-windows. It brought none of them back. It brought a curse. Under the colorless sun I felt parched and fruitlessly rich.

Nevertheless twenty-five dollars at length bought my passage.

"Why not?" said the driver, glancing downward with a mild show of acquiescence. Curiously pleased with the translucence of his pink knuckles as they lay, delicate, without vitality, like shells picked off a beach, over the halted wheel, he lowered a noble neck and the pale stretched cheekbones of the heir of some wondrous lost kingdom, aware, though not haughtily, of his sovereignty: he was a stark albino. "I don't mind," he told me cheerily. "Once I took a guy to Albany, he was suffering from nalmutrition."

"From what?" said I.

"Nalmutrition."

"Oh," I said, and leaned back. "I'm very grateful, though."

"Sure, that's all right. Listen, you know the name of that guy in the Bible that itched?"

"Itched?"

"Yeah, itched himself on this piece of old flowerpot. *You* know."

I did know. "You mean Job?" This was the harvest of the College Survey of English Literature.

"Yeah, that's the one, Jobb. Only you gotta announce it the right way for this saying I thought up." He felt my inquisitive stare rooted in his back and challenged it in his mirror. "Don't be embarrassed. Everybody looks at me, I don't mind. I got white hair like an old man, I'm only thirty-three. My grandmother's eighty-two, she got practically no white hair yet. I don't mind—I figure it's like everybody's gotta be famous for *something,* right?"

I agreed, but lacked zeal.

"Anthony Eden is an albino," he confided.

"Oh, I don't think so—"

"So was Mussolini. Anybody can tell you that, don't take *my* word for it."

It was plain that I had better resign myself to the fact of his conversation, and I reluctantly did. There are cultists who take the view that everything is Experience, no matter how mean, absurd, or inane, and that Experience has value for its own sake. I did not hold with this, being metaphysically flaccid; but, being flaccid, had no choice just then beyond

gaping out the window and thinking how odd the world was.
"You know the Supreme Court of the United States?" my
pilot demanded.

I admitted to it.

"Three of them judges."

"Really?"

"Albino. Take my word for it," he assured me, reversing
his rhetoric.

"Well, they don't look it."

"Don't look it!" he mimicked darkly. "*I'll* say they don't."
Though we were crossing a bridge, he glared around at me
and I nodded earnestly to get him to turn frontward again.
"They—dye—themselves," he pronounced with priestly
scorn. "Eyebrows. Eyelashes. The works."

He was so severe that I had to inquire, "Job too?"

"Hah?"

"You mentioned something about Job—"

"Jobb!" he corrected me impatiently. "I didn't say nothing
like that about Jobb."

"He wasn't an albino?"

"Where'd you get a nutty idea like that?" he yelled over his
shoulder. "I said Jobb, I meant about this saying I thought
up. Jobb from the *Bible*. My club, we wanna use it, you
know, like sometimes when we go collecting dues? You
know, a motto, like, 'Get on the Jobb and Relieve Our Itch
for Money.' You think that's any good, anybody'll get it?"

"It *might* be hard to get."

He pondered this lugubriously. "I mean it's kind of like a
gag?" he ventured.

"Anyway," I consoled, "it's not bad."

He brightened at once. "Yeah, that's what I thought. See, I
knew this guy once that itched as bad as Jobb practically. He
was a leopard," he told me.

"Is that so?" I said with interest. "Where?"

"Up in New Haven."

"New Haven, *Connecticut?*"

"Yeah, he was in a bad way up there."

"There aren't any lepers in New Haven," I protested.

"This guy was a leopard, *he* was from New Haven. One
night his whole jaw fell right off. He was brushing his teeth,
same as anybody would, and all of a sudden—pff! the whole
thing dropped bang into the sink, all them teeth and everything stuck straight in the bone, you know? All in one piece."

His rear-view mirror accused me sternly, damning me for a skeptic. "That's a medical fact," he concluded.

At these absorbing words, full of scientific connoisseurship, a settled good will, almost an affection, passed diffidently but wholesomely between us. He was a man of judicious parts, though young. His hair grew wispily long over his big un-ashamed ears, whiter than paper; his nape bore a crowd of strangely unpigmented mole-like speckles, too diminutive to be really ugly—it was as though he had been splattered with invisible ink. In someone else they would perhaps have been no more curious than freckles. I fixed on them, and they seemed to thicken; so, meanwhile, did our friendship; so, meanwhile, did the traffic. We had long talkative waits under stubborn lights, the motor slackened in expectation of the click that foretold green, and, all around us, the silver herd pressing near.

He had other acquaintances. They were all extraordinarily stricken. One—a resident of Teaneck, New Jersey—was a victim of yaws. Another, who lived in Philadelphia, suffered from trachoma, and had actually had to give up television, the flies got so much in the way. These cases were not in the least unusual. Rampant tropical diseases afflicted the East Coast of the United States, the most dangerous area in the world (he explained) for one's health. He knew of a malarial outbreak in Dobbs Ferry; he was certain of five instances, possibly six, of bubonic plague in the Consolidated Edison Company of New York. Presently, persuaded that he had plainly won both my confidence and my admiration, he in-vited me to join his organization, which was dedicated to stamping out yellow fever in the Bronx. Its slogan was "Don't Be Yellow—Join the Fight." He told me with a touch of con-ceit that he had invented this himself. "Of course you got to pay the dues," he apologized, "if you come in with us." He also offered further data on the world's hidden albinos. It de-veloped that the following were deficient in melanin: Princess Margaret Rose, John Foster Dulles, the young Aga Khan, two television comedians whose names I never did get right, and Booker T. Washington.

"*Booker T. Washington!* Oh come on, now you're carrying it too far. You can't claim *him*."

"You ever hear of Julius Caesar?" he demanded in easy re-buttal. "This here old-time king?"

"Him too?"

The pupils of his eyes—I now examined them for the first

time—were a deep red, but the irises were faint and milky and impressed the mirror so little that it scarcely gave them back. "You heard of Tommy Dorsey, right? The band leader?" he swept on, with a pink blink.

"All *right*," I asserted readily enough. "But Booker T. Washing—"

"Listen," he said, reaching out an arm (we had arrived) to open the door nearest me, "I got a list, nobody's found me wrong *yet*."

So I decided not to find him wrong, either: and took him for a philosopher for whom the world is cleft, like the devil's hoof, in two. His Yang and Yin were no more unreasonable than anyone's. Where my mother saw the powerful and the inconsequential, William the ordained and the immortal, Enoch the guilty and the murdered, and all the rest of the world parochial versions of cowboys and Indians, *he* apprehended albinos and the obscurely diseased. It was an opposition—whiteness beyond imagining, a transparency of the flesh that hid not a single capillary, an openness of the soul's entelechy; and, against this, inconceivable deformity both bulbous and agonizingly minute, scales, monstrous flaking rot, hideous scum—an opposition no madder than the truth. I put him down for a visionary and began counting out dollars.

"You going to see somebody in one of them buildings there? I knew this stockbroker, see, commuted down from Mount Vernon—"

"That one."

Double glass doors gleamed like slivers of mica in the base of a concrete mountain.

"—*he* got dysentery from a water cooler in a building right around here, over on Broad Street. Worst water in the world, this district."

But this warning of his (I supposed it to be a warning) stopped short. I held out the bills; attentively he accepted them; he put them pleasurably to his lips as though I had handed him a nosegay; and, uncannily, perhaps out of pure suggestibility, produced a modest but unmistakable sneeze.

"Bless you," I said sympathetically. "You'd better watch that. Sounds like pellagra."

Thereupon—but with gravity—he smiled. "Yeah, you're pulling my leg." Not merely the smile, but its sober acquittal, seemed at once unfortunate. A formulator of any sort—by which I mean a system-maker—ought never to smile at a conclusion drawn from his system, lest we think him a contradictory fool, whereas he is only being superior and tolerant; while to smile gravely is to affirm the worst. It is as though the ghost of that old Greek Anaximander, confronting his sole surviving sentence, were to say, "Yes, but that is not what I *meant*. What I really meant is in the part that is missing." All in a moment, blasted at a stroke by the flash of this taxi-driver's good strong teeth, Yang and Yin collapsed, the ideal image of contrasting pairs of essentials collapsed. Albinism and disease, whiteness and impurity—the two pillars crumbled, and the world they supported rolled away like a severed head. An elegiac solemnity informed but denied his unceasing smile: "You can't kid me. Pellagra, they only got that in the *South*."

His method—alas—had the occasional flaw of ordinary seeing.

In this fashion I came at last to William's office, where, to my uninstructed surprise, an engagement party was under way.

3

The party was for William's son.

"We've got gin and scotch and rye," said the girl at the desk. "The ginger ale's all gone. So are the paper cups. We barely had enough to go around, and now there's not one left. I watched *mine* like a hawk, but anyhow I ended up with somebody else's—look, what a *vile* shade"—she held it up to show the broad violet crescent of lipstick at the rim. "See? It must be one of the girls from the steno pool. I mean only a cow would wear a shade like that. A purple cow." She laughed, and, leaning over, spied my utensil. "A dipper! Hey, that's bright! Who sent you after it?"

"Nobody," I said. "I just came in."

"Mister Nobody and his brother. Anyhow it's just what we need around here. I *hate* these paper things—it's like drink-

ing from a deed, you know? With sealing wax on it!" She
snatched up the dipper and filled it from one of the clutter of
bottles on the desk—there were signs from the abundance of
fifths and quarts and forlornly soaked pretzels that it had
been designated for a bar. Behind the desk an empty tray lay
upside down on a chair, with a man's hat on top of it. "Hey,
do you have to be a lumberjack to work this thing?"—she
had the long handle by its end, and was sweeping the big
square spoon up to her lips: but through some error of balance the cup unexpectedly rolled over and spilled. "Now I've
done it. There goes somebody's perfectly good whiskey."

"There goes somebody's perfectly good hat," I amended. A
swimming puddle filled the dip in the crown.

"Flora Fedora," said the girl, "they used to call me in them
thar days. Well, oops. It'll smell better than hair oil, look at it
that way. Hey, if you just came in how did you know we
were all out of cups?"

"As a matter of fact I didn't know you were all *in* them," I
could not resist saying, looking around, but it was a shot too
high for her. "You can keep it."

"Keep what?"

"The dipper. It's brand new. You can have it for a present.
You can't ever get lost with it because it keeps pointing to
the North Star."

"Look, are you one of these cruds from Miss Putrid's?"

It was my turn for bafflement.

"That *school*," she explained.

"No, I've come on business."

This made her hesitate. "I think we're closed."

"Then you're not the regular receptionist?" I inquired, and
did not trouble to cover the gibe.

"An *hour* ago she left, old Prisshead. *Hates* office parties.
Hey, I've got the hang of it!" Out went the length of the handle, gripped by a row of knuckles; up rode the cup. She
drained it with aplomb. "I'm in filing. I could say you're
here," she told me doubtfully, "only it wouldn't do any
good."

"There's no one to say it to?"

"Well, they're *around,* but it's sort of a celebration. I mean
they've announced it already and the whole staff's applauded
and all of that—" She studied me speculatively. "Some of the
lawyers, the young ones, thought up the idea and then we all
had to chip in fifty cents. It matters to *them* because he

might get to be their boss, like a sort of partner, but if you
ask me it's pretty silly. He didn't even *graduate* yet."

Plainly she was speaking of William's son.

"Do you like her?" she suddenly asked.

"Who?"

"His *girl*. The one he just got engaged to."

I faltered, "I haven't met her."

"Lucky you, what a crud. Came down here this afternoon
with this whole pack of snots from Miss Putrid's—you know
what that place *is*? A *finishing* school, for God's sake! Pack
of putrid snots, *I'd* finished them for free."

"Maybe you'd better say I'm here."

She hoisted the dipper over her shoulder like a rifle and
saluted obligingly. "Okay. I'll tell them," and began pacing
off. But in a moment she had to dart back: "What am I supposed to say?"

"That there's someone here."

"No, I mean what am I supposed to *say*? Miss What?" She
plucked a squat flask from the cluster on the desk and
clutched it in her armpit, and despite the encumbrances of
bottle and dipper, which made her seem as many-armed as
Vishnu, all at once turned aggressively businesslike: "I didn't
catch the name," said she, a rather too positive imitation of a
movie secretary. "Miss Who?"

"I didn't give it," I said, and gave it.

"Wow!" said she.

"Go ahead," I urged.

"But she stood without moving and whistled instead.
"You're not the *daughter?*"

"No," I said.

She had taken me, in the usual way, for Nanette.

"Go ahead," I repeated, with a sigh. "It's only a case of
mistaken identity."

"Niece?" she insisted.

"No."

She stared. "But he's the Partner!"

"Right," said I. "That's the one I want to see."

"You don't expect me to go right *up* to him? I don't even
know what he looks like!" She took furtive steps away. "I
told you," she reproved me, "I'm in *filing*." I had begun, she
implied, with the wrong end of the hierarchy: a thing clearly
as offensive as speaking deferentially to a servant in an English novel. The girl had a sense of fitness. She had, moreover, a sense of "place," and—shifting her accoutrements for

comfort, the dipper hooked around her neck, the bottle grasped in front of her with both hands—she fled to occupy it.

Left to myself and unattended, I went peering after William on my own, but with a certain caution. Plainly I had turned up at the worst possible moment—a moment which, though vastly and ostensibly public (there might have been eighty or ninety guests), was nevertheless a private occasion. An engagement party, it did not matter who sponsored it, had the odor of a family event, an I believed that the sight of me, without warning, even in such a crush, could do no less than nettle William. Embarrassment and a sort of angry shame would redden him acutely. In this kind of situation I could expect nothing of him: he wouldn't be likely to tell me, without resorting to the coarseness of uttering it, that I had not been invited and had no business being there. He was severely conscious of protocol, but on my mother's account, as always, he would hold his reluctant peace. Under any condition he would have been sorry to receive me, but in the hour of his son's engagement I supposed he would be positively unwilling. He would regard me not so much as an intruder as a violator. It was an ugly notion—myself coming in the guise of an aggressor to disrupt the first unfolding of a filial joy. Anyhow William could never look at me, I imagined, without seeing me as an admonition. He would suspect in me nothing but bad omens. I represented for him a failed marriage—his own, undertaken with all the trust of youth. If I cared to do him a service I would go home immediately.

I became gradually aware of these unpleasant certainties, moving from cubicle to cubicle, each rather spartan and prudently secretarial, though vaguely airless and perfumed, and I avoided the large noisy interior room where I would be liable to attract notice. Twice I passed its door, and inside glimpsed a long wall of windows opening the glare of a dizzying daylight in giant patches to a multitude of blotter-brightened desks and torsos animated and stretched by the gestures of clever shouts and amused faces which the steady cooling of hidden machinery (now and then I encountered a vent overhead and felt a blast) had not kept from going generally pink with a more internal heat. The nearly hundred arms reached upward—a forest of paper cups—and, like a long birch in a pine-wood, a single aluminum dipper; someone was reciting a toast. Round plates of little colored cakes lay here and there on the desk-tops. There was a dish or two of thick cheese-yellow sandwiches. I was all at once sensible of being famished, and although I had already persuaded myself to start straight-way for the door and down the elevator, I suddenly hesitated. I began to reconsider. If finding me there were to discomfit William, why should I care? I had after all *not* come to a party; I was after all *not* a deliberate invader; I had come solely for information and it was my last chance to get it. In two days I would be with Tilbeck. The day after tomorrow I would be with him; he would have me; it was frighteningly close. I thought of it and it seemed unreal; and then once again bitterly actual, bitterly imminent; and then again false, a fantasy. Nevertheless I would stay. I had come for William and I did not mean to go simply to oblige circumstance. I helped myself to a sandwich and a cake and stood devouring them both. The cheese had gone dry, but the cake was good and I took another, wandering at my ease through the crowd. There were a great many young people and I recognized some classmates of William's son: they were the dancing partners he had brought down with him from law school sev-eral weeks before, as a favor for my mother. A pair of them, walking together, passed me with a faint acknowledgment, puzzled; but one in fact stopped and said, "You're not still *here!* Smokestack have a hole in it?" A fourth was civil:

"That was a nice party. I don't usually like charity balls but this one wasn't half bad." "What do you mean?" I asked in horror—"It wasn't a charity ball, it was for bon voyage." He was a little drunk but his laugh was kind, even respectful. "That's what you call it when they drag out the stags for an act of mercy. A charity ball," he explained through a watery mouth; "it's only an expression." The rest did not know me, or if they did they concealed it. I was not distressed; I was not indifferent, but I was relieved; if they had spoken to me I would have felt ashamed, not for myself but for my mother. I had no doubt they thought of her as an admirable manager. Her champagne was undeniably decent though it had not in-spired conviviality. Perhaps they said the same of me.

I did not see William. For some minutes I struggled through the mazy aisles among the changeable chattering groups, diligently watchful; and now and again I took to my toes to squint through the deepening smoke that swam in eddies from shoulder to shoulder. I did not see him. I felt as though I were pushing my way through a busy school-yard: the room was overrun with girls in their teens, each one sailing an ice-cube in a paper cup and drawing on a short cigarette as if it were a soda-straw. They smoked their cigarettes to the butt and at once lit fresh ones; they tapped their ashes to the floor with elegant little flicks, and drank roughly, in gulps. They wore their hair in extremes—either very, very short or very, very long, but in either case energetically burnished—and they all pronounced "o" as though it had an umlaut over it. Most of them were moderately tall—long, rather—with charming figures, though the mode just then was, I observed, the stringently flattened breast—and over this region of their anatomies they each had pinned a little typewritten card: GOOD LUCK FANNIE FROM FORM 7, MISS JEW-ETT'S. This interested me immensely; it was my mother's old school, a limited but reasonably venerable institution, fashionably small, but so absolutely "correct" that its reputation for getting its graduates into college was justifiably meagre. It was, moreover, a place I had clamored to be excused from attending after breaking my ankle as early as the first form. One did not usually break one's ankle until the third form (and then one spoke of it, airily, as only "cracked"); my precocity shocked me into defection, and startled even my mother, who, though in theory she always applauded rebellion, did not question the necessity of going to Miss Jewett's. Going to Miss Jewett's was, in fact, a family convention— *her* mother had been tutored (in ice hockey) by the original Miss Jewett (not the mere pastel niece), the genuine Miss Jewett, the aged and astonishingly agile Miss Jewett who was from the beginning Mistress of Fencing and whose second highest attribute appeared to have been simply that, in an adulatory era which celebrated anything even foggily English, she was a Londoner—what part of London remained a mystery. It was rumored that she was no more than an enterprising Cockney, a story which her muscular graduates, with unperturbed smiles, used neither to affirm nor deny. If Miss Jewett had been a Cockney, she had at any rate known the difference between a Cockney and a lady; and *they* were ladies. In my grandmother's time Miss Jewett, by then already very grand and elderly, had begun to walk with a cane, which she would raise without warning to bat a ball flying out of bounds. Her talent as a batter was exceeded only by her genius as a pitcher. She wore high collars of blue lace, culottes, and bifocals so strong they enlarged her eyes to the size of rather worn grey golf balls. When she died she left behind her a flourishing school. Her gymnasia had overflowed into the basement of the neighboring Episcopal church, and she

would have rented a nearby Presbyterian cellar as well, had
the minister not been a Scotsman. Her library was poor,
though perhaps merely eccentric: it was filled with old copies
of *The London Illustrated News,* to which she had never allowed her subscription to lapse, and seven complete, and
completely uncut, sets of Dickens, but little else. Her gym
closet held fifty-four volleyballs. Her last lecture had been
on the purity of the temple of the body, and against sweat.
She had designed her educational philosophy to foster athlet-
ics and motherhood among her girls; and it did, in that order.
She used to say that while her fencing stars had the healthiest
babies of all her girls, the baseball players had the most intelligent. It all had to do with the tension of the pelvic structure
and the stroke of the pectoral muscle. "A Sound Mind in a
Sound Body" was conspicuous on her letterhead, but if she
was attracted to the first half of this slogan, it was only because of the sound. The motto she preferred was "Play is
Work." For Miss Jewett's graduates a university was a vulgar
place. To go to one was a confession of moral, social, and
muscular defeat; it was a capitulation, and no one but the
failures in volleyball ever committed themselves to this igno-
miny. Her most notorious case had been a girl who had made
herself ridiculous by getting into Barnard, and afterward
passing; this creature as a consequence was regarded not only
as contemptibly disloyal, but worse, as unwomanly. The girls
of Miss Jewett's were trained for womanliness. They came
out, as a rule, in the fifth form, were engaged in the seventh
or shortly afterward (though "shortly afterward" carried with
it a certain mild disgrace), and married themselves directly
into the Junior League, where for a few months they quib-
bled over dates for charitable theatre parties until the arrival
of their predeterminedly vigorous first babies. My mother had
gone to Miss Jewett's; William's present wife had gone to
Miss Jewett's; and I thought it an orderly and proper thing
that William's daughter-in-law should shortly be an alumna
of the same school. It gave me, this propriety, nevertheless a
moment's pity for William's son; he had so readily surrendered. He had chosen a schoolgirl; he had chosen womanliness; he had chosen the very right thing. I felt despairing: he
had chosen only what his father might have chosen for him.
Yet it seemed he might have wanted something other than
the very right thing; it seemed he might have wanted talk and
even bookishness and even character. Oh, it seemed he might
have wanted—not me (not even my secret musings dared this

direction), and not even someone very like me (though I had frequently, and not without smoldering irony, contemplated such a turn: it was a kind of self-indulgent daydream, half-vengeful, half-vicarious), but, at least, not one of Miss Jewett's girls! Not one of them! They were all of them replicas of Allegra Vand; and it was useless to suppose, just because it was inconceivable they should, like her, leap at working-class causes, that they were not replicas. If it had been in the style of my mother's generation to have no ideals, to be sick of ideals, she would have had none, she would have been sick of them. If it had been in the style to go abroad not for world-improvement wobbly rallies but for self-improvement, she would have gone for that instead. Miss Jewett's girls were all alike, they were up-to-date; they were inhabited, though not inhibited, by the Zeitgeist. And if the Jewett-trained daughters quarreled with the Jewett-trained mothers, it was simply the Zeitgeist, and not Miss Jewett's muscular influences, which had altered. "Woman's physiology stays the same," Miss Jewett herself used to say; "it's only the times which are different." This was her argument, in my grandmother's day, against tobacco. It was the same argument which the girls of Miss Jewett's used to produce when my mother went there— only in favor. Now it is the young Miss Jewett, the original's seventy-year-old niece, they must answer to: but it is strange how they have come around to the old Miss Jewett's way of thinking. Today they do not much like tobacco. They smoke marijuana instead.

I learned this not—as it might be presumed—long afterward, but then and there, from *The Good Sport*. This—it turned out to be the school newspaper—had been left lying on one of the desks in that wide bright desk-huddled room, and when I flurried it open a photograph of a girl in a tennis costume jumped out at me, side by side with a half-page advertisement taken (I guessed in resignation) by William's firm: "Compliments Of" set in a sea of white margin like a craft fit for darker waters. "Beverly Ames Snearles Loses at Love," said the caption in twelve-point Bodoni Bold, "Wins Match." A tragically romantic notice: and here is Beverly in her white shorts and white thighs, laughing into the saucy camera and measuring her racket like an oversized salmon. "I've been smoking the weed for relaxation," she explains, "and it's definitely improved my serve." "Do you recommend it for other sports?" inquires the interviewer, identified in the by-line as Eleanor Bell. "I don't know about other sports," says Beverly

to Eleanor; "tennis is my game. But for tennis I definitely recommend Mary-Jane." Mary-Jane—the sweet weed itself—at
Miss Jewett's! Still, I had seen pictures of my mother in this
very pose, and if experimentation with the slow taste of
Mary-Jane had replaced experimentation with the class-struc-
ture, the essentials were the same: the throbbing bosom, the
clear chin-line, and an overwhelming belief in the omnipo-
tence of the present over the future. Oh, the girls of Miss Jewett's! They had, if nothing else, a perfect self-possession; and
this—not talk, not bookishness, least of all character—drew
William's son. He wanted the womanly child, the childlike
woman—in short, exactly what his father had married in my
mother.

This perception entered me like a cloud; and under the
weight and flavor of it I suddenly spied William himself, although I had already given up looking for him. His hands
were hooked by their thumbs across his grey back, and his
big waxy distinguished skull, disconcertingly like the heavy-
chinned head of Henry James or Edmund Wilson (without
their aura, which illuminates even the solemn photographs, of
amazement at the world's incongruities—for William was too
pious for wonder), cautiously wheeled toward his two companions. I was left with a quick vision of that broad serious
middle-aged brow, obscured now half by the shadow of his
retreat, an out-of-the-way corner, and half by the flourished
arm of the taller of the attendant pair, a narrow dark man
with unhurrying eyes close to the surface of a rather Tartar-
ish face (though grossly and even mediaevally lidded and
lashed), wherein courtesy hid covetousness. The shorter and
squarer one was plainly an Irishman, but not the ebullient
sort; he was more pale than any monk, though he seemed as
silently self-absorbed as a Trappist. Neither man had the
proper look or tone which might be construed as habitually
environmental for William, he was not casual with them, and
I supposed they had not emerged from the special air of his
clubs, or, going back still farther, of his class. It was not only
that they had the wrong faces. Even from a distance I could
tell they had the wrong point of view. The Irishman was too
detached, and the other, with his hand nervously slapping at
his thick-haired temples to emphasize a phrase, was too actively attached: he had a rapid joyless smile which, with no
warning of expression, he uncovered now as weapon and now
as semicolon. The Irishman merely listened—but dependably.
It seemed a conference of elders, dense as a thicket, and I

might have taken one or the other of them for the bride's father had either remotely struck me as Protestant.

While I stood considering, *The Good Sport* was snatched from my hand.

"Here, I've been looking for that, damn it."

The rough grab startled me. I turned, and subsided into a gradual absorption of a subdued aristocratic sneer, as certain and imperious as a head on a coin; a diminutive cigar, grandly squeezed; and the proud breast of an arrogant buffalo: it was William's son.

Without pleasure he took in the fact of my presence.

"This is a surprise."

"Your engagement?" I said. "Yes, it is. I hadn't heard anything about it. I really am surprised."

He rewarded me with a quick impatient artificial scowl. "I meant finding you here."

"I came to see your father."

"On business?"

"My mother's," I said facilely.

"I'm afraid business is suspended for the rest of the day."

He brought this out so gloomily that I was constrained to remark politely, "Of course. It's an extraordinary occasion."

"Well, it was a surprise to me too."

"Your engagement?" I said again.

He looked at me with open annoyance. "This party. It was sprung on me. I had no idea." But he gathered himself up, recovered, and gently lowered *The Good Sport*. "I hope you don't mind not being asked," he pursued, all at once summoning up an exquisite courtesy which, if it had been less acid and had more successfully concealed a contrary inspiration, might have resembled his father's. "Of course there'll be the official engagement thing later on, and of course we'll expect you and Mr. and Mrs. Vand. I'm told it'll be a supper party at the Burgundy. Mother was very careful to put you at the top of the list."

I hid my skepticism and thanked him.

But he had not finished. "I imagine you were simply overlooked, for today."

"Look, I didn't come for the party," I said, feeling warm. "You don't have to apologize."

"The boys here simply got together about it behind my back. Naturally they'd ask just who was most obvious. I mean they wouldn't think of you."

"I'm anything but obvious," I conceded.

"If I'd known about it I would have thought of you myself."

"Of course," I agreed.

"My father would have reminded me of it. Especially with all these fellows down from school. It's practically the same bunch I dug up for your send-off, you know."

"It was awfully good of you to do it," I said. "I'm sorry it was all for nothing."

"Well, I know, but my father insisted on it. To please Mrs. Vand. I guess she thought there'd be something in it for you." He must have felt how these words put him in the wrong light, for quite suddenly his high alert manner faltered, and his eye trailed consciously across the room.

"There wasn't," I said candidly. "It really doesn't matter, though."

"No? I heard you don't date much."

"Because I don't want to."

It was his turn to cover disbelief, and though his doubt was justified, I resented it. He took up again with a renewed effort: "It must have been a let-down for you, though. I mean not to get to go after all."

"I've *been* to Europe," I said: but with a certain sharpness.

"When you were a kid," he observed.

"Right after the war."

"It doesn't mean you shouldn't go again."

"I guess I will," I asserted, but hesitated to state what I did not credit. "Later on. Maybe when my mother's better."

This blinked him swiftly to attention. "Yes, how *is* she, by the way?"—but his curiosity was not so overwhelming that he troubled to leave a gap for my satisfying it. "You don't remember anything about what it was like over there?" he concluded without a pause. "I suppose you were too young."

"I remember a lot. But I don't think about it much," I said.

"Then do you happen to recollect a man named Pettigrew?"

"Pettigrew."

"Your stepfather used to run into him now and then. They were in different sectors but they came to know each other after your mother got into some sort of legal trouble over an automobile."

"Oh, marvelous," I applauded. "Now you've learned her file by heart."

"You don't have to be mad about it, it's not really all my

fault. I've been working in the Vs all summer—Venue, Validation, Vacantia Bona, Valuation, Vand."

"Perfect. I like the way you do your job—the only thing missing is Virtue."

"In your mother's file? You're too hard on her. And after I had the good grace not to mention Venality!" He bit on his unlit cigar and grinned on either side of it. "Pettigrew settled some sort of threatened suit for her, do you recall? It cost plenty. They had to buy the whole Paris police force. Not to speak of a complete hospital staff. It's quite a story."

"Is that the way your father does business?" I sardonically inquired.

"Oh, well, I've stopped thinking my father so all-holy. He put Pettigrew on it, that's all I know. Maybe it's the way Pettigrew does business. Or your mother." He shrugged. "The times weren't normal anyhow."

His whole tone was so slippery it was useless to accuse him. "You've had a profitable summer," I merely noted.

"Not bad, not bad. Educational." But he looked around with distaste. "Unless you regard today as its culmination. I don't care for all this crawling around. —You don't recollect him?" he persisted.

I condescended to reflect. "What sort of work did he do?"

"For a while he was Special Assistant under Marshall. That's when he knew your stepfather. When the Republicans took over they threw him out."

"He's a Democrat?"

"Pettigrew? Oh my God. A Roosevelt New Dealer actually." His smile was speculative and almost genuine. "You can imagine how my father feels about it."

"I *think* I've heard of him," I said, barely recalling it. "At least the name. He's the one who went to that dancing school, isn't he?—with your father and my mother, when they were little?"

"And *my* mother," he added. "He's been stepping on their toes ever since. Politically speaking."

"I don't know him," I admitted.

"He's going to be my father-in-law," said William's son.

This interested me mightily: within the propriety of the match, then, there lay a hint of discord. Curiously, this possibility appeared to amuse William's son; through his posture of vexation I saw his excitement in the promise of conflict. He obviously thought it something to enjoy.

"Will that be an obstacle?" I put it.

"To what?"

"Oh, I don't know. Family unity."

He laughed out his scorn at me. "Family unity! What a
prude you are—I don't care beans about family unity or anything like it. I've grown up on it, you haven't. It's only a contrivance, believe me." He offered me his derisive eye. "You
can't tell me anything about family unity that I haven't already seen in the raw. What else do you think they have between them," he asked, "my father and my mother?"—and
answered himself with a harsh nip of his cigar: "Family
unity, that's what."

This was so unexpected and perilous and fragile a subject
that I did not know how to reply. "Your mother is an admirable woman," I ventured.

"I admit it. So does my father. I guess he isn't inspired by
admirable women," William's son gave out; and, because I
had plainly failed to catch the sharp purport of his tone he
softened it to a confidence: "That's why Mrs. Vand is unforgivable."

"You always say that and it's not fair," I maintained. "You
forget who wanted the divorce."

"You don't have to remind me. My father is a selfish man
and your mother is as wild as Borneo. He was out to save his
hide. She would have run him to tatters."

"William can take care of himself," I announced.

"Do you really think so?" —It was half a jeer.

"He's a mountain."

"With a geologic fault. Or maybe it's simply a fault of
character. The point is he'd do anything for Mrs. Vand."

"No more than for the other client."

"Maybe not. But certainly more than for my mother." He
saw my alarm and came back quickly, "Not that he's negligent, of course. In fact I suppose he's what's called a born
family man. He's very good at being head of the house. He
presides over us beautifully."

"Then you can safely take him for your model," I remarked, afraid to say more yet unwilling to withdraw.

"Sure." He raised his chin sedately, an illusory movement
so very like William's habitual manner that it aged him thirty
years. "If I should ever decide to run after what I'd already
run *from*."

"William doesn't run after my mother!" I cried, tantalized.

"Do you think it's necessary for him to deliver her installment by hand? The firm could just as easily deposit it in her account and leave it at that. It's the routine thing."

"Then I suppose he likes to avoid the routine thing. He has a ceremonious nature."

"Exactly. And in ordinary matters it's the ceremony of the routine thing that he lives by."

"Then he does it as a simple courtesy."

"A courtesy, but his motives aren't simple. —Oh, I don't deny he's gallant!" he conceded.

I said severely, "There's nothing improper in being gallant."

"I told you you're a prude."

"I'm only precise."

"Precision isn't the same as truth. The truth is he's never attached himself to anyone else. He does his duty, but it's not duty that brings him out to look at your mother every other month."

"He likes to hear her talk," I admitted. Then I had a thought which made me lower my head before I could dare to speak it out. "But when you think of you and Nanette and Jack and Willy—and, well, Cletis is only *two*—" But my intrepidness embarrassed me; worse, it scared me. I felt as though I probed a sanctuary with a vulgar and broken broom. "I mean it wasn't duty which brought you all into the world," I threw out.

"Oh, what you don't know about family unity!" said William's son.

This high and prescient assertion, delivered with a not unfriendly insolence—and prescient because it seemed to point to a vision of my interlocutor's own marital future, as orderly ιs his father's—provoked me to surpass myself in pluck. 'Don't you *want* to get married?" I neatly wondered.

He remembered to resume his patronizing smile just in time. "What kind of comment is that?"

"It's not a comment. It's a question."

"Prig," he observed. "What do you think I bothered to get engaged for? You wouldn't expect me to cohabit without"— up went his mocking chin—"the sanction of the law?"

"No," I confessed. "It's only that you seem so cross about it."

"I'm mad as hops," he agreed. "I could wring her neck. I could hang her from the yardarm."

"A declaration of passion," I concluded.

He looked at me with a certain surprise. "You're a satirist, aren't you?"

"No," I said. "I'm a prude and a prig."

"I know. But besides that."

"What has she done?" I prodded.

"Oh God, plenty. Look at this." He spread open the pages of *The Good Sport*. "It's this damned ad. She badgered me into giving it to her under the firm's name. I didn't wait a minute before I suggested 'Best Wishes from a Friend,' something in that line, but no, it wouldn't do. It isn't professional enough—everyone's nasty uncle takes an ad in just those words. —Believe it or not, she's the business manager of this sheet. She multiplies on her fingers, so they elected her business manager!" he crowed—it was difficult to tell whether with affectionate pride (multiplying on the fingers being merely an adorable crotchet) or with clean contempt (the conforming masculine attitude toward the weaknesses of shining womanliness). "She was afraid 'Best Wishes from a Friend' could make them look tacky—as though they didn't *have* any friends. Amateurs hate to be taken for what they are, you know. It was the firm she wanted." His steady mutter dissolved into a confidential sigh. "Like a damned fool I gave it to her, and now my father's down on me," he complained.

The criminality in this exposition was lost on me; it had, in fact, the whimsicality of a joyously trivial, though conventionally impenetrable, mystery. Still, I was glad William's son thought me a worthy receptacle for these minutiae. It gave me a narrow opportunity to fasten on an image, theoretical though it might be, of his fiancée. The more I heard, the more I thought *her* unworthy.

"He's not down on you just for giving an ad?" I said, implying there was better reason: let him look to the girl for it.

"Isn't he though."

"Well, it isn't as if you'd gone and violated the Ten Commandments," I consoled, pleasurably detached.

"No—only Canon 27."

"I see"—though I did not.

"Of the Canons of Professional Ethics," he groaned. "My father's afraid the Bar People will be down on *him*."

"Is there something the matter with the ad? It only says Compliments Of."

"Nothing at all the matter. It's perfectly all right. There's nothing wrong with it," he disclosed with something like a wince, "except that it's a total scandal." He gave the ceiling a glance of direct and unpretentious comradeship. "It's unethical for a law firm to advertise at all," he supplied ruefully.

"In a school paper? It's only a school paper."

"My calculation exactly. That's why I took the chance of doing it. She kept at me and kept *at* me and, well, finally I gave in because I never thought my father would get to see it in a hundred years. It's not as though I put it in *The Wall Street Journal,* after all. And I paid for it myself, so Connelly wouldn't list it."

At the mention of Connelly—the meticulous accountant— this innocuously detailed history suddenly blossomed with importance. What had to be kept from Connelly had also to be kept from William. And what was kept from William, shrine of innocence, was undoubtedly not innocent. "Then William got to see the ad. He got to see it anyway," I hazarded.

"He wouldn't have if not for this stupid story about a tennis-player at Miss Jewett's"—belligerently William's son snapped his fingers against the guilty *Sport.*

"Beverly Ames Snearles Loses at Love," I recited. "Is it true about the marijuana?"

"What do *you* think? They all do it down there, for kicks. Anyhow it was partly Nanette's fault. She's been friendly all term with one of these girls from Miss Jewett's—"

"But Nanette goes to the Academy," I interrupted.

"—the one who wrote the story. Eleanor Bell," he pushed on aloofly. "They're going to be in the Junior Assemblies together next spring. At least Nanette will. The other girl was supposed to be in it, but she won't be eligible if she's expelled. God, I hate this gossip."

"My," said I, vaguely spiteful, "it sounds like Lowood, in *Jane Eyre.*"

He stopped long enough to rebuke me with a stare. "You have a literary reference for everything"—as if he expected me to apologize for it. "It's proof you don't listen."

"I *am* listening. I really am," I said quickly, afraid he would go away. "*Are* they expelling her?" I inquired, as a token of my attentiveness.

But he was moving energetically onward. "You bet they are. Not that those girls haven't been smoking it down there for the last seven months. Especially during the summer make-up term. Everybody knows it. It isn't a crime to know about it or to do it—it's only a crime if you print it. Anyhow"—he took a breath, and I somehow wondered whether he did hate gossip after all—"the girl's father—that's Bell, the broker—intends to sue the school for breaching its contract to educate his daughter, the tuition having been the consideration, although . . . It's a long story." He maundered off into meditation and when he came back to me again it was with an explosion. "Well, look! The upshot of it is he got my father to handle the thing. Legally it's pretty tricky. My father didn't want to touch it. He was horrified."

"It's a difficult case?"

"Not on account of the law! He's not afraid of the law. It was on account of Nanette—her being chummy with this Bell girl, though he wouldn't stoop to mentioning her by name. He didn't even have the decency to say 'addict,' which would have been silly enough. He simply came out and called the girl a dope fiend."

"Not to her poor father's face!" I exclaimed.

"I haven't any idea of what he said to Bell. I just know what he said afterward, to Nanette. She cried and cried—but she always does that, she likes to cry. And in the end he had to agree to his taking the case anyhow—because of me really."

"Because of you?"

"If they expel Eleanor, you see, they're liable to expel others—they're liable to expel all of them."

I marveled at the burden of this revelation. "Including your fiancée," I said. "The Disgrace of the Prospective Daughter-in-Law."

His unexpected half-smile, agitating only a part of his affirming lip, carefully neglected to answer me. "At any rate it was through Bell that he got a copy of the paper."

"And saw the ad," I summed it up.

"Oh, he didn't see it then. He overlooked it while Bell was with him. But when he came home that same night—this was only day before yesterday, you know—he found Nanette pretty stirred up. She'd heard that Eleanor would be dropped from the Assemblies. My father said he couldn't approve of it more; he thought the contamination ought to be removed. That made Nanette cry, of course; she's full of histrionics. I suppose he regretted having started her off: he usually does. Anyhow that's when he came upon the ad—turning over the pages while Nanette cried. My father hates tears."

"It's part of his code," I defended him.

"I'm sick of hearing about my father's code," he said dully. "As far as I'm concerned it's the code of the lion and the

Christian. Everyone seems to think my father is the Christian."

"He gives every impression of being one," I said.

"When actually he's the lion salivating in the arena, if you want to know the truth. He had it in for me, all right."

"It doesn't seem such a serious thing," I said doubtfully. "One little ad."

"It does to the ethics committee. The worst of it is my father is a senior member of it. It's pretty embarrassing. And now you can't get a copy of the *Sport* for love or money. This one's practically irreplaceable," he said, folding it up and digging it into his pocket. "It's the file copy. He wanted to know whether I intended to get him disbarred and then to cap it by marrying a dope fiend."

"And the tennis player in the white shorts?" I asked. "Will they expel her too?"

"No danger of it. She won a cup for the school."

"Ah."

"And more to the point, Snearles has already promised to build them a new gymnasium if they keep her. That's Snearles Contracting, you know."

"Maybe Bell will build a gymnasium too. Maybe that's what your father will advise."

"I've already told you I've stopped regarding my father as a holy of holies."

"What does that mean?"

"You know exactly what it means. He's not so virtuous as he appears. That Town Island business, for one thing."

I let this pass, or tried to. "And for another thing?"

"Isn't that enough?"

"One act doesn't imply habit," I said.

"If he can do something once he can do it again."

I felt myself on uncertain ground, and lowered my eyes.

"I told you I found out about my father's part in those expenditures of your mother's. The money that goes to the caretaker down there. I meant it when I said I always thought he'd kept his nose clean."

"That's a disgusting expression."

"Don't be so tender. *He's* not, believe me." He had put aside his cigar and was addressing me with the flattering earnestness I had always imagined possible between us, though I had never before seen it. It was like the conversation, I thought, of distant cousins at a rare family occasion—a fu-

neral, perhaps. We had in common certain asymmetrical relationships.

In response to this mood in him I was soft. "I don't think
your father's implicated in anything," I said steadily.

"Up to his ears."

"Did he tell you that?"

"We've been over this ground, haven't we? You know what
he told me."

"No I don't."

"You know all about it."

"No."

"When he asked me if I was trying to get him disbarred
with this damned ad I said he deserved it for another cause
anyhow."

"You said that to William?" I cried.

"And when he asked me if I intended marrying a—a 'dope
fiend'—good God!—I asked him whether his reputation was
any better."

"You didn't speak to your father that way!"

"How else was I to speak to him? You think it was easy
going through that?" His head twisted away from me, obscurely butting the misty room: a wounded bison in torment.
His voice was a blade. "It killed me to find out about him. It
killed me."

"Your father hasn't done anything. It's all on account of
my mother—"

"You *do* know about it."

"No," I said fearfully.

"You told me yourself—on the telephone. You said there
was a museum there. A marine museum."

"I was—only guessing," I faltered.

"You knew about the estate. Your grandfather's property
—where your mother grew up: You *knew* about it," he insisted.

"Only after you told me. I thought it had been sold long
ago." I hesitated before I brought out a sudden lump of rage:
"You're the one who knows everything! You're the one who
reads my mother's file. You're the son of the trustee!"

He said slowly, "What my father did isn't in the file." And
then, while resolutely I sought out his look: "The vital things
never are."

I stiffened.

"Even the divorce papers aren't there," he said.

"Neither of them?"

"What do you mean, neither—neither party's?"

"No," I said. "Neither divorce."

"Nothing," he quietly affirmed.

A passage of pity, unsure of itself and useless, uninvited yet unmistakable, intervened curiously between us: pity one upon the other.

He said, "This is no place to talk. Come on out," and I followed him through a sunless corridor, blind-dark after the brilliant and busy inner room, lit by those long daystruck panes, where we had conversed unnoticed under the weaving crowd's negligent eye, into one of the windowless cubicles I had earlier observed.

He shut the door and without delay told me a story.

I heard it and did not recognize it and half believed it and half knew it to be false and a fabrication, though thinking William ingenious still: continuing to suppose the tale a shield set out to deflect any suspicion of Tilbeck's presence in that place, and at the same moment wondering at the lifelike quality of the lie, a lie too like truth to be a true lie; a lie beyond the limits of an imagination as dry as William's, perhaps; or else a lie so extravagantly like a novice liar's notion of what a model lie should be as to be anything but a lie. For it was very strange that William, so unpractised, should be so ingenious; it was contradictory that he should have invented, to avoid the sordidness of one confession, another even more sordid. If, as I supposed, it was part of his recognizable code (to which his son had just yielded the obeisance of contempt) that to spare my mother the stain of Tilbeck he should by other means stain himself, then the dye he had chosen was unnecessarily melodramatic and dangerously crimson. It was a barrister's diversionary trick in a man who put far more trust in documentation than in oratory. Perhaps I could rationally expect him to have shown, for charity's sake, a moderate duplicity: but of theatrical art William had none; not from him had Nanette inherited her player's bent —his capacity for wholesale pretense of the passions so far went undemonstrated. In short, I thought him honest, without deviation, after all; and, very reluctantly, still doubting my conclusion, I began to think the lie false. There was too much blood in it for make-believe—though by the same logic was there not too much blood in it for truth?

I did not know what to believe. I pressed my hands together until the sweat ran along the channel of the palms in broken pellets.

William's son, indulging himself in the rhetoric of precision, began from the beginning. "My father told me this: your grandfather died with an obsession, maybe only an enthusiasm, about the property. He had supervised the building of the house from the first—badgered the architects, had the porticos copied from the cathedral at Ferrara, and went abroad to select the marble himself—he was a nautical sort all his life. When it was finished he had a fountain built around an anchor in the gardens and called the place Duneacres." Without hurry my narrator let down his straightened and narrowed fingers for a search in his pockets: on the way *The Good Sport* in one of them crackled so loudly it startled me. He came up with a book of matches and muttered through his teeth as he lit his cigar, "I'm trying to reproduce this in an orderly way"—he puffed futilely, working up the light—"since that's how it was given to me. You see I'm taking your word for your ignorance," he accused, "though it's perfectly plain you've heard of everything I'm saying."

"I've heard of Duneacres," I said, "the name. I mean—" reflecting, while the cigar caught at last with a cone of smoke and a little flare in its tip, how I had a dozen years before encountered that word, meant for an address and curled like a salt-worm in my father's hideous hidden scrawl.

William's son showed me his disbelieving scorn by omitting even the smallest pause. "Of course. You barely know the place, and then only by name."

"It's true," I said heatedly.

"Then to oblige you I won't fail to be explicit."

"You won't oblige me if you succeed. I'm not concerned in any of it."

He bit down hard. "You think you can do without the truth?"—and would not have waited for my reply even if I had had any. "At the end," he went on steadily, "when his wife was dead and his daughter married, he was living on the estate all alone, though with one of the largest household staffs in the country. At one point, I think, there was an ancient spinster aunt in his charge. She predeceased your grandfather by a year, if I'm correct. The fact is—" He turned on me. "What?"

"My mother's great-aunt Huntingdon," I murmured thoughtfully. "She's the one I'm supposed to look like."

"I'm sure you will some day," he said with a smoke-hung scowl, "if you can get longevity to support you in it. Though I understand that your grandfather was only in his sixties at his death. He died just seven months after the marriage." He glanced up purposefully, but saw with relief that he was not required to specify which marriage. "There wasn't anyone to inherit the place usefully; it wasn't needed—your mother and my father were all newly settled in"—would he say "our house"? or "where we live now"?—delicately he avoided it and instead grew civic: "Scarsdale. Not long before he died he fastened on the idea of turning the place into some sort of museum. His son-in-law, as trustee, was supposed to carry it out. The agreement was that the trust would cover the up-keep of the estate, in perpetuity; and on that basis my father got the county to sink funds into the plan. The trust, you see, was supposed to pay for the physical renovations, the guards' salaries, all of that—but the county had to hire the personnel. So they went out and chose a whole staff of experts, scien-tists, an unemployed curator or two—people like that. They weren't hard to find. It was the bottom of the Depression, you know."

"Oh," I assured him, "I've heard of the Depression. Though only barely. I've heard of it by name, so to speak."

He stopped short. "All right, you've made your point."

"I have?"

"Either you're without any knowledge at all or you're to-tally callous."

"If I'm allowed a choice—"

"If you knew anything about it you wouldn't laugh at it. They *have* kept it from you," he said gravely.

"Then do you think you should take it on yourself to re-veal it?" I inquired.

"You want me to have scruples, is that it? When only a little while ago you were advising me to model myself after my father!" He walkèd away, gave me his back, and con-fronted the drab wall. "The whole crux of the story is that *he* didn't have any," he said, from afar. "He never went through with it. He simply let the place go to rot. The county had to renege—they were left with all those commitments of jobs, and no jobs."

I was puzzled, though not yet affected.

"William must have had a reason for it," I ventured.

"Oh, a reason!" His spine quickened with spite and repug-nance. He spun and spat: "Listen, there was a bunch of let-ters from these men. Fifteen men all together. Grown men, and they pleaded like sheep. What do you suppose a job like that was worth to an educated man in 1933?"

"They must have got on somehow."

"Got on!" he threw back at me. "As a matter of fact fourteen of them did. They came; then they went back to where they had come from. The difficulty was that fifteen had been hired. —Though I shouldn't call it a difficulty: the arithmetic couldn't be simpler. I imagine even you can cope with it. They got on, if that's what you want to call being out of a job in those times—haven't you read, don't you have an ounce of historical imagination? —They all got on but one." He blew out a round and violent cloud: in that tiny room it had the smell of enclosure and wariness without hope. "His name was John Vermoulian. He happened to be the youngest of the lot, just out of school—it was the chance of his life." A vagrant and unsentimental snigger accompanied the last phrase; I was being treated to the iron in irony. But he went straight on: "It was a good connection, the perfect opportunity, and on the strength of it he was able to get himself engaged to a girl of a family which ordinarily wouldn't have touched him. They used to call that sort of thing a love match—in olden times," he sneered. "We don't have them any more. The girl's father was a doctor high in the community—naturally he wouldn't hear of it, it wasn't decent enough for him—the son of Armenian immigrants, after all —you see his point. Though they *did* have a little family restaurant which was hanging on nicely in spite of the times; it had seen the boy through college in fact. In a way they had their own hopes. It didn't help, by the way, that the boy had educated himself in a thoroughly impractical science—in the doctor's view of it, I mean. He was twenty-five; his own family was as practical as the doctor and their solution was to urge him to come and be a waiter in the business and forget the girl. Meanwhile on his side of it the doctor kept on resisting and warning—but when the job came through the idea of the museum won him over. It was honorable and it was *almost* a profession. And anyhow a museum has a classical sound to it." He broke off angrily, "What's the matter?"

"Letters—you said there were letters."

"Damn it, aren't you following me?"

"You didn't *see* the letters," I said uneasily. There was an alarming tangibility in this account. Though William had suppressed as figment the fact of the impious Tilbeck, reducing him negligibly and namelessly to hobbling caretaker, and now-and-then guardian of a weedy ruin, the drift of the tale showed it no longer likely that a simple figment stood in Tilbeck's place.

"It wasn't necessary to look them *up*," William's son proposed, "even if I had known where to look. My father admitted to them readily enough. He went and got them and threw them on the table and called them Exhibit A." I heard; I took my breath slowly; I credited it all. "After he had begun he admitted to every part of the thing. He didn't try to duck any of it, I'll give him that. What would have been the use? Foul is foul. And if he didn't withhold the end, what else could he have thought worth hiding?"

Tilbeck. But though I knew the answer I seized on the question. "The end?" I repeated, sharply wondering.

"There *was* an end. When this boy found there wasn't going to be a job after all, he went out into the woods behind the house and slit his throat with a fish-cleaning knife."

The sweat froze in my fist. I could think of no word to speak.

But William's son was narrow and quick and permitted no gap. He finished hoarsely, "My father had lost interest in the project. You ask for a reason. That was the reason."

Thickly I tried it: "Maybe it was my mother's fault. It was her inheritance, after all," I conjectured. "Maybe *she* lost interest."

He shook his head. "No. It made no difference. He was the trustee. It was his legal responsibility."

"He wasn't expected to be responsible for a man's suicide," I said without effect: and added the familiar, perilous, useful, baleful phrase of escape—"according to the terms of the trust."

But it was an unwitting mockery and whipped his face.

"No," said William's son. "It was only that he was responsible for a murder." Then abruptly he threw open the door and by a lift of his burning cigar he commanded me out. "That's what I know about my father," he said, and went off like the last of a dying species, his buffalo-head low, his buffalo-back sorrowful and unforgiving, leaving me standing there alone.

4

Or, if my metaphor is unreal (but is it? think how stoic is he, genus bison americanus, early victim of genocide, the remnant of a race that opened nostrils once wherever there were grasses, and now to please a mere remorseful Government must populate tame tufted showpiece fields, subdued, without hope of animal pride, enslaved in showpiece herds, labeled "extant" though marveled at as near-extinct, a thrown-out plains prince mourning his old genius)—if, then, staring after him as after a debauched buddha, I indulged William's son in an image too unlikely, inferior to his sadness, construable as insult to his reversed state, spite upon his blighted fortunateness, bad thread shaming the perfect plait of his elegance—whatever the cheap sigh of rhetoric is overquick in its whim to call that disfigurement-by-disillusion which stood plain in the face of fury William's son took with him—if I had chosen too ornamentally I changed and was simple. I watched him round a corner in the swagger of compunction with his pocket bulging and his smoke-trail thinning out and knew that I saw—simply—a proud dandy come down in the world: a moral dandy betrayed by the shock of dirt: a pretend-cynic wounded by the falling-short of pale and sickly virtue.

For myself, I opened my hands and blew them dry. For myself, I could rally. For myself, horror was only surprise raised to a higher power; and surprise was itself a component of the comic. Tragedy dates quickly, and then we have to laugh at it, as at films of forty years ago, with their irrelevant voiceless anguish, their trivial voiceless fright, their blows without impact. And when bitter at the morally unexpected, we always laugh. If the rationality of deliberate comedy is worthy of laughter, so much more is the irrationality of equally deliberate fate. What is hysteria if not fate's tears, too deep for thought? It is even possible to laugh at Lear—and who shall say that Hamlet's futile lunge at the arras is not designed to be partly laughed at? So I felt relief; I felt I had come far. Pity dwindled, though not ravishment. He was put down, William's son; dismayed; shamed. He was broken. I did not care. I felt elation at the straw of pride bent and rent; it brought him down to me. He had yielded up the secret history of our equality: now my mother, famous for scandal, silliness, duplicities, seemed no worse than William, who was tutored enough in Paulinism to see how wickedness differs from folly. The lily of deceit grew in William too; it grew well in him. I was glad the deed was old, and had preceded his son's birth and mine—the older, the more susceptible of wisdom's bony laughter; it meant we had grown up together with the deed, that death; it was our brother, our sister; we were born equal with it. Had I not heard Enoch declare righteousness a joke invented for dupes by confidence-men? And William's son was his father's dupe.

Not I. I supposed myself no one's dupe. Not only because I had no decorousness to be blasted (how elegantly he vanished, his head lordly though his long hands drooped!), but rather because I thought fraud my atmosphere, deceit my premise, hoax my modest axiom. I was used to them all, and comfortable with their divisions. I knew nothing of unity; of what William's son called "family unity" still less; in the impossibility of betrayal I had no faith. I had for a long time seen how my mother teased and catnipped life as though assaying a sort of acrobatic trick, and how she threw herself astride it like a circus rider, and how she bred me to her repute while, waiting for the almost-fall, that most dangerous of all tricks, I watched with suspicion, incredulous even as she righted herself with a recklessness of equilibrium dependent partly on luck and partly on wile and not at all on the spirit of the steed. What William's son suffered, I did not know how to suffer. The dissolution of balance was, for me, neither novel nor blown with fear. I preened myself on my familiarity with distrust, and recovered easily—oh, how easily, with the complacency of practised repugnance—from a mere tale of a young man's cutting his throat.

But not from the live young man who had told the tale. Once more he entered that wide inhabited room where his father stood conversing among the splendid mob of youth, while I lingered at the bottom of the dim corridor down which he had led me to deliver the chronicle of his father's

fall, already thinking it little, the sweat of horror already dry
in my palm, myself all unmoved by antique incident. It might
have been of the death of Priam he told me; old Kings and
self-slain boys were nothing to me. It was all history, and history, as Enoch and William's son had equally divined, did not
touch me. It was the live boy I cared for; it was the image of
the live boy that ravished me, William's son—who, making
his final disgruntled turn into the crowd and out of sight, left
my eye abruptly bare. —Though not so bare as his mere disappearance would have it: his head, both brutal and delicate
with defense, lay like another dimension—a tissue—against
my lid. It settled into my willing stare with all the immobile
persistence of a thin frail photograph; like a powder of gold
it acridly dusted my vision; I feared its beauty at last. All that
hapless unreachable beauty!—the beauty of valor, like that of
a Roman soldier surveying an English swamp for a road that
would outlast Rome's very legend. And not calculating valor
only: something in his contempt, once perhaps a schoolboy
affectation and now too bitterly justified by actuality, wrung
me: it was so like a leap into danger. It had all the stylization
of bravery and innocence thrown into the fire of deceit and
bad dream. I saw him as though on a frieze—one of those
staunch figures in buckler and helmet, leather scutum
upraised, stony calf taut beneath the military skirt—then,
above, grim graven face showing a pair of arched lips so unexpectedly soft, in all that stone, so surprisingly vulnerable,
that they might have been in the act of speaking a lover's line
by Catullus.

Well, look! I knew well enough what zeroes these romantic
and perilous fantasies held for me. It was perverseness that
drew me to the bliss of fancying myself in love just when that
bliss was most inaccessible. He was engaged; and, even if he
had not been bound by this not-quite-awesome compact, he
would not have been less inaccessible. It was a robbed bliss
and a robbed beauty I contemplated then—it seemed all the
more impenetrable, all the more puissant, all the more richly
luring, for its plain implausibility. He did not like me, William's son; he blamed me for being the daughter of Allegra
Vand. His look denunciated; his look scathed; his look was
full of taunting. And his voice was severe. His voice was savage. He was all savagery. He was not kind to me. It did not
matter. I expected nothing. When he was gone I stood and
blinked after him, warmed by his disciplined and purposive
confidence, though preferring to take it for savage and wild.

If he had spoken to me kindly he would have diminished my adoration. I leaned just on that scorn in him that reduced and denied his father. It made us, in a way, both fatherless. It leveled us. Now all freely I spun out the strand of love.

And tangled it curiously, a moment afterward, in the bright quick feet of the girl whose snare of kisses I had seen him ravel while I stood as witness in my dress of gold and silver, like a measure of those kisses' cost, in that midnight on the terrace.

She came running toward me down the hall; her shoes were not the same, no longer blue, and no blue strap went as isthmus across her instep now: instead an ordinary brown ribbon-bow bestrode the brown point of each darting toe. She halted, not certain of me—her berry-mouth was swelled like a pouch, full of cake; and then, when she had swallowed that obstruction down, recognizing me, it turned out it was full of a message too. "Hey!" she began. "Come on, you're wanted inside. You weren't *supposed* to be here, you know; but now he's heard you are—some little clerk told him—so of course he has to say he wants you."

"Well, thanks," I said, with a certain dryness, in no hurry now to present myself to William, no matter whether he summoned or not. His son had metamorphosed him into a stark criminality and the confrontation all at once seemed a prospect more complicated than half an hour before, when I had thought him a blameless adviser, my mother's lawyer, confidant, and even, in a blanched but lingering sense, husband.

But meanwhile William's messenger, grown suddenly lazy (or perhaps in imitation of those heroic messengers of Greek drama who, having arrived choking, breathe out the vital scene, and then collapse and die), leaned against the wall—or, rather, stood interestingly propped by a long papery tube which she thrust as a kind of supporting rod or flying buttress between her round flowered hip and the nearest vertical surface. The device, I saw in a moment, was only a rolled-up magazine; and with a childlike maneuver that was still more charming than the first, she lifted it to her eye like a telescope, let herself fall with the grace of a vivid stem against the wall, and squinted out at me. It was more startling than any open gaze she might have tried. "You don't have to tail it to him right away," she informed me while I watched her peer through her improvised hole. "He's not doing anything anyhow—just talking to a couple of men."

"I know," I said. "I saw."

"One's Connelly and one's Karp. I've been introduced to everybody!" she told me with a snicker of triumph—she clearly meant everybody important. "I might get Karp to put an ad for the Harvard Law School in the *Sport*, you know that? Anyhow I could try. *That* wouldn't be unethical, at least—for the next issue, if they don't ban it. You know they're thinking of banning the next issue?" she pressed, brisk with indignation, just as though events at Miss Jewett's occupied the universe, school facts being the world's facts. She even expected me to show my contempt for the censors, which I did, by means of the unwitting wince I gave while avoiding getting struck by her jutting scroll. "You know who Karp is? He's a *professor* up there," she went on. "So actually it wouldn't be unethical for *them* to advertise, would it?"

"But it might be unprofitable," I said mildly. "For the Law School, I mean. You don't think anyone from Miss Jewett's would apply?"

The rolled-up tube came slowly down and both her eyes looked frankly across at me. "Law's for *boys*," she told me unequivocally.

"What about Portia?"

"Who's that?"

"A famous woman lawyer," I admitted lamely.

"Look," she expostulated, "it takes brains." She was all reasonable patience. "In England they even have to wear wigs —they're all supposed to look like George Washington, don't ask me why. It's just wild! I know, I looked into the books once—half the stuff's in Spanish."

"It's not Spanish," I said. "It's Latin."

"Latin?"

"Yes."

She meditated briefly. "Ovum and Virgin," she said.

"What?"

"Ovum and Virgin," she daintily repeated. "Those are two Latin writers. We learned about them last term in Social Studies Past and Present. We had Past before gym and Present afterward."

"What about Future?" I inquired.

She answered me gravely, worried about the deficiency. "We don't have anything like that at Miss Jewett's," said she. "We have everything else, though. Maybe they give that at the Academy. They're awful sticklers there—poor Nanette even had to take algebra, you know that? I'd've died if my father'd made me go there, wouldn't you?—I mean your step-father," she corrected.

"My stepfather doesn't make me do anything," I said.

She emitted a half-envious cluck. "Lucky you—I don't get away with peanuts. They treat me like the Prisoner of Zenda, especially since all the fuss at school—you know. That's why I can't wait to get married, so I can do just as I please. When you're married no one can stop you from doing *anything*." But this seemed to remind her of something else: she picked at the cloth blossoms that grew out of her buttons and with an innocence almost clever fashioned her transition—"How come you showed up here, by the way?"

"I thought it a proper thing to congratulate William," I invented with a try at dignity.

"Why, what's he done?"

The straightforward orderliness of this question charged me with a secret mischief: what had William done! I could not get out of my head what William had done—it was all a new and horrendous gospel—it made me delay and delay. Nevertheless I was obligated to reply only to her meaning, and not to mine. "It's what his son's done," I explained. "What the party's for."

"Oh," she said dubiously, "I didn't realize you'd heard about it."

"The party? I hadn't," I confessed.

"I mean the *engagement*," she emphasized. "They *said* William would leak it to Mrs. Vand before anyone wanted him to—they're supposed to be very thick, he tells her everything, it's a shame—" She stopped herself guiltily. "Anyway they all thought you ought to be asked for today, but I couldn't see it. It's not as though you were related, or even *friends*. So then they didn't. I hope you don't mind," she ended civilly.

"I don't mind," I assured her.

"It's sort of my fault."

"It's really all right," I said, thinking her not so bad-mannered after all. Still, it was hard to forgive her; the pink flowers in her dress seemed to dance around her throat and multiplied in garlands at her knees—she swiveled her little neck and I discovered in astonishment a live tea rose dangling from a dip of hair behind her ear. "Did you help plan this? I thought the office people did it."

"Oh no," she protested, "it was my idea, the whole thing! They *paid* for it and all, but I'm the one who thought it up. It was my idea to bring down the Cabbages, anyway. The whole lot of them came down." She laughed at my incomprehension. "That's what we call our team, isn't it awful? The opposite team's Onions. And when we have a game it's called a Stew—that's all Miss Jewett's thing, it's the way it's done in England. Do you play volleyball?"

"Not much," I said.

"Really?" she exclaimed pityingly. "Don't you play anything?

"I used to."

"What?"

"The violin."

But her grimace showed how unfair this was. "What corn. I'd *die* if I had to. Nanette's got to take piano, William *makes* her."

"Maybe she likes it."

"*She* doesn't like anything but doing plays," my companion observed with a hoot of scorn. "That's why William didn't want her here today, on account óf Euphoria Karp—she bosses some sort of theatre up at Cambridge, and that Nanette! She'd badger *anybody* to death for a part. .Tears and all. You honestly wouldn't imagine a girl like that could have a halfway human brother, would you?"

"You approve of her brother," I interpreted.

"Well, why wouldn't I?" she wondered. "Ask the Cabbages! *They're* all disgustingly in love with him. He's not even handsome, you know that?"

I wretchedly obliged her: "You don't think so?"

"Oh, *I* think he's a brute, absolutely!" she flung at me with an enthusiasm so radiantly possessive it both puzzled and alarmed me. "Everybody does; don't you?"

"I agree he's halfway human," I echoed her.

She took this as she had given it—as the most sweeping praise imaginable. "Oh, I know! I adore him!" she rejoiced, letting her magazine snap down like a sprung window-shade in plain celebration. "Sometimes he can be pretty nasty, though—it might bother some people, but it doesn't bother *me*. You have to be that way if you're going into politics, like the Senate and the Board of Estimate and things. You know he might go into politics? William doesn't want him to—they never *have* in that family, except for one teeny alderman away back who doesn't count—but he'd be awfully good at it, he's got just the perfect voice for it, don't you think? And anyhow campaigning's terrific!"

And so was she; I drew back in awe. "You shouldn't call

his father 'William.' You keep saying that," I objected with all the resentfulness of an outcast whose last feeble privilege has been violated by a parody.

She stared. "What do *you* call him?"

"William," I said weakly.

"There! And you're nothing to him! —Even though everybody thinks you are."

"That doesn't justify *you*," I said.

"Oh, don't be so strict—what do you expect?" she struck back. "It's not as if he isn't practically my father-in-law already!" She indulged herself in a broad but modest preening; she peeped down the front of her dress, as though hunting for a dare. "I can call him what I please. And if I want to I'll even call him Willie!"

So I was left, after the disclosure, after, rather, the transmutation—it was quite like watching the cygnet turn into its true identity of princess—with nothing to pronounce but the blessing. "You're not the Pettigrew he's marrying," I pronounced instead, half-muffled by somber envy; "you're not the fiancée?"—not sparing myself, though sparing her: what else could the descending language of my startled melancholy be if not: Is it you? Are you the one? Not you!—still, even in my milder spoken version, showing no more than delayed perception, I felt a bungler, and overwhelmed. She had in fact moved the mountain: she was a sprite, all in flowers, all unexpectedly loosing her not-to-be-guessed-at influences, and whatever those massed circlets were in which she gleamed, lilies or pansies or some bland designer's abstract notion of a bloom, just the same she stood sheathed in them as if in instruments and magnets formidable, glancing out her fragile might.

"Well, who'd you think I was?" she demanded. "Didn't I just *tell* you I was getting married?"

"I didn't know you meant immediately. —Then the party's really yours," I concluded.

"Sure," she said. "It's tit for tat. Last time it was yours."

"This one seems more of a success," I said ruefully.

"It's because of the Cabbages—they're a riot! A while ago a bunch of 'em was trying to empty the water cooler so's to fill it with gin, did you see?"

I acknowledged that I had unfortunately missed this.

"It didn't work, though—they only got the whole back part of the floor flooded; I nearly died laughing! Did you ever see this really antique Clark Gable movie where they fill a gin bottle with water from the water cooler? You ought to, honestly, it's a scream—it's where the Cabbages got the idea, only in reverse. In the movie Clark Gable gets drunk just from *thinking* it's gin!" she shot out gloriously, and then in a darker voice, which, it struck me after a moment, was fashioned to console, began again, "Say, you want to know what was the matter with that bon voyage thing you had?"

"For one thing, there wasn't any voyage."

"Well I heard you weren't going, but that's not what I mean. It was the creepy music, right out of the Dark Ages, you know? The *band* wasn't bad, just the music. Nobody wants to dance to that stuff. That's how come it fizzled," she earnestly advised.

"I'm sorry about that," I said.

"Oh, *I* didn't mind, honestly! Because that's the night I found out," she told me suspensefully, dangling the statement for me to probe.

I went right after it, just as she wished, though wearily. "Found out what?"

"About getting married, silly! Till then I was just hoping. You saw how crazy he was about me, didn't you? I guess that nutty editor of your mother's, you know who, got him jealous, because driving home he all of a sudden said O.K., let's get *married*, for God's sake. And all I did was have one conversation with that Ed McGovern! I love to see boys get jealous," she said contentedly. "So for me that night wasn't really a fizzle, if that makes you feel any better about it. Oh come on, that's not being fair, don't look at my finger!" she cried, although I had all the while kept my eyes on my own sad wrists, one crossed over the other, "—because I don't have the ring to show yet, it's still on order. But it's absolutely fantastic—it'll *kill* the Onions!"

"Are any of them here?" I wondered.

"Any of who?"

"The Onions."

"Gosh no! We don't go to theirs and they don't come to ours. Anyway," she went on with a pleased sniff, "we're three engagements ahead of them this term—mine's the third. Didn't you see the signs? They've got Form 7 on them; that *includes* the Onions, which practically *peels* them anyhow."

"Those lapel things, do you mean? I did, but they all said Fannie, and I didn't think—"

"It's for short, like a nickname; we all have nicknames. I hate mine, but that's the idea, you're *supposed* to have a

nickname that you hate. Fannie's not so bad really, it's only
the end part of Stefanie. You know what the Onions call
Beverly Snearles, even though she's an Onion? —They call
her Reveille, isn't that wild? I mean the reason it's so funny is
because she's always late in the morning, she can't get up.
And you know poor Eleanor, who got kicked out of the Assemblies? They used to just call her El's Bells, but now since
all the fuss they call her Little Knell—with a K, like for
doom and all that!" she happily informed me.

"You all seem to have a sense of humor," I essayed.

"I know, we're a howl sometimes. Especially the Cabbages.
I mean some days we can laugh and laugh for hours."

This took from me no more than a lugubrious nod. Here
was fate arrayed and laughing, and here was fortune all smiling, quite as common speech depicts them: behold, in flutes
and flowers, William's son's lissome lot. Of myself, meanwhile, what could I gloomily think but "infelix Dido"?—out
of that poet known as Virgin to Miss Jewett's unconscious
mediaevalists. (For the Roman literati spelled it Vergil:
wasn't it the cabalistic monks who, in pious deference to their
Lady, echoed it into Virgil?) Oh, well, there—now parenthet-
ically I've shown what Stefanie Pettigrew believed of me. Not
that I stood mumbling to myself in a dead language! I only
mean that I knew acutely what she saw, that blithe girl, and
felt the soaring scorn of her half-justified assessment: myself
a mopish moralist, drab and yawning and pocked interiorly
with the mold of pedantry—while she, in contrast, petalled
all over like a paper flower-cart, or real daffodils in a trance,
leaned against that dark legal wall and lit it. The more I suspected her of holding this shrivelled image of me, the more I
pitied my standing there, starched by wonder, fixed on the single tea rose that sprang down to touch her flower-ear where
William's son had kissed. I gave myself out, then, as futility
coming before the judgment of a gleaming garden bent on no
verdict but beauty and vitality, and let down in resignation
the long, long vine of my self-grieving; I twined it all around
me, sad because I had none of that life of chatter and charm
and lyrical frivolity that splattered the corridor with ascending joyous shrieks. She was all undeliberate liquescence, a
wind on a pond, Miss Jewett's pretty Artemis, her arrow-
point nothing but the green stem of a water lily magicked
into power. "Well, if you want to hear about sense of
humor," she interposed, "you ought to come and meet Mrs.
Karp—she's a riot! I mean she writes the funniest poems—not

anything like Ed McGovern's—*you* know, just funny, about people's being sick and things. I just can't be bothered with poems," she brought out with the smile of a restless conquistador, "unless they're weird: you want to see?"

I did not; I wanted, rather, to go, but the passage was suddenly full of the flutter of the scroll's unfurling—the cover flashed by so quickly I could not tell whether it was *Harper's,* or *Harper's Bazaar,* or merely *Harps,* "the magazine for angels," the celestials being, of course, those glorious hosts of housewives who bought it. Whichever it was, the illustrious Euphoria Karp wrote for it, and in a moment, while Stefanie simpered beside me, I was staring at the wit of the wife of the Professor of Copyright:

OPERATION CYST
A GYNECOLOGICAL GARLAND OF VISCERAL VERSES

"Read it!" insisted Stefanie, and put the page firmly in my grasp. "You'll absolutely *die.* All the Cabbages did," and, so as not to survive alone in a Cabbageless world, I complied. The poem was in two parts. I read them both:

I

My life isn't as interesting as Madame Bovary's.
My trouble isn't lovers—just ovaries.
The Doctor said to Madame Bovary, "I'll kiss and squeeze ya."
The Doctor said to me, "I'll give ya anaesthesia."
Madame Bovary had a lover's tryst.
But *I* only had a cyst.

("Isn't it a *scream?*" said Stefanie.)

II

O Cyst, from thine ovarial perch descended,
Poor Cyst, arrested in thy bloom and apprehended!
Once happy parasite, no longer canst thou sit
'Mongst companion entrails, where thou wert wont to flit.
Poor abstracted Cyst! Ah, what fate could be sadder
Than to have to leave thy fellows—kidney, womb, and bladder!
But grimmest of all that heartless stroke, that sharp-edged blow
That cut thee from thy paramour—O woe!
Come, dry thy tears, good Cyst; in thy bitter grief take heart:
E'en the best of Cysts from his Ovary at length must part.
So the gods decree. Now farewell, O wistful Cyst,
Farewell—for thou never wilt be missed.
—Euphoria Karp

"I told you she's a riot!" my companion burst out as I lifted my eyes from these unusual verses. "She writes a lot of stuff like that. For all the big magazines. Once she did one on getting your arm broken and having to wear a sling, and once on a slipped disc. *That* one was an absolute howl."

"Are all her themes surgical?" I asked, not caring to dispute this literary passion. If Mrs. Karp's couplets were to be correctly classified as mock heroic, then my own heroism in having read them must be acclaimed as altogether genuine.

"I guess so. But even if they're not," said Stefanie, reluctant to disappoint, "she's practically famous anyhow, on account of *Skunk on Sundays*—that's a book she did once. It's supposed to be hilarious: even our school library has it."

"Writing a book doesn't necessarily make you famous," I countered. "My mother wrote one years ago. It was a bestseller but it didn't make her famous."

"Except in Russia. In Russia they even write *articles* about your mother's book. I've heard all about that."

"You have?" I exclaimed.

"Sure! What d'you think William's talking to Karp about? Come on, I'll show you," and she led me away, marching gaily ahead of me with her rolled-up magazine stabbing the air like a baton and her remarkable little feet spurning the carpet beneath them.

A morose curiosity made me keep up with her. We raced past all the secretarial nooks and dashed over the threshold of the clamorous room where the festive talkers swarmed; but no sooner had we plunged into the margins of the throng than the Cabbages converged. "Gimpy's looking for you, Fannie," said one; "Knell said you'd gone to the head; I told Beets no one was in there but some little coolie with a comb," insisted another, "and so you missed the best thing. You'll never guess!"

"You got the gin in the cooler," Stefanie guessed.

"Lordy, you're off the track! —Hoofy found a contraband Onion!"

"No! That's nerve! Which one was it?"

"Of all people, fat little Silverpants. She came right in and walked straight up to your fiancé and said she was from Miss Jewett's and her name was Sylvia Prantz and as a friend of the future bride she wanted to congratulate him—"

"What gall!" yelled half the Cabbages.

"Friend!" yelled the other half in disdain.

"—and so he actually shook *hands* with her," the narrator

concluded indignantly. "Hoofy saw the whole thing from start to finish."

"No kidding! What'd she *do?*"

"Quick called a war council. With everybody looking we couldn't throw her *out,* so Stookie said did she want some cake and old Silverpants said sure, and Stookie said well, there's none left out there and the rest's in *there,* through that door, come on, and bang! locked her up."

"Locked her *up!*" Stefanie squealed. "Where?"

"Right there," said one of the meeker Cabbages, pointing to a door. "She's been quiet as a mouse all the time. She's a good prisoner all right."

"Last time they caught one of *us* was at Toodles' Christmas thing, remember? When that New Haven creep threw up?"

"*You're* the morbid one, Hoofy," protested a very long Cabbage. "They nearly tossed me out the window. If Stookie hadn't called the Fire Department they would've, too."

"Good old Stookie!" applauded all the Cabbages together; it made a wondrous roar, into which Stefanie herself disappeared, while the room revolved its multiple head to see what it was all about; and William, who was far off under a window, turned too, and gravely took my glance.

I had to go to him, then, and made my way through Cabbages and clerks and novice lawyers and finally an unexpected puddle which the broadloom was wearily soaking up, to where solemn William glowered. "Water in the rug," I said with a try at a pleasantry, "has there been an accident with the water cooler?"

"Not an accident," he said grimly, and introduced me to his confederates.

There were three: Connelly; Professor Karp; and, thin as a crane, behind a ruffled jabot like a crane's breast, Euphoria Karp.

"I've just had a look at a poem of yours," I told the third. "I heard you're giving one to my mother, for *Bushelbasket.* I'm sure she's very grateful."

Mrs. Karp's teeth stood rapt. "It's the one about the placebo, yes, I couldn't sell it anywhere though it's very comical so when William mentioned it I thought it would be a nice gracious thing to oblige Mrs. Vand with it. She does so much for art."

"Well, so does she," said Professor Karp, explaining with a lift of his chin that he referred to his wife.

"Oh, not like Mrs. Vand. I'm not a philanthropist like Mrs. Vand."

"She's an organizer," her husband revised, still meaning Mrs. Karp.

"Euphoria has a hand in the New England Verse Theatre," William elucidated with a certain abstractness.

"You're very old-fashioned about actresses, William," Mrs. Karp chided him. "If you weren't I'd insist that Nanette come to us. She has a flair, you can't deny it."

"*I* call it the Worse Theatre," said Karp. "I prefer prose."

"There's nothing wrong with amateurs," Mrs. Karp said quickly. "Oh, that's an unpardonable quip, isn't it? And William didn't catch it anyhow. Pros—professional actors, you see?"

William murmured, "Oh, yes, I see."

—Whereupon Connelly gave a dour little laugh: a pond rippling obediently to the stroke of William's dropped pebble.

"But we weren't talking theatre, we were talking about the government," Mrs. Karp continued fluently. William clasped and unclasped his hands, and Professor Karp, noting this, momentarily shut his eyes in the plain hope that it would somehow initiate a similar action of his wife's mouth. It did not. "Mr. Connelly is very shrewd about taxes. Accountants are the poets of the Sixteenth Amendment, you know. They had a sort of instinct," she remarked, giving Connelly a wink of brilliant mischief.

The subject of her praise drew in so full a sigh that it puckered his melancholy forehead: if he had not already been created a man, he would certainly have been in that instant a veritable bulldog. His almost vertical little ruby-dark nostrils looked healthily moist. "The government is Bolshevik," he stated at last. "Doesn't make any difference, Republicans, Democrats. Tax the rich to keep the poor."

"Is that Lenin or Robin Hood?" Mrs. Karp wanted to know, disposing of her husband's hasty frown.

But Connelly had a notable frown of his own; it made him seem more anxious than ever. "The poor deserve their situation. People keep forgetting that," he said strictly. "The rich work for their money."

This was so indiscriminate a contradiction of what I had already learned of the world that I had to dissent. "My mother doesn't though."

"Your mother's money works for her; it's quite the same thing," he answered, not in the least discomfited. "It's not

taxation I object to, mind you, it's confiscation. They don't
tax in Washington any more, you know. They gave up taxes
years ago. They just take it all away. That's the opinion of
this office, and we've had the experience to back it," he said,
offering his round head to his employer's support like an austere pedestal looted of its fretwork.

William, however, just then showed no velleity to be identified with that establishment, ruined, as he must have thought,
by rivers of youths; instead he at once inquired how my
mother was.

"All her hair fell out," I said.

He nodded sadly; he knew it already. "Her so attractive
hair," he said, contemplating it. "Your mother is a great
beauty," he told me earnestly, as though reciting a Commandment which he feared any one of his listeners might im-
minently violate.

"A very handsome woman," Connelly piously rejoined.
"Her investments are striking. I can take no exception to any
of them. Though I didn't see the point," he added with a
touch of censure, "of Michigan Laminated."

"Good Lord!" said Mrs. Karp. "What a terrible thing to do
to Michigan."

"Beg pardon?"

"Laminating it. It can't be comfortable living there any
more."

Connelly exposed his feeble reluctant smile; the small tidy
squares of his dentures had a canine aspect, hiding a growl.
"Oh, yes, I see"—a fair rendition of William's tone, though a
shade more aloof.

Mrs. Karp nevertheless was constrained to take it as a
compliment to her wit. She took it, moreover, as applause,
and even seemed to hear in it cries of Encore, which she at
once set out to satisfy. "It's impossible to quarrel with your
views, Mr. Connelly, so long as they don't contradict Scrip-
ture. 'Blessed are the poor in spirit' is one thing; it doesn't say
'Blessed are the poor in investments,' after all, does it? And
as regards the unlikelihood of a rich man's entering the Kingdom of Heaven, well, you know, a camel *can* go through a
needle's eye. All that's required is a big enough needle. I suppose Michigan Laminated manufactures them?"

Connelly's grudging grace vanished and left a smear of distaste on his lip. "I'm afraid I can't pretend to speak for the
Church," he said sternly.

"Then speak for yourself."

"Not on a moral question."

"Very well. Then do let's discuss an immoral one."

"Now Euphoria," said Karp, out of desperation resorting to direct address.

"Now Jerome," mocked his wife.

"You don't want to navigate in muddy waters," he warned.

"Don't I? But it depends which way the wind blows my sails. I've got no independent volition in these matters—I'm just like Mr. Connelly. I check everything with 'Rome."

"Can't we leave Rome out of it?" Connelly said in a hurt voice.

"Oh, I wouldn't think of it. After twenty years of marriage? Not on your life! Besides, 'Rome has all the power in the world; he makes the first-year students tremble."

"Oh look," William said with a wretched display of gravity, "she only means her husband, you know."

"Oh—yes, I see," Connelly said again, but weakly. "How amusing."

"Euphoria is a very amusing manipulator," Karp grumbled —was it out of self-defense?—"of wit."

"Yes indeed," his wife confessed. "I'm a po-wit in fact."

"Specializing in witty lines on Poe?" I wondered coarsely.

She turned on me in delight. "I never thought of that! How charming of you; I must use it somehow. You know I adore puns. And more than that I adore puns on puns— they're even rarer. I do so appreciate people who have a sensitivity to humor. They're so few. But I really ought to be able to make something of that—" Her active clever eyes with their faint tendency to bulge, exaggerated this proclivity; she plainly strained: her moment was upon her, and loudly, rapidly, precisely, and without a single intake of breath she rattled out the following:

> Edgar Allan Poe
> Died of drink, you know.
> He lived his life in squalor
> And never had a dollar,
> Which news by word of mouth
> Reached the Deepest South
> Where they maintained it wasn't gin
> That did him in—
> "He sho'ly daid
> Cuz he war *po'*," they said.

"Good Christ!" Connelly pealed out in an access of amazement.

"Don't let it bother you, she does it all the time," Karp said, embarrassed. "It's really nothing to be perturbed about. She can't help it. She just happens to have that sort of brain."

"But it's not *good,*" Mrs. Karp said peevishly. "I don't like it. It's not worth writing down; it's not funny enough, is it, 'Rome? I mean it's too tritely philosophical: it only makes that silly old point about character being fate, did you catch that, William? And then all that build-up just for the play-on-words at the end."

"I'm afraid I can never understand dialect," he apologized; his ears were vaguely pink, and I pitied him.

"You mean you disapprove of it," said Mrs. Karp. "I believe you're a liberal after all, William."

"Now, now, no name-calling," Connelly said; this was *his* little joke, and he indulged himself in a marginal laugh, like the creasing of tinfoil, which no one shared, though Mrs. Karp looked ready to put her tongue out at him.

Nevertheless she refrained, and instead wagged it for another purpose: "Tell me, do you help out with *Bushelbasket?*" she asked me. "No? What a shame, I've got a revision of the placebo thing in my bag—that's the one I've already sent to your mother's editor, you see; I thought you might take the new version with you, to hand over to him. It's ever so much better now, you know."

"It's twice as long," Karp sighed.

"Which logically makes it twice as good," Mrs. Karp took up stoutheartedly. "Would you mind delivering it?"

"Not at all," I said, "except that he's in San Francisco."

"Who do you say is in San Francisco?" William demanded, suddenly attentive.

"Ed McGovern. My mother's editor. She gave him a check and he went."

"What the devil for?"

"I don't know. To spend it, I guess."

"To freshen his point of view, you might put it," Mrs. Karp said helpfully.

"Wastrel," Connelly muttered, with a quick peep at William. "Parasite."

"Printing costs are so high," Mrs. Karp added; she was, on principle, admirably pumping up the conversation. "I hear your mother saves on capital letters."

"She leaves them out," I admitted. "Commas too."

"How economical!" Mrs. Karp marveled. "Though I hope it won't harm the placebo," and reached into her big deep pocketbook, thick with scraps of paper, wherefrom, as though it were a pickle, she unerringly picked her poem.

I took it and saw that it was very narrow and very long. "My mother's favorite shape in a poem," I remarked out of politeness.

"Oh, 'Rome, you hear that, isn't that fine? It's Mrs. Vand's favorite poem! In that case she's sure to care for the new version, don't you think?"

"That McGovern fellow," Connelly interrupted crossly, brooding. "She pays plenty for him. Well, look at it this way: it's one of her questionable investments, same as Michigan Laminated. That's the only way to look at it."

"It's one of her pleasures," William corrected: which startled Connelly, who at once began to cast around for a qualification that would not sound directly like an apology.

"There's no money in pleasure," was all he came up with on short notice.

Mrs. Karp could not permit so manifest an opportunity to go by unpounced-upon. "But there's lots of pleasure in money!" she cried, and looked to me to join her in her gratification. "That's what wit *is*," she explained civilly; somehow she had taken me for her partner in metaphysics. "You have to seize on every chance. You have to *listen*. You know most people don't listen, not even to themselves. It's what leaves them wide open to becoming someone else's butt. That's why I always make a point of listening to myself."

"Sometimes you're the only one who does," said her husband.

Meanwhile I occupied myself with an investigation of William. The presence of the Karps, teasing around him like a school of carnivorous fish (only afterward did I suppose that the name had supplied the image: watching them, I simply derived it from the way they kept him cornered at the bottom of their part of the ocean, a place unfamiliar—too warm, perhaps—to his cool kind), rejoiced him so little that he had no disposition to feel anger at me. Though earlier I might have counted myself lucky in this, it struck me now that he was not merely "behaving well," as I had expected of him: he was hardly aware that I was there. He looked at me, and thought all the while of my mother—but not because I had come as a reminder. On the contrary, my mother was the substance of the Karps' surveillance. "About this Russian business," he said abruptly to Professor Karp, cutting Euphoria off without realizing he was doing it. She stood with her

long, meagre-gummed teeth glistening, eager to oblige him by
withdrawing—as some fish swim backwards momentarily before darting out for a bite of their victim's side. *"About* this
Russian business," he began, and Connelly pressed in, making
the circle tight against women and children: they talked of
visas, and officials, and then of "prospects" which Connelly
said were unfavorable until William said well, it couldn't be
predicted in advance—"oh," said Connelly then, "I don't
predict, I go by what's been the case for the last two decades," while Karp worked the two parallel ditches between
his eyes. William had endured trivialities long enough, apparently; he was after the issue, and could not bear the boredom
of the dance on either side of it and all around it. It *was* of
my mother they were talking, it developed in fact—of her
unpaid Russian royalties. I was surprised, though Stefanie
had warned me of it. "Out-and-out thieves," Connelly put it
without extenuation: but William listened steadfastly to
Karp. They spoke of the formation of a Commission. "Five
of us," Karp said. "In a quiet way. The lot that went over
last year made too much noise. You can't have an ex-candi-
date for the Presidency, lawyer or no lawyer, do this sort of
thing. It's got to be quiet and obscure, no known names,
nothing political, just plain lawyerlike negotiation—" Connelly asked what the money would be, in the aggregate.
"Well, we'd have to see what their terms are, after all. What
percentage they'd be willing to agree to. I wouldn't expect it
to correspond with their domestic practise." William said he
thought not. "Though I didn't get you down here for details,"
he murmured; "only for the general question. Pity it had to
be just today, in the middle of all this—" He waved a hand
of despair and censure into limitless fields of light overgrown
with Cabbages: the despair was for these, but the disapproval
was for Karps. "The young people," he said, somewhat more
loudly, noticing me as though I were a footnote authenticat-
ing this explanation.

But Karp loftily disagreed. "I'm afraid Mrs. Vand *is* a detail. You don't want to expect anything special. In a thing
like this there can't be special cases. All we can hope for is to
soften them a bit; to get them to acknowledge that we *have* a
moral case. We can't even begin to expect them to acknowledge the International Copyright Convention, God knows.
They translate everything and pay for nothing," he said, di-
recting this at Connelly, who looked first miffed and then
puffed with an interior monologue which the eager twitch of

his nose betrayed—he was only an accountant, and in the presence of lawyers he always felt patronized; all of this his damp nostrils seemed to signal, opening and shutting like flexible quotation marks. His nostrils, in short (though they were long), quoted his thoughts, and his thoughts were envious and scornful: lawyers believe in money and credit the way boys believe in kites—not as the very pillars of the world upon which the angels of Christ rest their elbows. Widening pridefully, narrowing aristocratically, those twin Celtic holes enclosed their final musing. "Talk to pirates about moral cases!" he said aloud, though his nose, rising as his large skull dispiritedly ascended, insisted he needed no elucidations— they might talk of copyrights if they wished, or of morality: *he* knew they were talking of cash.

So did shrewd Mrs. Karp. "And if you're not going for Mrs. Vand, what *are* you going for?"

"The principle," Karp said.

"Oh, the principle! The principle's nothing!" she contributed smugly. "William didn't ask you to come down for the principle, did you, William?" But she was too hurried to wait to hear. "And if we'd come down yesterday—it's *my* fault we're a day late; I admit to it; I made 'Rome stay for last night though he whimpered all through it—a regular cry of pain," she joked. "We put on a perfectly marvelous comedy at the Verse Theatre, all in quatrains, half of them composed by yours truly, you see; that's why. It was the premiere, if that isn't a misnomer for a one-night stand. The setting was a spaceship headed for another solar system—a sort of up-to-date *Everyman*; at any rate if we'd come down yesterday I never would have gotten my revision of the placebo into properly appreciative hands. You're just clutching it," she admonished me, looking to see whether my hands *were* properly appreciative; "aren't you going to *read* it?"

"Oh yes," I said weakly, damning her for her interruption; I was interested in Karp. He had quick unusual gestures; he liked to pat down his bold hair, and now and then he put a narrow forefinger to the side of his head, as though listening to the pulse there, or the machinery of his brain. It was easy to see that he respected that machinery, and ran it at its highest efficiency, without taxing it or abusing a single notch of its gears; also he respected it the way a man on a ladder respects the rungs that separate him from the hard ground; and in spite of his wife, he took one rung, or one notch, at a time. "I'll enter Mrs. Vand on our book-list, certainly," he as-

sured William; this was as far as he could carry the favor, he
implied. Though he gave himself out as acting only out of
principle, his manner contradicted him. His moving hands
responding to himself, even his captious but cautious face
with its slowly sliding eyes, seemed to expose something else
in him—principle, to be sure, but smaller principle, a sly
sharp private principle that he kept for himself, for his own
advancement. I all at once remembered my mother's remark
—they had dropped Karp from *Who's Who*. He was now
merely in the Index of Former Biographees, or however it
was designated, though when I looked it up afterward I discovered that fleshly red book both too polite and too brutal
for such an Index: instead they had tacked near Karp's bare
name a circle-within-a-circle, ominously reminiscent of Dante
—in this way, hushed, clean-handed, they consigned Karp to
the hell of the No Longer Prominent. He had ceased to be
important, and in order to be re-included had to build again.
So he was once more impatiently building, went down to
Yale for luncheon with the dean while Euphoria set herself
up for the afternoon like an influential icon among the drama
aspirants and the homely playwrights, and all in all collected
his bricks from the best quarries. The going-to-Russia Committee was very good, very fine, a bit obscure, but he had already made a virtue of that: he had the obscurity, he had the
machinery, the problem was entirely within his expertise;
membership in the Committee was excellent, they were all
five of them enterprising and scholarly. I sensed Karp's opportunistic calculation, against William's solid beating, that
he regarded William as his veritable keystone. William in
conjunction with the Committee!—I saw him feel for his
high dark hair with a nervous claw of knuckle, conscious already of laurel. Though he did not cosset, like that sad dog
Connelly, still he was justified in thinking of William as a sort
of trophy—it was William who had come to Karp, and not
the other way around. And it gilded his power that, distinctly
as it was worth his while to undertake a favor for William, it
was all really out of his hands: performing the favor was not
equivalent to granting the boon, which lay, abstractly and
only in conjecture, with some mustached, burly-cheeked
board of officials in Moscow. He might be the most vigorous
advocate ever to bombard that board; still, if on political
grounds they were beyond persuasion, he was helpless—the
caprice, or call it policy, of unknown men governed all. This
was delightful; it put Karp in the delicious position of disap-

pointing William while seeming with all his might to be working to satisfy him: it was very like the sympathetic pride of the court physician who must tell the king he is incurable —the diagnostician wears the purple then. For the man whom glory nurtures, when alas for him he is born alien to the ruling blood of the province, a chink into the throne-room can be found: if he would have his elbows rub nobler elbows, let him, half by imitation and intuition, and half by bribery, become a courtier. Clearly this was Karp's way. He coveted William—I mean he coveted him socially: a dinner party at the house in Scarsdale with William's Groton intimates and their unimaginable wives (how Karp longed to see whether Euphoria approximated these!—he had chosen her because he thought she did, but surely *they* did not commit verses—or, if she did not approximate them, he hoped to learn how, with a little coaching and no coaxing, she, a will-ing mimic, might be transformed)—this discouraging com-monplace was Karp's Eden. If William knew, he had no call to practise, the democracy of, say, a university circle (where-in Karp hobnobbed with a high administrator descended from Jonathan Edwards and a bright teaching assistant three years past twenty who was great-grandnephew to Woodrow Wilson); and this exactly, that he denied his cozier self, was William's allure, for Karp held that democracy cheap. He craved no entry where entry was generous, and it was plain in his tone that all the fraternal liberties and splendors of Harvard and Yale and even recalcitrant Princeton moved him not so much as a single tremor of approval in the eyelid of caste-iron William.

Caste-iron: how Euphoria Karp would have rejoiced in this equivoque!—which, for I do not wish to plagiarize, I had, even while I said it to myself, to credit to a gravely Utopian page in *Marianna Harlow.* In Russian, I observed, the pun must have been lost together with the royalties, and so I turned to ask in a voice that—since it sounded briskly to-the-point while not being on the point at all—might almost have been Mrs. Karp's: "It's not for literature you're going?"

"Well yes; why not for literature?" Karp said, taken by surprise. "It isn't just Mrs. Vand. It's Faulkner and Heming-way too. It's everyone."

But so far William's hallowed eyelid remained unblinkingly rigid. "What has literature got to do with it? I hope you're not thinking of going all the way to Russia for the sake of a frivolity," he said sternly. Each conscientious sentence emerged as cautiously and absolutely as a chess move; it was not the Castle (wherein gaudy sinners pursued their own amusement) William put forward, but rather the somber-visaged Bishop (the Bishop, it might be noted, on the Right). "If the Administration were paying for the trip I assure you I wouldn't expect better—only last month they sent some foolish pieces on tour, abroad, full of holes and deformities, sculpture, they call it—a quarter-of-a-million-dollars' worth of exhibiting to the world how we make monkeys of ourselves. All right, but if we're putting up the money privately, it's not to finance a depravity, it's for results, it's not for the flowers that bloom in the spring. It's for the royalties they've cheated her of."

"They've cheated all the others too," Karp said, downed by discontent and deprivation—he had not expected he would be called upon to argue. "The list we've prepared shows some very distinguished authors."

"Don't talk to me about your list. Your list means nothing to me. The point is there's no one on it who has her sales over there."

"She goes like hotcakes over there," Connelly morosely supplied.

"Russian hotcakes?" quipped Mrs. Karp, brightly blazing, and paying strict attention once again. "You mean Mrs. Vand's novel sells like *blini?* That's Russian for—"

But no one seemed entertained by this demonstration of the resources of linguistic humor—so, out of charity, before she had it all out I gave her a smile, for which I imagined I would have to pay sooner or later. From fellowship Mrs. Karp exacted more fellowship. "—for hotcakes," she finished doggedly.

Still, all this was behind the scenes, as it were; for meanwhile William had not paused. "I ought to say that the book itself is not at issue. I never thought anything of it. I can't claim that I've ever read it. I was never an admirer of its political tone," he said tautly; "but I haven't read your Faulkner and Hemingway either, and I don't intend to. When I want a taste of fiction I go to the newspapers and look at the editorials. Your 'distinguished authors' may be better writers than poor Allegra—though candidly and logically I don't believe there can be better or worse in nonsense and vice—but they can't have better sales. The fact is it's her sales I'm concerned with, not her book. She's been at the very top over there for a generation. The book itself is a puerile outrage. Which says something for the Russian public."

"Well, people tend to forget," Connelly embroidered with a pugnacious scowl of irrelevant wisdom. "They forget how Rosy-velt tried to pack the Court."

This counterpoint did not perturb Karp; he kept his gaze on William. He was not essentially interested in literature, or in royalties, or in Connelly. He was interested in what interested William. He saw that Connelly, who was generally flexible but not noteworthily intelligent, and who was in his more primitive fashion what Karp was himself—a fawner—did not interest William, whereas Mrs. Vand did. "The political tone?" he asked, though he was not essentially interested in politics either.

"They read her like a sentimental tract," William confirmed. "I'm told they read her in the high schools. She's the Soviet *Uncle Tom's Cabin*—it can't be helped, though it's a terrible pity. I admit to feeling a patriotic shame over it. I happen to regard it as an immense scandal, but it doesn't change the fact that she's entitled to her royalties."

"She's not a sympathizer?"

"She grew out of it," William said curtly.

"The country didn't," Connelly complained. "Bolshevik ideas even in the Republican Party, right today. They put the New Dealers out of office but kept the New Deal, so what's the gain?"

"I'm talking about Allegra," William said angrily. "I always knew she would grow out of that stupidity. She never had anything in common with it."

It startled me to hear from William so public a private declaration. Embarrassment had wrung it from him, and I discerned that, for the sake of regaining Allegra Vand's lost royalties, he was in the process of negotiating much more than it seemed on the surface; he was exposing himself, and bartering his exposure. His very negotiation seemed to support what he abhorred, even in memory—my mother's wild long-ago days; yet the more he expressed his abhorrence—so as not to appear to have partaken in her shame—the more he propelled himself into the unchivalrous appearance of proclaiming that shame. Conceit for his soul's condition and loyalty to my undeserving mother puffed his clean jaw with unendurable contradictions, and I recognized in poor proud William his old, sad, foolish affliction regarding Allegra Vand: *odi et amo*—or, if that is too classically burning

for such a disciplined heart as William's, say instead that he
suffered from a wound which had been suppurating for an
eternity, only because he would let no one (not himself, not
even, with all her fastidiousness and love of gardens, his
wife) bandage it.

His avowal made me meditate. "If you always knew it," I
said slowly, astonished to hear myself speak it out, "why
didn't you wait?"

"Wait for what?" Connelly asked, more callous than inquisitive.

"For the stupidity to end."

William closed his eyes.

"For her to grow out of it," I persisted, conscious of my
daring.

He opened them again, but not at me. His narrow look
pursued detachment. "You can tell your mother," he coolly
directed me, "that the Russian business is underway. It's
going to be taken care of."

"That's right, tell her William's hooked Karp," said Euphoria, demonstrating her special wink.

But William's hook dangled nakedly. It was not Karp he
was after. "Tell your mother," he said again, setting his bait,
"that the Commission will do much more than merely put
her at the top of its booklist."

"We'll do what we can, you know," Karp said.

"Tell her," William said, "that she's going to get a quite
distinct recognition. Professor Karp will acknowledge that
she *is* a special case," he said, "he'll insist on it, you see," he
said, turning to me at last, but only to avoid Karp. "So you
can tell her it's more or less settled. I'll be coming up to see
her myself in the next week or two—no, later: after your
stepfather's hearing. I'd rather not thrust this Russian business at her just now when she's concerned with the other—
it's an issue that's always gotten her I think dispropor-
tionately excited. Well, and no wonder," he expanded while
Karp watched him with the contempt of a man who when
rebuffed grows suddenly cruel, "she's keen on justice, she's always been keen on justice. Then you'll get it for her, Jerome?" he plainly commanded.

Not Karp but his wife answered—like a jester, she saw her
task as requiring her to jump in with praise for her lord in
the very moment of his humiliation. What she chose to praise
was his cruelty. "Oh you don't have to worry about 'Rome,
believe me! They had their chance once before to say no over

there; they won't say it again though, I can promise you that
—'Rome never gives anyone a second chance! Never, never.
He always attains justice because he never bothers with mercy—as a policy it's incredibly efficient. Imagine," she
laughed, "how many lives of freshmen he's blighted just on
account of being keen on justice himself! Freshmen *and* their
wives—freshmen in law school *all* have wives nowadays,
they're absolutely rampant, they even have to have them organized in clubs," she gratuitously informed us, valuing all
fact equally, "but you see what to Mrs. Vand is only an emotion is to 'Rome a working system, there's the difference. So
if his system can break the heads of freshmen, just think
what it'll do to the Kremlin! 'Rome never gives *anyone* a second chance," she finished with a shake of her ruffles.

Professor Karp tried to look modest through this discourse,
quite as though he did not wish to appear really as vain-
glorious as Euphoria described him; or perhaps he only thought
his wife talked too much. He had, nevertheless, nothing more
to say; and neither, it turned out, did William, who was at
that moment unexpectedly distracted by a particular screech,
higher and wilder than its companion-cries, which flew soaring across the room out of the throat of his daughter-in-law-
to-be. He bent his head with melancholy. "Your poor
mother," he murmured, and I thought it irrelevant to anything but the contents of his own mind until it came to me
that this radiant halloo (it had to do, apparently, with the
continuing political strategy of victorious Cabbages versus
captive Onion) which had no intellectual meaning but was
instead an open and joyous ringleader call of judgment on the
world that a bird in its simplicity might make upon the crimson cherry-bough—Stefanie's bright voice—reminded him
not of his son's misfortune but of his own youth.

"Then it's settled," he repeated to Karp; "you'll let me
know the date you fly," and Karp knew he would never see
the inside of the Scarsdale house, or the wives of the grown
Groton lads: William had summoned him not for himself,
but only for his usefulness; only for the blade of his brain,
and for the clever sheath of vanity that covered his merciless-
ness, though both had been honed in competition with men
better-born than he, men who were named for the dales and
fields and rills of a *place*, and not for the homeless landless
scavenger fish; William esteemed nothing in Karp, nothing,
only what was exploitable and at the same time execrable, as
though Karp were a mediaeval money-lender: only what

would bring about the satisfaction of the whim of Allegra
Vand, which he desired—why?

Because he remembered still the curious gathered-up
laughter of her girlhood—my mother's cry: that rod of white
fire with which she had struck him when she fled the house in
Scarsdale: which Karp was never to enter.

So Karp and I had *that* in common, though a negative, and
for reasons not different. Karp, however respectable his origins, had been in William's view born to the wrong father;
and so had I. In spite of it I sided with William against him,
and not only out of habit. I did not like him. I did not like
his wife. These two were proud. They were proud that Karp
had no compassion; that he oppressed the hearts and sped
and bled the years of young men and their brides; that like
fate he spited hope; that he used authority not for order, but
for a whip, to assure himself of his importance. They were
proud, they thought themselves important; pride and importance swelled and swaggered in their unextraordinary faces;
and strangely I felt a sorrow for their sorrow and their delu-
sion. How hopeless to yearn after William's tea-table!—William who by inheritance and conviction was, hence never
troubled to denote himself, "important." How like a pair of
voyeurs they seemed! And so they stood mutely pealing wanting and woe, while William looked past them, stiff as a figure
on a bow with wooden arms posed behind his back, thinking
out toward the horizon, himself wormy with impossible long-
ings, and these two below him not understanding that he had
ceased to see them. Whereas Connelly, the practised-perfect
acolyte, was already moving off, intuiting without having
been directly told when his duty was over. He showed, as he
drifted away, a sense of ceremony; his very physiognomy displayed it; ritually his retreating little ears continued to wait,
segregated like very pale mushrooms a decent distance to the
sides of his wide wet eyes. The meticulous accountant meandered, then stopped a far but fealty-filled space from his master, a lonesome squat man who crumpled his big square forehead and would not drink: odd duck, Irish teetotaler, who
had given up liquor perhaps in imitation of William, perhaps
for some private tragic cause he kept to himself, a sort of
atonement—his sister was a nun.

Meanwhile Euphoria Karp. Her husband brooded, imagining Moscovite revenge. Not she. "Aren't you going to read
the placebo?" Her mouth jagged with charm, she pressed me

for my promise. "Read it. Don't keep it from William—I mean read it aloud!"

And because I hardly knew whom to pity more in that company—the silenced Karp or this voluble Karp; the meticulous accountant divided between practical worship of Protestant success and romantic musing reverence for the other older success of the Eternal City; or William my almost-father, who would gladly have unstitched his central organ from his unhappy ribs to appease my mother for his having solemnly determined, after many and bitter trials, that she would not Do—wretched for their wretchedness I fell into an earnest confusion and obeying thin Euphoria I read aloud her Revised Version with as much incomprehension as I would have felt had I been adjured, then and there, to recite from Koheleth the Preacher. As I have said, this poem of hers was shaped like a tube, through which bravely I began to blow.

OWED TO THE PLACEBO

("Ho ho," said Mrs. Karp. "Tell them how it's spelled! O-w-e-d, not o-d-e. And don't go calling it doggerel, William—it's too frisky. If you must, call it pupperel. Ho ho, ho ho.")
And I said into the air what I saw:

> All hail to the placebo,
> The mild, delightful, effective placebo!
> Sing hoo, sing ray,
> Sing night, sing day,
> Sing while sitting in the latticed gazebo,
> Sing while with alpenstock upón Mount Nebo;
> Laurels and praise to the wondrous placebo!
> Though the placebo is a pill
> For the not-so-ill,
> It must never occasion your mirth.
> Small is its girth
> Yet what on earth
> From desert to firth
> Can boast the worth
> Of this radiant pill
> For the not-so-ill?
> This homely, familiar, not in the *least* exotic
> Device for the not-very-sick-but-somewhat-neurotic—

("Did your mother's hair really fall out? All of it?" Euphoria, though enraptured, allowed herself to break in.
"A lot of it did," I answered.

"Poor woman! Suffering from one of the ills that mortals fall hair to. Ho ho!" said Euphoria. "Don't stop, don't stop. There's more to read. Ho ho!")

I read grimly on.

There are pills which are drugs which have plenty of power
But when you eat them, alas, their taste is sour,
They give you a frown and a scowl and a glower.
But the sweet placebo makes nobody cower!
Of invisible strength it's a veritable tower!
How sly the placebo, how subtly deceiving:
It only pretends, but succeeds, in relieving,
For its recondite force, whether medical or dental,
Lies just in this fact: that it's nothing but mental.
If we hadn't the placebo for the hypochondriacal
The whole world would soon go quickly maniacal!
So you patients who are found to be fit as a fiddle,
You patients whose ailment's an insoluble riddle,
You patients neurotic, sulky, and cranky,
Give thanks for this medical hanky-panky!
And sing hoo, sing ray,
Sing night, sing day—

There was more, much more, and a whole column of even more ingenious rhymes, but here I not so much rebelled as faltered, having observed William in the act of unleashing his locked hands.

He spoke.

"Goodbye." he said to Euphoria Karp.

"Goodbye?"

"It was good of you to bring Jerome up here in the middle of all this. In spite of everything it's been fruitful, fruitful."

"It's been peachy," winked Euphoria.

Professor Karp led her away like a hangman dedicated to his work.

And William spoke again.

"Your mother's all right?"

Apparently he had forgotten that he had already asked this. "She coughs now and then," I said.

"But she *is* much better."

I nodded. "She even comes out on the terrace now."

"I'm glad to hear it. Though she mustn't be careless, you know. I hope she isn't planning to go down to Washington for that hearing?" I admitted I knew of no such scheme. "Those hearings can be nasty," he continued. "It won't do **her** any good down there."

"I thought it was open and shut. I thought all they had to do was confirm Enoch's appointment."

William's eyelid flickered for me, as it had not for Karp. "That's right," he said.

"Then why do you say nasty?"

"It's in the nature of politics," was all he would yield, and offered nothing more. His look hardened, quite as if not biological tears but a sort of chemical lacquer brushed his stare, and he listened once more to the voice of his daughter-in-law.

This reminded me of the duty of civility. "I've just learned about your son and Miss Pettigrew. How wonderful."

"Thank you, yes, wonderful," he lugubriously acknowledged it. "A charming child. Vivacious."

But he did not wish to be drawn into talk of his son. He was silent, and simply waited.

He waited: for me. And so, because I could think of nothing further to delay the moment of confrontation, I had to begin. "I came to see you," I finally undertook it.

"Obviously"—but he did not mock.

"I hope you don't mind. It's not a terribly convenient time—"

William did not palliate these excuses by dismissing them.

"—but I had no idea there was a celebration."

He answered with a mutter.

"What?" I said, straining.

"Your mother," he said again, in so low a tone I scarcely heard, "doesn't know you're here."

"No."

He appeared neither angry nor not-angry. He was controlled; more, he was indifferent. "I thought not," he said merely.

"I'm going away in two days."

"I suppose you are."

"To a place—it's a house, I don't know, Duneacres it's called. It's a place on an island."

"Yes," he said patiently.

"My father is there—it's where my father is. They're sending me to my father," I burst out. "My mother and Enoch."

"I see." He took me by the elbow. It was a spontaneous motion. In all my life before, except in a formal clasp. I had never felt William's hand.

"It's to see my father," I explained. "And they tell me nothing. They won't speak of it."

"Come," William said.

"I want to understand," I pressed on; "and they won't speak of it."

"Oh: understand"—as though understanding were nothing.

"I mean"—I half-pleaded and half-insisted—"I mean I need to *know*."

"Come," William repeated, exactly as his son had done earlier, expecting me to follow. In this they were alike, equally imperious, and each had a stride (William's less vigorous, a little elderly, not from physical weariness so much as from the moral fatigue of continuous authority)—a condescending stride dedicated to isolating an intention. I walked obediently after him along the periphery of the wide and tumbled room where already the dark purplish-gold of a late-summer late-afternoon was wearing down the flung energies of gaiety, and the noise as we passed through it seemed, though less abundant, shriller, blade grating on blade, until we came to a shadowed corner and a door.

The back of a metal office chair was jammed tightly under the knob.

"Good Lord," William said, growing redder, "what the devil is it now? There's no limit to it," and briefly tugged. The two rear legs of the angled chair screeched along the floor, fighting tautly for release, and toppled free with a high metallic clatter, like an armored knight clumsily unhorsed and clanging in a forest. A sharp corner, breaking the air, struck William; he bent with a wince over his stunned knee. Meanwhile all around the outer room those startled celebrants surrendered to a hush of watching, and shook themselves down into a staring assembly rooted on the mysterious doorknob; it slowly turned this way and that, tentatively, almost in resonance with the resentful rubbing poor William gave his pounded skin. Of its own will, it seemed, the door began to travel open, at first cautiously, but then with a furious push that slapped it against the wall; and without a word and trailing tears from a ghastly bitten lip, a small plump girl, full of fright and daring, rushed recklessly out.

Behind us the Cabbages whooped.

"It's old Silverpants!" And they all moaned together.

"William's let her out," Stefanie Pettigrew (unmistakably she) announced in disgust. "And bawling like a babe."

This was true. Old Silverpants, the captive Onion, had stopped in her tracks and was standing white as a real onion and as intimately concerned with the business of weeping. The drops paused on the little pale bulb of her nose before leaping off it to mustachio her scared and wretched mouth; for half a second she glanced without expression at William and at me, and threw a look back into her hour's prison; and then, more hopeful than cunning, she assessed the crowd and made a run for it.

"Get her! Get her!" screamed the erubescent Cabbages. "She's getting away! She's heading for the elevators! Stop her, get her!"

But the nervy Onion had escaped.

5

And William ruefully went on rubbing his knee. "There's no limit to it," he said. "Turned over the water coolers. Locked up a child. And probably broke my leg."

"The taxi-driver I came down with said he thought all the water coolers on Wall Street were polluted. He said you could get diseases from them," I told him, wondering whether he would smile.

But "Wrecked my office," he only grumbled; he had not been listening, and loomed on the threshold with a vague stoop, peering in. My grandfather Huntingdon's unbenign portrait scowled upon his erstwhile son-in-law from the far wall—my mother's father, one of the firm's great men, whose name was kept on the letterhead still. In spite of this piety the gold frame was black with neglect. The shades were down, and the remainder of the sunlight filtered through greenly: William's private office looked undersea, a lonesome submarine lost from the world of action and plotting against it. It was a place for conspirators—a soft and resplendent hideout. The fine gloomy oak desk with its leather rectangle squatted on elegant claw feet, aging moment by moment, glowing with polish, like a beautiful shining saddled lioness. Its back was smooth and almost naked, except for a standing photograph and a big clumsy crystal ashtray, wherein five

cellophane caramel wrappers lay crumpled: the Onion,
though a whimperer, had not been without the resources of
nourishment under siege.

"She's got everything sticky," said William with distaste;
"well, come in; come in and close the door."

In the greenish light the brown cushion of carpet and the
brown squares of paneling met imperceptibly. It was a room
which had a sense of generations: the portrait of my grandfather with his large English-style mustache stuffed in the narrow space between nose and lip like an extra handful of the
carpet which no one had known how to dispose of, and
downy brown thick wisps of it crawling up his nostrils; and a
yard behind William's splendid old chair (he creaked down
it with a sigh) the far-off true entrance to this confidential place, a tall door carved all over with strange leaves,
rubbed and gleaming and as dependable-looking as a discreetly turned back, through which who can dream what
great characters daily walked; and here now in spare isolation
on the surface of the desk the image of tiny Cletis sucking on
a fat watch docilely in her mother's lap, the unoblivious heiress of all the whispered moneyed intrigues of this citadel and
treasure-room. Meanwhile I came face to face with William's
wife. Her serious eyes did not accommodate the photograph;
they evaded it as though an obscure religious scruple, so that
she appeared intensely in a "pose," holding high the sort of
carefully unfashionable head one describes by the faint-
hearted word "distinguished';—this meant her hard will toward orderliness showed, somewhat perilously, in the uncongenial serenity of her long oval forehead. She was austere;
she was not so much her husband's guardian as his guard.

"Cletis is older than that now, you know," William said, interrupting my gaze. "We're grateful that she's stopped sucking at everything in sight. She's learned to discriminate—we
like to say she's acquiring tastes." Suddenly it was his old
tone, the one that idled over bits of news of his boys and girls
on those occasions when he was perforce thrown together
with me, awaiting my mother's step and in terror of what I
might choose to bring up. Instead he brought everything up
himself, thinking to stave off with Cletis whatever indignity
and shame might line my silenced tongue. But here, in this
retreat, under the cool aware watchfulness of the picture of
his wife viewing him with all the somber power of a talisman, he could rely on no rescue by Allegra Vand; and I understood that he spoke of baby Cletis now not to save himself

from what I might remind him of but to save his wife from my long scrutiny, stubborn with curiosity over this surrogate for my mother and redolent with obscure intimacies. It was the suggestion of intimacy—of intimate visualization—which dismayed William: he did not like me to look closely at his wife, and so he talked of Cletis. Perhaps he naïvely feared that I might require him to discuss whatever my eye fell wonderingly upon; and of the two, his wife and his child, Cletis was the safer subject.

Then while (to give him ease) I tried not to consider that brittle, glazed, and civilized madonna armed with offspring, I heard him say the terrible name.

"Tilbeck," he began: and so it was I who was startled and dismayed by the crudity of an intimacy. For he spoke it not as an allusion but quite as though he were horribly addressing me.

"You're here just for Tilbeck then," he said.

"Well, not for Cletis," I had to answer, alert and partly insolent with melancholy. "And not for your son either."

"They didn't ask you, the young people," he acknowledged; he was glad of tangents and digressions.

"I don't care. I told your son I don't care. I told Miss Pettigrew too. Really it doesn't matter. It's only on account of my mother that they would have asked me anyway."

"Your mother likes you to meet young people—you don't want to blame her for that. I recall you made a great fuss about not intending to come out. It was stubbornness, I told your mother that. I'm happy to say Nanette doesn't give us that trouble." He tried on a reluctant smile. "She gives us other trouble, I'm afraid. She has the Thespian call. She wants to be an actress."

"Perhaps Mrs. Karp—"

"Yes, Mrs. Karp might swing it. I do awfully dread Mrs. Karp."

I sat down opposite him and felt him survey me across the long space of desk.

"I hate a clever woman," he finished.

"So does your son."

"Ah, Miss Pettigrew," he said. "She has an able father. I don't care for his ideas. His ideas are irresponsible, but he's able enough. He used to have a job very like the one your stepfather is just giving up. Of course it was under the old Administration."

"She's very pretty."

"Yes, a pretty girl. Full of life. It doesn't surprise me that he's chosen a good-looking girl, though Lord knows"—his regret only pretended to be a pretense—"I didn't expect a Democrat."

I came out directly, "Then what *did* you expect?"

But he only shook his head. "No, it won't do, one must never expect things for one's children."

"My mother does," I said vividly. "She expects everything."

"For you?" He swung forward. "But she can't help it. Circumstances plan for her. She does what she's obliged to do. She wants you to be free."

"She's told me that," I bit off. "Is that why she's obliged to send me where she pleases?"

"She's not free to have you be free. I suppose you understand that."

"Oh—understand!" it was my turn to exclaim. "They don't tell me anything."

"And if *they* don't," he said rationally, "why do you expect it of me?"

I had to think. I was conscious of a flood of courage. An hour before I would have known how to reply to this. An hour before William had represented himself in my imagination as a distantly familiar marble certainty: a statue signifying nobility, which one has ceased to notice because its physical and moral nature is as reliable and unchanging as the lamppost. I had come seeking that monument like a native of a place bent on rediscovering old civic landmarks he has never before had the openness of wit really to *see:* but what I found was rubble. I had come too late. A disorderly affliction had razed that grandeur. I saw now what his son saw: the broken pile.

"I don't know. I thought"—I wavered and wandered, searching for what I really *had* thought—"I thought you were not like them."

It was so. I had thought William not like Mr. and Mrs. Vand. I had supposed him incapable of betrayal. I had believed him to be—oh, what I had believed him to be!—it was simple, simple, single and simple, and the multifold word stuck to my tongue, a stale pearl of honey: it was only that I had believed William to be trustworthy. Trustworthy!—that sculptured notion which his son had intervened to sully, like a boy daubing the blank eye-ovals of a stone god with an obscene leer painted all distastefully in the corners of the proud smooth sockets; or like time, rightly named inexorable, which cracks not men's works (for what that grows from the hand and not the mind is so perdurable that we can truly call it "works"? what is not waxen under the life's-breath of breeding time?) but their beliefs and wears them out and sends them down into decay. Time struck at William, and a dead boy, and hope died too: past time beat at him; an Armenian name, old though alien (alien though accustomed, used, relentlessly encountered), shuddered against his unmoved lips. The dead boy dead at the age of William's son, a spiteful age, dead in the defiled moment of the marriage-hope where now William's son stood hissing scorn and spite. What was William now? I looked at him and saw what his son saw, the terrible trader in kind who had exchanged trustworthiness for mean treachery, and had given over conscience for—what? for cynical neglect: the turning of his back. He bartered everything, this new despoiled William. He had bartered my mother and all her swift feeling for this calm wife who watched him with the grey assured eyes of a solemnly dangerous, household deity. He gave everything away for the sake of new shipments. And even Enoch, dealer in unnameable shipments, recorder of unrecordable goods, numerator, broker, collector and connoisseur of atrocity, in those days of his briskest commerce over the body of Europe had given nothing in return and took his loads as they were settled on him, and required nothing. So it was no longer sensible to hope for truth in William; even in William. He would give truth if he got something valuable for it, if he owed it as a payment: and now I suddenly believed his son, now I had unconsolable evidence, now I saw in him what his son saw, though with disillusionment less frail and without the pain of a noble loss: not having had a father, unlike William's son I had no father to lose. And yet, after all, I had William to lose (William, trampled grotto, violated shrine), and wondered whether I had already lost him (as when the spoliation of the lovely thing is still a rumor, though accepted and credited, and one hurries to the place to see the substantiation of one's hideous imaginings, by now as certain and believing as if the act had been one's own); and whether, since I supposed I had nothing to offer in exchange, he would give me what I had come for. It was the truth I had come for, though his own boy had ceased to hope for truth from him, though his own boy had told how he had murdered a boy, though he was capable of filicide, having murdered not only the long-dead boy but also his son's illusions, and (but it did not matter, it did not matter) mine.

So William tumbled down—a collapse (the collapse of trust, the collapse of time) I had come too late to witness. I had come an hour too late. Consider: a single hour earlier and I might in the unlucky labyrinth of that place have missed his son and his son's intervention and his son's tale of suicide, of filicide, and of the old old contrivance of a knife: but now, too late—the inconceivable hour of revelation had already descended into pest time, like the suicide itself, and I found that in reality it was not only this unkind hour which separated me from the chance of having escaped the crucial flick of the son's tongue, toppling the massive trustworthiness of the father. I had come not an hour but a whole generation too late. For it had all happened long before.

Everything had happened long before.

"No one likes to dredge things up," William said. "I can't condemn your mother if she doesn't want to."

"You don't want to either."

"I don't want to either."

"You're sorry to see me here."

"Sorry."

"And surprised," I persisted.

But this stopped him. "Surprised? Oh no no no no, not surprised." Wearily he put his fingers across his lids, contemplating me through them as through the bars of a jail. "The fact is"—and now slowly, very slowly, wearily and slowly, phrase by phrase he brought it out—"I've been expecting you on this very errand for twenty years."

For twenty years. So I was right: everything had happened long before. And perhaps I was predictable to William only because in some way my movements had been predetermined. The notion amazed me, and I waited to hear if he would confirm it.

From the imprisonment of his spread hands he said, "We live with possibilities, but mostly we live with consequences"; and confirmed it.

But it was not what Enoch would have said. Enoch, wizard-like, would have seen consequences *as* possibilities. My stepfather was a magician however. William was more practical; and was it not just for his practicality that I had sought him out?

So in the same vein, practical and sober, I put it to him: "But all the while I've been in the dark, and when you're in the dark it's nothing but a question of grasping at straws. It all comes down to that. And *you*," I told him, "are the last one left."

"Your last straw?" he echoed reflectively.

"When you don't know what's happened—when you're in the dark and you can't tell the difference," I pursued, "between a possibility and a consequence."

He was thoughtful. "You're intelligent," he said, "you're acute," and let it momentarily hang. I wished, in the interval, that instead of these he had merely called me innocent, but his hesitation had ended. "So you won't be distressed to remember that the last straw is exactly the one reputed to have broken the camel's back. And if I'm your last straw"—he looked at me shrewdly, lowering his protective fingers—"are you altogether prepared for that?"

I felt the involuntary rip of shock. "What do you mean?" —though I saw his deliberation.

"Yes," he said in a low hard formal tone, "if you have come here, if you have come to me, that is what you have come for."

"If I've come—" I began, but William did not allow me either crescendo or conclusion, and whatever my cry was to have been, protest or exhortation or plea, it fell away like a flake of cinder into that past time where truth was interned side by side with betrayal and death.

He cut me off—"Never mind"—and undertook to murder possibility with consequence. I mean by this that (like a missionary) he explained his intention and robbed my life of its axioms. "And now," he said, without haste, oratorically (like a missionary he was about to convert me, and did), "at your own request, if you please—at your own request"—he strangely emphasized this, as if to show how he abhorred forcible conversion, showing me instead the whole pale force of his round bright pupils, "I am going to break your back."

He did as he said. He did what every trader or missionary will do for a customer or convert when he expects to be well paid for it. In my cognition of William at that queer moment, trader and missionary appeared to coalesce theatrically—a twinning of vision unremarkable when you think of those altogether respectable Societies for the Propagation Of this or that faith which, behind the counters of their sleek and tidy shops on fashionable streets, will sell you religious articles or scriptural keys out of zeal for your eternal soul, but always collecting a good sum for the privilege of bringing you to the truth, as though their particularized and immediately vendable truth had, like pistols, a cash value. It was, in my mother's lawyer, an unexpected savagery. But had not his son, an hour before, been equally savage?—and then I had marveled at it, it had fallen across my perception with all the turbulence of a rough beauty, a sort of fantasy of manner, an intricate secret elegance, like the incalculable path of a spring happened upon in an otherwise orderly countryside by a party of unsuspecting tourists. It was nothing I could ever have guessed at; it was something to stumble over, both in the father and in the son—in the father especially, the countryside of whose face had always raised its contours in fine ruddy hillocks more melancholy and quiescent, as in a pastoral, than violent. But in the father I did not like that startling streak and rush. It oppressed, it cut through the design of his voice as though it wished to persecute; it hurt. Against the unreality of the masked dusk-light William ministerially raised a hand; the blazing translucence of the little webs of skin linking the roots of finger to finger frightened me: I was vulnerable even to that terrible vulnerability and delicacy of his thinnest flesh.—A breeze jangled the metal slats of the blind, and lifted it away; and through the triangle of window suddenly revealed I saw the sky shining like a polished copper gong. Immensely and hopelessly it seemed to toll in the far commanding firmament, a high clear signal of the marketplace, and below it William and I, tented in that silken room, tugged for a bargain in our inevitable exchange. He had received me into that privacy knowing me for what I was, a suppliant after truth; and he intended to give it to me —for a price. He did not mean to outwit me, only to exact from me his price. I looked: it was posted on his brow, plain to see—he meant it to be plain, he meant to have me see him in the guise of merciless collector. The cost of truth was my surrender. I would be indentured now to exile—I had to barter my freedom for the truth, and yield without a word. And I took in these lucid implications soon enough; they were familiar, they were close. It was the same surrender of myself which had bought for my mother, in all the ceremony of mystery, my stepfather's safety.—But now (just as the father had been annihilated by the son's tale) the mystery would be annihilated by the father's tale.

The errant window-shade, maneuvered by a contrary sheet of air, fell back aslant, and covered the gleam of sky. Between its bottom slat and the sill the round space of gong reduced itself to a golden hoop—the whole diffuse brilliance of that sky was concentrated into an intense circle spinning against the panes: it was the coin of sun, suspended in the valley of skyscrapers, about to drop away, as into a slot. And I, counting up the two clean sea-stained dimes fixed in William's seizing eyes, wished to slide down into that dark shaft with the vanishing afternoon, to roll with my humiliation out of sight: I was stunned by coins, coldly felt them all around me, in the unendurable disc of the hanged sun and in William's burning face and in the round round moons of my fingernails, and remembering my lewdly clinking dress (that dress which had made me ashamed to look with innocence upon William's son), jingling like a peddler's pockets, full of money, full of Tilbeck, full of noisy contemptible actuality —oh then, then, then, even before William (despoiled, my almost-father) spoke it out to me I knew what I was, what unspeakable mint had made me, and how like a piece of unclean money I could be passed from hand to hand, one day to pay for this, and the next for that, and to be bitten between cruel cynical teeth testing for the counterfeit.

So the transaction in that office was concluded. William gave me the truth, and I paid for it.

He said: "Now I am going to talk to you of your legal status and I will be obliged to use a set of legal terms. They will seem brutal, but they are what they mean. I trust you will accept them without commotion. They are what you will have to face. Afterward, if you wish—I suppose you will— we'll talk of their history. But first you will have to face what you have come for. You ask me about your father. But you ought also to ask about your mother. Your poor mother," he repeated, and it was wondrous that he did not falter—"the fact is that in the eyes of the law—and I am please understand a lawyer talking about the law" (but at this small point he faltered at last, and allowed a low phlegm-noise to be juggled in his throat, and then took up again) "—you are what is called illegitimate issue. You are," he finished, driving in with all unmistakable clarity his deep and iron nail, "a bastard."

6

The father's tale.

Once, long ago, on an occasion I have by now forgotten, Enoch said to my mother: "Hell is truth seen too late," and without giving it any thought I assumed he was speaking for himself. But my mother, shrewd and shrewish that day, said petulantly: "And what about truth seen too soon? You're not going to tell me that's heaven?" —And afterward I came up on my stepfather's remark in a book: it was a sentence from an English philosopher. He had been reading Hobbes. But his reply to his wife was characteristic only of himself—he answered not with a logical corollary but with a fresh tangent. "Oh no," he told her, propelled into one of his placid satiric moods, "Heaven is never to see the truth at all." And then, to mollify her—she had taken it roughly against the shield of her frown—he threw out, "if you see the truth too soon you naturally accommodate yourself to what you see; and by the act of accommodating yourself you change whatever the circumstance was when you originally saw it; and by changing the circumstance you alter the ground from which the truth springs, and then it can no longer grow out that same truth which you foresaw: it has become something different. So you see it is impossible to see the truth too soon, for when its moment of commitment arrives, it has changed its nature and it is already too late. The truth is always seen too late. That is why hell is always with us," he insisted on finishing, although my mother had long ago covered her ears and was shouting with vigor, "Stop! Stop! I can't stand it, I *won't* stand it!" And they ended laughing together, enigmatically, as though not the English philosopher, and not Enoch, but Allegra Vand herself had innocently convulsed them.

I think of this now, when I have come finally to the father's tale, though not *my* father's: a tale told by my almost-

father about my "true" father, signifying anything but fatherhood. For if, in my stepfather's phrase, it was for me a truth
seen too late, that story which William eventually related,
then let it stand that on a certain afternoon in the first days
of September, in William's darkly glazed private office, under
the painted eye of his brief father-in-law and the paper eye of
his determinedly permanent wife, I entered hell.

My observation upon arrival? Chiefly, that the place felt
familiar. In what respect? In this: that to enter hell and find
Tilbeck there was no surprise.

William, who had deliberately denuded my mother's file of
everything important, had access to the devil's own dossier.
And there were stored and stuffed all those missing papers in
the matter of Allegra Vand which William's son had vainly
coveted, to redeem, I suppose, his sense of historical order—
not a petty but a moral sense: for William's son, in his zeal
for personal history, appeared to invest a proper chronology
with morality, to wit, "that is good which follows"; and one
day, when he would have learned to transpose this uninteresting notion into a more politic one, viz., "that which follows is
good," he would indubitably grow into an even cleverer lawyer than his father—"that which follows is good" being a dictum of complete legal probity, especially when applied as
heading to a document full of brilliantly concealed tax
crimes. But this is digression, though purposeful. Only yesterday my stepfather had defined history as a judgment on humanity; today William's son saw it as a compilation of the
appropriate papers. As for William himself, his relation with
history lay in his not having any. How was this possible in a
mind concerned most of its sentient hours with the law,
where presumably precedent governs? But precedent did not
govern William's mind, for precedents are only relative, and
contradict one another now and then, and anyhow William
was a Calvinist, and believed in the foreordained: call it, for
brevity's sake, destiny. Destiny is individual, and what has
gone before, in similar cases (no matter how similar to, or, as
lawyers like zoölogically to put it, however truly "on all fours
with," the case at hand), is irrelevant. To William, the circumstances of my birth—how indecently priggish and Dic-
kensian that sounds! yet I succumb to this mean phrase out of
deference for poor William, who, after showing so much respect initially for the precise terminology and taxonomy of
his profession, reverted with relief to another show of respect, which he expressed insultingly in circumlocution and

euphemism—the circumstances of my birth, at any rate, implied for him not simple event but a destiny for which I was responsible in the first place and to blame in the second. And not only a destiny, but even a breed of soul which such a destiny might spawn. Those "circumstances," moreover, explained his aversion and clarified his evasions; and all delicately and exquisitely and secretly they gave me a sinister chill, as though, while standing solemnly in court, about to be sentenced, I had caught sight of the god Pan at the window, clutching a bunch of wild flowers, hellebore and jewelweed, and laughing a long and careless jingle of a laugh, like bicycle bells.

So it turned out that—as I have stated—it was the devil's dossier which contained the missing papers. At the same time let it be noted that the devil's dossier was altogether empty. A paradox? No. The papers were missing because they were non-existent. That is the way it is with the devil's file—it is full of lies, and lies, in an absolute sense, have no reality, body, weight, or substance. Lies, being what-is-not, are not there. There were no documents recording my mother's divorce from Gustave Nicholas Tilbeck because there had never been a divorce. There had never been a divorce because there had never been a marriage. If lies *had* reality, body, weight, or substance, there would not be room enough anywhere to keep them in, and the devil would have to appropriate the whole world for a safety-vault.

To this, Enôch—I can hear him!—would say: "Exactly. He *has* appropriated the world, just as you say. Why else is the world so stuffed with lies? The liars are all file-cabinets for the devil." Regarding all plain contrary-to-fact falsehoods perhaps this is so, but it is not so with the lie that is a lie only because the truth has not been uttered. The lie of omission, like the silent hollow within the flute's facile cylinder, cannot be put away, and will continue to plague the universe forever, by virtue of its formlessness, which is dependent on honest forms. An ordinary lie, because it is a simple opposite of what-is, can be contradicted by exposure of its contrary. But the lie of omission is a concealment contradicted by nothing, and bolstered, in fact, by the solidity of the revealed. That Tilbeck existed, I had been told; that he was my father, I had been told. From this I drew the assumption of a marriage; but it was an appearance: a nefarious illusion, worse than a made lie. Rumor and murmur come to kill a made lie; the made lie is tangible and can be cut down. But the omitted pertinent thing, the lie of illusion, falls like a damp pervading smoke. It was by illusion and trick my mother and William had snared me. And Enoch, who had been quiet, who had said nothing, had thereby had his part in it, and was a liar like the others: though a hater of liars.

William began: "The circumstances of your birth—"

"My illegitimacy."

"—of your birth have turned out to be highly useful to a particular individual."

"You mean to my father. Gustave Nicholas Tilbeck. Don't think I don't know all my father's names!"

If this was a challenge William did not rise to it, and only said, "In spite of that you have been protected from the beginning."

I said: "I wish I had been protected *from* beginning."

"Sophistry. I don't hide it from you that I regard it as a great pity."

"A pity that I was born."

"I refer only to your mother's behavior."

"My mother's *mis*behavior."

"I think you had better take a more serious attitude," William said.

"A more humble one, do you mean? Befitting my position in life?"

"Please," he said harshly.

"I believe I'm *not* going to weep."

"Excellent. I'm glad of it. I ask you to be serious, but not irresponsible."

"In other words, not to take after my mother. But I've been better brought up. *I* haven't been anyone's mistress," I told him, and added guilefully: "So far."

"I also ask you to speak of your mother with"—anxiously he chose the less obvious word—"propriety. I hope it won't be necessary to warn you against bad taste in this matter."

His gravity was both intense and fastidious, and therefore so absurd and piteous that, despite my declaration, I almost wept after all. I came so close to it that I laughed instead, and was surprised: what emerged was bitter shame. "And to think," I brought out, "I always imagined the divorce itself was the thing in bad taste!"

"There was no divorce," William said.

"What you mean is there was only one divorce and not two—one, I suppose, is in better taste than two? In that case

my father has improved on things. Unless the first divorce
was a sham as well?"

"I won't countenance this—"

But I would not stop for his remonstrance. "If only you'll
make it clear that *you* were never married to my mother either," I offered, "it would do away altogether with the taint
of divorce, wouldn't it? Think how clean the family escutcheon would be."

"I do not like this talk," William said.

"No. It's dirty, like the escutcheon."

"Look here," he said abruptly, "you don't grasp in what
capacity I've been willing to receive you. You will have to
understand that I have been your mother's lawyer for a very
long time—"

"And something else."

"Her lawyer. I speak to you in that capacity and in no
other," he finished.

"And in another," I nevertheless pursued.

"What are you after?"

"You've omitted something. You've been something else,
and it makes a difference. It's an influence."

"The trustee. Yes. Very well. I've been the trustee," he
stated without comfort.

"And the husband."

"Your mother's husband," he observed, "is a Jew named
Vand. —You needn't draw on any family relation where none
exists." All unwittingly his elevated arm had stretched to the
level of the mouth in the portrait behind and above him—the
confident, even arrogant, rather flat Huntingdon mouth which
my mother, but not I, had inherited. This mouth was the only
living feature in that fearsome yet curiously pallid representa-
tion of my grandfather; not Sargent, but an imitator, perhaps
a pupil, had given posterity those unconcerned angelic nostrils, too spiritual to breathe. But the mouth showed what the
man had been: it looked ready to spit.

In the presence of this icon-like carpet-mustached ancestor
I inquired of his son-in-law, "And where a family relation
does exist?"

But William had noted my upward gaze and intercepted it
with a force which made all irony of appearances ineffectual.
"Is is not was. None exists," he repeated, and became conscious suddenly of his hand in the air; he brought it down
and laid it on the desk and solemnly viewed it.

"Your son? I'm speaking of your son. You admit to a family relation *there?*"

"My son," he granted, "is a stranger to this business."

"A stranger?"

"He knows nothing."

"He knows plenty. He knows more than I know."

"I don't see what you're implying. He knows nothing about the circumstances of your—"

"—of my worth," I joined him mockingly. "But he's completely aware of yours."

"You had better be explicit," William said.

"Your son has already been that. I've heard how the trustee failed to live up to the terms of the trust."

"Ah," William said meditating. "He talked to you?"

"He told me about the death on the estate. My mother's estate. —The place they're sending me to, in fact. We went out to one of the cubicles and he told me," I said.

"That's quite outside the proper area of your interest in this matter. —He talked to you about it?" William said again. He continued to stare at his hand as though it had turned to bronze. "He has no discretion."

"He picked Miss Pettigrew," I slyly acknowledged.

"My son will have to answer for his own recklessness. In every respect."

"And you picked my mother."

"And answered for it."

"By losing her. But you know," I took up, inflamed inexplicably into vehemence, "I always believed you had divorced her on account of, well, on account of *Marianna Harlow!* The terrible Chapter Twelve!" I threw out at him all the infamous jeering incongruity of it: "I thought it was on account of politics! Because she was mixed up with Communists—"

"Communists," he echoed carefully.

Then very gradually and astonishingly I felt between my shoulders the beginning of a kind of jarring, a reverberation: without realizing it I had grown tremulous.

"Your mother divorced *me*," William corrected, essaying it with impeccable exactitude, as though caution might be relied on to keep his fist as stiff as cast metal. But he began to rock it thoughtfully, like a small bronze pony.

Though nervous, I had to scoff. "That's a gentlemanly technicality."

"However it's a fact."

"So," I said, "was her adultery."

The word struck like a stone against his eyes.

"Don't continue in that language, please."

"I didn't choose the language."

"You are remarkably sullen. I warn you," William said.

"It's Biblical language, isn't it? It says 'adultery' in the Decalogue—in that case I'm perfectly sure I can't be blamed for the language, can I? Though maybe you might blame Enoch."

He looked up wearily.

"You just *said* he's a Jew. They invented the Bible, you know. Blame *them*."

He did not move. "I blame the sinner for the sin."

"I hate religion," I said.

"Then you hate God."

"No," I said. "God hates me."

So we came to a standstill at hatred. We came to it quickly; and we stopped there. Where else could we have stopped? For William, hater of adultery, it was Christian duty. For me it was plain pagan philosophy. I hated William not because he had failed to become my father according to respectable plan; I hated my mother not because she had borne me in wildness and reared me in tame constraint; I hated my father not because secretly and fearfully I felt his alien and singing bravado in my intellect; I hated Enoch not because he addressed me always with the contempt of repudiation, as though I were a category or an opposite point of view—no, no, I was not so orderly in my hatred, I did not sniff after the weavings of the minor plots of past time. I hated my stepfather, my true father, my almost-father, my mother who had bedded with each of these, because they were the world. That was my whole, broad, and uncontaminated philosophy—scorn for everything that devoured my mind: for the world exactly as it stood; for all phenomena. In existence there *is* no might-have-been, though we contemplate it despairingly. God does not allow returns and beginnings-again-from-the-starting-place. What firmer sign can there be of God's cruelty? He has made the already-accomplished inexorable. We cannot go back to do it over again. There are no rehearsals. Each fresh moment is the real and final thing. Each successive breath is the single penetrable opportunity for its pitiable duration; there is no other, there is no beginning on the morrow, there is only what we have done yesterday, or what has been done to us yesterday; we live on our yesterday's leavings. To God we are inflexible

facts: he does not judge us, any more than we would judge
the barnward cow's round dung-tower in the field behind her.
Dung is fact. Man is fact. If God were not indifferent to us,
we might not be indifferent to each other.

7

With this indifference—it is the indifference of hopelessness, the indifference of helplessness, the indifference of the
badly born; go ask the cripple or the idiot how indebted he is
to the world! (God so loved the world that he gave his only
begotten dung)—I learned from William what he now began
to recount. It was—as I have said—a father's tale, to begin
with. I suppose he meant to justify those events of dereliction
and death which his son had given me; but rapidly and mysteriously what had begun as the father's tale became a lover's
tale. He told it so. He told it with a vocabulary of raw timidity—a lad's vocabulary. He did not own words of what is
called, foolishly, mature feeling. Feeling had ended for him
even before suffocating life had thrown the cloak of sentience
over my unguarded and blackguarded begetting. He did not
tell it as I shall tell it, with the crowding of chronology. In
fact, as I remember it, the end came first, and little by little
the end persuaded the appearance of its various preceding
vertebrae, till at last was reached the central matter atop that
story's spine; nor was it a long story. It was a story short,
slight, and common; but it was not vulgar. If the story had
been mine it would, I think, have been vulgar. Godlessness
inevitably produces vulgarity. Civilization is the product of
belief. William's story—that golden lover's tale, mythic as
Troilus'—was (though golden, though mythic) short, slight,
common, but not vulgar. Into William's ken my mother had
swum like an act of God.

8

In those days there were dances. They might have been thought of anthropologically—not that such a notion would ever occur to the dancers. Visualize the girls (women now, pitifully transmuted, arms and necks distorted, so that nothing glimmers of what was but the very inmost light of the eye-pupil, where the self knows the self)—girls in white dresses, my mother among them, in the not-quite-white of a gull's winter-subdued breast. A tea-dance: the cakes pink, the cloths pink, the young men's noses vaguely pink from the walk in the snow from driveway to house—and all of it anthropology, an engine, to put it starkly, for mating according to caste. Even indoors there is a consciousness of the snow. It heightens the spirit, like an incongruously cold liqueur. My mother—Allegra—is perhaps fifteen: a white perpendicular forehead and a white round chin magnificently formed out of snow polished and honed to the clever ice of perfect bone. Compare if you will Stefanie Pettigrew, a rougher sketch of the model, an artist's poor copy of the hanging masterpiece, daringly embellished with up-to-date technique. Is it youth does it? All of youth is beauty if one defines beauty as that which precedes blemish: but blemish is character, and a pretty brow without the scars of character signifies only youth, and not proper beauty, which is banded with marks and acts. This explains Miss Pettigrew, whose impudence the coming decade will have sandpapered into querulousness. Allegra is impudent too, but impudence is not yet a blemish in a child of fifteen. Allegra is subtler than Stefanie perhaps. (We are, you see, laying a swathe through the generations, and setting all the forms of youth side by side, as though they were for the moment immortal. And what a charm it is which allows us to think of Stefanie and Allegra as contemporaries!) You do not agree that Allegra is the slyer one? But already Allegra values freedom. Already her manner is wild. She is just a little more reckless than, in view of her station, she ought to be. And it is not the recklessness of simply lacking judgment, which will, like impudence, wear off into some more sober, or at least commonplace, trait. Not at all. Her recklessness is perhaps her most serious characteristic. She is one of those who have alertness without talent, intelligence without form, energy without a cause. She has come into the world prepared to believe in nobility. Consequently her recklessness will last. If she is disappointed by the betrayal of a dream of nobility—and through what dream of nobility does a traitor not move?—she will avenge the betrayal by further recklessness. Her extraordinary eyes promise swiftnesses.

And William? Very well, William. Visualize William next. He is twenty-five and at the tea-dance given by his mother for his two younger sisters he is everything he should be, though perhaps a trifle timid. Nevertheless he is aware that dynasty must be served. Unlike Allegra, he is naturally religious, hence effortlessly noble. He does not think, as she does, of personal sacrifice, though he is conscious of duty and purity, the latter far more difficult than the former while entirely dependent on it. He supposes that in three or four years, when he and Allegra marry, purity will become a thing to be easily stepped around rather than an aggression against duty. He will of course marry Allegra; it is both right and appropriate, and everyone is very pleasant about it, though no one mentions it. Only what is unsuitable is remarked, and who could be more suitable than Allegra?—if a bit too lively. It is as much a made match as any in India, but this is not the sort of idea that one contemplates for long. William's chief wish at the tea-dance is that he were not quite so afraid of talking to Allegra. He knows he ought to, and more than that, he longs to. She dances by; her quick knees flash their silk at him mockingly. But William is at this time what is generally known as "a poor chuck" in company. This implies a number of matters, all to his credit: for example, it intimates that he is as devout as his mother, whose custom it is to read aloud to her children from her collections of annotated sermons. It also bespeaks a rare wholesomeness. Consider, à propos, the influence upon William of rocks.

In past years William took it into his head that he must become a paleontologist and dig up fossils. At school he was actually secretary of the Fossil Club, which went on Saturday

tramps seeking bones. Instead the boys' shovels kicked up the
clangor of endless rocks, and the young William prudently
wrote in his minutes: "Saturday. A field trip. Chip of mammoth tusk found by Beale, engendering great excitement. Arrive at Natural History Museum just before closing to present
mammoth-tusk-chip to curator. Curator has already gone
home. Told by guard at door that chip is sea-pebble. Much
indignation. Two days later: mammoth-tusk-chip turns out to
be sea-pebble of highly interesting formation. S'cy of Club
presents brief paper on history of sea-pebbles, is both booed
and applauded. S'cy secedes from Club, achieving schism,
founds Geology Club with almost one-half of Fossil Club
members." This was William's earliest triumph of deflection.
In later years he was sometimes called, by disappointed lawyers fruitlessly seeking compromise, The Great Deflector. In
fact it was his continuing concern with rocks which gave William the revelation that enabled him to become a lawyer at
all. In the first months of the Harvard Law School he did not
do well. He studied without penetration. Perhaps it was because his father had considered geology an unrefined form of
nonsense and explained that it was William's *duty* to go to
law school. His mother, on the other hand, had reminded
him that to tamper with the stones of the field could scarcely
be God's plan for His children.

Thus William: "I have always disliked abstractions. It
might be said that I understood the law from the moment I
saw that it was real and tangible, as a rock is real and tangible, and that it was about real things, and not about things
which stand for something beyond themselves. There is nothing symbolic in the law, I am glad to say. Unfortunately my
son has taken a liking to jurisprudence, a murky and unlaw-
yerlike subject. I trust to the influence of the firm to clarify
his views. Law is not theory. Law is denatured geology, you
might say. A set of facts, like a rock, is derived from the various influences that have acted· on it simultaneously in the
past. There is no legal situation that cannot profitably be
compared to the history of the formation of rock. No legal
situation can be said to be more abstract than a rock."

This is direct quotation. (Poor William! I do not mean to
satirize him, only to reveal him.) It is from the newspaper
text—like the Fossil Club minutes, I found it among the accumulated bundles of my mother's papers: antique, mid-
dling-old, and merely stale anomalies folded in with all those
beginnings of earnest Ibsen-like plays and poemlets of her

"writing period"—the text of a speech William once made before a commencement assembly of a not-very-important evening law school, where all the students were men, not boys; but they tittered like boys over his doubtful remarks about his son. "I trust to the influence of the firm to clarify his views"—William's son was then stuttering sixteen, with Justice Holmes newly in the crook of his arm and ideal notions not yet emptied from his platonic pockets. His son, at any rate, unlike the audience of graduates (who during daylight were grocery clerks and bookkeepers), would not be obliged to comb fat midtown partners' offices for a job, jurisprudential handicap or no; and if *they* (the night-time graduates) had any geological reflections on the law, it was the knowledge that they would have to start from rock-bottom. In this, as well as in the absence of jurisprudence from their lives and studies, they differed from William's young son.

I have already told, however, how William was called upon to speak here and there. He spoke not always brilliantly; but he spoke his mind. It is not that age demolishes shyness, by the way—it is only that power conceals it.

But (to return to that old scene, where the half-child-self of my mother dances in her white dress): confronted with duty, with his sisters, with Allegra, with his own house festooned into strangeness, with mysterious and ritual waltzes, with all those clever little cakes that said "Helen" and "Marie" amid the snow of icing—William could not speak. He supposed he was to speak. Years were to grow her before they married—surely, in between, he should emit a word?

But she spilled out his name, flying by with a blond plump gay little partner who blew her like a flake round and round —"William!" she called—"William!" a second time, from the hub of her turnings. He felt sober, pale, clumsy; he felt old, old, old. For half a second he wished his height did not aspire to the ceiling, and that he knew how to make her catch up quickly. If the decade's gap between them were shut, he was sure she would not be so slippery. She came by again and was off again, more slippery than ever, and left her ridicule in his ears: "I told Vernon you looked exactly like a pillar of the church standing there, and Vernon said—" She was snatched away. He had to wait for her return before he could know what Vernon said. "—he said you're not just a pillar, you're a caryatid!" Her chin was lit with laughter—her partner's, who simpered into it.

They came and stood with him, and talked of Shelley. Allegra had written a poem. Vernon said it was as good as Percy Bysshe's—"symbolic images," he explained. Vernon was the protégé of a certain headmaster. Put it boldly: he was a teacher. It shocked his father, who was the grandson of a merchant, and did nothing himself, though now and then he put on his suspenders and went to a board meeting. Meanwhile Allegra, very serious (and who could be graver than the laughing Allegra?), darted: from poetry to philosophy. She liked Vernon; Vernon was a rebel. "I mean to live!" she told him, and gave her back, a lovely wall but still a wall, to William. "I don't mean just see the world, or die in a storm, or have my heart snatched from the pyre, or anything like that. I mean really *live*." "The Spanish Main is out-of-date," Vernon teased. "No, no, I mean it. You know my father's gone round the world." "Your father's old." "So's the world." "It doesn't count. It only counts to go round the world when you're young." "Oh, I'll do that!" said Allegra. "You know 'To A Skylark'?" "Certainly," said Vernon, as though he had written it himself only day before yesterday—"Shelley's or Wordsworth's?" "Well, we're *talking* about Shelley, for goodness' sake. It's *Shelley* we're talking about, isn't it? Anyhow that's how I feel. Just like that, that's what I mean. William wouldn't know what I mean," she threw out with a little mound of mockery bloating her lip. William agonized, knew he should answer, but could not. He supposed it was because *he* was only intellectual, but *she* was clever. Since he could not combat her, he forgave her instead; he told himself she was a child still. Vernon, on the other hand, was not; he was twenty-three. Vernon taught English grammar in a boys' school, however: so it did not matter about Vernon. "William must think skylarks are illegal," Vernon ventured; "perhaps they trespass"—still smarting over her having turned his erudition ("Shelley's or Wordsworth's?") back upon him. "William's coming to work for my father," said the skylark-emulator with sudden practicality. "He's going to have a little brown office all to himself with a picture of an American Bald Eagle in it." Vernon thought this remarkably funny, and patted his vest with hilarity. "Really. That's a bird of a different color. I mean how foul, f-o-w-l. What are you doing now?" "Clerking," William said, his ears blooming like carnations. "In Woolworth's, do you mean?" "Stupid," said Allegra, "for a judge. It means he doesn't do anything. He climbs out from behind his desk and says just-a-minute-please to people who've come to bribe the judge." "That's not—" William began. "Yes it is. That's just the way it is. And then you say, 'I'm sorry, but this is Righteous Wednesday. We don't take bribes today.'" "There," said Vernon, "it's a perfectly human fox trot for a change. Come and do it, will you?" "Pooh. I like marches," said Allegra. "Then you like the General." "Not the Attorney General"—sticking her tongue out at William. "I meant General Nuisance. Hurry up, it'll end before we get to the floor." "When I come out it'll be all marches." "Then they'll send you in again, miss." "No, I mean it. I hate this sort of stuff. It'll be marches." "Good heavens," said prissy Vernon, "not the Wedding March too?" and danced away with William's bride.

Afterward William looked up "caryatid" in the dictionary. Until then it had not been part of his vocabulary; thereafter it never left it. He did not really see the joke, but it did not prevent him from marrying her after all, and they honeymooned conventionally, though of course they did not know it. They were the newest honeymooners in the world, and they naturally supposed the business that occupied them had begun only with themselves. Cape Ann in September was agreeably deserted. They sat side by side in the shade of a rock (William identified it as calcareous) and Allegra read aloud, rather more brightly than William cared for; he was secretly bored by her favorites—they had been her favorites so long—and she read with a kind of abandon that puzzled and even shocked him. Why did her voice travel up and down so unashamedly? It was as though she sang without music. One sang only in church, and then there was an organ to keep one from making a fool of oneself. But he did not think he would be going to church as often as before; Allegra hated it, and called herself an atheist. Of course she was not. He would not have been permitted to marry an atheist. In the crescent of noon-twilight below the rock he heard his young wife's ardent soaring:

> "Like an unbodied joy whose race is
> just begun"

—self-captivated.

It had a noble sound, but he fell asleep; beneath them the sand was warm as a cradle. And then quickly he awoke: his young wife stood barefoot in the margins of the sea. A fan of little bubbles was shutting itself not far beyond her encircled ankles. She had thrown her Shelley in the water, and was

watching him drown. "You drifted off, you know," she told
the husband; long years afterward he remembered how her
mildness at that moment deceived him. He scarcely knew it
was the bitterest accusation of her life. "But it was the only
book you brought along," he protested, now that it was sinking. "It's all right. I've just decided I hate poetry anyhow."
"Fantasy has a limited usefulness in our lives," he assented in
his gentle but decisive way; it was his thirtieth birthday. Then
he stretched over the water for her hand and led her plashing
out. She sat in the sand and drew on her white socks and
shivered. In their room she lay staring with her head turned
from him—she pretended to search for the lighthouse that
was the most elusive note in the view. "Turn," he said.
"Dear, I want your face. Turn to me. Turn." But she could
not. He supposed it was some impulse of her innocence. The
race had just begun, but his joy remained unbodied. She let
him perform the duty which permits a man to step around
purity in order not to soil it. But she could not give her face.

Three decades afterward he thought of Miss Pettigrew, and
prolonged his melancholy. "Miss Pettigrew and my son," he
took up his minor theme (for the major I had to wait), while
I observed how a parsley-curl of white hair sprang sentry-like
from each blood-darkened ear. He was on the years'-edge of
giving way to these sad signs of accumulation. In that glowing little office where he opened history to himself and to me
he nursed his back against his chair like an old cavalry-man
imitating his early self, but some part of the seat betrayed
him by an unexpected bray of the springs: rider and steed
were aging together. "Not that I expect you to be anxious for
an institution of which you long ago chose not to be an
alumna," he persisted. "Nevertheless you may know (I will
trust you to allow me to continue in the dimension of complete frankness) that among Miss Pettigrew's classmates there
has been—something of a—" I saw him finally skirt the word
"scandal," though his lips had stretched to accommodate it
—"*situation,* relating to the, the taking of, I won't conceal it
from you, drugs, by inhalation as it were—" I confirmed that
I had heard of it, and headlong would have volunteered
more, but he was too much in pursuit of the present as a distraction and a relief from whatever old images were staining
his sight to allow me anything beyond a tentative assent. "It
is serious, it is of course very serious. Luckily Miss Pettigrew
is among the innocent. My son assures me she is among the
innocent. Nevertheless one must always take precautions, one

must always forestall even unlikelihoods, one must be prepared to intercept. In this connection—" his ready little cough punctuated briefly, and I had the sense that he would go on mercilessly talking of Miss Pettigrew quite as though she were Cletis, and for the same reasons—"I have seen to it that she will not be expelled. It would be intolerable if she were to be expelled."

"Particularly," I said sourly, "if she's as innocent as your son says she is."

"You speak as though you suppose her not to be."

"When really it's you who thinks she's not."

"Not innocent? Ah," he gave out, motionless with unease, "all this has made a very bad impression. Very bad. Her father—"

"Miss Pettigrew's father? The Democrat?"—but he did not know I mocked him.

"Exactly. I regret to say that though he had a hand in an Administration I was never able to regard as Constitutionally answerable, at the same time it put him in a position to do me a favor once with respect to your mother, a favor abroad some years back. Years ago, you see. I never imagined a reciprocal opportunity would arise. Of course it is a debt I had always hoped to wipe out, and now in this very special and very delicate matter it has become possible to correct a certain unfortunate impression—"

But with lawyers it is always necessary to translate. Perhaps because the stuff of their commerce is so hideous, they must overdress it in periphrasis. "A very delicate matter" is the jargon applied only to whatever is notably indelicate; and the continuous use of "nevertheless" is like the progression of staves along a rail: the fence of argument will not stand unless rooted in alibi. "I know that old story," I said promptly. "Your son was discussing it only a little while ago. You mean what happened that time in Paris. Pettigrew. He handed out bribes right and left. I don't mean only the little bribes to the doctors and the police that my mother gave. I suppose he even bribed the magistrates for you, never mind the Chamber of Deputies. He must have gone straight up into the Government."

William looked at me unwilling to receive my irony; perhaps, though unaware, I had blundered into what was not irony. "My son told you this?"

"I knew it before. I was there, you know."

"There?"

"When the chauffeur—"

"You were a child. A small child."

"But I was there."

"—and still a child. Your judgment remains childish. A negotiation is not a bribe," William said.

"A negotiation is not a bribe. Then it couldn't have been by negotiation," I concluded, "that you talked the school into keeping Miss Pettigrew?"

"You go far," William said. "See that you don't go too far."

"As far as you take me."

"I take you nowhere."

"That's a place too," I acknowledged.

"I am uninterested in psychological remarks," William said. "It diffuses. We lose hold of the issue."

"Illegitimate issue," I said. "—That's not a psychological remark."

"It is a very rude one. It is unworthy of your breeding, I think."

"I know how I was bred. Tell me how I was born."

"You've come here looking for a circus."

"Bred and circuses; but I want more than that."

"You want a show."

"A show of bravery," I said.

"Exactly," William said. "This is extremely distasteful, no doubt for you as well as for me."

"No doubt," I said.

"I am altogether aware of it. In consideration of your position, perhaps then it would be more useful on your part to display courage rather than defiance."

"I didn't mean on my part. I meant on your part. I'm brave enough. I am. I don't care what you tell me. But you —" His face held nothing for me, neither menace nor prod. "You're indecent about my mother. You're not brave enough to be decent about her."

"What your mother did was I am afraid indefensible."

"What you did was indefensible. You gave her the opportunity."

"Let us agree," William said, "that here at least your judgment is inadmissible. In this case you cannot claim to have been there."

"But didn't the trouble begin just because I *was* there? Eventually, I mean. Because if not for me she would have gotten away with it. I suppose she got away with it lots of times before I was born. Unfortunately I constitute solid evidence, don't I?—what in the movies the district attorney calls Exhibit A.—Embroidered in scarlet."

"I commend you for your allusion," William said heavily.

"Your son doesn't like literary references either. It's a good thing Miss Pettigrew doesn't know any."

"Undoubtedly she has other gifts equally abstruse."

"She adores Euphoria Karp—is that one?"

"I leave it to my son's ingenuity," William said, and he opened his hand out wearily, "to expose whatever qualities are to be found in his fiancée."

"If he exposes any, it won't be to you. He doesn't let you in on things."

"You are treading, I may say, in alien fields. I have never had any reason to believe that I do not have my son's full confidence."

"Is that why you thought it worthwhile to intervene with Miss Jewett? —I mean," I covertly mimicked him, "even after your son had assured you Miss Pettigrew was among the innocent?"

"I don't see what relation this incident has to my son. The simple fact is that my wife has a certain influence with the younger Miss Jewett which the Pettigrew family could not possibly have. Mrs. Pettigrew is a quite unextraordinary woman—she was schooled somewhere in California, if I am not mistaken, whereas my wife is of course an alumna of Miss Jewett's. I am afraid the atmosphere of the school has perhaps in general declined—Nanette, you see, goes to the Academy precisely because it is my wife's conviction that the atmosphere at Miss Jewett's has certainly declined; besides, there are far fewer theatricals at the Academy. Nevertheless there is such a thing as a standard of loyalty to be maintained, and Miss Jewett is just now campaigning for funds among the alumnae, I think it is for a swimming pool. Mrs. Pettigrew is not an alumna, and it is not to her that Miss Jewett would normally go—"

"A swimming pool in exchange for the Chamber of Deputies," I interrupted. "No one can say you haven't evened it out with Pettigrew."

"—a series of facts, in short, which bears no relation whatsoever to my son's veracity. I repeat, I have never had any reason to suppose my son avoids the truth with me."

"You have a reason now."

"I take it you are an authority on my son?"

"It's just that he's an authority on you. He doesn't trust you. He's stopped trusting you."

"I see," William said, and contemplated this. "Then he has been corrupted."

"By finding things out."

"I promise you he remains ignorant of everything I have told you here today. Neither he nor anyone has had access to any information about your, let us call it your origins. Your mother has been shielded from any shadow. We have always done everything in this connection that your mother wished. We have acted," he said, leaning away, grieving into the leather cry of his chair, "with as much circumspection as our position has required, and perhaps with more. We have acted with providence. It is not too much to say that we have acted intensely and perpetually for your protection. My son knows nothing of this business. The world knows nothing."

It was the first time I had ever heard William speak of the world.

"You sound like Enoch now," I said. "And Enoch knows, doesn't he? Enoch; and—counting today—myself; and you; and my mother. That makes four. Four's not the world; though maybe five is. If your son knew, then the world would know.'

"You think little of my son's discretion. But he knows nothing. He knows no more than the general impression: simply that your mother was married to this person—"

"To Gustave Nicholas Tilbeck. Those are his names. I know my father's names," I said.

"—and divorced. The impression stands. We have done everything possible to allow it to stand without hindrance. We have particularly contrived to foster this illusion in you. There was no intention ever to embarrass you by informing you of your actual status. Until recently there was no necessity to inform you of it. Your mother and I"—how easily this flowered in the soil of his cold and arid talk! "Your mother and I"—the unwittingly but unremittingly paternal phrase; at once he noticed it himself, and self-consciously divided the autonomous graft—"your mother, as you know, has desired all along to keep you clear of this disclosure, and I, as her agent, have closely acquiesced. We have sought silence. We have arranged for silence. We have nurtured silence. For a dozen years we have bought and paid for silence."

And in the silence William withdrew, and creaked the inglorious screw of his chair around to see now the crevices of the Venetian slats were startled into rods of wine: "Late, late, it gets late sooner these days," he muttered at timeless Cletis' morning-handed watch, remonstrating with his wife, who appeared to accuse the absent sun of having fled its post under fire; and reaching up to the plain lamp over the photograph he turned the switch and turned his lip: in the blast of quick light it shifted like a worm. "We have paid and we have paid and we have paid. It's nothing you or anyone could feel the way your mother has. Though in the early days your stepfather was known to tot it up now and then—to see what was left for himself, one supposes. At any rate we have paid. Up to last month we were still paying. We have paid and paid" —how cautiously he released this into the fan of brightness that came tilting over our twenty flattened fingers, and hesitated, and resumed, "and paid. And we never knew if it would do—the money—he wouldn't say how much, he left it all to us. In the beginning he would specify. He always sent a figure—that was in the beginning. He would say what it was for. Sometimes what he asked for was absurd—enough to buy a bottle of champagne if that was what he had a whim for, or a pair of shoes: whatever struck him at the moment. Or else he'd go out and rent a flat and fill it up with luxuries and send the bill. And once—on a postcard—I won't withhold even this—he wrote: 'Two dollars for Swiss tart.' I don't withhold even that. Torment and torment. Imagine how it was. Your mother had me write and tell him to name his sum and let it go at that. So he stopped saying how much and made us guess what he wanted. Spite. He wouldn't settle for a regular figure—I was ready to set up a monthly thing in a bank over there: he wouldn't settle for it. His reply!—if he had a steady income it would give the illusion of a steady job. He wouldn't join the bourgeoisie. I won't repeat all that madness, however. It suffices that he left it all to us: he wrote and asked and never named his sum, and we had to respond with conjecture. And we never knew whether it would do. Sometimes a little would do; at other times a very great deal wasn't enough for him. Torment! It was part of his whimsy. Your poor mother," William said, lowering his great naked brow under the lamp, "she never felt safe over you. There was no way of trusting him not to break through and show himself."

"And if he did?" I murmured, thinking of the locked room and the ledge where I had crept to hear the private visitor's terms. "I remember when he came that time. He had a blue bicycle, with bells. He laughed and laughed, and had books strapped to his bicycle in the rain. And one of them was full of flowers, and my mother threw it in a barrel. He was like a court jester. She asked Enoch if he had a knapsack."

"You were to have been kept free of him. Your mother paid him so that you would be kept free of him. She meant you to be safe."

"She locked me up. I never saw him."

"Or put it more pertinently: he never saw you."

"He never wanted to."

"Extortion isn't for the thing itself. It's for the use of the thing."

"Is that another of my father's names?"

"I beg your pardon?"

"Extortioner."

"Call him what you please," William said. Now the window had gone black. "Seven o'clock, and dark. September. But don't call him a court jester. He was never amusing. Your mother and I never found him amusing," he said. "Though your mother did. Then never again. Never again. She suffered. Under another set of chances she might have thrown it all off. Under a different star, so to speak."

"You mean if not for me," I offered once again.

"If not for you," he acknowledged finally. "She had to live it through. She has thought always how you must be kept safe from him. It has been her preoccupation. It has been her obsession. It has been her cross. He would have told you what you were."

I said, "What I am."

"It would have been unspeakable to do. It would have been hideous to do. It could never have been allowed."

"Until you could do it yourself."

"Until," he contradicted, "it had to be done." And I saw the worm of his mouth coil.

"I don't blame you," I said. "You've done it to save my mother the job."

"You were never to have been told. Your poor mother," poor William had to say again, lifting the weight of his head and mourning after some secret vision perhaps too literal for his tethered imagination to wonder at; but it was years too late for remorse. She had thrown the book of flowers, those vulnerable beauties, into the rain-barrel, she had thrown her Shelley into the tunnel of the sea, the black spray of flies flew up, the white flies of the foam flew up: ENCHIRIDION and the unbodied joy given water-burial, flowers and flower sent grotesquely down to swell; and the next day they saw her book floating just beneath the water's membrane like a cinder trapped under a finger-nail, the pages winging outward and bloated, the pages like the wavering limbs of an undersea anemone, waverings of print speckled over them as indistinct as filaments and anthers in a field. Did he think he could recall it now?—he who had nearly praised her for the loss, and chided fantasy out of existence? Did he think he could turn back the sea and its salt from the drowned wound? Did he think he could turn back her face from the undiscoverable lighthouse in the view? There is no retrieving, there is no redeeming. Her white socks left shapeless craters behind her in the sand. It was September then, and dark. The honeymoon endēd.

Then the new house, built for them by both their fathers, because she would not live in that other house, all empty and receptive, where she had grown up, though William was willing enough; he was fonder of his father-in-law than of his own father, that pleasureless man of meagre desires, who looked on life as a pyramid to be raised brick by golden brick, the whole to be rewarded by an angelic sermon from its peak on the Last Day, and by the solidity of the structure in the meantime. Allegra's father was something else: scoffed at Adam if not at Eve and marched eagerly up and down his beach, swinging the keys of his mansion from a chain attached to a polished seashell. He liked to think of himself as a mariner, though all he knew of ships was Cunard saloons and waiters gliding sidle-hipped by on the incline of a scarcely-felt crest. But he wanted his daughter; the very beach, he claimed, demanded his daughter; and he promised to build a wall through the garden and give her half for her private own, and half the house, and half the staff; or, failing that, to go away himself, the old aunt with him. But she despised that place, her father's estate, which he had made in pleasurable celebration of his voyages of pleasure—it was too gaudy, it was too splendid, it was a horrid oversized peacock of a house teetering on haughty skinny legs pointlessly at the water's edge, with its shining tail foolishly upraised. A foolish place—a whim and not a house, with all the goose-faced Kings of France jutting from dark panels in the dining room, and stuffed with a multitude of leisured maids and servingmen, and the aged aunt's tremulous night-shouts out of dreams, and the big marble anchor in the garden—a fountain

breathing shiny glassy sea-water up and down the anchor's
immense and pointless flank hour after hour, with a sound
like road-traffic. She despised her father's house; she did not
like to stay where she had been a girl; rooms in which the
girl has walked and stalked cannot be where walk and stalk
the perils and blisses of the world; and it was the world she
wanted. So they went instead to Scarsdale and the new house,
all triumphant oaken Tudor. But she could not praise the
new house, either; and, spiting the gift of father and father-
in-law, she had lived as though it had been drilled through
with secret passages. Her decorating notions were anything
but conventional; she re-invented. The beds had chalky posts
and purple canopies, the windows went without cloth or
shades to cover domestic tableaux, dresser drawers perpetually ajar hung out their tongues of sleeves, the young wife's
easels stood in doorways and had to be squatted under to
pass through, telephones came by twos in every room. Often
they all rang together. People called her up. Who, who?
There were muffled talks. Then almost immediately the vast
Arthurian table arrived from the East, and she split her shoe
in the spite of punishing it. Though it was still early autumn
there were no screens: she liked the sound of a buzzing hor-
net nosing the ceiling in the first sigh of morning. She ate
heated canned asparagus, the yellow tips fragile and buttery,
for a week at a time. The cook quit, and was replaced by a
Moslem in a sari. William yowled at curry on his lip. She
hated maids and hired an English lad to mop underneath the
beds, where a crop of luscious dust-curds bloomed like rose-
heads; she gave him a whole wall on which to paint a prehistoric mural—and there, at night, when the hornets returned
to their eaves, a crimson pterodactyl battered a turquoise horizon filled with mastodon and tyrannosaurus rex. Though the
English boy's style was true primitive, the room remained a
room and not a cave; and his mistress snapped her fingers angrily and told him he was a coward to be afraid, just because
it gargled, of a vacuum-cleaner. The thirty telephones—the
twenty? the forty? the fifty?—rang at once. Every afternoon
she hid away to write long, long letters, all benign. Answers
jostled one another's thicknesses in the mailbox: "I am
happy indeed that you so much liked my poem, 'Sicilian In-
tensities,' which was recently published in *The Toreador Review*. Rare is it, and therefore ravishing, revivifying, for a
New Mexico poet like myself to receive unbridled recognition
from so distant, yet so discerning, a reader; from a reader of

sensibility; and I will, indeed, as you suggest, telephone you at your residence if Fortuna, that unpredictable goddess, should ever bring me to New York . . . P.S. I am enclosing, for your *private* perusal, a sheaf of six as-yet-unpublished poems which comprise the early part of a cycle, 'Tiresias at Taos,' begun some fifteen or twenty years ago. Perhaps you recall seeing Strophe Nine, beginning (and also entitled) 'How Blind We Are to the Day of Our Death!' which was to have been printed in the November issue of *The Sweeper*. Unfortunately the magazine was only just discontinued in October. Nevertheless the poem is, I may add, explicitly antidadaist in theme and execution . . ."

"Have children," Allegra's father said; "have sons quickly." It was now too cold to stand for long on the beach. He rambled instead in those gigantic rooms, moving from window to window to survey the mutating color of the sea. His own skin was altering; it was rather too falsely ruddy a sailor's hide. He was tired. Corporations were corpses to him now; he left his affairs to William, who had a talent for them. "Have sons," he only seemed to joke, "then you needn't depend on the alien nature of a son-in-law to take things over. Because consider: if not for that brother of yours, not that I'm saying anything against Helen and Marie, they're both nice girls, if not for Max where would I be now? You don't think your father would've handed you over to me, just like that, if he hadn't had another to keep for himself—and who would I have at this stage of the game to watch out for my interests? Dynasty is destiny, keep that in mind! And tell it to Allegra. It's bloody threats from her if *I* say it. Some people grow sterile waiting for a good philosophical reason for progeny. There isn't any. Tell it to Allegra! She's an eccentric, you know. That's not the same as a Bohemian, though it may seem so to you. I've seen them all over the world, including the East—eccentrics, I mean. Bohemianism is the product of a society of wealth—meat to protest against: it's no use being a Utopian vegetarian among the Hindus, say—but even the poorest have their oddities, that's a fact. I'll tell you what makes an oddity." He liked to talk to William. He thought him a wary young man, he knew his daughter was a fool, and he was pleased and even excited by the possibilities in combining elements. The irregularity of it, when outwardly it had all the appearance of propriety, teased his fancy. He waited for them to mate. Curiosity made him long for grandchildren; he supposed they would be fools and prigs, though he hoped, provided there were enough of them, for a canny one in the lot. "An oddity is stuffed," he explained, leading his son-in-law into a tall downstairs cavern he had without humor named his Marine Room, "with wishing. It's wish, wish, wish from the day they're born. Look, you understand sin. Then I tell you it's a sin to be an oddity. It's to commit the Sin of Vicarious Living. It's wish, wish, wish—and for what? For a picture in the heart. There's no cure but distraction. Don't be modern, you hear?—have sons quickly." Table followed table: and on each an uncanny clutter of green bottles, fetid, murky, filled with round eyes and fog and dark blue smear—oh, vile, and like a laboratory-heart kept alive with all its robot valves exposed and dimly working. "Nice, see? Pickled fish," he said, "not that I have the things classified, though I wish I did. I wouldn't know how. You're a geologist, right?—but I'm only a beachcomber. It's not a *system* I am showing you, mind you—it's simply the occupation of my senile years. The poor old woman hates the smell—I tell her it's not the sea-things themselves, only the solution they're in. The pickle they're in, ha ha. My wife wasn't fussy—she didn't only tolerate, she admired. A good woman—my only friend, so to speak, I mean when you get down to it—she was sick for maybe fifteen years before she went. I meandered around the world without her now and then. 'She went' —I once heard a captain speak that way of a ship gone down. I suppose that's why Allegra grew up all fads and no religion: an oddity, my daughter, drowned in wishing. People are wrong, you know, when they talk of Mother Earth. It's Father Neptune who takes us in our last days. Not dust unto dust—never mind the Bible. Offended, boy? But blood is salt water, like the sea, which never left us though we left it. They say the dolphin has an intelligence equal to, if not better than, man's. All right—at least the dolphin had the sense not to throw up his sacred home for the ash of land. All of mankind's wrung with drunkard's thirst for the sea. In my view that's the explanation for religion. Would Sinai have been possible if it hadn't been preceded by the Red Sea? And all those fishermen, and water-walking and all of that, and loaves and fishes at Galilee! Did you ever look hard at the backbone of a fish? There's a crucifix hidden in the skeleton; make of that what you want. And Tao, where they say the Way is like water—it's there too, reality, I mean. Why does a man salivate? Why does he bleed? You're on the wrong track with those rocks of yours. Who cares how old the earth is?

It's all iron anyhow: a fleck of iron. Nothing reproduces unless it has sap in it: chew a weed for proof if you like, or smash a bug. Your rocks are tellurian ash. Sterile; sterile. What's wrong with my daughter? Have sons! I've given this place a secret name, you see. Duneacres because it sits at the seaside—that's only picturesque. But intimately between me and me it's Doomacres. I've built on silt. The sea will come up, the tide will come and pull it down. I give it twenty sound years—that's more than long enough for a sand castle, and the anchor won't tie it down, the anchor won't do it any good—the anchor's stone. Stone is ash; wishes are ash. Have sons, have sons!"

There was a swarm of servants everywhere, idling, idling: schools of servants paddling by on elaborate non-errands. He was lonesome, the old man. His skin darkened to grape, and he laughed it off, diagnosing his dying: "I'm marooned"— and spread his hands to show himself the fat incredible maroon veins. But the aunt died first, complaining how the place smelled of fish and disinfectant, wailing that the summer storms (it was January) frightened her—the crackle of lightning on the water so close it started static in her gold bridges. So he raised the anchor and lowered it, in between burying her beneath it—the ground opened, and the vaguely delightful stench of marsh weed rose up and hung. Hoar-frost and miasma tickled in his shoes. He thought how the house would be, death-abandoned, and the woodland around it and the beach and the dock below it. "There's only one good reason for children, and the reason's not philosophical. It's to fill the bedrooms. I married too late for it, my wife was old, then sick, maybe only the sickness of being too old to fill the bedrooms, but still, we had one daughter, an oddity, and *she* doesn't fill the bedrooms of her own house, except with telephones. Things being what they are, I'll give the place to the sea. Every room to be a mansion for Neptune—sea-nymphs everywhere. Thetis and all the Nereides—I forget their idiotic names. Go and get me scientists: experts, I mean, on sea-nymphs. Men with an idea of the majesty of wetness. Salt! Get brains with plenty of salt. Finny fellows, ha ha! Offices upstairs, galleries downstairs, or vice-versa. *I* don't know—get an architect who does. I want the outside intact though—the lines of the place intact, widow's walk and all, the garden stays as it is, no little city starting up on the beach, the wood left alone. I don't want the sand castle tumbled, you see? It's got to look as though the ocean could lap it up any time it felt like it. Which it can. Hours of talk between you and me, this means. A long story, vast plan, deep blueprints. The more I think, the more devoted I get to this magnificence. I mean it to be magnificent, you understand me? Big tanks, living things, but not just an aquarium, mind you. Let it be a History of the Origin of Life. You understand me? Don't you? A rock can't comprehend the wash of the tide. Then convert yourself. Right away. Salt and sap, that's what I'm after. Go ahead, draft the deed of trust. The will has it all to Allegra; but *she* doesn't want it; anyhow it's time I did something public. A public thing, this will be. A museum."

And died; died, the old man, hurrying after the anchored aunt. Of him were ashes made; and Allegra, multiplying the tear-salt sea, stood on the dock and at a sign from the minister—a Unitarian—threw into the water whitish earth of her father. "No one could say of him," said the minister, saying what no one *would* say, "that he was not a visionary." A pretty remark, suitable, but like all grave-side summaries only wishful. A visionary? That selfish old man who could not bear to see the circlets of spittle on his wife's half-paralyzed lip, and went out year after year to watch instead the spume of liners? But a man who foists on posterity a monstrous piece of real estate with the intention of compelling a hundred people to produce out of it what no one had remotely thought necessary, whether for public education or edification or elevation or enervation—what else shall he be called if not a visionary?—short of philanthropist, a word saved only for the really wicked. He had pretended, Allegra's father, to be one of those old buccaneers of business: he fattened his speech with fake coarse riches, and toughened his stride, and praised his bookish weak unhappy wife for loving Emerson, and did all those eager rough vulgar things one expects of a money-pirate in America, quite as though he had swiped all the money himself, starting from the plain scratch of ambitious poverty. He was as bold as any ruffian of the nouveau riche, and all to smother the fact that he had (like William's father) been born into seven generations of Hudson Valley railroad-padded burgher-pride; and he spoke of the old feeble spinster-aunt (who sweated in winter) as though she had been in early days a barmaid he had pinched away to a palace for the protection of her honor.

Yet Allegra mourned him, and complimented the Unitarian who had complimented her father who had complimented her mother for loving Emerson; in the end perhaps it

was simply her mother whom she mourned. For a servant
came upon a box of letters from her mother to her father
(they had to clear out the top of the house for the first crew
of renovators), in envelopes addressed to Eastern ports: letters which had never been mailed. And the bookish weak
semi-paralyzed unhappy lover of Emerson wrote accusation
after accusation—"fraud," cried the greenish-become ink in
ancient penmanship, "fraud and bigamist; fraud and polyg-
amist: Solomon not as to wisdom but to wives: how many
sons, offspring, progeny, boys, children, babies half-Asiatic,
half-Arab, half-Mongol, half-black, half-brown, half-yellow,
from those far-ranging loins?"—and every bitter violent letter
sealed into its envelope and stamped and ready to be posted
and never sent. Of course it was all a fantasy; and perhaps
her mother had even known it was a fantasy; but was it a
fantasy less plausible than her father's quixotry of a museum
of the waters? Her mother's mouth was twisted, and her
womb grown dry. The eyes of her remorse saw sons, none
hers. "You don't want to mind it, dear; don't mind it," William said of the letters, concealing his horror and his scorn.
Meanwhile they watched the servants dig into niches and
make small notes on where the stairs whined, and whisper to
the masons how the cellar ran with long-antenna'd silverfish,
quick-footed scum like insect-mice; and Allegra said, "I don't
mind. What if he did? What if he did? After she died didn't
he go sailing on someone's yacht with a black flag up for
grief? Didn't he go out to the Indies wearing a black arm-
band all the way? And anyhow love is for the taking—it's
nourishment, like wheat, and ought to be generally available." But William in the shock of that began to wonder
whose taking love was for. Never, never had she given her
white face to him, and she kept, besides, a careful calendar
of when in the month's length he lay with her; and she went
habitually to dangerous lectures, and told him afterward what
the speaker had declared, that love bound by the chains of
duty was not free. "The chains of duty?" he echoed her—he
whose Sunday lesson had always taught that the truest freedom of all was doing what one must. But she would not say
more, and instead battled with him about what was being
made of her father's house. "It's evil, evil," she said, "all that
effort and all that money for something that won't do a bit of
practical good in the world! If he wanted to do good why
didn't he at least pension off the servants? The *kitchen* people
at least—after all those years! I want to give them pensions.

Fix it so I can give them pensions, William. That's the whole
point of Social Security!—then the Government would do it,
and it wouldn't have to be just charity and being at the
mercy of the capitalist conscience. In the Soviet Union *all* the
workers get pensions, it's only fair," and while William listened without hope, she told of strikes and scabs, and riots
against management, and employers with iron rods: all that
drab lexicon of her tedious clubs. He knew about those clubs;
even at Miss Jewett's she had gone to Social Justice Teas, but
he had always regarded these as more than innocent, even as
exhilarating—she wore a jumper and held high a banner with
bare fists and wrists and arms so delectable to the very nerve
of his eye, that, contemplating her, he felt a breath from his
cautious lung could disperse her, she hung like a spider from
an insubstantiality, the sun provoked her wandering sign into
silk. It said "Colonialism is Napoleonism Made New" or
"The Amalgamated Peoples of the Earth Decry Mississippi
Miscegenation Laws," or "The Aspiring Negro is Our
Brother," or "Honest Labor is the True Aristocracy of America's Future" or "Greed for Profits is the Workers' Loss: The
Bosses' Gain is Labor's Cross" or "What Shall it Profit the
Prophets of Management?" or "PEACE PEACE WORK
WORK." The words pirouetted like Pavlovas; the poles spun;
the band-aid signs purported to heal what William's God had
not healed in all the centuries of obeisance; the band-aid
signs rose and descended, aspired and denied themselves; William's breathing rose and descended, aspired and denied itself, and he pitied her error for being not error, but fleeting,
and he pitied his own love for its brief captivity in the fleeting sheeny skein of her error. He pitied and he loved: the
banner-mobbed moment belonged to her youth, it would not
come again, the sublime error of her upraised arm would
never come again. The rasp of aberration scraped on his regret: Allegra dared, and he had never dared at all. She pulled
down propriety: father, mother, right and rite. Her arm lifted
like a spear, and her father's fury and her mother's pique,
punishing, forbade her the white dress of coming-out. William sorrowed for her, remembering his sisters' coming-out:
the crest of the nubile hour. Lucky Helen, lucky Marie! Unlucky Allegra! She got herself (in retaliation) engaged to
Vernon: it was the stamping of her foot. William looked on,
ambushed by terror; but Vernon was too fat and too pedantic: he criticized the position of the commas and semicolons
in her poems, so that she asserted she would prefer to marry

even William, who never criticized her at all. True, true, all bewilderingly true: William did not criticize her even now, though he despised her clubs and had no taste for the visitors who came an hour short of midnight without hats or coats or neckties, slouching and laughing and eating dripping fruit in the living room, where the hearthrug was a real polar bear, though dead. Some of them were midwesterners, unmannerly; worse, he suspected among them a Jew or two. Why had the signs and banners not vanished, like the young wife's jumpers, like the girls of Miss Jewett's? Why had they not melted away into the ache of an old mischance which one recalls with a perversity of yearning? The signs and banners of the mind: the alternative which is not really an alternative, the zealous error which is not zealously pursued, the playing at piracy by children—he was puzzled, puzzled. There was a queer knot in the young wife: the thread did not pull smoothly through, as it ought. She was clinging too long to resistance, too stubbornly tediously long to error; she was playing pirate in grown-up's clothes. Vaguely but patiently he wondered who was to blame, and saw again the bulbous pages swaying like fleshy blades under the water, turning in the water, diving and rising in the water-rings around her ankles. He had fallen asleep. She had thrown her Shelley in the water. He was wronged, he was innocent: he could not love and pity error unless it swam up refracted through the wave of an olden time: the way his sight quickened in spite of itself at a mediaeval spire, pin-thin at the top, though he knew it belonged to the Dark Ages of superstitious faith and lacked the homely cleanliness of Bible-things. The long-ago existed for the sake of pity and love; one was young in order some day to forgive oneself for it. Willingly, wittingly, as an act of cherishing, he forgave Allegra her parading years. But she did not forgive herself, she did not relinquish herself, she did not defy herself. She continued, she continued. Still he did not criticize; but fifteen holding companies inextricably entangled with one another intervened, and drew him away like Theseus in the cave, unraveling. The polar bear's head ran with pear juice, and afterward Allegra, poking at the last log of April, confronted him with prongs and defenses: "the subject," said she, "is bears," and laughed until he laughed too, and then said "forebears," and defended her dead mother against her dead father because her mother was right and her father was a fraud; and defended her dead father against her dead mother because love is not a cage; and defended the working classes against the leisure classes because the members of the meeting had proved their case; and said to the young husband (who longed to kiss her hair, close and valorous as a helmet in the log's glint), "Who do you think can go to museums? And on an island, an out-of-the-way place like that! They'll have to run a ferry, the train stops two towns away, he didn't think of that! And not even pensions for the kitchen people! And all for the sake of whales and things! What good is a whale to the workers? The workers don't go to museums! It's only a scheme to set up a capitalist monument to unreasonable profits, that's what the members said tonight; we talked it all out tonight. Who do you think can *go* to museums? It won't be the workers, it'll be the rich!"

And William's reply?

He took the poker from her and sat her on the polar bear (a peach-pit in its muzzle) and touched the slidings of her hair with a single courteous finger (how tentative, how jocose, his finger on the margins of her skull): "We," he said, "are the rich."

"I"—the young wife began mysteriously to weep (was it that she felt how he feared to strain beyond courtesy, she felt how tentative, how jocose, the finger of his hope?)—"am mankind," Allegra said. And meant to leap from him and stand; but she had called herself mankind, and him a capitalist, so he kept her down; he kept her down and would not permit her to break free. He oppressed her then, tasting salt in her eyes. "Allegra, Allegra," he said, exploring her name for consequence, for motion; and she turned, and for the first time gave him her face (always afterward he thought of its look then as gilt, bronze-poured, religious), and said, "I think I'm pregnant, William." Power held him holding her; he gave a shrug of ecstasy. She licked herself, her arms, like a long cat, licking tears: "I hate it, I hate it. It could be you, I think. It could be." Was she honest? Ought he to doubt her doubt? She mumbled, muttered, murmured, wept. "It could be," she said once more, licking, and fell away from him the way a petal falls when some rough hand has made the stem shudder: a hand, not the uncaring wind.

("She was mistaken," William bluntly announced twenty-five years later: to me in his office. "Luckily. Luckily. I thanked my stars and still do. It was not my ambiton to be the father of a child whose father I was not. I meant to rear my own. I thanked my stars.")

But it was confession, revelation: she was not safe: he

could not trust. "Trust, trust," she moaned back at him (often they argued it), "what does the trust matter? I mean if you let it go just one summer? You take everything so seriously, William, just because it's written down. Everything's the Divine Word to you. And just one summer! There's nothing in it that says you have to start it right away, is there?"

The document lived in his mind, like all documents. "As soon as feasible from the date of execution," he quoted; it was already halfway through May. She was asking for a single summer. "He meant to see it go up in his lifetime. We've already got an oceanographer coming to look things over," he objected, staring.

"But just this one summer! After all, the property's *there*, nobody's going to use it, and they all say it's ideal. The house for meetings, the nucleus group indoors, the overflow in tents in the woods—"

"Tents in the woods," William said. She was not safe, he could not trust, she was lost to him. He saw her bent over her notebook. It was the first version of *Marianna Harlow*. She no longer wrote those queer little poems that never rhymed: she told him that art without immediate relevance to society was wicked. What a moralist she was! He asked, "What's it about?" and put on his straw hat, though the band was too tight and pressed his brow and stained it with a red thong-mark.

"The revolution of the workers."

"Yes," he said. "And will he be here today?"

"Who?" But she knew.

"The one from Pittsburgh."

"He's not from Pittsburgh, he's from Chicago. I don't know, I can't telephone. The telephone company took out all the telephones this morning—I made them. I can't concentrate with all that racket. I don't want anything ringing in my head but these voices: the sisters, the foreman, the workers. Wait till I read it to you, William!"

He waited, and went in a ferry up the Hudson to a reunion of graduates. He wandered across the quadrangle under ancient eaves in the greenyear time of the newest grass-tips and squandered his eyes on the horror of all those boys' faces grown rigid with maturity. In his clubs in the city he never saw how those same young men had brutally grown less young: but here the travesty of dark scooping line and dim steady frown shook him with the gloom—was this Henderson, was that Blackfield? What a secret cuckold time was! He walked and talked—but even their talk was different from the usual maundering of the clubs: here they all seemed conscious of the danger of making themselves out for fools, they talked almost innocently—and heard a speech from the new headmaster and left a promise for a check and came home again at dusk. The young wife sat as before.

"I've got as far as Chapter Three," she cried out. "All in one day! It's only a draft, though. —Was it all right up there?"

Thirstily she emptied the last of a bottle of milk while he watched. How white the milk was! He had never before noticed the density of its color: it was thick as the moon. "I shouldn't have gone—it was a bore. It's always a bore. Same thing as the last time. It's only to ask for money. They're going to build again." He was dizzy with too much fresh air. He said, "I saw Manning. They've just made him a major. He's balding. Imagine, he's almost bald, and he's a year younger than I am."

"Listen!" said Allegra, not listening.

She read what she had written. It was a long lying account. It was non-event, non-fact; it was even anti-fact. None of it had ever happened; it was grotesque. It was false, false, false. It was full of false principles. He thought of Henderson and Blackfield as they had looked nineteen years ago; he remembered them in their football uniforms. He remembered their teeth. "What's that Chicago man do?" he asked.

"A journalist"—but her answer was a hiss of rancor. Why, why? She was bitter. He had nothing to say about her chapters. He did not comprehend them. They were either absurd or insane. At best they were trivial. "You can't feel it, you can't identify. You hate what I think! You hate my *mind*," she charged him crossly.

"A journalist? Is that all? I thought he was a professional organizer. He gives that impression."

"Well, why not? He's Youth Leader."

"Youth Leader?" he repeated stupidly. (And Manning was already bald. And Henderson and Blackfield had daughters and sons. One of them was old enough to read *Uncle Wiggily*. Henderson said: "The old rabbit gentleman, if you want to know. That's who Uncle Wiggily is." And the others smiled down innocently at the brilliant grass. The tragically mutilated boys talked of their children: strange! It was not the spasm of vanity that pricked William. He believed he had a duty to exacting time; it made him hate philosophy. "Have sons!" the ghost of Allegra's father called from out of the sea.) "He's a bit long in the tooth, that fellow, to see himself in that category," William protested.

"He's Youth Leader anyhow, it's his title. Just like Manning's being a major."

She knew Manning. She had danced with him at his sisters' parties. "Manning, well," he said, "he earned his title in rather a different species of organization."

"Rather a different," she was quick to mock. "Now he can train gun-fodder for the reactionary imperialists, can't he? Rather a different!"

The country-air, the lawn-air, the air in the shadows of the school-founder's statue: he had pocketed it all in his clothes. It had the fragrance of fresh milk in a density of whiteness. He closed his eyes and saw points of yellow dandelions; he saw a waterfall of milk, and an old rabbit gentleman wearing a hat. "The fellow influences you," he accused, "he mesmerizes you."

"Because he can do anything, I've told you, in a political way. He's a sort of genius."

"He has no background."

"You're always looking to put people in classes!" she shot back.

"I don't put them there. It's where I find them."

"*We* think about a classless society." —She screwed on the top of her pen.

William argued impotently, "You let him be your ventriloquist in fact," and discovered, in the moment of opening his sight to the absence of dandelions, that he was wishing for a different life. Was it too late? was it too late? The barbarians were scarring her mind. O Allegra! He meant to have her back; he gestured at her closed notebook. "All mad ideas," he said. "Mad ideas attract you." But that was not the way: the more he condemned, the stricter her scorn for him. "They won't last, these notions," he essayed.

"Nothing lasts," she answered speculatively. "That's the whole point in having a revolution—to see that nothing lasts."

"Is he planning a revolution? Is that it? He's going to overthrow the Government?"

"Who?"

"Your Youth Leader," he said: but with a secret daring danger in his caution.

"Well what do you think all the discussion is *about?*" she

sneered. "Only naturally it's important to lay the ideological groundwork first. You just don't go out and start a revolution."

"Ah," William said. "He's not a mere hothead then."

"If you're going to be sarcastic—"

"No, no," he retreated, "I'm simply looking for information. You spoke of a camp. I believe it was a camp. —For what purpose?"

"I *told* you. To discuss ideology and things. To train for the future. They're talking about having a World Youth Rally —that's just an example of the kind of preparation we'd need. It would be all the races on earth congregated in one place."

"I see," William said. "You're not thinking of bringing all the races on earth down to your father's beach?"

"Oh William! Will you, will you? You'll let us have the estate then?" she crowed; he had given himself away. "Oh look, I don't mean for the Rally—the Rally's not till next year, and anyhow it's going to have a million people. It might be Moscow or it might be Stockholm, we haven't heard yet. But we're hoping for Moscow. It's the logical place to celebrate."

"Moscow," he repeated. "To celebrate what?"

"*I* don't know—I can't *bear* lawyer-questions. I guess peace and freedom, things like that. Revolutionary things. Because the world's changing!" She flew out of her chair. "All we want is the camp. Just for this one summer! There's no rush about that museum, it doesn't matter about that museum—it's a crank idea, that museum! Oh please, William. Just June and July and maybe August. Fix it up!"

"It can't be 'fixed,'" he said thoughtfully. "There's the trust."

"The trust, the trust!" She whirled around him, spitting words. "I hate that trust!"

"I hate your camp," he said.

"What do you mean?"

They stood assessing one another.

"I mean it's abhorrent to me. It should be abhorrent to you."

"It's what I want," she said stubbornly.

"It won't last. It will burn itself out."

"Not the Movement!"

"Your devotion to it."

"My devotion is to justice."

"For whom?" he asked calmly; he was in control now; it

was very like an examination before trial; he felt the root of his confidence.

"For the downtrodden! For the workers!" she threw out.

"And what about justice for your father?" he inquired.

"Oh what's that?"—impatient: as though he were a fool.

"To fulfil his plan. Not to betray his wishes. Not to betray the trust."

"The trust again! A piece of paper! He was rich, now he's dead: *they* don't need justice, the rich and the dead. You see?" she said sourly, "That's just the difference between the capitalists and us. It's the workers *we* think of."

He was against argument—as much dispute with a cloud. But resignedly he said, "Then you don't think far enough. You don't think beyond sensationalism into sound economics." He finished: "The conversion of the estate will open jobs that never existed before."

"Jobs for fish!" she scoffed.

"Jobs for men."

"Pie in the sky!"

"What an adept you are," he said tiredly.

"You're reneging. It's just that you don't *want* the camp."

"No," he agreed. "I don't want it."

"You don't want anything," she said acidly.

He looked at her. Her eyes shimmered like a pair of tea-cups.

He said, "Have the camp. Just as you wish."

But he felt her confusion. He felt her suspicion. "June and July and August?" she demanded.

"June and July and August," he assented.

"All the house and all the grounds? The beach too? The woods?"

"All," he pronounced. "Just as you wish."

"You can really fix it?"

"I can ignore it. I can postpone beginning. I can wait," he said.

"Oh, if you wait for us to burn out you'll wait a long time!"

"Perhaps," he proposed, "you won't ignite at all."

"Pooh," she said. "People always catch fire at a camp, if it's enthusiasm you're talking about. It's because nowadays there are techniques. The Youth Leader knows them all. He can start anything from scratch."

"A firebrand," William said warily.

"Oh, an inflammatory, call him what you want, *we* don't

care. It doesn't matter—just so long as there's progress. Call it sedition!—the main thing is having the camp."

"I thought the main thing was peace and freedom."

"Well of course! But there's a different thing for each different condition. It's important to be practical and expedient as well as just idealistic," she gravely explained.

"I see," he took in. "Your Youth Leader is a clever man."

"I told you, he's a genius at political things. I *know* he looks perfectly ordinary, but really he's very smart. He makes everything pay for itself."

"Excellent," said William. "And so do I. Your father's property is worth something."

"It's worth only as much as what can be achieved in using it," she said neatly.

"On the contrary. It's worth what the trustee decides."

"Oh the trustee!" she jeered.

"Myself."

"Ha! You."

"—And if the trustee, on his own responsibility, arranges to dispose of the estate, even temporarily, against the terms by which he is bound," William said slowly, "he ought to have some compensation."

"Oh look! You're not asking for *rent?*" she said in disgust.

"No."

"Well I don't know *what* you're asking for. I can't understand that gobbledygook, it's too impersonal. Are you giving us the camp or not?"

"On a condition."

"I thought so! It isn't rent? We can't pay rent, you know. They never would've asked me to ask you if they thought you'd be that materialistic."

"They aren't materialists themselves then?"

"*Dialectical* materialists. It's different."

"Ah," William said.

"Then what is it? What *is* it?" she persisted. "You said you want something, and now you won't say what."

"Oh I want something," he remarked vaguely; he was aware of a quick red heat behind his vision; he feared he would stammer. "I want loyalty," he said finally.

"All right, but after all it isn't what you call a *betrayal*, it isn't being disloyal to my father just because—"

But he interrupted. "I don't mean your father."

"You said loyal—"

"To me."

She gazed. She understood. "To you? What a euphemism! How funny you are, William! You're scared of a few tents!"

He could not speak.

"No free camp, no free love! One or the other! How funny! Is *that* what you want? A sort of bargain?"

"Put it as you please," he said hoarsely.

"But it's a *bribe*," she cried, humiliating him with an access of laughter.

It was a bribe; he meant to keep her. He looked on her zealousness as some curious erraticism of his own; it was not that he permitted—rather it was that he did not dare to forbid. He meant to keep her. It was a bribe. Yet who was to judge who had succumbed to whom? He bribed for love, she for zeal: it was a bargain they had struck. The odor of the contract-seal invaded obscurely: as the price of keeping her trustworthy, what would he not have bartered? So he gave in, and gave up—only, he warned, for June and July and August —the dead man's trust.

And in June and July and August the tents went up; and in June and July and August they came, the campers; and in September and October and November they came. And in November the son of Armenian immigrants came, imploring his livelihood; and in January came again; and there, in February, in a morning wind, behind the empty tents beating on poles frozen immobile in the ground, abandoned by the campers who now slept on cots in the house, upstairs and downstairs and along all the narrow corridors, there within earshot of the planning meeting for the Moscow March For A Better Future, the son of Armenian immigrants (whose father and mother had seized the confusion of war to leap like fish from the oppressive fist of Moscow toward the sea's escape) cut the future out of his neck and fell without grace among leaves, rusting their rust with the knife's rust and the special rust of a young man's blood when air has turned it brown as leaves.

The knife was rusty from stem to point. It had lain the whole winter on a stone. All summer they had cleaned fish with that knife. All summer they had fished, and cracked open clams pried from under rocks in the little cove, and every night sang—O illusion of illusion! thought William— with a fine robustness around a campfire. William saw it—the fire—and it smote him like a theory. It was artful, and it was artless, and he supposed it was another of the Youth Leader's contrivances, like the uncaptained cooking committee, everyone taking turns, and then the hideous mass feeding, like cattle in a barn. But the jolly fire and the jolly songs obscured the meanness of it all—the cots, even in the gate-house, beside which he had to leave the car; and the noble gate bent, as though it had been swung on for a game; and the road blocked with cartons. He looked into one; it was heavy, and filled with cans of peas for the next day's cooks. Then he heard the singing, and thought it was girls' voices only, because of the lifted thinness, like a light hammer on far far metal; but when he halted in the oak-clump at the top of the hill the sound thickened and mingled with darker sounds, and it was the men who carried the words. So he gave in to the path; it took him sullenly downward toward the shadow-blotted fire, and a whitish smoke that the moon clarified, and a braid of smoke that divided black from black across the water, beginning from the beach and smearing out for the middle of the sea: it was the moon's trail, as liquid-ivory as though pressed that moment from an udder. And meanwhile the singing assaulted the air, imposing joy on the night's heat. A stereotype of illusion! What did Allegra want here? Now gladly she slept in the house, but when her father had asked her to sleep in it she would not; she would not live there; now the house was given away to the mob and she lived in it with the mob. What, what? Why? The song said: "I dreamt I saw Joe Hill last night"; it said: "alive as you and meee"; it said: "I neverrr died, said heee"—and William stopped to see the life of the place, all as Allegra had promised it, but troubled with a plague of falsehood. They had put the fire in the rose-garden: the trellises hung weighty heads by the hundreds, like a gallows. The roses were not for night; they dangled ashamed in the artifice of the camp-fire, and their clots of sweetness fell guiltily and steadily, like a strangely delicious and dangerous gas. On the black lawn the singers had thrown themselves against the dampness, form by form, leg by leg; tangles, it seemed, of lovers; and then, without warning to the trespassing eye, torso and head and arms of Allegra—on the margin of the fire, feeding it a stick as though it were a dog that might run with it and return. And the little loops of flame ran with the stick and returned, then ran again; then came tamely, then suddenly reared up barking; and in the tall light that the quick high fire built, William saw the naked back of a Negro, with lean jutting shoulder-blades; and against this Allegra, wearing over her blouse a man's shirt, sat propped, easily and lightly, spine on spine, close

close against the man, the thickness of a thread between their two skins. William called her name. She sang and tickled the fire and did not hear. He called her name, but the absurd noise streamed to its climax and overwhelmed him. He felt dumb; he felt deaf. He felt he had fallen in among brigands, vagabonds, gypsies, robbers, beasts; a roiling, lazy, clownish lot of deceivers. And Allegra? Was this what pleased her—to sit chanting on the cold ground of her father's ruined garden like a Hindu on a patch of burlap? She offended him; she outraged him; she insulted him. "Is this it? Is this it?" he said to her, and she, startled, knocked with a knuckle on the brown man's bony back as on a door, to make an opening for him to come. So he came, and sat like the rest of them with his knees in a mound before him, and sat in the middle of their thievish hilarity, and grieved for the spoiled grass, and the unpruned trellises almost audibly cracking, and the lush waste of rose-heads (his mind ranged them nobly in milk-glass jars on the window-sills at home, stacked instead with Allegra's abandoned notebooks): agitatedly he took in how a month of unguarded unruly summer had smothered with jungle his vision of what had been before. Jungle and jungle and jungle: he saw the Negro laugh without circumspection, and like a savage put passerine fingers on the round belt of skin inside Allegra's openly hanging sleeve—and she jumping away as though violated: "Hugh, it hurts!" He had forgotten, and pressed her tender sunburn. Brigands, vagabonds, gypsies! A fellowship of savages: but "No," Allegra said, "of philosophers. You don't know how to see us, William." He scowled at her "us"; she left him out. And again he pleaded, "Is this it? So this is it? The air that makes you happy? What you want? And how long will you want it?" "Until I don't want it any more," said his wife. "I won't come again," he told her meditatively. "You said that the time before." "I won't come again, though." "Yes you will. You want to sneak up to see what we do to the property. You don't trust us," she said into his ear, like a secret. It shamed him, the demeaning act: into his ear, as though he were a conspirator, and cared only for the property, and not for his own fate.

Oh, his own fate! It was to stand astride a cleft in the rock; a fault creaking wider by the moment. Quickly he had to choose, or else fall to the limits of vacancy: Allegra solidly on one side, a fresh empty field on the other. He leaped—his fate leaped, his will leaped, every imaginable force of urgency leaped: for Allegra. It was Allegra he wanted—she who taunted him with wanting nothing at all on the crust of the world. He wanted her, but obscurely altered; he could not say how: to be just as she was, but qualified—the vitality without the mockery, perhaps; the sober stern sureness without the improbable commitment—he did not know. "Oh, there, *now* they're at it," she said, aroused; "watch them, William, if you came to see sinister rites!"

The Negro yielded another cannonade of laughter to the frosty air. "Who said a bar sinister had any rights?"

"What's a bar sinister?" demanded Allegra.

"A saloon with a bad reputation."

"Oh, *Hugh!*" she whimpered, faking peevishness. And then: "Is it, William?"

He began feebly, "It's a term of law—"

"Then never mind; *don't* explain it—you get so long-winded when you start on law, William. Anyhow I don't care. I only care about what has to do with real things that happen, don't I, Hugh?"

"Real things that happen," said Hugh, obligingly. "Virginia reel things."

"What?"

"That's what they're doing."

"No they're not, it's that Highland business."

"They're all the same," said Hugh, "derived from your primitive tribal ancestors. I bet the Virginia reel used to be a rain-dance."

"Oh for Pete's sake! If there's one thing it does in Scotland is *rain,*" Allegra said in disgust. "Sometimes you're so *arrogant*—my God, it's insufferable." —Oh, just as she was! Just as she was! The energy of her hauteur charged and charmed. Her malevolence, her spite: they drew William like spells and sparks; like arrows of wind; like a golden collar. She bit, but she gleamed. She was seized with wishfulness. The wishfulness gripped and turned her the way a lathe grips and turns, shaping, shaping. She was incomplete; she was an experiment in search of a potter. Then it was not too late to alter, to qualify; to *have* her. And meanwhile on the lawn the campers had risen because of the cold, and were rubbing on grass, and stamping numbly with both feet so that a tremor seemed to muse and loiter in the ground after each blow; and two by two between a column of hand-clappers they bounded and slid; and then all rotated mysteriously, shrieking out a kind of breathlessness that did for a tune: it loosed a barbaric shudder in the trellises.

"Do you do this all the time?" William asked. "Every night?"—because it seemed to him that even the dance was a tool, and had the power to shape and shave, and could lop her awry.

"No—sometimes we do laundry."

"Or pudding," said the Negro.

"We have lots of jobs," Allegra said: with a snap of practicality in her teeth. "Everyone does everything. You just go ahead and do whatever falls to you."

"Ah," said William; he was looking awkwardly for a tone to take. "That's your Equality, I suppose."

"Not quite," said Hugh. "We never really get them equal —some always end up lumpier than others. You meant the puddings? You couldn't have meant the races?"

"Sly! Then you ought to mix the batter harder," Allegra said, performing a culinary frown. "It all depends on how hard you stir."

"You *do* stir," Hugh said. "You stir *me,* girl."

"Ball and chain," Allegra said. "Beware."

"Who?"

"Him."

"Is that the one!"

"I *told* you, didn't I?"

"You didn't tell me. You kicked me. But I guess that's a quibble. I *do* declare," said Hugh. "I do absolutely declare. Do you duel?"

"I beg your pardon?" William said.

"Sir, I ask if you duel. Choose your blades."

"Blades of grass," Allegra tittered, chewing one.

"I am in love with your wife," said the Negro.

"You see?" Allegra said helpfully. "Now you've *got* to kill him, William."

"That's your Justice, I suppose," the Negro said.

"There! That's William to a T," Allegra cried, admiring the other's mimicry. "He's all for the dead hand and things."

"And life, liberty, and the pursuit of property," said Hugh; "add that."

"Oh pooh! Really, is there anyone vainer than a black man? Talk of property!" Allegra said. "Nobody's pursuing you any more."

"That's what *you* think, girl. Enoch is."

"Is he? What'd you do?"

"It's what I didn't do. Sin of omission. Those notes on the Scandinavian organizations I promised him."

"Haven't you sent for them yet!" Allegra marveled. "If it depends on you we'll never get to Moscow. —Lazy and shiftless you are."

"Terrible indolent race, us Swedes," the Negro said. "Here, gimme my shirt to sweat in. That's another reel starting—carries me back to old Virginny, where my old black grandmammy used to mix arsenic juleps for the Squire. *There* was a revolutionary!" He jumped to his feet and offered a slim hand to William. "You want to come, man? You look's though you could *use* an aeration of the blood vessels. 'Legra won't, she's got the curse."

"Go ahead, William," Allegra urged. "You know how to do it. You can kill him in the do-see-do, when his back is turned. —All *right*. Damn it, Hugh, *take* your filthy shirt."

He plucked it on the fly—"My corpuscles are as white as the next man's, miss"—and swung off into the pack of dancers.

"Hugh's awfully defensive about being educated," Allegra explained.

"Is he?" William said.

"Terribly. Being so defensive is what makes him act that way, sort of self-attacking. You know. It's because he's so defensive."

"Is he educated I meant."

"That's his whole trouble, he's *got* a Ph.D.—he's older than he looks, lots of their men are. Anyhow he's afraid people will get to thinking on account of the Ph.D. that he's forgotten all about the sharecroppers down South."

"And he hasn't?" William said drily.

"Well look, if he had, he wouldn't've joined the Movement, would he? It's social justice we're *after*, isn't it?" Indignation lit her; triumph lit her. "And you know what? Hugh's practically the only person in the whole Movement who can write Swedish! At least around here he is, isn't that remarkable?"

"I suppose it immensely increases his value," William murmured. "When the millennium comes the black races will recite the Eddas to the white races."

"Don't be nasty, William. We have lots of correspondence with Stockholm, I told you."

"I thought it was Moscow that was the Mecca," he said; his knees were beginning to ache.

"That doesn't mean we can't have anything to do with the Stockholm groups, does it? We have groups everywhere," she announced positively. "All over the world. Even in South America and Africa. It's because we're against the imperialists. You have to be really international to fight the imperialists."

He sighed. "Allegra."

"Hugh sings in Russian too. But Enoch said his accent's no good."

"I think it's been enough, Allegra. I think you ought to come home," William said.

"I *am* home."

He could not contradict her. "Then I think you ought to come with me."

"*You're* not going anywhere."

"And you?"

"I'm going everywhere!"

"It's definite then," he said.

"It's definite about Moscow anyhow. As soon as we got coördinated with that Swedish bunch. Enoch's trying to negotiate a date with them. The Norwegians are O.K., it's just the Swedes, they don't see why people don't like to go North in winter."

"I didn't mean Moscow," he said heavily.

"You asked if it's *definite*—"

"That this is what you want. This kind of thing." He waved out at the patterns of the reel and the trellises croaking with every thump and the voyaging moon, and meanwhile Allegra shivered; her skin was sleeveless now, and broken out into tiny moles of cold—it was the wind that blew up from the beach, full of sea. "You don't know what you want," William said.

She kneeled forward. Then she stood. "But I know *that* I want," she told him. "I want and I want and I want and I want."

"I won't come up again."

"You will. I bet you will."

He said quietly into the diminishing fire, "I don't like the life."

"Or the liberty. It's the liberty especially you don't like. All you care for is the property, what I said before."

But he cared for his fate. It was his fate he cared for.

"They've chiseled initials in your great-aunt's monument," he said.

"Stupid stone anchor! It's not her monument, it's nothing

at all. Anyhow she was a loon; didn't know one season from
another."

"Neither do you."

"What?"

"Know one season from another. —I have nothing against
what people call idealism—"

"And *you* call it what?"

"Folly. Entrapment. Time-wasting. Escapism. Illusion. Illusion above all."

"But you have nothing against it!" she scoffed.

"It shows a spirited will, I don't deny it. All that's charming. Charming. But it's for children. It's for children. I say
it's enough, Allegra. It's time you came away."

"Time!" she threw back at him.

"Time," he said again. "All things in their season."

"Well, am I ripe yet? Am I supposed to drop from a tree
like—like I don't know, a coconut?"

"Allegra," he said.

"Don't try and sympathize, William. You're even nastier
when you sympathize."

"It's enough. It's time you came with me."

"What for?"

"To stay."

"What for?"

"To be what you ought to be."

"I'm not what I ought to be?"

"You're self-indulgent. It's a fantasy you live here. You
prolong it. The world is different."

"The world is different," she repeated.

"The world is not a Utopia full of reels and puddings."

"Of course not. Utopia is the house in Scarsdale."

He did not acknowledge this. "You're too old to play at
Brook Farm."

"Utopia! Mecca! Brook Farm! Where do you think you
are, William?"

"I like to think I am where I belong."

"*I* like to think I belong where I am."

"You won't come then?"

She gave a cunning smile. "Afterward. When we get out of
here. Right now we're settled in."

"Afterward?" he said wonderingly.

"There's so much to do it wouldn't be fair to leave in the
middle. But I'll come if you want. I'll come in October."

"You mean September. The end of August, the beginning of September," he said.

"But we're settled *in,* you see, and Enoch thinks he needs at least another month. It isn't easy to find headquarters large enough, especially once you're settled in."

He said gravely, "The contractors are coming in September."

"Oh put them off another month! You can do it. You can do anything of that sort, William, if you want to. You *can.*"

"The county has hired the men already. They're arriving in the middle of September."

"Oh the men! Who cares about the men!"

"It isn't a thing to do, they're fine museum people—"

"Another month, William. What's another month? The museum will be forever, won't it? So what's one month to forever?"

Afterward, she said; forever, she said. And afterward she would come to stay with him forever.

"And meanwhile?" he asked.

"Oh, meanwhile I'll be good."

This seared him. "I didn't suggest—" he began, but wheeled from it in distaste. He had forgiven her. He was certain he had forgiven her. "What is this Enoch?" he said instead.

"A Jew."

"I mean who is he."

"Well, you said what. I thought you knew *who,* for goodness' sake. He's the Youth Leader."

"Is he old or young?"

"Old, like you. But you've seen him! Oh look, you don't have to be jealous of Enoch! Enoch's nothing."

"You speak as though he were everything."

"Because he is. He's a genius, I've explained it to you a hundred times: I mean at political thinking. That makes him nothing and everything at the same time."

"Is that a sample of your dialectic?" he said bitterly.

"He's everything to the Movement. To himself he's nothing. There's nothing in him that doesn't belong to the Movement, that's all. It isn't dialectic. It's the way he is."

"A prophet."

"Oh, a prophet!" Her dark mirth wooed his dismissal. "There, now you can go in peace. Nobody can be jealous of a *prophet,* can they? People don't elope with prophets, do they? I told you you didn't have to be afraid of a few tents!"

He went, though not in peace: he drove onto the hooded
deck of the thick-sided little ferry, glistering even at night
with paint new as its franchise, an oval pink toy bobbing absurdly in the River Styx (though it was only a bay in the
Sound) while Charon grumbled at his empty boat. William
kept to his car, and kept to the wheel; the pilot kept to his
high cab and kept to the wheel in it; but the ferryman came
and put an elbow on the fender and complained, with an old
green captain's eye on the tamely kicking moon-white water,
that he had been cheated: "First they said they'd have the
place finished by the middle of the summer; now they say
fall, and meanwhile to keep my franchise I got to take her
across and back at least once a week. I got to take her across
and back, and nearly empty, except for a kid or two from
over there, or I don't protect my franchise, and still no
museum over there, and never mind gas and oil, I got to pay
my pilot, don't I?" And whined against the fender. An old
river man, he said he was. He had a dog called Shep that
barked from beginning to end of the journey. He had
hoarded up his life to put it all into the Pink Lady.

And still no museum over there. William put off the contractors; he put off the curators; he put off the county
officials; and did it all for the sake of elusive afterward and
risky forever, and did it because Allegra had told him she
would come to him in October. And in October she came,
but only to take away a bundle of sweaters and woolen skirts
and to shop in the city for fifty blankets and to beg him to
see about letting them have coal for the furnace.

"Coal?" he said, disbelieving.

"Well, you know, maybe try the regular people who used
to deliver for us in the old days. *I* wouldn't know. I told
Enoch you'd be able to look *up* a thing like that, you could
fix it up for us." She opened out her hands to plead with his
stupefaction. "Oh, don't be mad! It's not as though there isn't
a *reason*. What happened was, well, we've had a turnover.
The summer group was no good, they were nothing but the
fun-and-games type. They never cared a hoot for ideology,
and we planned for them, and they fooled us: they never
cared at all, so now we have to begin all over again with the
new ones. Enoch's taken it better than you'd imagine—he
says it's that way in any organizing effort, you have to lose
the many to discover the few. He says it isn't only the leaves
that turn their coats in the fall. —Oh look, William, it's just
the winter months we want! And in the spring we'll be out,

the Rally's definite now for spring, and anyhow if the place isn't kept heated in winter the water-pipes freeze and crack, you know they do."

He marveled at her new proletarian enterprise. His imagination, heartless, pointed out the daughters of plumbers naked in their tents. Dully he said: "It's impossible. I've postponed them twice already."

"Then a third time will be easier, you'll be used to it."

"It can't be done."

"Yes it can."

"No," he said. "I won't do it."

"A few heaps of coal!—As though coal were gold!"

"Impossible. You have to get out. I'm in too deep, I'm obligated too far. I'm committed."

"Oh committed! Committed to what?"

"To the trust," he said reluctantly: the word hissed between them like an old practised familiar spite.

"To fish-bones! To bones and bones. To my father's bones. But never to flesh and blood."

"The contractors are flesh and blood," he said. "The curators are flesh and blood."

"And me," she said. "Me, William! What am I? —At least not a bone like you, available for any public gnawing! You're willing enough to feed the flesh of contractors and curators and . . . *curates*—"

The literary consciousness of the last did not escape him: the innocence of this affectation, in the heart of her savagery, made him distrait. But he missed its cruelty. He thought it an honorable, though mistaken, accusation. It recognized, though it did not reckon with, the moral position in his strictures. "You don't see," he said. "You don't see. Here's a letter—a letter, it arrived this morning—from one of these people, midwesterner this one is, an ichthyologist, young fellow —he's waiting, he's *been* waiting, he has no other employment—"

"Yes," she jeered, "I know how good you are at documenting feelings. And then you mark each one with an asterisk, See Attached Sheet, only when somebody looks it turns out to be only another instructive Bible text. I know! It's pieces of paper you feel obligated to. —And when I've *told* you we'll be out of there by spring, we *can't* stay beyond April: we'll be in Moscow the early part of May—look, do you want me to write it down for you in a sworn statement and sign it? Is that what you need?"

Her mouth radiated contempt; afterward and forever dissolved there. He saw; he saw and grieved.

"Do as you please," he said.

But she was bolder than that. "You won't interfere?"

"I'll put them off. I'll put them off," he said.

"Ah, you won't regret it!" she told him joyfully, and swept up her notebooks. "The one with the red cover? Did you see it? I've got the *whole* outline for the middle part in it, it has a sort of red cover: William? —Oh, here it is. All the dust made it look brown. But even if it *did* get lost it wouldn't really matter, because I've got lots of new ideas now. I had plenty of plot before, but I felt ideationally empty—that's why I quit. Now it's going to be a Thesis Novel: political and economic, instead of amateur sociological. Did you ever read *Jews without Money?* Neither did I; Enoch says I ought to. Do you know there's almost nothing to read in that whole place, except what Enoch's lugged with him all the way from Chicago? William, my father's library is a *shame*. It's full of absurd things on the Merchant Marine, and sailing ships, and all sorts of piscatorial debris. One of the new people actually found a volume of memoirs called *The Fish, My Finny Forbear*. That's the one who's set me going on the novel again. He's changed the whole tone of the camp. He pokes around corners in ways nobody else would think of."

"A thief, I'm sure," said William. "He'll burglarize the walls."

"Well let him then!" she said indignantly. "What I mean is he *stimulates*, don't you see?"

"Isn't that the job of your Youth Leader?"

"Enoch's all brain. He invents. But he's too difficult, and he talks too complicatedly; and sometimes he bores, he really does. He's amused but he doesn't amuse. That's why half the camp left as soon as they woke and found all that slippery ice on the tent-poles after a night rain. Nobody wants to freeze for intellect. But they will for a good show. Enoch says that's why there are more Christians than Jews. He's a terrible chauvinist that way. He says that's the reason God sent Moses, a writer, after all—he wrote the Tablets—to the Jews, but sent an illiterate fisherman to the Gentiles. And if Paul didn't always keep on writing those letters, the illiterates might have made *him* the Christ, which he was sort of angling for anyway."

"A corrupt, impious, sacrilegious, impertinent rascal."

"Saint Paul?" said Allegra, her cheeks drawn in with pleasure.

"Your Enoch."

"Well, he's not *mine*. I don't own him!"

"Exactly, exactly. He owns you. He owns your mind."

"He does *not*. 'Die Gedanken sind frei.' Hugh taught me that. 'Nothing human is alien to me.' You know who said that? Karl Marx! 'My mind to me a kingdom is.' That's Sir Edward Dyer. Nick does that one; he does it very well. He does lots of poems and songs and things, not that he's literary *himself*, but he penetrates. He penetrates right into Literary Theory without the bias one gets from practising it oneself. He always knows exactly what feelings to have; most people don't, did you ever think about that?"

"No," William said.

"According to Nick they don't. I didn't realize myself how vague I was about even my *opinions*. I quit writing because I didn't know how to feel implausibly. I was too logical; it made me tentative. I became certain only when I gave up certainty. It's all Literary Theory, William! And just what I needed—I had to be prodded out of obstinacy, because it led to self-mystification; I had all the wrong attitudes."

"And now you have all the right ones?"

"Well, I'm speaking of literature."

"*I'm* speaking of reality."

"Reality's nothing but attitudes too."

"According to Nick?"

"According to Enoch."

William faintly groaned.

"Nick thinks writing a novel is simply a matter of burning to do it. But not for sensible reasons, like wanting to get famous; it has to be a burning you can't imagine the cause of. Like a mysterious heartburn, and you haven't eaten anything bad."

"If it's only a question of burning—"

"It's only a question of burning," she vividly assented.

"Burn here," he said.

"Oh, don't start that again! I'm going back, I thought we settled it." Her laughter judged him ludicrous; in its minutest vibration he felt the current of his own despair. "The point is Nick means to read all the bits and pieces so far, and help me get perspective. I couldn't do it without him, don't you see? If I tried to do it here, I'd burn all right!—I'd burn the manuscript!" she bleated, high-frequencied and absolute and all at once in earnest: "Because he sees how to utilize the given—that's not just myself saying it, it's how Enoch characterizes him: he embroiders axioms and pragmatizes artistry—isn't that interesting? He distributes, he popularizes. Also he makes merry."

"I suppose you mean by that that he drinks."

"He drinks *in*. Oh look, he knows how to experience things! You can tell just by the turn of his eye: a sort of lazy but discreet eye. And the fact is nobody thought he'd stay when Hugh brought him up. Anyway Enoch didn't. Enoch said he was just a looker, he'd look and go. Which is what happened," she insisted, "in spite of his being a friend of Hugh's. Enoch said he didn't have Hugh's motivations. —Enoch's always talking about the motivations of the American Negro; it's one of his *topics*. But the second time he stayed."

"Having acquired motivation," William intervened.

"Call it what you want, *I* don't care. You never *used* to be so cynical, William. The whole point is he got to asking a lot of questions, about how the Movement got hold of the estate and so on, and he ended up interested."

"In the Movement or in the estate?"

"Well, in me! In *Marianna Harlow*. Because I told him about all the notebooks I left behind in order to come up there. I told him I had to come anyhow, out of socialist principle, even though the whole place used to depress me when I lived there before. I never meant to go back to it for anything in the world. The way it used to throw me in a *mood*—"

"You told him a lot," William observed.

"Well?" —She waited belligerently.

"You ought to show some reserve, Allegra."

"Oh reserve! Federal Reserve! You think I'm some sort of bank, I ought to be kept locked up all the time. I'm not a bank! I told you, I'm flesh and blood!"

"Flesh and blood," he repeated obediently, like a litany.

"Well yes, flesh and blood," she sing-songed back at him, to press her mockery. "—Like most people."

"You are not like most people," William said.

But she would not let him go on. She was afraid he would talk of the trust. "I am, I am! Yes I am. I'm exactly like everyone else up there, all that heiress business doesn't make any difference to them. Not to them!"

"Not to Enoch? Not to Nick?"

"Not to anyone." But she was evasive. "Anyhow not to

Nick. He *asked* me was it different up there—I said different than it used to be, and better; and Nick said he didn't think he'd mind it without the mob, all that space and the feel of the bigness of everything; so then I told him why I came, I said the mob was the reason I came—"

"I thought it was socialist principle," William reminded her. "Or is that the same as saying mob?"

But she missed him conveniently. "Without the mob it's a haunted house, that's all it is. I told Nick that. So of course he wanted to know haunted by what, but I didn't feel like saying, so all I said was capitalist greed, which is perfectly true anyway. Every brick someone else's underpaid sweat—"

"And the real ghost who does the real haunting?" he wondered blandly.

She hesitated; she fingered her collar. "I don't know. An old copy of Ralph Waldo Emerson maybe. Maybe that." She apprehended his puzzlement but purposefully ignored it; perhaps she was as puzzled herself. "You know what Nick asked me? —Whether what I was writing was autobiographical or only about a sort of random fate, and if I was putting my father into it, and what my father was like, and where I lived before the camp got started; but he never asked about mama, though I told him she was the one who died first—"

"And what else? What else?"

"What do you mean, what else?" she said angrily.

"Did he ask how much you get a year?"

"Oh, fine, fine! You think he was smelling money, you're always suspicious without cause—but you see how wrong you are, William? He didn't even ask about you! It never entered his mind: who you are or what you are. Not even where you are, so you see? He isn't petty, he's *large!* Which is why he didn't want to stay. He told Enoch he despised *all* cells—molecular or political. Do you know that made Enoch like him right away? —I mean Nick doesn't go swallowing everything whole, like some of the ones we get. Some of them you can make believe *anything.* Tell them Friedrich Engels is a Chinaman, and they'll believe you; and afterward they're the first ones to beat it when you're getting together a floor-mop committee, or you have to send some pickets down to New York. First in the vanguard, last in the homeguard—that's what Enoch's always saying; he hates enthusiasm. He says it's the clearest sign of the gullible, and political revolution is no business for the gullible."

"It certainly doesn't seem to interest anyone else," William said.

"It interests *me*," she assured him stoutly. "And Enoch is the least gullible person ever created. You know what he told Nick? He said if he didn't like cells he'd better devise a way to get out of the Milky Way, since the whole *planet* is just a cell of the galaxy we're in. Then Nick said it wasn't the galaxy that bothered him, it was the rhythm of the surf—it got into his stomach and made it queasy. But Enoch told him that was perfectly all right and no obstacle, he could assign him to the scullery where he couldn't hear it over the pot-scraping. (We have an idiot who always burns the pots.) So then poor Nick looked cornered, and laughed, and said he didn't have a vocation for the Movement anyhow, and was against the workers because he was against work, and if he stayed at all it would be on account of the Empress of Russia."

"Merciful Lord," said surly William.

"He meant me!" she jubilantly declared.

"Take it to heart, take it to heart. When the Czarina was surrounded by Marxists she was shot."

"You twist everything. He simply offered to be my Rasputin, don't you see? —And help with *Marianna!* He was *interested*, don't you see? You know who Rasputin was? He helped the Empress with everything. If she'd had to do a novel he would have helped with that too. Don't you *know* about Rasputin, William?"

"A sorcerer," he obliged. "And the Czarina was his dupe."

"Twist, twist! Nick hasn't asked for a penny, whatever you think."

He conceded with a frown. "Rasputins don't ask. It's not their method. They prefer you to ask them."

"Ask them what?" said Allegra. But she was too impatient to pretend reasonableness; she thought him literal; she thought him stupid; she preferred the advance of her story to his qualifications and digressions. "Never mind. You weren't there and you didn't see. Anyhow it was delicious; a victory: in jumps Hugh, and makes Nick admit he'd have to move in with the rest of us if he was really serious about being Rasputin. And you know what Enoch said after that? He said Hugh had pulled off a literary coup, because Omar Khayyam had met his Fitzgerald at last, though of course the analogy wasn't exact. —So then I absolutely kissed him, out of gratitude."

"Hum," said William, figuring it out. "Kissed Enoch?"

"Can you imagine anybody's kissing *Enoch?*"

"Kissed Nick," he ventured then.

"Kissed Hugh! *He's* the one who persuaded Nick to stay, after all. And people don't go around kissing Rasputins. Nobody ever accused the Czarina of *that,* did they?" she inquired pointedly. "—Oh look, he's white, if you're wondering!—just because they're friends, Hugh and Nick . . . You ought to see them together. You ought to see Nick. He has white-watery hair: a *real* blond. And fantastic eyes, oh unbelievable eyes—"

"Then you had better not believe them," William advised, and would hear no more. The rest of the visit was financial. He agreed to release money for the coal delivery; he agreed to see about the bill for the blankets. The voice was the voice of Allegra, but the hand was the hand of the Youth Leader. "If we had a really big refrigerator, you know the kind, a giant one like they have in hotels and restaurants and places like that, we could buy our meat in large quantities at one time, and get it wholesale, and save plenty of money." So he agreed to this too, though it cost the equivalent of half a year's salary which might have been paid to the anxious young ichthyologist with the Armenian name—what a queer complaining letter the fellow had written! He said he was engaged, and spoke as though the marriage depended on the museum's getting started, and on the job. Not on the money simply—and, truth to tell, the money wasn't much—but on the very job itself. William thought of his father-in-law, and marveled how the biology of the sea could so fascinate some men that they valued it as much as marriage, and mixed the nature of one with the nature of the other. Was he himself, then, a deviation among lovers?—he was as ardent as anyone, but he wanted a simple life and a simple wife, and nothing more: all as plain and solid as a stone, and as free of philosophy. Then and there he felt himself an enemy of philosophy; hence of philosophers—hence of the one called Enoch and the one called Nick. He hated them because they theorized; Enoch, at least, theorized; the other perhaps only put it on. And if theory had not magnetized Allegra, she might never have succumbed to Enoch and Nick, that pair of exploiters, vagabonds, nobodies. Or regard it vice-versa: if she had never encountered these two, she might at this moment still be unsurrendered to philosophy. And what he wanted was Allegra without the abomination of her notions; Allegra sans

philosophy; Allegra quick with zeal, but over nothing more
serious or terrible than a houseplant. He wished she cared for
flowers; he had a pretty vision of a pliant little wife who
could tend a rock-garden and keep her window-vases filled.
Instead she let the nobodies come and ruin her father's arbor.
One of the trellises had given way weeks before, and fell into
the fire with a wet hiss and the crackle of thorns. An auto-
da-fé: they had burned next year's rose-crop on the stake of
their ideology; property was a clot of blood to them; it was
quite like burning up the future. And she told him it was a
bad business, he ought to send the gardener away, because
the man was always cross and called them reactionary names
and got in their way. Here and in this at last William's tone
would not be opposed: "It was your father's idea to keep the
ground intact. You can't dig tents into a lawn and expect
grass to grow. Your Youth Leader's brought in the deluge,
and the gardener's our finger in the dike; the gardener stays,"
but the gardener quit. She pointed out how foolish it would
be to hire another—the grounds were already too far gone: a
tractor would be more practicable than a gardener. It no
longer mattered to him. The fuel and the blankets and the
freezer and the charred vines and the still-unmarried youth
continuing to pelt him with frenetic letters (he was threatening to come and agitate for his job to begin) were footnotes
to William's greater venture: he had extended a lease which
he had no right to grant to begin with. But this time he was
aware that she had promised him nothing in return, only
what he knew already: that she was flesh. She piled her notebooks into a suitcase, meanwhile quoting something else
Hugh had taught her— "Ich kann nicht anders," she said; "that's
Martin Luther"—and left him to kick the polar bear's
head in isolation. But he too could not have done otherwise;
and he had yielded only the winter months, she had not
asked for more than the winter months, and what contractor
would care or dare to ferry across to an icy isle to plaster up
a partition in the middle of the winter? He knew she was
flesh; it was the worst assurance she could have given him.
Yet it was only until January. Meanwhile he would see about
the feasibility of constructing a bridge.

And in February flesh turned to stone: stone beyond the
purview of any geology. He went on the ferry to see. There
would never be a bridge. There would never be a museum.
There would never be a marriage. The girl came, and the doctor her father. The doctor looked around him and said:

"Awkward location for an aquarium." The girl would not speak at all. She wrapped the knife very carefully in her handkerchief to take home with her; she had asked the coroner for it. "Irregular," the coroner said, but he gave it to her; only the day before he had drawn it from her lover's neck. William felt curiously obligated about the funeral. He went on the same airplane that carried the body, and was astonished at the emotionalism of the burial service. There were Armenians everywhere, they swarmed around the grave, dark fused eyebrows over angry drowning eyes. The parents took him to their restaurant and gave him dinner. The father said his son had tried to overreach himself. It was education that had killed him. It was the doctor who had killed him. He ought to have stayed with his own people, in his own people's business. It was the museum that had killed him, and the museum did not even exist. Her recurrent weeping made the mother's English indistinguishable. "You don't have a son," William thought he heard her say; her accent was a deformity. He was glad to take the train for home; Allegra was there now. The boy's death had scattered the camp, and it was still twelve weeks before the Moscow March For A Better Future. It was a year since she had sat on the polar bear and declared herself to be mankind. It was a year since he had known for himself that she was flesh. She had arrived at Chapter Eight. She occupied herself with writing.

9

"And then?" I said to William.

"And then nothing."

He made a curious gesture. I had seen him do it several times as he spoke: he brought his fist upon his heart. It was curious, it was primitive; I half expected him to beat with it there. Instead the raised hand came down to the desk again, where it lay, apparently not penitential, but separated from whatever will drove it.

"In May," he said, "she went to Moscow. A boatload of them went, not nearly so great a crew as they had hoped for, however. The ship-fare stopped them."

"And the time in between?"

"Insignificant. Quarrels and so forth. She scarcely left the house, I might say. —None of it concerns you in the least."

"No. And Moscow?"

"Oh, a vast mess and fuss, everything in the newspapers of course. —I don't doubt your mother's still got the clippings. I used to mail bits of the *Times* to her, all hideous. I did it because she asked me to. The whole affair impossible. Insane and subhuman. It can't be adequately told. A streetfight once —the Scandinavian contingent against the South Americans: everybody drunk on all sides. That was Moscow. —And parades. Right out of the trains and into the parades."

"I didn't know my mother knew him in Moscow. Enoch, I mean. —When the fact is she knew him longer ago than that. She knew him far, far back." I absorbed this. "She traveled with him?"

"With him and the other fellow. Greek ship, the *Croesus*. The other fellow was seasick all the way. The Negro was with him as usual. Also a decent little chap, couple of years behind me at school, good family, name of Sparrs. I don't know how he got himself mixed up with them. There was a pack of very foolish girls, as I recall. How many fares she paid I never found out, though I wrote the checks myself. —The upshot of it," he grimly provided, grinding my questions out of the atmosphere, "was that she never came back. Not as my wife. Right after the Moscow thing she went off with him. She went off with him."

"With Enoch," I concluded, thinking he meant to another Rally somewhere.

William coldly looked the other way. "No."

"With Tilbeck? —Ah," I said.

"At last," he blew out, scorning the slowness of my comprehension. But I was slow because *he* was strange. "The pair of them together. Not that I guessed it at first. There were so many parades in so many cities. At every point I had letters explaining the necessity and importance of each. One was for establishing one thing, another for abolishing another thing. Sometimes they abolished in one parade what they had just established in the previous parade." I wondered whether this was a sort of angry joke, but his voice pealed disgust, and was not indulgent, so I followed the stern entrapping fold of his spacious brow in puzzlement: it could not be said that he suffered. There was in his manner the modest shiver of self-gratulation that always accompanies ritual disapproval. "It was the words she loved," he continued. "Reform. Advancement. Equal Distribution. Their mythos."

"But all the while she was with Tilbeck."

"Don't suppose he was to be distinguished from the words. He had other words. He was a cult in himself."

"The cult of art," I said, "the cult of experience."

"Neither," William corrected. "The cult of the cheat. They went to Petrograd. They went to Stockholm. I wrote. She wrote. She wasn't ready to come home, oh not in the least. I wrote. She wrote. Then she gave the reason: Europe was better for finishing the novel, she had to stay until it was done. That meant Nick, so I did the only feasible thing."

I was hopeful he would say what the only feasible thing was.

"I ceased to write," he announced.

"Did she?" But he had disappointed me.

"Letters in flocks. Bundles of them. Long long letters. Oh, they gave themselves airs. Travel letters. She must have assumed they had the sort of literary value which even I might recognize. Genre writing, you see. I imagine I was supposed to save them. She sometimes slipped into a when-these-are-published vein. But I tore them up. They were unanswerable. Unanswerable." He wandered off into meditation, speculation, recrimination. I waited. When he came back to me his speech was altered by a mysterious rheum: "Italy," he said queerly. "They went à trois—took the colored boy with them. They went on down to Rome and left him behind in Milan. They went to Switzerland and Norway and Germany, in that order. Well, in Germany it was the New Order, and a row they cooked up, and it turned out they just skipped out of there in time."

"The Nick of time," I said, pleasing myself.

William appeared offended. "In Munich he got hold of a Fascist shirt and put it on, all smeared over with calves' blood. They had gone to a slaughterer's for it, with a bucket."

"You read this in the papers?"

"Oh, better than that. I received the consul's complaint in the mail. She was listed as a provocateur by the Nazis and I was requested to get her out for her own safety."

"A protest against the regime it was," I surmised.

"On his part? It was the most scandalous act he could conceive of in that place, so he did it."

I examined this. "And all the time she kept writing you, and you never replied."

"I don't say I wasn't sending her checks as she requested them," he informed me. His eye sharpened abruptly. "I wouldn't permit any other arrangement. I admit to that. When she was out of money she had to ask for more. I considered myself financially responsible for her."

"As trustee," I gave out.

"As husband."

"She hates not having her letters answered," I said, marveling how with these two liturgically parallel phrases, trustee and husband, these opposites of lawchamber and bedchamber, we mirrored our talk's beginning—though, as in a glass, our mouths stood pertinently reversed: where earlier, claimed as the husband of my mother, William had enjoined me to seek my stepfather for that place, now with the stroke of my stepfather's name I brought it to him that his old rights, even his negligences and omissions, had been usurped. "Enoch never answers her letters, and she hates it. He doesn't answer anything except emergencies. He never even answers her cables."

"Ah, but your mother is prolific with those," William said.

I agreed it was her habit to send a great many cables.

"I meant emergencies," William said. "She has always been prolific with emergencies."

"She likes excitement."

"She likes crisis. She likes it well enough to fabricate it. She learned how long ago."

"She doesn't fabricate," I objected, more defensive than convinced.

"She doesn't need to any more. I'm afraid the crises are all thoroughly genuine now. Your poor mother," he said; it was a figure that succeeded with him. "She used to run after mirages of agitation. You see they made these things up. They made them up."

"The crises? The emergencies?"

"In those days," he assured me spitefully, "there was no evil in the world that they didn't make up."

"They didn't invent the Communists," I said.

"But they invented the masses. In fact they went all over the Continent looking for this particular invention of theirs, in order to stir it up. After Germany," he persisted in a thickness of pursuit, "they went to London. Vand was organizing there. A terrific riot afterward, I never got it straight why. Something about Poland. Little Sparrs got the worst of that one. Finally in the middle of the summer the two of them went down to Brighton and took a cottage. By then they had been traveling more than a year. A year, more than a year, a year and a quarter—"

I interposed in surprise, "You let it go on so long?"

William pinned me with a derision so acutely spurning that I felt beggared and demeaned and had to persuade myself not to fear those fine milky triangles that, by their innocent contrast on either side, burnished the abscess-like roundness of his eyeballs. His intention was to humiliate. "My—dear—child," he lilted at me with a kind of contemplative danger, "exactly *what* would you have had me do? What, what, and then what? *They* had me"—he turned away and I wonderingly saw how the danger crumpled like a paper thorn—"they had me wearing horns."

"Then you ought to have horned in on them," I said at once and without pity. "You let them get away with it. You could have gone over there and stopped it."

"You like to speculate," he said harshly. "It couldn't be done. The difficulty of—the implausibility—I was at the time in no—" he twitched and switched away—"position to leave my affairs unguarded. The incident, its occurrence on the property, had brought on—"

"You mean that boy's suicide," I said.

"—certain investigations, there were a number of contrivances, I was forced—"

But this aroused me. "Oh, that's good Business English: affairs that can't be left unguarded. And *her* affairs? Hers?"

He wearily rubbed his forehead with a single moist finger. "This won't do. I am not accustomed to arguments of this nature—"

"If *she* had an affair you could leave it unguarded!"

"You sometimes have a distinctly coarse way of expressing yourself."

"Maybe it's the subject-matter that's coarse."

"The subject-matter is one I notice you chose for yourself," William said.

"You could have written to her then. You could have," I insisted. "But instead nothing. No claim, no protest. Not a word. Nothing! —The subject-matter was too coarse," I flung at him without the support of ridicule.

"You want to blame me."

"It's just as fair, isn't it? You're the one who let her get away with it! If you'd said a word, a single word—"

"You want to accuse. You put your teeth into it." And there was his odd stiff fist against his vest, seeming to clutch at a button. Then quite suddenly he told the truth: "But it was too much."

"What?"

"A single word," he repeated. "I had lost the faculty."

"Of licking a stamp."

"Of speaking."

"You do it well enough now and again, according to the *Times*."

He separated his hand from his body, and opened out the knuckles with their stretched whorls like shut eyelids, and turned the wrist, and set it down upon the desk as though all of it—the taut fingers, the thumb purplish at its fatty base, the palm with its private linear text—offended him by certain betrayals. This was bizarre: William was not given to obvious gesture. "When we met again—when she came back," he said, obscurely apologetic, "we shook hands. It was all right, you see, eventually."

"Yes," I said.

"There were a great many matters of essence that had to be attended to."

"Yes."

"I'm referring to her return. We had a number of necessary conferences."

I said caustically, "The faculty returned when she did."

He began, but discovered he was hoarse.

"I mean the power of speech came back," I pushed on.

"I addressed her," William said through a clot in his throat, "as a client of particular value."

I did not ask him value to whom: I feared he might say to the firm. "It's always possible to speak to a client," I said merely; but I saw in his cheek a visible snap of discipline; of recovery; and I laughed. "You know Queen Victoria's complaint about Gladstone? —She said he addressed her like a public meeting. I read that in Lytton Strachey. Of course," I modified, "he was only the Prime Minister, he wasn't married to her."

William looked over as though he were about to compliment me on my astounding grasp of British Constitutional History. Instead he remarked testily, "You choose cynical authors for false applications."

"I wasn't comparing you to Queen Victoria," I said.

"Perhaps you read too much."

"I don't have anything else to do. I've been going through the newspapers all summer. They're full of crises and emergencies that nobody's made up. It's really remarkable. What happened in Brighton?"

"In Brighton?"

"You said they went to Brighton. —Your client," I explained it, "and her novel-in-progress."

It was plain he despised me for this. "I haven't mentioned her novel."

"Yes you have. You said it was the reason she was staying in Europe. —There," I pointed out, "if I put it that way you can't say I'm being coarse."

"She finished it there."

"In Brighton?"

"Yes."

"The affair?"

"The novel," William threw out, blazing.

"So he was right. Nick. He got her to do it."

"It was simply that she stopped traveling. She settled down to it."

"He got her to settle down to it."

"She settled down," he contradicted impatiently. "Before that they were joining up with Vand at one place or another, wherever he claimed to need them. She took the cottage expressly to finish. No moving about and no interruptions, only that Vand stopped there now and then."

"She wrote you that?"

"She wrote everything."

"Well it worked," I said. "She finished it. She's never finished anything since."

"You have very curious values."

"—It's only that I believe in finishing things." I might have said marriages, I might have said divorces, I might have ventured love. I might in fact have said anything, but I just then preferred the safety of ambiguity. *Odi et amo*, that vague old squeal: he had kept her on as "client," but he had kept her on. He had kept her, he was keeping her yet. It gave him an intimacy without the requirement of intimate address, that lost faculty for terror he mourned.

"Excellent," he pronounced without a pause—it was his old tone, the speaking monument. "You believe in finishing things. Then let us suit your creed to our interview."

But awe for William had abandoned me. Let me be granite: that scorn did not command me. We faced one another in that exceptional nakedness of equality which now and then afflicts fathers and daughters—a relationship I entertained in contemptuous metaphor only.

"So they lived on what you sent," I summed it up without a blink.

"I don't know what they lived on. Air. I sent half of whatever she asked for."

"She had to ask."

"She asked enough for two. I sent enough for one, poverty for two."

"It was her money."

"My wife's money. I saw no reason for my wife's money to support anyone other than my wife. She was still my wife, you see. I wasn't out to subsidize a lapse in morals."

"It wouldn't have been the first time," I said.

"You refer to the camp. Yes. The unfortunate incident. The Armenians are a very rash people. Irresponsible as Italians, and none of the Italian frivolity of nature. A heavy-natured people, a peculiar sullenness in them—"

"You make it sound like a national movement."

"You think I make it too great?"

"You make it too little. A boy died."

"Killed himself."

"Was murdered."

He gave the stare of Zeus.

"Your son says it that way," I supplied. "He lays it all at your feet."

"I see. —My feet."

But I found I could be brutal. "He thinks they're made of clay."

"My feet," he said again. He turned aside. "Plausible. I won't contradict."

"He doesn't trust you any more. I told you. On account of finding out *that*. He holds you accountable."

"And you?"

I exhaled a token of a breath signifying detachment. "What do I care? You're not *my* father."

"You don't hold me accountable?"

"Not to me."

"Then you think morality is between persons only? If you are not offended in yourself, then there has been no offense? One can't offend against a tenet?"

"All that's theology," I said.

"Precisely."

"It's why you let my mother starve."

"I didn't let her starve."

"Poverty for two you said."

"I didn't let her starve."

"You weren't out to subsidize a lapse in morals."

"You misunderstand. I had no wish—after the camp—to encourage—" He stopped. "They were investigating the estate, it was with the greatest difficulty the thing was kept out of court, the county wanted to litigate—"

"Spite. You wanted to make it hot for her."

He regained himself. "I didn't intend to let it seem that I would abet a further breach of trust. The camp was enough."

"The boy was enough."

"You keep insisting on that boy."

"Theology again. Or maybe I imitate your son."

He struck the desk-top with an extraordinary vitality— startling after that pizzicato of guilt. "Leave my son out of it, can't you?"

I reflected. "All right. History did, so I will. *He* wasn't in Brighton. What happened in Brighton?"

"She wrote."

"You said that. Wrote and finished."

"I don't mean the book. She wrote a letter."

"And you never answered it. You've *said* that."

"It was as long as any of them. A long letter, so I went ahead finally with the divorce. —I mean to say I arranged for her to be divorced from me immediately."

"Over a letter?" I marveled. But it was not so wondrous after all: once I had believed it was over a chapter. And whether a letter is more substantial than a chapter is moot, particularly when a novelist has written both.

William said: "She told me in it that she was several months short of having a child. I was not its father."

"No," I agreed, "not you," and closed the openness that had been between us. For hostility is openness; it is at least dialogue; but narrative is a fence-making to keep out the other.

Then I heard how I was born.

10

When the child was born the father vanished. Not immediately, but by degrees, like a barometer measuring weather.
Italy was warm, for example; he measured that. He began
merely by talking of Italy, because the coast of England was
turning cold and dull and tedious. The cottage walls were the
color of the inside of an eggshell, though more porous. In
summer, when they first came there, the house was a creamy
hump in a nest of green weediness, a place to tumble about
in with a frying-pan lid for a cymbal; and Allegra was a joke
on herself: "I'm a helium balloon!" "Then you'll be kept
from floating off," said Nick, and tugged at her hair, which
grew and grew like weeds, till she thrust it round out of her
way. "Work," said Nick, and went to sleep in the narrow
bed; he liked to sleep, and afterward reported the long adventures of his dreams, in which, oddly, she appeared only once,
and then subordinately. But he dreamed often of Hugh, who
was still in Italy. "Work," he said, and since he was asleep
(he had finished the wine), she read a little in Oscar Wilde
("That's to prime the pump," said she) and went to *Marianna* with an elegant and erotic chameleon-pen, and wrote
of flowers like an aesthetic druggist, meditating in a botanical
handbook that told of vegetable cannibals, savages, and Mac-
beths. "Quit it now," he said, yawning himself awake; "come
and show me what you've done." She showed him: "Is it awful?"—because he laughed. "It leaves me full of awe," he answered; "it's Walter Pater crossed with George Eliot." "But I
meant it to be Socialist Realist." "Then that's just what it is.
You've bred a hybrid, and have every right to give it a name.
If only Dickens could have tried his hand in the middle of
the seventh month!" "I don't see what *that's* got to do with
it," she said haughtily. "Everything, everything. The female is
an engine." "Well, my *mind's* not an engine." "True, but I

wasn't speaking of your mind, I was speaking of your imagination. It's involuntary, like parturition. The male ought to be prevented from writing at all. Male literature ought to be abrogated for its wishy-washiness. There ought to be daily burnings, beginning with Voltaire, and including all the male poets before and after. I don't leave out Sappho, though he was unwillingly a woman. True literature is obscene, and only women know how to be truly obscene; they can't help it. Rabelais only imitates the talk of women when they're alone in a room together, and Lawrence goes a step farther by trying to *think* like a woman—Joyce too—but it's hopeless. No one, no matter how talented, can be as obscene as a female about to bear. Now look, that means I'm sure this chapter's better than the last—it's got more social justice for the unemployed lovers in it—so go and get the darts." They had no target, only a round bit of scallop on the cornice, with a worm-hole for a bull's-eye, and Allegra's throw went out the open window and pierced a little tree. They swore to one another that they had heard the dryad shriek. Every day for a month or so they wondered if she would shriek again to show she was not dead. But she was dead; it was winter; they never heard her. Then a shriek, howling and long, after all: and the child's head was born that moment.

The greengrocer was a far walk. The butcher was dear, the milk repulsive. The child shivered when the mother's hair fell down into its queer face—like pygmy notches carved into a wedge of coconut meat. "I *can't* drink wine, I'm not supposed to," said the mother, pale as milk. Then there was no safe place to keep the child, so they put it in a packing box begged from the grocer. "It smells of apples," said the mother. "It smells of sourgrass," said the father, "and if the money goes for milk we can't have wine." "He'll send the money now," said the mother. "Now? Why now? You said he was certain to send at least double the amount when you first told him, and that was months ago." "But it wasn't born then." "It's born now, and where's the money?—I tell you what, let's to to Italy, Hugh's living it up in Sicily on nothing at all." The child yowled. "Oh we can't go to Italy!" said the mother; "what's it yelling for? Look, its head is sort of funny, do you think I broke it off? Aren't you supposed to hold their heads a special way so they don't fall off?" "Can't drink wine," said the father, "can't go to Italy, can't get cash. Trust him not to send the money even now." "But it's freezing, that's the trouble! Can't you do something about the fire?

Its lips are purple." "Oh damn its lips," he said, and fiddled
with the hearth—"nothing's coming from America. Why
don't you write him again?" "He never answers." "Well damn
him." "Maybe if Enoch gets rid of the manuscript to a good
London publisher—" "Hurray, you've got the Noble Outlaw
for an agent. They're bound to treat him very respectfully at
Chatto and Windus. They love their agents in Grecian sandals at New Year's. I say damn him." "—then I'd get an advance on it maybe, and we'd have some money right away.
Anyhow it's not Enoch's fault he can't wear regular shoes
with his feet in that condition. It's ever since the last Peace
March, it's no joke from Glasgow down to Manchester, it's
one of the longest they've ever done." "And the typist he got
you was five pounds hard cash." "I had to have it *typed*,
didn't I?" "Then damn you too. Give me your wallet, I'm
going out." "Where?" "Where! To bring some breakfast.
—Doesn't the thing ever shut up? We'll all end up deaf. Is this
all the money there is?"

And went, and dawdled a bit on the square, then dawdled
in the train station, then dawdled in the carriage; and, by degrees, departed.

But when the child fell asleep—a thing that occurred
abruptly, with an exhausted and queerly narrow snigger of its
lungs—he was still on the square, browsing in a newspaper
stall. And he had only just gained the station when Allegra,
restively blackening her thumb with the carbon copy of *Marianna* (since Enoch had taken the original away to London
to find a publisher she read in it every day, marveling and
doubting in turn), suddenly seized out of the morning som-
nolence a new scene, brave, lubricious, carnal, and at once
sat down to write it into its logical place, which was Chapter
Twelve. That was the chapter, and this the scene, that afterward caused a New York reviewer, the well-known Orphew
(nicknamed Off-Hue) Codpress, to call the author, with a
prurient sneer, the Wunderkind of Eros (he said this sedately
to his wife, however; in print he said "shameless," "shocking," "boring," "tedious"). And in the Soviet edition that was
the chapter, and this the scene, that subsequently had to be
almost wholly omitted, on the ground—according to *Litera-
turnaya Gazyeta*—that only the paragraphs celebrating the
workers' council were actually relevant to the novel's great
and primary theme of Capitalist Plunder Exposed.

But all that was afterward, and commentary; the scene itself she did not imagine in a single moment, as she liked later

to pretend, though what she gave out in that hour of her only genuine inspiration was a unity of sensuality not, after all, the sole product of inspiration so much as the grafted fruit of inspired tutelage, the tutor meanwhile paying for his ticket out of her alligator-skin wallet, a long-ago gift from William. If there were ironies in this, the baby's interruptions (the baby itself a sign of the novelist's interrupted Sangerian subtleties) were still more ironic, since the baby (which normally whimpered, even in slumber) interrupted chiefly by not interrupting: lay in its box motionless and ominous. Its cold rubbery little hands were curled up like snails, which Allegra conscientiously felt; then, just as conscientiously, she listened to see if it was still alive. It breathed, so it was. But Allegra, reminded by her own hoary puffs to shiver, and drawing on a pair of socks over a pair of socks to effect an elephantiasis of warmth, slanted her mind from the subjective being-fondled of the fictional breasts of her heroine to the now-dry mammary vessels which Nick had forbidden to suckle; breast-feeding was then in disrepute; it was not, like the appearance of the baby itself, avant-garde. She rehearsed an address to Nick: "Look, a revision, rich, rich," was the whole of it. And his reply (which, since by now he was boarding the train, he never gave): "You ought to've revised before, if you were going to revise at all; I told you Twelve was a sermon preached by Enoch and needed a slippery slavering tongue, but you wouldn't touch it, and now we'll have to pay the typist to type over, and how—with a certain New York lawyer stitching up his stingy pockets—how, my dear poet, do you think we'll get the money?" It was perilous when he called her poet; it meant he was hungry. Then she observed to herself that he was long in fetching the food. He never cared that *she* was hungry; *he* would buy himself a bun on the way: so she found her pen (it had dropped into the baby's box and stank slightly) and filled it, and emptied it in long scrawls, and crammed all the chinks of Chapter Twelve with arrowheads and goat-hooves of Venus and Pan, and wished she had a bun with frosting on it. Finally the postman intervened, hastening and truncating (though he did not know he was improving anyone's style) the anticlimax, and bringing a letter from America fat-cheeked with documents. The money was at last assured, but by then, of course, Nick was already halfway to London, and asleep in his compartment with a crumb on his lip.

11

The divorcée's reply:

February 2, 1938. Dear William, I wrote my name wherever you marked the blue dots. I also got your note that came separately about your not wanting me to get labeled Adulteress. You don't seem to mind lying any more. Thank you for hoping I will always be very happy. I can't drag the coal in and I am *cold* and nearly *dead* and yesterday it *hailed,* right on top of the old snow. If you hadn't lied the way lawyers know how to do better than anybody I bet you would say I am getting the wages of Adultery, but now all you cay say is that I am getting the wages of Incompatibility, or whatever it is you fixed me up with. I didn't read all those papers—I just signed wherever you put the blue dots. They couldn't put me in jail, could they? I'd rather be an Adulteress than a Prisoner. Enoch's in jail right now, and it's awful, it's not a bit like the time I learned how to play cards. There's a man named Mosley who's got a Fascist gang, and they made some trouble out in the East End against the Movement, and somehow everybody got away but Enoch, and he didn't raise even a stick. They were nice to him in the police station but the jail is as bad as this house, if you want to count dampness. The reason I'm still here is that I have to wait till Enoch gets out. He's coming to help me pack up, but he won't be out for two more days. I'm going to London, I can't stay here alone. There's the rent owed anyway. If not for Enoch I wouldn't have survived everything. He was here a couple of days before the Mosley thing happened with *Marianna Harlow* in a box like a coffin. I hate Chatto and Windus, and will try finding another publisher with more intelligence when I get back to America. Anyhow I wrote some extra parts for *Marianna,* and one whole section is so exciting now and up-to-date that I expect to get famous from it, not that you care. The enclosed (I'm sorry, but it had to be in handwriting) is a copy of Chapter Twelve the way it is now. Your blue dots came when I was in the middle of doing it, and I'm sending it to you so that you can learn something about love-making in case you ever decide to get married to someone else. It's a sort of advance wedding present. I hope you don't find it too literary, though it's not Shelley. Have you got any publishers for clients? I want an American publisher now because Enoch said I should go home right away on account of the baby, also the World Situation. I don't know what else to do. Enoch doesn't like the baby much, but I don't blame him, neither do I. You always wanted a baby and I don't see why. This one isn't very good-looking so far, I suppose they get better as they go along. It's allergic to something, it pukes all the time, nobody knows why. We used to give it wine like they do in France and those countries and it puked and now I always give it milk and it still pukes. That time I wrote you about, a couple of months ago when Enoch was here for that parade and his bad tooth flared up and we made an ice-pack from snow on the window-sill, well, what happened was he had such a terrible pain we had to give him the bed, and it was so cold that night we had to put the baby in with him under the blanket to keep it from freezing, and that's just when it decided to puke all over *Enoch*. So you can see it's a terrible baby. I'm going to use your name for it and I'm going to keep on using your name for myself too, I'm supposed to drop only the Mrs. William part. That's what Abby Lywood did—you remember Abby from Miss Jewett's, who was the second to get engaged in our whole class? After she and Walter were divorced she stopped writing Mrs. Walter Paine and wrote just Abby Paine, and that's what I'm going to do. Not because it's what I'm *supposed* to do, I'm not doing it because it's what you used to call right and proper. If I always did what was right and proper you wouldn't have sent the blue dots. Well, if it were up to me I'd go right back to being Miss, why not? But Enoch says the baby's got to have *some* sort of name, so it might as well be yours, there's no other that's currently available. If I sound resentful it's honestly not on account of the blue dots. It's all right about the blue dots, I don't blame you, except you were stingy about the money to spite me for Nick. He's in Italy now I think, he kept talking about Sicily, maybe only to mislead. *He's* the one I'm bitter about, not you. I have to go home to America now, not just because Enoch thinks I ought to be

where I can get good advice, but I somehow really want to
now. Everybody keeps worrying about a war, not that it isn't
perfectly plain it's all a bluff. But there's nothing to *do* in Europe any more, and England's ten times worse. I hate Brighton. Brighton's the place I hate, because the happiest summer
of my life happened right here, even though the baby was
coming in me, it didn't matter, it just made everything hilarious and sentimental. There were lots of things this summer I
didn't write you about, I know you don't think I have any
decencies but I wouldn't have written at all except that Nick
made me, on account of there not being enough money. You
should have sent more or else you should have answered. All
I can tell you about the summer is flowers—I mean you like
gladioli and ugly formal things, things for funerals, but *we*
cut twigs of red berries one day—not to eat, they're dangerous to eat (I looked to see in a little book I had that tells
about poisonous plants)—but to keep part for a bouquet and
part for a sort of garland. You wouldn't have thought of that,
in fact you wouldn't like it, you don't understand Sacred
Beauty. For instance, there's such a nice tree, not too tall but
sort of thin and holy-looking, just outside the window. You
wouldn't look twice at that tree, that's what I mean. You
wouldn't even see its connection with holiness. Most trees are
atheists, but not this one. Once in July all the sheets were off
the bed for washing and I noticed that even the *mattress*
looked religious. It had a pocket in its middle and you could
imagine a guru sitting cross-legged in it. There's a frying pan
with a copper bottom that's like one of these Oriental gongs
Buddhist monks hit with little hammers when they're calling
the rest of the monks to prayer, and even the *frying* pan's
connected with the tree. There are connections everywhere
that you don't know anything about, and it's not even your
fault, it's exactly what the blue dots say, Incompatibility, me
with you (according to the blue dots) and you with Sacred
Beauty. If you want to know what I mean by Sacred I mean
anything that's alive, and Beauty is anything that makes you
want to *be* alive and alive forever, with a sort of shining
feeling. That's why I brought up the gladioli and the red berries: to show you it couldn't be helped, so you oughtn't to feel
bad. It's as though I was destined to feel one way about the
tree and the frying pan and the guru in the mattress and you
were destined to feel another way about the blue dots. In a
certain sense my way is a lie, and your way is a lie too. I mean
my way is Pagan, and yours is Presbyterian, and maybe not-

lying and Sacred Beauty come somewhere in between, and are where people really belong. Nick's the one who discovered I'm a Pagan, and half the summer he called me an ancient Greek, and made a face whenever I said I was a modern Marxist. He said you couldn't be both, you were a heathen or you weren't a heathen, and I was the clear-cuttest heathen he ever saw. But Enoch was down from London then—he was practically always down from London last summer, because there was all that trouble, the strikes and all, and told Nick he needed a haven, but Nick said what he really needed was a hideout. All he did when he came was sit around and read things like *The Psychological Basis of Social Economics*, and weed. He did a lot of weeding, isn't that funny? It's because weeding is very good for meditating and thinking through your position —you bend the knee and you disembowel, and it's veneration and violation at the same time. (Enoch said that and I copied it down.) Anyway, I was telling you, one particular time when Nick called me a heathen Enoch gave one of those secretive laughs he's capable of.

Nick: Aha. The whinny of consent. You agree.

Enoch: I'm agreeable, at any rate.

Nick: That's questionable.

Enoch: If you want to call her unredeemed—

Nick: She has no morals. She's a pre-Christian.

Enoch: Ah, but if she has no morals she's a Christian.

Nick: She's what I say she is—heathen.

Enoch: Exactly—Christian. All Christians are heathen, but not all heathen are Christian. Still, if she isn't redeemed, it doesn't mean she's not redeemable.

Me: Oh, I don't want to be redeemed!

Enoch: You will be. Historically the fate of the heathen has always been conversion.

Nick: To convert 'em you need a missionary, and at the moment there aren't any missionaries in Brighton. Unless—

Enoch: Don't look at *me*. I'm not out to convert her to anything.

Nick: You already have.

Enoch: You mean the Movement. But it didn't last— she's a heretic. She's gone over to your sect.

Nick: I have no sect. Sects are exactly what I'm against.

Enoch: People who are against sects form a very large sect.

Me: But don't you see! I'm not *open* to conversion.

There's no missionary representing *anything* who's
clever enough to catch me.

Enoch: The missionary needn't be clever.

Me: Anyone who could change *my* ideas would have to
be clever all right!

Enoch: On the contrary. Even illiterate. Even ignorant
in toto.

Me: *That* sort of individual wouldn't affect me.

Enoch: That sort of individual will persuade you.

Me: To what?

Enoch: To become what you were always intended to
become.

Me: What's that?

Enoch: A member of a class.

Nick: Ho hum, Karl Marx again.

Enoch: No. Anton Chekhov.

Me: What class?

Enoch: The one you were born into. Your husband's.

Me: It would take pretty powerful missionary ways to
bring me back to William's ways!

Enoch: The opposite of powerful. Helpless. Illiterate.
Ignorant in toto. *There's* your missionary, mewling
in its box.

—He meant the baby, which was so funny and absurd that I
had to laugh, but Nick didn't. I don't see how a *baby* can
influence you in anything—*you* control *it,* not the other way
around, after all. The reason I put in about "William's ways"
for you to see is that I want you to understand positively that
I don't *mind* about the blue dots. I know you think it's a disgrace to be divorced, just because nobody else in our families
ever was before; but I don't mind, I wish my mother had sent
blue dots to my father, instead of those horrible suspicious
half-crazy letters she nearly sent. I'd rather be an Incompatible
Adulteress than *dead* in Scarsdale, with gladioli on the window-sills and no guru in the mattress. And in spite of what
Enoch says, it's not on account of the baby I'm going home,
it's because I'm sick of this place, and it's so cold, and Nick's
gone, and the baby's a nuisance without a nurse for it. I'm
sure I can find a nurse-girl in London (they call them Nanny
like in Peter Pan) when you start sending the money. I hope
you start sending it *very soon.* It was awful having the baby,
but really it's even worse taking care of it. I thought you
would send the money after it was born, that's why I wrote
you about it; but in a way there were two births in this cottage, you know?—one the baby, and the other Adam Gruen-

horn, which is an alias Enoch thought up in the summer once
when he was here and reading Adam Smith. (Nick made fun
of him for that, but Enoch said Adam Smith was in effect the
Karl Marx of the Mercantile Era. I don't know what that
means, maybe you do.) The Gruenhorn part is sort of silly-
nice, it comes from a little green horn—a cut-off bit of
branch all covered over with moss—that sticks out from the
tree's belly. Nick used to hang the garland of red poison-ber-
ries on the green horn whenever we didn't want Enoch to
come in, and sometimes when he was just fresh down from
London and saw it there he went right off and stayed with an
old lady down the road who had a spare room, and never
came round till the next afternoon. He was really very good
about it, even once when he had to keep away three whole
days in a row because the red berries were on the green horn
all that time. "Enters the intruder," he said, "because you let
your garland down." And everyone laughed, it was so theatrical to hear Enoch trying to do a pun. He has no sense of
humor, except in certain unexpected cases. For instance, right
now, you see, it's not *Enoch* who's in jail, it's only Adam
Gruenhorn. That has all kinds of metaphysical implications
concerning Identity. It's what Enoch calls an Ontological
Question. I mean if you're not able to pretend you're someone else, then what *are* you? Sometimes I like to pretend I'm
married, *really* married, and then I begin to feel splendid, as
though I *owned* someone beside just myself. Freedom isn't
when you own just yourself, it's when you own somebody
else. Enoch and I were discussing that, just before he left
here to go to jail—he had an *appointment* with them, they
were very nice and gave him two entire days on his honor
before he had to go back to get incarcerated. He said anyway
he was just as free inside a prison as out of it, because he
didn't have any human relationship that counted one way or
the other.

Me: That's the first unpolitical thing you've ever said.
Enoch: Not at all. Freedom is the most political subject
    there is.
Me: But you weren't talking about political freedom.
    You were talking about freedom in human relation-
    ships. That's what you said.
Enoch: Oh, in human relationships *by definition* there is
    no freedom.

—I don't know whether I agree with that or not, because
marriage is a human relationship, isn't it?—and I think if I

were married, I mean to Nick, *I'd* feel free. I wouldn't have to go *do* anything, I'd just sit still and be happy, and now I have to move around and go to London and then America and pretend it's on account of War Clouds I'm doing all that, when it's not at all, I don't care about war or no war, I *hate* patriotism exactly the way you hate Roosevelt, because it deprives you of *personal* self-interest and possibilities you can make up for yourself. I think about being married practically all the time. I mean married to Nick. That time I went to Cape Ann with you I thought it would be a certain way, full of eternity and freedom and Sacred Beauty and a very, very delicate sort of owning. I thought it would turn out like that no matter *whom* I married, it would come just from being married. Like the Doctrine of Grace the way your mother once read it from a sermon in a book she had. Also I believed everything *felt* should be *stated*. That's why I took along the Shelley—to state it. But I was dry all the time. I was just dry, so I threw Shelley in the water and watched him drink, but still I was dry in myself, and I never felt Grace till Nick, and without being married, so it proves you don't need to be married to feel it. But still I wish I were: not because I'm a nail and want to nail him into my side. But it would be a Statement, do you see? Oh, I want to be married to him! All day long and all night through I think how it would be, Greek if he wants it Greek, Pagan if he wants it Pagan, Socialist if he'll let me, and free, free, free, the baby in a little cart of its own being pulled up a hillside all furred with daisies and susans and marigolds and smoky-headed dandelions, though I suppose after a while it would grow *up*, and start running around on its own. The question is what am I to do all the time it's growing up? I can't just sit and watch it, I'm not the type to carry off loneliness by naming it motherliness, I don't know what to do. That's why I'm coming home, to think out what to do, and where he's gone. He's gone, he's gone, I don't know where, Sicily he was thinking of. If I came to talk it out with you it could be fixed up for a legal thing, couldn't it, finding Nick? I could say he ought to marry me on account of the baby, I could say it didn't matter before, but now it really does, wherever he's gone, maybe Italy, maybe not. I thought you could know how to find him, you could send him a warrant or whatever they use, you could call it Desertion or whatever they call it, you could call it Abandonment. I'm abandoned, I'm deserted, it's a desert here, nobody here, nobody, just myself abandoned. It sounds terrible to say that word, like people who live in the slums, but what's legal is legal for all classes, and it can't be legal for Nick to go off to Italy when there's a baby left behind, can it? There must be something in International Law that you would know about, something strict and stern about paternity and infants, I know in law there aren't lovers, so let it be fathers and daughters, whichever way you want to do it: the trick you did when you fixed up Incompatibility instead of Adultery, fix it up fathers and daughters instead of lovers, which ever way you want to do it. Only help. You have to help, you can't help helping, it's part of the trust that you have to help, isn't it? I asked Enoch if he'd watch the baby for me, the tiniest sort of vigil while I went to Italy to look myself, to look for Nick wherever he is, but Enoch thinks whatever can be done you'll know how to do best, because of the trust. It means he doesn't like the baby, but after all he's right, he doesn't think you'll mind—I told him I don't believe you have very bad thoughts about me, at least not the way I have terrible and evil thoughts about Nick. About Nick I have terrible and evil thoughts. I want to put a nail in him till he bleeds. Into his eyes: even that, even there. The trouble with a person who has impressive and extraordinary eyes is that they never look distracted—they're all eye, and all aye and yes yes yes, and all Now This Minute, and later on you find out it's nothing but a sickening fraud on you and they were plotting an Afterward that disgorges you. Plain average eyes can't dissemble like that, they're too naked, if they leave you out you know it right away, a smudge of color and a lid and a look and that's it, no horrible deadly polish on them like the sun if the sun were blue all around and inside itself and throwing the blue of itself on itself. What I'm saying is he didn't betray a waver and he didn't waver when he betrayed, he just walked off right in the center of happiness and took it with him. Afterward when it was nearly night and I had your blue dots and there was nothing but a tin of tuna fish and pabulum I felt blind, it was like all at once turning blind. He took away his eyes and I couldn't see. That's the truth, even though it's only a metaphor. And now the first thing is I have to go to London and stay in Enoch's room—he owes me a hideout he says, but oh it's a haven I need, and such a tiny room it is—I stayed there once with Nick. The baby's *box* would take half of it. That's because it's a greengrocer's box; a chemist's box Enoch thinks would be more compact, in certain ways he's very practical, so I'll get one. I put the address

at the top of this letter, in case you finally decide to answer
—don't forget to put c/o Adam Gruenhorn, *not* Enoch
Vand. It feels so queer here right this minute, I can't explain.
I don't really mind packing and unpacking, so long as it's
done thoroughly, all moved in or all moved out, everything
settled and nothing by halves: it's *what* I pack that kills. For
instance, a print I got in Moscow of this fantastic old basilica
with domes like onions that's a museum now, I just put it flat
at the bottom of a suitcase and stared straight down at it,
which sort of turned it into a photograph, with that archaic
look even recent photographs get pretty soon. There weren't
any people in the print but I *saw* people, all by thinking it
was really a snapshot—Nick and Enoch and Hugh and
Dickie Sparrs and me bundled together trying to keep warm
in the plaza in front of this gigantic oniony church on the
day we had that awful quarrel—I wrote you about it, Enoch
saying we hadn't any loyalty and were damaging the Movement by going off, and Nick arguing he'd be more useful as a
contact in different places, and Enoch answering that was
Hugh's job, because Hugh's a linguist—it was almost autumn,
and all our breaths were standing still in the air in front of
us. I remember that because the moment I was actually in the
middle of that incident, with everybody's voices all mixed together full of meanness, and foreign flat-nosed Tartar faces
going by giving us mean and hostile looks, it *felt* like a snapshot. I thought: this is me, this is Moscow, this is Nick, we
don't dare sway or we'll blur. The print is sort of blurred
anyway, it's got that mistiness of line artists use when they
want to make a thing seem very remote and ideal: it's as
though they're withholding, they're not really *telling*. But to
me a thing isn't real until you tell it. (That's why I brought
the Shelley that time.) Enoch said: The Movement doesn't
care who anybody lives *with*, just so long as it's assured what
he's living *for*. If he's living for the cause, we're not interested in his cohabitations. In spite of that Nick and I left, we
needed to—though I made us go with Hugh, so Enoch would
see we weren't leaving the *Movement,* just the crowd. And
for months and months afterward we helped with all the rallies, and Nick wasn't against it because at first I was getting
enough to cover taking trains to different places very comfortably, but then you cut the money down to practically
nothing and we had to sit still in one niche, so we came to
Brighton and were glad after all. Not that Nick wasn't really
immense at these rallies—sometimes he had absolutely bril-

liant and fantastic ideas, like the amazing incident I told you
about that happened in that hall on New Oxford Street—but
he said the Movement cramped individual invention, and he
was right, for instance I didn't touch *Marianna* for a year or
more while we were marching in parades and things. And he
said it was foolishness to march in parades anyhow, and he
was tired of it. So I said the *Greeks* had parades, and Nick
said they weren't ordinary agitating parades, they were religious processions for Dionysus and Demeter, and when the
ancient Greeks dealt with agricultural output they meant
wine and fertility instead of bloodless ideas like land value
and commodities per capita, and when they dealt with industrial potential they were thinking of Penelope at the loom,
patient for the return of Odysseus. And he said the Greeks
weren't afraid of getting drunk, like Enoch and all the other
Jews. And he said he didn't like Athens, where Socrates was
always wandering around the streets lecturing people, but
cared only for the goddess of the coppice, and that's how we
began to throw darts at the tree I told you about, to make
her cry out. And sometimes, if you closed your ears with
your palms and listened hard, she did. And all the while it
was really only Brighton we were in, so we hung the print of
the oniony Moscow church on the wall, to remind us how
some people in the world have to live without dryads watching their doors. The frame is only celluloid, and cracked, so I
haven't packed it—still, it's odd how an empty picture frame
on a cold white wall, with the screw showing exactly where it
snakes into the plaster, seems spooky when you're all alone in
a place you're not accustomed to being sad in. It got sad toward the end. You never sent the money and the baby kept
screaming, and Nick swore it was screaming Money Money
with the consonants left out; it really sounded like that, and
then out of the blue he went off, while I was writing all about
how love in bed makes you feel, private and all sweet. That's
the part I've put in here for you to read after you finish this
letter. And he took away my ENCHIRIDION—my lovely
tiny book full of poison flowers, and lovely perfect drawings
of the red hard shiny waxy berries we used to hang on the
green horn to make Enoch go away, and he went away. I
don't know why he took it, I guess it just happened to be in
his summer-jacket pocket, and he went out wearing his summer-jacket under his overcoat, because of the cold; the last
time we went walking to get berry-twigs it was still October
a whole year since we left Moscow to go everywhere together

and amaze ourselves with ourselves. That's Nick's, that part: "we'll amaze ourselves with ourselves," and it came true, and now he's in Italy, or maybe not, with my flower book I bought in Southampton coming into England in his pocket, and out the window there's nothing on the tree but an old stuck dart with dirty snow on its tail, and I think how happy and gorgeous it was here, all green, and how it was with the tree and us and the coppice-goddess, as though there could be a goddess in Brighton, or a dryad! So Brighton's the place I hate, in the whole world I hate Brighton most of all, you always hate the place you were happiest in. Poor William, poor you, I guess there isn't any place for you to hate like that. But you're lucky too, it means you don't hate any *person* either. I told Enoch I'm sure you don't hate me, you only have contempt for me, but that's your religion and you can't help it, you think I'm fallen. And you know what Enoch said?— Presbyterians have contempt, but Pagans have babies. In spite of not having a sense of humor or laughing much, Enoch doesn't really take anything very seriously, except Social Justice. He feels about Social Justice exactly the way Nick feels about Sacred Beauty and ancient Greece, but Nick laughs all the time, he laughs the most marvelous lonesome laugh, as though he were seeing visions nobody else ever saw. It's silly to keep imagining he left his laugh behind in this room (oh I hate this room) when it's only the baby that's awake and jiggling some walnut shells Nick twisted into a paper bag for a rattle. Rustle, rustle, it could be Nick's laugh but it's only the baby playing, he took his laugh with him and his eyes with him and my little ENCHIRIDION with him, everything, and I think of him right now on that Island of Sicily, spread out on a beach in the sun the way I used to watch him spread out on Brighton beach in the sun and getting practically as black as Hugh, or rowing around in a boat with a foot overboard in the water, and I get so full of wish, wish, wish I begin to believe wish, wish, wish will break whole out of my skeleton and work on him, on his long foot in the water and his long hand trailing in the water. I mean I wish he would die. After that boy, I can't describe my feelings but this even you can take in exactly and give it out again without a lawyer's lie, after that dead boy and what I saw, and how it happened because of the trust, the trust *made* it happen, I really did *swear* (just as though I believed in God) I would never again wish anybody's dying. Because before then I sometimes used to wish people would die: I wished my father would die, and he died, but left that horrible horrible trust, that murdering trust that killed a boy with its inflexibility. The trust killed that Armenian boy. And that weird widow-girl who came and took the knife, as though the knife killed him!—I *told* you you should have given her the trust to take home instead of the knife, but instead you went to the funeral, all because you thought it was the right and proper thing, on account of his family's being poor; and you tried to give them money, I know you did. Wergeld! —That's what Hugh said it was called, paying off the family for the body. The body was awful. I remember the hands up at the neck, like the baby's when it's asleep, there and not there, because I touched one of them, just the fingers, just the dead thumb really, and how it was. And even in spite of that, even in spite of that, I feel it now, in spite of that I feel it again, wishing a dying for someone, because there's Nick all black-skinned in a boat down there, laughing and laughing in that hot place full of sun that goes down there right through the water, shimmering dropped through the water spread-winged, and after everything me here freezing alone after Brighton after freezing after everything it's no wonder, I don't wonder in spite of that boy I wish he dies, I hope he drowns, for all I care let him drown down deep there. Because of Brighton Brighton Brighton. Because of Brighton.

William's answer:

February 14, 1938. Your inordinately diffuse letter and enclosure, marked "Air Mail," due to insufficient postage for its weight arrived by ship. Consonant with my duties as trustee, I am ready to make immediately available to you whatever funds, in accordance with the arrangements separately attached, you may authorize, from the date of this letter forward. Pursuant to this I have asked Mr. Connelly to set forth in detail necessary procedures for you to follow. You will find, together with his explanations, a list of thirty-two European cities, including London, in which various banks are now open to your signature. Mr. Connelly has, I believe, anticipated any questions that may arise, particularly in the matter of drawing checks and opening further accounts. Mr. Peat and Mrs. Charlottine of Nothham, Peat and Mr. Charlottine of New York will assume direction of the properties listed on the enclosed sheet marked with their letterhead. In all other categories I have retained personal discretionary powers, according to the terms of the trust, and continue to stand ready to aid and advise in all fiduciary and financial matters. Yours sincerely.

Allegra to William:

March 22, 1938. About the nursemaid. Mrs. Amy Mealie. She's Welsh. I want to bring her home with me when I decide to come but don't know how to do it and what she's got to do to come. She's already applied for a passport. Will there be some stupidity about bringing in an immigrant? She says the baby's been starved, I wasn't feeding it right. I *knew* that, after all. She took it to a specialist, there's something wrong with its inner ear, that's how come it pukes so much, but it's supposed to get better gradually as it grows up. It might be a hereditary condition, not from me. Mrs. Mealie gives it liquid vitamins. Connelly didn't write how to fix it so Mrs. Mealie can write checks on her own when I'm not around. Because sometimes she needs things in a hurry and she's very strict in her morals and doesn't believe in credit and meanwhile there I am away and out flying all over London in different places doing this and seeing that, and everything's just the opposite of how it used to be when we came just to march. I ride around in a hired car the whole day and my hair is cut very short (in Brighton it got to be like a serpent) and you can't tell me apart from any old eccentric Countess. And last week Enoch went to Spain. It's to assassinate some Fascists there, not that I think he can really *shoot* anyone, even though I saw his gun. It's tiny and black and looks fake, but isn't, which is very sinister. He went as a sort of correspondent for this Liverpool paper that wants biographical sketches of the Falangist leaders for a column they have, called "Notes from the Land of Quixote." They print maps and follow the war from day to day. Enoch thinks if he can get to some of these Fascists through this job he can shoot them. It's terribly dangerous and naturally he's very brave but honestly I think war is too stupid to bother with. Sometimes I feel I'm the only real pacifist left in the world. Enoch used to be the most *passionate* pacifist you'd ever want to meet and was always talking about beating swords into ploughshares and all of that, and now he's not a pacifist even about Spain. None of the pacifists are any more, it's peculiar. You don't say anything about finding Nick. I keep waiting for you to say something about *looking* for him. Please note the new address above. It's a very nice flat, very big—it has so many rooms the whole Spanish Civil War could be fought in it and you'd never notice. I hired a man to cook. He cooks Viennese, he's a refugee from over there, not that he's a real chef or anything, in fact he used to have a china factory, but they always gave dinner parties and he was what in German he calls a praisecook, it's a gourmet who cooks to get the applause of his guests. Everything is always a bit greasy, but otherwise he's all right. He wanted me to take his wife on for the baby, but I already had Mrs. Mealie who's very good and besides I didn't like the look of the wife, too withdrawn and fragile. As you can imagine they were well off over there and one could see she didn't care for being a servant only on account of Hitler. The class-consciousness of the bourgeoisie is the most offensive sort, they despise work. Two different Jewish families in Manchester took in their boys and I don't know where the wife is now, he never says. You find refugees scattered all over London with their horrible broken English, and they're not cheaper, they're more *expensive*, in fact. I'm glad about the money, but you should have sent it before, in Brighton.

Allegra to William:

April 12, 1938. Did you find out anything about Nick? I saw Dickie Sparrs two weeks ago and he heard Hugh was in Sweden. He doesn't think Nick ever joined Hugh in the first place, since Hugh hasn't been in Sicily since August. Dickie's mother mails him *The New York Times* wherever he happens to be, with messages along the sides of the international-news columns telling to watch out for this and watch out for that, and not to go here and not to go there, and to avoid getting mixed up *socially* with Hitler and Mussolini and Franco and Stalin, so that's how I saw the announcement about your engagement. I didn't know Sarah Jean *too* well at Miss Jewett's, she was part of a clique that stayed out of everything except Saturday afternoon horses. I remember she used to be very religious, especially about the New Testament. Once when I asked her to demonstrate against something with us she said render unto Caesar what is Caesar's. I didn't agree with her then but I do now, on account of what happened to Enoch. It's too stupid, he didn't get to see the Falangist leaders or *anybody*. Going across the border they attacked the bus he was in and stole his gun and kicked in all the windows and fought with pieces of window glass and cut practically a pound of flesh from his left arm. It wasn't even Fascists that did it, it was Loyalists. There was a person on the bus they wanted to kill and they killed him. Somebody fixed a tourniquet after they left or Enoch would be dead now.

It's really too stupid. Marching is one thing, but after all when you think how many innocent babies there are in the world, on *both* sides of any cause, no cause seems worth killing either side's babies for. Nick once told me the reason he was against the Movement was that it judged the world by every possible value except the personal ones, which are the only sort that count. (Not that he's acted as though they count to *him*.) And you know my thought on this? It's that surely nothing is as personal as a baby—something I've just learned, and I learned it by myself. Enoch's opinion is that I got sentimental about the baby the very minute I stopped having anything to do with it—he gives Mrs. Mealie the credit for my caring about All the Innocent Babies in the World (he's very sarcastic about it). He and Nick *always* used to disagree about Personal vs. Abstract. Enoch said swords-into-ploughshares was an abstraction, and the greatest idea on earth; and Nick said Jesus-raising-Lazarus was a personal happening, and the greatest idea on earth.

Enoch: *Off* earth, you mean. It certainly didn't happen here. Maybe it happened in heaven.

Nick: Here, says the story.

Enoch: Heaven isn't here, you'll agree to that.

Nick: Modest! Only until you fellows bring it, I suppose.

Enoch: We fellows aren't such ninnies as to want to duplicate the Christian notion of heaven. It would obligate us to infer hell, and having inferred it to condone it. We're not that barbarous—at least not so barbarous as the average preacher, you see. Besides, the answer to Jesus and Lazarus is dust unto dust.

Nick: Some state the same thing vice versa, and call it just as true. The answer to dust is resurrection.

Enoch: The most successful religions are those that tell lies in the most picturesque way.

Nick: At any rate the answer to swords and ploughshares is rust unto rust. And when a man lets his Things rust, he slips back into prehistory.

Enoch: Only into the prehistory of Things. Only into the prehistory of *homo faber*. *Homo sapiens*—which is to say man when he has acquired moral possibilities—has no prehistory, he has history only. Technology progresses. A flint hammer becomes a bomb. A cave becomes a skyscraper. This is *homo faber* progressing—man the maker. We call the Things we don't remember his making, prehistory;

and the Things we seem to remember, because he described them for us, history. But *homo sapiens* doesn't progress. He is always the same. He was modern from the very beginning. We date him from the moment he learned that killing, which didn't bother him, and being killed, which did, were really the same act. That moment is when human history began. It began when *homo faber* became *homo sapiens*—when manufacturing man became moral man. Having made, he thought about what he had made, and what he ought to do and ought not to do about what he had made. Moral man has no prehistory, because before history there was no man, there were only beasts. One never speaks of the history of beasts, though some, like the beavers and the birds, are very fine manufacturers of their own environment.

Nick: A beast can't make a telescope.

Enoch: It's only a beast who does. A telescope is the eye sharpened. But it is only the eye. It isn't something *other*—it's the beast extended. The naked eye is the telescope's prehistory. You won't discover the nature of man in the little bundles he carries with him always—they're only his mess of pottage. His birthright is something else.

Nick: His birthright is personal—you can't deny that.

Enoch: It belongs to him personally, he personally must act on it, but in itself it's an abstraction. His birthright is a message against killing; against killing as a theory and a methodology. Of course you can't prove that the message is *there*, the way the telescope can prove the distant stars are there. That's because we don't know whether the message proceeds out of ourselves, the way the telescope proceeds out of ourselves.

Nick: Watch it, you're on the margin!

Enoch: The margin of what?

Nick: Arguing for God.

Enoch: God is an abstraction that can't be proved.

Nick: God is a person who was never born.

Enoch: Now *you're* on the margin. You're about to make out a God as tangible as a mess of pottage. I call that idolatry.

Nick: So do I, and gladly. But a God like a mess of pottage isn't tangible enough—he's too mushy. I want a God I can touch with a clang! That's why I've had

to settle for gods. There's one Allegra knows
about, in the tree, a goddess with a hide as firm as
metal. We haven't seen her, but we've felt her. We've
struck her. She's there, all right.
Enoch: Mess of pottage.
Nick: Better than a pot of message.

—I still laugh when I think of that! They used to talk like
that on summer nights sometimes, always like that, and it's
queer that afterward Nick was quick to leave tree and me,
and Enoch was just as quick to buy his little black gun. And
all in spite of how they talked. I remember what they said,
but I can't remember *how* except through a kind of membrane. I don't know what the membrane is, maybe time,
maybe only having had to listen to them through the baby's
crying. It never cries now, and looks smooth and healthy, and
sometimes even bleats out a noise that sounds like me-me-me,
which Siegfried says stands for Mrs. Mealie. It's still not awfully good-looking but Siegfried (the cook) thinks it shows
high intelligence and is going to begin talking very early. I
don't know whether he means it or not, he's very sly and says
things just to ingratiate himself. He hasn't mentioned his wife
again but now what he wants is to bring his oldest boy to live
here, there's a school nearby that's offering scholarships to refugee children of a certain age. He promises he would keep
him in the kitchen and quiet and out of sight, but I've had to
decide against it, it's the old story of the camel and the
Arab's warm tent, pretty soon it would be his wife and the
two other boys (who I understand are practically only *babies*
—you can imagine what a nuisance that would be), and
there wouldn't be room for *us* to *breathe* in. Mrs. Mealie
wouldn't like it either. They're awfully pushy people, I have
to admit you used to be right about that aspect. Of course
Enoch is different. When I told Enoch about Siegfried, you
know what he said? —Moses was really an Egyptian, Jesus
was really a Samaritan, so Siegfried must be really a Jew.

Me: But they're all Jews, I know that much. Siegfried
especially.
Enoch: *Especially* Siegfried, since he's absolutely indistinguishable from any other Viennese of his class.
Nothing is what it seems—that's the first rule of
tyranny—and if it seems to be what it is, then
it ought to be disproved by logical schemes grounded
in false premises. Better yet, it ought to be abolished
by force.

—I don't always follow him when he's being sardonic, and since that Spanish business, and his arm, he's hardly ever *not* sardonic. I think the reason is he's reading philosophers now. Also his arm *is* still in bad shape and very painful, the doctor said it's a wonder it didn't have to be amputated. He stays in his hideous little Adam Gruenhorn room practically day and night, all bandaged up, reading like mad. He's reading Materialism and Idealism. What it means, you see, is that there are two sorts of philosophers, Materialist and Idealist. One thinks the world is bad and really there, the others think the world is good and not really there. The Materialists—the ones who think the world exists but is bad—believe in God, but hate him for creating a bad world; and the Idealists—the other camp—are atheists who would love God if only they believed in him. Anyhow that's how Enoch explained it. Then I asked him what you would call a person like you, for instance, who thought the world was both good *and* there—whether he'd be a Materialist or an Idealist, and Enoch said neither, he'd be a fool. So then I gave him the news about your engagement, sort of to make the point for you, and he warned me strictly not to omit congratulating you. I suppose that was sardonic too. Though it really *is* a thing to marvel at: the way life works out. I mean it would have been perfectly sensible if you had *begun* with Sarah Jean in the first place, and then you wouldn't have had to feel ashamed and degraded because of the divorce. I hope contemplating this doesn't make you terribly sad, if you *do* like me and don't hate the irrevocable for *being* irrevocable. I do, I wish I could have the past back, not to do things over again in a different way but to realize while I'm living those things that this is my only chance at them. Because you don't recognize till afterward which moment of all the moments you've experienced is going to be the great high full one; and by the time you've sorted it out from the rest, it's gone. You can *think* about what's gone, but you can't *live* it. I wish there were a signal system that said: Now, it's Now, so look with all your might, and taste with all your might, and feel with all your might, and *be* with all your might; it's Now and it won't ever come again. A signal, not a thing like a chime but a familiar human voice, because think!—you might that very minute be taking it all for granted, you might be distracted by a fly in the room or an itch in your toe or a sign on the road, and never at all be aware you were in the prime of your one and only deep and beautiful hour. I wish in Brighton I had heard

a voice I could trust say: "Brighton"—just the one name, like
that, not "Europe," not "England"—just: "Brighton," and I
would have understood. But there wasn't a voice. Or maybe
there wasn't a voice I could trust. Or maybe I was feeling too
happy to listen. The trouble with happiness is that it never
notices itself. Enoch looked queer when I told him that, and
said it was enough of a burden on mankind that we *always*
notice our unhappy times. Then he said I ought to be a Pil-
grim Father like you, so I'd never worry about the irrevocable and would just accept it under the heading of Predestination. And then he snorted like a walrus from behind his
bandages and asked me if I'd ever thought how interesting it
is that people who believe in Predestination are also obliged
to believe that God is a very bad planner—taking for example your having to marry and divorce me in order to marry
the sort of person you ought to have married to begin with. I
explained it isn't exactly Predestination you believe in, only a
vague sort of idea about heaven's will, though you probably
never even *think* about it, it would embarrass you if you ever
did. And you know what Enoch answered? —Since we can
realize our destinies only after the fact, determinists should
never speak of heaven's *will*, but only of heaven's *was*. —He's
terribly clever, but over my head, and sometimes I get a *little*
sick of always having to think so hard when I'm with
him. Oh look, after all Enoch's warnings I'm nearly forgetting to tell you Congratulations after all. It's really the best
thing you could have done, and very nice for poor Sarah
Jean too. It was such a humiliation for her when Alan Pettigrew broke their engagement—it must be five years already!
—to marry that lively girl from the West that nobody ever
heard of. Everybody thought it a tragedy, but fate had something else in mind. Life! *C'est la fille!* Anyhow Alan Pettigrew was always a devious little boy. Even way back in dancing school he was always changing partners on his own, and
never kept the one Miss Lamb paired him with—remember
Miss Lamb's pairing system? She listened to all the old gran-
nies. Sarah Jean and Alan Pettigrew, me and you. And see
how different it all is now! P.S. I've just read this whole letter
over. You won't like the philosophy parts. But really believe
me in spite of them I'm much graver-minded than I used to
be. You can't have had and lost Brighton without ending up
a lot graver-minded than you started out. P.P.S. Let me know
what to do about Mrs. Mealie and the $$$!

Memorandum from Connelly to Allegra:

April 17, 1938. Bank of London, Ltd., has been directed to honor checks bearing signature of A. Mealie up to the value of £5 each. For problems of similar degree, it will be convenient for you to make arrangements with Mr. Ian Makin at the bank. Blackburn and Tweddly, Solicitors, have been instructed with regard to this individual's emigration. Yours very truly.

Allegra to William:

May 1, 1938. This isn't a letter. Today is May Day, and even Enoch's ignoring Labor. He has to, or his arm won't heal. Still, May Day without a parade! We're going to get ourselves driven all the way up to the Cotswolds to see some May Dancers. The Green Park is full of green, it's true, but the country is the country. One ought to ogle low stone walls. This is only to say how surprised I was to hear (from little Sparrs, who got it from his mammy) that the wedding happened so fast. And so quietly. I suppose it was a great sacrifice for Sarah Jean, letting it all go with a hush, and not getting to be a bride with all the gala. I don't know why you slipped into it like that, it makes you seem so *mournful*, like a widower. Doubtless you knew what you were doing. —I was going to say something about staying on a few more months, but here's Enoch leaning on the bell, so goodbye, we're off for maypoles. But the bank sent a mysterious little message. I guess you know about it. The upshot of it is you want me to keep away till you're settled down. Just like a widower faced with an unlucky ghost! Well, if you want to correspond through the bank until you're settled down, I don't object in the least. The trouble is the bank doesn't care whether they find Nick or not. The bank's given up, and advises me to do the same. Everything's dead to a bank, you know, it doesn't matter how many ribbons are going around how many maypoles. —Enoch's in, and yelling like a madman. I *said* this wasn't a letter. No, there's not the tiniest stick or thread I want out of the Scarsdale house. It's all Sarah Jean's, with my blessings. (Is it all right for me to say that, or do I have to whisper it to the bank so the bank can whisper it to you?)

12

My mother's letters. If only it were possible to call them incredible! (And thus evade them.) But by their tedium they compel belief. Not that their impulse shows a want of vitality—they have, after all, the flute-note of purity: a distinction which some persons, probably including my mother herself, ostentatiously like to toss into the category of Subjective Truth. Tedious her letters undoubtedly are; but they are not *merely* tedious. Think of music—some delectable sonatina, say, small yet brave—and imagine it played in the next room. Imagine it played in the next room for five hours. Even the marvelous, too long sustained, can be charged with tedium as absolutely as, in another part of the mind, the folklorist Toynbee kills our trust with his deadly progressions of distortions, any one of which, alone, we might smile at, as upon a weed grown up in a Japanese rock-garden. Here, however, I find that I am quoting Enoch. "Not only endless quiescence, but also endless excitation, produces the torpor of tedium," he said the day I brought out the bundle of my mother's letters; "the most celestial hymn, uncelestially prolonged, will do it. Not for nothing"—sly Enoch! to achieve this last and my mother's laughter he threaded through a lacework of ornately balanced prologue—"not for nothing do we speak of the Te Deum."

I have stated that I brought out my mother's letters. This means they existed. How did they exist? William said he had torn them up. The stern historian, remembering this, will accuse me of having reconstructed them from my mother's public mode of writing (I avoid the word "style," though the innocent historian might not) in *Marianna Harlow*. And indeed such a forgery would not be difficult. The letters as they stand have many of the characteristics of her fiction—so much so that, having tested one's soul in these, it is no longer

necessary to try oneself more profoundly in *Marianna*. Here,
in the absence of novelistic device, are all her devices: more
than one panting reader has noted how the whole of *Marianna* appears to have been conceived of as a single paragraph. And here is her adoration of dialectic, and of dialogue, and of Intellectual Matter not her own stuffed naïvely
but diligently between rapturous sheets so as to make a mattress upon which to rest the astonished and violated ear. The
metaphor of the mattress is not by chance. And the guru in it
is undoubtedly what my mother would term the "philosophy
parts"—though the same historian will perhaps blame me for
having invented these out of the logic of history, which always personifies. Even in the dialogues of Plato (easily as
theatrical as my mother's) we have representations not of hu-
mors but of the dual political history of the race. ("The ma-
jority of the beasts, if polled, would vote Rightist." —Enoch.
Or again: "Lambs are born liberals.") But the mattress has a
kick here, and a sag there, and is, besides, noisy with the
claims of phantom voices: sometimes Enoch's, more often
Nick's, now and then a solecism adapted from a foreign
idiom introduced to my mother by that Hugh who, though
this may not be the place to tell it, finally earned his daily
nutriment abroad by dressing in Arab skirts and singing romantic Russian songs in a Georgian accent (not that Georgia
where Stalin was born) and in a very fine near-soprano. The
accent was partly perforce, and partly to deride—not the
songs, but his audience. Sometimes he liked to tease a male
auditor (whose spoon hung amazed at his lip) by declaring
himself a rival for the male auditor's wife's affections, and
this in a country where there were no miscegenation laws.
But what Hugh really liked was the skirts: they hid him.
They also revealed him. After the war he turned up where
Nick turned up; they often traveled together, a pair of min-
strel dominoes or dice, white imposing on black, black imposed on white. Or they split, usually by night, each addressing his own scarred piano in his own fork-flashing winey pro-
vincial cellar. Their daylight sins were not the same. Nick
roamed beaches, found what he had not sought (he prided himself on never petitioning), and afterward submitted to physio-
logically-oriented interrogation in several languages, including
Dutch, by his fellow piano-player the walnut-veneered Ph.D.
If the woman was my governess, and could be had therefore
only in the unfocussed depth of morning dark, while demons
clanged, the questions would be Dutch, the vicarious fancy

would be Dutch, Hugh in his long Arab skirts would dream himself deliciously Dutch, and then go make excuses for Nick in Nick's café to Nick's employer, in French. He would say, in French, that his friend had been kept away the night before by illness, and would be kept away tonight by the same malady; the malady was a Dutch malady, and continued until my mother cured it by sending away the carrier, poor wrathful exiled Anneke, who saw cruel Palestinian wastes in the sands of the beach where Nick came rambling in indifferent hope of discovery: and discovered my governess, dozing on a flat wedge of stone. Meanwhile far below, among the smaller wavelets with their heads dissolving into little pools of white spittle, I was catching the ringworm from Jean François. Like a pair of courting lizards, Anneke and my father (my father!) flirted on that stone and arranged their brief opportunistic future: one spoke of the nasty child she had to tend, the other of his nasty piano. And Hugh was sent to tell them at the Palatin that Nick could not play that night. Well, let this be said of Hugh: he knew all the white man's languages. Never mind mere Romance, Kelt, and Slav; he knew all the varieties of the Germanic tongues—Low, High, Middle; Scandinavian in its several guises; Flemish; even Yiddish; even Afrikaans. Afrikaans yes, Bantu no. He had the round, beautifully-turned foreskull of a Johannesburg sweeper; few American Negroes are negroid enough to have retained that lordly arc of brow. Let this also be said of Hugh: though knowing all the white man's languages, though agonized by the longing to be white, a white man he did not long to be. The white man takes. Imperialist colonialist brute, the white man takes. Hugh wanted to be taken.

But all this is by the way. Be assured that I did not get it from William. I was musing on my mother's letters. I did not get these from William either. Yet innumerable letters glutted William's files. He had letters from architects and from contractors and from engineers of bridges. He had the young Armenian's violent letters. He had the cautiously polite but impatient letters of the fourteen other prospective curators. He had one primitive letter, in capitals, from the ferryman. He had repeated letters in a hideous pastiche of near-English from the young Armenian's parents, in which they refused the indisputably generous sums proffered for their son's life. He had a sympathetic and perhaps too graceful letter from the doctor who had escaped the acquisition of an Armenian son-in-law. He had letters from the county threatening suit.

Oh, William had letters! (All lawyers do.) They were kept in a file in Connelly's charge, marked Miscellaneous. His son had read them all.

But not my mother's letters. These William did not have. These his son had never read. Why? Because they were in a cardboard ladies' stationery box, with gold stripes across the cover, secreted at the back of the third drawer of Enoch's locked desk. He gave me the key and told me where to find them and ordered me to bring them out. There were the letters I have reproduced here (and not from imagination or speculation), and a few others. Each was encased in a pair of envelopes, the inner one fragile and crackly and zealously scratched over in my mother's hand, the scratches pointing furiously toward America, the outer one of a thick opulent paper and prudently directed toward an English bank. America had read them all, and America had returned them all. Strange, strange! There were, besides, the letter from William I have already given, and a dozen or so memoranda under Connelly's name. Oh, strange! I held them and weighed them and sniffed their ancient emanation, vaguely of sea (but most had gone by air), and regarded them as my mother must have regarded her mother's madder letters, never mailed, which the maids had brought down to her long ago: it was the same; I thought them intrusive; I thought them obscene; I thought them monstrous. For a short space I intensely believed them to be forgeries, or, lacking that, some incomprehensible hoax understandable only to an irrational generation, now luckily dead. I saw them creased, unfolded, re-folded, sealed and unsealed and then again sealed, here and there yellowishly gluey or dimly patched with brittle tape; but their horror for me was not that they were old. They were old; it was not age which opened out my bitter fright. It was that they were evidence; they were in effect witnesses; by their changelessness they confirmed, they spited. Worse, they showed how the devil contrives to keep his dossier empty. They existed without seeming to have existence; like all witnesses and testimonies they were not the thing itself; they were *about* the thing, and could err. Behold, the thing itself has vanished; place, time, circumstance—all vanished and vanquished. Only the witnesses and testimonies linger. They come on stage Indian-file, superannuated, redolent of rejected moonings, and wearing out-of-date garments everyone now finds as ridiculous as a costume for a slightly stilted play. That my mother, today placidly conjuring herself mis-

tress of the Embassy, should yearn to marry Nick, a drifter, a
piano-player! Obsolete, all obsolete. It was as crude and absurd as though she should suddenly declare a passion for Ed
McGovern. I could not swallow it: my mother as young as I,
my mother in her wild old days. Her letters stank with their
imposture; they denied the stick of time along which we willingly enough appear to jump, insanely, notch by notch; I despised them. No wonder the devil's dossier is always bare!
There are no wedding-congratulations in it. There is no philosophy in it. What has been uttered has been forgotten.
What has been written is disgusting, and no one will believe
in it. This is how he maintains his flexible versions of what-
was—the devil; this is why his briefcase is unburdened. Everyone helps him. What exists, or existed once, is said not to
exist, or never to have existed at all. And if evidence should
all at once emerge, and testimonies, and witnesses, by their
own force, by their own radical and improbable nature they
are discredited. My mother's letters! She, it turned out, did
not remember having composed them; and when, obeying
Enoch, I confronted myself and her with their unarguable
quiddities, present in, of all undeniables, her own unchanged,
hence undeveloped, handwriting, she professed more vigorously than before never to have written them. She claimed
she very plainly did not feel that way, therefore could never
have felt that way; she leaped hindward from improbability
to impossibility. And I with her, daydreaming they were a
fraud, like my mother's second marriage and divorce, sup-
posedly to and then from that Nick who courted my governess on the beach of Europe and afterward bargained for my
ignorance of his being. And achieved both; Anneke by night;
blackmail by day. He always achieved what he was after;
probability never touched him; for him, without danger, everything could exist, all things were permitted to exist. Meanwhile in a backward fancy I fixed on Connelly, the meticulous accountant: saw him standing, head large and clean,
neck a clean slice of cylindrical pudding, at the harbor of
New York, hailing steamers; or in the middle of some undersized Nineteen-Thirties suburban airfield, cattails innumerably
waggling behind the landing strip, waving down a shimmering noisy wing. In all that distance of twenty years he seemed
not smaller; rather, enormous, excessive. His great thick fingers plucked my mother's letters from the sea, from the air; I
felt his dread intercepting frown. What came to William's eye
William's hand tore. He tore, he tore; and tore. But Connelly,

meticulous, had never torn a paper in his life; he offered to
establish a private file, a smothered file, a file open to no one
at all, not even to Connelly. William murdered the proposal
with a twitch: a descent of the eyelids, trifling and sudden,
but to Connelly meaningful and stupefying. He hung from
William's look like a spider from his tenuous chain, on which
the mesh of delegated strengths rely, through which all connections merge. His employer did not quite seal upper to
lower lid; only pointed his glance as near to himself as possible, hoarding what he might finger there. The solid spears of
my mother's childish alphabet ripped the caves and cushions
beneath his sweating knuckles. Then inexplicably he ceased
to tear her letters: inexplicably he ceased to open them. He
gave the envelopes, virgin, to Connelly. He spoke: "Read, review, consider, administer, reply to what requires reply. Then
discard. Discard." Connelly, well-instructed, read, reviewed,
considered, administered, replied to what required reply: then
doubted. The bookkeeping mind does not discard indiscrimi-
nately. It discards either what is altogether irrelevant (this
comes under the heading of finished business) or what is only
too relevant (unfinished business of a suspicious nature). My
mother's letters, with their devious tangents and tiresome dis-
courses and irrational intrusions of scenes and slyness, escaped either category. They seemed not to count for nothing,
but neither did they count for too much. Here and there, in
scattered parts, they were plainly business, and carried the
voice of injunction typical of clients of a certain magnitude;
yet they represented, in a particular area pertinent to Connelly's employer, a business unmistakably finished. They were, in
short, neither trifles nor threats—what was to be done with
them? Not for the first time obedience quarreled with private
judgment in Connelly's exacting universe. He forsook the
Rome of William's command and made a Protestant decision: he delivered up those laden envelopes, white and terrible as wedding-sheets, padded and flaunting shame, delivered
them up preserved, to William's desk, where his employer,
coming one morning from his second marriage-bed, met them
all in a row, like violated pillows pinched by use, or say instead like dead fattened swans, ready to be eaten. But he despite outrage could no longer tear them: Sarah Jean, who
lived her piety and recommended mercy in all things, was
certain one disposed best of the ungrateful past by showing it
a gentle hand; she produced an apt epigram from the Epistle
to the Corinthians, which coaxed a secret quiver from her

husband's larynx, and induced in her own soul (she was certain she had a soul) a firm superstition that men who marry twice are as the lost sheep who will be gathered in. But William caught himself that minute in a recurring guilt of contrast—he could neither endure it nor elude it. The new wife's shrewd Pauline maxim, succinct, all wide white glass in its clarity and charity, all touching, modest, and persuasive, soiled his mind with its perfection. It shook out in him resonances; he scarcely knew whether it was her disciplined niggardly bosom in its spare dull-silk frame that embarrassed his early eye, or some peril of longing seeping somewhere near his collar-bone, as though he had just swallowed something queer but familiar. Gladioli stood serenely in vases. Was it this, a kind of dream of order realized, that made him all unexpectedly, all astonishedly, oh criminally despair? And here nearby were Sarah Jean's books, brought from her parents' house—impeccable ancestral sermons and collections of hazy brown photographs of Sussex parsonages. There was a harmless Episcopal strain in that family, a tendency toward genuflection among some of the older aunts; Sarah Jean had not yielded to it. She established faith, then left the rest to behavior. She thrived on advice—projected, not encountered—and advised William that error could be brought to penitence only through the medium of sincere pity. He thought she mentioned Mary Magdalene; it startled him—but then she might only have been speaking of the Cambridge colleges, à propos of her current absorption in an ecclesiastical history of England. She read with now and then a pleasant obliging sigh of discovery, like Queen Victoria examining an official compliment from her Prime Minister (Disraeli, not Gladstone), and consenting to recognize it as true. William found it prudent to be attentive to her attentiveness, so precisely solicitous was it toward his views, so totally bending was it to his preference. He uneasily felt he did not always deserve the plenitude of her attention when she addressed him (meaning—he faced it vaguely—that he did not always give her his). She was grateful to be married; she was very clear about that; she did not hide it from him. Her reply to everything was simply and modestly to hope she might be good. She *was* good. She was persistent in her goodness, she was above all certain in it. Her goodness was founded on an altogether modern distaste for self-deception. She explained she would try not to forget that she was a successor, a replacement, a second thought, in William's life, if not in his present mind. She said: "We must not be afraid to name things by their names," and supposed it was hardly reasonable to expect that William could obliterate his treacherous and unhappy failure. Together, therefore, they would agree to fix on the past, to take it in and turn it round and observe and perceive and comprehend whatever unendurables it might throw up in the stir. She contended that it was they whose duty it was to swallow the past, lest the past swallow them. No one should ever blame her for not allowing William the opportunity for purgation. Freedom of the feelings was with her no mere mildly-acknowledged tenet: she believed in it actively, and was ready to listen to whatever William might wish to rid himself of, all old miserable tales of what had happened to make him stumble.

He could, he must, tell her everything about poor Allegra; it would help him to tell it all, and then, as convenient by-product, it would help *her:* from it she would learn exactly what she must not do to stain his hope in her. For example: one day he had praised her punctuality; and she, fiercely fearlessly direct, all bravery and therapeutic theory, inquired whether Allegra had not ever been punctual. Curious how he blushed! She had to prod: "Was she? You must *not* evade. It's better for you to air old annoyances, dearest, no matter how trivial. Haven't I told you again and again how awful it was for me the day I got that telegram from Alan from out West? *That* was trivial, too—adding another girl I didn't even know to the list of wedding-guests. And then"—but Sarah Jean's humor was of the too-conscious kind—"marrying her instead of me! There, you see how I've purged all that? You must do the same. *Say* it: Allegra wasn't punctual." "She wasn't—very," he concurred feebly. "You see! There now! Don't you feel better already?" said Sarah Jean, and punctually conceived the germ of his son to show him she would do for him whatever Allegra had not done, as well as vice versa. The point of things was to give right names. God was God, and had a Son, who was Our Lord and Saviour; the past was the past, which meant not that one never thought of it, but—on the contrary—that one owed it something, probably reformation; and (finally) bad behavior was bad behavior and had to be accepted for what it was if redemption were to be properly understood as a real process in God's scheme. What this signified practically was that William was not to think it necessary, on Sarah Jean's account, to

sever his acquaintanceship with poor wretched Allegra: oh,
by no means! One day soon Allegra would come home, and
then, of course, she must be treated as a Christian would
treat anyone. She must be seen, interviewed, aided: the bundle of pitiful baby as well. Above all, William must not *avoid*
Allegra on the gentlemanly supposition that a confrontation
might enliven something like jealousy in his wife—*she,* after
all, was his *wife:* how humiliating for her if by such a delicacy he implied, however obliquely, that he thought them *the
same*—equals who could be compared one to the other! Instead let there be, for decency's sake, an open trafficking of
Christian mercy between William and poor mistaken Allegra.
Did she assail him with wearisome demands in every mail?
(A guess. Sarah Jean was a sorceress at guessing.) He ought
to answer her, of course, and *personally:* only contemplate
her situation! Alone, abandoned, alien to all the world's ways!
William's wife, still riding the majesty of her newly-bought
bed, gave the fullness of her sincerity to William's tie, which
he was knotting. "What? No, I didn't say *Mary* Magdalene,
what made you think of that? I said Magdalene—did you
know Peter was on their crew?"—referring to some obscure
younger cousin who had been sent abroad to breathe in a
Church-of-England education. "You know what they called
him over there? Peetah. He came home with it and now all
the time he pronounces it *Saint* Pee-tah. It's one of the names
on my list. We've used it a lot." "Names?" said William with
heated nape. "Dearest, for the child. You must start a list
too"—how tractable, yet how .confident, she seemed in the
new bed!—"and then we'll see where we match." "If we don't
match at all? —I don't care for Peter." "We'll match somehow, wait and see. We're bound to overlap. One always does
overlap with lists of names." "I thought of William," he said
shyly. "Dearest, whatever you like. Though *we* never did go
in for Juniors. They've simply clambered down. It's the kind
of thing the Irish do nowadays. But never mind, it's to be
whatever you like, William. Still—" she spaced them out: elegant smile, yawn, elegant smile—"isn't your office man, that
Connelly, isn't *he* a Junior? I mean just to prove my little
point?" He nodded; in him something shuddered open like a
bleakness, a chasm. "Well then! Whatever you like," she
beamed. Whatever he liked: it jumped, half-wooed, half-re-
pelled, a live tendril round his neck, the suddenly recognized
thing garlanding him—the anti-sermon her docile eagerness
aroused and then suppressed. She removed herself from the

throne of bed in her stately way, and came and put her face
upon the knot in his tie. She was taller than Allegra; her eyes
were too close to his. "We're to make up for everything, I
mean disappointments in the past; I intend to manage that we
will; and we will, if we plan and pray," she said into the
place where his voice coiled in hiding. He could not uncoil it;
it resisted with a gasp. He had not heard his wife, though she
heard him, and wondered. The unbodied joy had him by the
throat. Its race had never begun. He had drowned it, he had
dashed it into a wave. And now it had him by the throat.
"What's the matter?" said Sarah Jean. "Do you think it's
wicked to put it that way? All right, let's pray first and *then*
plan," she reversed herself submissively, releasing the piety,
like a blue milk, into her propinquant eyes. She was twenty-
seven and nearly happy. Already a strict little duet of lines
like linked semaphores lauded the indivisibility of marriage in
her high bridal brow.

And William asked Connelly, "Is it do you find a very
common custom among Roman Catholics of Irish extrac-
tion?" Connelly stared, expecting anger and the violent dropping, all eery noiseless click, of William's white lids: the letters lay arranged and revealed. His employer did not look
down. "Naming the son for the father, I mean." "I'm Jim,"
said Connelly, "my old dad was Jim. I don't know about the
rest." "I see," said William—and attached: "these. I see these
are surviving. A tedious collection, I've told you. What am I
to do with bulging envelopes? Why haven't you torn them
up? Look at the dates—have you kept them in a crypt?
You've at least taken care of their insides?" Connelly assented: he had done it all, read, reviewed, considered, administered, replied to what required reply. "Then discard," said
William; "discard; I say discard them, I don't want them, get
them out of here." And kept his look wide, wide: with his
hand curled on his chest, as though he were about to cough
up a lodged bone.

And Connelly? Authority weighed; but authority sighed at
its loss. Connelly, meticulous, could not, by his own hand, destroy paper. In hell the accountants will be made to tear all
the letters they have ever written, and all the letters they have
ever received; and the howls of the accountants will exceed
the bleats of those who for their sins the God of Dante condemned to roll throttled in the river of excrement. Still, Connelly was not technically disobedient. To get rid of a thing is
to discard it. The letters came at last into the keeping of the

English bank, which is to say they came into no-one-in-particular's keeping, which is to say they were, at last, nowhere. And if they were nowhere, how could they be said to exist? And if they did not exist, how could they fill the devil's dossier? And if the devil himself has no evidence, who then has?

The question is not rhetorical. The answer is Enoch. He was not what we mean when we say idealist, and preferred Job's shard to Plato's absolute. Perhaps this is the explanation for why he chose a smoky August day in 1939 to move my mother out of England. He himself drove the hired car (in those days he would never ride behind a chauffeur) to the queen-ship, a tower dimly speckling the fog with flags limp round her smokestacks, steaming with the cautious breathing of the refugee rich. He shook hands with Mrs. Mealie only because her stern Welsh wrist jutted like a log at him; but he refused to kiss the baby, which was held out for goodbye. "Farewell," he told the baby. "Go home," he told Allegra. "I've left a mess," she complained, "nobody knows what a mess I've left, all sorts of stuff, Siegfried still packing the littler trunks, God knows what he'll steal for his wife. And papers and papers of one sort or another at the bank mixed up with William I guess or that Connelly, I haven't the slightest notion, all the money-arrangements and things, after all I never go there, I tell them to send me the money and they do. You're just pushing me out, you know that." "Out of the way." "What, I'm in your way? And who's come practically every day and read that idiot Kant to you in that idiot hole of a room so you could listen with your eyes shut? I can't understand it, if you're so mad at the Germans, and you go right on reading that idiot German—" Like a troubling echo in a deep deep cave, the ship's whistle boomed. There was a rustle among the passengers. "Well, it's not *cannon*," said Mrs. Mealie, disapproving of the stir; there was fear in it. "Me-me-me," mouthed the baby, switching its small ugly eyes upward toward the marbled ceiling of the cabin. The cabin was indistinguishable from an English parlor; there was even a fringe on the lampshade. Mrs. Mealie moved from table to table, patting things admiringly. She had never seen the inside of a ship before, and she was not yet certain whether it was really moral for a ship to seem exactly like a parlor. "What am I going to do about the *bank?*" said Allegra: "I mean if they keep on sending the money, and there's no one in the flat but that Siegfried—oh, I forgot to tell you, Enoch, I'm letting him stay there; after all, the rent's paid for months. I

don't see why *you* didn't want it instead of that hole. I told
him he could bring his wife if he wanted to, and the whole
Viennese ghetto if it suited him. He was pretty obsequious, it
was disgusting, they don't understand about democracy. I
don't like them when they're grateful and I don't like them
when they're ungrateful. Well, look, you're not going to tell
me they're *all* like King Solomon or King David or somebody
—" But the whistle had begun again, a long sharp groan, as
though a very large creature had been wounded. Under the
wine-colored carpeting vibrations faintly beat. "Goodbye,"
Enoch said, "it's all ashore that's going ashore." "Well, dash
away," said Allegra—"abandon me to the sea's bowels. You
made up the whole war scare just to get me out of your
room." "Get you out of Europe," Enoch said. "London isn't
Europe, not a soul ever thought it was. Anyhow it isn't as if I
didn't read aloud *perfectly* satisfactorily!" "I don't quarrel
with your elocution," Enoch said, "but it's not the sort of war
you're meant for. You'll be better off at home." "Oh, better
off, better off! What do you know about better off?" she
wailed at him while the cabin shook. "I know *I'd* better be
off," said Enoch, and ducked out the low door. ("There's the
engine!" cried Mrs. Mealie; privately she was noting that no
decent parlor in her experience had ever had floorboards that
wobbled.) "But the bank," said Allegra; "can't you do something about the bank, Enoch?" She had followed him into the
corridor. "Shall I blow it up?" he offered, showing her his patient genial ordinary scowl. "I mean," she explained, "I've
neglected everything, *such* a mess, I didn't even telephone
them to say I'm leaving, it's *just* the sort of inefficiency William hates—" "Ah, if you're out to please William, that's another matter," he concluded nicely: "I like that. It's touching,
a loyal spurt of conjugality-after-the-fact. You make a model
wife—provided the precaution has been taken of divorcing
you first." A steward came through, pressing himself past
them against the tube-like walls of the passageway: "Gangplank's coming up, sir. Gangplank's coming up. Last call."
"Go home," Enoch said, "America needs you." "Oh, I know.
America craves me." "Go home, prove by your presence it's
still the land of the spree and the home of the idle rich. Have
a good time. Let us leftovers here have our little European
war to ourselves. Go home and be an heiress." "It's nothing
but a silly fight over refugees from perfectly awful ghettos.
Nobody's going to fight over that. Only," she said with a
gloomy absent look, "if there's a war I'll never find Nick.

Never, never. Therefore there won't *be* a war. And if there isn't a war the bank will think I'm acting like a damn fool for running out. William will, anyhow." "So let's have the war to save your face," Enoch said. "But take care of the bank, will you?" I'll settle it all, I'll see to everything," he told her mildly. "You'll settle it all, really?" "Yes." "You'll see to everything?" she insisted. "I said I would." "But you only mean the bank, don't you?" "What else could I mean? I'll settle the Nazis, I'll see to Hitler? Bank on it, I meant the bank. The bank, the bank, the bank. Bank on it." "You didn't mean Nick." "Oh hell, you bet I didn't mean Nick." "Then I'll never marry," she said in furtive despair; Mrs. Mealie stood righteously at the curtained porthole, shrugging the baby to the inconvenient rhythm of the swarming engines underfoot. It was plain from the tilt of her shoulder she had determined it was *not* moral for a ship to seem exactly like a parlor. Luckily she had not been informed that the baby she held was societally amiss (a phrase the baby would have enjoyed had the one been uttered and the other been awake to hear; for, already human, it was beginning to like to imitate sounds and to create semblances of word-noises, some rather complex), or she would have regarded the baby as she now regarded the ship: tolerable for the length of the journey, since there was no avoiding it, but not to be personally acknowledged, since it was an impostor. The baby in particular was an impostor: Mrs. Mealie had been told (it was Enoch's idea to tell her) that it was the child of divorced parents; she thought it was being taken to America to be seen by its father. The baby had a passport all to itself: in this and in the ship's register it was already passing under William's name, the first of innumerable similar impostures. This too was Enoch's plan; incalculably, Enoch believed in respectability. Nevertheless his departing words to Allegra were irritable and not respectable: "Oh go home; what do I care if you marry or you don't marry?" But this woke her into a gleeful sneer —"As long as you settle me, as long as you see to me! I'm banking on you!" she shouted after him while the returning steward, come to give the last alarm of all, stared.

The next day two things happened: a pair of mustached men (one lip wore an inkblot, the other a bear's elbow) settled it all and saw to everything—Europe, that is—and named the myth they had made between them a Pact, to keep the cynical peace; and Enoch walked into a certain grey structure of the kind that is usually called "imposing" and

presented himself to a spectacled person grown up to be like
an asparagus—limp, lean, vaguely pale in a mottled and
moldy way, and his fingertips just moist. "Mr. Ian Makin?"
"Quite," said the asparagus, but was imperfectly cordial as
though he suspected a daylight robbery, until his caller explained that he had come in behalf of the American lady of
whom Mr. Makin would know a very great deal; and would
Mr. Makin kindly take effective cognizance of the fact that
the lady had gone home to America? "A pity," said the asparagus, who had regarded Allegra as one of his most profitable international "arrangements"; he had very generous
terms from William, and almost no service at all to render,
beyond the mailing of a check and the maintenance of a
vault. The vault was a bit of a nuisance; he had instructions to
see to it that none of its contents (of a certain nature) was
ever permitted to travel back again to the New World's in-
hospitable shores. The patroness herself, of course, he had
never seen. For more than a year she had kept aloof; she
seemed to look on every communication from the bank as an
insult. Now and then a paper came from New York imploring
her signature; the paper entered the London mails, received the
lady's chill child-like scribble, re-entered the London mails,
and was quickly posted back to New York. But this was rare.
Still, Mr. Makin had observed from these operations that
New York appeared to wish to deal with the lady as impersonally as possible; and this was exactly what outraged her.
She blamed the bank for allowing itself to be put in the middle, and for behaving rudely. Mr. Makin felt a particular
kind of moral discomfort, as though he were a keyhole peep-
er, whenever he entered the vault and with his own hand
placed in their assigned compartment a new batch of envelopes which an accompanying note from a certain Connelly
had described as unreturnable under any circumstance. Being
a banker, he was a suspicious man, and it seemed to him that
the lady's own letters were flocking ungallantly back to her.
Luckily or unluckily she had never called for them—perhaps
because the bank had failed to mention in any specific sense
that they were there. The bank said merely, "Here are some
new papers that have come for you," and the lady said, "Do
I have to sign?" and when the bank said no, the lady did not
reply further. But now here was this gentleman (who somehow did not look *quite* a gentleman: perhaps it was that his
shoes were not brushed enough) telling him that the lady
would not return to London at all, that everything was to be

severed; certainly they would have to wait for a confirmation from New York, but meanwhile it would do no harm to withhold the checks, as the ungentlemanly gentleman was suggesting. Doubtless there was going to be some difficulty over the vault—did the lady desire everything to be transferred to New York? *"She* doesn't desire anything," Enoch answered, thinking how, after a whole year, she still desired Nick. "Ah?" said Mr. Makin, and turned over a wan hand; "then we're to wait on word from Mr. Connelly?" "I don't know any Connelly," said Enoch, who had more than once encountered this name emitted in wrath; "I suppose you'll be hearing from the trustee as soon as she docks. He doesn't know she's coming." Mr. Makin thought this odd, even uncouth, and very American; it made him more uncomfortable than ever. "What do you make of the news, sir?" he said in a thin voice, deflecting a discussion which puzzled as much as it embarrassed him—"I suppose if she'd known it was coming, she wouldn't have been so quick to escape poor old England, eh? There won't be a war now, you know, and in my opinion we're safe as houses, just as long as those great fellows keep things down between themselves and leave the rest of us out of it, eh?" But Enoch had only just awakened from a sleep begun late that morning; he had read—i.e., had not read—all night, in an anguish of insomnia; between leaves the objectionable baby jiggled in his brain as it had jiggled on its nurse's shoulder in the ship's cabin. He thought he despised it because it could not talk philosophy, which was true enough, though he did not suppose that was the real reason. The real reason was that it was Nick's. But that was not the real reason either. He did not care that it was Nick's. He cared that it was Allegra's, and fettered her. Meanwhile this silly asparagus was wanting to know whether he had read the newspapers. Of course he had not read them; he had not even read his Wittgenstein. "Peace is all, sir, made it all right between them, those two," elucidated the asparagus, "who'd believe it only this morning, eh, the surprise of the century! Hitler and Stalin in bed together? Well, give an inch to the Reds and they want to pull everything down, but I've never had any quarrel with Mr. Hitler myself, and now here's the evidence just today that Mr. Chamberlain's been right all along, in spite of the way some quarters show themselves partial to slander. I don't say there's any soul can do no wrong in politics, but he never said worse than that Hitler wouldn't go to war, and I say the proof of the eating is in the pudding

—" But here Mr. Makin had to pause. He was now certain that his visitor was not a gentleman: he had not smiled at his wit in turning round the proverb about the pudding, and, worse, Mr. Makin half believed he had heard the fellow enunciate a phrase popular only in the gutter. "I daresay you're one of these leftist warmongers," Mr. Makin did in fact not dare to say; instead he thanked Enoch for stopping by, and said how very sorry the bank was to lose one of its valued American patrons. Having brought this out—it was a clear dismissal—Mr. Makin paused again. He was remembering the difficult envelopes. If the profitable "arrangements" had indeed been terminated, as his caller claimed (and Mr. Makin admitted to himself that the man seemed remarkably well-informed about everything relating to the American lady), then the unchivalrous vault would have to be vacated. Plainly the bank could no longer keep watch over property no longer entrusted to it. Banks, after all, whatever they may be morally, are legally rigorous. But neither did the bank—in a pinch Mr. Makin often interchanged his own mind with one belonging presumably to that grey height of stone—neither did the bank care to send the interdicted letters back to New York. Not the bank but Mr. Makin had received certain warnings from Connelly, whose position over there was unascertainable: he was possibly a person of influence, from whom might flow further opportunities for equally profitable international "arrangements." Mr. Makin slightly flexed the asparagus-tips which were his ears. "Mr. Vand, may I ask," he asked, with all the shrewdness of a country person (he *was* a country person, though he did not know it; even while their genes roar in us we seem not to remember our great-grandparents), "may I ask your relationship to our erstwhile patroness?" Apparently this was precisely the right question. A look of absolute attentiveness stiffened the visitor's rather plump face. Mr. Makin noted to himself that he was not mistaken in his formulation of what could logically be expected of human nature, including his own. "There *is* a little matter," he continued, "which we should find just a bit sticky to dispose of at long distance. We here deal in cablegrams, you see, and cablegrams—heh heh—tend to confuse absolutely, as Lord Acton didn't—heh heh—quite put it. We of the bank so much wish the dear divorced lady had called on us before her departure. It would have simplified indeed. Not the least thing against these war scares is the way they, ah, *scatter* people. *So* unnecessary. The bank, you see, is in possession of a *particular* group of papers—" "Oh, that's all right," Enoch said, "I'll take them if you want." "*Personal* papers, I should perhaps add? Though it's only a perhaps unwarranted suspicion on the bank's part. These are the bank's suppositions, you understand. As a matter of fact the bank would have no way of knowing—" "Perfectly all right," intervened the visitor, whom Allegra had been consistently refusing for fifteen months, "the dear divorced lady in question is planning to become my wife." But they had never found the town where the May Dancers were supposed to weave. Instead she made the chauffeur drive into an opening in a yellow meadow (it was the last time Enoch ever consented to go with a chauffeur), and left him to swelter in the brilliant black limousine near a nodule of incurious cows while the two of them went to sit on a wall. It was low, in the ancient fashion of that landscape, and made of round and flat and angled rocks ingeniously fitted together, and all without mortar. They marveled at the decency of a pair of shady trees, and at the long-ago stone-maker's dogged eye and hand; then unexpectedly Enoch declared himself to be not a stone wall. "Nobody ever said you were," said Allegra. "And even if I *am* a wall don't think I have any objections to mortar," he retorted. Whereupon his companion reasonably complained that he ought first to decide whether he was or wasn't a wall, and then she would see, if he persisted in metaphor, what "mortar" signified. "Anything that sticks," he said at once and nastily: "I have in mind wedding-glue." "Blood's plenty stickier than that," she told him. She said she meant the child. She owed it its proper father. She would never marry—oh, never again!—unless she married Nick; it was simply a question of learning where he was, only no one would help her, not Enoch, not William, not that fool Connelly, certainly not the bank, which she regarded as no better than the parakeet house at the zoo. (Their architectural styles were undeniably similar.) In spite of all William's practicality, concerning the bank she was wiser than he; she knew perfectly well the bank wasn't responsible. It had written to her insultingly: "It is not in our province to conduct a missing persons' service, particularly in today's Europe, with its shifting populations." As though a man were a population! As though Nick were a refugee! As though she could go and marry anyone, when she had Nick's own child to think of! As though Enoch could even *dream* of getting her for a wife! She chided his effrontery with regularity. Meanwhile he had to live, and went to work grubbing for a freshly-organized encyclopaedia company, which hoped to prey on the respectability-urge of poor people, and assigned Enoch the article on Metaphysics, History Of. He felt his eyes deteriorating when night after night he dug into his library load. So Allegra came to Adam Gruenhorn's hole and read to him; he saw the light on her hair, and tried to be amused by the mechanical spate of her mispronunciations. When she went away he had to study all over again what she had sung out to him. She was bored, and he pitied her boredom, but kept her motives alive: she supposed she was a Samaritan nobly assisting him, and gloriously yielded everything up in a garble of non-comprehension. But in the matter of wedding-glue she was steadfast, and refused him all the way from the pre-Socratics through David Hume. Hope of Nick had made her puritan and body-shy: in Adam Gruenhorn's room Allegra read, and Enoch pretended to take notes while her voice swayed among the sentences it knew how to turn into mysteries. They never touched fingers. She refused him and refused him. In Adam Gruenhorn's room she refused him; she refused him through Hegel and Kant; she refused him on the ship in the last hour, while Mrs. Mealie jiggled Nick's daughter, for whose sake alone she said she hoped in Nick. She commanded him not to dream, and refused him again. Despite her strictures he had his dream, though at first sight a bank may not seem a likely place to speak one out. At first sight only—for articulated dreams are lies, and lies have been uttered before in banks. "Oh, very good indeed! Splendid for the bank!" lied Mr. Makin, hearing Enoch's dream (he meant splendid for himself, seeing he was to avoid a predicament with Connelly), and led his caller into the vault—"of course if you are affianced to the lady, in that case, sir, though I confess it's a trifle irregular, I can entrust these entirely to your discretion? Actually, these days most things aren't being played exactly according to Hoyle, are they though? We jolly well wouldn't have believed it this morning about the Reds and the Germans, would we now? In the same bed? Still, the main thing is keeping the peace, isn't it?"

So there were two tricks played that day: one to get hold of my mother's letters; one to get hold of Europe. Perhaps it will be claimed the latter is really wicked, the former not very. Yet power motivates great and small. It is something to slice up Europe like a whipped-cream cake, through which the brute knife flies. But it is also something to steal the let-

ters of a woman who will not marry you, though the mouth
of a new May has swallowed the old May's tail, by pretending that she will.

The letters disappointed. They stimulated in him no sense
of power over her privacy; he felt only the sort of obliging
and embarrassed pity one accords a vaudeville act that fizzles.
They were the last of her letters he was ever willing to read,
including those numberless texts and tracts that afterward
came to him legitimately, and came, and came, and came. In
the first place, he saw at once that her letters were not really
private. She had composed them not for William, who would
be blunt to their experiments, but for that multitudinous
readership we call Posterity, as though it, unlike our poor
selves, cannot be startled by the irrational and the sudden.
Those abstractly creeping dialogues, as whimsically intrusive
in the life of the letters as a rumor of lava, were certainly for
Posterity: they were stiff and priggish, as if to say: "What
clever young men I was acquainted with in my prime!" She
had left out all the profanity. She made everything arid, respectable, and tidy. She had contrived to have Enoch sound
like a silly philosopher, so that her lover would show up juicy
by comparison. But all the same he did not emerge as juicy:
Posterity, being better-read than Allegra, would tick off all
the influences; it would label Nick "derivative" and toss him
off as a husk. Even his Greeks were not *his* Greeks; he had
picked them up along the way. The dryad was gypped from
an English novelist. All the effects were staged. The romance
was Romantic. The jeering was puerile, and was unrelated to
humor. The wit was a bore. The only note of reality was the
baby, which had somehow eluded inhabited trees, garlands,
spooks, and even myths about the sanctity of beauty, to come
out of it all still a baby, leaky and unpleasant but at least not
illusory. It had vomited over his leg while a lightning screech
of toothache slammed the innermost nerve of his skull. The
baby was real beyond all. Everything else was Imagination,
which is useless in society, and weakens the Ideal by infecting
it with its own unreality. But Enoch had determined that the
Ideal is the opposite of myth, because it always belongs to the
future, and owns thereby the reality of the possible; he took
Ideal as a synonym for Real, and scorned that frailty in Allegra's mind which had chosen for a Golden Age a tawdry little episode called Brighton. Imagination entered her second-
hand from Nick, who himself had it third-hand, because Romance meanders from peddler to peddler, holding itself out

for what it is not and defrauding the be-glamoured and credulous world. Here was Enoch coming down from London
once upon a time covered with carbon-smuts the dirty train
had liberated into its passengers' pockets and lungs; he arrives
dusty, tired, but undefrauded; and when, hoping for a cot
and a meal and a tease from Allegra, he sees instead that absurd sticky circlet of berries hung upon the tree, he does not
think: "Ah, Romance." He does not think: "Ho ho, Imagination." He does not think: "Aha, an idyll, pastoral or otherwise." He thinks: "Sex, damn it, and it's me shut out and
bound for the old robber-witch who keeps roomers down the
road," and would in fact have turned back to London if he
were sure his best friends there weren't likely to sell him to
the police for a license to storm the Cenotaph, and if there
were in London a square of earth he could line his fingernails
with. He was in Brighton to dig up weeds and scheme a future: nor was he deluded by the notion of a future which can
compel lion to lie down with lamb. *That* is Imagination, *that*
is Romance, and offends against the given genius of lion and
lamb, which the Ideal, scrupulous and preoccupied with the
Real, will never do. Ideals and idylls do not recognize one another. An idyll twists nature, and spins us lawns and pipers
where life delivers a marsh and toilers, and, ignoring a rapa-
cious commerce in slaves testifying to other things, gilds us a
Greece of athletes, leaf-crowned, beautiful. But the Ideal is
tougher than hoaxing Romance, and was never designed for
the gullible or the stupid, and works in anger with the grain
of nature, rotted grey, split and splintered, old, old, hammered, tragic. The tragic grain of nature! The Allegra of the
letters missed it; she thought sadness a lustrous form, like an
objet d'art, a vase with its dark dread hole kept secret and
small, and the round sides all one and all dazzlingly patterned, and all fathomable; and the whole to be held to the
light for an unimaginable and always absent flaw, the eye
never to be put to the lips of the black entrance, as though
nature had no bloody underside, and grief had no ugliness,
and fact had no dirt in it. The stiffness of a thumb: that was
death to her: that and nothing else: carcass: not unintelligible unspeakable affront committed by a criminally Godless
universe. He sat amazed at the untextured flatness of her vision. The culpability in her innocence snagged and rubbed
him: that very smoothness of her apprehension was precisely
what he acknowledged to be the coarseness in the grain.
Meanwhile the walls of her flat, where he had come directly

from the bank as part of the gesture of settling and seeing to
the traces of her departure, were broadened by a spill of sunset, which increased the volume of everything. Nearby the
head of the servant seemed huge and golden; the diffused
blaze perched for a moment on a bristle half-visible inside his
nostril, and thickened it into a brazen bar. He was folding
sheets into a trunk, urging one knee against a leather hassock. "Siegfried," said Enoch, "you look like an armorless
knight. I hate to see a man kneel. A passerby might take it
for worship instead of packing." "Bitte, nicht so schnell zu
sprechen," muttered Siegfried, matching corners; he pouted a
cigar upon his lip, a practise his employer had forbidden: it
gave his jaw a mournful slant. "I need a box," Enoch said,
"for a hundred fat letters. A parallel action to yours: a trunk
for these sheets. Ein Sarg, you see? Find one." "Bitte?" "A
box. To keep dead things in. Nice and roomy, you understand what I mean?" The head veered into shadow and was
reduced to that of a sullen man: "Ja, here is somewhere one
she finishes yesterday," and vanished into what two days before had been Allegra's bedroom. The door opening like a
sail pressed out an acute startling perfume. "This will be?"
asked the man, too deferential, presenting a fine deep fancy
cardboard cube: "so much letters she has made, there are
also others empty-standing should you require." "No, just
right; this one. The perfect coffin. —Siegfried, what will you
do now?" "Bitte?" "You'll stay till the paid rent runs out?"
"Ja." "And you'll bring your little boys?" "Nicht possible,
they are residenced already with Englisch families, I give for
this monthly the money, also for my small child." "But you'll
bring your wife all the same?" "Nicht möglich." "Ah, too
bad. She's got a job somewhere, is that it?" "She is in hospital." "Filthy place to work," Enoch remarked, concentrating
on cramming a fool's letters into a cavity. "Nein. She will die
there," said Siegfried, but contradiction was not in his voice:
he had with a whole heart entered the servant class.

Allegra never knew. She would have considered a cook
with a dying wife the worst of all morbidities; she would
have dismissed him. Often enough she accused him of releasing a morbid atmosphere into the house; she said refugees
brought a morbid atmosphere wherever they appeared. She
would certainly have dismissed him, so he hinted at nothing,
and pretended muteness was his character, though he wished
that earlier, when it mattered, he might have had his oldest
boy to live with him. He would have reined him and held

him very still, but she would not agree. She feared he would ask to bring the younger pair, as if he did not know they were too little and difficult and as if he would think to keep them. But in the evenings he would have taken the oldest child to see the mother. How expensive in England simultaneously to die and to board boys! At first their tragedy was formal and decorous and even mincing; there was no haste in it; the woman in the bed described the processional of her suffering as segmented, like the parts of a stained glass window, each invented shape of agony added to and confirmed by the previous one but separated from it by a leading of morphine: a mosaic of bright pains. That was her first joke in English (at home she was the family clown); she kept English children's books, whirling with colored illustrations, in the bed with her to learn the language well, until all language unlearned itself in the wall of her shocked mouth. "The boy can come *now*," Enoch said, "there's no obstacle to his coming now." No use: she was never conscious, two weeks already never awake at all. How expensive in England to breathe like grass and to be drugged and to wait! He intended to wait in this great carpeted apartment until the dry breast stopped its subtle journey of fractional ascent and hesitant descent; meanwhile would wait below a high ceiling not very different from the ceilings of Wien, under which his incredible stews had glowed and serving-maids fled to fetch trays of pastries lambent with spiced honey. The view was not the same; in Wien fountain after fountain after fountain, but they had robbed him and forced him naked to play underwater like a whale for them. How a country is traitor to a man! A whole nation turned seditionist! A government betraying its own citizen! Then the escape, bribes, Switzerland, Italy, a filthy boat, Portugal, England, the man, the woman, three sons, alive, alive. Survival!—stilettoed by what? fate? irony of fate? fate sans chivalry? Never trust. Trust is a word for the firing squad. In the end a germ is fate. Dessenungeachtet, as a servant (he did not say as a man: what is man?) he was grateful as a dog to his employer for the gift of allowing him to remain without paying in this grand place. It was a bed to sleep in. He would prepare himself for his orphans. Poor Rudi! Leon! Berni! Berni with his six little teeth! The rent he saved would be the price of the coffin. "She has told me she has offered to a friend this flat, but he would not take it, he has not wished it, for me how fortunate, where should I in the last hours go?"—kneeling to lock his employer's trunk.

The lid swept down with a wheeze, setting off a fidgety dance of the grit on the window-sill: it lifted and stirred and rained itself down once more. Grit is one of the eternals. The chimneys heave their laden bladders, the grit is spawned out of a domestic cloud in the lowest air, the black footless ants appear on the sill. Brush away, mop away, empty buckets with zeal; grit returns. Everything is flux; grit is forever. Futility is day after day. Time is not what we suppose, moments in an infinite queue, but rather a heavy sense that we have been here before, only with hope, and are here again, only without it. "Your luck will not change," says Time. "Give up, the world has concerns of its own," says Time, "pain is biologically discrete," says Time, "woe cannot be shared," says Time, "regret above all is terrifyingly individual." And Time says, "Take no comfort in your metaphysics of the immortality of the race. When your species has evolved out of recognition grit will be unspoiled. There will always be grit. It alone endures. It is greater than humanity."

But it is not greater than humanity; it is the same. We join the particles in their dance on the sill. It is the magnificent Criminal plan, to shove us into the side of a hill, mulch us until we are dissolved into something more useful but less spectacular than before, and send us out again in the form of a cinder for some churl of a descendant to catch in his eye, cursing. The tragic grain of nature! The sadistic whittler, insane with repetition and muddy bungled extirpation! Contemptuous of decent extinction! Who can revere a universe which will take that lovely marvel, man (after all the fierce mathematics that went into him, aeons of fish straining toward the dry, gill into lung, paw into the violinist's and the dentist's hand), and turn him into a carbon speck? Imbecility of waste and conservation!—every atom of matter economically converted for miserly reuse, and the single unrecoverable unduplicatable mind switched out of existence unlike a dream, less than a dream, for a dream will sometimes recur; thrust out of being as if pulse and kidney were all. Is mind a neural synapse? Is this smudge on Siegfried's knuckle as he leans on the window-ledge for traction in pressing the trunk-lid tight the total remainder of a thought Adam had when he beheld the angel with the flaming sword? Siegfried, wiping the dirtied back of his hand on his trouser-leg, erases Helen's emotion during Paris' caress. Meanwhile the carbon specks are still gyrating on the sill; high on a wave, while the seasick baby vomits, his employer in the saloon of the queen-ship is already writing to Enoch to learn whether the bank has been settled and seen to; the banker over his five o'clock tea is still pleasuring in gossip of the Pact which the dictators have fashioned for cunning peace; secretly one of the dictators is already mobilizing to trample Europe and the other dictator to ash; and exhausted Europe curls under her fields with her belly slack, a receptacle for a million million carbon specks about to be manufactured by the apparatus of Romance.

And in that moment Enoch sees.

"It is fastened," said Siegfried, straightening himself.

Enoch saw. Put it that he saw. He saw the refugee shutting Allegra's trunk to send it to America. He saw Europe open, open: an impatient trench. He saw May Day pledged to Walpurgisnacht. He saw not Lucifer but all of Paradise fallen. He saw the inkblot and the bear's elbow foamy with the same lustful brew. He saw commissars and storm troopers linked. He saw—to state it in the unhallucinated prose he later told it in—a number of obvious political facts, and understood that he had been duped, like all the rest: not, like Allegra, by the sham temporal delight of those high-flung shouts and banners, the sober martial evangelical exhilaration of the parades, the camps, the songs, the whole lovely lore of utopian idolatry, the gods like darling grandfathers, the liturgy the sound made by sheaves of wheat in the instant of their scything, the bodies of youths in rings round squares, statues, pillars of parliamentary office buildings, picketing with long sturdy cheerful yells intending to warn the millennium it was about to be scabbed by human glory: not Enoch! He did not hang from those shining strings, being (he thought) himself puppeteer, and acquainted with the artifice and danger of philosophy applied. But duped all the same; duped every bit as much as the lightest head in the parade; duped and fooled by fraud, hoax, and duplicity.

"It is loosened," he contradicted Siegfried, who did not comprehend. He meant he had loosened the ropes. He meant he was free of the Party. He meant he was done with the idyll of trust in heroic governments. Henceforth he would oblige himself to stick to history, which knew where it had been, and could neither promise nor betray, and was clean of hope.

It was, in fact, one of those moments of spiritual clarity men like Enoch tend to be skeptical about. But spiritual clarity is nothing more mystical than disillusionment, and no more magical than the separation of dupe from charlatan.

The Red Sea, we are informed, went to all the fuss and in-
convenience of dividing itself only to make the same commonplace point: simply that a man must abandon what has enslaved him. If he does not, then he has acquiesced to evil, in
the manner of the Christ when he rendered unto Caesar Caesar's evil unmodified, and when he condoned the blow by
turning toward it a second time, and aided the torment by
aiding the tormentor. Ah: I should have mentioned long ago
that even in that early time my stepfather was flatly against
Christ. Christianity, along with piety in general, he equated
with the Normal Behavior of Mankind, and so had a rather
pleasurable contempt for it. But Christ was one of Enoch's
great villains, and for a reason competitive rather than theo-
logical. He believed the divine ought to keep hands off, and
not send messengers to meddle with affairs they know nothing of: he insisted God ought to stay what he is, a principle
which it is blasphemy to visualize. And he chose Christ for
enemy not merely for his cruelty in inventing and enforcing a
policy of damnation, but more significantly for his removal
of the Kingdom of Heaven to heaven, where, according to
Enoch, it had no business being allowed to remain, by the
Saviour or anyone else, and ought instead to be brought down
again as rapidly as possible by the concerted aspiration and
fraternal sweat of the immediate generation. A Kingdom of
Heaven stowed away in heaven is a perfectly useless fact,
though pretty, and can do no good for anyone who does not
happen to feel the force of such a fact; meanwhile, he observed, oppression and murder continue below with exactly
the same frequency as though there had never been a Saviour.

So Enoch was—as I have said—against Christ; against Romance; against Imagination. Not these but the Ideal, with its
unforgiving knowledge of human nastiness and its aversion to
prettifying it or blinding it fancifully out of being with a
phantom sheen of generalized love or pretending it can be redeemed by anything other than the personal and individual
act of a man covenanting on his own behalf, had drawn him
to the Party. And the Ideal, when at last it was forfeited by
the Party, which gave to a conspiracy of subjection the name
of peace, drove him out: and he was left like Adam to know
his shame. Still, even in a moment of spiritual clarity, even in
the press of crisis, one has to say something.

Enoch said again: "It is loosened."

"But I have just fastened it. It is quite secure," the servant objected.

"Oh look, I'm not talking about that damn lock on that damn trunk. Didn't you just say it yourself? You can't have an attachment or a commitment in the light of that. It *has* to be loosened."

Siegfried did not comprehend, and blamed his slippery grip on the English language.

"Oh God damn it! Trust! You said it yourself! Trust is a firing squad! You said it yourself a minute ago, didn't you?"

Siegfried admitted he had said what was attributed to him; but he did not comprehend.

"You said God is a germ."

"Oh nein! From me this thought never," Siegfried responded excitedly, though he considered emphasis and emotion to be unbecoming to a servant, and in his opulent flat in Wien had always been cool to his own when he caught them trembling, "nicht Gott, aber das Schicksal, ist ein Keim! —Fate I think you say? I express fate to be the germ—"

"They're not the same? Fate and God?"

"So unequal my Englisch, nicht possible to give out myself," and gave himself out forthwith to be a faithful second-generation Lutheran who prayerfully hoped he would be saved through belief; who despised Moses as a worldly legalist; who felt extreme moral shock at hearing the Christian God indelicately compared with that microscopic saprophytic wolf which was ravaging his wife; and who was, as a natural consequence of the foregoing, puzzled at being beaten for a Jew. "Bitte, bitte, sehr schwer für mich the Englisch, my wife only has many tongues, in Portugal she has spoken once many times—"

"Your wife," said Enoch, "has lost her tongue and will die. So they are the same, fate and God."

"Nein; nein; ich bedaure, in diesem Punkte mich Ihrer Meinung nicht anschliessen zu können!" exclaimed the refugee: "Not the same. God is good. Surely he is good. The bad germ which kills is not the God, it is the fate which is bad."

"I understand," said Enoch. "Fate is what we experience. God is what we do not experience. Fate is certainty, it is what really happens to us. God is legend, and has never happened," but did not laugh, not out of tact—he had no tact—but because it came to him then that he stood outside his old home; that there is no Eden without its secret coil of treachery; that he had ruined his brain by fastening it to a legend, and never to fate. It was loosened; he had loosened it now; and where was his fate, and where should he in his last hour go, and what was there for him to do in the broken world?

He did the thing that was left for him to do: he married.

He did not think it could be accomplished immediately; and it was not accomplished immediately. But in the end, curiously enough, he did not have to persuade. For a year he had tried to persuade, and with no success: she had refused him and refused him. The letter she wrote on the queen-ship came; a fool's letter; he grumbled in his little room (it was addressed as usual to Adam Gruenhorn, who no longer existed), and threw it in the fire. On the day Hitler sank the first boot into Poland she sent him a cable, but so garbled by the overseas frenzy of rushing messages that he could not read her meaning; it was enough to see that she did not mention the war; and that satisfied him. No war was hers, neither moral nor actual wars. She represented for him not earnestness but—he had already explained it to her—spree, and wars are not the province of fools, whatever the pacifists may think. But he felt himself eclipsed, because war eclipses a man who is not in his own country in exactly the same way a man is made to seem a child when he must speak introspectively in a language that is not his own.

So he attached himself (in the blatant argot of my mother's salvaged clippings) to an heiress. It was what he had intended, and he was surprised to see that his intention, privately arrived at, was publicly observed. She had money, that was the point of it; she would always have money, it was uncountable, it was undiminishable, it was not even money in the ordinary sense, it had survived the Crash, it would survive stock-markets both as temples and as concepts, it was likely to survive everything. Here is the charred waste of this piteous planet, and here nevertheless are Allegra's money and the carbon grits that danced on the sill for Siegfried, companions in ineradicability. Both are mercurial elements, and readily change their guises, and follow Einstein's law of conversion—or call it instead Enoch's rule of animadversion. He hated money; had never had it; objected to thinking of it. It bothered him to think of it. Far behind him lay a black Chicago alley. In the Party he would have found the liberty that money famously confers useful. Out of the Party he found it imperative. In the Party it was possible to go on writing pieces for seedy encyclopaedias. Out of the Party it was necessary to stand on a foundation. ("It is necessary to stand on a foundation," he said to himself.) In short: he required money in order not to require it. That is a commonplace, not a subtlety. The disillusioned will understand. When hope is gone, it is good to be able to fall back on money.

And he did not even have to persuade her.

13

"She did it for the status of the thing," William told me. "There was the child, of course. She had to marry *someone*. Still, it was not like being married at all. They took him, you see, for the Office of Strategic Services—"

"O.S.S.," I said familiarly. "I've heard he began there. The Order of the Secret Spies was it?"

"Dirt. Unsavory stuff. Most people wouldn't have touched it. He had all those unpleasant connections over there, everybody under foolish aliases, nothing respectable, undoubtedly just what they require in intelligence. No one denies the war made patriots and heroes out of the worst malcontent element. One imagines they had to have them for jobs of that character. Misfits, sly types."

"You like him now, don't you?" I countered.

He let this slip by, whether for acquiescence or demurral I could not tell. "In Washington they thought well of him. I had to shuttle back and forth myself in those days, and I would hear things. There was a general down there who said he didn't dare violate security to tell the thing, but in view of a certain incredible incident he'd stake the country on Vand. (He's retired now; General Tassel; he's one of the witnesses the Senate wants.) Lord knows what he did in those years over there. Whatever it was, it was grisly. He got to be one of their key men. General Tassel told one of the Senators recently how Vand used to answer everything with a maybe, and then bring it off. That's just the gist of it—the full statement was given to me in confidence by the Senator. The relevant fact is that he was over in Europe almost the whole time. He had one trip back—that's when they married. In fact from '42 to '44 they never met at all."

I thought this over. "Was there a wedding?"

"Thank God no. Sandy Clemens did it. District Court Judge he was then. Appeals now."

"Formerly of Miss Lamb's," I guessed, taking on his abrupt and angry eye.

"Don't smirk. As a matter of fact the entire party was of a piece—call it a piece of Miss Lamb's if you like to be pert— all but the groom. He was bright-eyed enough—grasping well beyond his shabbiness and even open about it. Fat little figure, starting one of those bookish paunches, looking down and out and every bit insensitive to the criminal absurdity of it. My wife and I stood as witnesses: Vand requested it. Oh, astonishing; I'm exactly aware of it. It was both obvious and sly of him—and in combination disgusting. On Allegra's account we had to consent, though my wife came to the ceremony without her gloves. She always shows her point of view. If he expected to grab an identity for himself out of it he was mistaken. Sandy did a quick job of it and had the delicacy to leave out the amenities. I believe he was as much repelled, really, as any clergyman in his shoes would have been, though he wasn't very fond of clergymen in those days. He's come round since, of course. Quite naturally *they* didn't dare think of a minister."

"Maybe Enoch didn't want one," I said. "Because of his religion."

"His religion! My—dear—child, are you obtuse? Or merely vulgar? Would you have expected your poor mother to join him under a greasy Oriental canopy to be jabbered over by a little whiskered Shylock of a rabbi? His religion! The man was an atheist."

"Well if he was an atheist he wouldn't have wanted a rabbi either. You can't be a Jew if you're an atheist, they're mutually exclusive, aren't they?"

"Not having mastered their Talmud, I don't know," William said, backing his cold formidable head away from the light. "I assure you Vand managed to be aggressively both. I was against the marriage, I won't conceal it from you. My wife and I were both against it. And on the practical side, I may say, your mother was left without any protection to speak of. He went right off. He had no address. For months at a time she never heard from him. It was not—as I have said—not really a marriage. It was quite as though there were no marriage at all," he reiterated. He now seemed extraordinarily revivified. "I took the opportunity occasionally to call on your mother to inquire after her welfare, and I may add that except for the attentions of this office her interests were virtually neglected. She was practically abandoned."

"But it wasn't anyone's fault. It was just the war, wasn't it?"

"She was well-warned beforehand."

"About his being in the war?"

"It wasn't the war which separated them," William said. "It was more than the war."

"I can't think of anything that's more than a war," I said.

"You have very little experience. There are matters which precede and exceed war. One, he didn't come from anywhere. Two, he was a Jew."

"Three, my mother didn't care."

"Ah yes, *she* had had experience, hadn't she?" he said in a tone that (had the words been mine) suggested we were once again on ground he would have termed "coarse." —"It wasn't merely that she didn't care. She had actually a positive opinion. If he didn't come from anywhere, she supposed that was all the better: it gave him somewhere to go. She confessed to the attraction of ambitiousness. As for the Jew-thing: agreed that they are reported famous for the stickier paternal qualities—one sees them kissing adult sons in the streets: oh, manly!—still she had to have it that they're 'family men,' unquote. That was presumably for you. —She married him, you see, for *your* sake."

"Enoch's not interested in family," I interposed.

"More to the point, he's not interested in you. He never took to you. Oh, as a marriage-motive you were a great failure," William said with satisfaction. "And as to family! Let me not enter upon what his family might be! The Senator recalls some source or other on the father: one of these usual immigrant items, the little Yid tailor; Tassel corroborates, and adds night-watchman besides; no opinions on anything, grubbed midnight and morning, died at an age younger than the son is now, probably of insufficient sleep (that's Tassel's joke); and five offspring to boot. —Oh look here, let's not touch on family!"

"My mother doesn't care about all that," I repeated sullenly, and privately counted William's offspring. They came to five.

"Put it that the Senators care," William said. "Every trifle, you understand, has been gone into with diligence and without scruple, rag or tag, well in advance of the public hearings. These things are not worn on the lapel, after all. You will observe how considerably I understate when I say that all in all it is not precisely the kind of 'background' one hopes for in a United States Ambassador. One hopes rather for more typicality. Representativeness, portrayal of the general culture of the sending nation—"

"You mean," I burst in, feeling odd, "he won't get it? They won't confirm?"

"Oh, in that sense his history is not at issue. In emerging from it, in fact, he has acquired a certain very recognizable subtlety of contrivance. As the Senator says (the Senator is a Californian), he knows his way around. He's a fond persuader. The Senators are not indifferent to his merits. The post is a working political post, more than (some would say less than) honorific. It may be inferred from this that they want him. They will settle for him. The President has been most pressing. The Vice-President has been most mollifying to the opposition party. Needless to say Vand will have his price domestically. But the committee as a whole will settle for him. They have settled for him already, in spite of everything, everything being his history. Nothing now remains but the assimilatory processes of the hearings themselves. The nature of these should be clear to you by now."

"I think my mother's afraid of a fuss," I said. "Will there be a fuss?"

"They will suppress. What they do not suppress they will minimize," William continued. "They intend to suppress whatever will publicly disturb, they intend to minimize whatever will publicly offend. They have anticipatorily resolved to pass over the tasteless and the ignoble. Put it that there are, metaphorically, tailors and night-watchmen among the Senators themselves: the committee is a reflection of the larger body, and the larger body as it is nowadays composed is not above the tasteless and the ignoble. They have examined, they have investigated."

"If there's a fuss he won't get it, is that what you mean? My mother wants him to get it more than anything." But I said all this repetitively and with a certain dullness. It seemed he had concluded the father's tale; the lover's tale. He had given out the usual climax, a marriage; the rest I knew. The rest was only Enoch and my mother. But I had not come for

Enoch, and not for my mother. I had come for my father: and here was that middleman William leaving off in the middle, marking time with me almost as he had marked it with Mrs. Karp a while before. Perhaps he suddenly felt he had told too much. But if he had not told all (all continued to be Tilbeck, Tilbeck continued to be all) he had not told enough. "My mother wants Enoch to be Ambassador more than he wants it for himself," I took up. "It's the central point for her."

"It's the central point for us all."

"Not for me."

"Especially for you."

"It doesn't matter tó me what happens," I persisted. "It doesn't count. *They're* the ones who want to grab—my mother more than Enoch, I told you. *He's* content as he is."

"He's content, yes."

"With his views, I mean. He lives on his views."

"Some would say he lives on your mother."

"He says so himself. That because his views are—I don't know—oh, bleak, I think you would call them."

"Oblique?" said William. "Perhaps. Then let *me* be direct." And would have pressed on at once with the substance of his discourse as he had pressed on with it against Euphoria's placebo, never attending to my dissent. What I might speculate just then could only hang weightless, since towards the substance itself he had a brutality of attentiveness that showed him unmoved and purposeful, as though concentrating on the ingestion of a pill so repellent of flavor, odor, and appearance that no one observing it trapped in his teeth could possibly take it for a mere placebo. He spoke of generals and senators precisely because they were real powers, and not speculative, and not oblique.

But I said: "*Be* direct."

"If you will permit me," William replied in his tethered tone.

"You don't give me what I came for," I accused.

"I give you nothing else."

"You don't. You keep on about committee hearings. What's it to me, all of that? If Enoch gets to be Ambassador or not? You began about private things, and now you keep on about public things."

"I keep on," William said, "about the things that are pertinent."

"What you mean is pertinent to the body politic. Public

things," I repeated. "It's *my* body they're shipping off, isn't it?
And I'm as private as Tilbeck is, and Tilbeck's been kept so
private all along he's nearly a secret, and still they ship me
off to him—"

"Everything has been done that could be done," he said in-
scrutably. "The committee hearings are public." And then:
"We have been forced," he appended.

"Forced! A drifter, a piano-player, and you talk of forced,
and you drag in those hearings, everything public—"

"We have been forced to come to terms in a way that was
never contemplated."

"Because the committee hearings are public!" I threw
across at him. But in spite of spite I wondered at his words:
long ago my mother too had had to speak of "terms."

"Precisely," William concluded. "Hearings of this sort are
entirely public. They are self-righteously public. In public the
committee represents a formalism, though not quite a formal-
ity. That is because political decisions are arrived at neither
formally nor publicly. The witnesses will have been selected
with a view toward the presentation of the most favorable
impression. Put it that the witnesses will lean, they will have
a particular tendency. They will argue a long and admirable
record, which exists. Which exists: don't mistake me. Undeniably such a record exists."

"You tell everything," I taunted. "You tell everything but
what I came for."

But he did not pause. "The other matters they will pass
over. They will pass over whatever in the record is less favorable, because privately and informally the Senators will already have passed over it beforehand. Before, you understand, the public hearings."

"Then there *won't* be a fuss," I gave out, irritated with his
surface mood. "How nice for my mother, how nice for
Enoch, how lovely, how delicious, I mean for the two of
them: but what difference does it make to me? They've *got*
the Ambassadorship: say they've got it, William. The President wants it, the committee hands it over, and isn't that
enough for them? To run half the Western world? You'd
think that would be enough even for *her!* But on top of it
they've got to ship me off, and nobody'll tell me why. *They*
won't tell me why."

To my surprise I discovered he had been staring at me all
the while. "The plan dismays you that much? You dislike
going that much?"

It seemed it was the first time he had thought of me.

"Oh, I don't care."

"You don't care? Please, you contradict yourself now."

"What else would I be doing anyhow?" I said limply. "Sitting perfectly still. Reading the papers."

"How sullen you are," William reflected, as though capitulating, and dropped his hand flat. "You are not like your mother. At your age she had enthusiasms."

"All the Action Committees, and being a revolutionary. Ho," I said. "Hum. New Oxford Street and Adam Gruenhorn."

But he was unexpectedly stirred: "Undoubtedly she was carried away, and I will not say I could ever approve it, yet it's to her credit in a way. I acknowledge that. It speaks well of her intent."

"It's all so silly, it seems so dated. —My mother especially. She comes out of it a bore."

"The opposite. The opposite. It gave her a spiritual vividness. To be mistaken out of hopefulness hardly mitigates the wrong, yet unlike so many others of no background she was not mistaken out of malice. The rest wanted to avenge themselves on the privileged, as though any position of privilege in society has not been well-earned. But through it all your mother had a sense of herself, she had the self-esteem of numerous industrious generations that is not egotism but is inbred, she had a fancy in favor of engaging herself to the significant act. She had a willingness for good, in spite of a tragic definition of good, and you see all the tragedy that came of it. She has that same willingness today, she will engage herself vitally, she is capable of trying on diverse forms of life—" He stopped, and relieved himself, by means of a destroying blink, of the long attachment of my amazement. He had fallen through surface into whirlpools. He was loyal still. He said: "That is why she wants the Ambassadorship." He examined me. "You are not like your mother."

"Am I like my father?"

"See for yourself."

"Go without a peep, you mean. Get shipped."

"If you value your stepfather you have no choice."

"Oh, value," I said—but this was merely filler, and I might just as well have muttered "Oh, choice," and been as meaningful.

"If you value him as Ambassador."

"That's the way *she* values him. Don't expect the same of

me, I'm not like my mother," I reminded him, "you've told me so twice."

"How rude you are. Rude and sullen. You will go if you, value your mother."

"And should I value. my father too?"

"I beg your pardon?"

"He's the only one who seems to value *me*."

"Yes, he has always established a price on you." He all at once evaded the contents of my face. "Understand me. I don't purpose to make a wound, but here as with most things of the world we are confronted by a business exchange which requires the business mind. You should demonstrate an attitude in accordance with that."

"Gustave Nicholas Tilbeck doesn't have a business mind," I intervened, inexplicably defensive. "He's no good for business. It sounds like he was good for the Action Committees before he got tired of them. Maybe he was good for New Oxford Street and all those parades and Moscow and Sweden. That's all he was good for then, and now I guess there's nothing he's good for." I considered. "Do the Senators know about New Oxford Street and the Action Committees? And Adam Gruenhorn? And my mother? And Gustave Nicholas Tilbeck? And everything years and years ago?"

"They know it all. They are familiar with everything."

"And it's all right? They don't object?"

"The business mind never objects when its own advantage is at stake. Not all the Senators are tailors and watchmen, even metaphorically: which is to say that not all the Senators are fools. They have recognized these items as topically inflammatory but topically worthless. They pass over New Oxford Street because it is too tangential to count, and too dangerous to bring up. The public is interested in the worthless and the inflammatory, but the Senators are interested in what is useful. They will not take it on themselves to bring the worthless and the inflammatory to the notice of the public. They are not ignoble. They regard Vand as a proper candidate not for his biography but for his usefulness. They regard him as sound—sounder than most. He's been through the mill, as Tassel says: knows the other political philosophy first-hand. If he doesn't like it it's not because the Government tells him not to. He knows why he doesn't like it because he has been in it. He has been in it and recanted. Moreover he recanted years before it was the fashion to recant—*that's* in his favor. He has been through all the blandishments, and come out on the other side. Not clean: to my mind nobody can come out of that philosophy cleaner than one who has never been attracted to it: but of course the Senators are not interested in lifelong purity; they are interested in usefulness. The pure and the useful are not always identical. Sang-froid is an acquisition to be earned by a journey through dirt, so to speak, and the dirt has clung. An Ambassador, like steel, should be an alloy."

"I'll tell that to Enoch. Good alloys make good allies, he'll say."

"You're laughing," William observed.

"Because you're not. A minute ago you were complaining he wasn't typical enough, and now you praise him just *for* that. And you don't see the joke."

"The necessities of politics praise him: I don't. He has talent, he has merit. And his talent and his merit are wonderfully attuned to the necessities. If they were at odds with the necessities it would be a comedy perhaps. But there is nothing absurd or comic in the congruent. Furthermore there is another vitally congruent element: he has money available to him. There is no joke in money. There never will be. In this case the money is part of the merit—they wouldn't have him without the money. The post is one of the more expensive ones—surely that's plain on the face of things. It couldn't be run on talent alone. Merit can't staff an embassy building. Luckily he is as well-known abroad for the availability of the money as he is for having had, all these months, the ear of the man who has the ear of the President. In the past he has made both those ears ring. No doubt you have followed that for yourself. But you continue to laugh. I believe I am offended by it. I amuse you?"

"No. The money does. There's a joke in the money after all." A shrewd intimation, an inward scar of awe, lifted me beyond the lamp, and I saw not William's but my grandfather's mouth, sea-obsessed. Had it been live flesh and not oil —sailor's lore that oil and water do not mix—it would have watered at my thought. I said: "She's buying him the Ambassadorship."

"You offend. You offend very much."

"Now there's nobody she hasn't bought."

"Vand was bought—'bought,' if you will—to be a father, as I have said, for you. An unsuccessful transaction. As I have said. The locution is vulgar and I don't accede to it. But she has bought, in that sense, no one else."

"You," I said. "She pays you."

"She pays her attorney. I am her attorney."

"Well? But she pays."

"In my capacity as trustee of a difficult estate I encounter and disburse your mother's money," he answered, but with an anger too small to arouse him. Or perhaps, since the subject was business, he kept himself businesslike: "In spite of that the nature of my relationship to your mother is wholly fiducial."

"Financial?"

"Fiducial. A matter of faith."

"Of commerce, you mean. Every word you say to her she has to pay for. You get your cut out of everything. And now if she has to buy the Ambassadorship for Enoch there's nothing to choose between you and him. She just goes ahead and pays everybody. Up to now I didn't think Enoch had to be paid for; and now it's even Enoch. She pays for everyone. She pays the whole world. She has to pay to keep alive. She has to bribe the air to let her breathe. She has to pay for what other people get for free. It's better to be poor. It's better to be poor and be a blackmailer. It's less humiliating."

"I assure you that for your mother nothing would be more humiliating than not to be the wife of the Ambassador. What she provides she provides willingly. A poor man cannot be Ambassador. An Ambassador cannot be poor."

"He can't be poor, he can't be pure," I recited. "Does that cover all the requisites?"

—He sealed his eyes.

"He can't be dour? But Enoch's thoroughly dour. I told you, he's bleak. You thought I said oblique. But oblique doesn't always fit him; only sometimes; when he wants to he can go straight to the point, I've heard him. Sometimes he goes straight to the point and he's a boor. My mother says so. She tells him he attacks his soup like a boor. He tips his plate the wrong way, that's all. Does the committee know *that*? He's an impure dour poor boor—who'll tell the committee that? I bet that's something they haven't found out! And you say they know everything. He eats his soup like an ex-Communist dupe—"

"If you persist in hysteria—"

"It isn't hysteria, it's rhymes, like Mrs. Karp. I'm accumulating character traits for the Ambassadorship. My mother's money, Enoch's brains, the President's assistant's ear—"

"—and a host country that wants him. I suggest you hear me out finally. I suggest it very seriously."

"Sure," I said, mainly because it rhymed with pure, poor, and dour.

He did not trouble himself to finish the various adornments of his frown: he simply proceeded. "The Foreign Office people over there are unmistakably after him—it's still another factor immensely in his favor that they want him, they are distinctly eager to get him. I have this from the Senator; it is undoubtedly true. And there has been, in addition, a hinting note from the Prime Minister actually, though usually he likes to keep hands off for fear of being misunderstood by the Senators. But the Senators are not fools," he brought out for the second time, in a voice burdened by an unwilling urgency that filled eerily with echoes of itself. He had said all this already. It was as though he were insisting all over again, and more ominously than before, that the committee hearings were public. He had made it intensely and perilously plain that they were public. "Not all the Senators are fools. If they are left alone they will pass over whatever needs to be passed over," he ended, but without the tone of ending.

I marveled at his repetitions. "If the Senators are left alone?" I asked. "You mean by the Prime Minister?"

"I mean by Gustave Nicholas Tilbeck," he said, and now at last I heard him carried down by the sound of ending, and he ended what he had set out to say, and gave me what I had come for.

But what I had come for was no more than what I had come with: my father's names. We were all at once cast back from the public to the private: notch by notch along the greedy wheel of things we had arrived once more at my father's names. Meanwhile I observed that the wheel was rigged, like a lottery disk at a cheating carnival, which brings the same number always to the member of the house: but the member of the house, though a conspirator, is masked like myself to represent an innocent, and summons not through luck but through artfulness.

William said: "He wants to throw it all open."

"All?"

"Absolutely everything."

I began to enumerate: "The Action Committees, New Oxford Street, Moscow—"

"That isn't quite everything."

"But if the Senators *know* everything—"

"The public doesn't. He has made detailed promises to secure that the public will. Your stepfather has had assurances from him."

"There was a letter," I said, "and Enoch wouldn't let me see it. Was that the one?"

He ignored me. "He has named three prominent newspapers in three cities. Each is a hostile and influential political force. Whatever the Senators are willing to overlook, you may be certain that figures connected with these newspapers will not. What has been kept down for twenty years will emerge in an afternoon. In an hour."

A scrub of enlightenment ascended in me: "Because the committee hearings are public," I said.

"Everything will become public. Nothing will be omitted. The public will eat Mr. and Mrs. Vand alive."

"*Mrs.* Vand?" I said.

"They will lick her clean."

"Mrs. Vand doesn't have any politics."

"Neither does the public. You don't imagine the public has the remotest notion of how the Senate goes about qualifying Ambassadors? Or cares? —Politics will be the least of it."

"And what will the most be?" I said in bewilderment.

He gave a great heave. "Even the Senators are not aware of it. We have evaded scandal ingeniously. About you the assumption has been the usual one: the child of a second marriage which terminated in divorce. Don't you see," he pressed out, "we have tried to keep you free, we have done everything for your safety, we have never permitted his breath on you, we have paid him and paid him—"

"Oh," I said. "You mean Brighton. He'll tell about Brighton."

The criminal phrase disgraced the air.

"It might have been regularized. It might have been minimized," said William, moving in his chair. The leather writhed and bleated. "If Vand had adopted. From the start I recommended adoption. But he refused. He could not be persuaded. As a result the matter remains as it was. As it was. Yet something might have been salvaged. You would have had a name."

"I have your name."

"You have no name."

His fierceness was that of a flagellant. He hoisted himself; he rose; he stood mortified, his arc of forehead shining absurdly. A photographer would have powdered it; a painter

would have made a still life of it: it seemed a purposefully
barren bowl awaiting the stroke of a single leaf. Then I saw
on the white flank of the temple an apparition of leaf: the
fuzzy elm-like oval of a track of sweat. He said: "I think
there is nothing left now. We are finished. You have it all."

Seeing his fear I was afraid. "He won't take money? Tilbeck? Can't he take money? Why not money?"

"He will always take money. This time money is insufficient. He wants you."

"I know that. I know, they've told me that. But why there?
In *that* place? Does he live there?"

"He squats there. He comes and goes, there is no one to
stop him. It is an empty house. It has not been kept up. Perhaps it tumbles. He does as he likes."

"He's the one who's free," I said.

But William had pulled the chain of the lamp. The doorknob whined at the neck. "He used the place often before we
learned of it. The first we knew was when he directed the
money to be sent there. He has the caprice of a demon." The
darkness, though enlarging him, presented me with a pudding
of William, wavering against a distant tiny light. The room
beyond was vacant and warm and smelled spent. Paper cups
lay glinting in the aisles between the desks like Viking debris
in a deserted hall. The engagement party had dispersed itself:
Cabbages, Onions, law clerks, all those young men who had
once come down in vain from Cambridge to wish me bon
voyage. "What he wants," William said dimly, "is to harass.
That's all he ever wanted: to harass. To a man who has no
power harassment is power. He envies power. He works on
whatever the occasion offers. I hear a sound. A tick." Tick
tick tick. A minuscule mammal chirp.

It was the sodden nap of the carpet, seeping.

I said in the doorway: "Someone ought to harass him
back."

"Don't take it on yourself!" William answered.

"Oh, not me. I'm only barter," I said. "I'm ransom. I
might as well be a sack of money."

—"Is someone there?" someone called. "Anybody left
over? Who is it?"

At the mouth of a far cubicle, sharp as though inked there,
a pair of tombs embraced.

"Now it's clear," I pursued. "They're sending me to save
Enoch."

"I bet it's a joke. I bet it's a trick. It must be a left-over

Cabbage. They hide out for a surprise. Hey! We can't see you. You a Cabbage out there?" A metal dipper came whirling like a spoke down the corridor; it missed our pioneering shadows by half an inch and fell clattering against a desk. "Go home!"

William's voice emerged from the reverberation: "To save the Ambassadorship."

"To save my mother, if it comes to that."

"Cabbages go home!" The tombs leaned apart, then joined in a single new shape: an uneven obelisk. "Privacy's wanted!"

"It has come to that. It has come to that," William said.

"Oh listen," cried Miss Pettigrew, "it's your father I think."

A noise of scrambling; overhead illumination; exposure. A vale of sandwich rinds.

"Good Lord," William said, "it's a graveyard."

"They left an awful mess," his son confirmed. "I thought you were gone. I told Mother so. She called on Connelly's line. Cletis swallowed a button."

Stefanie's tea rose was pasted to his collar.

"Oh Willie!" she exclaimed, shooting me a lofty crafty look, "see, now you've gone and embarrassed my only fiancé! And we weren't doing anything I bet *you* didn't do in your prime either!"

She had, by that easy abbreviation of his name, fulfilled her dare. He was to be her father-in-law. She reduced him to an intimacy. She claimed him.

"Oh my father in his prime!" said William's son through his neutral withholding smile; and addressed the subject of his apostrophe: "Only it turned out to be a Canadian penny. With an engraving of the Queen on it actually. Cletis *said* it was a button," and recounted how the doctor had held Cletis upside down until the coin shook itself out.

"When I was little I once ate a stock certificate," Stefanie volunteered.

"You'd better not eat any around here, they're mostly Mrs. Vand's," said William's son. "That's why her daughter turned up today—on business for Mrs. Vand. That means she's checking her mother's files for teeth-marks. Show your incisors. Stef; let her see if they match."

"They match yours," I told him.

"Or my father's in his prime," he muttered.

But William was retrieving the carol of his daughter-in-law's laughter from the whorled air as though he could hear in it the beating of his prime; he did not attend. The nictitation of his slow lid seemed underwater, like that of a diver oscillating in a still pool: his reaching fingers widen to comb the sea in hope of catching the snarl of an eddy he remembers, in which something, he does not know what, falls and falls.

Meanwhile his son wheedled a bonfire into the snout of a new black cigar. The act was a drawstring that teased his pupils along a comical slide toward their mutual confrontation; then he lifted his martial head, freed, for a mocking even view of me. "Talk of teeth-marks! Has he been chewing you over? He has to give advice, you know; it's his living," he observed. "No! And still you've come out of there looking martyred?"

"What's martyred?" said Stefanie.

"What they do to saints," William's son supplied, "when they're ignorant and illiterate and have impoverished vocabularies."

"Then it won't ever happen to me!" she crowed. "Will it Willie?"

William glared at his wristwatch, then at his son.

"St. Stefanie," said the latter, "martyred *circa* 1957 A.D. for the improper severance of a proper noun."

Beneath his imaginary helmet I seemed to see the lost flower breathe into bloom.

"I would never do a thing like that, would I Willie?" shrieked William's daughter-in-law-to-be, entwining us all in her joy.

PART FOUR

DUNEACRES

1

It is only the secret reasons which really account for a marriage.

Why did my mother marry Enoch Vand? Not for the reason William held—that public and plausible justification of an unjustifiable suddenness which, like the rest of my mother's fabrications drawn up to satisfy William's respectability, William gave out to me as conservatively as if he believed her lie. It was to himself he lied. Without having to be persuaded, and after so long resisting persuasion, my mother married Enoch Vand: but she married him not for me. In name or act he would not feign fatherhood. He thought me an impediment—not to freedom, but to honesty—and my mother knew it; also William knew it; I dimly knew it, feeling behind Enoch's self-conscious indifference to me a more encompassing indifference. He had the disregard and detachment of one who has given up, yet perversely retains a metaphysical interest in the motions and motives not of the abandoned thing, but of renunciation itself.

This brought my mother to him. A marriage can be a sacrament of despair, and a seal on loss. Or say: it is possible to get used to a revised sense of the self.

My mother (it was remarkable) revised herself and chose Enoch. The war slammed down like a guillotine between America and Europe: she revised, if not her vision, her commitment, and fell almost comfortably into a defense of bad marriages. "If I don't like it," she told William's wife, who after the ceremony stood with her peeled-looking pink hands like the narrow bony heads of carnivorous hawks, "I can always lump it. Following William's example, you know. What the law hath joined together any old divorce court can put asunder." Sarah Jean was heavily pregnant, and in a conscientious voice of meritorious accomplishment reminded the bride of the claims of Divine Law. "Well," said the bride, with a smug tug at the virginal coil of her turban, "if Divine Law doesn't recognize divorce then it's got to recognize polygamy, that's only logical: ask the Heavenly Judge when you get there. What William's done with you he's done with me, don't forget it; and did it like a stick, I don't know how he is with you, but I've had better than that, I've had living blood" —this unholy phrase being the last Sarah Jean was ever willing to receive from Allegra. She turned the arc of her belly like a reproof flourished within a parenthesis, and presently sent a servant to the door to accept Allegra's gift at the birth of William's son; but it was a servant who brought it.

My mother married Enoch, and in the end without having to be persuaded, because she had given up expectation of renewal. The war slammed down like a guillotine; like an electrified gate; like an oven door. Europe was inaccessible. Nick was irretrievable. He could never be found, he would never come back. Who would find him? He was lost, he could never be found, Gustave Nicholas Tilbeck, in all that tangle of time and armies. She felt time on her. Brighton was devoured. And if it was a Hundred Years' War? What would that bring her? She mourned Brighton, but felt time; and married Enoch.

He was willing to succumb to the ordinary. He was workmanlike; he handled actualities; he met conditions (he said) pragmatically. His pragmatism lay in his seeming to think unpragmatically, without regard for consequence. "We share the empty aftermath," he told her, "of the extraordinary. Have you been betrayed? So have I. By what? By a beautiful commitment, in my case; in yours by a commitment to beauty. Now I am the opposite of beauty, as you may have noticed. I don't mean physical beauty; I'm no Nick; but I don't care about that. I mean I wouldn't want you to be harboring wrong notions that I'm somehow immensely worthwhile 'within.' I am not. I'll tell you now I'm not ambitious, and don't care about influence; but I don't expect you to remember that more than a minute; appearances will be against the truth of it. I used to believe in influence; I really believed that good influences make the world good. It's not true: that's why I have no ambitiousness left at all. In spite of that I want to go as high as I can, within my powers. And that's

another thing, my powers—they're not what you think. I'm
not a philosopher; not even a hack philosopher who chews
over someone else's tangent and makes a little name for himself as a tangent-chewer. I'm not a philosopher or a political
scientist or an economist or a historian. Nothing. A dilettante
is all. What I mean is I'll never be a professional *anything*. I
used to be a professional revolutionary, I admit it; I admit
that's the thing that had me at the vitals; at the vitals is where
it lost me finally. I was never more innocent than in my
crafty plotful days; lately experience shows me how to sham
purity of heart, so I'll go far. Far and high. Why do I want it
if not to satisfy ambitiousness? if not to gratify a will for influence? I don't know. Maybe it's academic curiosity. A
zoölogical inquisitiveness. I want to see how high and how
far absolute rejection will take a man. By absolute rejection I
mean absolute revulsion, absolute cynicism: in my amateur
fashion I profess that. At revulsion I'm not a dilettante, I'm
an expert. I want to learn how far and how high a man can
go believing that the world is innately evil, without doing
more than mere contributory evil himself. Call it an experiment; and remind yourself now and then not to confuse it
with ambitiousness, which is not an experiment with an unknown outcome, but a commitment in which the results are
anticipated. If they let Jews be President in this country I'd
aim for that; and I don't omit the possibility—there was Disraeli, after all, a more extreme impossibility. Meantime I'll
take things space by space, at my own haste, which isn't the
same as speed, doing a job at this and a job at that: the evil-
ler the premise and the principle, the better for my investigation. You want to avoid illusions about me, you see what I
mean? I have to go into the high life to look things over, and
see how they rob and murder up there with clean legal hands.
I've seen how robbery and murder are done down below;
now I want to prove that the world is of a piece, top and
bottom. I want to demonstrate how creation is an unredeemed monstrosity."

It was their wedding night.

Allegra said: "But what *for?*"

"Why bother, is that it? Everyone knows it already, is that
it? —A meagre question."

"No," she said. "That's not what I'm asking. I'm only asking why be so mean? Enoch, you're *mean*"—at that moment
establishing exactly the vocabulary and the tonality of the

kind of affection—comradely and hearty and faintly plaintive —that was to characterize them ever after.

"Because," he said, "I'm a disappointed religious. I expected another species of God, why not? Before my birth (it's time you heard the facts): before my birth (the facts, properly selected, account for everything psychological), I contracted to lead a virtuous life if only I could be born into a world where virtue was possible. Never mind probable. Probabilities are practically the same as certainties. But when you say a thing is 'possible' you give the world a chance to change itself overnight. By saying 'possible' you agree to adapt to the way things turn out, even if they lean against you, you see that?"

"Go on with the story," said his wife, yawning.

"Now the next question is what did I mean when I said 'a virtuous life'?"

"You meant the Party without hierarchical totalitarianism."

"Too involved for an unborn infant."

"Nothing's too involved for *you*," she brought out with a suspect sweetness. "If something starts out uninvolved you fix it up so it *ends* involved. Look, there's a white hair. No, two! Right over your right ear. I'm going to tweeze them out, hold still."

"Age doesn't hold still. I'm ten years too old."

"I don't care, so was William, compared to me I mean, not that that's any recommendation. Age wasn't his trouble. —Tell the part about the virtuous life, will you? Hold *still*. Can't you talk without wiggling your head like a bear?"

"Would you like to hear a story about bears instead? Once upon a time there were Three Bears, and one was too cold, and one was too old, and one was *just right,* and his name was—"

"Shut up," she broke in. "I don't care about that, I want to hear about how you were going to live a virtuous life."

"His name was Nick," he finished.

"Oh Goddamn."

"Exactly what I said I would never do."

"Hm?"—hunting with the tweezer's jaws ready to spring.

"Damn God. I even promised—ouch, I can't spare so many hairs, you said there were only two grey ones to go—"

"*White.* There are eight million four hundred and six billion, and all the rest pure scalp. I'll pull till I'm satisfied. Don't say Nick any more or I'll pull and *pull.* Go on."

"If you had a razor instead of a tweezer would you nick instead of pull?" he said meekly.

In response she gave a ferocious yank and came away with a snarl like mist. "Poor Enoch, you're going bald like a rocket. Just fleece or feathers all over. Puff and it's out and gone."

"I'm a very unattractive man. Unsuitable for a husband. I never planned to be a husband. You know I thought I would be a monk."

"Jews don't *have* monks."

"Precisely the problem," he acknowledged with enthusiasm. "I made a pledge: let God be the kind of God who would allow the sort of world in which it is possible to lead a virtuous life, and I would repay him by dedicating my days and every so often my nights to constant praise of his holy name. No Goddamns to speak of. A sort of friar I would be. After I grew up, of course."

"And then you grew up."

"No. Then I was born—look how you lose the chronology, you're not attentive. First I was born, and found the world the way it is, and myself a Jew, and God the God of an unredeemed monstrosity, and well, just as you said, Jews don't have monks, so it was easy to see something was wrong immediately, but so naïve was I that I didn't despair or suspect—"

"Yes you did. Jews are cunning."

"—and in my simplicity I thought that whatever you come upon that seems unredeemed exists in this state for the sake of permitting you the sacred opportunity to redeem it. I used to have a crooked idea that man finds the world unwell in order to heal it, I had the presumptuousness of thinking myself one of the miracle rabbis. Charlatans and deviations those were, and as cunning as Methodist Bishops. But afterward I became wise, and learned how the world isn't merely unredeemed: worse worse worse, it's unredeemable."

"You have no sense of humor," said his wife.

"That was meant to be a joke."

"All of that?"

"Yes."

The tweezer dropped to the pillow. "I don't like long jokes."

He laughed aloud. "And that's a short joke."

"I don't see why."

"Not seeing why is the point of the joke. Sometimes a joke is a joke only if someone doesn't know it's a joke."

"Oh Enoch! How mean you are!"

"How rich you are," he countered.

"*I* can't help it, can I?" But she was all at once infiltrated by a sulky meditation. Her gaze moved interiorly. "Did you see this afternoon how that small-minded Sarah Jean came without any gloves? —Just because it was a civil ceremony doesn't make it right."

"Civility was expected to be an attribute of the ceremony, not of the witnesses," Enoch observed.

"She did it for spite. If it'd been *church* she would have worn them with a decency. But my God, did you get an eyeful of William's work?—it looked as though any minute Sandy might have to follow up with a christening. If judges do that."

He said, "You'd rather it was Nick."

"Nick?" She was fearful; she was petulant.

"Instead of me. Instead of me."

"Well what's the difference? She *still* wouldn't have worn her gloves. Anyhow I settled long ago it wasn't going to be Nick."

"You settled it wasn't going to be me," he contradicted.

"But that was before."

"Before? Before what?"

"Before we gave up finding him."

"And if we find him now?"

"What do you mean now? Now there's a war. You don't find anyone in a war. William said so. You said so. War's the end of finding anyone."

"But if we did?"

She picked up the tweezer and bit the air with it. "I've given it up, I told you."

"It? It? And what do I read for *it?*" he demanded.

"Hope."

"Ah, that's something else! Hope isn't Nick. You give up hope, you don't give up Nick. Nick you don't give up, is that the idea?"

"I give up what I please, who knows if I'll ever see him again? So it doesn't matter. For God's sake, Enoch."

"It doesn't matter? What doesn't matter? It doesn't matter that you'll never see him again or it doesn't matter whom or how you marry as long as there's a certainty you'll never see him again?"

"For God's *sake*, Enoch. I can't follow any of that. You married me for the money so *think* of the money. Concentrate on the money and leave Nick out of it."

"All right. Out he goes. Put the child away."

"What do you mean, put her away?"

"In a school. Or whatever."

"A school! A baby three years old! And melancholy enough to begin with!"

"The point is you look at her and think Nick."

"Liar. You mean *you* do. All you think is Nick Nick Nick. It was supposed to be the money you cared about!"

"I care about signs."

"Dollar signs you're supposed to care about!"

"If you gave up all hope—"

"I have, damn it. Talk about signs, what's this bed?"

"The first time isn't typical."

"I know what's typical and what isn't," she threw out with a roar, "for goodness' sake I'm no virgin."

"Plainly," he said: which softened her.

"The way a thing begins is a sign anyhow. I believe that. The way it begins is the way it stays. So if you want a sign that I don't think of him you've had it."

But it was not enough. He said again, "If you gave up all hope of him—"

"I have! Go to hell if you can't tell that I have."

"No. You would give up all sign of him. That's all."

"The child stays," she said with a finality. "She goes with me wherever I go and she stays with me, and *that's* all."

"Because of Nick. She's Nick's, there's the reason. Open and clear."

"She's mine, that's why."

"She's not mine. Just remember that. Don't have any expectations inconsistent with that."

"You don't have to tell me what to remember! I know what to remember without slogans!" she delivered up with the wrath of humiliation, and released from her covetous grasp the wrested puff of his weakling hair: it ascended on a thrust of draft from the open window like a horde of parachute-seeds preparing to fertilize the hotel-room carpet. "Don't think I don't remember things without your advice! I remember how I got her, I remember how and where and when. Brighton! You think I can forget Brighton just like that? You think it's easy to forget Brighton?"

"Naturally Brighton. Brighton would stick to you," he answered, "like an icicle. He left you to freeze and went to warm himself God knows where. Reminisce about freezing while you're at it."

"I never reminisce," she said proudly. "I hate the past."

"Carpe diem. I married an American."

"Don't talk foreign languages at me, it's gauche."

"All I said was tomorrow we die."

"That's how *I* feel. Entre nous, that's just how I *feel* about things, Enoch, don't you?"

He said solemnly, "Let us vow to agree about everything."

"Don't think I don't know when you're being sarcastic!" But she had subsided. "All right. As long as I have my way in everything."

"Oh, you will, you will," he saluted her, and went his way, and let her have hers: so that it was difficult to see that their ways were divergent, they agreed so well. The next day he departed to resume espionage, his trade then, and she stayed to invent his future. "His future" became the thing they agreed on. It suited them both, like an eclipse to watchers satisfied to see their equal moon-borne shadows cover the parts that had been too light to bear.

2

Exposition of this latter scene was my mother's, when I finished reading her letters.

"Of course it was a fib—Enoch's saying he didn't have any ambition. That was his way of covering up. He always has to cover things up, he's terribly complicated. It's right in his temperament, being negative about things. Negative and proud. The more negative and proud he is the more he's craving something. I ought to *know* him by now! Take my word for it: he's got a hollow craving in him, more than anyone: more than I have. That's why he's the only person I

could have married, logically speaking," she concluded
haughtily.

But this, I must be careful to explain, was afterward.

Also to be noted: before this statement, with all its rococo
belligerence and artful defensiveness, she flung herself upon
herself, she tore histrionically at her own skin; she performed, in short, a largeness of weeping, an avian elegance of
screech; her elbows declared themselves two muses of grief.

But this too was afterward: after, I mean, I returned from
William's office; and all because, arriving, I said I had seen
William.

The significance of this was not at once plain to her.

"And what did you there? Frightened the mouse that was
under the chair," she sang out. It was night and half-past
nine o'clock, but she was brilliantly dressed and cheerful; she
was engaging Enoch in enforced judgment of a hat in the
shape of a cowl. "See? With the brim up I look like the
Seven Dwarfs and with the brim down like Lady Macbeth.
Which? Enoch, which?"

"Down," he said, and stiffly down also went his mouth,
bored.

"No really, pay attention. You're not paying attention.
Up?"

"Up is fine."

"You just said down! Because there might be photographers, and really I want to hide the ravagements just in case.
From all that coughing I'm turned into a crone. Well hello,
home is the hunter, home from the—look who's here. Wrinkled you are, the back of your skirt, what a pity you never
give a minute to groom yourself. The least you could do for
yourself. What do you think?" she greeted me. "Brim up or
down? Enoch can't make up his mind."

"The Lady Macbeth way," I offered.

"Well all right, better a murderess than a Mother Superior.
Just so I don't get taken for a nun. They have such blank
eyes, nuns, but they wear things on their heads exactly like
this. It covers, that's the point. Where in the world did you
run into William?" she took up.

"I didn't run into him. I went to his office."

"On purpose? Oh I forgot, that's right, his boy's engagement party. That little Pettigrew spawn. Was that today?"

I felt in awe of such omniscience. "You couldn't have
known about it?"

"Of *course* I knew about it."

"But it was a surprise."

"To William's boy it was. Not to me. But I heard they had no intention of inviting you—they didn't want to embarrass you, really their motives were perfectly reasonable, all things considered. The same nice group of them down from Harvard Law, that's why, and not one took you out the time before. What a waste, that bon voyage! —It's because you have no bosom. You're not social either. It's sickening, with you it's brain brain brain. Oozing brain all up and down the *side* of you."

"You mean of course the maternal side," Enoch said.

"Viper."

"Wipe her yourself," he only seemed to capitulate: "she's yours. Send not to ask for whom she oozes, she oozes for thee. As for me, I'm ready for compulsory gaiety"—laying aside a broad book—it was an atlas—with a sardonic sigh.

"Now don't say compulsory. Enoch, it's mean to say compulsory. If I *ask* you to go with me it's voluntary, isn't it? —Good God, if there *are* photographers! Won't William feast on I-told-you-so, he thinks flashbulbs fell with Lucifer. Only let's take the subway."

"The subway?" He was incredulous.

"Well why not? I haven't ridden the subway in years." Flailing, my mother collected her burgeoning gown at the knee; energies bickered in her throat. "All those loops hanging from the ceiling. I *like* the subway. What if someone threaded a big wide shiny ribbon, Virginmaryblue maybe, and satin, right through all those loops, right through the whole train, from one car to the other? Like a horizontal maypole, sort of. Wouldn't it be beautiful, all that waving and twisting underground? I *like* tunnels." She displayed a silvery face innocent as a plate. "You know where we're off to? Guess. You'll never guess."

I forfeited my guess by declining.

"A club, that's where," she said, her elbows pink with satisfaction. "I suddenly couldn't stand all that reading, I suddenly couldn't stand *bed*, if you want to hear the truth. Static! Viscous! Another minute of it and I would've been ready for Dr. Freud, so I decided the way *not* to be sick was not to be *sick*," she explained. "Mind over mattress Enoch said it was, so here we are going to the loudest nightclub on the map. Oh look, you're not taking *that* damn map? Not *with* you? Think how it'll look in the papers, just in case, and the hearings coming up! —I mean if there are photographers, columnists," she said joyously, "there are *always* columnists, vermin—"

"At the appropriate moment I will retire to the men's room," said my stepfather, "a palatial nook of Byzantine splendor and Roman proportions—"

"You and that map. Really. You don't have to memorize every *village*. Those stupid Senators aren't going to get you to tell the population of every little dump in the whole country, are they? It's bad publicity to be seen studying."

"Depends what the man is studying," Enoch said. "In this case, on the eve of my possible aggrandizement—"

"Not possible. Definite."

"—I'm learning how small I am. An atlas is a source-book for human insignificance. Puts you in scale, full of oceans, oceans full of islands, islands full of sand, sand full of infinities—"

"You full of stupidities. *I'm* not interested in feeling small, just remember that. Those damn Taj Mahals round my ears, I was so depressed—what *I* want is to go out and get noticed. I admit it! It's not as though I'm afraid to admit it. I've been cooped up too long, I intend to feel something *great* before the night is out. I mean an experience. Like the haying scene—"

"The haying scene!" said Enoch, delighted. "The haying scene in a nightclub! And then stack it all up in Washington Square?"

"Well I meant the emotional *equivalent*. You *know* that's all I meant."

"The hell you did. It's the pitchfork you're after. To each his own."

"I just want to feel something. I haven't *felt* anything in such a long time." She turned unexpectedly desolate, lifting her hooded head to the mirror and absently addressing my image in it: "You mean you got invited after all?"

"No," I said. "I just went."

"Rude, very rude. Did you dance?"

"There wasn't any music."

"Of *course* there wasn't any music," she said contemptuously, as though the idea had been mine. "Too many desks in the place. How did he look? Happy?"

"William?"

"Fool. His *boy*. William hates that Pettigrew girl. Afraid his boy won't be the first. William puts a lot of value on being first."

"She's very pretty," I said.

"Pretty, pretty, what's pretty? At that age it's no trick to be pretty. I was pretty too, what's pretty? For you it's a trick. I don't know how you manage to look practically thirty and no bosom. People ask if I had you at ten. I tell them certainly: she was ten at birth. Some people are *born* a hundred years old. It's the effect of what do you call it, Enoch? That word like the name of a German newspaper? That Eddie put in the—"

"*Weltanschauung*," Enoch said: "Come on, if we're going let's go."

"No not that one. The other word that Eddie—with the ghost in it."

"*Zeitgeist*," he obliged, and settled back into his chair again.

"That's the one. You know I heard from Eddie this afternoon. Already. I knew he could be trusted, whatever Enoch said," she informed me. "Two telegrams delivered together, one from last night when he landed out there, one from this morning. He flew. I let him fly to get him back here on time for the next number. Here."

She handed me two yellow paper squares and I read on one:

> GOLDEN WEST GOLDEN WEST
> I WILL MAKE YOU QUICK
> AS HAIKU OR SOME GIRL

and on the other:

> IN SAN FRANCISCO
> THE ZEITGEIST BLOWS THROUGH SNEEZING
> FROM ITS ALLERGY

"Teasing!" my mother said.

"He sent them collect," I observed.

"Teasing!" she repeated. "Of course as *theory* they're too rigid, but otherwise as *poems* they're not bad. Surrealistic. If you stare at them long enough they expand out of their superficial meaning into a deeper meaning, can you see that? —Never mind, I take it back, it's no use asking *you*. *Wordsworth*," she pronounced, haughtily and heavily. "We don't print any of that ilk in *Bushelbasket*, do we?" She appealed beyond me to Enoch.

"Good God no," he mumbled from inside his atlas.

"Would kill the tone. Here's a town named Cheatyourboss. Believe it or not."

"What country?"

"California."

"Oh *you*."

"Word of honor. Population two-hundred-and-sixty-three."

"Two-hundred-and-sixty-four," I suggested, "now that McGovern's out there."

"That's what Enoch *meant*. Don't abet the man," she admonished me, pleased that I was trying to: but Enoch was oblivious. "Anyhow I was *telling* you—early this evening I sent out to this shop for some hats and well, they brought a pile of them and I picked this Mother Mary one and just then who should walk in with the milliners walking *out* but this same Western Union boy! Not a *third* one I said—"

"Not a *third* one," I interrupted, and took it from her:

IN FRISCO IN THE FALL
THEY HAVE NO RATS AT ALL
EXCEPT ON TWO LEGS

"This one is really very good," my mother said. "I may decide to let him go ahead and print it when he gets back. If there's room. Of course that business about counting the syllables is such a bother it's hardly worth it."

"Then *don't* count them," Enoch said, momentarily emerging.

"Silly! If you don't count them how can you tell it's a haiku? —What have you got there?" she demanded out of the middle of her triumph: she was watching me dip into the pocket of my skirt.

"Do you have room for this? It's a present from Mrs. Karp."

"Mrs. Karp? Euphoria Karp? What a coincidence! I mean here we are talking about verse forms, and in you march with, with a—"

"Placebo," I said, surrendering it.

"Imagine." She snatched up the page and marveled. "How in the world did you get mixed up with *her*?"

"Her husband's going to Russia to see about getting you royalties," I provided, "with a delegation. The humor's for *Bushelbasket*, none of the harpies would have it, so she's giving it to you. It's supposed to be humor."

"Those gangsters," my mother muttered, but this was

merely automatic; having made her obeisance to justice, she
was free to resume her astonishment. "Certainly her verse is
humorous, it's *known* to be humorous. What is it," she said,
examining the placebo's contours, "a suppository?"

I recited: "William says not to worry, Karp will do what
he can."

"You met her at William's place? Karp too? What were
you doing over there in the middle of a business conference?"
Under the eyelid of her cowl my mother's eyelids blinked
suspiciousness.

"It wasn't business, it was a party."

"What was Karp doing at that boy's party?"

"He came a day early," I said, not very diligently searching
after Mrs. Karp's story. "No, a day late I think it was."

"A day late for what?" my mother said sharply.

"That Russian thing. Making them give in on your royalties. William asked him to come yesterday and he couldn't.
They had to stay over in Cambridge for Mrs. Karp's play."

"I know that type. They pretend to be your closest friends
when they know you need them for something, and then they
impose. William should have made him cool his heels," she
said. "It's rude to show up when you're not wanted."

"I bet that'll be the Kremlin's view of it exactly," I agreed.

"Smarty, you know perfectly well what I'm talking about,
I'm talking about you. You shouldn't go where you haven't
been invited. Were you invited?" she probed again, not out of
forgetfulness; she distrusted.

"No."

"No," she echoed with the satisfaction of bitterness. "So?"

"I was expected," I said, which shocked me: not for its peculiar sidewise truth, but for the tremor which, for the second time that day, my voice was unfurling like a signal in my
back.

"You were expected all right. You were expected to stay
home and not go where you weren't asked. How many
chances do you think those boys—"

But Enoch's speculative eye had joined us. He brushed his
book from his thighs and came to stand beside my mother,
his thumb stabbed into the thick core of his cheek. "You
were expected?"

"Yes. Sort of."

"William's *boy* expected you?"

"The whole thing was a *surprise*," my mother broke in, insisting. "Weren't you listening? William's boy wasn't expecting *any*one."

"Then William," Enoch pursued. "William expected you." He was soft and quick, concentrating, like a man pulling away the skin of a delicate scaleless fish.

"He wasn't surprised to see me," I said. "He told me that."

"Not the same thing," my mother drew out of herself, slow with scorn. "Bad manners from *her* wouldn't surprise a demon out of hell."

"So you were expected," Enoch concluded. "Let it stand at that. But not necessarily today?"

"Not necessarily."

"And not necessarily this month?"

"No."

"And not necessarily this year?"

"No," I said.

"What *is* this?" my mother leaped in. "Cabbalah? A Zen catechism?" She was viewing me disgustedly. "As if it wasn't enough to embarrass yourself in front of those boys by running *after* them, you had to go break up a *very* important, possibly valuable, *legal* conference that might decide my entire future with the Soviet Union! —You can't deny you injected yourself right into the middle of it? You *know* how polite William is, if he saw you there he'd take you right over to him no matter what he was dealing with at the moment, he'd simply break it up then and there—"

I defended myself: "But they were halfway through when I got there—"

"Halfway through! Those gangsters! Halfway won't get me my royalties, will it?"

"Allegra," Enoch said.

"Are you listening to her? Are you listening? Halfway she says!"

"I think it was the whole way."

"What?"

"Take off that idiotic visor, helmet, whatever it is, that piece of stupidity," he commanded her; his gentleness was not protective. He chose not to disclose the sources of his reasoning, yet he continued to reason, and this made him seem dangerous even without provocation. To me he said: "What did you go there for?"

"What do you *think* she went there for?" my mother intervened. "To humiliate herself and grab trouble! Those boys wouldn't *look* at her the first time, and then at least I had her *dressed,* and will you just please observe her now, that awful skirt with *pockets,* all ribbed up like she's been on horseback the whole day in it, *now* she's after those boys! She heard those boys were over there, that's why she went. Those law students, perfectly *acceptable* boys—"

"I didn't go on account of the boys," I said.

"She didn't go on account of the boys," Enoch said. His repetition of this, his tone very simple and in spite of simplicity reverberating with ominousness, brought a glimmer of bewilderment into my mother's mouth; a startled bubble blew itself up at the delta of lips and cheek. "Take off that headgear, will you? You're got up for a duel—I told you before I won't be your second in this, no matter what."

"But we're going out in a minute—" All the same she complied, pulling off the connected segments of her hat like a sausage moulting; meanwhile directed erratic disputations at me. "I don't know why *you're* so complacent, I'll bet you're not even packed properly; leaving tomorrow and disappears the day before and not even packed—"

But here, perhaps because by yielding to my stepfather she showed herself vulnerable, exposed to dread—her scalp obvious in patches through insufficient hair had a piteous spark, like a candle by day—I slid out the thin point of my accusation: "But there wasn't a divorce—"

Her look, coming to take me slow-motion, emptied itself en route. "Oh, is that it? Is that it? What everything's about?"

"Because you were never married," I completed it, and waited to feel the blow I had cast against my own frailty subside.

But she held on; she was all skilful deflection; or else all opacity. "Well we *were* married at first. We had a honeymoon and everything. And just because William likes to keep up a, a *relationship,* it doesn't mean he doesn't feel just as divorced as I do. It's a funny time of the night to want to start a discussion about William," she said, striding off to stand behind Enoch's chair as though the back of his head had answers written on it, which she was even now consulting. "I don't deny it's a *subject,* the way he sort of can't let go, let go of *me* I mean—I suppose you bumped into it over there today? Well look, it doesn't bother me, I'm not the one it really kills, and it's not that we're not on speaking terms either, nothing deliberate like that—I'm talking about Sarah Jean—it's just a kind of accident, really, we simply haven't managed to meet in all these years . . . who brought it up?"

"William's son," I said, amazed that her obtuseness—wilful or genuine—should hit on a fact so squarely.

"That boy tries so hard not to be like his father. It's why he's never shown any interest in you: you *represent* me," she brought out: she had a trace of Enoch's manner, half abstraction, half mockery. "Look, do you want something explained? About how a honeymoon stops being a honeymoon? Well I know, I mean it's absurd at *your* age: but Enoch, she's always been backward, not mentally speaking, socially I mean, always since she was little. You'd know that without my saying so if you'd ever paid any attention. —Because if it isn't sex relations you want to hash over, right in the *shank* of the evening, really we ought to get started—"

"Allegra, you're perfectly stupid," said her husband.

"Am I? Am I?" A power entered her voice. "*I'm* willing to talk to her, or haven't you noticed? If I'm so stupid why don't *you* talk to her for a change?"

"It appears not to be necessary," he said mildly.

"Nobody has to talk to me," I said.

"Then what sort of an issue are you trying to raise? Damn it, she disappears the whole day, she barges into somebody's *private* engagement party, she ruins the Soviet Union for me —those gangsters, and then out of the blue she brings up *William and* brings him up *and* up—"

"Nobody has to talk to me."

"Then what in God's name is it all about? What's the *issue?*"

"William said issue," I said.

"What?"

"William said issue. He said issue to me."

"Come to the point, will you?" she directed, loud with anxiety, and dropped her forearms over Enoch's shoulders. They came on him with a roughness, pressing down as though she could smother scorn with the weight of her wrist-bones, hooped gaudily with a twist of bracelets scribbled there like a spring. She had turned her sleevelessness into a foliage of chatter and glister fit for the vermin of photographers, implying racket, implying improbable volitions, implying scandal. "Is there a point here? Come to the point, can't you?"

"He said issue and I said illegitimate issue."

My mother released her hold and jangled her hands fearfully around the paleness of Enoch's intimately-scrolled ears. "What in the name of Christ Jesus is she talking about?"

"Me," I said. "Me me me."

"She's been told," Enoch said.

"I'm talking about me," I said.

"Pig! You you you. That's all you ever think of. Little self-ish pig," my mother brought out: she walked round and round her bed.

"Wrong animal," Enoch said. "The plaint to the slaughterer. Though no pig. Ram. The ram demands to know why he, also God's own creature, is less worthy than Isaac. Everybody worries over Isaac, and then the ram substitutes under the knife, and nobody cares. A subject the Commentaries leave unexplored."

"*I* don't leave it unexplored," my mother said raspingly. "Don't give me rams, I'll ram rams down you! I want to hear things in plain English! Who told her what? Nobody told her anything! There's nothing to tell, it's all been kept down—"

"William told her," Enoch said, flattening the atlas from thigh to thigh, like a bridge; over it he flexed his fingers, fisting and stretching. Then with a subtlety: "Are you afraid?"

"Told her what? I'm not afraid. Told her what? You think I'm afraid? I'm not afraid, there's nothing to be afraid of! Talk!" she ordered me.

"Tell what you've been told," Enoch said.

"It's not news."

"It's news that you've been told."

"What do I care? She knows it already," I protested.

"What what what!" my mother screamed. "Talk!"

"She's brought back a dirty word and that's all there is," Enoch responded; a series of hyphens composed longitudes in his lap.

"Pig! William said something? He didn't say! He didn't! He said something?"

"Allegra."

"He said something!"

"He told her."

"He told her," my mother breathed. Her breath was a dog's breath; it was audible; I discovered myself in shame for its naked audibility; it was audible, it was pitiful. "He told her, Enoch?"

"Somebody had to tell her," Enoch said.

"I know, I know," she murmured, consenting, "I know."

"You delegated it and it was done."

"I didn't delegate it, I only decided with William—"

"The agent performs, the proxy acts. The trustee is surrogate. A case of behalfs adding up to the whole."

"Oh *please* don't start that sort of talk—"

"Myself neither gear nor cog in it, I warned you. When I favored the whole it was cloth I meant, whole truth being partial error, if I may reverse Lord Shaftesbury and Pope." But he was perfectly unsmiling.

"You, you're so detached," she flung out.

"Say it again if you want. Detached."

"Pedantic in a crisis!"

"A, there is no crisis. B, what other crisis behavior do you think plausible?"—and he suddenly began to chant, his big head listing piously:

> Don't be pedantic
> When in a crisis.
> Do be frantic,
> For it stimulates your vices.

My mother halted in the middle of her circuit: "Enoch, you joke, you carry on, and meanwhile the whole world's changed—"

"Nothing's changed," he replied soberly.

"Mrs. Karp's better at it," I remarked.

He inquired, "Better at what?"

"Instant rhyming."

"My dear child, I have spent the last twenty years perfecting that verse. The only thing instant about it is your mother's disapproval. Nevertheless after removal of all visible syntax, I intend to submit it to *Bushelbasket* for editorial consideration. Not your mother's—her representative's: following her example, you see, with regard to responsibility."

"Enoch, will you *listen* to me? I did *not* delegate it, I only said if ever some day it had to be dealt with, I mean if it came *up*, if we *had* to, well, *you* wouldn't do it, and so he said, William said, if it happened *he* would. If we *had* to only."

"I recall it. I fail to see the logical 'we' in it. You should have done it yourself."

"It's a problem of law, it's for lawyers."

"I should rather call it a problem of family," he said lazily.

"All right then! Family!" she cried. "You're in it same as anyone if that's the case!"

"Ah, you're a step beyond the actual case," he noted.

"You could have told her yourself. I mean if you think it's so terrible about William doing it. William's nothing to her!"

"*I* am nothing to her."

"You're her stepfather, damn it!"

"Precisely the step too far I had in mind," he bit off.

"Oh, you're cool about it," said my mother, folding her lip in tight upon her teeth, "*nice* and cool, aren't you? You're in it same as anyone! Deny it! You're the one said to pay him off in the first place, deny it! Eleven, twelve years ago, that time we talked the whole thing through, you came out with it right at the beginning—"

"You're missing that money? You're in need of it?"

"You're the one who made me give in to him."

"But we didn't have reasons, did we? *L'acte gratuit* it was. We did it for the love of him."

She stabbed feebly, "Oh stop it, don't say love like that, you're the one who made me."

"And viewing it retroactively, you would have preferred exposure? We didn't have a motivation good enough for Allegra-after-the-fact? You want to forget how we looked at every side and into the future and all around the thing?"

"Well she's pigged up anyway now, so where's the difference?"

"Twelve safe years is the difference."

"But now she's pigged up anyway."

"I'm not pigged up," I said.

"The hell you're not! I should never have given in to him in the first place. That was the mistake of it. Never give in to a thief." With dull guile she addressed my stepfather: "You're the one who made me give in to him in the first place. It's because I gave in to him."

"You gave in to him," he repeated. He often repeated phrases of hers, but with a conscious change of intonation which turned them sinister, even when he chose, as now vaguely yet too calculatedly he chose, to laugh. "Still," he considered it with the whole clandestine energy of his cleverness, "it depends on exactly which point in history you refer me to. As for our present circumstances, you're perfectly right, they wouldn't have their interest for us now if you hadn't given in to him in the first place. Only," he concluded, all wondering outstretched palms, "was Moscow the first place you gave in to him in? Or before that, the camp? God knows Brighton wasn't the first—"

She spat out at him full and fierce: "Bastard!"—and a jewelled smear of spittle stood upright, webbed over her still open mouth, a flat skin of terrible shining bubble, like a valve.

I did not hesitate. "William's dirty word," I said quickly, to punish her.

But "I didn't mean you"—she took it as undeliberate, as a wicked accident of the feelings, as hideous confessional misappropriation, as every horror—"I didn't, I only meant oh God oh God," she sent out, grinding crescents into the carpet on humped knees, sinking her head into the bedcovers. Her eyes, going down in milky shadow, yielded momentary points of warty light and drowned. "I meant I gave in to *pay* him. I mean that."

I said impatiently, "I know it. You paid him and paid him."

"It was to keep him away."

"I know all that."

"We kept him away, we kept his *name* from you—" She carried her face up for a second's surveillance of mine. Her nostrils appeared briefly to collapse, then muscled out to leak streaming transparencies: "And for this, for this!"

"I know his name. Plenty of names he has," I said.

"For this," she gave out, swallowing deep among sheets. "I thought you'd be free of that, I always meant you to be free, you were supposed to be free," and clanged out a fearful drone: Enoch jumped with alarm.

"The stupidity of this," he urged. "Get up. Don't be a fool, Allegra. Stand *up*," and stood himself: the atlas flashed down between his legs like a fan or hand of cards, flicking out nations, pink, purple, orange, green, and lavender-blue waters anchored and split by hyphens; suddenly it showed Brazil, brownish, bloblike, supine under the chair, and Enoch leaned and spoke into flesh bunched under one horrified eye: "How stupid you are."

My mother answered with a live tone like a tuning fork. "Oh God oh God oh God," she snaked out with a queer clamor, half noise half voicelessness, "why now, what I want to know is why now, after a lifetime why now?" And then began that wailing, never-to-be-forgotten, which inhabited her for minutes without rest, without insistence but rather as an immanence, as though by right, and therefore curiously tiresome, which in fact I have already described: how she dashed herself upon herself; how she splintered fingernails into tissue; how she bowled bracelets up and down her arms; how her elbows declared themselves to be two idols of fate,

knifing air and bed and Enoch; how she played out her long
lung in bawlings that coarsened her speech for a day; how
she wept, how she wept, because I knew she had paid and
paid, and had never been divorced because never married to
that father who had plenty of names but none left over for
me: because I knew; and she wept for an hour because I
knew. "Why now, why now, just *tell* me, after a lifetime why
now . . ."

And Enoch said: "Whose lifetime? Yours? Not yours.
Think, allow yourself to think."

"Still, still, after so long keeping it down, we kept it down
so long, it doesn't make sense why now—"

"If not now, when?" my stepfather said at the end of it.

My mother raised herself. She was ugly. Her lids were fat
as lips. She was silent.

"He would have told her all the same," Enoch said.

"Nick? Nick you mean?" she wondered, straining to chirp
at him: "That's who you mean?"

"Probably it's why he wants her. To give it to her in his
own way."

My mother brought up a single sound without meaning;
she kneeled lower and straightened her ankle so that a nervous snap clicked in it. "Ah, but it's terrible now. To send
her knowing," she croaked from the mattress-heart, "it's
criminal to send her knowing."

"Criminal," he mocked, "to send a daughter to a father?"

"It's not just a daughter to a father any more. It's sending
her *knowing*. Look, go ahead and simplify, the more you
simplify the more complex you make everything."

"I am not without my gifts," he wearily agreed.

"Sending to a father is one thing, when you send that way
it's all right; but now it's sending to a crook, just like that,
out in the open, nothing to cover it up," my mother pursued,
"it's exactly like making her into an accomplice—"

"To whom?" he challenged.

She suppressed her answer under a fragmentary whine.

"If you mean to us—" But he did not finish; instead he
threw out at her dangerously, "Well then *don't* send her."

My mother looked at me with what I recognized as a new
timidity.

"I'm going all the same," I said.

"Ah," she pronounced, and took in Enoch with pursy violated eyes. "There, hear that? She wants to, hear that? There,
she wants to, for your sake."

"For his sake," I said, crafty to mislead her.

"You see, Enoch, for your sake," my mother repeated.

"No: for Nick's sake," I amended. "He's the one that wants me."

"Oh, he wants you, all right," my mother said, snuffing up a spasm of breath. "It's perfectly plain he *wants* you. Only don't get the idea it's all for your own sake—"

"For *God's* sake," Enoch objected, slapping his hands to his temples.

"But you see? I *said* accomplice. Twitch an eye and isn't she ready to join up in a minute on the other side? Sweetheart," she parried, "he's a *crook*. He always *was* a crook. Look how he's threatening Enoch—you know about this business don't you? I mean now you understand all about it, right?"

"Maybe he does it just to get me. Nobody ever let him get near me any other way, so maybe he does it just to get me. Because he wants me," I said again.

"Idiot. He doesn't want *you*, it's me he wants to get at. He wants trouble. Well look, what he really wants is revenge," she stated, "on me, don't think I'm going to be *obtuse* about it. He thinks he has plenty to get even with, that's why. —That time in Europe."

"What time?" Enoch said.

"The whole time. The whole time he was in Europe. The whole war I mean."

"Sure. You made the war just to spite him."

"Well indirectly we all did, that's *your* idea, isn't it? To spite ourselves. Humankind brutalizing itself. So I suppose I was in on it too. Don't ridicule, he's never forgotten and never forgiven, you *know* that." She scrambled herself erect and confronted us with her mouth pointed into a deliberate argument of openness, like a trapezoid. "I came safe home myself, that's why, and never got him out of there, and ever since what's it been but a simple case of getting even? That's all he's after. It was a simple question of, of"—she swiveled quickly to shatter Enoch with her high ruined declarative—"abandonment. Say what you want, it's true, that's just what it was, abandonment. Nothing else. Because I left him there."

"You left him there," Enoch admitted.

"Well it's true, go ahead, try to deny it. There I was safe in America and there *he* was God knows where."

"Sure," Enoch said. "Nobody denies that."

"And I don't feel bad about it even one little bit. I would do it all over again, the same way if I had to. The point is" —she fixed on me, ,daring me to be indifferent—"well the whole *point* is I could have got him out of there if I tried harder, well not *just* me, but this bank I had dealings with at that time and William didn't lift a finger either . . . not that that's why I decided to abandon him though. He was a crook, out and out. He wasn't *worth* getting out of there. —You remember Anna? That girl we had for you when you were little? When I marched you over there right after the war?"

"Anneke," I said, distracted that she should suppose impermanence in me of a vividness of fear.

"That's the one, you always did do her name with a good accent—she practically made a foreigner out of you anyhow, the way you picked up the language over there. Of course you were *born* on that side of the water, that probably has something to do with it. You remember we sent her away? He was pumping her for information, naturally at that age you wouldn't realize that. Once a crook always a crook, that's the point, you follow? He came right up to us and right out with it and asked for money, that's the calibre he is, you follow? Well I *knew* all that, practically from the beginning. He didn't make a fool out of *me*, maybe out of plenty of others, but not out of me. Out of the blue I went home and left him. Pure and simple out of the blue. He never knew what hit him, you see what I mean. You don't get over a shock of that nature, and ten years later he turns up nearly insane with spite, *not* a normal man by anyone's standards, and asks for money. As far as that girl goes, well that was all vicarious, that's what I mean by not normal. What do you call it again? Enoch? In psychology?"

He waited with nostrils shrewd and stretched wide. "Call what?"

"Something standing for something else."

"A stand-in."

"That's *movies*. Psychology I want. It's a *term*."

"Metonomy."

"Is that it? It *sounds* Freudian, but not exactly, I don't know, maybe it's Jungian, is that why? Metamorphosis? Anyhow *she* was working for *me*, so it gave him this feeling that if he influenced *her*, he was getting at me—"

"Ius primae noctis," Enoch said.

"I'm sure that's not it. Look, never mind, will you? It doesn't matter what it's called, it's what happened."

"What happened was you paid him," I said, but she did not hesitate.

"We got rid of him. It was a nice little wish-fulfillment thing he was acting out with that girl, a cheeky type anyhow. I don't know how he worked up an image of me out of *her*, but that's how they do it. There doesn't have to be any moral resemblance, let alone physical. Fetishism. Her attitude was the world owed her a living. We got rid of them both. The only reason I'm telling you this is to show it wasn't the first time I had to get rid of him. The *first* time I just came home. Left him. Look, it's what I just said, plain ordinary abandonment. Maybe he would die in the war, maybe he wouldn't. Naturally he survived. That type always does, they're indestructible. In this world the worst always triumph. I could give ninety-three-thousand examples. I don't say I *wanted* him to die, it was just a bet I had with myself."

"You ought to quit lying," Enoch said.

"I'm not lying. It's a fact, why should I want him to die?"

He ignored this. "After all she's going to him."

"I know that. I know who she's going to."

"Then quit lying to her."

"I'm not lying. You can't contradict one single thing. What happened happened. Now listen. Was it abandonment pure and *simple?* Was he an out-and-out crook from the first *minute?*"

"Allegra."

"Allegra Allegra. Did I run from him the way you run from a plague? Cholera? Malaria?"

"Allegra," he said. The name, or his voice giving it out in succession, sounded like an object: a table, a book. "You don't save anything this way."

"You think I don't realize? I realize that. What's there to save? How do you think I feel, her getting it like that—the Goddamn bloody way he picked to tell her: that word. I didn't think he'd do it that way. I mean not that *word.* I thought he'd do it with plenty of embroidery, *decent* words at least. I thought he'd do it like a lawyer, damn it."

"Credit him for doing it at all, will you? Don't dream," he said. "If it had been left to Nick—"

"*I* don't know, how should I know how Nick would do it? Maybe better, maybe worse. How do I know how he's going to act with her? What I'm getting at is William at least was supposed to make something fancy and legal out of it, not plunk plunk hello you're a so-and-so. He could have said it in a, well I don't know, a figure of speech."

"There are no figures," he sighed, "of speech."

"Yes there are. Bar sinister, there's one. Hugh taught me that years ago. It was part of a joke once when William came down. To the camp."

Enoch said, "Don't you see you don't change things by changing them in your imagination—"

"He didn't have to say issue either. Illegitimate is bad enough, he didn't have to say issue. It sounds like out of a nineteenth-century hospital where the doctors don't wash their hands. Leeches and things. Sores gushing. A run of bad blood. He doesn't *have* any imagination, he could have done a fancy legal job, never mind this hacksawing."

"It's not William's imagination that's at fault," Enoch said.

"Because he doesn't *have* any, I just told you."

"The most ruthless words are the legal ones," Enoch said, "they have the vice of accuracy."

"Now tell me something new. Tell me about the decline and fall of the Roman Empire. You think I don't know that? You think I haven't had any experience with legal words? You take a perfectly *beautiful* word, you give it to a lawyer and it ends up meaning something just the opposite, ugly as sin, oh but *terribly* exact, you have to walk right down the middle of the white line the pirates draw on the gangplank for you. I've had plenty of experience! You'd think if somebody gave you a trust it would mean they trusted you, but what it really means is they *don't,* they think you're deaf and blind and don't know the most obvious things about life."

"Namely," Enoch said barrenly, "that in life nothing is obvious."

"I hate that word."

"Obvious?" he guessed. "Nothing? Life?"

"Oh stop. Imagination. Damn it, what do you think we're talking about? You don't listen to me. You listen for a minute and then you quip and then you don't listen. I *listen* at least. You were just telling me you don't change things if you imagine you're changing them, true?—so then please explain how we happened to give her twelve safe years, you said it yourself, you *said* twelve safe years, and didn't we change things by letting her imagine something that—well, that divorce business, say. It changed things for her, didn't it? It kept her free all that time, right? And the whole thing was imagination, right?"

"Al-*leg*-ra," he enunciated with drained patient toneless-
ness.

"You want to make me hate my own *name*, Enoch? Say
leg like that again and I'll kick you with it."

"Don't feed her fairy tales."

"What fairy tales? *What* fairy tales? He didn't come sucking around that Anneke ten years after? He didn't get stuck
for the whole war over there? Look, I don't remember any
hordes of lawyers and bankers and ex-Youth Leaders running
around in circles trying to find him and get him out, do
you?"

"I think," Enoch said, "she should read now."

"Read what? Enoch, you're crazy. What she *should* do is
pack," my mother argued. "I've had Janet standing by for
days just *for* that, every grip in the house wide open, there's
not an article of hers that isn't ironed and ready. She doesn't
have to do anything but point a fingernail at what she wants
to take, and *that's* too much for her . . . as it is she reads
more than what any sane person would call normal. Before
you got home she was reading newspapers like a fanatic.
Mental health columns, everything."

"She should read," he repeated, "history. Here," he told
me, "third drawer down, compartment in the back: a little
history of àbandonment: cardboard box with foolish stripes
all over it, the whole thing holographic and incredibly ancient, you can't miss it," and held up the key to his desk, a
short brass bar crowned at one end, club-footed at the other,
and, it turned out, body-warm. He had been fondling it inside
his pocket all the while.

"What are you up to?" my mother asked; already it was a
plaint of denial. "What are you *giving* her?"

"Hell," he answered, a noun, and tossed the key for me to
catch; it came winking down near my shoe, attached in flight
to its little ring, and displaced in me, even before I bent to
take it from the carpet, a ferocious image. "She's entitled to
it same as anyone," Enoch said, while I dived and tapped yellow metal teeth: the touch of points restored me to shock, as
though this room were that old other room where my mother
had locked me into freedom, naked as birth, and really as
though this small sweated key from Enoch's hand, tinkling
along its ring, could chink out reluctant contemplations—a
blue bicycle cradled in a hedgè shaped like a duck, able to
rattle, doomed to clatter and chime, a belfry of mobile violence, each wheel-hoop a spinning coin great as a gong; and

the key itself indistinguishable from that old rusted giant
which had lain like an icon in my mother's palm, cold as
cash.

3

So I found her letters, and read them through against the
scratch of her long argument, and was soon done with them
(having skipped the philosophy parts), and knew as little of
Brighton as they gave—my mother meanwhile protesting, declaring she had never seen them in her life before, calling
them phony contrivances, calling them forgeries, denying her
own handwriting, blaming me for looting, for snooping, for
attacking her privacy, for crushing the box, for stealing the
key, for misunderstanding her feelings, for being unable to
conceive of the nature of Brighton, or the nature of those old
early days, or the nature of Nick, or the nature of Enoch,
whom, she ended, she could easily have had arrested for burglary.

But she was watching me with eager looks: "Now you see
how it was! Exactly what I said. He was swallowed up right
into the middle of the war. So I left him. The chronology
doesn't matter. Who left who doesn't matter. The main thing
is I didn't marry him. I couldn't, not with the war. Otherwise
I would have. I would have, Enoch knows that. But I had to
leave without him, on account of the war."

"Hear it," Enoch said, "how the maze of pride writhes
around a new corner. Let it go, Allegra. Drop it. Let it stand.
You don't need to try this—"

"Try what? Try what?" she appealed. "I said just exactly
what happened. I *said* abandonment."

"You don't have to justify yourself," he finished hopelessly.

"I'm not justifying myself. You think I'm justifying myself
to bourgeois morality, right? That's what you think? Well I'm

not. I say the hell with bourgeois morality. I've always felt
that way. It's been my position from the beginning."

"We're not at the beginning any more."

"Then what are we at? The end? I don't know about you,
I'm not at the end of anything. I'm just starting! You think
an Embassy is nothing? Anyhow I'm *not* justifying myself to
bourgeois morality, I'm justifying myself to *her*."

"It's all the same," he said.

"No it's not," I said.

"There!" said my mother, snatching me for sudden ally.
"See? She's not as shallow as you make her out to be, at least
she's capable of understanding what an Embassy means. Only
when the time comes," she warned me, "you'd better change
your attitude. I'm not a liberal any more, if liberal signifies I
have to tolerate gossip. My business is my business, nobody
else's." She hardened: "Respectable boys don't take out running sores, they don't marry issues, remember that while
you're deciding to be so liberal."

"I'm not respectable enough to *decide* to be liberal."

"Oh fine, listen to that! Enoch, you heard that. You heard
it for yourself. Where's an attitude like that going to lead?"

"You are whatever your mother wants you to be," he told
me: "Apparently she wants you to be respectable."

I laid the bundle of letters on the bed and said nothing.

"I don't want her to be anything," my mother remonstrated, "except free. As long as she's free," she said, but this
was mechanical: it was not her thought. Her thought was
something else. "*We're* free," she explained. "Free as kings."

"An Ambassador," Enoch observed, "is not exactly an absolute monarch."

"I know that," she said demurely.

"An Ambassador," Enoch observed again, "is not exactly
left to do as he pleases. Neither is his wife."

"I know that."

"Then our freedom, you see, is not what you imagine."

"Yes it is," my mother said. "We're free to take the Embassy."

He said slyly, "You wouldn't trade the Embassy for Brighton?"

Her gaze floated over me.

"That was fake crying before," she gave out finally.

"I took it," Enoch said hollowly, "for grief."

But she was swift to pin him: "Is that why you called it
stupid?"

"Fake is stupid," he blew back at her.

"You didn't know it was fake, it's just that you don't care what I'm feeling," she complained. "You don't take me seriously, you're always clowning."

"I am the grin," Enoch said, "in your chagrin."

"See?"

"I don't like your blasphemy," he said: "It's blasphemous to simulate despair. There's plenty of the original in the world."

"Oh, the world!" she said in the shrill consummation of her disgust.

"You weren't feeling it," he accused.

"No," she admitted.

"You didn't feel a thing."

"It's wrong not to feel a thing, isn't it? I don't feel anything at all about any of that, it's peculiar. It's all gone."

"Brighton?" he asked.

"Nick," she heard herself reply.

"Ah," Enoch said, and sealed in that enclosing syllable their unanimity, self-amazed. It drove a gate against me; wedding-glue had cemented shut the seams at last. I foresaw the Embassy, a sandstone palace in an alien nation with an iron gate coiling up its scrolled crest through shimmering queer foreign winds, and staves like spears or lances, and myself never in it. I would stay behind, I would never enter. It was Enoch's house, that Embassy, bought for him by my mother, paid for by my surrender to my father; I would never enter it. I had never entered William's house; I foresaw I would never enter Enoch's. Did they pity me, those counterfeit fathers, false Enoch, false William, who gave me for hostage so that my mother in her appetite might take an Embassy?

I went to pack.

"—Wait a minute, will you?" She stopped me on the way; fatigue narrowed the bone of her nose; her nostrils seemed to waver independent of structure. "Now listen here, I never told you any lies at all, you follow? I mean look—suppose I'd married Nick, you think I could *stay* married? To a vagrant, a bum? An out-and-out crook? I would've divorced him in the end anyway, you follow? It comes to the same thing, you see my point?"

But there was power in the room: Enoch exultant under its plume, a crease of elation in either cheek, his forehead heavy, white, shining with relief. He had her now. She had sloughed off not Brighton (and what was Brighton after all?),

but Nick. He had never feared Brighton, he had never feared
me: only Nick. And he had her now, and was, as she said,
free as a king. He had her. She reminisced for him; she was
telling how, the very day she married him under William's
high jealous shadow, in the flesh-gleam of William's wife's
scorning glovelessness, all the while she was missing Nick.
The fractional cut of diffidence she had earlier opened to me
left no stitch or ridge or fissure: she was whole, he had her
whole.

She missed no one.

To me she said: "Of course it was a fib—Enoch's saying
he didn't have any ambition. He said it the first night we
were married, it turned out it was his way of covering up. He
always has to cover things up, he's terribly complicated. It's
right in his temperament, being negative about things. Negative and proud. The more negative and proud he is the more
he's craving something. I ought to *know* him by now! Take
my word for it: he's got a hollow craving in him, more than
anyone, more than I have. That's why he's the only person I
could have married, logically speaking."

My stepfather responded to this with an uncommon glimmer of smile. "Logically speaking," he began, in a voice so
given over to mastery that I was sure he was about to disclose a conspiracy of advice for me to take with me, "there
are neither lies nor fibs. Lies and fibs contradict the truth,
and contradictions don't exist in logic"—it was only another
conundrum, one of his jokes; he had nothing to tell me. "And
you," he told my mother, "crave nothing at all," which, while
never touching himself, penetrated her exactly. She missed no
one, she missed nothing.

4

In that place there was a short tree crouched over its short
trunk, not much higher than a bush, and with a full misty

mane like a bush, and all its comb of yellow leaf stained through by sunlight, the wide wash of day narrowed gunlike and spat out in points of magnetic shimmer on each tremulous lamina, the whole blown head of it coruscating like a transparent great net of caught fishes: the little caught tree wriggling, and with every wriggle enmeshing itself still more inescapably in its bag of light; every breath it dared to take sluicing it in a supernal flash—tossing itself there, on the edge of the swamp, back and forth, dazzling, darting.

My mother's chauffeur said, "This looks like it, miss. A bit of dock left here. I was told a bit of old dock," and put my suitcase—I had taken only one—on a nailed-together pattern of soaked colorless faintly noiseful planks. "Must've been deeper here once—deep water—if a ferry ran. They must've cut in deep here, for a ferry."

"It was long ago," I said, looking out at the long grasses up to their knees in water.

"We been out of the Bronx only ten minutes, that's the amazing thing. All new roads up around here that didn't use to be. Don't know the neighborhood, miss, or we wouldn't've got so lost. Sorry about that, miss."

"It's all right."

"You want me to wait with you, miss?"

"No, it's all right."

"Perfectly fine with me, miss, whatever Mrs. Vand said. Maybe Mrs. Vand didn't realize what it was out here, swamp—"

"You'd better go, if she told you that."

"Trouble is maybe they come by to pick you up and left, us being so late and nobody here," he said, changing the position of his sweated cap and worrying over my mother's story. It was, of course, a bucolic; a false bauble; one of her fancies of what my life might be, if only I were free, if only I could have been what she called "normal"—a squad of school friends coming down a sparkling little stream in a chartered excursion boat heavy with its party of incredibly eligible boys handsome as lords and loyal steadfast girls in butterfly skirts hanging over the rail, shouting steering directions at the patient cheery captain, crowing out my name when they spotted me signalling with both arms aloft on a painted toy pier, surrounded by valises. "You know maybe a boat couldn't get through any more, what with all them weeds growing around, or we got the wrong place could be." He drew from his breast pocket a scrap of inky map, which Enoch had made for him the day before, based on a gasoline-station highway guide and obscure sources of his own. "Up there's the throughway, and we left the car *here,* up near the clover-leaf, which by the way we might get ticketed for, I *told* Mrs. Vand, and here's this little road we just come by . . . it looks right, miss. What with the dock, it looks like what they said. You sure you don't want me to wait a while, miss? Till they get you safe on that boat?"

"Not if my mother told you not to."

He frowned at this, and walked for a step or two, and then took off his cap and let the line of wet dammed by it descend; he was an old man, and had an old man's chicken-neck, each crowded fold a limp ring of heat. "What if you're stranded, miss?"

"I'll be all right, really."

"You're late now? Mrs. Vand said one o'clock positively?"

"You'd better go," I told him, unwilling to accede to that tentative kindliness of his which, like much of the kindliness of people who find themselves servants of the old sort in a democratic republic, was subversive. He meant to enlist me against my mother's recklessness. He thought it wrong to leave a girl alone in a swamp, and the tender backward-twisting glimpse he snatched of his boots scalloped with mud up to the heel was intended to entice me to conspire with him against my mother's idiocies. I watched him go up the thread of path, surprised there *was* a path at all; he vanished between spears of man-tall weed, and then re-appeared in parts, sometimes only a slice of pink neck meandering like a fly. He was circling to avoid the sudden ponds that sprang into reflections as soon as the ground was pressed. He was vain of his boots. Now and again he bent to wipe them with his handkerchief: I could see him dip and rise, dip and rise, the cloth sliding like a white face between the green high bars, and from the top hairs of the embankment heard him call down: "There's a police 'phone up on the highway, miss, about a quarter-of-a-mile down aways, in case you get stranded in there—all right, miss?"

"Right," I said—this leaped up briefly in the stillness like an animal bark and shamed me. He stood awhile, looking toward the water, squinting down under the awning of his cap. My mother had told him one o'clock because Tilbeck had told her two. She plotted to give me over unobserved by anyone, even by her driver, who was less than anyone. Her driver lingered, not daring to call again, though his shadowless noon figure, the sun a bright blot in the middle of his chin, continued to grow curiously out of the hill into the sky. Finally he trod away without crackle or splinter; up there he had clean clover under his feet.

I arranged my suitcase flat side up and sat on it. The dock stirred with an indoor creak like a rocking-chair, and I thought of the Pink Lady, salmon-shining, clicking its vigorous optimistic engine, arriving to meet the landing with a proud and caressing exactitude, and William—an aggrieved William already not very young, made patient by hopefulness, and neither patience nor hopefulness the natural properties of his mind—that early sorrowing William driving right off her back onto a once-upon-a-time road as buried now as Caesar's, the paving worn to pebbles and woven over by an irreversible plait of reeds and rushes and mud and years. Years, years, covered that place. The quiet was tumultuous with insect chatter: the works of a perpetual-motion machine which had been going on forever and ever, from beginnings no one remembered or believed in: the grasses had sung out their riots for my girl-mother on this spot while she waited to cross the water home to Duneacres. My lique-maniacal grandfather had kept motor-launches for that purpose, each maneuvered by a butler of its own: and, after that stupefying climax of abundance, came the practical puritanical Pink Lady stuttering back and forth to serve my grandfather's museum, which never was or would be. There were two waters: the far and the near. The far was a streak of white brilliance; the far was a shawl of lightning pinned down. The near was fecund, a black skin pinched and mottled by barnacles of glitter, tranquil except when something—a frog? a grasshopper?—jumped. The near was teased by leggy eels half an inch long, and gauze flies like fragile volant tubes of grass, with green wings like grass, and just-visible green feet like separate airy grass beings.

In the middle of this the tree blazed. Lens upon lens burned in the leaves with a luminosity just short of glass and nearer to vapor; the veins were isinglass ducts swarming with light, running knife-bright into stems, and the stems pursuing twigs, and the twigs branches, and the branches hurtling into the bole like rays recaptured, undoing refraction: the whole short powerful trunk a prism in remorse gathering in its tribes of beams, all imaginable exiled light flowing and flowing home to the mother-light.

In the penumbra of its anti-shadow I felt myself an object

of meditation. It seemed I was watched. It seemed I was contemplated. A consciousness dangled. An eye pondered. I viewed; I was viewed. A radiance lifted itself from the shoulders of the tree and hung itself, by some unknown manner of passage, close against my face, so that, to see, I had to stare through a tissue of incandescence, and saw in a spontaneity of concentration the lit water, the far and the near, the far stream of white and the glint-pointed near, the revolving veil of mites and motes in their inexorable gold whirl, and showering the swamp's edge with elusive sparkles, the extraordinary little tree. The tree was an eye. It observed me. The tree was a mind. It thought me. The tree lived because I lived. It burned for me, it leaped all whiteness and all light into being, and for me; for me it consumed itself, because I had made it, I was its god, my gaze had forced its fires, the sanctity of my wonder had quickened its awe; it had found me out in that grove of grasses, and knew me as a holy interloper; I appeared like god or goddess on a platform in that waiting water, a miraculous preparation, unaccountable in that place, undesignatable and unlooked-for in that place, and I came to the wooden lily-leaf to sit upon it and stare, as once the Buddha sat and stared, and, seeing, showed himself divine; I was nymph, naiad, sprite, goddess; I had gifts, powers; and the tree worshipped, because I could conjure flame in it, I could snuff it, I could bore it through with a devouring torch, I could deliver it into its own night, it was in my hand, having aroused it to transparencies I could at will shadow it and snuff it.

Then it was snuffed. The light went out of it. The sun slid down and away, and leaned a long leaning, so that the far water and the near water were the same; and the light went out of the tree. It stood there drab as toad's skin, and commonplace, already browning with autumn intimations. Its posture was undistinguished, it had an awkward foot with a rooted burly toe, it climbed out of the bank of that marsh—if a marsh, that most gradual of ideas, can be said to have a bank—a larger and more ragged yellow weed in a habitat of weeds. It did not notice me. I knew myself to be profane. It neither reverenced nor perceived. It was blind, it was dumb, it was a dwarf which could hallow nothing. The gazing light was dead in it. The sun had carried off its consecrations. On the rooted dock that had survived the Pink Lady I sat all the afternoon, waiting for my father. I equipped myself to converse with him. I began by introducing myself, and discov-

ered an embarrassment, not in him, over William's surname.
To counteract this I spoke to the tree (which out of convenience represented Tilbeck) of the tree: "A dryad," I said,
"is an optical effect." But this was false, and not to the point.
"A dryad," I said, "is one of us, ourselves. I have been," I
said, "a dryad. I have given life," I said, "to a tree. Today.
Here. In the swamp. At the ferry dock. Before the late afternoon." But this was fey, and full of spells, and uncertain to
attract a thief and crook. Or perhaps he would not remember
how they threw darts in olden times at the Brighton dryad,
Allegra and himself, or how the Brighton dryad was extin-
guished by a cry exactly in the moment the baby's howling
head was born, so that it seemed the Brighton dryad had died
of her own cry. To the tree representing Tilbeck I said (but
none of this aloud: solitude, so as not to be self-suspect,
makes dignity), "You are not punctual. It was early afternoon when I arrived, now it is late afternoon. I have observed the passage of the day's center from a point just behind this recently looking-glass tree, silver-backed by the sun,
in which I nearly saw myself, and *would* in fact have seen
myself had I not been distracted by suddenly turning holy, to
a hollow over there behind those very high, very erect cattails. And still you have not come. And the tree is now perfectly opaque, and even drops a shadow. Clarity has waned."
This was better; it was at least explicit, and left out dryads,
which he might, after all, think a stupidity if not a madness,
never reminded of that Brighton dryad of his own discovery,
or invention, or more probably plagiarism; but I had the
fresh advantage of my mother's letters. For memory, he
might apply to me. Old imaginings I could provide, but if he
had no new ones he would likely not recognize the old. Perhaps through thievery, through crookery out and out,
through blackmail perhaps, imagination had left him and
play had left him and all the woodland flowers listed in the
ENCHIRIDION had leaped with their limp stalks safe out of
his buttonhole.

When he came, he had no buttonhole. He had no shirt. In
surprise I heard the crisp plummeting of oars—I had thought
he tillered a motor. Plash followed plash. The middle water
chirped at the slap of the blade and trilled at its lift. Steady
margins of interlocking whirlpools touched at my raft. I
stood to see over the grasses. A naked back glided, tensed,
again glided. Naked arms slowly propelled themselves up and
around and down in a cleverly timed, infinitely leisurely, su-

perabundantly self-possessed orbit, and at each rise I spotted an arc of unexplored skin reaching from under the armpits to the waist, where no passion, not even the sun's, had ever lain.

I was no private visitor. The boatman was a boy.

5

He was not a very large boy, but he was master of his craft. He drew one oar in and raised it dripping over the side and set it down in the hull, doing all this with a single competent thin-wristed hand; the other held on to the second oar. Then he took the second oar by the handle and altered its angle to that of a paddle, and turned the boat efficiently within the narrowest possible radius, and coaxed it toward the dock, whispering it through the grasses, and blinking out now and then an eager little nose supporting eye-glasses twinkling light like semaphores. He moved in his craft like a Viking child, or like a sort of Norse centaur, the top half human, the lower half presumably the parts of a boat; his arms circled as though air were a familiar kind of pool, and his boat circled skimmingly, as though water were as yielding as air.

Twice I heard my father's name. Was it boy's voice or water's voice? "Tilbeck," I heard. And again it came: "Tilbeck."

"Hello," I called.

A scared green frog no longer than a hairpin landed in front of my feet, gave me a primordial glance, and shuddered into a flying arc when the boat bumped.

"You want me?" I said.

"Mr. Tilbeck does. He said to look for a lady on a dock and yell his name so you'd know who I came instead of." He stood up; he had legs after all. He said critically, "He didn't mention a valise or anything."

I handed it down all the same. "In that case he doesn't think very practically. No, if you take it that way you'll overturn."

He took it that way and did not overturn. "Yes he does. He's *very* practical. That's why in the end he decided to let me come. You don't have to be afraid. I'm a good rower. Put the other foot in first. Hold on to that old rusted ring sticking out from the side there. Of the dock. That's all right, don't worry if she tips a little. She'll be fine once you're in. That's the way. You'll be safe with me. I'm a good swimmer too. I've already got my junior lifesaver's certificate. I don't mean *with* me. Next year I get my senior lifesaver's certificate. That's the one that says carry on person at all times to prove competence. You have to be thirteen to qualify. My birthday isn't till next April. Actually I can qualify for it right now, if you don't count age requirements. I'm not saying that for self-praise though. My father says never indulge in self-praise except when absolutely necessary for the purpose of reassuring others. I just thought you'd like to know you'll be pretty safe with me. Safe as if Mr. Tilbeck came himself. He didn't on account of the motor."

"Safer maybe," I said, settling on the plank seat in the bow, next to the suitcase. It was crowded.

"Well, I wasn't thinking of *that*."

"You weren't thinking of what?"

He said proudly, "*I* never get sick on water."

"I hope that doesn't count as indulging in self-praise," I said. "Does Mr. Tilbeck?"

"Well, I'd hate to say. I think I've *heard* him say things that sound like self-praise now and then, but I might be mistaken. It's hard to tell what's just plain self-praise and what's reassurance for the safety of others. Anyhow my father hasn't mentioned it to him."

"I meant does he get sick on water."

"My father never gets sick. Oh, I see. Mr. Tilbeck you're referring to. Once in a while he does. He told my father. He said 'I get sick on water, but never on anything stronger.' Actually that's a sort of joke because even though my father didn't laugh my mother did. She says all ministers are humorless. When my mother laughs at anything it means it's Over My Years. The first time I ever heard her say that I thought she meant *ears*. I used to feel up around my ears to figure out what was over them. I was afraid something funny was growing there, that's why people were laughing."

"Is your father a minister?"

"Oh no, but I'm going to be, D.V. D.V. stands for Deus Volens, it means God willing. Don't you know my father?

He's not very obscure. He's Purse the paleontologist. Oh wait, you'd better not. She's kind of puddly down there." I was lifting the suitcase with an uneasy jerk, setting it down on the bottom, out of the way. "Here," he ordered, "I'll put that right up with me, there's plenty of room. I'm very narrow at the hips. That's all right, I've got it. I'm very strong."

I said, surveying the damp-darkened floor, "She *is* pretty wet, I didn't really notice. Have we sprung a leak?"

"It's just general splashing from before. Kick-back from the motor."

"But there isn't any motor."

"That's the whole point. They've been trying to fix it all afternoon. They oiled it and everything. It starts and sort of splashes all over and then stops. When it stops it makes this very peculiar noise. Mr. Tilbeck told me it's just exactly like the sound eunuchs make between their teeth once a month to convey a message to the sultan. That's just a figure of speech. He's never really been to Turkey or any place like that. Of course there are very few sultans any more. He was referring to a time before they had modern democracy. I don't know if they ever had sultans in Pakistan though. You've heard we're going to Pakistan, haven't you?"

"I don't remember your mentioning it," I said, "so far."

"It was in the *Times*. Do you read the *Times*? It's this very famous dig they have out there. This bunch of archaeologists found these very interesting humanoid bones. They nearly went crazy. Jotham—you know Jotham? Jotham the anthropologist?—well he said Piltdown all over again. Fraud. Of course they don't *know*. They're having this terrific argument about this toe-bone they found. You know you can tell by the toes what their posture was. Do you read *Popular Ancients?* It's having this terrific argument with *National Antiquity* because *National Antiquity* had a special color photograph of this toe-bone and under it they had 'Creeping Shikarpur Man.' *Popular Ancients* put 'Bending Shikarpur Man.' Anyhow that's why *we're* going. For all *they* know it could be a marsupial toe. They have to have my father out there right away. He got a speed-up on his Ford. Do you know what a Ford is? It's money. I bet you thought it was a car. Shikarpur isn't even where the dig is, it's only near, but we have to start out from there. It's a city. They named the bones they found after it. All nine of us are going, even Dee. The visa man said we've got the longest papers of 1957. Two feet at least.

Dee's my brother but only a baby so my grandma thinks it's awful."

"Is she going too? Your grandma?"

This made him laugh. "*She* never goes anywhere except to meeting. She's too old. She had to have this wheelchair, so my mother built her one. It's an invention. It can climb stairs one by one all by itself. It's got a motorized ratchet on it. It's set for an eight- by six-inch step. The thing about our meeting-house is it has all these stairs."

I leaned to search over the water for the dock: it existed as an invisible point, a platonic hypothesis, below a small smudge of decaying cabbage-head, which I took to be the little far tree. A white line of highway sat like a rigid hat on top of the swamp. Where we had been yielded to distance. Where we were throbbed with progress. The boy rowed his toy. His feet were wedged against its sides as if in stirrups. He commanded it the way a rocking-horse is commanded. We pursued our arc of advance seriously and without whimsy, fitting the crescent of our keel to hollows beneath us, the water rapidly vacating like a cheek drawn in. "She's moving beautifully," I told the boy.

"I'm a very fast rower," he acknowledged.

"Is it far?"

"It took *us* only fifteen minutes. We came over from New Rochelle in this very small launch my father hired. You know New Rochelle?"

"I was there once," I asserted without grace.

"Well, you know Polygon's Boat Yard? It's right off Echo Bay. That's where we got this launch. It's named *The Polygon,* after Polygon. We just about all fit. It's really pretty small for a launch. You can't squeeze everything into a purse, but you can squeeze a Purse into anything. That's a joke my mother's always saying about us. Polygon's man is coming back for us in a couple of days. We've been here practically a whole week. He's a Japanese man, but Polygon's a Greek. Did you ever see him? Polygon? He's very fat, that's why I ask. When *we* first saw him my mother said he'd had all his angles filed off, but then he wanted to charge us a whole lot and she said he *knew* them all just the same. Then Polygon said he had to charge us so much because he charges per passenger, but my father said with nine of us it wasn't fair, he should charge us just for the launch and the Japanese man to run it. Then my mother said it was injustice for Polygon to fill his purse by filling *The Polygon* with Purses, because you could put a Purse in a Polygon and still make a profit, but if you put a polygon in a purse it would stay just as flat as before. So then Polygon laughed and said lady that's Greek to me. And then my mother said well, Polygon has a point, *several* points in fact, you can't deny that if you put *Mr.* Polygon in a purse it would turn out nice and round after all, points or no points. Then the Japanese man said lady don't try to bargain with Greeks. Then my father paid."

I observed that he was panting slightly.

I asked, "You mean he paid per Purse?"

"He had to. Did you ever read *The Odyssey?* Greeks are very hard. You know my mother has this sort of riddle she invented. 'If the money in parsimony can be seen it won't be perceived' is how it goes but it isn't wonderful until you hear how we spell the last word," and he recited aloud capital letters and hyphens several times over until I had captured understanding. "You see how wonderful it is? 'If the money in parsi-money can be seen it won't be Purse-sieved.' Harriet Beecher printed the whole thing on a chart. You see when my mother and father got married they took this vow that they would never spend more than fifty-five cents a pound on any cut of meat. And they never have. The first joke my mother ever said to my father was 'When meat is dear, Purse-severe' "—and very politely and perseveringly he spelled out the joke for me, which, however, I was this time able to seize at once. Mrs. Purse, it seemed, had a great many jokes, but, analyzed according to their dominant principle, they could be reduced to a single crystalline substance, what some would call an article of faith—she believed she had married a man with a comical name; and, further, she believed this placed her under a certain obligation to the muse, whom she unflaggingly Purse-secuted. But this I was not able to conclude until afterward.

"Your mother," I said diligently, to please my navigator, "must write the slogans on buses," and dipped a forefinger over the side to feel the current.

"Oh no, my father wouldn't let her," he told me gravely, "he says *never* deface *any*thing, especially library books. He was really pretty bothered when Mr. Tilbeck explained how he used up the beds."

"The beds?" I said.

"Well, *he* sleeps in the kitchen, on a green sofa with little French people doing these minuets all over it in the embroidery. Mr. Tilbeck likes to have a roof over his head. He said that to my mother. That's why he stays in the house even though nothing works in it. The stoves don't work and the faucets don't work and the electricity doesn't work. Nothing works in the whole house. That's how come there aren't any beds. The radiators don't work either."

"I don't see the connection," I said.

"Mr. Tilbeck chopped them up for the fireplace last winter. All the beds in the house."

"Oh," I said.

"There's plenty of other furniture upstairs though. Only there's this very unusual sort of purple mold growing over most of it. In the kitchen there's this tremendous old refrigerator that doesn't work and *it's* full of purple mold. Harriet Beecher and Al and Foxy all climbed in to see if they would fit but Mr. Tilbeck said they might die in there if the door closed on them. So they got out. He's very nice to children, you know."

"Who's Harriet Beecher?"

"My sister. We say Harriet Beecher for short. Her whole name is Harriet Beecher Stowe Purse. When my mother wants her to keep quiet she says 'Harriet Beecher, Stowe your tongue in its Purse.' That's because Harriet Beecher is an unusually talkative girl."

"The price of being a Purse," I noted. "Extravagance of language. Money talks."

He appeared to appreciate this, though not much. "Well, I'm quite extravagant that way myself on occasion. Basically that's the reason I'm the one who turned out to be the family black sheep. They thought Foxy was going to be, but now I guess I'm the one for sure."

"But didn't you just say you're going to be a minister?"

"I said I'm going to be a minister D.V."

"Oh I see. Your mother disapproves of a Purse with initials on it."

"She disapproves of a minister," he said gloomily, "because my father does. He says it's nothing but self-assertion. Our meeting doesn't have a minister. We just have this quiet and you can say things if you feel the spirit but I want to be a real *pastor* with a flock and everything and a pulpit and these very long sermons I like to make up. So that's how come I'm the black sheep."

"In this case the black shepherd," I observed. "What was Foxy's offense?"

"Self-assertion, same as me."

"Another minister?"

"Not Foxy," he said scornfully. "Foxy's against ministers. You see he thought he ought to act exactly like the person he was named for, or what was the use of his being named for that person, and he said he had to wear this black coat without a collar and this big black flat hat and everything, and say thee to everybody, to be true to himself. But my father said it was all just wilful self-assertion, and the reason they named him after George Fox in the first place was so he'd be courageous within but meek of mien and very plain and not go make a circus of himself everywhere. And Foxy said well Throw's worse, he wants to put an altar in the meeting and be a bishop and make people cough up their sins to him, and my father said well at least Throw doesn't put thee in his English compositions and get D in grammar."

"You're Throw?" I inquired.

"Henry David Thoreau Purse," he said grandly, "and Dee's Mohandas K. Gandhi, and Al's Bronson Alcott, and Manny's Walt Whitman, and Sonny's Ralph Waldo Emerson. We're all named after someone great. It was my father's idea. At first my mother thought it was pretty shocking. She even told my father it *might* be self-assertion and maybe even self-praise not to call one's children just John and Mary and Susan and plain names like that. But my father said it wasn't for self-assertion, it was for inspiration. And then my mother's whole face lit up and she said, 'Yes, that *is* a good thought, because you certainly can't make a silk Purse out of a sow's ear,' and so they did it."

"It's a remarkable story," I admitted. "I've never known any Quakers before."

"That's just what Mr. Tilbeck said. When he asked us to come and stay with him he said he wanted to be able to tell himself just once that he'd tented a Friend in need."

I watched the oars rise and mused in a corrective spirit and finally muttered "Tended."

"Oh no, tented, that's why my mother laughed so much. She laughed *very* much at that. It's a joke. You see Quakers are really called Friends."

"I know that. I read it in the *Times*," I said.

He devolved on me a wronged look. "It's not a very good joke. The real reason she laughed," and I took this as I was meant to, for a rebuke, "is that my father says always respond adequately to your host as long as a principle isn't being violated. You know all those old tents he has?"

"Who has?"

"Mr. Tilbeck. He dragged them out when we came and slammed the dust and plenty of caked mud out of them and put them up and now we sleep in them. He put them up right near this terrific sort of spring that comes right out of these real woods back of the house. It's terrifically sanitary. We brought our own soap. You wouldn't expect that primitive living could be so sanitary. My father says it's very good preparation for Pakistan."

"Oh," I said, enlightened, "tented a Friend. Yes. Did your mother top that one? It would be a Big Top, of course," I offered blandly.

He rewarded this sally into Mrs. Purse's inmost pouch with the stern avoiding gaze of an archbishop about to reprimand a poacher on ecclesiastical precincts; he missed a stroke of the oar, clapping wood on wood—the hull gave out a blank sound with no overtone—and for a moment we weaved without direction. "I guess she did," he informed me, and I thought he was patronizing me until I heard his reply, which vindicated his manner and humbled my own. "She said 'If you'll permit me to coin a phrase, Mr. Tilbeck, rely on it that you will always have a Friend in a Purse.' Then you know what Mr. Tilbeck said to that?"

"Bravo?" I asked.

"What?"

"He said bravo?" I ventured again. "*I* would have said bravo."

"No, no, he made a joke. He got the hang of it. Eventually everyone does. He said 'For a coin like that, go to a Purse.' That's not bad, you know."

"For a beginner," I agreed, "it's not bad. It didn't violate any principle? I suppose your mother responded adequately?"

"Oh yes, she laughed very much. We all did. If it wasn't for Mr. Tilbeck, who knows *where* we'd be—he's the one that saved us. My mother said he snatched us right out of the jaws of despair. She said we were all really very lucky to have met a Purse-snatcher."

I told myself privately that if they ever hanged Mrs. Purse for her wit, I should like to have charge of the Purse-strings.

"You see," explained my pilot, "the people we rented our house to had to move into it a whole week before it was time for us to leave for Pakistan from Idlewild Airport. You know Idlewild Airport? It's right near New York City. We were supposed to stay in this hotel in New York City for this

bunch of days in between, before we had to go to Idlewild
Airport. My father arranged it all in advance. He wrote for a
room reservation and everything. But when we got to this
hotel we had the reservation for, the manager came out and
looked at us and counted and said we couldn't stay there unless we took two more rooms. Then my father said it wasn't
fair and he didn't see why he should be forced to undergo all
that extra expense for no good reason. Then the manager
said because there are fire laws, and you can't have nine people in one room. Then my father said we certainly didn't
intend to set fire to the hotel. Then my mother said it was injustice and not the fire laws at all, because we were a united
family and the manager was just trying to divide one Purse
three ways to get more money. Then the manager made this
awful sort of demon's face and said he was very sorry but he
was pretty sure he didn't have any extra rooms anyhow so
would we please clear the lobby. So then we spent the whole
morning going to different hotels and they all treated us the
same way. My mother said New York City is very hard on
pocketbooks and Purses."

"But you were rescued all the same."

"Well, my father says expect the unexpected, that's how
come," he affirmed. "We had to give up after a while because
Dee was starting to holler, so we went into this Automat
place and sat down, the whole nine of us, and my father was
thinking maybe we ought to spend the money on the extra
rooms, we had to stay *some*where, and all the time we were
talking it over, there was this man. We didn't even notice
him. In New York City you never notice anybody, and this
man kept on sitting drinking coffee at a table and sort of
eavesdropping. It was terrifically discouraging. In spite of everything my mother made a joke, she said we reminded her
of the Children of Israel, we were so dis-Pursed, with no pillow for our wanderers' heads and no place to sleep. Then all
of a sudden this same man that was drinking coffee comes up
to her and says why not sleep with me, madam, if you people
would like to I could set up these tents for you on this property I have. He said it was on this island that's called Town
Island and there's no town on it, but if *we* came, right away
there'd be a whole population. Then he told us about hiring
Polygon's launch to come over with, because he had only this
one little motorboat that wouldn't hold us all. He said if we
didn't mind roughing it we could stay the whole week and
he'd be glad to have the company."

"And you accepted?" I marveled. "Just like that, out of the blue?"

"Sure, we took the train right out to the boatyard."

"They weren't afraid? Your father and mother?"

"Of what?"

"Of a stranger. It might have been an ambush. He could have robbed them. He might have been a murderer. His whole idea could have been to fleece them."

"Not Mr. Tilbeck!"

"But they didn't know."

"My father says never turn down an angel of mercy. My father says trust in your fellow-man and you trust in the Lord."

I murmured, "That sounds very nice."

"But it's true! It hasn't cost us a penny since we got here, that proves it. It's *much* cheaper than any hotel. —See that sort of bend in the shore line up ahead? No, across." He pointed and listlessly I followed his finger toward the green. "That means we're practically there. It isn't taking very long, is it? Even without the motor."

But I was preoccupied with a meditation: Gustave Nicholas Tilbeck as angel of mercy. "It hasn't cost a penny?" I repeated.

"Not even for the groceries. Mr. Tilbeck bought everything. That was when the motor was still working. We cook things over a campfire, like cave people."

"He hasn't said anything about money?"

"You mean *asked* for it?"

"Like rent," I said. "For putting you up, for instance. Or for anything. Money in general, I mean."

He shot out a quick scornful whistle. "Mr. Tilbeck's *rich.* He's got tons of money. He's got this whole *island.*"

"But he burns beds, washes in a brook, cooks in the open—"

"Well, he doesn't think it's worthwhile to rehabilitate the place. He told my father that. You see he doesn't really *live* there. He doesn't live there permanently. He's a traveler. He lives wherever he pleases. He has islands with old houses all over. He has an island right off Greece, right in the middle of the Mediterranean Ocean."

"Crete?"

"He didn't say its name. You know some islands don't have names. But he owns them all over. He's terrifically rich.

Somebody that rich wouldn't ask for rent, especially not from us. With nine of us it wouldn't be fair."

"It wouldn't be justice," I said. "Does your father believe that story?"

"My father says never look a gift horse in the mouth."

"That's new," I said. "That's one I never heard before. What about your mother?"

"She said it was bad manners to worry about anybody else's situation. She said we should just keep Purse-spective on our own."

"That makes sense too," I capitulated.

He spelled out c-e-n-t-s, and explained that his mother, being a Purse, insisted she was always full of this. "But my father told my mother confidentially one night that Mr. Tilbeck might be a counterfeiter," he informed me. "He has all this money. I saw it myself."

"Well, the question is did you see the minting machine? —To be fair, I mean."

But he had anticipated me. "Harriet Beecher and Manny and I looked all through the cellar and couldn't find it. He might keep it on one of his other islands though. He might keep it on Crete. You know what my mother said?"

I was afraid to hear; I dreaded Purse-iflage.

"She said confidentially to my father that Mr. Tilbeck is a habitual liar."

"And they don't mind that?"

"My father says it isn't necessary to believe the word of anyone but the Lord. Mr. Tilbeck told Harriet Beecher he might buy her some new dresses before we go to Idlewild Airport. He might get Al an accordion. Al's dying for an accordion. He might get my father a brand-new traveling case."

"Maybe all that's a lie."

"We *all* saw the money," he assured me, and I had a mournful yet comical intimation of how they, in Purse-suit of the schnorrer's famous golden fleece, intended to fleece the fleecer. "Schnorrer," I must in spite of awkwardness here interrupt, was a sly gift from my stepfather, flung down in my presence for his own mischief and his wife's mystification, and chipped from a language which he had once elucidated to my mother (who hated it) as being both remarkable and homely; but equally she hated knowing that he knew it, on account of which he had sometimes slipped me a word or two of it—"di goldene medina," he taught me to call America, whether with or without irony I was then too young to estimate—and vulgarly she warned him that he might yet forget himself and use his mamaloshen in direct address before the Senators: at which he nodded with the gladness of spitefully-overlooked incongruity—"Aha! Parasites and spongers! Do-nothings! Swillers at the troughs of drunken lobbyists! Take Hundt, that schnorrer—if he leaned any farther to the right they'd have to fish him out of the Atlantic Ocean! Take MacElroy, another schnorrer classique, with an absentee record as long as the history of the, the—gypsies! —Thought I'd say Jews, did you?" he cried and crowed, and the inimitable word tumbled into my possession to await its moment of attestation—which struck, surprisingly, in this boat that crossed a bay to take me to my father. I saw then, and with perfect conviction, the simultaneity and constriction of scope of the world's schnorrers—a Senator or two nibbling at this company and that, Tilbeck nudging, grasping, gleaming, menacing, the homiletic Purses out after the smell of convenience, cash, lodging, loneliness. Did my mother's money support them all? Did the blatant swelling of her investments, like the breathing of some gigantic horn-armored but entirely mythic creature—the gryphon, perhaps—nourish on the crest of their inhalations the whole dependent universe of schnorrers, the high and the low, the whole gratuitous grating ungrateful gratuitant but above all ingratiating company?—since, at least at first meeting, schnorrers are without doubt the most charming persons in any society, and attract deliciously before they prey. Did she, unawares, sway the companies that several of the most charming of all the Senators milked in return for certain insignificant exceptions, scarcely noticeable, in certain negligible bills? Or, to take another aspect of the same radiant herd, how many courtesies and generosities and canny gifts and little girls' dresses and rings for ladies and little boys' thingamajigs had she year after year unwittingly bought to please those charmers who chanced to please Gustave Nicholas Tilbeck? Plain that Connelly's account-books were the organisms on which now even this mob of nine lean Purses fed, and meanwhile—meanwhile? O shock of happenstance—curls of water poured off the oar-blades, and the boat without loss of tremor seemed not to move on the tremulous platter that moved beneath us.

"Why did you stop rowing?"

The boy had his fists secure in his lap; the wet paddles shone high in the air, dripping grandly. And there we were in

the middle of the bay—not, so far as I could see, a matter
yet of land ho.

"We're nowhere near a beach," I objected.

"How do you know there's a beach?" he caught me up. "I
didn't tell you there was."

"I *assume* there is," I said. "I was thinking of the footprint
in the sand. Robinson Crusoe. Don't all islands have beaches?"—but if I had assumed a beach it was because of that
other shipwreck in my brain, where early early and from the
start I had figmented a sandbar the color of gold, and a yellow shoal glowering with mist, and rocking there a figure
tugged and secreted like a sculpture by tide, or like the raised
effigy on a coin of some overrun civilization, the lineaments of
its caesar's profile swathed in undersea moss, the eye a
rubbed freckle, the noble nose worn to a snub, conquest sea-
dyed pale dead tan. My father's body lay in my brain, and in
the same sea-vessel yet elsewhere on still another beach the
body of my governess spread itself flat on a flat rock, sport-
ing motionless; and here is the lizard of my father's tread,
crouching; and Palestine burning; while beyond, in the water,
as they join, a book opens wings without lungs and drowns.

We sported motionless; the boy, the boat. "Bring down the
oars. Let's go on," I commanded.

But he had stopped to look me over.

"What does he want you for?"

A question that knows its own answer is a lie. "Who?" I
lied.

"Mr. Tilbeck. You didn't just go and invite yourself? He
asked you, didn't he?"

"Well, not exactly," I said. "I asked myself. It's a story.
You see I have this very rich mother. Not as rich as Mr. Tilbeck maybe, but still very rich. Extraordinarily rich. If you
put all the people who live on her in a spaceship the earth
would be left a bare skull. And one of the things about my·
mother is this: she wants me to be free. —You care to hear
this story?"

"Is it true?"

"Quakers don't lie."

"You're not a Quaker," he said.

"No," I said. "I'm a coxswain. Some coxswains lie and
some don't. You want to know what my mother means when
she says she wants me to be free? Bring down the oars or I
won't tell."

"Tell or I won't bring them down."

"You're taking advantage," I warned. "I won't just sit here."

"Will you get seasick if you do?"

"I never get seasick."

He thought this over. "Mr. Tilbeck does. I told you. But not when he's got a motor. It's on account of this Ménière's Syndrome he has. He says it might be a psychological disease or else he was born with it. It makes him throw up after he's rowed awhile. He thinks it's the way your arms have to keep doing these circles sort of. You get a steadier ride with a motor. —I like to sit still in a boat, don't you? I like the way it goes up and down, don't you?"

"It's antithetical to progress," I said. "Bring down those oars. You've got them sticking through the sky. Suppose you dropped them? And lost them? Then what? We'd go up and down forever."

He wondered at me. "Are you feeling sick? You won't throw up?"

"Not me. Look, don't annoy. I'm not Tilbeck," and discovered in the act of pronouncing it yet another lie.

"I think you look like him," he said, and a demon lurched in the boat—it was my suitcase falling flat with a bang.

"He sent you to row for him? Then row," I yelled. "Everybody looks like everybody. Mankind is one."

Beautifully, he brought the oars down. "Pity this busy monster, manunkind, not."

"Where'd you get *that?*"

"Mr. Tilbeck sings it."

"You mean recites it."

"Sings it. Pit-eee," he sang, "this biz-ee mon-STER," he sang, "man-UN-kind," he sang, "NOT. That's the way he does it."

"To do anything you want to in the whole world," I said, my half of the bargain having been to tell my mother's meaning: "That's free."

He slapped the gregarious blades on either elbow-side—they cleft the water, churning spittoons of whirlpools. We skimmed, we fled. "Is that what you do? Anything you want to?" he asked.

"For instance," I said, "this summer all I wanted to do in the whole world was read newspapers, so I did it. And my mother said is *that* all you want to do? You call that being free? So I said all right what *should* I do? And then I said all right I'll visit all the islands in the world, so my stepfather got out his atlas, and I went to Majorca, Minorca, Iviza, Formentera, Sicily, Rhodes, Cyprus, Formosa—"

"Crete?"

"—Crete being among the first I went to, then Buru, then Santa Cruz, Samoa, Guadelupe, Ellis, Staten, and plenty of others. And after all that there was nothing left in the atlas but Town Island. It's the only island in the world I haven't seen. Duneacres is the only house on the only island I haven't seen. Mr. Tilbeck is the only man in the only house on the only island—"

He intervened: "It's a joke, isn't it?"

"—I haven't seen. And since I'm the only person in the world who's visited every island in the world but one, Mr. Tilbeck—encountering me one day on Ellis Island, which, you know, is absolutely empty, a genuine desert island right off the East Coast of the United States—Mr. Tilbeck, you see, walked up to me with his coffee pot in his arms and invited me to live in a tent on his great decaying island estate—"

"I know about Ellis Island. It used to be for immigrants. We studied it in American History. You couldn't've been on Ellis Island. It *is* a joke," he said.

"You mean a lie?"

"Mr. Tilbeck *said* who you are. He told my father."

But I was sharp and quick: "He told your father *what?*"

"Who you are."

With my whole mind I considered it. And finally: "Who *am* I?"

"His daughter."

"He told your father that?"

"And my father told my mother."

Wondrous! Everything that Mr. and Mrs. Vand had striven to conceal from me all my life Tilbeck yielded in a word, and to anyone at all. What the Senators were never to discover the Purses already knew. What the trustee had paid and paid to bury, Tilbeck lightly disinterred to laugh at. What jeopardized the Ambassadorship—my mother's great lustrous prize—fell like a glossy scrap—a bus transfer, say, a snappy shiny ticket, of no more worth than that—into the Purses' casual pouch. He belittled the private not by making it gloatingly and efficiently public but by scattering it among those for whom it had no significance. If a tribe has not known gold, it will kick it underfoot. He was less blackmailer than all-around charlatan. He was a tremendous clown, and mon-

strous: he was audience for himself. Oh, he loved himself!
He was amused!

"And did they," I lengthened my breath, "believe that?"

"Well, why should they?"

"You mean because he's what your mother called him? A
habitual liar?"

"He *can't* have a daughter. He's a bachelor. He hasn't got
a wife."

"He might have had," I said, "once."

"You don't understand. He doesn't *get* married." He
looked at me oddly—as though, that is, *I* were someone odd.
"I know what they mean but I can't say it to you."

"Can't you?"

"Not to you."

"But didn't you just tell me I looked like him? A daughter
might."

"Everybody," he came back, "looks like everybody."

"You don't think I'm his daughter?" I pressed, amazed.

"Oh no no," he said, dropping his head toward a creak in
the oarlock, "I know you're not. We *all* know it. But it
doesn't matter to us. We're very liberal. My father says always be especially indulgent toward those who are most self-
indulgent. My mother said it wouldn't be the decent thing to
treat you like a Purse-ona Non Grata. So you see you don't
have to worry about *them*. Some people you would have to
worry about, but not them. *I* know what they mean. My
mother said it was Over My Years, but I know what they
mean. He only *says* daughter."

"But it's true," I said tentatively, afraid of what was true.
"I am."

This pumped into him a sudden jollity, half shy, half aggrieved, as though an embarrassingly easy puzzle had just
then come out absurdly right; our bow bounced on the huge
triumphant splashes of his thrusts. "They *said* you'd be in on
it! They said you'd corroborate the whole thing! They said he
probably does it *all* the time, tells people daughter when he
means—"

He stopped dead.

"Means what?"

"I can't say it to you."

"Can I say it to you?"

"What you are? You wouldn't!"

"If it's Over Your Years maybe I shouldn't."

"I know it anyhow!" he shouted. "They said it confiden-

tially but I know it anyhow! —Hey! There's the beach, see
it?" There it was; I saw it—a faded string before the green
began, like one of those sacred threads Brahmin boys are
given to wear across their chests until they die; the beach was
initiation. A woman knelt there. She seemed to knead with
her hands. Objects littered the sand, some mobile, some not.
From afar, it was a view of the pristine and the not-yet-cor-
rupted: Eve in Paradise on the world's sixth day, surrounded
by the forms of nature.

Then the mobile objects began to dance and wave.

"There's Sonny," said Throw. "There's Manny. Look at
Al! The other one's Foxy. See Dee? Dee's the one that's digging. The one with the bangs, that's Harriet Beecher."

"I can't see bangs at this distance," I said.

"But you can see her waving, can't you?"

"I can see them all waving."

"Except Dee. Dee's digging to China. Dee doesn't know
anything anyhow, he's too little. But Harriet Beecher and
Foxy and Al and Sonny and Manny, *they've* all been waiting.
They're practically purple from waiting."

"Waiting for you? They feel the pinch of an absent
Purse?" I dared him.

"Waiting for *you*. It's what you are," he said apologeti-
cally.

"Whatever I am I'm nothing to turn purple for."

"What you are to *him*," he amended.

"The most unlikely people have daughters," I assured him
coolly. "Daughters turn up everywhere."

"Sonny said we ought to call you the missing link," he reported; his voice fled falteringly upward, but he strained to
keep his look down, as though an earnest appreciation of respectability had to be centered in nether parts only. "Sonny's a
sort of humorist. He's supposed to take after my mother."

"There's nothing funny in that," I said with gravity.

Desperately he emptied a cyclone from his lung. "It's not
the part about missing that's humorous. You're not missing
any more. I mean you're *here*."

I acknowledged I was where I was; it was the least I could
do to relieve him.

He was not relieved. "Sonny said you're a link because my
father said something that sounded almost like that."

"Sounded like a link?"

He assented with a kind of shamefacedness. "What a link
does," he explained.

"Let's see," I said. "It's a shipboard game, is that it? All right. A link does what?" —I considered. "What does a link *usually* do? A link connects. All right? Is that it?"

"It's what you are," he miserably repeated.

"Dense is what I am," I said. "A link connects, whatever you want to say about it. I'm not a connection?"

"No."

"Well, that's where you're wrong. A connection is a relative. I *told* you daughter. So did Tilbeck."

"It's not the way my father said it."

"Oh, your father! Isn't he simply expecting a Neanderthal dressed in dinosaur teeth if he said missing link—"

"*Sonny* said missing link."

"Then what did your father say?"

He sighed until the whole Purse of him swelled; he blurted air, and in the air a word like the chug of a far-away locomotive. "Attachment he said."

I took it alertly: "Is that it? What you couldn't say?"

"It's what you are," he brought out in vindication. Then: "Well I *said* it."

This left me meek though pugnacious. "That's it really? It's what they think?"

"It's why they can't wait to see you. Foxy said it's like a Bible story—"

"You never heard of the Scopes trial," I halted him. "There aren't any missing links in the Bible."

"—like when King David was old and cold and they wanted to warm him up in his bed—"

"Oh, *that* story. And your mother and father too? They think I'm coming for that? They're convinced?"

"They don't *blame* you. I told you."

"You told me," I agreed. But the Purses' false coinage rang out against reality with a stroke euphoric, frenetic, lunatic, marveling, credulous, mad—I laughed, in short. "Because they're liberal!"

"Because they think you must be doing it for the money," he improved it.

"Then they're not Purse-spicacious after all," I said with satisfaction. "Unless Tilbeck's old and cold like King David?"

But he was undeflected. "He *isn't* paying you to come?"

"I came of my own free will. Because he wanted me to. So then *I* wanted to."

This made him blow out hard on his working fists. "I suppose that makes it worse."

"If I came because he was paying me would that make it better?"

"My father says the wilful deed is repugnant to the Lord, but if you do something for money you're not doing it wilfully, you're doing it for a perfectly sound reason."

"Your father is wonderful," I said. "Your father is a casuist."

"Paleontologist," he absently rectified, and set his spine for the final lap: the water blossomed from the oar's penetration like enormous dissolving lettuces, or the labyrinths of the human ear. "We *had* the Scopes trial," he protested. "In Community Civics. —See that lady with all the motors? On the beach? That's my mother. In a million years you wouldn't guess what she's doing right now."

"Yes I would. Punning. *She's* wonderful too," I said.

"She's an ex-prodigy," he confided. "Didn't I tell you she invents things? She likes to say this joke about how she's only im-Purse-onating Benjamin Franklin or somebody. She's very mechanical."

"Ah, she takes after her jokes"—*sotto voce*.

"She made Mr. Tilbeck drag out all these old motors that were in this sort of shed—it used to be a boathouse. It's left over from long ago when there were lots of launches going back and forth all the time. Mr. Tilbeck found sixteen motors in there. Most of them are all rusted together. They look pretty hopeless, but my mother's been fooling with them all afternoon. She said she's going to produce at least one working motor before the day is over."

"Suppose she produces something else? Accidentally invents an unexpected machine out of old parts?" I speculated. "Think what a robot Purse would be like!"

He construed this as the kindliest flattery and matched it: "Well, just on account of her being so handy with the motors Mr. Tilbeck said she was an inspiring resource. And my mother said what Purse isn't."

"Never mind," I gave in. "There already *exists* a robot Purse."

"You mean the way I handle myself?" he eagerly put it to me; "I told you I'm fast!"—but my allusion was merely to Mrs. Purse's Pavlovian responses; the reticule of her repartée was truly bottomless: how rich she was in pertinent riposte; how she had for every line an overwhelming answering line —indeed how well-lined a Purse was she! "In fact," said my oarsman, distracting me, "if they had a prize for such a thing, I bet I could row against a motor-boat and win hands down."

"And palm up for the money," I reflected, accusing him: "Spendthrift you are—in self-assertion and self-praise. Behavior unbecoming a Purse. Your father would moralize about it if he heard. Your mother would Purse her lips with displea-. sure at braggadocio per se. P-u-r-s-e say," I enunciated.

He listened—or did not listen—as soberly as a congregation. "You won't let them know, will you? What I said?"

"Trust me. Upon my word as a coxswain."

Nevertheless he lifted a worried mouth. "—Because they don't want to let on about any of it. They told us"—but did not this spurt of anxiety seem out of proportion to the mere sin of bragging?—"we ought to treat you with the respect a daughter of a benefactor would deserve."

"Daughters again? Is that what you're talking about?"

"You won't say I said it to you?"

"I won't say you boasted. A boasting Purse is an empty Purse."

"I don't mean about rowing fast, who cares about that? I mean what I *said*"—exasperated. "About you. They don't want to let on about you," he insisted.

"I don't want to let on about me either."

"Then do it the way you started to."

"Establish the connection without reference to any attachment?"—sly.

"Stick to being his daughter and leave it at that." This unboyish directive came in puffs between pulls; it was not the homiletic Purse that spoke in him then, but the one who knew how to accede to circumstance, how to follow like a gleaner to catch possibility. He gulped air with an athlete's rhythmic thirst for it, and the little voids that this violence made gap in the metrics of his words forced devious hesitations into my understanding, so that he seemed not merely hot like a child, but more, an evasive witness before a committee confident it has uncovered a spy. "Besides," he panted into spume, *"we* don't care. My mother said the Purses would be pound-foolish-penny-wise if we walked out on Mr. Tilbeck just to show we had a moral sense. Mr. Tilbeck's going to get my mother this very expensive drill she's always wanted, with about twenty different kinds of fancy bits. He's going to get my father this whole terrific fourteen-volume set of *Evidences of Lateral Femur Development in the North European and Sinaic Mastadon*—it costs over a hundred dollars, and three of those books are nothing but Bibliography and Index. My father says he's always aspired to owning that set and inscribing a motto in it, for inspiration—Perstare et Praestare. It's really the motto of his university, but my mother says it will do nicely for us in particular if we think of it as P-u-r-s-e-stare et P-r-i-c-e-stare. So you see it doesn't matter *what* you are. Not to liberals and humorists it doesn't. My father said Mr. Tilbeck's visitors are between Mr. Tilbeck and the Lord."

"Is that a comfortable place to be?" I wondered—"between Tilbeck and the Lord?" and meditated on that limbo place; my birthplace, in fact, where Allegra Vand, presumptive Ambassador's Lady and erstwhile attachment, had discovered herself long ago; and in that place—between Tilbeck and the Lord—was abandoned by both. Thereafter my mother never again knew love or religion. There is a way to know both, and simultaneously—let self-love be one's religion. But never again did my mother love a man or adore a philosophy. If now she had a religion, it was Enoch, or else (should religion, in the modern manner, demand definition as infatuation with process rather than object) Enoch's advancement; but one cannot love a man who in one form or another constitutes one's whole piety. Nor could she love herself. Who can love bank or bursary? Perhaps one of those pathological misers with dollar-stuffed mattresses and sleeves bulging with dollars and sewn-up trouser-cuffs ballooning a crackle of dollars can; but my mother was prodigal and wastrel, and what she spent she loathed. She loathed herself: universal bank and leaking bursary, leaking leaking cash, purse to Purses by virtue of (but the connections of history are long, are tedious though synapse-like: leave cause and effect to Aristotle and Tolstoy)—by virtue of having hung a garland of red berries on the twig of a tree in Brighton. Hence, by logical and presently effective links, these schnorrer Purses. Hence, by a final causal snap (as of a purse clicking shut), their imputing to me my mother's old rôle and crime of attachment—as though I were a schnorrer after a connection I had never committed, but which had nevertheless spitefully committed me to life. But all the same, and by the same logic of ultimate causes, as if the primaeval atom had schemed it, I came to that place as daughter, and meant to see in Tilbeck not my mother's lover, and not the germinator of my being, and not bank or bursary of sperm, and not trickster, blackmailer, beachcomber, fraud, and not parasite and schnorrer upon whom sub-parasites and sub-schnorrers fattened, and not a pocket for Purses to pick, and not incubus and appetite upon my mother's secretions (her money-perspiration, her money-excretion, her money-exhalation, her money-sneeze, the money-wax that appeared in her ears overnight, the money-cakes in the corners of her eyes when she woke, the morning money-coating on her tongue, her money-belch, her money-fever affecting various thermometers, her money-bile and money-acids, the pits of her money-pox)—nothing I knew I purposed to see in Gustave Nicholas Tilbeck: but the one condition unimaginable. I meant to try him out—oh, in the ordinary way!—as father. Oh, in the ordinary way! I thought —supposing he did not have yellow spoiled teeth and the graininess of the knock-about and vagabond, and even supposing he did—I thought plainly I would kiss him. Oh, in the ordinary way! For often I had seen daughters kiss their fathers.

But we were already bounding dog-like for the Purses' benefactor's beach, that sliver of my initiation into daughterness—and in the shallows, look, hymning out in unison a pulse of alien sound, the little Purses were noisily pullulating around us, as though a very large bag had suddenly spawned.

They were counting in Urdu—all but Mohandas K. Gandhi Purse, who held a tiny blue shovel and dug, dug, dug.

6

Behold the woman who kneels on the beach. Distance, abetted by H_2O (this formula signifying, we are romantically told, the elemental mother-fluid of our planet's life-germ)— had sentimentally cast her as the First Woman. But then *we* were bobbing, and *she* was remote. Now nearness and dryness convert the portrait. More sinister or less? How does one reckon Eve, who produced self-conscious lust, beside Circe, who rewarded it? And did her children frolic on the beach the moment after Circe changed Odysseus' crew into pigs, boars, peccaries, razorbacks, wart hogs, swine of every sort and continent? Homer does not tell whether that magical lady was a mother. And yet why not? No mention of Cain and Abel occurs until *after* their progenitrix (and ours) sinned with that unholy apple; and presumably those rivalrous siblings were not yet born while their parents were innocent; that indeed is the point of the story. The connection between Evil and the birth of the next generation is intimate. Evil must have a means wherewith to perpetuate itself, else it would not be hourly earning its notoriety for everlastingness. That is why children are created ubiquitously and eagerly— so that there may always be fresh skins for Evil to dress itself in. It is logical, then, to think of wicked Circe as maternal and loveful to a herd of little girls and boys, all her own, each one begotten by a visiting sailor before his human snout lengthened, at a thought from that wizard beauty, into piggish muzzle. —Therefore the capering of that company of Purselets did not contradict the possibility that Mrs. Purse was Circe modernized, extemporized, and finally mechanized, which was the image that pressed itself on me while I shook her oil-slimed hand—she laid down an ogre of a wrench to effect this greeting—and heard her explain that *all* the Purses were learning how to count their Pakistani pennies, that Urdu was the language of the place they were going to spend their Ford in ("Purses *can* be af-Forded, they're not clothed in alligator," she put it mystically but beamingly), and that the best way to make linguists out of Purses was to begin with them while they were very young—"while they're still only wallets, you see," she said, and actually horribly winked.

She was surrounded by the victims of her spells: unlucky mariners or just ordinary visitors who had been cast up on that island to be lured by her and then to be changed into something appropriate to the age. And she was too skilled and too practical for sties or stockyards; or perhaps disliked the odor of pork; or was perhaps vegetarian and a hater of the animal kingdom; or perhaps believed herself to be an aesthete, hence quite naturally anti-pig. Whatever her motivation, metal came to her as to a magnet: metal metal everywhere. Her enchanted prisoners, transmogrified, ironized and then oxidized, nutted and bolted and riveted, lay scattered in the sand: this one turned into a starter-battery, that one into a fuel tank, and behind her a whole navy bewitched into ignitions, levers, gear-shifts; here at her right one doomed fellow

finds himself a lowly gasket, and there at her left some great
hearty chap is reduced to a poor little piston; and here a rod,
and there a ring, a cylinder, a muffler; clutches, shear-pins,
propellers, carburetors—they sprawl like so many limbs and
souls. And Circe plays with them all with a kind of tactile
healthiness, as though she handles important fragments of
men; their hideous old rust ruddies her hands so that they
seem just now lifted out of entrails newly-opened and dripping automatic oils. And me she considers with an easy, welcoming, assessing, trifling, and barely puzzled smile—the look
with which no doubt she confronts everyone, wondering what
variety of machine-part the newcomer might best make. In a
flash I felt myself fitted out—a screw-thread here, a nozzle
there: she had without hesitation refurbished me as that Attachment I had been warned of. She was ready to hook me
up to anything. "*Such* a racket," she began, all apology for
her children—"they have these terrible tongues, every one of
them. And Throw's the worst. Did he talk your ear off coming? I tell him he has *such* a tongue people will take him for
a shoe instead of a Purse. He won't like that, you know! He'll
have to go around in laces!" she admonished, gleaming away
at me, her wrench restored to her grasp, her wrist experimentally twisting in air, pondering what corner of my apparatus
might most readily respond to tightening. "Now look here,
Dee, stick to your digging and keep out of my tool-box! The
superfluousness of certain Purses!"—giving me to understand
that one good hardy screwdriver was worth more than ten
Mohandas K. Gandhis, and that the animating impulse of
this last Purse of all (breathing, climbing, scrambling) had
come about perhaps through a mechanical oversight, an accident of the assembly-line, a case of over-supply in a region
where demand was already fully satisfied. Her tool-box, I observed, was deep enough and wide enough and generally spacious enough to swallow a small Purse, and even, for that
matter, a quite large one; and there was Dee, with cheeks
afloat around his nose like swelled rubber bladders, straining
over the brink of that portable machine-shop to exchange his
toy spade for a clever wire-cutter. "Well you see," Mrs.
Purse explained, following my eyes (as if she thought they
needed a slight rotary adjustment), "they don't have anything
like our standard of living in those heathen places, you know
that. We're not going unequipped! It may be a wrench for us
to leave America, but we aren't leaving America without a
wrench," and threatened the last Purse of all with that self-

same implement. By now the Urdu-counters, having arrived
at their limit (I later received it that they could go up to
eleven, which, reckoned in Mrs. Purse's cents, seemed a natural block to extravagance), had encircled us altogether, and
stood among the enchanted machinery like a set of pale
gnomes. And if those captive sailors retained within their
steel marrows some shade of human consciousness (as Circe's
swine kept theirs), how that heap of complex hardware must
have trembled at such paleness! It was the paleness (the sailors had known it in their fathers and mothers, and that is
why they ran off to sea in the first place) of perfect priggery
—the paleness of the justice who has spoken unappealable
condemnation, the paleness of the new priest who has taken
the unalterable vow of celibacy, the paleness of the sober sa-
loon-keeper, the paleness of children who have learned too
much and suspect even more than they have learned. Mrs.
Purse, it remains to be said, was also pale, and that was very
curious, because I had stubbornly imagined (on the principle
that all humorists share a standardized clown's jaw) that she
would resemble dark bony crane-like Mrs. Karp; but no, she
had her own way and her own paleness and lightness, different from the lightness of her progeny—she was big and
blonde, the blonde, when you came close, already half-white,
and she was ample and buxom and plump and laughing and
very young-looking, and she had the sort of smile which
shows gums over short teeth located much lower in the face
than they ought properly to be expected. She did not in the
least remind me of Mrs. Karp, but the sailor-souls in their
cold capsules at once disputed my surprise. "You are in
error, of course they are alike," said those spellbound mariners in their cages and cells, "most people are more alike
than they are generally rumored to be," said those magicked
beings locked up in their bits of outboard motor-parts, "take
us if you want an example! The uniqueness of the individual
is one of your benevolent democratic lies. Take us! Take us
for uniformity! The characteristics of mankind," said the ignitions, "run in schools," said the starters, "and the true races
in men are shown," said the cylinders, "not by the amount of
kink in the hair," said the piston who had once been a great
hearty chap, "or by the length of the head as measured by an
ethnologist's callipers," said the rod and the ring, "but rather
by the undeniable evidence that there are biological nations
of prigs, and of wags, and of fools," said the shear-pins and
the propellers, "miscegenation among whom produces mon-

strosities of prig-fools, or wag-fools, or, worse yet, prig-wags,
polluting," said the lowly gasket, "the purity of the original
strain," said all the bits of motors together; they had the
unanimity of steel, and glinted on the sand where they lay dispersed, imprisoned and full of hatred for the paleness of the
Purselets' perfect priggery. "Purse won't like that," Harriet
Beecher meanwhile cried—"better not let him hear you say
it," with an ear to Throw, who was bloating himself with
confidences, telling how well he had rowed, how fast, how he
had rowed me there like a shot, how they had me now plain
and clear for inspection. They inspected me, all very pale,
Throw among the palest, Foxy deadliest-pale, Sonny and
Manny and Al sufficiently pale to frighten the sailors hidden
inside their utilitarian tombs. "She did it," Manny told
Throw. "Ten minutes ago she did it," Al told Throw. "Got it
to work," Sonny told Throw, "but Mr. T. was bored watching
so he went up the hill with Purse." "What for?" Throw
asked. "To get on with the game, you stupid," said Harriet
Beecher under her pale bangs. "Cut a wire, cut a wire," Dee
sang out just then, pounding a rusted carburetor with his tiny
spade. (The carburetor was actually an old sea-salt with one
eye, famed for having once eaten human flesh. He would
have eaten Dee if he had not been metalicized.) "I'm a terrible cannibal," Mrs. Purse opened, "you see we had this one
sound motor to begin with, and a terrible sound it made, ail-
ing you see, so I cannibalized all these pitiful old things for
bits and pieces and now it's all right, though they *did* resist
with a fury. Rust fuses and thereby *re*fuses. The thing won't
last forever, but it's all right until the new one that's on order
comes—it's all a makeshift, I admit, but poor Mr. Tilbeck—
Manny, don't you dare call him T to his face, at least not T
square to his face" (here she paused for Ralph Waldo Emerson's titter), "he'll think you're a little savage, and that's just
what you are—*poor* Mr. T. doesn't know one end of a brace
and bit from the other, he thought *oil* was the trouble, the
lovely man. I suppose oil is more literary, that's why. *Lovely*
man, you know the children are all so attached to him, I suppose you are too," she ended, and sprang up from her knees
to look me over levelly, letting the hammer of her scrutiny
decide what hook or catch in me would best suit for purposes
of Attachment. She was speedily satisfied. "Throw"—
commanding—"you *are* lazy, take that luggage, won't you?
You'll likely never again carry anything so fancy—Purses
aren't up to alligator, and if we don't get up the hill soon

we'll be eating past sunset and in the pitch and with mosquitoes in the cheese. —It's very primitive here, it's all a ruin and heartbreaking to see the waste, but we find it thrifty, I suppose Throw told you? My goodness, that's *genuine* alligator, isn't it, it's certainly not plastic? Purses are nothing if not plastic," she marveled, "very flexible to adjust to different standards of living," and reached a tool-hardened finger to feel my traveling bag. "But that must have been very expensive! Mr. T.'s responsible for that, isn't he?"

"Mr. T.'s responsible for everything," I said, and straggled through a hill of sand with Circe and her pale herd, leaving those crippled bound sailors to brood on the final equality, not of the machine, but of man. The resuscitated motor, revived through dismemberment of the others, was somewhere among them, and indistinguishable to the innocent eye.

7

Mrs. Purse washed her hands—with soap—in the brook. The seven Purselets washed *their* hands in the brook. Under the trees there was a table, very stately, approached as in a gavotte by chairs, very stately. It was not a picnic table—by no means. Instead it was a ponderous indoors table carried, for whimsical or practical reasons, and certainly with difficulty, outdoors. The chairs were fully carved: from the wrist of each arm grew a little wooden long-nosed face, and out of the back of each popped another such face, clown-featured, king-costumed. All the little wooden heads wore little wooden crowns, but had to look mournfully down on bursting puffy slit seats. Chateaux were washed away. There had been figured velvet to sit on once, with moats and rosy pages openmouthed below the turrets. And now it was a fairy table under trees, left to rain and droppings both vegetable and avian. In reality the table was not very clean. In reality the chairs, the whole dozen of them, were not very comfortable.

But it was a charming scene, like any tea-party. I drew—no, felt—two comparisons: Alice of course, and that glowing and classical moment in the world that begins imperishably with: "Under certain circumstances there are few hours in life more agreeable than the hour dedicated to the ceremony known as afternoon tea." The sentence is celebrated for its civilizing atmosphere; and surely the very fact of a table under trees—especially when there are set on it a platter of red plums and one of white cheese and one of a golden roast chicken yet to be dealt with, with the steaming spit still lancing it through—brings to mind whole civilizations. It did not matter that a smoky smell of fowl hinted at something in the air more primitive, intimation of the hunt, or that the kitchen was a fireplace made of round stones in a ring and supplied with forked branches in wonderful wild-west fashion, and the fire nearly out. It merely seemed as though Fashion itself, in the person of courtiers, was at masquerade for its own amusement—as though civilization, as represented by the table and its kings, had come out to tease and be teased. Behind that flat victual universe, and held in the brambly basket of the treetops, was an enormous scarlet globe, perfect as the rich yolk of an egg: it was the late sun, caught in a hedge and delayed. And between the table and the sun, only much nearer to the sun than to the table, two men played a game.

There was no net, though there were poles from which a net had once been strung. There was no visible court, though there was a kind of floor out of which hairy weeds wandered. The two men swam in the brush. A tan ball darted from bent racket to warped racket. Sometimes the ball lost its way, and dipped into the pool of fine tall grass. And then there was a wait; and then suddenly the ball could be seen again in arc, like a moth lured to the circle of the sun.

I left the brook, and came to the table and breathed gnats, and left the table and the gnats and headed for the players. They were farther than they seemed; I had to walk through a heap of straw—it might have been a formal garden once: decayed trellises and dead thorns all over, and a thicket of cancerous runaway ivy smothering flagstones; and in the center of a sort of grove an astonishing stone ruin, broken like a Greek shrine. It was the remains of a fountain. A hollow finger of pipe protruded from the ground; and a long thick ugly serpent-like chain meandered near it. The chain led to rubble—a stump with kicked-away points at either end: it was an anchor of stone.

They played without conversation. They were governed by the ball, which raised their right arms high, and they were joined by the ball, which brought the blow of one to the blow of the other. They beat the tan ball back and forth. Their faces seemed boiled by the light and concentrated in pursuit. One was still a young man, though he had the clefts of use descending from nostril-margin to mouth-margin; the other was not young. The one who was not young was the taller and the more agile. The one who was still young was the more decorous, and stamped through fiercenesses of weed-growth like a clever circus horse. They kept no score—at least not aloud—and seemingly had no rules beyond the limitations of thigh-high clumps of straw spears and crazy blistered rackets, so I was struck with wonder at whether this earnest breathless gaming pair, like the motors below on the beach, had suffered sad and profound bewitchment. Or perhaps had the dancing sickness and could not end their match until some unendurable unheard inner music ended. Or had a bitterness between them that needed victory in this odd way.

In a little while one said: "Fee fie foe fan. I smell an Ameri-*can*."

"*Damn* it, you're deficient in imagination," said the other. "You go all over the lot. Can't you imagine a net?" —But neither man turned.

Phung, went the ball. Phung, back again. Phang!

"If you please," said the man who was no longer young, "don't stare. If you please, young lady."

"Watched pot, hah? Nervous! —Well, never mind, it's only a tourist," and the speaker, short of breath, vanished for a moment under a mat of greenery. At length he gracefully emerged. "She's got to be shown around. I authorize you."

"The view's worth showing of course."

"Terrible idea. Show her the wine cellar. Pick—out—something—nice."

But neither man made any move to leave off playing. Phung. Phung. Phang!

"Tell her," continued the man who was still young, "to take a handful of kids if she won't try it alone. I need my wine with my dinner."

"They've *been* downcellar, most of them."

"Well, tell her to pick a glorious hero out of history who *hasn't* been yet and go downstairs with it. Then dump it in the spring."

"You're offhand with glorious heroes," the other grunted.

"The bottle I meant. To cool. Last month I lost a beaut that way—cork was loose. Washed out. Fresh from the cellar too. Some lackey must've nipped it once. Water turned"— phing!—"claret. Matched the house-mold exactly. Pity to see —perfectly good—spring water—diluted."

At once I knew him. Tilbeck was the one who needed wine.

I was afraid to look at him. I looked at the other man. The other man, whom I had taken for old, was not old. It was only contrast that made him seem so. He had a mouth stern with rigid piety—a hollow mouth, full of teeth but hollow-sucked all the same behind lips puffed and womanishly budded. And a step too quick for a young man, since young men are unashamed about not always showing their nimbleness. They will show it if it pleases them. Yet Purse sped, as though someone had doubted how nimble he could be; he dashed and darted, vigorously in training. It made him seem old. The other laughed and sauntered. The other was lazy, and went after the ball casually, like one of those self-mocking tropical divers who greet incoming holiday-ships with a nonchalant crash to the bottom of the harbor, and all for the sake of a penny. He laughed, and he strolled, and he stuck a toe out to kick the invisible net, and he missed his serve, and he ducked, and he held his racket like a feather-duster; and he panted recklessly all the while, until he vaguely reeled. But he was at play, and Purse was at work. Frenetic repetitions rather than exhaustion aged Purse; he looked what he was, a father. Not so my father. I stared with the rot of disappointment at a man not yet forty who had the enamels and graces of a man not yet thirty. Heedlessness—his shoulders demonstrated how little he cared for anything but the soft inch of pleasure; he did not even care for triumph—heedlessness perhaps it was that had left him immune; but he was not *that* immune. Time must overtake before it takes away the whole of a man's earliness, and no one had told me how Gustave Nicholas Tilbeck stood with respect to the touch of the withering finger. It had not tapped him. There was still something unrecounted about the stink of my first cell. Dejection seized me. Shame heated my legs. Not even William, sordid puritan, had had the courage of this sordidness. I viewed my father. He might have been a decade younger than my mother; half that surely. Then and there I had to swallow what I was: the merest merest whim. Oh, less and worse: it was not that I was the flaw of chance. Others belong to chance, others have

sprung from caprice. It was not that I had never remotely
been intended. It was simply that I could never have been seriously believed in. It is bad to fail, but to succeed beyond
one's genuine imagination is terrible. It is the spurt of a too
great precocity. It surpasses what is decently normal. A boy
of seventeen had made me.

"You! Tourist!" he called to me two-and-twenty years after
that moment of his singularity. "I need my dinner. I need my
wine. Bring all those counting-houses up from the beach. Tell
them their papa laid everything out like a French chef. His
missis done? Fixed my outboard?"

"They said it's fixed. They're washing," I answered, and
watched the ball go wild.

"Good. This is Purse the digger," he announced. "When he
digs into a purse it's not his own. Joke." And then: "This one
is my girlie. The kid get you over all right? Didn't soak you,
dry enough I see. Though not a looker. What the hell, I like
my girlies lookers. Expected a looker, the odds were for it.
Show you around all the same. You show her," he nudged
Purse, and snatched the racket from the other's grip and
threw it with his own into a bed of rushes. They fell with a
sound like a distant sneeze.

"I'd better see to the hand-washing," Purse said nervously.

"Right you are. Germ gets into a Purse, never gets out
again. Give that one to the missis with my compliments.
Doesn't come up to her standards, I'm only an amateur. The
professional product—how can you make a small purse
count? Answer: Teach it. Topical joke, unquote Mrs. Purse,
so help me sweet baby Jesus."

Purse bolted like a racer, with a noise in his nose.

"Sacre bleu, blasphemed again. Keep forgetting not to. It's
all right in front of the kids, they're hypocrites, but it hurts
the pa's feelings something awful. Though he won't say anything—I made him promises. He'd recite all the devil's names
for the price of an encyclopaedia and a new tin trunk. Fast
on his feet, look at that. It's not hands he's going to super-
vise, believe me. Prayers. That gang never consumes a Goddamn crumb without first spitting up a blessing. Wear out
God that way. You religious?"

"No."

"Believe in God?"

"I don't know. I don't think so."

"Which means Yes. Don't have your mother's shape, now

do you?" he said critically. "They teach you something in that college to make up for it?"

"Latin mostly."

He whistled. "Let's go get the bottle. Show you your bed on the way."

We avoided the wilderness I had come by and followed a little path past three large and dirty tents. "Here?" I said.

"Put you in the house. With me. You're no tramp. This way—back door. Through the kitchens. Show you *my* bed."

It was a sofa pushed nearly into a fireplace. Minuet dancers paraded on the cushions in bubbles of frocks the color of grass. Grass underfoot nipped strangely, in knots, out of gaps in the tile. A lobster glow prowled through the windows; some were boarded; here and there a few glass teeth still hung. On the lip of the hearth lay a silken pillow ragged with raveled rosettes. Black enormous surfaces of stoves stretched into mediaeval distances. There was a bad smell—dampness, feces of mice. Wax candles leaned like stalagmites. Under the sofa a heap of charred table-legs. Against a rotting wall something—a cube the size of a cottage, with its door swinging free; perfectly square; gigantic; breathing caged heat: a terrifying refrigerator. "Pantry. Laundry. Back there the bakery. Rows of sinks like elephant troughs, see 'em? Burned all the bread paddles last winter. Break your heart, hah? All dead and finished. See that clump? Behind you. Right up through. No basement under this part of the house, that's why. The power of grass. Takes over in the end. Gloria was sick on the bus last Monday, you follow?"

I did not know how to answer.

"Tourist! No? Don't get it? Thought you had Latin. Sic transit gloria mundi as they say. Come on, I'll show you the kings."

The kings matched the kings on the chairs under the trees. Grotesque noses, awkward rough little snarls, wicked wicked foreheads leering with the minute grain of the crafty wood; he went from dark guileful panel to dark ingenious panel of an empty room, empty and immense, empty and inhabited by the heads of kings. He polished wooden foreheads with his wrist-bone. I pursued him through a litter of newspapers and peered upward: "There must be three hundred of 'em—*I* never counted," but he did not mean the prisms that showered from the chandelier like a brilliant bundle of kaleidoscopes; "see?" he said, "up near the ceiling? That whole row up there? Half a dozen of 'em? Those are the Six Philips of

France. Heard of Philip the Fair?—that's the crackpot-look-
ing one: crosseyed. On the other side—there's plenty of light
left, come on—those are the Five Philips of Spain. Murderous, hah? The way I understand it the old man imported
these walls direct from somebody's Hungarian castle. Filthy-
minded old man. These are only the heads—figure for yourself what they would've done with the torsos. Well, come on,
I'll show you a piece of filth!"

Now a room larger than the last; a bereft drawing-room
plainly; a hall. Sky, zodiac, cherubim and seraphim; trumpets, scrolls, lofty harps encrusting the vault. But unlike the
room of the kings, this one is furnished. A piano and a sofa.
The sofa is identical with the kitchen sofa, only the dancers
here wear red boots, red bodices, red waving ribbons. A
woolen blanket is folded on the arm. "You sleep here. Quite
a little instrument, hah? Ever see anything like it for filth?
Works all the same. B flat below middle C nice and dead, but
you'd expect that, leather gave out. Miracle all the rest are
O.K. Sounds like a trapdoor slamming half a mile off." He
struck a key: out flew a quick tiny metallic cry. The eigh-
teenth century flocked across the piano's grand flanks—courtiers and courtesans, princes and dogs, orchards and mazy
streams, all in gilt and pastel, the buckles gold foil, the wigs
all silver, the rouge on every cheek a delicacy of brushwork;
and lions on the legs, and bronze claw feet, and green fields
and mounted hunters dreaming straight across the music-rack.
"Filth!" he said. "More of the same upstairs; sailor's filth."

I was moved to speak: "You're not fair," I said faintly.

"No? You want to prove it with the upstairs? Elevator
cage is nice and dead. Full of stuffed birds anyhow. Two
flights up though I can show you a dozen dressing-tables that
this damn piano doesn't nearly come up to for filth. Genuine
filth. A tourist, I knew it!"

"You call everything filth," I said.

"Why not? This place look better than filth to you?"

"I don't judge places."

"That's nice. Tourist's view—pure. All the picture postcards have the same value. You're a pure one! What do you
judge, people?" he demanded.

"History," I said, and thought of Enoch. "Records."

"They tell you to come with that? Look, don't try on
masks with me, I see right through them. I might surprise
you, I might not be what the high and mighty Mrs. Vand

says I am. The high and mighty Mrs. Vand could be one high and mighty fake."

The frightening familiarity of these words shocked me into memory; he had said the same long ago, while I crouched listening on the ledge of Europe. He had come for terms and said these words; it was history I was hearing, and a record emended to eliminate the laugh. He was not laughing now. He stabbed the piano with a finger: down went a black bar, but it was silent. "Don't say high and mighty," I begged.

"Don't say filth, don't say high and mighty! Who are you, girlie? Not a judge, only a general. Tell me," he said, "you don't think I've got my side of things too? That's all you have to know about people, their side."

"I don't want to take sides—"

"That's right, the disinterested observer. Sit in the center. It so happens that most things can't be seen from the center. You have to go into the thick of one side or the other to get the truth. Nothing's really disinterested but logic, and what's logical isn't what's true, verstehst? There isn't any disinterested truth, there's only partisan truth, comprends? What do you know about your grandfather?" he said suddenly.

I looked with shame at the harps on the ceiling. "He tried to get my mother to live here after she was married. But she wouldn't, she didn't like it."

"So? —That's it?" He waited.

"Well, then he traveled around a lot. Toward the end he got interested in science—sea things. I don't know much else," I faltered: "he died before I was born."

"After you were born."

"No, before—"

"All right, see what I mean? There you are in the center, keeping your mitts nice and clean behind your back, and you don't know a damn thing. *After.* When I tell you after better take it as gospel."

"But it isn't true, my mother had only just married William—"

"Your grandfather was a Swedish longshoreman and he died frozen drunk in the streets of Seattle in 1946. Now tell me different."

I said hesitantly, "Your father, you mean? That's who you mean?"

"Don't try to step back from it that way. Blood is blood. Gustavus Tilbeck. He couldn't read a word of any language on this earth, but he was named after a king and me he

named after a king and a czar, so you can see he had the
imagination of an aristocrat. Your mother never told you
that?"

"No."

"All those lawyers and accountants she has, they never
mentioned it?"

"No," I said.

"People like that avoid what's interesting, that's why. Me it
strikes as something interesting that the high and mighty Mrs.
Vand's girlie is all mixed up with a Swede with the proclivity.
I've got the proclivity myself, but I stick to wine. Kings I like
too, you've noticed it. Did you know about that, that I was
named for a king and a czar?"

"No," I said again.

"Because actually I was named for my father and for a
dog he was very fond of in his boyhood. Dog's name was
Nick. A wolfhound. My father spent his boyhood on a fine
wholesome prosperous farm just outside of Upsala. He was a
graduate of the University of Upsala, as a matter of fact."

"But you said he couldn't read—"

But now he gave a long laugh I queerly recognized. "Nobody who graduates from the University of Upsala can read.
They don't teach reading there, they teach theology. Old Gus
couldn't swallow the Trinity, so he settled down on the docks
instead. The reason he picked the Seattle docks is because in
Sweden they advertise American opportunity. Well, it's a success story. It hasn't embarrassed you?"

I said: "You're not the way I expected."

"Better, I hope. This is a first-class shirt I'm wearing. Observe the fine stitching. Observe my excellent shoes. Extraordinary knitted socks. Observe the structure of my knees
below my fashionable tennis-shorts. Superlatively hinged
knees. The entire costume courtesy of the high and mighty
Mrs. Vand, clothier by appointment to my humble origins.
Except for the knees, which are also gratis, but from another
source. God. Now you have it all."

I persisted, "I thought you were older. Enoch's age."

"No, no, I've got a few years on the Ambassador."

"But you must have been very young—"

"You mean you want gossip. Right. I was an absolute boy
when I slept with your mother. Does that satisfy? I wasn't of
age, I had to write home for permission. My father stirred in
the gutter and said Go ahead, my child, which made my
mother and sisters weep for a month. Your grandmother and

your aunts. All members of the Lutheran Ladies' Aid Society, though one of them gave up tea and converted to Mormonism. My mother always read to my father out of the Sunday supplements and he was shocked at the modern neuroses he learned about that way. That's why he told me to go ahead and pursue the rich. The illiterate are very clean-minded. You're sure I'm not embarrassing you?"

"I think you are," I said.

"Tourists are easily embarrassed, especially by just the thing they've come to see. The scenery isn't antiseptic enough for you, that's the trouble? You don't like the smell of the ruined abbey? You want the reconstructed cinderblock replica with indoor plumbing for visitors?"

"Why do you keep calling me tourist?" I asked.

"You hate a place where you have to do your duty behind a tree? Is that what's embarrassing?"

"No," I said. "It's not knowing what's real and what isn't."

"A philosopher-tourist!" he cried. "You're like your mother in that. They're the worst."

"Some of what you say isn't real—"

"—and some is. Brilliant beginning. I put a cinderblock replica and a ruined abbey in everything I say. The ruined abbey is real."

"No it isn't, not if it's kept that way just for show, like a museum—"

"A museum? You've heard of that? They were going to turn *this* place into a museum, you've heard of that?"

"Yes," I said.

"And a man killed himself here."

"I know."

"Briefed. Perfect! Tourist-with-guidebook, knows all principal points of interest beforehand, knows when guide skimps on tour, behaves honorably all the same, tips guide even though he cheats, but vows privately to boycott Rome next time round. I know the type! You think Rome misses you, girlie? All right. On with the tour. What other sights did they tell you to look for especially, hah, tourist?"

"I'm not a tourist," I said.

"The hell you're not. Allegra sent you to look around. The high and mighty Mrs. Vand, an old hand at tourism. Hasn't got the nerve to come and see for herself. Can't look me in the eye. Wants a report. Tell her"—again he laughed his long laugh, a chain of laughs—"tell her I'm finally letting the grass grow under my feet!"

"She didn't send me for that."

"No? Not to get a look at Nick? See if he's comfortable and all? Check on his health?"

"No."

"She feels guilty about me, y'see. She owes me a lot."

"She's paid you a lot."

"Aha. Just what I said. I knew there was something else you might mention. A quotation from the fine print—a renowned spire, so to speak, that they've made famous for you back home by keeping a picture of it framed on the wall. Or a picture of the ravens that come to nest in the vine-covered nave of the ruined abbey. So to speak. You've heard of those? You've heard of everything then. You've got a very good guidebook, pictures aside. Who wrote it? The Ambassador himself? —No, no, your mother's a woman of honor, she pays her debts, if she's paid me a lot it's because she's owed me a lot. Right from the start. In her whole life she's done only one thing on her own, and she didn't do *that* on her own. 'Hollow Marianna: The Girls' Own Das Kapital.' Or: 'The Double-X: Se- and Mar-.' You think that treatise would've gotten done without me? She'd've had the discipline for that sort of thing? I kept her at it, I made her do it. It's a tutorial fee she's paid me. That's how she ought to look at it. It's how *I* look at it. —Getting dark. Around here you need a flashlight. You bring a flashlight?"

I shook my head.

"The Purses know where I keep 'em. Ask the Purses. Meanwhile I'll descend for the bottle. You like port? No, out the other way. Front door, excellent sample of Mixed Renaissance filth. Take you right out to the Purses at prayer. You might be on time to see them pass the plate. Mrs. Purse has soap if you want it—they brought their own—she probably made it out of tallow in a vat. Slaughtered an ox herself to get at the fat. Undoubtedly forged the steel for the knife. Fine woman. If you have to do your duty, pick a tree."

He vanished behind a brown door, and I heard his languid pressure on the stair. I went the way he had pointed, and discovered the Purses ranked palely around the table under a sunset of rose and purple smears, clouds like colored ships, each child with a king's snout in its back. The spit was restored to the flame, and a second fowl dripped its fragrant shine from it like a candle dripping wax. And there was Purse carving away at the bird on the board, delicately—a man who knew his bones and meant to keep them in order.

The children sent up a babble. Mrs. Purse looked all around her and smiled and smiled; then she stared at her fork as at a captive. "Oh why won't you all be *quiet,*" she murmured to the air—"it's bad manners to jangle Purses in public," "public" being her salute to me as I came up; one child only responded with a quick shrill howl.

It was an idyll.

8

The child who laughed was Ralph Waldo Emerson Purse, the humorist; he laughed again when Mrs. Purse, handing round paper platefuls of chicken parts, moved her short teeth and low gums into shadow and observed (this too was for my entertainment)—"We like to keep our Purses well filled, you see." "A thought we've already digested," responded the humorist. "Oh shut up," said Harriet Beecher crossly. "I want a drumstick," said Throw. But Purse said: "You know Dee always has the one, you shouldn't be always claiming the other. That's greed." "It's greed in Dee. He gets one all the time." "Dee is only two, remember that." "Is that why he eats for two?" said Sonny. "It's my turn for the drumstick," Foxy said. "It is not." said Al; "I haven't had one ever." "Liar!" said Throw. "Lyre has nothing to do with it," Sonny said complacently—"all he cares about is lute. He wants to grab the l-o-o-t." "If you're going to be silly and wrangle—" Purse began. "They don't wrangle, they *jangle,*" said his wife. "—nobody at all will get it," he ended severely, and took a greasy bite of it down to the bone. "There," said Mrs. Purse, banging her fork: "That's what happens to a bone of contention. Nobody at all gets it," and looked at her husband as if she were looking at nobody at all.

The wine having arrived—two bottles sprouting like antennae from under Tilbeck's arms—it was set to swim in the spring.

"You'll have the water in its cups," Mrs. Purse chided brightly.

"Can't I have you the same?" asked her host.

"Ah, but we don't, you know."

"We don't," said Purse with emphasis. "It loosens the will."

"Chacun à son goût. Better the will than the bowels."

Purse frowned terribly. He was jealous of his wife.

"Here's your dinner," said she, holding out a plate to me. "Do you like to hear singing? Mr. Tilbeck has a charming repertory. He sings epigrams. He makes up the tunes."

"He sings Robert Frost," Throw said.

"Sing Robert Frost," Mrs. Purse wheedled.

He sang: "HOW are we to WRITE the Russian NOV-el in America a-a-a-as long as LIFE GOES on so UNterrib-LEE?"

"Oh, that's funny. That's really lovely and hilarious," said Mrs. Purse.

"I would like—" he had a mouthful of wing—"to set Plato's Dialogues to music. It's one of my ambitions. Only—" here he swallowed—"it would make a very boring opera."

"I don't see why."

"Too much recitativo."

"Sing Robert Frost again," Harriet Beecher said.

"Harriet Beecher, don't you nag. You let Mr. Tilbeck eat his meal."

"I don't see that life goes on so unterribly in America," Purse demurred. "The problem of social justice remains, in spite of supermarkets. No one can say it's altogether solved, even in America. Pockets of unemployment all over the country, to take only one aspect. Or take the situation of the migrant workers."

"Ghastly situation," said Mrs. Purse. "Babies in the fields right alongside the pickers. They suckle them in the furrows. That is *nothing* like roast chicken in the open air."

"Or take the moral situation."

"Ghastly moral situation," said Mrs. Purse, discharging a cucumber from a basket. "Have one of these, Mr. Tilbeck— you already have our gratitude. I hope it's not too soon to tell you what a lovely and hilarious week this has been."

"The conventions are loosening. The seams of society are opening. God means very little to the young. We're breeding atheists. The idea of love has lost its sanctity."

Mrs. Purse said coquettishly, "My husband thinks you might be an atheist, Mr. Tilbeck."

"If a lady can make a motor out of chaos, surely God

could make the úniverse," Tilbeck said, "out of similar material."

"There, you see? Of course you're not an atheist."

"She got it to work," Throw said, "I told you she would."

"The universe? I shouldn't wonder. Though I did notice the Milky Way out of kilter last night. A little oil maybe? Observe the twilight, Mrs. Purse. A shade too dark for this hour. I hope you'll do something about it."

"End of summer," Mrs. Purse murmured. "Charming. We'll miss your teasing, Mr. T."

"More and more," said Purse, gnawing at the knob at the end of his joint, "the old values fall. Honor becomes the appearance of honor. Authority becomes the appearance of authority."

"For one thing," Mrs. Purse said, "your shear-pin was broken off clean. The universe is more reliable than that."

"Reliability becomes the appearance of reliability."

"Ghastly," Mrs. Purse said. "Rinse your chin, Walt Whitman. Who wants more?"

The second bird was brought to the table. They all wanted more. Further disputation over distribution of two drumsticks. Mohandas K. Gandhi got one. Purse—reserving decision in an access of fairness—got the other.

It was nearly night.

Mrs. Purse addressed me: "Your father is a charming companion. Delightful."

Purse said, "Generous. Very generous."

Mrs. Purse said, "I look forward to a charming correspondence."

Tilbeck said, "There I'll fail you. I don't write much. As a rule."

Moths were solemnly revolving.

"Here," Mrs. Purse explained, "we follow the universe slavishly. We go to bed with the stars."

"There's nothing else to do," Tilbeck said.

"The habit of electric light makes one forget the ordinances of the Lord," Purse said. "It's very black without a moon."

"Fine moon tonight," Tilbeck said, watching the children dance under it.

"The moon makes them go wild. They look so primitive."

"It's only Dodge Ball."

"But they use a stone. Poor Dee. He always gets trampled."

"I should like to've known you in the Stone Age, Mrs. Purse. You would have advanced us to Iron in a month."

"Charming. What a pity you don't correspond. My husband writes voluminously."

Purse dug. Then he put down his spade and began fo bury the debris of dinner. Into the hole went the bones of two chickens.

"A paleontologist like yourself might dig all that up in the Fourth Space Age," Tilbeck said, "and then what?"

"Maybe by then this island will have disappeared," Mrs. Purse reflected.

"Where could it go?"

"Oh, Mr. T., don't throw your bottle in."

"Empty—"

"Yes, but the children would so like to put a note in it. And give it to the tide. Harriet Beecher asked me specially to ask you."

The bottle was spared burial. Purse covered over the hole. "I think it's time now."

"Yes, it's time," said his wife. "Though the moon is like the sun."

Stones were dropping one by one into the brook.

"We're coming," Bronson Alcott called.

"You'll play again tomorrow. Manny, is your chin clean? It's time. Where's Dee?"

No one knew. —A search. They found him asleep under the table.

"His mouth's all funny."

"It's purple."

"It's the color of the house-mold."

"Make him walk."

"He won't. He won't wake up."

"Why does he smell like that?"

"He smells nice. He smells like Mr. T."

"Ah."

"He was in wading."

"He helped himself, didn't he?"

"Wasn't the cork in tight?"

"I think," said Tilbeck, "you've misnamed the boy."

Purse said: "We meant him to emulate a saint. Self-restraint and discipline, discipline. We had in mind that sort of saint."

"But he wants to be a god," Tilbeck said.

They carried Bacchus off to his tent.

"Good night, Mr. T."

"Good night, Miss Tilbeck."

"Good night," I answered, startled.

"Good night."

No one had intimated it would be an idyll. Not Enoch, not William—not even my mother, who knew.

9

Curious: in color there is a difference between what is pale and what is light. We dark heads are notorious for our attraction to you blonds, whom the sun has honored with imitative pigment. In my mother's family we were all black-haired; occasionally—like my grandfather—carpet-brown. It was the Scottish element—or so my mother analyzed our Italian looks: she blamed it on Caesar's legions. "Mediterranean types on Sauchiehall Street," she liked to say of Glasgow— "short dark little wops of women," and on account of the Roman invasion she had always gone to the pale. William, milkishly pale, turning pinker and pinker, the underside of a white cat's tongue lapping milk. Enoch, white skin, hands very white and square, like geometrical abstractions, eyes pale as theories. He was one of those blond Jews of whom it can never be said that they remind us of the prophets. The golden-bearded Jesus of the North, that mild blond womanish lamb of the calendars, is a sham. So outwardly was Enoch. Two thousand years' absence from the Near East had left the curve of his mind intact, but had colored him differently. He should have looked like an Arab. Instead he was the perfect Pole, the perfect Ukrainian, the perfect Shtchepan or Ivan of the Russian provinces in the Pale—urbanized and scholarized out of farmer strength and sinew and farmer hulk and bulk. Call it, with the biologists, protective coloration. When the creature enters the environment, the environment enters the creature. But it never protected. The true Shtchepans and

Ivans knew which faces to smite, in spite of the faces' having become like their own. Enoch's paleness was not William's, though only history, not the spectrograph, can tell us the reason for it.

And here at last was Gustave Nicholas Tilbeck—a very blond man, son of a Swede (if he was to be trusted)—looking into the fire, which sparked like a live wire on snow (reigniting itself on remnants of grease), muttering good night to nine pale Purses. The sun, when it chooses to honor its northern people with paleness, makes them pay for it with fear of the sun; they shun what they reflect. Perhaps the sun is jealous of its rivals, even when it has appointed them itself. But it might be otherwise. The paleness might signify fatigue rather than favoritism. What of Prometheus after he stole the fire? Presumably he was tired. It was his one great act. Nothing could equal it, not even his noble passivity afterward with the vulture. So with the passive blonds of the North. Having seized the color of the sun to live in their hair—through what exhausting scenes of mythological prowess or brawn or cunning who can say?—they have exerted themselves as far as they can. They have taken the sun for beauty, and it is the end of their obeisance to beauty; there can be no obeisance without impulse. They have done themselves in. Their pale heads and arms faintly tissued with pale hairs droop across the northern cap of the world. Race-justice does not allow us to criticize the Danes and the English and the Germans for their spiritual languor. It is no small task to have leaped into the copper pot of the sun and come out dyed with the eternal gleam. If, having done this much, they have no energy left for the other masques of brilliance, who can blame them?

None of this describes Tilbeck. He was not pale; he was light. How explain the difference? The dark heads of the South have taken their sober colors from the black shadows under a congregation of trees; yet they skip with vigor, and compose themselves into beauty aimlessly and easily. Perhaps, having opted for the wood, they have learned the wood's powers of secret quick growth and hasty composition, and the lush lesson of the sap. Perhaps, having opted for the wood, through which the sun is strained and enters poorly, they have had to learn to generate their own profuseness. No one knows the answer, though Tilbeck wore the answer in his skin. Animation—a collection of vitalities, all harbored cautiously, none wasted (as pale Purse, running, wasted his)—gathered in him as in a headquarters. He had the authority of a nodule or centrality of light—not alone the centrality that issues, but the centrality that receives. The firelight charged at the fair fine flat tongue of hair that lay across his foreskull as though seeking a brother. He took what he took as though he were capable of taking more and even more. I thought of the tree in the swamp and its appetite for light, and just then he gave a savage spit into the fire and told me he was part Greek. It justified the Nicholas.

"Like Polygon then," I said, bewildered into satire. "Greek like Polygon who owns the boatyard who brought the—"

"Sure. Polygon's my cousin. I always send him business."

"You're not Greek."—And put scorn for liars in it.

"What's the matter, you don't like being Greek? What I am you are. And *I* dreamed up the Parthenon."

"Slaves built it."

"I wasn't a slave."

"In Greece? How do you know?"

"Because I know. A man knows when he's free. That moon means business. The size of it. Means autumn."

"But it's hot." I had decided to be peevish.

"Hot," he echoed, "as hell. This place is good for another month, I figure. At most."

"Then where will you go?"

"Somewhere else."

"Don't you ever plan?"

"They're the slaves. The planners. You've never known anyone but slaves, hah, girlie?"

"I suppose." Then I gave in. "I suppose you mean people like William. Did you ever meet William?"

"Never had the misery. The Ambassador I knew well. Prize slave of them all."

"In Egypt."

"Hm?"

"Enoch always says he was a slave in Egypt." An interval. Finally I put it to him: "Would you have spoiled it for Enoch? Wrecked the Ambassadorship? —Told those three newspapers," I stated.

"Mm, now you're getting subtle. Probing."

"But would you really? If I hadn't come?"

"Oh you," he said vaguely. "What d'you have to do with anything?"

I would not let go. "The bargain. I know every detail. I really do. Tourist with guidebook."

I was touched that he did not laugh. He smiled instead, the

kind of smile that trembles gradually into being, so that for a
long while it seems to beat in doubt of its own self-creation:
imagine Buddha in the moment *before* that arch-moment by
which he is usually represented. —Were his teeth clean? It
was too dim to tell. "You have possibilities. Self-comprehen-
sion. At your age Allegra was obtuse as a wall. A drop of my
Greek in you maybe."

"But it *was* a bargain."

"You think I care if they make him Ambassador to the
Court of the Angel Gabriel? If he wants it let him have it."

"My mother wants it."

"And he wants her. If he wants her let him have her. The
high and mighty Mrs. Vand, Queen of the Universe."

"You don't like her."

He said narrowly, "Keen of you to spot that."

"I hate sarcasm," I informed him. "Why don't you like
her?"

"Same reason you don't.'

"I like her," I protested.

"Did you say something before about not being able to distinguish between the real and the unreal? Be humble, girlie."

"But I do like her," I said. "She's an interesting woman."

"She's a stupid woman. She's obtuse. She wants everything."

I looked around for logic. There were only the trees, the
table, the kings, the white moon. "Well, you want everything
too. You said it yourself."

"I deny it."

"You said a man knows when he's free."

"Being free isn't wanting."

"Being free is doing anything you want to in the whole
world."

"A line not your own—Polly want a cracker?"

"I said that once before today," I apologized. "I said it
coming over in the boat. I was telling that boy about my
mother."

"And preparing him perfectly for the hypocrisy of the pulpit. That's your mother's Philosophy, I recognize it. She's an
ass."

"She's a bigger ass," I flared, "to go against her philosophy
if that's what it is. You've never let her do what she wants to
do. Or me. Always intervening. She locked me in a room in
Europe because of you. I would be in Europe right now if

not for you. I'd be in London and Paris and Copenhagen and Rome."

"Europe? You wanted that?"

"No," I said, ashamed.

Musing laughter.

On account of it I emphatically resumed: "You've always been in the way. A schnorrer with your hand out. What gives you the right?"

More laughter. "You."

"You just said I had nothing to do with anything."

"Not with me. But I can't help it about them—if they've always been afraid because of you. You've made them afraid."

"You've made them afraid. You're the one."

"You. You're the issue."

"Don't say issue. You've threatened and threatened—"

"Now and then I tell them I might come up to town. Is that a threat?"

"And badgered them from one end of the earth to the other—"

"The time we met by accident in France? That was just a coincidence. That Dutch girl that used to take care of you— you remember?"

"I remember," I said.

"I saw you on the beach. Couple of times I saw you. An ordinary little girl. Talking French to another kid. I wouldn't've noticed if *she* hadn't said who you were."

"I never saw you. I saw your bicycle. Bells on it."

"Bells! That's right," he said, impressed.

"I found your book."

"What book?"

"A little handbook of wild flowers."

"—What a bitch," he said reflectively.

"Anneke?"

"Also true. But I meant Allegra."

This time for some reason I did not contradict. The remnant of the fire sputtered. He took out his flashlight and stood it on its head on the table.

"They all think I want things from them, but they miss the point. They think I have a terrible ego. But the whole point is I don't. I'm the new man, modern man, Man without Ego. What I mean is this: I don't want anything. I don't want anything. *They're* always wanting something themselves, so they can't believe it, they can't understand it. That's why they can't cope with me. I can make them do anything I seem to want because there's nothing I really want. That's the secret, and it isn't a secret at all—excuse the paradox. It's just that the plainer a thing is, the harder it is to see it. Not wanting anything is what makes me perfectly free. *I'm* never angry, and your mother always is, day and night. It's true, hah? *I* never lose my temper. Why? Because I'm never disappointed. Why? Because there's nothing I'm ever wanting. There's not a thing in the wide world I want. Or ever wanted."

"You wanted me," I said.

He made a little noise, through his saliva, like the scratch of a match. "A second one way or the other and you might have gone the road of all the other dead cells on the planet. Is that what you call wanting?"

"I mean now. You wanted me now," I said with a hardness.

"Now?"

"In exchange for leaving Enoch alone."

"I didn't want you," he said distinctly.

"But I'm here. I'm here!" I wailed to the twelve kings' heads on the chairs. Some were in silhouette, like elves, with open mouths in profile, ready to quarrel. With my outrage they did not quarrel. It was incontrovertible: I was there. "It wasn't magic that brought me," I mocked, "was it?"

"Depends what you mean by magic."

I said: "Blackmail."

"Ah, you're a roughneck to use a word like that on a fellow like myself," he said softly. "Black magic maybe. Not that the laws of human nature get suspended. They get applied deeper than ever. A bit of pressure makes people become themselves all the more, haven't you noticed? —A piece of psychological poetry—that's all it is, and interesting you'll admit—and look at the bad name you pick for it, hah?"

"You didn't write to my mother?" I pressed. "You didn't scare her half to death to make her send me?"

"I wrote her. It doesn't mean I wanted you."

"You were ready to take everything from her—"

"Look, girlie," he broke in reasonably, "what d'you think I could want you *for?*"

I had no answer. "But she sent me," I murmured, "all the same. You made her send me."

"If she sent you it's *her* doing, isn't it? Don't try to shove it off on me. Besides, you know why she sent you, don't you?"

"So you wouldn't ruin things for Enoch," I said promptly.

His laughter turned along the shape of a boat: it began flat, and ended pointed.

"Girlie, she doesn't give a damn for Mr. Vand. It's plain as God and always was. Would she come herself? Could she? Oh no, it wouldn't do. The high and mighty don't -come themselves. They wouldn't dare—it's too honest. It's too close to the truth to come yourself, so you send someone else. Be indirect, that's the whole principle behind an ambassador, ask any authority on the subject." He stated: "She wants to get the taste of things."

"What do you mean, the taste?"

"The taste of me!" he finished gloriously.

"You think all she cares about is you?" I shot out.

He waved this away, and at that moment the moon entered him. It poured into his eyes and tried to seep out again under his fingernails. On the hand that looped upwards five glinting hoof-shapes battled. "And you know why you're not in London and Paris and Copenhagen and Rome? You know why you came? For the same taste. Coercion's only a pretense—a trick of pride. You came and she didn't make you come. She sent you and I didn't make her send you. You wanted to. She wanted to."

Anger slid in me. "None of that's true."

"True as heaven, plain as God. *I* didn't want a thing. I never do. I've explained."

"If I tell her that—"

"Tell her. Tell her everything you see. I know she's relying on you exactly."

"—you'll never get any money out of her again."

"Won't I though?" he sang at me.

"If she takes you at your word."

"But she never takes me at my word; I wonder why," he said slyly. "Not wanting, by the way, isn't the same as not needing. I don't want her cash. Never did. Why should I want her cash? But I need it. It's my needs she's been supplying, not my wants. You tell her that. Make it clear." He stood, unexpectedly yet not suddenly—the whole of him rose, but without simultaneity, as though he were arranging himself, as he stretched upward, in alphabetical order. He was a tall bellyless man. His silver thumbs hung from the pockets of his shorts. His eyes seemed silver, rooted deeply into his face like a startling pair of flowers: the thick lids an inch of leaf, and the effect of this was to give the bridge of his nose a vividness of solitude. Under the ascending moonlight I saw at last his undistinguished teeth—the ordinary human article, and he meanwhile must have felt my investigations, because he lowered himself to the ground and sat, looking up at me with a simplicity. He had changed the level of our two seeings, and it changed somehow the level of his tone. It came straight to me. It intimated an alliance. It invited me to his side of the argument. "Tell her," he picked up amiably, "it makes no difference to me if she's the high and mighty Mrs. Vand *in* the Embassy or out of it. No difference at all. Tell her I don't envy her husband if he's looking to get more of the world on his back. I don't envy anyone with the world on his back—not that esteemed lawyer fellow either, who I put the horns on twenty-odd years ago. Not if they steer the universe. So what if she's rolling in it, tell her—I live in her house when I like it, I drop her cash when I like it, in fact I'm quite a squire around the old place by now, I've got it humming, tell her, nearly like the old Bolshie days. Import kids to tickle me—kids tickle me, the way they're all phonies —and coolies in a pinch to do what's over my head, in this case a bum outboard. I've had all kinds though. She'll want to know such items, your mother. How I'm getting on and such. Now watch it while I spit." He did spit. "No apology, when my stomach's roiled I spit."

"You think that sort of thing'll bother her?" I said. "What you do around here? It's nothing to her what you do."

"Well, you tell her. Tell her and see. Tell her how surprised you were."

"Surprised at what?"

"Well? Say it yourself. You say it. What were you surprised at, hah?"

Expecting the infernal Dante, I had found the Virgil of the Eclogues—a green land with a shepherd in it: this was not my answer. "Nothing," I answered, but without sullenness. I moved into the sense of being subdued. He was slow, and spoke inefficiently; this pleased me. He was leisurely, he did not mean to overrun. He had the wastefulness of a natural force. He was mediaeval, but not like a knight; he was like the horse the knight rode, and that at once made him modern, not a social factor, but a factor of earth. It struck at me: I had feared him always; it was against the facts to feel this invasion of spirit and delight. I was afraid of his three dread names, I was afraid of the globe of his forehead not far from my knees, with its cold flat blades of light sunk in the hair. The fire was crowing with cinders, grainy and ending. Hints

of terror rambled like a faint familiar fever. We did not stir
in that plain summer heat, but from the buttonhole of his
static lips laughter opened out like a magician's trick bunch
of flowers: a great flossy abundant head. It made me laugh
with him. "Surprised at youth," he called out to me, though
he was not two feet away—it was nearly a shout, and set off
a sort of reverberation, a little moan among the tents. Some
of the smaller Purses were rustling in their sleep. "What a
very young man he turned out to be! No one told. They
didn't tell, hah? A surprise, hah? Vestiges. Your mother'll like
to hear it, it'll interest her that I've still got a face. —Fact is
I'm a ruin, a bagful of wrinkles, but never mind. She's not
here to see for herself, she's got you to rely on, isn't that
nice? You tell her all that."

"Man without Ego," I announced to the flashlight.

"It's nothing to her what I do?" he repeated, a speculative
finger on his nose. "You go ahead and tell her everything all
the same."

"All the same," I took up, rocking, "She doesn't care."

"I'm an enemy?" he said pleasurably. "An enemy. So be it.
Tell her I'm free. Want nothing."

"Want what you need."

"Get what I need. A distinction. Tell—no, mention. Mention Mrs. Purse. Right into the inner flap so to speak. Not of
the tent. Sand's where she does her work. Every night but
one. This one."

It flew from me—"Mrs. Purse!"

Laughter: long, long, long; until I bent my body away
from it. "I get what I need," he said. Was it fantasy and lie?
The mother of seven asleep beside the nuptial pole, under the
nuptial canvas tongue? Or was it Circe wandering nighttimes
among her motors, her toes straining sand, her pale neck
gleaming? "Not," he said, "that I don't have a settled life,
that's what they call it y'know, and proof of it. Evidence!
Full-fledged family man. Have that in common with Purse. A
father. The time comes when you need to express that. Show
what you have to show, if only to yourself—claim what you
have to claim. The descendant of Vikings and Greeks, and it
doesn't stop, it sits in the genes, the time comes to look into
the mirror of the future. Young, young, young—you I mean:
like a warrior's girl on an amphora—" He put forth a hand
slow as water and gripped my ankle. "Hers was thinner. Nice
foot she had. Ankle like an arrow, not this blunt thing all
bristles. Don't you shave your legs?"

"Yes—" A whip of throb danced in me. "Why do you compare me to my mother?"

"It's natural, I only do what's natural. Lend you my razor if you like. How long're you staying?"

"Until after the Senate hearings," I said firmly.

"That's trust!"

But I hesitated. "I thought how long was up to you. We all thought it was."

"All right. Let's say it is. Throw the Senate to the sharks for all I care. Up to me, all right? Want to go beddy-bye like the rest?"

The parallel knuckle encircling my ankle climbed like a ladder of bone: Laocoön seizing a live column. He withdrew the clamp of his power. It was as though he had willed himself back into the mere myth of being Gustave Nicholas Tilbeck. I scorned his Vikings and his Greeks. They were severances and pastiches. They had no whole existence. But his hand was the hand of a man.

"I'm wide awake though—"

"Good. So am I, and so's the moon. A boat-ride, how about it? She got the motor to work, they all say, so how about it? Try it out. When the going's good motor feels like a heartbeat. Prime it for tomorrow, what d' you say?"

"Now?"

"That's the word to live by."

We stumbled downward toward the beach. But it was only I who did the stumbling, caught here and there in a trench, or bang against a stubborn tuft of weed, which grew black as hair in the dark—he walking plainly down, taking his time, in lucid progressions of logical movement without complexity, like a chromatic scale rather than a chord. His walk was as real as his hand. "Damn—the flashlight," he said when he saw me baffled by what might have been a crater or a mound, uncertain how to spring it; the moon killed perspective. "I forgot the damn flashlight. —Did you get one for yourself?" I had not. I looked behind: there was the shining silver stick upside down on the table where he left it, a miniature Doric column far off, a tourist's souvenir of the Parthenon.

But without a beam he could not distinguish among the motors. Shadows of shadows confused their shapes.

On the sand I found a rectangle of clear polished light. It was a little pocket mirror. I held it up to let it flash; instead it blackened into invisibility. A thread of hair clung to it. "Mrs.

Purse's," Tilbeck said. —I brushed it clean of granules. Circe on the beach, combing before she lay down with her lover. —But he said: "Clever woman. She was using it to get a back view of some cramped area in one of these machines. Like a dentist's mirror. —I'll be damned if I can tell in the dark which is the one she fixed. Bunch of cripples is all I can see."

He went from object to object, puzzled. Machine parts sprawled as in the aftermath of a massacre—members and torsos. Among the mutilated bodies of motors a white fog of moon crept, and going down on his knees Tilbeck crept. His waist and legs disappeared behind the curious form of a machine. He looked like a faun—half man, half motor, the sort of faun a modern imagination might invent. And for a moment I pondered the bright image of the boy coming in the boat, his lower half magicked into keel, meandering toward me through dark swamp pools.

"Should we row instead?" I called.

"With the motor ready? What's the point? Anyhow you've had your fill of it today." And his hands reached from turret to turret, like a blind man's.

"—Throw said rowing makes you sick."

"No, only a little vertigo." He spat toward the sea. "I give up."

"Can't you find it?"

"There's the material for fifteen, sixteen motors here. Only one of 'em's whole. Don't ask me which."

"This one? How about this? This one right here." I tapped with the corner of the mirror on a squat collection of crenelated bars and ridged planes and deep jagged iron mysteries, and in the tilt of the glass accidentally happened on my face. There in its tiny window I saw my sudden mouth. The milky drizzle of moonlight spattered it. The skin of my lips shone.

"You're only guessing. She's disguised it," he said wrathfully.

I wore the gleaming membrane of my mouth, and turned the mirror to conceal the dazzle. My mouth was a shield; idiot words battered it. "But couldn't this be the part—" it was necessary to speak as if I had seen nothing of myself, and did not know—"it could be the part that attaches to the back of the boat—"

"Stern," he said.

"Stern," I acquiesced. He was crawling toward me. Crystals of sand sheathed his moving haunches like a moon-dappled mail. "This hooked shape here. This sort of halberd-thing. You see it, Nick?"—and tapped again. I had never said his name to him before. A brief hollow music stood in the air; something stiff let out the thin clean line of a ghost—the mirror cracked along the line, and came away in my hands like broken bread, or like the two remembered halves of the vernal ENCHIRIDION.

"Nick?" he said. "Why not Thor? Why not Loki? Why not Apollo?—No, that's not the one. It's got its crotch missing. That other pile two yards down is short a nose. Can't spot Lazarus among cadavers by night. —Sit down yourself, and I'll tell how they named me wrong. I was named all wrong. More's the pity. Well, in my time they didn't call babies Zeus—"

"Or Pan." A hot wetness fled quickly out of my finger. "Stupid—"

"What is it?"

"I cut my hand, it's bleeding—"

"Let me see." He strained close and touched my palm in its crucial center to support the hand. "Bend down, I have to see." I bent, and smelled the floweriness of wine in his shoulder—swiftly he licked the long shining narrow stream. "It's what they do in Sicily for first aid, the country people—to stop a virgin's bleeding, obtain the fresh-sucked saliva of the head of a family—" Another wetness wet my finger. Instantly the air dried it. The same wetness came on my lip. I tasted his saliva on my lip. The taste of the blood from my finger mingled faintly on the inner skin of my lip. Carelessly and silently he entered my mouth. His eye giantly near my eye was a great lily. His hand massing at my ankle was a tower. The faculty of taste altered and became skill. Carelessly and silently an evanescent tissue of the wine's floweriness opened a deep secret room. Unseeingness unlocks. Strange and new, I breathed the minotaur.

Then ran.

Up the bleached hill of sand, to the weedy black lawns, to the black wood where leaves like white tongues jittered, to the brook, careless and silent, swirling the gilt yolk of moon, to the three tents compact, intact, folded in, inviolate, to the panicked kings, to the table dense with civilization, ran, ran from the faun, head of a family.

A triangle of brilliance pouring from the flashlight led me into my father's house. It was dark and a ruin. I took off my shoes—their clack on the tiles was like pursuit. A grass spear

licked moistly up from a crack. I walked on grass and into
the room of kings and into the room where the haunch of
piano crouched. There was my bed, alive with minuets.

Following slowly up out of the beach, a small laughter
came from the beautiful man.

10

The next day I slept late on my sofa. When I awoke the
sun was dangling from the top of the sky and nothing had a
shadow. Tilbeck was gone.

"He's taken the boat to fetch some more groceries," Mrs.
Purse explained.

"Has he? But last night he couldn't tell which was the good
motor and which were the castoffs—"

"Oh?" said Mrs. Purse. "Were you down on the beach with
Mr. T. last night? I attached"—very lightly she paused over
this word—"the motor for him early this morning and he
left. Harriet Beecher went with him."

"To drop the bottle," Throw said, eating an apple.

"With a note in it," Manny said. "To drop a note you have
to be pretty far out."

"An ocean liner would be good," Al said.

"Or a plane," Foxy said, as if mentioning the devil.

"Maybe on the way to Pakistan," Throw said, "we could
open a hatch and toss one out."

"Or paint the note in red ink on Dee's bottom and toss
Dee out," Sonny suggested.

Mohandas K. Gandhi lay on the grass, naked and languid.
He lay like a meditating plaster cherub executed by a disciple
of Michelangelo; perhaps he had fallen off a frieze. His tiny
fat buttocks looked shockingly white. His little blue shovel
was stuck deep into the ground. The handle had no shadow.

"That'll teach him that Purses weren't made to hold wine,"
said his mother. "The silly thing woke with what I suppose

must be a hangover. He cried all morning and after he stopped crying he got like that—detached. I had to take off his clothes to cool him. Have some biscuits," she offered, "I'm afraid we've run out of breakfast cereal. Jam?"

They watched me eat.

"She doesn't say grace," Foxy observed.

"Ssh," said Mrs. Purse.

"She doesn't say Stella either. Maybe she doesn't know any Stella or Grace," Sonny said, sustaining a grin like an advertisement.

"I wish you wouldn't be so derivative, Ralph Waldo. You can't ring changes on your old mother forever. She's long since stopped being a belle. Though *some* people find her attractive enough. We're out of instant coffee too. Would you mind a tea-bag? Throw, stir up the fire and put the water-pail back on and don't dare take it off until there are plenty of bubbles. Speaking of tea," Mrs. Purse addressed me, "what in the world did Mr. T. lure you down to the beach for in the dead of night?"

"He thought I might like a boat-ride."

But there was an unconvincing overtone in this, as though I were myself aware of some fantastic element in what I said even as I dared arrogantly to say it. Shrewdly Mrs. Purse picked at my absurdity: "Mr. T. loves going fast," she reflected.

"So do I," Throw said. "She's already *had* a fast boat-ride, I gave her a dandy."

"That's pride in you," Foxy said sourly.

"It's not Throw's fault, it was pried out of him," Sonny said.

"Derivative," chided Mrs. Purse. And to me: "Couldn't find the motor could he? That poor man doesn't have enough resourcefulness to fill a hub-cap. He nearly tried to go off without any fuel—he forgot about fuel. I made him put the oars in just in case. He never thought of taking them—said he had full confidence in my repairs. Confidence in the fixings of a Purse, I told him, is subject to change. *Change*— nickels and dimes, you see—well, I really enjoy hearing that man laugh," she crowed. "And then what did you do?"

"When?"

"After you gave up about the motor."

"Came back up," I said.

"And talked, I don't doubt. Talked a good deal. A lot of family catching-up to do? A lot of that? I shouldn't wonder,

father and daughter—charming. I understand you haven't
met for some years? A reunion of sorts?"

"A reunion," I agreed. Walt Whitman and Bronson Alcott
were wrestling in the grass; I pretended to be distracted by
their shrieks. Over'and over they rolled, the poet on top of
the philosopher, and then the philosopher in the ascendant
position astride the poet. They shrieked and they rolled, their
pale heads full of scraps of straw, their pale joyous barbarian
faces patterned with clinging mud; they rolled right over the
sculptured baby, they rolled hugging one another right down
the hill, they rolled right through the froth of high-grown
Queen Anne's lace until the horizon toppled them out of existence.

"Those two," said Mrs. Purse. "They stick to each other
like Damon and Pythias. Excuse *me,* like a demon and a python."

"Derivative!" yelled Sonny.

"Derisible," Mrs. Purse said modestly. "Children are such
animals one almost prefers machines. Of course you need
switches for both."

"Di*RI*gible," Sonny interpreted.

"What?" Foxy said, but it was less a sign of incomprehension than a syllable of contempt. He followed his father in
being a spiritual, rather than a mechanical, Purse. It pleased
him that he had never heard of a dirigible; in morality machines do not matter, and clearly he was in favor of keeping
a mind clean of man's folly.

"It flies," Sonny informed an ignorant world. "You fill it
with gas. Not gasoline—*gas,* like laughing gas. Then it goes
up, it's lighter than—"

"Incorrigible. What I *said,* Sonny, was 'de*ri*sible'—"

"You said incorrigible."

"Oh, I'd like to flatten you! Purses *should* be flattened
when they come as empty as you. *Di*rigible, you mispro-
nounced it anyhow—well, go fly like one. I'm trying to have a
conversation with this young lady, can't you see that, Ralph
Waldo? Flee, if you please," commanded his parent, "flee,
flee—"

He took it properly—i.e., like a proper noun. "If I can find
a dog to light on," he acquiesced, and fled.

"Purses are capital, but too many at once!—give me an occasional bankruptcy. Look at that one there. If you leave a
Purse lying around someone's bound to pick it up." The
sculpture on the grass, hearing itself mentioned, suddenly

came to life and stuck its thumb in its nose. Mrs. Purse made
a sad face. "Your mother's dead? Now that's tragic. Mr. T.
told us she died very young, only twenty-two or so, over in
England. In Brighton, he said. Isn't that a sort of beach
place?"

I abandoned my biscuit with fingers stiffened by shock. Tilbeck dared anything. He dared the lie that plays with life and
death. He trusted, I saw obscurely, in a God like a man—interested more in the phantasmal re-arrangement of justice
than in justice. For the sake of a story he struck my mother
dead; it gave his story a color to tell it that way. A greyish
curl of margin appeared on the surface of the table, just
under the biscuit. A shadow. Afternoon was on the point of
beginning. "I've never been there," I said. Then I remembered that I had. Jaggedly I amended: "Though I was born
there."

Mrs. Purse chose not to remark on the contradiction. Perhaps she decided that to have been born in Brighton was not
the same as to have *been* in Brighton really; full consciousness might have been her criterion. Yet I had the sensation
—it was more than a suspicion, and could almost be witnessed physically—that she had made a small note for herself, and tucked it away. "Such a lot of travelers you are!"
she breathed out with a moment's absent brightness; then resumed funereally, "Mr. T. said he actually had to farm you
out—he'd tried keeping you, tried nursemaids and so on, he
said, but it didn't work. He told us he finally had to give you
to the Peruvian Ambassador's family to be brought up in."
She was very polite; she looked to me for corroboration, as if
she nearly expected me to believe she believed this.

"Not Peruvian," I said dully.

This encouraged her. She gave out a facsimile of eagerness: "But I suppose you speak Spanish fluently?"

"Not fluently."

"That's your modesty doubtless," she acknowledged with
disappointment. She had been hoping for total denial, not
ambiguity. By "not fluently" did I mean "not at all"? She
could not tell. "I wish you'd transfer some of it to Throw—
we have a terrible time with that boy's ego. Throw!" she
called. He was skipping stones across the brook. It was a
sport which Foxy would not partake in: stoning was contrary
to the creed of harmlessness. A water-bug might get hurt.
Throw thought Foxy thought Foxy might get hurt, and said
so. Foxy resented this; it confused compassion with cowar-

dice. Throw replied that *he* didn't think doing good meant doing nothing. The two sects competed in argument. Argument proceeded to obstinacy, obstinacy to conviction, conviction to crusade. Stones were hurled, not at water-bugs. Arms and shins and a feature of the face were struck. Martyrs' yells rose up piously. "Throw!" Mrs. Purse pounded on the table with a missile that conveniently came her way. Nothing happened; the Friend continued to war with the minister, D.V. *"Will* you see about that water? Bloody nose, good Lord!"

Henry David Thoreau departed from the field of action and peered into the suspended pail. Mrs. Purse's offspring were complaisant, if only gradually. "Boiling like mad," he said.

"Are you sure? Well *don't* bleed into the pot. Are there bubbles?"

"Sextillions."

"You know how you irritate Purse when you exaggerate. You *know* he thinks you use that word only because it's got sex in it."

Foxy looked affronted and stroked an elbow. A bruise glowed in it like an interior flower. "Purse is in the woods," he warned.

"If you don't mind," I said, "I'll let the tea go."

"Maybe you're right. It's too hot for this part of the month. It's too hot for tea and *Lord* knows it's too hot to drink blood. *That* must've bled a lot. That cut on your finger? It's since yesterday, isn't it? My boys turn into thugs when Mr. T. isn't here to organize them—George Fox is Caliban himself. Bloodshed's common enough here. I see you've not only noticed it but experienced it. Well! Do you find him an affectionate father?"

Bewilderment caught me. She had intended it to. —I said: "We're strangers—"

"That's just what I'm driving at. In spite of that, I mean. After such a lengthy separation. It must be hard. Though he's such an easy man to get on with, isn't he? So lovely and hilarious. Day after tomorrow we'll be gone and you'll have him all to yourself on a Purseless island. Prospero and Miranda—Mr. T.'s words. Pretty!" Her forefinger shook at me comically but grimly. "Without Purses the wages of sin never get paid. It *is* a sin to be a poor correspondent. He writes to *you* though?"

"To my mo—" I began, and stopped.

"Hm?" said Mrs. Purse. "I didn't catch—"

"Sometimes he writes."

"But not often enough. I see. Well, in your case it hardly matters. Blood is thicker than ink. In our case we're likely to lose him forever, though not, if you're with me, not the case itself: Mr. T.'s getting my husband a new *traveling* case actually—isn't that kind? He's remarkable about giving gifts— very sensitive to one's circumstances. I hope he thinks of alligator—I was enamored of your alligator thing the minute I set eyes on it. It shows he's just as sensitive about his own flesh. A wonderful man. It's *himself* he gives, like so few of us. Lord knows how many people have abused the privilege and taken advantage. Now Dee, get up, rise and shine. Make him get up, boys."

The warriors were sulking under a tree.

"He looks asleep," Foxy said, "with his eyes open."

"Maybe he's dead," Throw said.

"What's it feel like?"

"To be dead?"

"No. Drunk."

"It feels like a surprise," Mrs. Purse said. "I speak first-hand, a few of my wild oats were sown in moonshine. — Don't tell Purse that. I'm not a cradle Friend," she explained to me. "Purse's family all are. Temperance people too. I turned myself inside out when I turned Purse. —Isn't that indolence for you? That's just the laziest baby I ever saw. Look at that, a slack Purse. George Fox, aren't you always harping on being your brother's keeper?—when you're not bloodying his nose. Henry David! You're daydreaming aggrandizement, I can just see it. Carry him off, boys."

Accordingly the Mahatma was raised between them as on a palanquin. Halfway down the hill he squirmed free and waddled frantically away. They tagged him. He tagged back, screaming. They encircled him. He screamed, laughing violently. He sneaked under the fence of their arms. They overtook him. The sun oiled him with a white glaze. He was permitted to escape. Confident of his perfection and of the perfection of earthly joy, he jogged off. They pursued the burnished body of the little soulless god. Then all three were invisible. Plumes of noise chastely ascended, with no source but lungs. The god had a belly, buttocks, a neck like one firm finger, holy genitals pathetic in miniature; the god had grandiose lungs.

"Well it stands to reason you'd *be* more worldly than

most," Mrs. Purse chirped on, "growing up that way in an Ambassador's family. Did Mr. T. say Ambassador or Consul? I can't remember which—I imagine the difference in way of life is significant?"

"Not significant at all," I said reassuringly.

"You *are* worldly. How refreshing that is."

"Not refreshing at all," I said. And: "Here's your husband back from his walk." —Purse was emerging from a wrinkle in the green curtain of wood. He scampered out with the urgency of a man shaken underfoot by the pressure of millennia striving upward against the soles of his tennis shoes like great prehistoric nudging elbow-bones. He was reminded of time by the lower geological strata and what they might hiddenly contain: it made him break into a run. He arrived with his mouth hollowly sucked in, concealing puffs. "Good Lord," said his wife, "you carry on *exactly* as though you'd found an old bone in there. Have you ever known any paleontologists?" she suddenly asked me.

I thought of William: William as incredible boy. And what if bones had taken him in the end after all, instead of rocks? Would he have gone in for the marrow of things or finished just the same, on the rock of the law, on the hard outside surface of feeling? "No," I said, "I've never known any."

"Well," she gave out decisively, "they're snoopers. All of them. They have this fixed idea that you never can tell *where* you might hit on a mastodon. You didn't find a mastodon in there?"

He sat down on one of the kings' chairs and silently breathed.

"You didn't find *any*thing in there?"

"Groceries," he said.

"In the woods? Now what in the world—"

"Dozens and dozens of cans."

"Oh, well, *cans*. It's no trick to find empty cans—"

"Not empty. Full. All rusted through and years old. Piled up right behind an old gate-house. I cracked one open just by standing on it and out came a mess of green peas." He pressed his forehead on his hands. "A real stink to it."

"Boy scouts," Mrs. Purse guessed.

"And stakes pounded deep. For tents. I counted thirty-eight, that means better than a dozen tents in and out of the trees."

"Well, there you are! Scouts."

"A funny place for scouts," Purse said, "on private property."

"Don't think about it. You don't have to bring your conscience into everything. Just pretend it's a public park," Mrs. Purse said consolingly. "Try and feel at home. Meditate on one hotel bill times nine."

He glared at me as though the dishonest suggestion—conversion of the private to the public—had been mine. He was not unlike William. Perhaps all paleontologists, the proto- as well as the perfected, have the drive toward stern moralities uncontradicted by frequent (though impersonal) spawning. One remembers those mediaeval scholars who kept skulls on their tables to speak of the disintegration of the flesh and the eternal glory of the spirit. There is something of the ascetic in men who deal in tangible human parts. (Was he Purse's son, the splendid savage child tagging on the nether slope of the hill? —Ecstatic howls still flew, like the caw of a bird. —Or had Circe coupled with a hero while Purse lay bound in the snores of an aging athlete?) A faintly celibate odor—like snuff—came from Purse: the smell of the bossy Inner Light? unbelievably moving fragrance of the prehistoric, which can survive only in the pitiable thinginess of fossil? —Enoch had dealt in smoke merely, which escapes us; therefore he could remain engaged and engrossed in the world. Not so Purse, who pondered a concrete mystery. "Someone died in there," Purse said. "Did your father tell you that? There was a death in there."

"Was it those bones you were looking for?"—gently.

"Ghastly," Mrs. Purse clattered; it was the tone she kept for "Charming." "Really you shouldn't joke about it. It upsets Purse considerably."

"We're living in a cemetery," Purse said.

"Not *living,* just visiting. Think of it that way. And day after tomorrow we'll be gone."

"Some of us will," he said; he took me in with swift covert accusation.

"There'll be a poor showing," she agreed, "without Purses. You don't think the boy scouts did it?"

"Did what?" said Purse. "What boy scouts?"

"Killed someone in the woods. Though it'd be against their oath. It wouldn't be a *good* deed. Maybe," she speculated comfortably, "Mr. T. did it. You see that's what Purse *really* believes, though he won't come out and say so to Mr. T.'s face. Now if Mr. T. did it, he wouldn't've told us about it in the first place, would he? It stands to reason he wouldn't. Unless you're thinking of the Reverse Psychology of the Boastful Criminal."

"Bah," said Purse, and leaned down to pull Dee's spade out of the ground. "The fact is he *didn't* tell us. Polygon's Japanese did, and when I put it to Tilbeck he couldn't deny it. You can't deny what's public knowledge "

Mrs. Purse clasped her hands like an opera singer, signifying pleasure. "It's just that Purse suspects your father of romantic things in general. —And a murder would be so lovely and hilarious. —Oh look, now you've gone and yanked off the handle, Dee will be wild. Give it here, I'll glue it back— I've got some glue in my box. Well. Let it wait then—I'm afraid my box is still down on the beach. Did you see it down there last night? My tool-box?"

"No," I said.

"I left it right down there in the middle of everything. Father and daughter," she explained to Purse, "they were down on the beach last night together. I knew it wouldn't rain with the moon up like that, so I just never went to bring up my tools. Just left them out. I wonder how you missed them."

"There was a mirror—"

"Yes, yes, then you didn't miss a thing. —She didn't miss a thing down there. —Do you imagine your father's capable of anything like that?"

"Like what?" I said coldly.

"Oh, you know, what the boy scouts did in the woods. Though *I* feel perfectly safe with him, no matter what Purse insinuates. —You don't mind this sort of talk? It's all in fun."

"All in fun," Purse echoed. "Fee fie foe fun."

"Now don't be spooky with Miss Tilbeck. That's all very well with Harriet—"

"Miss Tilbeck," he said with slow invoking care. "Do you answer to that?"

"Purse," said Mrs. Purse.

"Miss Tilbeck. You jumped last night."

"*Purse.*"

"Now never mind. Did you or did you not jump last night?" Grimly he invigilated me. "I said good night to you with perfect cordiality and in return for it got a jump like a shot."

"I'm afraid that's right," said Mrs. Purse. "You did jump a little. Now that it's been brought up we might as well look right *at* it. I wouldn't explore this at all if Mr. T. were here,

you understand that. We don't like to embarrass him—he's
been so good to us. —I wish you'd remember that," she
hinted at her husband. "There's no profit in embarrassing a
Samaritan, you've said it yourself often enough."

The appeal to restraint was without effect. " 'Good night,
Miss Tilbeck'—that's just what I said, no more, no less. And
you jumped. You don't deny you jumped? You're never
called that? It's unfamiliar to hear yourself called that? Taken
by surprise? Not used to it? —Well, don't go!"

But I was already yards away. Behind me a dialogue
floated up clearly and slowly, as though written on those
pinkish, tissue-like, airy and undulating ribbons dirigibles
used to trail from their whalish rears: the picture of the
Zeppelin, the famed *von Hindenburg,* which burst in the sky
while my mother sat enunciating Kant in Adam Gruenhorn's
hole, carrying after it a sign like a cloud of light or blazing
afflatus, *Heil Amerika* or something just as glorious—more
seriously than surrealistically the idea of this slow, clear,
speaking and pursuing great balloon had ladled itself inexorably out of the jargony nonsensical lingua franca of Ralph
Waldo Emerson's badinage (Emerson the humorist), and
though I made a rush downhill for the saving edge of the
horizon, the terrible banners of the monstrous Zeppelin—a
vast navel creating the sky—flapped close and sent their subtle winds slapping and dipping after me: "He lied about everything," said the wind that came from Mrs. Purse, "you
ought to've seen her face. Contradicted every word. She's no
daughter—nothing to him." And Purse's wind said, "There's
a resemblance still and all," and Mrs. Purse's wind said,
"Yes, they both have the usual number of arms and legs.
Doubtless made use of them too, last night on the beach,"
and I hurtled out of the path of the talk freighted dirigible
listing with surmise, and ran beyond the caress of its awful
ribbons (bearing a heraldic crest marked Purse-stare et
Price-stare), and flung myself among the tag-players under
the hill.

The little hypocrites would not have me. They had been
friendly enough with Tilbeck there, but alone they would not
have me. I lay flat and motionless on a rock, as years before
Anneke had lain, and saw what she had seen over Europe:
the sky, blue only in imagination, full of whiteness rather, the
tone and color suggested by those plentiful textures white can
assume—here a sort of grainy mat, like clean new sensuous
water-color paper, elsewhere swirled like the top of a bucket

of cream, and sometimes flashing and hard, enamel of an immense tooth: square bold incisor turned on its back; and sometimes the white of an eye so large that iris and pupil and upper lid were too far to be descried, and fine red branches, not blood-vessels so much as a whimsical embroidery, spread across its oddly animal shine. Meanwhile the children wove their games on the beach and would not have me. It was hide-and-seek, and squatting and squealing among the motors, but they would not have me; it was catch with a tan tennis-ball and, though I importuned, they would not have me. And mysteriously it seemed that Henry David Thoreau, who had, after all, piloted me there and confessed the life of that family on the way, was leading them against me: once when the ball came by and I threw it back into the pale garland of players, he let no one snatch it from my shy aim. They had decided against me. Throw had told them I had been to all the islands of the world, including Staten, Ellis, and Crete: they disliked islands and lovers of islands. They disliked this island. It bored them. They ran back and forth on the beach like bright-maned lions on the floor of their cage. They knew every shell and every track and every tuft. They wanted out. The tide moved up toward my mossy rock and Mrs. Purse moved down to us. She brushed glue on the little spade's handle; then she reached again into her wide box for a hammer and a nail. The dirigible's banner had escaped; the metaphysical Zeppelin had blown up in the very air of its birth. She hardly spoke. Tapping the nail had her attention. "Purse has gone up to the second floor," she murmured, "to see Mr. Tilbeck's books. There's a library up there, you know," and tried to wiggle the handle. It was rigid and satisfactory. She tossed the spade on the sand near my feet, and at once, like a dog to a bone, Dee came, a flopping merman. The others called him away from me. "Ah," Mrs. Purse reproached with a crucial deliberateness, "don't you take Miss Tilbeck into it?"—and reluctantly and formally the ball was submitted to me, like a letter. Then it was Dodge Ball again. No one explained the rules, and a tan sphere pounded with a wicked suddenness into my thigh. "Oh fie!" cried Mrs. Purse, not minding; her eyes were on the hill, and Purse racing glumly down it. "Fie," he said, "fee foe fum. A sailor's books up there. What you would expect. What a sailor would read. Pseudo-science—self-educated. Fish books." "Fish? He knows literature," Mrs. Purse said, frowning, and by means of two strong bare arms hoisted Dee above the fracas: he hung there, shimmering like an old copper fountain—at any moment an arc of colored water would spurt from his inflated cheeks. She took him into the great wide legs of her lap with the superior calm of a madonna: "He knows all the poets, all the novelists. Is *Moby Dick* up there?" "There aren't any poets and novelists up there," Purse said. The idyll was beginning to pall. The tide was getting into Purse's shoes. Then the ball was lost to the sea. Waders ventured after it, but another tide commanded it farther and farther away. Some distant magnetizing tug was contending with the waves' certainty. The deeper bay, well out beyond the waders, seemed inhabited; there was a swell, as if from below; as if down, down, underneath, Neptune stirred his huge teacup; or stroked with immense strokes, in front of an undersea microphone, the back of a purring sea-mammal. The dark purring amplified. The water vibrated. The whole surface of the water swung, as though someone had suddenly given the globe a twirl; the sun did not swing—only shrank back into its own stubborn blaze, staring. "What is it—that noise?" I said; the Purses had leaped up to look across the bay. A white froth of Purselets stood vaguely rocking—beating time with the sea—in the white froth of the shore. "Motorboat," Purse said. "He's back."

Then we saw the boat—a crazy far fleck, violent and random. It shot stupidly to the right and to the left—stupidly and ignorantly. It could not find the land. "Is he drunk?" Purse said angrily. "Look at that." A muteness had taken the children. They grew out of the shoal like surprised marbles. "Look at that," Purse said again. The boat was circling the broad wild rim of its own wake. "Ah well," Mrs. Purse said, "let's wave him in, the sun's in his eyes no doubt." They all waved. "Does he see?" They waved in long languorous sweeps. But this only seemed to frighten the boat—it roared straight away, multiplying parallels of scallops and sending rough ebbing kinks to wobble against the waders' white ankles. "What the deuce," Purse said, "is he going off again? Can't the idiot see?"—but no sooner was the imprecation loosed than the boat knowledgeably turned, powerful with direction. Someone had changed his mind. "There," Mrs. Purse said, "he's coming straight in now. Wave, dears There. He sees us all right. Coming straight in. Do you see something white? Like a flag?—" "A corner of a dress—why doesn't the child sit down? It's Harriet Beecher's dress—" "She left wearing *pink*," Mrs. Purse said in a voice of triumph—"he did

just as he promised, bought her something new. It *is* a dress?
A white dress?" "Why doesn't the child sit down? She'll fall
into the motor, does she want to get caught in the motor?"
"Queer," Mrs. Purse said, "I can hear it all right but I can't
see it." "See what?" "The motor. There's no outboard on that
boat—look, a sort of open cabin I think—" "It's not him,"
Purse said sharply. "It's someone else," Mrs. Purse said.

The cabin's windshield, divided by a rod in the middle,
shot across our view with the precision of a slide under a mi-
croscope, but hid its microbes: the sun stood doubly on the
glass, then blurred off. Under this hot film of glitter two tiny
beings rode. Foam rushed from the prow. The creatures hurried near on spitting suds—now obscured, now raised to a
tiny eminence. Behind them a scroll of wake opened out,
splashing serifs. The level focus of our concentration magni-
fied two tiny faces above the fleet thing's flanks; it cantered
on the water; it had a cabin streamlined and syrup-colored;
the water under its solid sides seemed frail as crumpled tin.
Bay and sun and sight yielded before it. It came like the dolphin whom my mother's sea-crazed father revered as the
equal of humankind; confident and lovely as the dolphin it
came, smooth and skimming as the dolphin that grazes its
breast on the water's breast, as rich and well-formed, choosing the straight way with arrow-calculation, elegantly rolling
out shavings thin and curled from the sea's lathe, carpenter,
astronomer (so keen is the reputed intelligence of the dolphin), dolphin, but with a throat full of exploding bullets,
and serious as the hilarious dolphin is not. It had almost decided not to come at all. It had changed its mind. Something
the island did not fulfil for it. Still it came, as though it had
forgotten to arrange an alternative destination; it had failed
to reason out another path if the first happened to be obliterated. The dolphin does not provide itself against every even-
tuality—in this too it is like us, but not from choice, for in
the sea there are no paths; not for nothing has the poet called
it trackless. In the sea there is no road not taken. All roads
are one. Down the one road came the brilliant boat. It grew
as it came, enlarging according to a movie-sense I knew well,
so that with the abruptness of a cut in the film it revealed,
without visual or kinesthetic preparation, its exquisite figurehead: not on the prow, but within it, contained by it—a
laughing girl. Her face led to her form. Each was a perfect
flake, individuated in grace. The girl's form was delivered up
to the boat's form; inevitably her waist gave way to rooted-

ness. Only her arms were free in space: and these were fixed
in an eternal woman's resignation: she recognized, she made
do. She adapted with a gesture, laughing. The boat's intent
had suffered the wild awe of broken expectation. Yet land is
land. Shore is shore. The needle-bow snorted into the shallows and insinuated its tip into the halting pools that whin-
nied at the margin of the sand. Agitated whorls struck at the
waders' pale ankles—they glimmered like crystals in a sudden
berylline maze. Docile, dockless, the boat permitted itself to
be moored. Intelligence fled it as it put its will under the
yoke. Tamely it discharged whomever it carried. The Purses
watched. Sweat fell from them. Heat rose from their blazing
armpits. A young man stepped from the boat. He pulled after
him a burden of rolled-up wool. He turned, and at his turn the
figurehead in a white suit descended. Her thighs moved, alive,
banded by a surface of cloth that barely moved at all, so near
and taut upon her trunk was it stretched, and therefore her
clothing seemed for the moment alive too: with both thighs
tense she stood on the rim of the boat, and the current of
tenseness entered her slick niveous skirt, and she jumped, like
a cat in its catskin, to the bubbling sand. Her voice began.

"Well in that case I don't see why we bothered to bring the
sleeping bags, all that fuss for nothing—I thought this was
going to be an *un*inhabited island," Stefanie Pettigrew complained, "don't you ever keep a promise? —Well for sweet
Pete's ugly sake!"

She had recognized me. So had William's son. His face
looked oddly vulnerable. Then I knew why. Something was
missing—the helmet of power. He had come to this place because he had uncovered evidence of its putative emptiness.
He had come furtively. An old notion shifted in me: loss. I
felt that I had once loved him, but no more. Still the prong
of love picked in me. Whom else then did I love?

11

The Purses. They never were part of this story (this ostensible father's tale), and here they take leave of it. But no. Both statements are wrong. Charon the ferryman is part of every story; a Purse had crossed me over. Nor do I mean that the Purses will now vanish out of the event. Physically, they remain. Physically, here stands Purse himself inside his rubbery athlete's bag, always faintly panting, always faintly purifying. Four nights in a row his wife, abetted by his own healthy sleep, has betrayed him. If Mrs. Purse should conceive an eighth child, perhaps it will be halfblood to me; perhaps not. The question is of no moment. The Purses will last, as Purses, forever. Occasionally they will throw up a little god who will intuit that the Inner Light must never be covered over with matter. The Purses love matter only. Purse loves money and bones. Mrs. Purse loves money and flesh: flesh of her flesh, and that other indwelling flesh that is necessary to incite and begin flesh of her flesh. The Purses are, as we say nowadays, monomaniacs. Mrs. Purse has her one deathly joke. Purse has his one deathly bargain-hunt: that the cost of nine should equal the cost of one. Neither of these consistencies is what makes them monomaniacal. Mrs. Purse, after all, though a bit of a fool, is admittedly an ex-prodigy, a genius, an uncanny machinist and inventor. She has invented more than that automatic stair-climbing wheelchair for her aged mother. I learned, but have not the wit to describe, the impressive nature of many more of her inventions, all practical, homelike, essential, enduring; all duly lodged with the United States Patent Office. And Purse, as his son affirmed, is not very obscure, at least not to other paleontologists. Though not a genius like his wife, unlike most men he is intimate with Hyracotherium (the little eohippus, whom Harriet Beecher Stowe Purse would have delighted to ride, had it only survived into our Cenozoic Era); he is one of the few persons alive privileged to have looked upon beauty bare in the remains, like a suggestion of necklace, of the Eocene Coryphodon; he can infer a quality of brain from a quantity of skull insides; he can identify a whole huge remote fossil animal from one small bone of one of its most casual toes. Plainly, the Purses count, and must be taken seriously. Therein lies their monomania: they take themselves seriously. But they must not expect that we will.

The Purse children. Of these it can most profitably be said that they *are* children. Let me explain. (Hold. Are you impatient for knowledge of my love? Unlike you, I have infinite leisure. A paradox: for "you" can mean only myself; I am my only reader. Then let me explain.) Children, though they are always becoming older, hence always becoming someone else, someone other, do not know this truth about themselves. They think themselves static, they think themselves eternal exactly as they are. This indeed is the real, not the imagined, condition of elves, and is why we fear them. (Do we believe in elves? No. In the concept of elves? Assuredly.) The static is what we fear in life. Stasis is itself a monomania, and children, who believe that they *are* and hold themselves altogether apart from becoming, are therefore natural monomaniacs. The Purse children must be repudiated even more decisively than their parents. Moreover they are uncommonly verbal, in the manner of children and elves; they adore words, but not for their uses—rather, as magic-in-themselves. (*Cf.* Rumpelstiltskin. *Vide* lyre and lute for liar and loot, where music, and rogues are indistinguishable; or derisible-dirigible, wherein the substitution of a single letter can produce a flying machine out of mere mockery.) Magic is inanity, is imbecile, and exists for its own sake; so do children; so do elves. And we fear them all equally. And equally they all despise us when they know we fear them. Even in setting it down I have trembled at the terrifying chatter (word-love) of the Purse children. Stasis. They do not progress. What they say leads endlessly, leads nowhere. I have ground my teeth to hear them speak. Charon plying his pole talks all the way. Beware. The Purse children, who would not have me (as elves keep from us the secret of their arcane lives), torment me. I fear the quotation-marks that come like signs out of their mouths to warn me they will speak. Seeing those two small tongues curled in air I crave escape: deafness, blindness, only let me not be obliged to put down a magic as obvious as Purselets' speech; I dread and despise these Purselets. They are repudiated out of the tale. I am glad to see them go.

I see them go. Purse takes them away, herds them up the hill. They are not talkative now but queerly dumb, dumbstruck. Purse takes them away because ("Look who's on the welcoming committee!" Stefanie says) he senses an impropriety in the amazed confrontation on the beach. We all sense the same: Stefanie and William's son, in search of a desert island, have arrived on this populous one to sleep together, in bags or otherwise. Purse shuns adultery. On the other hand, being "liberal," he resolves not to take note of it. He snores through his wife's. He shuts his eyes to his host's. But here it is, raw and open. Too much is too much. The children must be removed from this animal heat. He guides them slanting upward along the slope, sand metamorphosing into grass; he guides them into the house where it is cooler than the bottom of the sea. Here they will be safe from the animal heat of the sun. They file through the pompous door. And immediately a strange mushroom-like smell tenses and teases, bitter but obscurely pleasurable, so tantalizingly vague that it is nearly inaccessible to their struggle for it: it shudders on the bare threshold of acuteness, and will not disclose itself. Mold. Minutely it gauzes and grazes the refrigerator's, the sofas', the piano's backs and legs and undersides. The first day-heat has inflamed it; its bluish velvety steam is like the licking path of a tongue. Now it grows remote, too withdrawn for the coarseness of a fingertip. They cannot recapture the paradisal smell, and regret consciousness.

In this way Purse leaves the tale. He is spiritually fastidious: and the lovers have arrived. Hence the tale (a lovers' tale) repudiates him.

Hereafter the Purses are present, but accessible to matter only: though spirit may rule the island.

12

"You always seem to turn up," Stefanie rushed on at me without a second's gap, "first that office party thing, and now, when a person wants *privacy*—"

Mrs. Purse intervened by sticking out her manly hand. "Ethel Purse. Hostess-surrogate for the island's boss. So far as I've observed he doesn't turn anyone away. Stay for a meal, dears, whoever you are."

"Well for goodness' sake we've *come* to stay. For *days*. We certainly didn't expect to find a whole mob."

"The mob are Purses. By their myriads shall you know them. This is private property, dears."

"For goodness' sake we know that. We weren't looking for Yellowstone Park. We weren't looking for a place that's advertised in the *National Geographic*. It's your fault," she told William's son. "You said if there was anybody at all it'd be some seedy old caretaker who maybe wouldn't even *be* here, and if he was we could pay him to get out—"

"Ah well," Mrs. Purse said gaily, "I'm afraid bribery won't work with us Purses! The catch is we're not due to leave here for another day or so—you know all Purses have their catches, and *we* keep ours tight shut against monetary temptation. And when *we* go that'll still leave Miss Tilbeck, and heaven knows when her father'll decide he's had enough, I suppose not until the cool weather sets in—"

"You mean there're more?" Stefanie said, staring up the hill.

"Yes dear. The Tilbecks, I said the Tilbecks. And one more Purse, not included in the recently departed pack— Harriet Beecher, who at this moment is writing a letter to Eternity upon the faceless deep. Bottle with a note in it," she explained, all good humor.

"Well isn't this really ridiculous. Till *what?* I mean," Stefanie lectured, "Anybody who's *on* this place is really trespassing. That's law. I hope you all realize that."

Mrs. Purse's radiance paled before this plain hostility. "That's gall, dear. *We* were invited."

"*We* know the owner."

"He appears to know multitudes," Mrs. Purse noted.

"It's not a he, it's a she." It was clear that the girl had recently accumulated certain limited facts. Outside the world of Miss Jewett's long rows of file cabinets suddenly loomed and fled, and at their end William's son, a steadfast centurion, dangled his doffed helmet. "Unless you mean the trustee?"

"Oh shut up, Stef," William's son ordered. "How'd you get here?" This was aimed, enveloped in a furious growl, at me.

I borrowed from the nearest Purse. "I was invited."

"Bully for you," Stefanie said, and kicked at a pebble like an egg. "You usually show up even when you're not."

"Not what?" Mrs. Purse wondered.

"Invited."

"Ah but she's the guest of her father—there's such an attachment between those two. Very touching, considering they're strangers. When he gets back be sure to watch for it. Loyalty and so on."

"Look, she doesn't *have* a father," Stefanie corrected.

Mrs. Purse said. "Hm."—A syllable of indication leading to vindication.

"Well she doesn't. Unless you mean her *step*father. And he's in Washington."

I demurred quickly, "He isn't. Not yet."

"For goodness' sake my own *fiancé* told me, you think he'd lie? Your stepfather had to beat it down there early this morning because this *coun*try he's supposed to go to's in trouble or something."

"But the hearings aren't till—" I broke off and looked at William's son, who at once looked angrily at the sand.

"Till, till," Stefanie parroted. "Till *what*, I keep asking."

"Til*beck*," Mrs. Purse provided craftily. "You're gazing right *at* one, dear. If you don't mind my saying so I should think you'd know this young lady's name. You certainly seem to know *her*."

"Sure, we go to parties together all the time. Though that's not her name, what you said. 'Sfunny, she's got the same name *he* has"—and arched an immaculate thumbnail backward toward William's son. He stood glumly; a mouse of violence ran in his eye.

Mrs. Purse repeated loudly, "Tilbeck?"

"That's not their name, I just told you."

"Mm." Vindication Number Two.

"All the same they're not relations, it's sort of funny."

"Ah, they're not," Mrs. Purse murmured.

I burst in insistently: "What do you mean Enoch's in Washington?"

"They've started those hearings." But this was a surrender to despair: William's son, I saw, did not care to speak to me. Astonishment victimized him as it did not victimize his fiancée. She readily adapted to perplexities and surprises. Like Tilbeck (how quick and strange the parallel!), she took them for natural forces, and took herself for the same. She appeared to love to be confounded, and to confound. But William's son was a disillusioned moralizer. It had not yet settled in him that I was there. He had expected nobody. He dealt badly with chimeras, wrong turnings, breakages. Abruptly he threw out at me: "They got them going extra early."

"The hearings? Why?" I demanded.

"Oh *don't* start talking politics, it's *such* a bother." Stefanie allowed herself to slip into a shadowed hollow in the sand. Her stretching rubescent arm found a ledge of motor and she leaned deliciously, rubbing a powder of rust into the pocket crease of her elbow; henna glowed on henna; the curve of her wrist yearned downward like a rosy swan. "Look, I didn't come all this way in that damn ship just to listen to politics."

But Mrs. Purse was fascinated. She was fascinated by Stefanie, who seemed stuffed with vindications. "That's a handsome little craft you've got there," she said placatingly. "Twenty-footer?"

"*I* don't know."

"You measure fore to aft on a straight line parallel to the center line, excluding sheer. Don't count bowsprits or bumpkins. Looks to *me* like a twenty-footer. I see you don't have any sidelights on 'er. Not required to, probably, under twenty-six." A joyous cordiality lit her.

"That's man's talk," Stefanie said disgustedly, "and if you ask me it's just a bother. That ship's an engagement present from my father and that's all I have to know about it. He didn't say I'd have to join the damn *Navy* to ride in it. I hate boat-talk like that even worse than politics."

Mrs. Purse reflected on the collapse of her comradeliness. "That's your loss, dear, if you don't want to gain something out of a Purse. From the way she sounded coming in I'd say she needs a bit of a tune-up."

"That ship's brand *new,*" Stefanie said, miffed.

"Is it monogrammed?" I asked.

"Monogrammed? Well for Pete's sake you don't monogram a ship."

"Boat!" Mrs. Purse cried. *"Boat,* not ship."

"You don't monogram a broom either. Engagement present, is he *that* rich?" I said, mimicking a memory.

"Who?"

"Your father."

"Oh—" A bruise of recognition swelled her mouth. "You mean about that business at your bon voyage thing. What I said that time? You still mad about that? I always have to ask how rich people are. My fiancé"—untypically she mocked the word—"doesn't think it's polite. William thinks I get it from my mother, it's all because my mother didn't go to Miss Lamb's or Miss Jewett's. Well for goodness' sake she *couldn't,* she was in California. I mean even *William* says Miss Jewett's is full of nouveaus nowadays anyhow, and he doesn't send *his* kids there, so how come he blames my mother for never having gone? I mean if he wouldn't send his own kids? I mean look at Nanette—"

"Oh God. *Stef,*" William's son groaned. "Cut it out, will you?"

"She's mad because I once asked her how rich she was. Well I know your father's always telling me I have this tendency to assess money-value, not that it's so bad if I do. If you ask me so does he. The only difference is I do it out loud."

The pods of Mrs. Purse's eyelids split wide. "Obviously no one *here's* ever been in want of a fat purse," and punched the jolly flesh of her padded jowl. "I'd say three thousand, thirty-five-hundred for that little job?" she guessed, gliding her tongue toward the gold-brown of the cabin. "Though no one can match Mr. T. for generosity—" Did she hope someone would make her a gift of the boat then and there? She had a humorous afterthought: "A terrible lot of fathers in this conversation—I wish I had a penny in my purse for every one of 'em! Including," she added, "your stepfather. I didn't know you had a stepfather, what with your mother passed away—"

"Her mother?" Stefanie said.

"She's dead."

"*Her* mother's not dead."

"Hm," said Mrs. Purse, unfazed by resurrection. "I'm glad to hear it."

I burnt my ships. (Ships, not boats.) "And Tilbeck lives off her," I told her for no reason other than danger.

She did not grasp this.

"He doesn't have any money of his own. It's all hers. If he gets Harriet Beecher a new dress, *she's* the one who's bought it."

"Who's this Tilbeck?" William's son asked finally.

"The caretaker," I offered, presenting Mrs. Purse with Vindication Number Three.

But it was less welcome than the others. She said heavily, "That makes sense. Someone employs him to live here? Your mother employs him? That makes sense." She sighed like a falling tree. "*We* were never taken in. Though it'll be a shock to poor Purse. Promises made and so forth. He had hopes. Well, I have to see to my hungover baby," and made a little distance between us.

"Hopes!" Stefanie said, uncomprehending but only briefly bitter. "Everybody has hopes some time or other. We had hopes until we got here." She turned up a pleading palm to William's son. "Come on, pussyhead, sit with me. Right here. The sand's so nice and warm under my fanny. Quit looking mean, *you* couldn't know the Marines'd landed."

But he did not respond. His legs spread with deliberation. I saw the bluish globes of sweat on the breast of his shirt, extending meridians down from his armpits and up from his navel and groin. "Exactly what're you doing here?" he put it to me.

"Vacationing."

"Cut it out. You gave up Europe."

"That's right," Stefanie accused. "She gave up Europe."

He persisted: "Last time we met you swore you didn't know this place existed. You didn't give up Europe just to come *here*."

"Why not?" Mrs. Purse intervened, showing a glint of vengeful little tooth below a fatness of gums. "Could be she's here for the same reason you are."

"Oh, not her! Nobody even dates her! She never looks at *any*body! Ovum and Virgin—dead Latins, that's all *she* likes," Stefanie blew out; her nape yielded to flatness and she spread her hair among seashells, laughing.

"You haven't seen her look at the caretaker," Mrs. Purse

called back—she had begun to climb away from us. Her
words dissolved: "Wait'll you've seen"—the gossamer tail of
the dirigible came sailing out, and it might have been "Mr.
Implausibility" that she smeared across the sky; or might not.
Perhaps it was only "Nicholas T.," with the orphan Gustave
unthreaded in air.

"Mr. Generosity!" I yelled up the hill to Circe, spitting
malice for malice. "He gives himself, like so few of us!" She
thought me her dark rival in covetousness, not of cash but
flesh. Ponderously she gained the earlobe of the slope, then
its mound. The sun spattered her out of sight; little by little
she faded off.

"Horrible thing, talks like a garage," Stefanie said. "What
were all those horrible kids before? Bunch of ghosts."

"Tilbeck salvaged them out of the Automat."

She tittered. "What happens if you put a nickel in that
woman?"

"She brings forth," I said, "a child, a machine, or a pun on
pocketbooks. They're practising Urdu for digging fossils in
Pakistan. I've only known them"—this was melancholy—
"one day."

"What a day!" But she had already given up thinking of
my acquaintance with Purses, or its length; she was rejoicing
in life and weather. A sudden mood sat her up. "Did she
mean you're in love?" she asked in awe. "With that what's-
his-name—"

"Nick," I said. "Nick's his name. The source," I told
William's son, "of Mrs. Vand's miscellaneous expenditures."

He took this meditatively. "You really *do* know everything," he said. "You did right along. That's quite an act
you've been putting on."

"No act. He that increaseth knowledge increaseth sorrow."

"For Pete's sake, if it isn't politics it's got to be poetry. I
just can't be bothered with that eth stuff," Stefanie said.
"When even somebody like Euphoria Karp puts in an eth, I
tell *you* they lose me. I go as far as a wilt, but believe me I
draw the line at eths." But she screwed her face to cultural
duty, as though all at once reminded that her fiancé's tastes
required it of her. "Who wrote that anyway? That eth business you just did?"

"Oh, just some Preacher." To William's son I said: "I got
it all from your father."

"What do you mean all?"

I stated: "All."

"Knowledge she means," Stefanie said intelligently. "Anyhow it looks as if your sorrow didn't increaseth. What's this Nick like?"

I said abstractedly, "Young—"

But this made her scowl. "I don't like 'em young. *How* young?"

I was reluctant. "I guess around forty."

"Forty! Jesus Christ, I bet you think Methuselah's still in diapers. D'you put yourself to sleep counting wrinkles? I mean aren't men absolutely *dry* by then?"

William's son said, "Let it go, Stef."

"Well why?"—belligerent.

He mused unhappily down at his long feet. "You're in a glass house, that's why."

"Well my goodness! *You're* not old, and not too young, or anything. You're just right," she crooned, and reached up to pull him to her.

"Not that particular glass house."

She was genuinely baffled: "Well what other one is there?"

He addressed not her but me. "I know what you think," he said.

"I think you're brave."

"God, how I hate a satirist. God I hate 'em. Listen, you think I'm not like my father, right? Don't live up to the old family purity. You still think my father's got that old family purity."

"*What* glass house?" Stefanie insisted.

"I told you I wasn't a Christian gentleman. I told you that."

"Congratulations," I said, "on your fall among mortals," and to the girl, "Won't they miss you at home?"

"I'm out camping with old Beverly Reveille. Allegedly. (That's law again.) And pussyhead went and told William and his mama a regular bitch of a story. He's getting really good at stories. He's a *beautiful* liar," she praised.

"I'm getting more like the old man every day," he acknowledged.

It was true. Already he seemed domesticated. Obediently, familiarly, he laid his head on the sleek glissade of her lap. She had tamed the buffalo.

"*I* don't think you're like William at all, whatever anyone else around here says. —I bet your father never went away with your mother before *they* were married. —Oh." She bethought herself. "Is that what you mean by glass house?"

"Drop it, Stef," he begged. "Get your teeth out of it."

"You and me and her and this Nick forty, fifty years old? *I* don't see any resemblance."

"He's *young*," I said distinctly. (Obscenity—no, constancy, of the past. The hideous threat of constancy! —A boy of seventeen had made me.)

But she was looking wilfully around her. "Don't apologize, pussyhead. You really don't have to. A secret's a secret. As far's the *world's* concerned, we might've come just because we're shell-fanciers or something. Or for the scrap-metal. Or —I know!—because we're crazy about dense populations—" Her nostrils opened to challenge me. "*I* don't care who knows what."

"Me neither," William's son grunted, and threw a narrow brown trouser-leg over her taut linen thighs. "You dared me to it," he told me. "Cohabitation without benefit of the law. It has other benefits."

"It's not as though we weren't *engaged*," Stefanie said.

—He had lost the imperial mark.

"Look, while I'm on the subject—"

"*I'm* on the subject," William's son interrupted: he pressed his warm weight down, and granules loosened beneath her, sifting, hissing.

"—of engagements I mean, remember that weird man, Governor or somebody, *you* know, the night we got engaged after your bon voyage thing—"

"McGovern? My mother's editor?"

"That's who. That weird man. Him, the one with all the bedtimes. Does she still keep'm around?"

"He defected to California," I said.

"He was a weird one though." —Her program of domestication included a certain playing-off of one bull against another. It was curiously effective. Her fiancé seemed calmed, even comfortable. She had transmuted rage to a coziness. "William thinks California's a slum. Anyhow I adore weird men, don't you?"

"She's made an example of me," William's son said accommodatingly. "Talk about weird. Head of a cat—"

"Oh come on, pussyhead, it's just affection. Besides I don't care what your *head* is like"—she stroked it—" 'slong as your legs and stuff are all right. You have *such* nice legs."

"You too." He shut his eyes easefully. The sunlight beat a tune on their intertwinings. I felt, in their company, always obliged to play the part of *voyeur*. Such a part had I played

on the terrace, watching the two of them kiss while the river
darkled in ambush below. "Head of a cat, legs of a human.
Centaur in reverse, that's me," William's son said.

As usual he compelled me to cheap philosophy. "In the
end everything reverses itself," I vapidly announced, thinking
how he had declined. Once she had called him halfway
human: it was a clairvoyant celebration of her desire and her
skill. —He had lost the imperial mark. He mewed. The tragedy of the halfway human: half power, half victim. The boy
in the boat, force and gross potency of prow, bland boasting
muscle of child. Or Gustave Nicholas Tilbeck crouching on
the beach—the terror of the human head, the vital fork and
member machined, made mechanistic. This island turned men
from what they seemed to what they were. Plumed helmet
shadowed little soft snout of a cat. My grandfather knew well
how the place, on its own, would breed a museum: he had
his will, though not according to the terms of the trust. I remembered how admirably the centurion had spurned his
fiancée's arm, shining ochroid arch of horn, as we walked
forth to the terrace; and the masterfulness of his "encore un
peu" in the roseate circlet of her ear; and then, shutting me
and all the universe out, his long peremptory kiss. Now his
forehead was in the shade of her chin, and she twiddled in
his rough dull hair; it was a weakness, and new in him. Head
of a cat. He had abandoned the sneer of the helmeted centurion, keen and glorious, for sensuality. He mewed for her.

"Oh look, never mind reverse, not my pussyhead I hope! I
mean I *love* cat's heads, the way they have their ears all velvety, but I could do without the crawly of their legs and their
spooky tail and stuff, thank *you*," Stefanie said stoutly, giving
out one of those sprays of laughter, like so many flying
florets, that had recalled broken-hearted youth to her father-
in-law-to-be.

But something in my statement recalled William's son to
himself. "Speaking of reversal—" He flopped lazily erect,
pulling torso from torso with exquisite reluctance, as though
some fierce sticking plaster, with all their hairs embedded in
it, hair of head and leg and puberulent niche and cache of
arm, had kept them close and dedicated. "—You know why
the Senate moved up the date of those hearings? Very interesting."

"Interesting like a crutch," Stefanie said, left alone with
her bosom. "Somebody's crown's loose over there, that's all.
Not a real crown," she explained. "It's not as though they

had a king or anything. If they had a king I could at least *stand* it. I'm crazy about royalty—"

"The regime needs bolstering," William's son confirmed.

"—especially queen's clothes. Tiaras kill me."

"What's that got to do with the hearings?" I asked.

"Government's suddenly in a terrific hurry to get an Ambassador over. They figure a quick application of pomp and ceremony should do the trick. —That's according to a Senator pal of my father's. You know how my father's always crawling around horses' mouths. Trouble over there, dissident elements—"

"Communists," Stefanie said positively. "Bomb-throwers."

"—so now we want to get someone over as fast as we can."

I wondered. "Pomp and ceremony?"—and thought how my mother's lust for these would be fulfilled at last.

"Show 'em the power of the U.S. The mighty fist. Show 'em we're right behind the regime. They won't dare anything if we're behind it. That's the theory."

"Pussyhead, come back," Stefanie said.

I had to wait while he let himself be gathered over her impatient glitter. She licked the peak of his nose, upside down, and seized his fingers and made him dabble them in the mysterious crevice of her collarlessness.

"It'll be a shoo-in for Vand," he finished, absorbed in Stefanie's small clever luring fist, indifferent to the mighty one behind the regime.

But all brightly the note of her voice struck: "Who's your father? How come that woman kept saying father? I never knew you had a father."

"She doesn't, stupid," her lover answered.

13

Up to a point love is plagiarism. If no one had ever remarked a pair of lovers—how they dazewalk through the streets of cities in the shelter of their wound secret arms, how they dawdle interminably in their chairs, how they pick and slap at one another, how they stare and laugh, how they talk incessant trifles, how they stand at stalls studying the five-cent candies—the ritual art of flirtation would be unknown. None of it is instinct; all of it is imitation. Who invented it? Ask who invented the wheel. What spread it? Rumor, the mother of convention.

There are twelve kings' heads; but thirteen live on the island this night—an island well-named by the hopeful Dutch, who called it Dorp, supposing an inhabited future. So, being thirteen, we make the place a town after all—"the Last Supper," someone says (Tilbeck, probably), counting citizens; there is one seat short, of course. "Now if we can just get a betrayal going here, that'll eliminate *one*—" "The Holy Book should never be parodied," says Purse. But the atmosphere has altered: a shudder of thunder, miles and miles away; the vast table somehow askew, plundered, dirtied, piled with cartons; Mrs. Purse punlessly manipulating a can-opener; no fire; the xanthochroid children ludicrously feeding on tinned fish, while all around live fish presumably breed and brood out their underwater lives; the sunset spoiled; Dee unwilling to relinquish his chair for a fraternal lap; the two newest guests in a single heap consequently; Harriet Beecher returned in the same dress she left in; Tilbeck reduced in status from patron to non-patron of Purses.

And in the lovers too there is something ritual. It is as ritual for William's son to show virile embarrassment as it is for Stefanie to spoon new jam between his lips. It is as ritual for her to bleat at a tiny blade of lightning as it is for him to deliver scientific consolation. Ritually Stefanie sways on his knee. Ritually she first unlaces and then thieves his shoe and begins to run with it into the trees. Ritually—a little wearily —he runs limping after her. They penetrate the wood. Perhaps they kiss there; perhaps not. At any rate we hear them scrape and scamper; leaves already dust the ground in there; the hum of thunder brings a gust; they come out with red and yellow leaves shaken onto their hair, quarreling and calling animal names. "You skunk." "You raccoon." "You motheaten." "You chewedup." "Dirty old bear. "Five-toed sloth." "Blind as a bat." "Gnat." "Nit." "Double that and eat it." "Triple on you." "You began it." "You did." "I didn't." "You did." "All right then I'll *get* you for it—" And once more the ritual swiftness is on, and no one's will at work: the patient

assaulted trees take them in and shoot them out: they dart
and shriek in the immortal chase. Obeying art, the girl pursues the boy into the grove. Obeying art, the boy flees. Rites
are always witnessed: the Purses watch, I watch, Tilbeck appears not to watch—his neck is stretched up, the bottle's neck
is upside down, the funnel of one activates the funnel of the
other—but all the same secretly watches through the ruby
window of wine. A tree hides the girl, a gap reveals her, she
stalks, she vanishes, she reappears, she is seen running, a
great thick old trunk blots her out, her arms hug a thinner
trunk (but she has stopped behind it, so that what we merely
mortal watchers note is a little tree wringing its wild human
hands), she runs again, screeches, embraces a mightier tree;
its root grows out of her parted leaning legs. After her the
tired buffalo lumbers, scolding. She heeds not him but the
wood, and lets herself be caught. Kicking up the long red
stems of big leaves, her tongue visible in the corner of her
open mouth, simpering like a saint, out she steps to be
claimed. He claims her. And here a single inquisitive scimi-
tar-edge of light slices through the ruined and flattened sky,
and picks out the two of them (but only one of them spent)
emerging side by side, each dangling the other's shoes, barely
touching shoulder to breast, wrist to neck. "A man died back
there," Stefanie calls as they come.

"We know that," said Harriet Beecher: with the plainness
of complacence.

"*I* think it's just too creepy—"

"And well you should." Tilbeck persuaded the wine from
his mouth like a cornetist quitting his instrument during the
chorus of violins—a temporary separation for the cause of
art. "His ghost lives in that oak. The not-so-skinny one. The
one you put yourself up against. You poked him in the bellybutton I think."

Purse said quickly: "No one knows who did it."

"This little looker did it," Tilbeck said. "Poked him in the
bellybutton."

"Who killed him, Purse means," Mrs. Purse amended.

"Who kill Co' Robin?" Dee asked loudly, and went back to
sucking out the wooden eye of a king.

"Nobody. It was a suicide," Stefanie said. "This Turk just
went and killed himself."

"Shut it, will you?" Her fiancé had run himself out. He
was breathing painfully, like an old engine. "What do you
want to tell that for?"

"It was an Armenian," I settled it.

—They all turned to look at me: all but William's son.

"That's what I meant," Stefanie said accusingly. "An Armenian. They have those funny black eyebrows right across their *face*. Why would a Turk want to kill himself? I could understand an Armenian. I mean if *I* had eyebrows like that *I'd* kill myself." And to William's son, clandestinely: "You're right about her. She knows plenty."

Throw heard and swelled. "We *all* know plenty."

"Aha!" —His mother pounced. "In times of plenty what Purse doesn't? But nowadays! Nowadays—"

"Not a nickel's worth. Didn't bring back a newspaper," Purse submitted. "Not even that."

"—we could do with a tiny bit of good will here and there. It isn't as though we weren't on the verge of foreign parts. It isn't as though you weren't a traveler yourself and didn't know about expenses. The poor child, you said a little dress, no hand-me-downs for *her,* only girl in a mob of brothers . . . We counted on you, Mr. T.—"

"Count on the Lord," Purse said severely. "Never count on man. The unstable element is the human one. Never count on a human caretaker." —His wife, it seemed, had sufficiently filled his ear. "The Divine Caretaker keeps us always in mind," he finished; the notion made him brave but dismal.

But Tilbeck it made bright. "Right you are. As caretaker of that little commission I believe I'm a failure. Ah forgive it —a failure. Forgot to get you a dress, Harriet. Chalk it up to distraction of maritime composition. It drove out all garment thoughts but those of"—how deep, how insincere, his sigh! —"the Wet Green Garment of the Earth. We wrote to the world, this child and I."

"Mr. T. wrote," said Harriet Beecher. "Then we threw the bottle overboard. Nothing I thought of was any good."

"Seafaring notes about pirates," he chided her, "are redundant. Who's to find it but a pirate anyhow? And what good would that do? Poor fellow, be like looking in a mirror for him. It wouldn't enlighten. A very sad tautology." He spoke to Purse: "I avoid newspapers. Except to light fires with. There's a surf and scum of 'em in the house if you want."

Purse considered. "Look here, you put yourself out as a traveler," he said finally.

"I've been around. Right."

"A man of means."

"Means, you bet."

"And an owner. An owner? You own this land?"

This inquisition caused Tilbeck to elevate the wine once more. "Everyone owns the Dry Green Garment of the Earth," he purred after a moment.

"If everyone owns something no one owns it. That's why Purse is against nationalization of industry," Mrs. Purse noted, with no special relevance. And then, with particular relevance, "What a long swallow that was!"

"We should nationalize *you*, Mrs. Purse," Tilbeck said gallantly.

She took this haughtily and without pleasure. She meant to punish him for his impostures and his failed promises. Undoubtedly she saw in him now simply a man tainted by sentimentalism. He liked children, and what was that to her who made them? A caretaker on a little salary, what was that? Where was Harriet Beecher's new dress? And where the twenty bits of her own splendid new drill? And where poor yearning Bronson Alcott's dream of an accordion? And where Purse's alligator traveling case and the fourteen volumes of lateral femur development to be wittily inscribed Purse-stare et Price-stare? Ah, all prizes flew. Imagination. They had all seen the money. A petty larcener. A grand one, perhaps. She supposed the money was given him to keep the place in repair. For plaster. For shingles. For disinfectant. Silverfish swarming everywhere. The kitchen a wreck. Burning the furniture bit by bit. Nothing was re-plastered, nothing re-shingled, nothing disinfected. He spent it any way he pleased. A betrayal. Bought friendship. Bought girls and women. Bought her. She saw a lecher on a little salary; a habitual liar, she told Purse; told Purse, then crept away while he sleep-wheezed, to put her spine on the cold night-sand—she, the mother of so many cradle Friends: only to be abandoned for a tedious Attachment. Mrs. Purse's meditations sprang out; her long gums curiously but potently revealed them. Full of the energies of an anti-sentimentalist, her rebuttal fell on me: "I'm not an industry," she retorted, all at once brilliantly literal.

Tilbeck hardly compromised. "Ah yes you are," and patted smooth Harriet Beecher's cotton-white, thread-thin bangs, which a wicked wind was disarranging. A terrible gesture just then: to lean a hand out like that. "You're a whole factory in fact," he obliged her.

"Don't bother that child," Mrs. Purse began, and worked her way toward inspiration; instantly she found it. "You

seem to think a Purse is always good for a touch!" she
yielded it up, but with a sadness—almost with a carelessness.
Disenchantment was her worm. She was wearied.

Purse brushed away his wife's crescendo. "Ethel. Will you
let *me*. Now look here. Either you do or do not own this
place. Either you are or are not an owner here."

"Sure I'm an owner," my father said.

"He is *not*." Thus Stefanie—suspending a toothpick an
inch from her readied teeth: she was absorbed in spearing
tunafish out of a can. "What a roach to say he is," she muttered; then sniffed hard, as if the stuff might not be fit to eat.
Though daughter of a mother who had never had the profit
of Miss Lamb's or Miss Jewett's, she did not often dine on
democratic fare. Or so the prickle in her nose suggested.

But Tilbeck had his answer. "I own myself," he said mildly.
"Then you should control yourself," Mrs. Purse advised.

"Right, leave it to you, perfect rule for a factory"—he
roared this straight into Purse's untriumphant jealous scorn.
"For a factory absentee ownership's no good. If you don't
keep your eye right *on* it it gets away from you. You've noticed that, hah? You've got to be on the spot every minute or
you lose what you've made, right?"

"Exactly," said brave Purse. "Never trust a caretaker. I've
already shown that. The Divine—"

"Made a poor job of it too," Mrs. Purse intervened, in
hope of avoiding what was likely to be a further exposition
of the Divine character, or, more perilous yet, a divination of
her own. "He doesn't keep the place up. Everything neglected, you just have to look around. Grounds a pure Hades.
That broken fountain. Everything mechanical gone to rust—"

"Mildew in the library," Purse contributed, effectively
deflected.

"—and gets paid for it, more's the pity. All that money—
we all saw that money—and he doesn't lift a finger."

"You like what I lift, hah, Mrs. Purse?"

"Ah, pig," said Circe.

Purse dug on. "I say let's get to the record. It's been a
falsehood. A fabrication all along. If you put yourself out as
caretaker—"

"As caretaker he *doesn't* put himself out," Mrs. Purse loftily reminded him.

"Ethel. *If* you please. The guests of a caretaker would of
course be trespassers. It seems to me we were inveigled into
law-breaking. Deliberately inveigled."

"Now Purse," said his wife. "Don't be illogical. There's no reason they wouldn't *let* him have visitors. They may very well let him."

"All right. For the record then. They allow it? The owners? Comings and goings on the property? —For the sake of the record this is."

"There aren't any records," I heard myself contradict; and shunned a glimpse of William's brooding son. In me, meanwhile, a maze; depths; complicities.

"That's right," Tilbeck said. "This girlie's got it right. There aren't any records. Changed your mind, hah, girlie? First word you threw at me was records. Got the point now? —all that's a fake. The latrine in the ruined abbey, I told you. Figured out what's real and what isn't I see; got the taste I see. —*I* never said caretaker," he informed Purse.

"You don't put yourself out as caretaker?"

"No sirree. You don't catch me acting valet. Not to persons, not to places."

Purse speculated, then ventured. "Then what *do* you put yourself out as? There must be something."

"Roach," Stefanie said. "Nasty old roach. Pussyhead, you didn't even let *on* there'd be roaches up here. Pussyhead? Wouldn't Willie have a fit? People just going around saying they own what doesn't belong to them?"

Tilbeck vaguely studied her; she was plucking an ivory flake of fishflesh from the point of her toothpick. He watched her chew. "We settled that," he said indifferently. "A father. That's right. No more, no less. Same as Purse. I put myself out to be the equal of any daddy alive. That's all right, I hope. A father!" he ended.

Earnestly Purse emptied himself into the other's noise. "I'm sorry to hear you say that. Very sorry. No candor at all. I regret the example given."

"Example to who?"—but he kept his look for Stefanie.

"The children."

"Ah, *those* toadies!"

The toadies were listening alertly. Their heads in attendance composed a row of bleached skulls. Behind them a smudged sky palpitated. The transported fingerprints of a bureauful of government clerks moved steadily past the chipped chimneys of my grandfather's non-museum.

"Never mind," said Mrs. Purse, determined on consolation: "We'll be out of here before you know it. We'll be out of the whole Occident, in fact. Wait and see, Harriet Beecher'll be Stowed away in a pair of those flimsy Pakistani pantaloons they wear under their dresses over there before you can say boo."

"Boo," Stefanie gave out experimentally. "If you ask me, it's going to *pour*."

Purse continued depressed. "Taken in. Taken in," he announced. "I tell you I don't relish being taken in by a fellow with nothing but the breeze in his pockets. Fourteen volumes! Colorplates! Bibliography and Index! And then he doesn't even bring back a five-cent newspaper. Not even that."

"Right, me you don't catch at the papers," Tilbeck said. "What's somebody else's news to me? I'm my own Current Event, don't y'know." And amiably re-tilted his jaw for wine. When at last he brought his eyes down they came on me plain as marble. "*You* know how I lay off the papers, hah, girlie? Never go near 'em. Wouldn't swat a fly with 'em. *She* knows it. I keep out of the way of the papers, that's a fact."

"Two-faced," Stefanie flung out. "You just a *minute* ago said you use them to light fires with—"

"Sure, I use 'em to make things hot—right, girlie?" — Laughter of the usual sort.

A muffled male voice humbly requested tunafish.

"Ooh, pussyhead wants a *fish*," Stefanie warbled. "Next thing he'll be wanting *mices*—and didn't I bet you we couldn't keep zooming back and forth for meals? See? I told you a great big pussyhead gets hungry in no time at all! And there's nothing in that ship but a quarter of a Hershey Almond Bar. Yum, yum, open *up*—" William's son obediently displayed his uvula, and toward it a laden toothpick came charging.

"I thought you society kids lived on canned pheasant," Tilbeck said.

Stefanie leered. "Watch it, because we really live on guts. The guts of roaches I mean."

Laughter not of the usual sort. Blooms proliferated from the marble. "You want to know what I light those fires for? To signal. A man on an island keeps a bonfire going day and night y'see, and when a ship finally turns up that's got a mind to take him off, you think he goes back with all those fancy captains and stewards and ship's bursars and big Hershey Almond Bars? No sirree. Not on your life. He sticks to where he was. He sticks to himself. You think he's been signalling all that time just to go and get stuffed like them, to get nice and dead and filthy like them? Not on your life. He took those newspapers and he made that fire, and it's just to show 'em what it is to own yourself. Show who you belong to. Me, I belong to me. Those captains who run the world, you know what they are to me? Valets. Believe everything they were brought up on. All those big lawyers, all those ambassadors —"

"Hilarious," Mrs. Purse commented bitterly, "lovely. Ask him how he gets to all those other islands he's supposed to be boss of if he's never rescued off this one. Rescued is right! He couldn't manage it on his own, hasn't got the hands for it.— Ask him if he could, just ask him! Voyager! A man who doesn't know a motor from a junk-heap. And feels it in his stomach if he turns an oar in an oarlock more than ninety degrees! —Rain," she finished wrathfully.

"Ouch, I'm hit, I *said* it would pour," Stefanie cried, the first to jump up. She slanted her head to show us all. There, violent in her dazzling cheek, a great clarity of a drop had broken. The ribbon of wetness fled upward into the puzzling caves of her nostrils, indistinguishable from the trail of a tear. "D'you always talk like that?" she challenged, wiping and wiping.

Purse darkly supplied the answer: "Always." But the question was not for him.

"Well I think it's dumb to talk like that. It's really dumb. I don't go in for ghosts and dead people in trees and trees with bellybuttons and people belonging to themselves and ambassadors getting to be valets. All that's just stupid. Nothing but a silly bother. Hey, come on, let's get *out* of this mudbath—"

A force of winds pursued the early lone drops. Singly they knocked on leaves, then joined in companies, then made a streaming phalanx for descent. The Purselets tumbled cartons, seized the cereals, abandoned the cans, overturned the kings, and escaped ululating into Duneacres. But William's son followed cautiously after, hobbling in his unlaced shoes; saving his lit cigar in a fist inside his pocket; pecking tunafish from a stick; solitary.

In the dark house my father asked craftily, "She go in for anything at all, this kid?"

"Sports. She goes in for sports. Just give her a ball," I said.

"That's right. Just give me a ball," Stefanie affirmed.

14

They said they had no ball. They said they had lost it in the water.

"Well d'you know how to play Rumptag? You don't need a ball for Rumptag."

They did not know Rumptag.

"How about Castlemain? You can use practically any old thing for a ball in Castlemain. Anything that rolls."

They did not know Castlemain either.

She proposed to teach it. In seconds she had them organized. Cadres of Purselets drilled before her. Castlemain, it developed, was military. Its rules were deducible—it could not be undertaken without a missile—but its theory, if it had one, was arcane, probably irrational. No ordinary or extraordinary human satisfaction could be recognized as the object of the game. It was like a pessimist's philosophy: an energetic futility concluding in a vacuum.

Accordingly Mohandas K. Gandhi was drafted to be the ball.

"Just get all *round*," she instructed, and bowled him furiously down a line of boys representing the collective mouth of a cannon. The Castle—this was Harriet Beecher—was immediately and suitably knocked down. The collective mouth of a cannon cheered.

"Stef," William's son called. "Come on. Come on, Stef. Let's go look at the upstairs."

A wing of lightning threw a tender, irregular white feather at the window. The Purses' flashlights surprised the ceiling seraphim. Celestial love turned the pallor of the smiles of these angels to silver: it was as though a fasces of old awarenesses had beaten them into ecstasy, or into a belief in the cognition of chandeliers. Under the black self-rubbings of the unlit chandeliers Purse and Mrs. Purse sat, not close, on my

sofa, sunk into the heap of blanket, a mythological pair lost
in the early vengeance of middle age. Where I had slept my
virgin sleep their pressed and lowered thighs brooded on the
principle of sensation. They felt themselves separate, already
cooled, already inaccessible, shut away, unremarked, univer-
salized into the unnecessary. They were burned out. In that
decaying room the lovers were taking breath after breath in
an anticipation of the lubricity of their act. The air was an
envelope of secret waiting. And the Purses, flakes of ash,
scraps of white soot, were no more than trifles of granules
the lovers would find and flick from the inner corners of one
another's kissed eyes when they woke from love's sopor: sand
from the love-god's slipper. In this room of gathering love
the Purses now seemed sacks of sand, sacks of ash; sand and
ash weighted them where they leaned, their hands loose and
self-forgetful, the white clay of their covered thighs inert.
Meanwhile the skins of the lovers were divided by vastnesses,
those skins that would grind fiercely, those skins that would
seek and seek friction, those skins that would grow metaphysical and gardenlike, those patient ineluctable skins—how divergent they were now! The Purses, bags of sand, yet kept
their consciousness of that divergence. They knew how love's
confluence would flatten them. Let love connect, and these
vessels of ash lose human shape and collapse. Yet love is destined for this place, and the lovers await their moment. The
Purses await it too, resigned—they see how at the instant of
connection it is all over with them, at the instant of connection they must vanish. A commonplace spell. Nothing remains of the man or the woman—two low uneven heaps perhaps, grainy underfoot. For first lovers, middle age is not. It
refuses to be. It is not there. Hence, in the moment of con-
vergence, the disappearance of the Purses. Let no one be astonished. And—God forbid!—let no one go and look for
them.

Meanwhile they merely waited. Oblivion was not yet.
Meanwhile the skins of the lovers were divided, and by vastnesses. Here was William's son in a soaked shirt, morose, on
the piano-bench next to Tilbeck—where else in an absence of
movables could he put himself down? And there, far, far
over, an immensity away, under the high silent harps, there,
all movement, was Stefanie, Stefanie seen in typical rapture
of the chase: she was trying to prevent the ball from running
back to its mother. The ball's frenum was bleeding.

"It won't happen if you keep your *mouth* closed. All you

have to do—now look, you want to spoil the game for *every-body?*—sort of bunch up, that's right. See, I'll show you again. Get all round, didn't I tell you?—that's the way, do what I do. Stick your arms out and *punch* when you get there. All right now! Let's get going!—Hey you. Manny? Al? What's-your-name, you. You be the Castle. Not you. *You.* The rest of you be the cannon. O.K., everybody line up now. Fine. Here we go. Pow! Let 'er rip! Bunch *up!* There we are! Watch it now! That's it, that's it! Got 'er! Great, that's great! —Watch that cannonball, mister! Use your *foot,* stupid, give it a shove!—Well look, you can't be the ball if you bawl. Oh shut up, Sonny, I didn't say that to be funny. Always cackling. Just for that you have to be the Castle next time. Well *I* don't see what difference it makes if you've *got* a moat or you haven't. Pussyhead, you'll just die, they're so spooky, he wants to know if he's been de-moated. I swear you're all out of the molasses pot. Just line up now. Try it again."

The accents of Miss Jewett's won them. Strain and worship marked the slabs of their faces. She railed; they adored, turning tenderly black-and-blue, bruised, scraped, lacerated. The dust of decades drizzled and whitened their whiteness; the gumminess of inhabited cobwebs stopped up their noses. Through a respiratory racket, gluey, raspy, they celebrated her conquest. They took her in, they volunteered, for her they assumed everything, they were willing to be bats, mats, ladders, poles, goals, straps, burdens, carriers, walls, balls, subject, object, it, athletic equipment of the most complex and versatile powers. They were hers. (And me they would not have.) She bellowed, yelled, howled, moaned. Oh, her glorious gymnast moans! She moaned like a populous stadium in the bliss of agony, and in return they sacrificed one another to the muscle of her pleasure, and would have lopped off their sibling heads if the mistress of games (so Miss Jewett might have styled her) had commanded it. And she slapping her drenched, heavy, seal-like hair into the void, sent it streaking before and behind her, and followed it the way a hunter follows a trace, or a gleam, or a glimpse, or a stench, and was all the while innocent, and thought she was waiting for the rain to end, and whipped the blood in her innocently, and thought it was exercise and games. But she exercised in preparation for her moment, she waited for her moment to begin.

And then a vibration, not thunder, not the herd of feet, though minute as that delayed and glassy thunder, close as that stampede: a note, two notes, ten notes, fifteen tumbling grim chords.

"Stef! Come on. Come on, Stef. Quit that, cut it out, let's look around, come on," her lover wailed.

She fled the game.

"I didn't know you could play the piano."

"Sure," my father said.

"I mean that's *good*. You're good."

"Sure," my father said.

"You could even do it for a living, you're that good."

"You go in for music?"

She said doubtfully, responsibly, "We went to a concert last week. Bach and all."

A chord that laughed.

"You don't go in for that, hah?"

"My fiancé does, don't you, pussyhead?"

A chord that snickered.

"Dancing's what I'm crazy for. Dance music kills me. *She* had a party, nothing but marches. Like a funeral. Can you play Latin stuff?"

"Mm." He played a layer of Latin stuff.

"Come on, pussyhead, let's go round the floor. Terrific for dancing, all that space—"

"No," pussyhead said.

"Oh come on. He's *great*."

"Fine, a minute ago you said he was a roach—"

"So what? I like a tango-playing roach."

"Then it's not me you like," Tilbeck said, turning the tango into London Bridge.

"Ooh! Aren't you a riot! Pussyhead, he's a riot."

"Look, do you want to take a look upstairs or not?" William's son said.

"Nothing up there," Mrs. Purse called in a voice like a bit of tissue behind the Zeppelin.

"A library," floated up vacantly from Purse.

"I don't care about any old library. I want to dance," Stefanie said, and stamped. But this was the signal for the Castle to take position. It did. "Oh go away! Fall out! Forget it! Nobody wants the whole pack of you hanging around like that. *I* want to dance."

Instantly the Purselets clamored to be taught to dance.

She capitulated, but not to them. "All right, let's go and *look* at the damn house, what's the difference?"

"If it's a favor never mind. You just go back to Physical

Training. Go back to those kids, that's all," William's son said.

"Lovers' quarrel," said Tilbeck, and tinkled out a sigh from the Wedding March.

"Oh pooh, we never fight, spite isn't fight, don't think you're so smart. Cut out playing that. We *came* to look around, why not? This place might have been my fiancé's in*her*itance if his father hadn't gotten divorced. That's all you know about things. C'mon, puss, let's go up. Just get rid of these godawful brats. Scat!" she told the ball. Rebuffed, it ascended its mother's lap. She took the Mahatma up coolly, her eyes on the stairs and the climbing lovers.

"So that's the lawyer's boy?" my father said. "Got himself a looker, hah?"

But I would not answer in that din of Purselets begging tunes. London Bridge rose and fell, and they all came swarming at the mystical sounds. He raised the bridge twice over, and then Three Blind Mice fluttered out, and then A Bicycle Built for Two, and then Home on the Range, and then Clementine—he was glad to be restored to their esteem, and rejoiced in their fickleness. "Defected from the lady athlete, see that?" he said into the disorder of their high-decibel cawing; none of the Purselets could sing.

"Do you need the B flat for any of those?" I asked. "The one that's broken?"

"I use the key of C," he said proudly, "the people's key. Any requests?"

I said: "Rhapsody in Blue."

He loosed a trivial chord, like a shrug; down went the B flat, mute. "See? Can't be done with a dumb note. What's ancient doesn't necessarily revive. I don't go for the dipped madeleine, if you get me. Guidebook's out of date, hah? What d'you want me to do? Re-run an old movie of your mother's life? No sirree. Whatever you think I am, that's what I'm not."

"I don't know what you are," I said.

"That's the beauty of it, neither do I. Except now and then. Right now what I am is the Pied Piper. Couple of rats've left already, you noticed that? Well, if they think they'll find a preacher up there, those two, all they'll find is plaster dust. Pastor Dust," he amended, "marries nobody."

"And no beds."

"That's right. No beds up there," he agreed, grinning. "Watch. The Pied Piper—Pie-eyed Piper? Fried Piper?—

what the hell, the Stewed Piper of Do-Neck-'Er lures the Affianced Couple down.—Get that!" he announced into a river of lightning; on the quickly lurid keys his stunned hands were made unready.

It came on us like a blot of swift but total seeing, turning lips electrically vivid, nearly blue with vividness, the veins x-rayed to a sudden deep visibility; the image of my father's mouth like a carved silver bar froze in my mind, part of a torso. I saw him not like a photograph—though half the vividness was in the stillness and stiffness of him registered in surprise, preserved—but solidly, thickly, one of those small haughty straight-backed Egyptian figurines, all silver, a god of the Nile reduced to a curio. It was not he who had shrunk; it was the world—that hardening shrinking world which withdraws, age by age, from its fierce little gods. My mother's fantastic lover! And now thunder was bursting out of the keys, as though something had exploded in his fingertips, producing—behold!—Stefanie herself, howling into spaciousness. "Hey, that was a close one! Did y'*see* it? Shook the Goddamn roof!"—she: hanging dewy and plaintive over the bannister.

"Thor at the clavier," my father said. "He—I, understand —he presses the note long silent, and presto, the voice of God in B flat."

"Don't give me that, that was no piano," Stefanie argued from the stairs. "That was real thunder."

"Bad thinking," Tilbeck said. "It leaves out a possible alternative. Never leave out a possible alternative. It might've been the piano *and* thunder, in conjunction. A duet. Gustave Nicholas Tilbeck and God making music together."

"Oh Christ," she threw down.

"Is Christ God?" Tilbeck asked, and began, in waltz time, Onward, Christian Soldiers. "Dance, children, dance!"

But the Purselets had, at God's great stroke, vibrated toward the front door. It was open; they clustered on the sill in admiration of the shining storm, above which my grandfather's uncommon romantic imported lintel made a kind of Gothic picture-frame. And faintly, a far growl, we heard the rain grunting against the canvas cheeks of the tents. A draft like the devil's breath seized the room.

"Shut that door!" Purse called.

"Colds! Colds! You'll all catch colds!" cried his wife; slung between her legs was a baby like a white snail; curled, porcelain, bruised.

Tilbeck asked, "Where's the lawyer's boy?"

"Looking around," said Stefanie.

"Come down," he invited.

"Come up."

"I know what's up there."

"Books. Filthy old books. Phew, dust makes me sneeze."
Languidly she hooked her shoulders over the rail and dangled
her bright arms loose as a monkey's. "You're not the only
one, my pussyhead knows what's up there and he's never
even *seen* this place before. He knows all about it just the
same. He even found a part of a new wall they started to put
up once."

I broke in, "You want to bet he's seen the plans? Snooped
everything out of the files, even the blueprints——"

My father viewed me. "Don't hold a brief for the lawyer's
boy, hah?"

"Yes she does. If you ask me she's crazy about him. Admit
it!" she dared me. "I could tell the first time I ever saw you. I
can always tell when somebody's jealous."

"I'm not jealous."

"Aren't you though," she mocked, and switched to what
she supposed me jealous *of*. "You know where we're putting
our sleeping bags tonight? We were *going* to put them in the
woods—like Indians—only you don't catch me in mud up to
my ears, thank you. So pussyhead said O.K., then let's spend
the night in the upstairs part of a real house, just like when
we're married. We're supposed to move into this *house* when
we get back from our honeymoon, it's this sort of town
house. Know where we're going? Venezuela. It's all arranged,
it's part a business trip we have to do for Willie though. Anyhow now all we need is to pick out where. Which room I
mean. There're thousands up there. You want to come help
choose?"

"All right," I said, but it was not I she was appealing to.

"That's the way," Tilbeck said. "Bed 'em down. Watch 'em
at it."

"You've got your nerve," Stefanie clucked, but she had no
indignation. "You I mean. You coming up? The two of you."

"The two of us?" Tilbeck said acutely.

"*We* like to do everything together," she explained.

"Is that why you're downstairs and pussyhead's upstairs?" I
said.

"Smarty." She blew out a loud breath. "Well it's *such* a
bore. All that oceany stuff, I can't be bothered with that stuff.
There's a whole moldy old shelf full of maritime law or

whatever you call it and he's all squatted over it with one of those flashlights. First he says come look around and then next thing you know he's drowning in some stupid moldy old book."

I said sympathetically, "Maybe they won't have any books in Venezuela."

This somehow struck her. "Say! Isn't that where your stepfather's going to be Ambassador?"

"No," I said. "Not Venezuela."

"Venice was it? Vienna?"

"No."

"Well I give up. It's such a bother remembering those countries with those *names*. I don't know how anybody who doesn't live in America remembers where they live."

Tilbeck was delighted. "They have special propaganda for it. They write it on billboards. You'll notice this when you get to Venezuela, watch for it especially up around the rain forests where the natives are more primitive and can't read. In other countries they have to actually tattoo the babies at birth. You take a place like Czechoslovakia, if the baby's foot's too short to hold it, they tattoo it right down the shin for easy reference when it gets to be an adult—"

She said suspiciously, "If you ask me that sounds Fascist."

"No," he denied, "it's just fair and equal. Reduces capital punishment in fact. I knew a fellow once had 'Bermuda' in red, white, and blue, right across the palm of his right hand, and there he was, standing in front of a firing squad in the noonday sun, they were going to shoot him for spying for Luxemburg. He puts up his right hand to get the sun out of his eyes and then they see he was born in Bermuda. So they abandoned the whole project. He's alive today."

"I don't believe any of that," Stefanie said. "Luxemburg might've *paid* him to be a spy. Maybe it didn't have anything to do with patriotism or anything like that, he might've been doing it for the money."

Tilbeck gleamed. "She's O.K. Don't kid yourself, she's got the world figured out."

"I never heard about any of that," she was insisting. "That tattooing business."

"Look, you don't learn Realpolitik in finishing schools. If you don't trust *me*, ask the Ambassador."

"He's going to *be* Ambassador," I bit off.

"To Bermuda?" Stefanie cried. "You mean your stepfather?"

"Well who said no?" —My father blinked bluntly at another stitch of lightning. But each time there was a lengthening interval before the catarrh.

"Enoch's going to get that job," I said, "whatever you do."

"That's right," he obliged.

"No, it's true, whatever you do. It doesn't matter about you. It's too late."

"It's always too late. That's philosophy," he said mildly.

"He's probably already got it. They had the hearings this morning. By now he's got it. It doesn't matter about you. It doesn't matter about any newspapers either."

"You get this from the lawyer's boy?"

"*I* told her," Stefanie said, in the voice of Realpolitik.

I finished: "The main thing is it doesn't matter about me."

"It never did, girlie. I thought we settled that. I thought we talked all that out."

Stefanie noted coolly, "They probably ask her advice on every little thing down in Washington. *You* know. They probably do."

"That's right," my father said. "That's the way. —She's O.K., this little looker, she's got the world figured out."

"They get her advice on every little *thing*," Stefanie repeated. "That's how come she thinks she matters so much."

Tilbeck said happily, egging her on, "That's it. You've got it. You tell her."

"*He* doesn't think you matter either," Stefanie pronounced, swinging the weight of her wet darkling hair. "And he should know, shouldn't he? I mean if *he* doesn't know—"

"He does know."

"Know *what*, for goodness' sake. Now I've lost it. You two keep making me lose track—"

"Why I came," I said gravely.

"Oh that! I know that. Everybody knows that."

Tilbeck was pleased. "A public issue, hah?"

"Oh pooh, I'm not shy about it, believe me—anyhow I know why *I* came. And you," she bellowed down at me (mistress of games once more), "you came for the same reason! I would've known it even if the fat lady hadn't said so. Plain as day if you ask me."

"Plain?" said Tilbeck: with a honeyed look.

"Sex," Stefanie yelled against the acoustical cherubim. "Sex sex sex. That's the reason."

A stifled wheeze flew out of the region of the sofa. The Zeppelin halted horrendously in midair; then began to fall, slowly, slowly, its filmy banner twirling like a braid, hissing. Someone had stuck a pin in it.

"My God," soughed Purse.

"Now, now," said Mrs. Purse. "All that shouting down those stairs. Young lady, you don't care who hears what. Now look, you've scared Dee right out of his nap."

The baby glared, it seemed, at nothing; then released a virtuoso aromatic belch.

"Good boy," said Mrs. Purse, and permitted the Mahatma to slither out of the grip of her thighs. "The secret of life, and he's hit on it."

Wretched Purse sniffed. "They haven't been loading him with spirits again, have they?"

"What happened yesterday, dear, was he loaded him*self*," his wife demurred.

"Sex," sang the games mistress, drumming on the rail.

My father's great laughter mounted high and brilliant; he piled chord on chord out of huge and huger lung, and hawked up another thunder that pounced on all the ceiling host—on angels in narcotic bliss, on those bundles of bobby-pins that put themselves out for harps, and his head reared wonderfully back, like some sky-white horse, Job's horse, who saith among the trumpets, ha ha!

And what my mother knew once I knew then.

Stefanie softened; I saw her marveling at modifying, multiplying, mystifying circumstance; she marveled and she mulled: how queer it was that things never turn out as expected; and whether the secret of life is truly nothing more than a belch; or (because her mind was more original than most people guessed) the equivalent of a belch.* "And you know what?" —She tackled the riddle. "Back at your bon voyage thing I thought you'd never even been *kissed*. Hey! It's getting to be shreds of daylight again. You two coming up or aren't you coming up, well?"

My father spoke. "That's a good reason. That's a fine reason. I told you that's what you came for, girlie," he said. "A taste of it."

"Come *on*, anybody traveling around up there with us, yes or no?" demanded the mistress of games.

"No," said my father, reaching out to pluck the baby from the hollow of the room; lo, the godlet, wrested from its niche, meandered, stony dust of pedestal powdered on its naked heels; it carried the acrid holy odor of the grove.

"I will. All right," I said, and went by the Purses, who

were, I observed, still there. Goosepimples bristled in the central draft. Behind them Tilbeck had dumped Mohandas K. Gandhi on the piano keys and was feeding him black fudge-babies out of his pockets. Mouth pushed out and open for more, the sacred Mahatma knelt and stretched savagely after chocolate babies to chew, and all the while his scraped prayerful knees were inventing merciless discords, scrape on scrape, friction on friction.

But the Purses were still there. In spite of everything they were there. No lovers' moment had so far wiped them out. They were there.

15

And then they were not.

But I will tell about that later. First I must tell how we wandered, we three: the lovers and I. We wandered, we three, through the upper tracts of that ruin, and for no plain reason and in no real direction. We went—that is my impression of it now—round and round and round; I have an underwater sense of it, a flailing against veils and weight, a viscous floating memory, as of sailing somehow with limp limbs through some queer thick medium, a lake of honey, yellow, mellow, rich, heavy, yielding but reluctant, repentant, slow; and in it we slowly revolve, we let ourselves be turned this way, that way, our heavy legs in their heavy motions seem both to swim and to be retarded, as in dreams of perversely languid urgency, or with the dumb violations of some disbelieving slow-motion camera, unreeling strangeness and remorse.

That is how I remember it now; but often I think it is not this scene I am remembering, but something less certain, unlikely, intuitive, perhaps even occult, yet all the same real: that birth fluid in which I swung and turned, my mother just then throwing a dart at a tree and I just then crouching in my vast amniotic pool before the god of my habitation, whatever it might be: the braided totem of the umbilical cord perhaps: the thing or spirit, whatever it might be, that connects us to the certainty of life.

Nothing happened. We walked through room after room. I observed minute repetitions: William's son suddenly duplicating that habit of his adolescence—a book squeezed under an arm; William's son striding in the lead, Stefanie and I lolling behind side by side like a pair of sisters—so we had crossed a ballroom once, so we now took the top of that house. We took it and took it, and still there was more; odd walls, partitions, cube beyond cube beyond cube, bureaus, dressers, wardrobes, chiffoniers, chests, escritoires, some with their sides hacked away (we actually came upon the saw balanced across two square chunks of fallen plaster)—the whole bulk and filth of it dead under a fresh moist skin of living mold, and all of it darkened to the dark of venous blood. Over the mirrors the webs looked as well-used as fishermen's nets. It was an uninteresting place. No one had ever really lived there —young servants, perhaps, homesick—and the museum offices had never finally come into being. Some houses are a memoir, but this was not. There was nothing private in it and nothing public. Nothing had ever happened there; even Stefanie felt it: "That Turk or Armenian or somebody," she began, "who committed suicide, wouldn't this've been a lots better place than the woods?" "The place doesn't matter," William's son said, but it seemed untrue. Places matter: or if not the place, then what has happened in it. Nothing had happened here but the breathing, in sleep, of youths: first the wistful squads of servants, then the planners of the Moscow March for a Better Future. But most had slept under the eaves, in tents, in the woods, in an idle niche, under a trellis. Not many were willing to mop or march. The mold marched. The mold mopped the brow of rot. The purple mold mopped and marched and was its own memoir. "How funny," Stefanie said, "all these ridiculous fancy old pieces and no beds. Didn't they use beds in those old days? Your ancestors I mean?" "It wasn't ancestors," I said, "for heaven's sake it wasn't that long ago. He burned the beds, that's all." "Who?" "Nick." "How funny. I mean how sad. I bet your grandfather's turning in his grave." "The sea turns all the time," I said. This excited her: "You mean he was buried at sea, your grandfather? I saw that once on television. They drape the coffin in an American flag and the captain's allowed to be

sort of like a minister, then they slide it down this plank—"
"It wasn't like that. It was done from the beach down there.
It was just ashes scattered." "Ashes, that's weird though, isn't
it? Isn't there a law against that? What with pollution and all?
Pussyhead, isn't there? You know, like sewage." She ran forward and shook his arm. He dropped the book like a tree
dropping fruit; I glimpsed it in descent. It was called *The
Law of the Sea.* We all three bent for it, but Stefanie was
quickest. "Red in tooth and claw?" I murmured into William's son's curiously heated eyes. Stefanie admonished,
"Look, don't tell he took it, O.K.? Especially William. You
know Willie, Willie thinks everything's stealing. Pussyhead
took it because he saw it, it's from seventeen-hundred-and-
something, that's why. Finders keepers. It's no-man's-land
here anyhow, so who'd care anyhow? You don't see many
like that. That book's valuable, you know that?" I said I did
not. William's son said nothing.

We continued in the strange light. It was the quality of
light that is filtered out of the sieve of a storm. Through a
translucent blackness of panes came the sun new-born into
evening, and where the windows were toothless and knocked
down to just the spare warped gums of their frames, small
narrow golden old-ladies' tongues full of the spittle of sparks
slipped timidly in and out against the knobs of desks and
chests, cluttering the air with eccentric little glints. The storm
sailed on. It sailed like a woman in long silky hems across a
brush-hard lawn; at uneven intervals she stoops and we hear
the burred movement of her gloves across the ears of the
grass—all that is left of the thunder is this sly caress, and all
that is left of the lightning are those erratic senile imbecile
winks and licks.

The rain dripped thickly from the tops of things. It had a
slow ripe sound, as though each globule waited to be gener-
ated from a dot into a soft fatness before it could swell off its
shingle and fall with a plump pop downward.

We circulated, we wandered.

We went round and round and round.

The light was different now. It seemed sourceless. The sun
had rolled away like a boulder, leaving a long ditch, the way
a moving snowball leaves its furrow in a wide flat field of
snow; and brimming out of the sunball's trough oozed the
light, a fluid light, like the mucous lining of an egg, diffused
rather than diffracted, running over the banks of the sun's
lane, smearing even the papery edges of the sky. And we

three penetrated to the egg's center, a crucial pith, an innermost room, and there all at once all around us the yolk broke and spread. We were in a yellow sea. Our nostrils filled, the rooms filled, the rooms were separate cups of that glutinous liquor, and we passed from room to room breathing thick gold light. A heaviness of hands and feet slowed us; we dragged on and on. "Is this where?" Stefanie said; "this is a good spot to put those bags, right?"—but her voice was like a chime through fog, pulled out of shape: "How about here? Behind that highboy thing? I mean for privacy what more could you want?" No one answered her. William's son did not speak. "Which room did your grandfather have? Where did your great-aunt sleep? Could this be your grandmother's place?" I did not know. I had forgotten that these were the rooms of the Huntingdons. It was only the servants I remembered. It was only the campers I remembered. On one of these surfaces the mother of my mother, hardening her paralytic lip, had bent hard on the pen of her hatred. On one of these surfaces the father of my mother had leaned over watery maps to dream the deep cells of fish born without eyesockets. In these lit square foyers my mother's whistling ancient violent aunt had knocked her shoulders between the walls, sweating and shouting at the summer snows, the January typhoons. I had forgotten about those lives without consequences. Where there are no consequences it is as if there had never been happenings. The rings of the handles of the madwoman's coffin rusted under a rusting anchor below a broken fountain. And those fish that had eaten at my grandfather's vitals (what else were they to eat at in that lonely seafarer?)—had they spurned the char of his bone? My grandmother's crippled foaming face had gazed on that beach: without consequence. My mother had proceeded to marry: without consequence. The servants had proceeded to mop: without consequence, for here was the indefatigable victorious mold. The museum had failed. The revolution had failed. The trellises were burned. The beds were burned. In the failing burning light we went round and round—how many rooms there seemed to be! how mazily interconnected they were, with their little foyers, and interior balconies, and piazzas suddenly suspended from a window, and surprises of corridors, and chinese-box doors, and agglutinations of writing-desks, and velvet borders of mold! Something private grew. It began in the mold, in the smell, it expanded in the thinning unfurling inexhaustible light: widening like a plate beaten flat and then flatter, always seeming less and always becoming more. Particle clung to particle and made a swimming brew of light. In it rocked the pit and seed of the private thing, privacy itself, folded in, lap within lap: a potent controlling engine for our strange passage over those glowing thresholds. Why, why? Why did they turn and turn again, the lovers, in this desert of garbage, of vestige, shawled by light, like bedouins, sinking into heat as into a layered cushion, yielding their necks and waists and ankles into the languor of their queer slow purposeful circles? With my terrible patience I stalked them. Why, why? A tactile pressure came down upon us. A spasm of some intention propelled us. We were instruments of a scheme of permutation; a quest for consequence. Something would happen. "It will move," one says of a muscle; then a fist closes, an arm embraces.

A fist closed. An arm, a pair of arms, embraced. "For goodness' sake, you're always doing that. In *front* of her," Stefanie mumbled, then dissolved into concentration. They were kissing. Under our feet the piano drummed, but no tune emerged; wine ruled it, the divine small Bacchus rolled heels and hips over the teeth of its alligator smile wide as octaves. A door blared shut like a swear.

Something had happened. Dusk. They were kissing in the immobile dusk. The flashlight jutted between them in a closed fist. *The Law of the Sea* separated their torsos like a grid. Only their heads preyed one on the other, they nibbled then grabbed, they meant to swallow and eat one another; they were two blind fish at the dark core of the waters, at war, at war. The last web of sunset fell to pieces thread by thread. Yet I still saw their heads, black against the coming black, and their locked profiles, head invading head, butting, biting, bitter. They battled to eat one another, not for the bitter taste but for the sensation of the contest. I knew this. They kissed without complicity. Without complicity. I knew this. It was curious that I knew it. I was initiate. I knew it. I knew the taste of complicity. Nick had put it on my tongue like a pellet—complicity, amazing first-knowledge of the private thing, privacy itself. A commitment. I had acquiesced in the conspiracy against myself. I was what my mother had accused me of hoping to become: my father's accomplice. Her fears had destined me. I had joined up on his side at the flick of a tongue. It came into the inner room of my mouth, where I had thought only speech lived. No. Nature is more resourceful than that. The house of the word is where one learns how the word is superfluous. Taste; no word. Yet there was no memory of a physical flavor or even of the capacities of the inventiveness of a sense-organ. It is never sensuality that remains (I know now and glimpsed then), but the idea of sensuality; so that, finally, it is as though a word has been spoken after all—in code; and only a reassertion can decipher it. Feeling cannot be stored. Neither can pain, so it is nothing to regret. The nerve gives only the now, and is improvident. Now *The Law of the Sea* fell like a gavel. This time no one stooped for it. A candle of dust exploded out of the impact and yawned back down. In the nub of the cloud the book lay on its spine with pinions extended: the exposed pages had the look of black blocks. Here in the black was this further black, like iron doors. It was only a law book. They had cast it from between their ribs. Nothing now kept body from body. Their bodies pressed—but experimentally, conscious of use, conscious of the absence of the book's intrusion like a confessional grid between them. They pressed and kissed without complicity. The privacy of complicity failed them. Under closed lids the bulge of their restless eyeballs traveled from corner to corner, raising question after question. They were watchful. They watched one another in the secrecy of sensation. They felt penetrated by a witness. I was not their witness. They struggled to elude their witness; they drew back; the witness drew back; they drew in; the witness drew in; they breathed cautiously, so as not to be noticed; the witness noticed.

I stood, but was not their witness. I did not see them. I saw Nick. I saw myself. We lay crouching in one another's mind: private. In me private knowledge grew like a worm. No one observed.

Someone observed. In the conscious presence of each other they went on kissing with the dedication of spite, spiting the observer. They were the observer—they observed themselves. They were the watcher and the watched. They witnessed themselves. They spied on themselves kissing. They despoiled their complicity by listening in.

It was a curiously public scene.

In me meanwhile knowledge of the private thing: knowledge is the only real event in the world, and something had happened. In our slow voyagings through those ruined laden upper rooms, through the swimming light, something had happened. The lovers kissed; a law book had fallen; nothing would come of it. Yet something had happened—not in them. In me the private thing turned: knowledge turned, love turned, what my mother knew I knew.

And navigated around the staring lovers. They had sprung open their eyes; they wondered at one another, watching, listening; would nothing come of it?—a thwarted anger inflamed their lips glistening with spittle; they would not yield, they would not forget, they witnessed their exchange segment by segment, tooth by tooth and claw by claw. Ah. Nothing would come of it. Nothing. I stepped over *The Law of the Sea* and went to my father.

On the way I passed the Purses. They were there; they were there. And yet they were not. They were there and they were not-there. Their heads had rolled backward on the sofa. Their shoulders diverged and did not touch. A periodic and garrulous eruption rose in a reverberating column straight from Purse's nose. He snored. Mrs. Purse dozed fragilely— she had struck the wooden blanket to the floor. It lay in furrows like a brown sea slung between the sofa and the piano. By now I could comprehend the dark. It was night in the house and blue evening outside of it. The Purselets had escaped into the last of the blue. I heard them loudly bleating among the tents, muffled, aimless, violent. What game did they play?—out of the center of their barbarian voices came the high pure cry of the little god. Perhaps they would kill him. A god must die his little death or he is no god. At the piano I could see the phantom whiteness of a rod going up and down—it was Nick's finger on a key, going up and down. He was still there, trapped by the problem of silence. The key loosed a mechanical sigh and nothing more. He played it and played it—with concentration: the single unheard note. He put each finger of each hand to it in succession, as though if not one surely the other would call out the note's voice, if only he were patient enough. Patiently he played the note. No voice came. The Mahatma's voice came. It came and came, clean small screams, uttered with the concentration of a whole soul, like prayer.

The Purses did not revive.

"Tourist," my father said. "Now you've seen the works. What did I tell you? Filth. The whole thing filth."

Up and down went the mute key.

"Why don't you get Mrs. Purse to fix it?" I said into the flowery air.

"Fix what?"

"That dead note."

"You believe in the Resurrection? I knew it. A Christian. Look, this note's the only thing in the vicinity that isn't filth. At least it holds its tongue. Only item in the house that does. —Who, them? What about 'em? I did it with Brahms' Lullaby, I put it in A minor. —That little looker coming back down?"

I saw with astonishment that he had all the while been waiting for her.

"She's busy," I said.

"That's right, occupied. Full up as we say."

A long flute-like shriek toiled out of the tents.

I said: "They're murdering that baby."

"What's one more or less, she can always cough up another, call it Fabian. After the Fabian Society."

Like a fool I fed him. "They're not Socialists, they practically said so—"

"All right, then she can call it Thomas Malthus. That'll do it, fine old capitalist. Utopian enough for a whole population. You know why they slid off to beddy-bye? Wasn't Brahms. Embarrassment, I'd say. Lovers went up the stairs, that walloped Purse. Faded right out, just like that. Meanwhile *she* spreads the blanket nice and cozy on the floor, an invitation, what else? Declined it with party manners—had my hands full of babies, chocolate and otherwise. She's all right, Mrs. Purse, ready at the drop of the old man's· eyelids."

"Then what put her to sleep?" I challenged.

"Shock," he answered, "when she sees me shake my head no. Poor woman passed out cold. Meanwhile the baby's so upset at catching his ma flat out he unfolds his wings from inside his diaper and flies right out the window like a butterfly. Doubtless they're sticking a pin through the middle of him this minute. Or a nail, crucifixion, why not?"

"Somebody ought to wake her—"

"No use. I drugged her myself. A little saltpeter for the nerves. For a woman of her years I always recommend celibacy. You might pass that along to Mrs. Vand. Though maybe she doesn't need it, considering the Ambassador, hah? Hard in the brain, weak in the leg. The middle leg. An old saying y'know."

Still the Purses did not wake. They reclined like big straw dolls, ludicrous but stern. Their feet were tangled. Their hands were vacant. One would think they had fallen asleep from some extraordinary fatigue. A magic had hold of them. A robust presence restrained them: love was in the house.

Love enervates the loveless. Love blots out self-love. Hence the Purses' dimming; blazing first-knowledge had stunned them into the beginning of dissolution. Already they seemed half-erased. They sprawled in the darkness, incapable of malevolent peering, vaguely glimmering, like a pair of whitish smears, yet *there;* still there; palpable, visible, real. Nothing had been consummated. The instant of love's consummation had not yet struck.

"A fraud is what you are," I told my father.

He did not turn. "Evangelizing. A Christian, didn't I just say so? I can always spot 'em. St. Paul on the road. Five minutes ago she doesn't know what I am, all in the dark y'see, and now she knows."

"I do know."

"And now she has to tell. They always know. And when they know they tell."

"A fraud," I said.

"That's right, repetition makes truth. Look, fraud's your mother's theme song, it's dogma by now. Always expect dogma. Straight from Mrs. Vatican, what else? Only say it the way you said it before."

"I didn't say it before. I didn't know it before."

"Did. The Gospel according to St. Allegra. I don't notice any new revelations. Yesterday you said blackmailer."

"No," I said, "I don't mean that."

He lifted an ingratiating shoulder. "Well why not? Girlie, I've sucked 'em. I get what I can—if it wouldn't be Nick it would be someone else. Remember that. It's the balance that counts, not who's in the scales. They do it for the balance, not for love, you follow?"

The word stopped me.

He saw that it did. "Love," he said, "you've got a point there. That's right, so say they do it for love. Especially the Ambassador, he's the biggest lover of 'em all. Not that he loves people—just ideas about people. You think he can feel anything, that politician? Cold and hot out of the tap's about all."

"Enoch isn't a politician."

"Isn't he though. You want me to believe he's that much different from the old days? Well, I believe in change. The world changes, girlie, that's a fact."

"You don't."

"Who says so?"

"You're just the same."

"That's nice. Same as what?"

I could not answer.

"Look," he said, "Mrs. Vacuum told you fraud, you go ahead and stick to it. Be like me, stick to a thing."

I said intently, "She believes everything you tell them. She thinks you mean what you say."

"Sure. I tell the truth about what's fake."

"You don't mean any of it."

"All right, so I tell lies about what's true, is that it? Girlie, take your pick. Either I'm a fraud or not a fraud."

"Not."

"Ha," he said, "not. I like that. First yes, now not. Not not, who's there?—not the same is what you mean, right? Changed like the rest of the sons of bitches."

"The same," I said. "The same now as then. The same for my mother and the same for me."

He said with a revival of interest, "Your mother mistook an episode for a principle. Then yelled fraud. D'you know I've been doing Mrs. Valiant a favor all these years? Been giving her an opportunity to express her strong feelings of principle." And now at last his intricate gargoyle-filled laugh —a laugh a cathedral might produce. But he suddenly cut it off and recovered. "That's why she's against me. Nobody likes to be kept to a principle."

"You do. You keep yourself to a principle."

"I don't."

"You do."

For a moment we seemed to echo the flirting lovers in the wood.

"I don't," he said again. "What fraud would?"

"A fraudulent fraud."

Loud was his groan; it buried the screams from the tents.

"A fraud *cares*," I said.

"What about?"

"Consequences."

"Go to the devil. Trash. That's only a word."

"You don't care what happens to anybody. You won't *make* anything happen. You don't care if anybody believes you or not. A liar likes to get people to believe him. But you don't mind if they do or they don't. You don't mind anything. You wouldn't even have minded if I never showed up. If you never saw me. It wouldn't have changed anything. A fraud tries to get things changed—"

"Listen to her, out-and-out homage to fraud. The Woman of Principle should hear you."

"It's not that you're a fraud," I said, "it's that you like everyone to think you are, and *that's* a fraud. And all the time they're afraid you're going to do what you say you will, they rely on you to do it and they're afraid, and all the time it's only an impersonation—"

"Ah. That's the principle, hah?"

"If they hadn't paid you you would have stopped asking. If I hadn't come you would never have gone to those newspapers about Enoch. You never would," I said.

Footsteps overhead. The lovers were tramping down. In the dark I heard him spit.

He said: "What bothers you is you can't understand anybody who doesn't give a damn. For power I mean. That's what bothers you, girlie. The lilies of the field bother you. They toil not, neither do they spin, they get it just like that."

I took the smallest breath. "Enoch says having no power corrupts."

"I remember that," but his look went toward the stairs. "Hasn't he said anything new in twenty years?"

"Haven't you felt anything new in twenty years?"

To my surprise this pleased him. "You want me to improve? Look, you ask Mrs. Viscera if she thinks Nick needs improving. Because if I'm the same now as then at least I haven't deteriorated, see? Only if I'm the same for you as for her it's only by reputation. *She* didn't have dermaphobia, not Mrs. Vaccination."

I stared.

"Fear of membranous contact, call it. Well here's the little looker. Right off the amphora."

"Right off the what?" cried Stefanie in pique.

I said jealously, "He thinks you're a warrior's girl on a Greek jar. He collects Greek jars."

"Good God, you talk just like him."

"I *am* just like him."

"Well bully for you. You go in for ghosts in trees too?"

"You're wrong," my father said solemnly, "it's the gods I collect."

William's son said, "It's too wet to walk down there. Mud knee-deep. Forget it, we'll use the sofa."

"*She's* got the sofa. And anyhow it's full. Asleep at the switch and meanwhile those kids are playing Chicago slaughterhouse. We saw 'em from the window up there. What a racket. Pussyhead, if you didn't leave those damn bags in the *ship* where'd you *leave* them?"

"I don't know. Out near the table I think."

"You think. That big lawyer's brain and all. I bet they're soaked. I'm not going to sleep in a soaked bag, you can bet your life I'm not. The zipper could rust and we'd be like the Man in the Iron Mask. Look, you didn't have to go and forget to bring up the damn *sleeping* bags for goodness' sake. I'm not supposed to spend the night in a Greek olive jar, am I? Don't get the idea I'm going to sleep on the floor either," but she did. That night she did sleep on the floor.

"Well you want me to go down to the beach and look?"

"*I* don't know." She snatched her fiancé's flashlight and shone it all around. It washed shockingly into my eyes and then slid off, and in a half-blindness I saw that William's son had remembered to take away his plunder. *The Law of the Sea* was lodged in his armpit. The coin of light wavered, then found the Purses. "Your house is on fire and your children will burn. They don't budge, look at that."

She stood fixedly over them, marveling. Tilbeck came beside her. The two of them looked at the Purses. The tips of their elbows grazed. Purse shuddered. Mrs. Purse snapped one eye and yawned. Somnolently they rose. Yawning and shuddering, light as sacks, emptied, they were borne up, they levitated, they floated slowly out of sight. It was as though someone had rubbed them out.

"You'd think they'd *say* something," Stefanie complained.

Beyond the house, among the tents, nothing was heard.

"They're all dead. Everybody's killed everybody."

"Why not?" William's son said glumly.

The lovers had touched. The lovers had touched at last. Their skins had touched; the friction had begun; the Purses were expunged: something had happened. Love. The private worm; the same. What my mother knew I knew.

—I loved my father.

And the union of the lovers was about to be.

16

The union of the lovers takes place on the floor, between the piano and the sofa, on the brown blanket Mrs. Purse has thrown down. There is the night sound of wind. The wool is the color of earth. Into the cavern of the dining room a weak moving light swims. It swims in like a fish, with short unsure darts, nudging an eye into life, a cruel honed nostril, gouging a murderous chin: the kings' heads are swarming in conclave on those walls. What is it, what stirs the mouths of monarchs?—a tremulous candle beating all the while, and now and again a stick of brightness cutting' through from a flashlight. Someone is reading in the kitchen—I hear a page turning, I hear the fleshy creak of the reader turning his body into the night. The turning of a body is what has wakened me. I huddle on my sofa, hiding myself. The wind breathes as a sleeper might. I feel stiff with life, and lean my face between my knees—I can see my ankles, bad straight ankles with no indentation toward the heel. Above the heel a stubble snags my rub. The arms of the sofa shrug upward into shoulders, the shoulders into back. On the back the dancers dance. Behind it the lovers couple. I crouch on the ledge of the world and am their witness.

And I see her moulting, she crawls from the white tunnel of that skirt, her knees flash calisthenic. pockets, in her neck two ropes pull and fall, the plane of her face grows negligible, her head feels out the floor slowly, like the tenderly lowered head of a patient. Then hands rise—her own—and through cleavages in the cloth the butting noses of buttons force themselves, her jacket springs open like mechanical wings and her shoulders lift grinning their strengths, her fingers acquiring eyes maneuver valorously against the ditch of vertebrae and the white sails over her breasts fail and sink to her belly. Then in a kind of loneliness, with the subtlety of feeling watched, she shows sportsman's skill, bets on herself, begins to slide, as with an itch in the upper back, and with a quick comic football dig has freed herself into whole naked- ness, never once raising her body from its surgical lassitude. Arrogant on her dimensionless platform she lies stretched to his view and dares his daring. In her right thigh a dent like a scar but not a scar, a sulfurous soap-colored birth bruise, mocks the long strong highway of her haunch. With the vengefulness of the knowledgeably imperfect she throws her elbows crisscross over her head, displays the tangle in the armpit, and in a gesture almost scholarly closes one deft leg over another, obscuring the lower tangle. Then with buttocks nailed to the floor she rolls from the waist, twists out a bal- loon of flesh at the bending-point, presses to the wool two brown valves like weights dragging her breasts to their taper- ings, and reaches to shove away her clothes. He sees his chance, takes hold of her hipfat like a lever, and pushes her over—the solemn seal of her legs breaks, her chinbone grinds into the floor and her buttocks, pulled separate, crash into air like a pair of helmets. At the nape of each, on either side of her spine, there is a depressed pan; into the left one he fits his palm and sucks out the noise of vacuum tugging at vacuum. The hollow of his hand flees this place and seeks something round. "Roach," she says, "you nearly cracked my jaw." He gives no answer, travels with a forcing finger down into her bellybutton, he can tell how her muscles are carrying her ac- commodatingly higher for him, he bumps upward over the rhythm of ribs and is about to collect the candle-end of her nipple when she smashes herself suddenly down on his hand underneath her, so that her skeleton toils into his knuckles. "That hurt, you bitch, let go." "You roach. You cockroach," she says calmly, and heaves down to hold him. But somehow under her heaviness he has regained action—I can see from the minute but regular twitchings in his shoulder that he is in control of his wrist again, he has converted the soft hand of cautious searching into a fist with one uncompromising finger pointing straight out, a hand on a signpost, and how he aban- dons the upward direction, switches it round like an insect antenna, and probes down hard, punching with the ball of his finger as he listens to her anger, wiggling it down down among her whiskers, and slowly slowly of her own will she ripples her weight away from him, he is untrapped and free to wander, a bridge of strength grows from the root of her neck to her calves, her buttocks strain into squares, she seems

to hang upward from the cord of her side, her bones gather
themselves into a hinge and for a moment the leafy hillock
that caches her cleft swings up, rears, dominates like a fortifi-
cation, an acropolis, then from that second's ascendancy
dives—her high place is razed, the Y of her slaps into an I,
she closes like a compass, the hairy mound of love is re-
claimed and reduced by the primary mound of the belly, vanishing almost, she is on her back, shut, but his touch which
has risen with her, turned and fallen with her, clings for its
life to the cliff, grabs at brush to keep itself from slipping to
that belly-plain and its deep abandoned sexless pock, recov-
ers, arches its hard knuckles, protrudes the resuming finger of
excitation, and thrusts it laboring into the secret wood. "Quit
that," she says bitterly, "I don't need any help from the likes
of you, never mind those Chinaman gimmicks, believe me I
can just cross my legs and break your arm off," but her voice
runs with a moist sluggishness, the surfaces of her eyes are
leathery as calluses, he has tripped some strand linked to
other strands, some voluptuary wire in her brain tightens, he
has caught the drawstring of her frame, her thighs knot and
shift, the wicks of her nipples stiffen—"If you're waiting for
tomorrow skip it," she mutters—her upper lip is hoisted, her
nostrils knead themselves. But his body is away. "How d'you
like that, bus without a driver," he says, "you going to get off
before I get on?" "You'll never get on," she rasps. Again he
does not answer, his feet curve under him like communing
antlers, the absurd knots of his buttocks pile up on his heels,
he angles forward a little and from his cluttered fork just
then lowers a lopsided basket like bunches of grapes in a
wineskin, the round weights dragging heavily and unequally
in their loose pulled bag. Hairs spring from his shoulders and
he shows himself to her, leaning his tongue on his lip, then
quick and crafty plunges it into the furrow of her breasts. His
tongue scribbles figure 8s in a wobbling track—"I ride my
own way, nobody tells me how to ride," and I see what he
rides, I see the neck of the animal he rides kneeling, it
stretches to escape him but is docile, its long straight neck
yearns from its ruff and collar, it is a thick-flanked headless
beast and new to me. —I think of Enoch and the door always open to insult my mother's delicacy, and I coming by
one day and seeing how his stream falls from a tender fat
creature with a short neck scalloped out of the head, and in
the head a pouring cyclops-eye—the Jews are different. Stefanie laughs, mutedly they laugh together in fear of being

heard, exposed—"the Leaning Tower of Pisa," she calls up to him, "whyn't you try Perma-Starch?" and I see how under the whip of her dispraise his steed hardens its headless neck, all sinew and maneless muscle, all sudden brutishness and power, its will surges out of his thighs, it bears him up on the crest of its canter, he climbs sideways to her side and still that stallion stays high in an arrested leap between his thighs, it strains outward as though it would shoot free, a slow wax tear glistens in its blind cup—"are you dressed for this?"—he turns his mouth and spits into the dark. "What d'you think I *came* with," she answers him, "I'm stuffed to the gills, I'm not *stupid*," down now to a whisper, and he falls on his flattened hands on either side of her, and encumbered by the life that prances out of his fork he falls to his knees astride her haunch and suspends himself above her like the tent-skin that goes from bone to bone of the wing of a bat. His wrists and shins are the bones, and his ropy body hangs like a hammock between them; meanwhile his steed paws her belly. Then strangely—her face is very still—a fulcrum moves in her spine, her hams revolve and lift, her legs climb for their embrace like arms, she takes him like a caliper around the waist of an ant, her ankles are locked into his armpits, she divides herself to bag him, she cleaves herself wide for him, his stud charges and misses, retreats, assesses, charges, misses, their sighs sing together, he grabs for her buttocks and shoves them higher, she teeters on the base of her neck and props herself for him, he dangles her now from his neck like a wishbone, his sides within the crook of her urge her wider, she tears thigh from thigh, she opens herself, she is split beyond belief, his blind beast's thick muzzle lumbers down, vanishes. Ah. Reappears. She cries out at her loss of it, but now he has caught the sense of her track and goes to her straight, keen, with a cleanliness of skill and space, I hear a small brief grateful sucking, now he is like some woodcutter with a great bole before him and he must cut it down before night, and he begins, little by little, with his tempered saw, afraid of time and of magnitude, but snaring courage from the courage of the stroke, and driving in, in, toward the tree's deepest inner thong, each thrust to the center exacting an equal retreat to the farthest margin, the retreat feeding on the thrust and the thrust each time seizing more and more elasticity from the release that follows, so that the tree seems to labor in its own cutting, the tree devours the saw, together the tree and the cutter strive for its felling, the sunball leaps

down and still the tree offers its opened side to the saw and
the saw dives crucially into the wound, and they hurry, they
hurry, if they do not meet in the crisis of the stroke they will
forfeit the victory of time, if they do not match will for will
they are lost to time and crisis. Time and crisis sweat in
them, crisis claws time, time waits: now something huge;
huge, taut, distended; some enormous dome of absence
swelled by the squeeze of hope looms, intrudes, shoulders itself between the fitted halves of woman and man, untender,
cunning yet blunt, now her mouth strains to stretch flat, the
muscles of her cheeks squeeze now not hope but demand—
now it is demand and demand, she demands the hugeness,
she sweats for it, the huge freight of toil, she toils and demands, she demands what sharp birth she will bear, she toils
and demands—"You lousy little independent," he tells her,
"you've got plenty to learn," and she, bleak with fear of early
triumph, bleats, "It's you not me, just try and catch up,
grandpa," and suddenly both are motionless: motionless: a
photograph of the tide: then the reel begins to run again, but
too quick, berserk, backward, he flashes backward to his
knees, I see his wet breast rise like a column rebuilding, he
undoes gesture and posture, the trail of sweat shining downward climbs from the inner elbow to return itself to the armpit, he retrieves himself for himself: then reaches a single
vast hand curved and spread to contain her and takes the
swell of her crotch and fast and brutally, before she can
sprawl, he flips her over. And penetrates. A noise of pain
creaks from her—her arms are pressed crooked and tangled
under her ribs, her palms show helplessly the wrong way up,
like the pale backs of leaves, she is captive, twisted, his teeth
pull on the skin of her nape and the heel of the hand that
threw her over leans deep into her iron resisting belly, she no
longer has her will, she is heaped below him and cannot turn,
he keeps her stiff and still, his bottommost leg pries apart her
calves and angry knees, she will not widen herself for him
but inch by inch he pries with his invading knee and shin,
now he has her wide for him but stiff, his fingers creep to cup
themselves and push flat her nipple and breast, she is stiff but
wonderfully wide for him, she sinks for the blow of his sinking, she burrows her hams in his grizzly triangle, she claims
nothing, she is curiously manageable and quickly soft, he
rides with her and rocks, as on a sea-toy, he rocks and rides,
he slices the top off each smooth wave as it shrugs into being,
the waves shrug themselves tall, the sea-toy swells to scale

them, the waves are walls, his rocking slams the sea like a door, the tall water has walls and doors like a room, he rocks in the room, the small room shrinks, the walls tighten, he cannot rock so he beats, he beats, he does not rock or slide but he beats, beats, and slow-motion through the density of her spine the tender doors fall away of themselves, and behind one is another and beyond that another, door after door after door, and all the doors fade away into openings past openings, and he rolls from her, annulled, and she rolls slowly round, taking the curve of her flank prudently and slowly until she is on her back, her hand on the hand that dents her high nipple, and I have the sense that a mirror has peered into a mirror and viewed infinity, and I the witness of it.

From the beginning they never kissed.

17

They lay whispering.

Then I understood that they were making their plans, so I hung back to hear—a witness has no resources and no stratagems. But it was uninteresting. They were only wrangling over something nautical. Where they would go and what they would do seemed too well agreed for argument. And anyhow it was a very short quarrel, full of this boat and that boat; immediately they slept, so I started after the light. The light led from them. On the way to it I felt I had witnessed the very style of my own creation.

18

In the kitchen a gaggle of candles lit *The Law of the Sea.*
I said, "What are you reading in that?"
The flashlight drew a bead on me. "Piracy. What're you doing creeping around?"
"I thought that book was rare."
"Well?"
"Piracy isn't."
"I know that. I know what there is to know," William's son said, and vengefully blew at the flames: they all went out, but one unexpectedly revived.
"Long John Silver," I said. "The black flag."
"Oh shut up. Don't be a damn fool."
The flashlight circuited space and caught a mouse running into a cavern—we heard its feet slip in panic on the refrigerator floor.
"What do you expect me to do?" he said finally, and I was startled—William had asked the same, though retroactively. Certain questions, like fortunes and misfortunes, pass from father to son. "Apply the Unwritten Law? Go in and kill them?"
"You could start with local precedent," I said, and sat down next to him on the green silk sofa, my father's bed, where green girls danced. Our heads were nearly in the fireplace. "What this place demands of all its lovelorn. —Head for the woods like a red-blooded Armenian. You could always do *that.*"
And I made the gesture of the knife.
"Very funny."
"She isn't worth it?"
"He isn't."
I asked, "Do you make a habit of insulting fathers?"
"What?"

"First yours. Now mine."

"What did I say? I said he'd be a shoo-in—"

"Not stepfather. Father."

"I haven't said a word about my father. —All right, so I said I'm getting like him. Every day little by little, more and more—it's something you can feel. If I keep it up I may yet qualify for a trustee. Unless I decide to stop short of murder and stick to robbing banks."

"You could call it off."

"Call what off? My probably inherited criminal pattern? The grapes that the fathers have eaten shall set the teeth of the sons—"

"Getting married."

"—on edge. You don't turn back from the edge." He said fiercely, "I can't call it off."

"Why not? You think she'll quit? She's practically just got started."

"You don't just call a thing like that off. Not a wedding. You don't know the machinery. It would kill the families, they'd die."

"Of satisfaction. I mean William. I bet he'd do a jig. He doesn't like her."

"He hates her. Look," he said, "I told you once, you don't know a thing about families, not one damn thing."

"I remember—family unity. Its a sort of rule, like parliamentary procedure—has to do with giving people the floor." I took the flashlight from him and meditatively switched it off and on; then off. "Your fiancée's on the floor right now."

"Go to hell."

"You'll marry her anyway?"

"You bet I will."

"So's not to embarrass the families?"

He had scooped up some of the soft candle drippings and was rolling out a little wax ball.

"That's tame," I said. "Tamer even than William. *He* was capable of divorce."

"Do you admire my father?" he said bluntly.

"No. Do you admire mine?"

"You want me to testify before the committee?" he threw out. "What do I care? You don't have to remind me what my father's capable of. In fact I may go him one better, why not? I've had his example after all. I've had my mother's example my whole life. There's a lot to be learned from family unity."

"Never look on the floor," I suggested. "Never call a thing off."

"You prig. I don't give out credos. My father called off plenty, didn't he?—never mind that marriage to your mother, I mean this so-called museum and God knows what else. And called off all his Goddamn credos while he was at it. I wouldn't call this off if I had a written guarantee signed by her in blood that I'd find her on the floor every night from now till doomsday."

"That's loyalty. That's love. *That's* no credo."

"I'll tell you what it is, it's utility. It's making do. It's the lesson of family unity. If I called it off she'd get away with it. She's made a monkey out of me and she's not going to get away with it. My father let your mother get away with it and it made a monkey out of him for the rest of his life—she did her job on him and then just went on her way and never paid for it."

"She paid and she paid and she paid. You saw it yourself. You snooped it out. —Connelly's ledgers," I said.

By now the wax ball had ears and a nose. He said steadily, "It's not going to be that way for me. What I learn I apply."

"Aha, you'll make do."

"You bet. I'll make it hell for her," he announced in his deepest lung, and with the nail of his little finger he dug out a pair of eyes.

"Ssh. You'll wake them."

He gave a hiss: "The sleep of the just."

"My father's a pagan, he doesn't have a sense of justice."

"Oh hell. Let the Senate worry about it. He's a shoo-in, I told you. Quit worrying about it."

I said, "Why do you keep talking about Enoch?"

"You brought him up."

"I brought up justice."

"Well drag it down again. I'm not in the mood to hear about what doesn't exist. Shove metaphysics."

"Sometimes," I said warily, "you think something doesn't exist and then it turns out it does."

"Honest to God I'm not in the mood."

"Like Nick. He exists."

A draft annihilated the last candle. "He exists," he said in the black.

"And you didn't think I *had* a father. See, I know something about family unity on my own," I said.

"What's this all about?"

"Boats. My father is asleep on the floor. In the morning they're going to take a boat—"

"What's this all about?"

"I'm explaining. I," I said, "am issue of the floor. You," I said, "are issue of the nuptial couch."

He almost yelled. "Come on, what's this all about?"

"Please don't wake my father," I said.

19

In the end it turned on the issue of who he was. I said at once he was my father, but the Purses denied it with so much seriousness they were at length believed.

Town Island had become a town. There were goings and comings; and a doctor; and large boats with crews and special machinery; and men with notebooks; and a man with documents full of dotted lines and boxes to put crosses in; and men without uniforms who said they were from the police; and men wearing caps like sailors who were not sailors; and Polygon's Japanese; and some county politicians who walked everywhere and called the house "the old museum," as though it was a well-used phrase among them; and a helicopter clattering spoons into the sky.

Polygon's Japanese found the bottle with the note in it. It had washed up overnight; the tide had swung it far up on the beach, and it rolled into the crevice of a motor. A wave knocked it against a carburetor (it happened to be the one-eyed old sea-salt) but it did not break, and in the afternoon Polygon's Japanese, heading back to his launch without the passengers he had come for, caught the wink of sun on glass and picked it up. It was only an empty wine bottle with the cork left in, wreathed with seaweed, so he threw it down on the sand again and fled to call the Coast Guard.

I knew my father's alphabet. Water had seeped into the bottle and blurred the letters—that made them all the more recognizable: ah, my father's name in a smear of glue, inside an envelope, hidden: the letters wild, quick, overtaken. The hand that set the letters down heaved cartons, pushed off hulls (I saw what rough force had snapped the B flat dumb) —that hand is surprised by pens and pencils, little narrow quicksilver things too subtle to catch hold of solidly. The hand of a man. The mind that set the letters down loved no one. Love broke in me: infatuation, and I would have scratched the signature in hope of touching him. There was no signature. When you write to the ocean you do not leave your name. Gustave Nicholas Tilbeck does not leave his name for the ocean or for me. The lip of the bottle smelled of wine but did not taste of it. I gave it a lick. It tasted salt.

A Letter from Harriet B.S.P.
To Poseidon M.D. (Master of the Deep)
By an Amanuensis

The god of love is always
a baby.

Cupid! Christ!

It was the unmistakable voice of *Marianna Harlow*, Chapter Twelve.

At evening shouts spouted from the middle water. Over the distance the heavy calls of men came to us reduced. Tinkle after tinkle—the men roared their find, and we at last caught the high light flake of a syllable.

At evening they took him up in a net, like a fish.

They laid him on the sand. The net was tangled. They cut it away.

The Purses swore he had no next of kin they knew of.

Then in the full red of sunset a man wrote words on the dotted lines and drew crosses in the boxes. He took close note of everything, and tried to be accurate about weight and length and color, the way a fisherman who views his day's catch tries to be accurate. Among much other information, and below

Eyes ☐ blue ☐ brown ☐ other,

he put down that my father's hair was dyed blond.

My father's body was covered with vomit; but this required a separate paragraph.

20

"The point was to go out all quiet, well what in the world d'you *think* we took it for? He's the one said the other rode like a nymph, he said nymph and he said the wood looked like out of silk—he said things like that. He said Almighty God himself knew it rode like a nymph, and I said if you ask me it's just like splashing around in a lawyer's office, all brown, anyhow I hate that ship, my father picked it not me, I *said* what I really wanted was a little thing, you know one of these little free things that look like they don't belong to anybody especially not a lawyer and you can practically sail them in a bathtub, not that that was the *crux*, the crux was to go out all quiet—"

In long strokes, like a swimmer, all that afternoon Stefanie re-told her story. She sat on the flat end of one of the motors and talked while the men wrote. Then another boat arrived, a wire was pulled across the sand, a man tapped a microphone, and she had to begin again.

The county men came back down to the beach from the house. They had gone into the cellar and seen the wine. They had climbed to the top and seen all the dressers and bureaus and chests and finally a room full of books. They had seen the piano and the ceiling harps and the kings of France and Spain. They said the place would never have stood up as a museum—the foundations were no good. Built on piles, they said, into sand, and you know sand. Never expect anything from sand. The story was the old man meant to bring in a school of whales, live ones in a tank. One whale in the pantry, they said, and before you knew it you'd have your whale bang in the cellar. The floor wouldn't hold. Sagging bad enough already under that refrigerator—talk of things outsize and whalish. Dangerous place. Vandals. Attractive nuisance.

Tear it down, sell it for scrap. —The county men murmured; the men with the notebooks wrote.

Into the microphone Henry David Thoreau spoke a sermon: it seemed to be mostly about a junior lifesaver's certificate, but it was long, and soon it was about a senior lifesaver's certificate. The man holding the wire asked, "You believe it could have been prevented?" and another man laughed and said, "Get the kid out of here. A blowhard. And wasn't there. Get the girl back." Purse looked at the sky and said, "Our plane." Mrs. Purse said, "Well that's plain, we'll miss it if we don't start" and Purse said, "It's all over, there's nothing *we* can do." One of the men in uniform and one of the men not in uniform surrounded them: "Where will you be if we need you?" Mrs. Purse said, "How lovely and hilarious, I've never actually heard that *spoken,* not outside of a murder mystery movie—" Purse said, "Shikarpur, Pakistan." The Coast Guard officer said, "Good God." William's son left Stefanie's side. "It makes a difference, it hits on what they do with the body," he said. "I'm afraid we're of no help there," Purse said. "We've identified him sufficiently," Mrs. Purse said, "we don't *know* him, after all. A stranger. A fraud. We know his name. Maybe it isn't genuinely his name." The Coast Guard officer frowned: "Get in touch if you hear of any relatives or connections, will you?" Mrs. Purse frowned equally and said nothing. "No connections we know of," Purse said, "a stranger you see. A confidence man. We met him in the Automat." "Among the nickels and dimes," Mrs. Purse noted. William's son said, "He has a daughter." "No no," Mrs. Purse said, "no daughter. No connections at all. A man alone. A tramp. A cheat and swindler. An immoralist. —About the dead nothing evil however." "No daughter," Purse said, "that was only for protection. Cover-up you see. The Lord knows what's in a man's heart. There's no good in pretense. Well, the dead don't need protection," and Polygon's Japanese took them away.

William's son said: "Tell them who you are."

"I did tell them," I answered, "over and over. I said what I am."

"Say it again."

"I have no respectability. Nobody listens. They don't believe me."

He said sharply, "You want potter's field for him?"

"In a way he was a potter. —That's all right," I said.

He misheard in the din. Polygon's launch roared. "A pauper?"

"A potter too."

"Look, if you don't care what they do with him, all right. Otherwise you better get your mother to come out here pronto."

"What for?"

"To claim him."

"That's law school advice," I said. "My mother has her own lawyers. My mother has William. She claimed what William tells her to claim, right? It's in *his* discretion—you told me that once yourself."

"My father doesn't as a rule send persons to potter's field. He doesn't have that sort of clientele."

"No, William doesn't have paupers," I agreed.

"He doesn't have potters. I'm telling you, you better get your mother over," William's son said.

I said again, "What for?"

He scowled with exasperation. "To give some decency. The whole thing is sordid enough—good God, to bury the man."

"She wouldn't do it. William wouldn't let her do it."

"My father doesn't get in the way of what your mother wants."

"Right," I said. "She wants the Ambassadorship."

He turned to view Stefanie—she was sobbing noisily into the microphone.

"It would ruin Enoch," I said. "That's the whole point of everything—not to ruin Enoch. It's why I came."

She was explaining how her skirt was rent to pieces in the water. She had lost it finally. The county men and the man in charge of the microphone looked away, reminded by the drying rosebuds on her underpants. Her naked thighs were slick with oil.

William's son said: "She's worse."

"Who?"

"Your mother."

"Worse than Stefanie?" —I thought he would wince.

"Worse than my father." But he was bold merely. He said, "My father killed a boy to please her. But he went to the burial. *She* won't even bury a man."

"She won't bury a Muse. Nobody does that."

He said disgustedly, "The Muse is a woman."

"A male Muse he was. Nick."

"That beats it. Cant. What it comes down to is she won't bury the man."

"Then she's *not* worse than Stefanie," I said.

"You go to hell. That poor kid cries and cries. She's cried five hours straight without letting up. She nearly drowned herself trying to keep him up and out of it. And all that muck. I say she's a heroine. How about this quiz they're putting her through? You ought to get down on your knees to her—it's *your* father. I don't give a damn whose Muse, but he's your muck, and she nearly saved him—practically saved him, so don't go around saying she buried him."

"Not him. Somebody else. You."

Now he did wince. I saw it—a current of shock in the nostrils. "That poor kid's a victim," he defended himself. And hesitated. Then: "What she's been through today. A martyrdom. Use your eyes. A martyr to muck she is. She's been through hell today."

"St. Stefanie," I reminded him. "Patroness of housecats, *floruit circa* 1957 A.D. Pussyhead, you make William look like a lion."

"A man died."

"And you were the one who was going to make it hell for her!"

"She's had her hell," he said, subdued.

"The water-power of a tear exceeds the sea. My stepfather says that. What will you do?" I asked him. "*All* her lovers won't die," and watched him return to her side. My envy had nothing to take then but the back of his neck. She would have other lovers. None of them would die. None of them would live. It is no light thing to have intercourse with the Muse. Afterward there is not taste for this or that. The planet's sweetmeats fail after a nibble at vatic bread. The grove without its genius is bleak and chill. The spirit of a happening, like the spirit of a place, has no wants. It is we who want *it*. Think of the man who slept with a mermaid and learned her unearthly singing: when she at last, no longer amused by hot human love, and suffocated by hot human flesh, flopped from the beach where they had lain to the cold base-depths where he could not swim or follow, he was smitten not with grief of her abandonment but with unexpungeable longing for that singular absent music: he goes home, pursues composition, labors all the rest of his life to duplicate her clef and scale and system, never so much as catches the spoor of any of these, and is acclaimed a master of the newly weird, of art, of beauty, of the illimitable into which few can penetrate; but he breathes failure, loss stuns him. How changed he is from his days of gold!—*then* he wore a gold beard, and saw its image in the mirror of her burnished scales at that shining delta place where the human female's in-between would be, *then* he listened to the inhuman scales of her song, neither archaic nor Oriental nor twelve-tone nor diatonic nor chromatic nor like the lightly grave hendecachord of Ion of Chios, but unlike all, cold, multisegmented, isolate, phantasmal, neither color nor graph nor emotion, yet ghastly, ghostly, more lovely and less bearable than that hendecachord of Ion of Chios (which no living ear has ever heard), and the beat of it homologously suggestive of the rational wash of one's own blood in the arteries, when the ears are stopped by the sea in the instant before drowning—phylogeny connects that music and this, as it connects gill and ear.

So now Stefanie. She would change. I listened to the tissue of her weeping: she spun it out and spun it out. It made a grey net over her voice. The florets ceased to fall in her voice. She went on weeping and weeping as though joy were done forever. The county politicians sighed with boredom. All who have not had intercourse with the Muse, female, or male, sigh with boredom. The Coast Guard officer sighed with boredom. Ditto the doctor. Ditto the man holding the wire. Ditto the men with the notebooks—still they dutifully wrote. (The motors did not sigh.) Her flowerless voice told the future—how she would go from place to place, looking for Duneacres, as my mother had flown from place to place, looking for the bird of the world and secretly thinking it Brighton: and now thought Brighton might somehow lodge itself in an Embassy. William's son sighed with boredom. He had achieved his father in blunted tooth and shaven claw, and it could not be said it was against his will. All who had not had intercourse with the Muse, female or male, achieve no more than their begetters. The begetter of William's son acquiesced in the law of prey. So at last did William's son. They acquiesced in themselves as prey. But the Muse does not prey: no Muse commits the act of love upon a domestic animal, and she will never touch William or his son. Not that the Muse is extraordinary—extraordinariness in passion is a modern fallacy. Besides, the Muse is in charge of artifice (as no nature-acquiescing creature of prey can be), and artifice is never extraordinary. Our phrase for the marvelous is *natural* wonder. The sun is extraordinary, but the white blaze of my father's head was not. A dye. Ah, tawdry, tawdry, yet why not a tawdry Muse? (It must be a tawdry Muse to call forth Allegra's *Marianna* or Stefanie's tale of death and puking.) Tawdry, to hope to bring to life one of those boys on an amphora, bright-haired, goat-legged, with a little tibia-pipe poised and halted for laughter, among those love-exalted girls? A dye! Aha, my mother's fantastic lover, potter, Muse, charlatan, insincere blackmailer—somewhere and sometime he had to bend, grimace, crouch (crouched on the beach: mechanized faun, neck curved), dip his whole head into a vat of fake youth—there is no other way to get a good result.

The thing was visible. Impossible, after all, not to have seen it—sea-change at the scalp. The man who drew the crosses had noticed it at once. From my father's body, green with a moss of dried vomit (or green as one of those antique bronze statues divers now and then pull out of the sea), nothing shone.

(I interrupt for Enoch, though his turn is not yet. Reading *Anna Karenina* aloud to my mother, he one day began to talk of characters in life and literature. In literature, he said, a character is interesting because he changes. Fiction, despite its professions, cares only for stabilized types, and fiction amazes when it produces a person who plausibly reverses his nature. Not so life. In life, where not plausible but shocking reversals are commonplace—if only we are clever enough to witness them—it is just the opposite: in fickle life nothing amazes more than unchangingness. That is why, he said, we are so infrequently surprised by the people we know.)

The skipper of the parenthesis will have missed Enoch's cool half-paradoxes. Never mind. I thought my father more splendid than any other being, and not because he amazed by never changing. He never changed; he did not amaze. I had been amazed to come on a boy knocking at a ball in a ruined field, but what would I have felt to find a man like William or a man like Enoch?—it would have contradicted and corrupted all that I imagined of my mother's early time. My father devised and invented himself, and chose to stay at the crest: the same for my mother, the same for me. And the splendor of this was its perfect naturalness and logicality: what else shall Gustave Nicholas Tilbeck be if not a boy? I forgave him his devices; I would have had him yield more. Let them discover that his heels are split, or that he carries in his pocket a half-eaten mushroom (the flyamanite, with its visionary properties), or anything else incredible and magical—that his eyes are agate, his nostrils wrens, his teeth the horns of pygmy deer; that his nose hangs on a pivot; that he wears rings; that limb by limb he can be pried apart and kept in a jewelled box; that his death too is sham and he meanwhile merely hides grinning behind a tree, commanding that company of investigators to feast on his torso. Anything: I would believe it, and envied Stefanie who still steadily and liturgically wailed, talking now of suicide: "I could kill myself, really I mean it, I could die this minute"; but plainly she would live to be old, thin, resentful, duped, sly. Suddenly no one was bored—not the doctor, not the Coast Guard officer, not the audio man, not the men with the notebooks, not her fiancé. Just then she gave out a sense of raw presence; of totality: she had had her life, now it was over, she needed no more, the rest was commentary. All at once everyone acceded to her cry. No one denied it, no one told her it was nonsense. Envy had them in thrall—the girl had had her moment. She had it and it was gone. Faith in her claim showed in their faces. They looked religious. They were believers: her moment had passed, it would never come again. William's son knew it; it subdued him; they all knew it. Some careless secret, already lost, already half-forgotten, nothing extraordinary, marked her mouth: perhaps it was joy, perhaps it was an adventure, perhaps it was neither. She scarcely remembered. What has happened and will not come again is easily recognized by everyone, but the moment of recognition itself is unique and terrible, like birth and disclosure, and like these cannot be re-experienced. Once is all. Over that cluster of men and motors the irretrievable passed its stale wing.

She spoke again of the two boats. They had taken the little boat for the quiet. The quiet was the thing—so as not to wake the Purses. At dawn there was one star left over. The rest was clouds, long and spread out. Then came the sun, not gradually, but all at once, plink! He never wanted the little boat, it was her fault. She was afraid of the Purses. The big boat might churn them out of the tents and down the hill, it had a burr like death. She imagined them all lined up on the sand, the whole mob yowling and ogling. She wanted to row away, quiet and private in the new air. The moon was gone. With the oars rolling out it was like beating on cotton. No one heard. No one woke. There was a little hard wind that smelled of morning and of autumn. She slipped down into the hull to escape the spray and the cold wind. They were going for the middle of the bay. The idea was to get far out and then switch to Mrs. Purse's motor. She wanted cake for breakfast. They were going to tie up for breakfast at a fancy place in Rye, half dock half restaurant. He said again they should have taken the launch and had their comfort, no one ever tied up there in a shabby little tub, not even tub, bowl. He asked did she want to row awhile. No, no, it was cold, cold. He spat over the side and went on rowing. His arms hoisted like wheels. The sun drifted nearer and nearer, splattering in the water. He spat. She looked over and saw the foam of his spit fall into the hole in the water. The oar made a dark deep hole. Then the water whorled up and filled it from below, and the sun ran in. The motor now, he said. No, no, too soon. Everybody could hear, even pussyhead. Poor pussyhead, to see them fly away, at least he would be having the launch for himself, still he'd be mad all the same. We should've taken the launch, Nick said. No, no, stupid noisy ship it was, all those kids would hear and then the whole world would know where they were at. He spat again: the motor now. She held the oars for him while he turned to pull on the string. Why d'you spit like that? To catch fish with, nothing draws them like human spittle, they come down from Alaska and up from Peru, the flounder and the salmon, for a whiff of human wetness. I want cake for breakfast not fish. The motor did not catch. He pulled on the string again. The motor did not catch. I think it's too soon, we're not out far enough, they'll hear us, you better wait before starting it up. No, he said. And spat. He looked angry. Why d'you spit like that? Nothing, don't talk. Are you mad at me about the other boat? Nothing, don't talk. He pulled on the string and the motor brayed. There. She came out of the hull and watched the fork of their wake. It was seeded with gold. That's better, he said, talk if you need to, I was afraid the damn thing wouldn't get started. The blades drilled the water and now they began to take on speed. She laid the oars like a pair of crutches down at the bottom under their feet. He was holding the steering handle and she saw his teeth biting at the wind. He shouted, but the noise of the motor was too loud and she did not hear. She crawled back to him and yelled into his ear, See, I told you, we could wake the dead with this thing and the other one's even worse, I told you, but the wind almost plucked her tongue out, and she felt her words leap away as though they were energies of their own. They sat close in the

stern, and if they looked straight forward to the prow they
could not see the water, the boat's point rode so high. They
made their own waves behind them and slicked head after
head off the waves that kept getting in their way in front. She
decided to try screaming at him again, and let out as few
words as possible, very near his face: You're not mad about
not taking the big boat any more are you? He shook his
head, but now she did not know whether this meant No or
merely that he could not hear. She saw his teeth again, and
realized from his funny unfurling mouth that he was not
answering her, it was singing coming out. The water's like a
nylon stocking, we're making a big long run in it, but she
knew he could hear her as little as she could hear him. She
wondered what he was singing. This is much better, I hate
that ship, it doesn't feel like this, I'm so hungry, I feel so
happy, I wish I had that Hershey Bar we left in the other
boat, I want chocolate cake. She leaned against him and
could tell in his chest the vibration of his singing. It was like
a buzzer in an electric alarm clock, it was as if she could turn
it off if she wanted to but she was too happy to stir. Across
the water there was a fringe of green and brownish-yellow. It
was autumn turning. She reflected that autumn always came
after summer, it was never any different, why was that, why
did it always happen in the same order like that? Other things
didn't always come off in exactly the same order every time,
though some things did, for instance first you were engaged
and then married, never the other way, first you were young
and then old, even though it didn't *have* to be that way, for
instance a baby didn't have to be a baby, it could look like
ninety years old when it was born and then get better-looking
and stronger and all, and then when it was really ninety years
old it would be ready for sex and everything, and then it
could die when it began to look like a little baby, that would
be interesting, that would mean only little tiny coffins and it
would even save a lot of room in graveyards so they could
use some of the graveyard space for more tennis courts and
things. Swimming pools and even stadiums.

She was hearing her thoughts very clearly, why was that?
The sun was flat and clear on the water. Everything was still
and clear, and when she looked over again at the brownish-
yellow trees on the shore, they kept very still and never even
fluttered. Why was that? Damn damn damn, Nick said, and
she heard him because there was no motor.

William's son had resumed his cigar. The men on the

beach were listening silently. The doctor slapped at an insect
on his neck. "Motor failed," the Coast Guard officer said,
and the men with the notebooks took it down.

It isn't the fuel, we had plenty of fuel, damn that woman,
it's gone foul again. Who, Mrs. Purse? It's no good. He
pulled on the string. The motor had no lung. It's dead, he
said, not a spark, nothing. He pulled on the string. Nothing.
Damn her, she fixed it with a shoelace, nothing. That's all
right, we can *row* up, I like rowboats, I don't mind. We're
going back, he said. Back where? Where we came from, it's
the shortest, I'm not going to get stuck in the middle of the
Sound with nothing but a pair of posts, get down, will you?

As he rowed he spat. His arms went up and shuddered
downward. He seemed to be making a frame for the tall sun.
He rolled around the sun and contained it, then it rolled off,
then he contained it again.

She did not know what was the matter. His face was perfectly closed. His forehead was smooth. She was afraid to
speak. He rowed as though the water was an altar. The oars
spooned up bubbles. He continued to spit. Foam flew down
into foam. The oars came up like terrifying candlesticks.

He went on spitting. She did not know what was the matter.

Something shimmered past. At the side of the boat a stick
slipped into the water. It ran off toward the sun. He had lost
one of the oars. The other was pulled tight against him like a
chinning bar. He was exercising against it in midair; his
head was stiff over it; his eyelids were stiff. His squeezed
eyes shot a dozen scallops of skin across his face. Webs were
emitted from his nose. The bridge of his nose contorted verti-
cally. It was very strange. She did not like to see him pinch
his eyes, it made his chin unpleasant, the jowl of a toad. It
ruined him, he was ruined. He exercised against the oar. She
was certain he would drop it, they were in the near middle of
the bay, she bawled at him not to drop the oar. He did not
drop it, but it was suddenly as flexible as a finger, it turned
alive, it insinuated itself under his chin and then stretched off
like an impudent wrist, it seized itself from him and dived
in at the paddle-end, flat on the water, so that the splash
washed them both. Then he began to retch. Matter fell from
him.

The Coast Guard officer said, "Loss of sculls due to illness," and the men with the notebooks took it down.

A brilliant skein flowed over the top of the water. He

leaned after it. He braced a leg on the rim of the hull. He accommodated the hinge of his back to the flux. He hung howling. His issue escaped him, and unwillingly he followed it over.

Like any of Miss Jewett's girls, she had no physical fear and went after him at once, and for a long time they danced together in the sour water, but in the end he took a turn she did not know and he lost her. The skein had clotted into islands of tender putrid greenish flowers, and his falsely bright head was covered.

21

When I came home my mother was deep in grief which had no signs. She seemed just the same—she ranted, rambled, bellowed that my hem hung wrong, criticized the cut of the collar of my blouse (though it was her own choice and gift), documented by a line at my nose how I was sure to age early, and showed me that my quick return was in every way an offense to her: she was objective.

But all the same I saw, in certain absences, vacancies, distractions, omissions, in all that she had formerly professed and now failed to perform (for example, her eyes were perfectly tearless), the truth of her grief. She was stricken. Her grief was dark and genuine and contained a quietness. Behind the plain misery of our confrontation, her little quiet lurked. She had already had the news for some hours. She told me it had come out of the radio—Nanette's radio. "She locks herself up in her room to follow all the stage tunes, they don't allow it, and well, to make a long story short, Mrs. William passed by and heard the name. The name of shame. The name of blame. She hasn't been that excited since she got herself jilted. Well, about that, she asked for it absolutely— piety begets jilting. So behold, she permitted the name of shame and blame to leap from the purity of her lips, never

mind excited, call it exalted, I've always thought she'd make
a good priestess or vestal virgin. I don't suppose they were
really virgins you know. More likely a convention, a way of
speaking. —And reports."

"To you?" I said.

"To me. Direct address. Telephonic communication."

"Sarah Jean?" I said. "She called you up?"

"Talked to me. I'm trying to tell you. She hasn't talked to
me since the day I married Enoch, nineteen years almost. But
gave way for the sake of the name of shame and blame. She
recognized it, imagine that. 'Allegra, is that you?' 'No,' says
Janet. 'Allegra,' she says finally, 'I've been trying to get William, but all the lines are busy, Connelly's line too. It's something your lawyer should break to you after all. It's a thing
really a minister should tell you, but you don't *have* a minister. Bread cast on the waters, when you need one you don't
have one.' And then she pronounces the name of blame and
shame that came out of Nanette's loudspeaker. Contraband.
They think they'll keep that girl off the stage but they won't,
you know, it won't work. How did you get back, in the police
launch?"

"No. They took Stefanie in it."

"Aha. They'll want to question her at headquarters. That's
how they like to do it."

"No," I said again, "they finished all that, it's just that she
was upset, she wouldn't come with us. They might put her in
a hospital for a while. The doctor said that."

"Us? Who's us?"

"William's son and me. I came back with him. In that boat
they have."

"Not a thing on the radio about that boy. The papers may
or may not go into that kind of detail, why should they?
Local news, a nonentity gets drowned. Typical summertime
reporting, it's not what you'd call a story with a *name* in it.
'Allegra,' she says, 'a shocking thing. The name came out at
me.' She wouldn't've opened up after nineteen years if that
boy's name came out. Poor William. Mrs. William can take
it, but William! Maybe they'll leave out the boy and concentrate on the heroine angle. 'Debutante Ducked in Derelict
Drowning,' I know the style they use. My God. A crowd on
that place, it sounded like."

"There was a family."

"You'd think William would do something about the squat-
ters. He treats that place exactly as though it wasn't there. A

family! What was he doing with a family? Never mind. Milking and bilking I suppose. I always knew he'd drown. It was a fantasy I had about him. Full fathom five. Listen to me in life everything comes out exactly the way you always thought it would, that's the first rule of being. What did you talk about?"

In a fit of fatigue I threw myself on the carpet. It was after midnight. The boat's lights on the water had printed black points on my vision. I said resentfully, "You. We talked about you from morning to night. All he ever talked about was you."

"William's *boy?*" she marveled; she had not even thought of Nick. "In the boat? Coming back I mean. The two of you alone. He wasn't embarrassed?"

I turned over on my belly and moaned. "Why should he be embarrassed?"

"Well they didn't go up there to picnic, did they? Did he ask you not to tell William?"

I was startled; she had come near to the truth. "Tell William what?"

"What went on up there."

"He asked me not to tell *you.* On the principle that telling you would be the same as telling William." But I did not say what it was I must not tell. A commonplace. First crack at the bride's crack would never any more belong to William's son.

"Birds of a feather, that's William all over. Indirect, everything through Connelly. *I* think it's sound. Premarital trial run. If I'd done it with William we wouldn't have gotten married in the first place."

I said, "You don't just call off a wedding—"

"Oh don't you?" she sneered. "Where'd you get *that?*"

"William's son wouldn't."

"You mean it wasn't satisfactory? A failure? It didn't work out? He didn't"—she seized it—"tell you the *details?*"

"No," I said.

My mother was thoughtful but avid. "Of course he's younger, not that that's an obstacle—"

"He's not younger, he's lots older than she is."

"Who's talking about that Pettigrew girl? You I mean. I had you before Sarah Jean ever came into the picture, well didn't I? I used to think it would be such a funny ironic thing if he fell in love with you. William's boy. It would make everything respectable again, not that I gave a damn about that sort of thing. But he never did."

"He never did," I agreed.

"And you, you never fall in love with anybody," she accused. "Well go to bed if you're that tired, you *look* like an old maid dumped there. I'm staying up, Enoch's flying in. I wish you could wear clothes. You can't wear clothes, that's only part of the trouble. What *about* that family?"

"They're gone."

"Thank God for small favors. It's a nice empty island again, maybe I'll go and live there." The little quiet lay under her face. "The house?" she asked. "How did it look?"

"Big."

"Big, that's right. Big as an Embassy. I really ought to go and live there. That'll be a solution. Oh, sit up, sit on a chair like a person."

"He burned all the chairs," I said.

"Who?"

"Except the ones with the kings' heads. Nick. And the piano stool."

"Don't talk to me about Nick will you? I have to figure out my whole life. I have to *re*-figure it out. What do I care about kings' heads? They go rolling in the end, that's, exactly the point. That's where you just don't seem to follow. You don't know a thing, not one thing. You think just because we're rid of a threat there's nothing more in the world to worry about, all the rest comes easy."

I said, "He wasn't really a threat."

"Look, are you going to go on and on about Nick? Is that what you're here for? To go on and on? He wasn't *really* a threat, oh that's very nice, I expected that. You've always been on his side. I realize that. The reason you were born was for him to have somebody on his side. Celestial design. Look, he's dead, what's the use of going on and on about a dead blackmailer? He sweettalked you, I realize that. That's his *way*. You can't see that. He convinced you, right? Well he was *out* to convince you. That's why he wanted you over there."

"He didn't want me."

"That's right, he's got you now. You swallowed it and he's got you. The Man of No Desires. I know the whole thing, I've got it all by heart, please don't bother me with it. There's not a thing he wants, he doesn't want a thing. Just like the Buddha after nirvana. A holy man. What I want to know is how come these holy men always want to sit in a temple full of virgins? He *told* you he wasn't a blackmailer? 'Me? I'm no blackmailer, right? Is that what he told you?"

"No."

"No. So?"

"I could see it. He wasn't that way."

"He wasn't that way! She could see it! He sweettalked you and you believed every damn stale word. Don't tell me how he looked while he was doing it, I don't want to know, I'm not interested. Eyes like blueberries, nose like on a statue et cetera et cetera. Don't start on me with that. Then you'll say it wasn't just his looks, it was his soul. Well there is *no* immortal soul. Some people don't know a horsethief when they're in the middle of smelling the manure." Her look was maimed by anger. She was insulted. Then it came to me that her tone was formal, traditional, a fiction: she spoke not of a man but of a legend, a theory, an ancient familiar crotchet. "I don't say it isn't pitiful. I mean even if it was a complete stranger and I read the report in tiny type somewhere that a complete stranger got drowned somewhere I would think it was pitiful just the same. Even for a crook to die. I'm against capital punishment, you know that. I think all death is pitiful. I'm against Death."

With this proclamation she told her grievance. She still believed in her own duration, her ascendancy, even her perpetuity; she still meant to snatch a coruscating feather from the breast of the world. She was against Death; her grievance was against Nick; but her grief skirted both. Her grief was not for Nick. Nick was as little to her as Death. Nick and Death were the same. To my stepfather she had whimpered the very truth: she felt nothing. It was not grief then when she had mourned my impossibilities and what I was issue of and how I would not be freed: not grief but fabrication, grievance, pique. Fake, fake, every tear a fake, a theatricality, a fraud, hoax, and profane replica of loss. Her hysteria was only an expert indifference: she had never cared whether I was free or how I was made or where I must go. What she cared for was the Embassy. She was not in pursuit of my freedom but of a palace. I knew this, and from the beginning; therefore wondered why now behind the clamor of her grievance she hoisted the terrible small silence of disaster.

She said: "The Senate has confirmed."

Her voice had a certain lapidary uncompromisingness, like an epitaph.

"When did it happen?"

"The minute Enoch got there. *Before* he got there. They called him up and told him to fly out right away, and when the plane came down it was practically all over Washington. They met him and they told him."

"Fast," I said.

"Oh, fast, you bet. They rushed it through. The fastest confirmation in Senate history. It's made him a laughing-stock. A figure of fun, it took no time at all. They didn't ask him a single question. He did all that reading up on rainfall and cows and all their juntas"—she said the j of jugular for this word—"and it all went for nothing. A clown, a Punch-and-Judy show, they practically banged him on the nose with it—"

"It means they like him, doesn't it, if it went like that?"

"It means they were in a hurry. It's made him a fool."

"What's the difference *what* it's made him if it's made him Ambassador? That's the main thing, isn't it?" I watched the cautious point of her tongue. I said: "Now you have it."

"No I don't have it."

"All right"—I thought her pedantic—"Enoch has it."

"I'm in the middle of re-figuring out my whole life, I told you, can't you follow that? My life is changed. The whole basis of my life from now on, can't you follow?"

"You'll have to do something about your geography," I agreed. "And go to Berlitz for irregular verbs."

"Is that what you think's involved in changing a life? Is that what you think a turning-point is? Look, I'm at a turn-ing-point, can't you understand that?"

"So am I," I said.

"You?" She was blank.

"Someone died."

"Well what's it to you? Hypocrite. Don't start telling me you've lost a father, you never had a father. What was he to you? Not a father. Don't be a hypocrite. And for God's sake get up off the floor. Don't tell me in two measly days you found yourself a father."

"Not a father."

"Then don't talk about turning-points! You don't realize."

"You have it," I said. "I realize. Now you have it."

"I don't have it. And don't say Enoch again. Nobody has it."

"Nobody has what?"

"Idiot!"

"But if they confirmed it," I protested.

"They confirmed it, I just said so, didn't I? Blue in the face trying to get through to you. They confirmed it yesterday."

"Yesterday William's son came in the boat. A thousand years ago it feels like."

"Two thousand. Well then you *know*, he told you, you saw the papers."

"No papers up there. He said the hearings were moved up and all of a sudden Enoch had to go to Washington."

"What do you mean, no papers? I suppose he burned up the whole library too? A Vandal coming down on Rome. A Visigoth. That library's not intact, is it?"

"Mostly." And for honesty: "Not intact."

"See? Sacked I bet. Pilfered."

"William's son took *The Law of the Sea*." Her surprise was limpid; she had never heard of that law, and did not think it was for the taking. "One of those old books up there," I explained.

"Stole it? *Took* it? Didn't ask? Well, who *should* he ask, after all." She considered. "That makes it worse. If there was no one to ask he should have left it. Sarah Jean and all that holiness, and what the whole thing adds up to is just another —lit-tle—crook."

"He has ambitions as to size," I said. "Wait till he gets into the firm."

She jumped on this. "I despise the tale-bearers. Is that what he told you not to tell me? That he swiped a piece of museum? You didn't have to tell me, what do I care about that fish-house? Well at least the sea *has* a law apparently. Land doesn't. Land's always up for grabs, you know that? With a gun you can get practically anything you want in this world, especially a country. First he calls me up—"

"Who?"

"You *are* dumb. Enoch. From Washington, and says get ready right away if I want to go with him, I had to start out that *minute*. Well I said how could I, I had to have *clothes* didn't I, I had to choose what to pack, and he said let Janet and the others do it, it didn't matter, or else I could have a dressmaker from over there do me up quick after we got there. Any old dressmaker! Didn't matter! I've got a dozen closets full of Paris and I'm suppose to march into the Embassy looking like Macy's. I *told* him that. Not that he listened, he said he'd wait for me only until the seven P.M. plane, otherwise go himself, even though the Vice President

said it would be better if I went too, from out of Washington
not New York. The idea would be the two of us making an
entrance." She released a small snort of homage. "The Vice
President's *been* there, he knows what impresses those people."

"Wasn't that the time they threw guavas at him?"

"Cucumbers. Guavas was a different country. And two
hours later he calls back. Well I had to take *some*thing. I was
getting my underwear together after all, I *had* the maids running in circles as it was, Janet even crying—anyhow I was
sure what he was mad at was I hadn't started out yet, he
sounded mad all right, too damn calm. You know the way
Enoch gets," in her old habit of pretending an intimacy between her husband and me. "And that was it. The end, finis."

I did not comprehend.

"Ignorance, that's just plain ignorance!" she tossed out.
"Don't you understand anything about prestige? If a government wants power it has to have prestige. Well where does
prestige *come* from? From *us.* Enoch explained the whole
thing. When one of those governments over there's in trouble
all the United *States* has to do is go right over and pat it on
its head in public and that does the trick, all the revolution-
aries run back into their holes. That's how it operates. It's
what an Ambassador's *for*—diplomatic notes and keeping
communications open and all that, but mostly to show everyone we're friends with whoever's in power. And that *keeps*
them in power. That's why Enoch was supposed to hurry and
get there. For God's sake." She lowered herself to the carpet
beside me with a squeal of hopelessness. "O.K., so let us sit
upon the ground and tell sad stories of the death of queens.
That doesn't sound right."

"Of kings."

"Poor Enoch. The whole District of Columbia's in stitches.
You know what they're calling him? It's humiliating, I can't
repeat it. The Two-Hour Ambassador. Actually he was Ambassador for exactly two hours and forty minutes, if you
want to be perfectly accurate about it."

Bang against her wrists an emulative laughter spiralled up
obediently, as though a hypnotist had directed her to withhold it until she should sense his accessible sign (what was
that mark or sign?)—this silently coërced noise of hers rattled like bangles: her forearms trembled but were bare. She
was unadorned. She wore a flat black beret to cover her few
poor thistles just beginning to spring out with an aberrant

kink altogether new (mutation? an underemployed under-study gene suddenly given its chance?); and below this un-comical cap the left-over pinch of her reading glasses whitened.

On the other side of her body, halfway under a chair, I saw something brown.

"You mean they changed their mind? The committee?" Su-pine I reached over her and pulled on the thing. A wiggle of dust came with it. My mother's glasses fell out of a leather folder pouring loose typed slips. "What's this?"

"Confetti. I'm saving it for your wedding. Well they had a junta down there, that's what," she supplied loudly. And re-tained the jugular j. For a moment she scratched at the floor. "A notebook, what does it look like? Don't be a fool, they don't withdraw confirmations just like that."

"Hoonta," I said.

"I don't give a damn *what* you want to call it, the point is it's as Red as this rug. They held up the presidential palace about five P.M. our time—look, this is only *last night* I'm talking about—and who do they put in but a General who's as Red as a ruby. Surprise surprise. They're *all* Reds, the whole bunch. The Minister of State's a Red, the Minister of the Interior's a Red, the Prime Minister's a Red, and the Cardinal's as Red as a monkey's buttock. (That's the Vice President verbatim my dear.) Well hand that stuff over, will you? It's Enoch's business what he writes down and none of your own."

I said, "It looks like a list."

"Not *my* list. He keeps his own lists. Bits and pieces. Drop by drop, like blood. Poor poor Enoch, he's absolutely *dead* politically. Nobody'll touch him. Pariah. Taboo. Look, the *first* thing the President did was break off relations down there and the second thing was fire Enoch. I mean they're not even *recognizing* that ditch, so how can they send an Ambas-sador? It stands to reason. For God's sake."

Meanwhile in the fan of slips I read a word. It was Enoch's and a private one and was not "child"—how near now the private visitor's first note reverberated! how distantly his briny last! Babies did not inhabit Enoch's vows and views. He would never have smelled divinity through the diaper. He said: sentimentality is a limitation of the intellect; so the let-ters that joined my eye were unlyrical. "Is it poems? No," I decided, arranging the slips corner to corner. The lines were uneven. I handled prose. The word was "sinner." I asked, "Can't they give him something else instead?"

"Now what would you suggest?" —Scorn.

"Assign him to another country, why not?"

"Why not, why *not?* Who, the Two-Hour Ambassador? You should've seen the cartoons in this morning's papers, that's all. One had this picture of Enoch in the shape of this very fat *mouse* running down this *time*-clock, you know, and out of it comes a hand with a scissors that's supposed to be cutting off the mouse's tail, and the caption says 'Hickory, Dickory, Docked.' The face was Enoch *exactly*. And another one had him sort of riding astride this big rocket, only backwards, and looking scared and holding tight to his briefcase, and the rocket has 'Boomerang' written on it and it's headed right for the Capitol dome, and underneath it says 'Fired.' Oh, and that's another thing, by the way—the Russians actually put up a *satellite* today, a Goddamn little moon, I mean it's really come to that, they *did* it actually. Gangsters. Robbers, Karp won't get anywhere with 'em, now they'll be cockier than ever. And besides, all those cartoons make Enoch look so fat, that was the meanest part, he's not *that* fat. Well he's had it. Look, nobody's going to make an Ambassador out of Mickey Mouse, he's finished, can't you follow that?"

—Not Death but deflection was her grief.

The bird of the world fell to a sandy place, and no arrow in his breast. No arrow could have entered. He had no chink or plaiting; he was made of iron painted trompe-d'oeil, in an illusion of translucent membrane. He fell gaudily and with a clank: his works had run down.

My mother's finger rasped at the leg of a chair.

"What will he do now?"

The finger rasped. She did not answer. She did not know.

I said: "Not that he *has* to do anything."

"He'll do something," she called to the ceiling.

I lifted myself and watched her. She lay flattened and nearly breathingless.

"Something political?"

"I *said* taboo, didn't I? Pariah. Dead." The finger rasped. "Nothing public. Something personal. Something with me left out of it."

"If it leaves you out it can't be personal," I said.

"Oh shut up. Once and for all shut up. I hate a logician. You talk like a Goddamn little Jew. How do *I* know what he'll do?" But she appended with authority: "He'll write history."

"But he might be good at that—"

"Might be good at that," she drilled out singsong. "Of course he won't be good at it. If you're meant to live it you can't write it. And don't give me Julius Caesar. *One* Latin rebuttal out of you, just one, and I swear I'm fit for gore and murder. Lady Macbeth, I mean it this time. Besides, there's nothing *in* history any more. Nothing"—she hurtled to her last effect—"for me."

"Nobody ever got into history by being an Ambassador's wife," I said.

"Oh didn't they! Well you don't know *me,* I don't give up like that, I don't want to just get *into* history, that's what I call burial, I want to climb up *out* of it, I want to survive!" My mother teetered in a crouch; then with hands forward and heavy she thrust herself into the chair. "It's *Madame* de Sévigné not Mademoiselle you hear about, and Medea was somebody important's wife, ditto the aforementioned Lady Macbeth so don't tell me position doesn't count, in the sands of time spinsters don't leave tracks. And don't give me Emily Dickinson either, I'm not talking about mystic types and so forth, I mean people like myself who panteth after the world as the hart panteth after the brook or something. Is that Enoch coming in down there? I thought I heard—" She blinked. "Look, I have to feel I'm somebody more than just, just, I don't know, you think I want to be nobody? You think I could stand getting submerged in a century? Or a generation? That's bad enough, already you hear people matching me up with the Radical Thirties so-called, you should see William's ears get red at that. Or even a Goddamn *country.*" She was all at once tearing at her neck. "Hives, damn it, I've got these hives again. You know I thought that was Enoch down there. Well the fact is I'll die if he just crawls home into a corner and starts writing like Immanuel Kant or somebody. Basically all he's got are these ideas, you know what idea Enoch has, I mean about me? I'm an American, that's what he thinks. He thinks I'm an American! What he always wanted was an American. Well I'll fix him, he'd be a fool to go just on that. Oh God how I itch. I want to be more than the best heating plant in the whole world. Not just hum awhile and then die like the Great American Refrigerator—"

It was, plainly, her great speech of capitulation. She recognized she had gone down, and irretrievably. It was her

mourning song—protracted, like the mourning songs of the
Chorus of Women in the old old plays. Mockery remained.
"You can't be an ancient Greek," I noted.

"Oh bla bla bla. I know where you got that. Same old corrupted conniving blather, Nick all over again. Well I never
wanted to be Greeky, you follow? His idea not mine. All I'm
saying is I want something more than just my exact home address on my death certificate. A person should mean something. That's right, go stick your head in the rug, just like
Enoch, you don't think I can think. I don't care who said it
first, I say it for myself, only louder. You take all these feelings in the world, who knows how many feelings, you see my
point?"

"No," I said.

"Because some of them don't have people attached. I think
every feeling should be represented by a live person, every
feeling should have somebody to stick up for it, you see what
I mean? I'm not just talking about emotions, I mean *feelings*,
you see the difference?"

"No."

"Lost on you. On you it would be. Look, you *know* when
you're having an emotion, there you are living right in the
middle of it, but a feeling you might not know about until
long afterward, a feeling might go on for years before you
realized anything about it." She stirred; she knew her passion. Alas, she could not remember its name. "Like a sense of
destiny—"

"You could begin a list," I said.

"What?"

"In order of appearance. Emotions: rage, outrage, jealousy, love."

"Oh, you're cold. You always *were* cold."

"Types of sense of destiny: visionary, practical, prophetic,
missionary, American evangelical, Napoleonic, messianic,
world-love—"

"Cold cold cold. Don't say love, any kind of love don't say
it."

"Love," I said.

"You've never *had* a feeling."

"Recently," I informed her.

She showed an amazement not genuine. "Not that boy—"
I let the word stand.

"That *boy?* I can't believe it. Imagine that, put her on an
island and boom. We were *talk*ing about that boy practically

two seconds ago, and not a word out of her. Not that you ever had half a chance with him, but good for you, naturally when *you* come round to a thing it's too late. Pettigrew's got him."

"Water's got him," I did not say.

"He's taken taken taken," my mother said, "and when you get right down to it, so what?"

"Taken," I said, "by water," and never again spoke to her of her lover.

But she thought me, like herself, preoccupied with the trip home and its diversions. "Never mind water, it could be a helicopter for all the difference, in or *out* of a boat what can you talk about to a boy like that? Glum, no conversation. Carbon copy of his father. Not a smear of charm. Leave it to you to pick someone without any. I like a man with charm. He used to have *some*. That stutter years ago: fake but a style anyhow. Law school peeled it off. For your own sake I wouldn't consent to it," she announced, exactly as though William's son had just asked her for my hand; she raised one of her own like a perverse madonna retracting a blessing. "William might like the idea, I don't know. History repeating itself—not that it ever does. Or maybe he wouldn't, he's got this funny feeling about you—he thinks you're tainted." Her recurrent blink, like an automated doll's, had grown compulsive. Below it her nose was beginning to leak. "My God, I never dreamed I'd be telling you a thing like that."

"Enoch thinks the same."

"Not Enoch, William I said. Look, if you want some advice, just forget about that boy. When you have a feeling about someone who doesn't reciprocate the best thing to do is forget it. That's what Enoch would say. Enoch doesn't think anyone's tainted. Well he thinks the *world's* tainted, but that's another story. I admit Enoch never had charm, but he doesn't need it after all. If you're a political genius all you have to *be* is just that." She descended into herself. Something half-analytic possessed her nostrils. They went on watering. "If he doesn't write history he might write philosophy," she told me.

"You know he won't."

She said defensively, "He'll do *some*thing. He has this idea for an essay—actually it's a Jewish sort of essay, he was explaining about it and then, right in the middle, that Washington call came and he left. —Don't stare, I can't help it, it's hives, I *have* to scratch. —It's called Pan Versus Moses. It's

Moses making the Children of Israel destroy all the grotto
shrines and greenwood places and things. It's about how
Moses hates Nature. Enoch said the Jewish God is the Lord
of Hosts but it's the Lord of Guests who really keeps the
world. The Lord of Hosts lives in his house and calls 'Come
in, Come in,' but the Lord of Guests lives anywhere at all
and says 'You're already here.' " My mother excavated for a
handkerchief and blew volcanically. "He'll never write it, and
even if he does, so what? Nobody cares about that, Washington isn't looking for advisers on holiness lately, you know.
He'll sleep, that's what I'm afraid of. All he'll do is sleep.
He'll never get up all day if he hasn't got something to do in
the world. He *needs* something to do in the world."

I said, "Needing isn't wanting."

"Wisdom. Maybe that means something, to me it doesn't
mean a thing. A pensée. All right, then read Enoch's. I was
just looking at them myself, I dug them up out of his desk.
Well *he* didn't do them. Adam Gruenhorn did, not that you'll
know what I'm talking about." She had forgotten her letters
and what I knew. "They're sentences. Interesting, but no genius in 'em—that's because they're not political. Years ago I
had them typed up and sent them to *Atlantic Monthly,
Woman's Day, Country Gentleman, Esquire,* and *Harps.*
(*Harps* is where Euphoria K. has her things.) They all rejected," she concluded sadly. "Enoch won't let me use them
for *Bushelbasket.*"

So I spread the slips on the red rug and entered the mind
of Adam Gruenhorn, political genius, failed Ambassador.

Most of his maxims were personal:

22

To attempt to extinguish self-indulgence by the application of just a little more self-indulgence is like lighting
a match in a room that is already blazing with fire: the

big fire is neither diminished nor increased; the little fire will not frighten away the big fire; the little fire will not tire the big fire; the little fire will not conquer the big fire.

To make oneself believe that one really exists; to make oneself believe that another person really exists—which taxes credulity more? To achieve the belief in the real existence of another person one must first achieve the belief in the real existence of one's own being. But how does one persuade oneself that one really exists? By persuading oneself that the other person really exists. Hence psychological realities are interdependent.

Not a solace, not a refuge.
What then was broken?
The solace which was not a solace,
The refuge which was not a refuge,
Or an illusion?

1. Do not belittle others as you would not have others belittle you.
2. Do not aggrandize others as you would have others aggrandize you.

a. One who says, "I can't help it" means "I want it."
b. One who refuses to rebel condones his slavery.

To want to be what one *can* be is purpose in life.

Time heals all things but one: Time.

The cosmic system, oddly enough, is not to be found in the pit of the stomach.

Resentment is a communicable disease and should be quarantined.

He who cries, "What do I care about universality? I only know what is in *me*," does not know even that.

A blasphemer: He who laments his lot without sufficient cause.
What is sufficient cause?
What seems sufficient not to oneself, but to others.

1. There are no exterior forces. There are only interior forces.
2. Hope directed toward luck is not hope but superstition.

One's sense of "Self" is not relevant to the world unless

one considers the world relevant to the Self. What does this purport? If everything outside of the expression of your own feelings does not exist for you, or if it exists but is of no consequence to you, to whom and to what will you express your feelings?

He who cries, "All right, then, I'm selfish—so be it!"—does he think confession is absolution?

The continents of desire and wisdom lie beyond the membrane-meridian of the self.

The difference between sorrow and petulance is the difference between having cancer and having a temper tantrum.

Aspiration and complaint come in successive breaths. One is the catarrh to be expelled by the other.

1. Feelings of "constant distraction" occur when one refuses to allow oneself to be distracted even for a moment—from oneself.

2. An "inability to concentrate" is the result of excessive concentration—on something else.

a. A little discomfort is better than a great deal of gratitude.

b. But there is a great deal of comfort in a little gratitude.

Unmitigable depression = mitigable self-indulgence.
It is useless either to hate or to love truth—but it should be noticed.

1. Before you blame a person for not understanding you, first ask yourself whether he is obliged to do so. (If you have lent him money, he is.)
2. Before you blame a person for not weeping for you, first be sure that his tears are not needed elsewhere. (If he has lent you money, they are.)

He who squanders talent praises death.

Ego should not be condemned. Ego without imagination to evaluate ego should be.

The difference between thirty-two and twenty-five is not seven, but a generation.

Do not choose for sympathizer your psychological twin.

A sense of proportion presupposes an interest in the size of the universe.

Exploitation, whether material or not, is reduction in the guise of swelling.

Dedication to one's work in the world is the only possible sanctification. Religion in all its forms is dedication to Someone Else's work, not yours.

Not God but fashion compelled the fig-leaf. God would have contrived something that did not have to be pasted on or held by the hand that should hold the plough. It is not our nakedness that God intends us to cover, but our notions of dress.

Riddle:
Who is the starved traveler who chooses the longest road, carries the weightiest baggage, and hardly ever arrives? And should he arrive, he at once loses not only his whole equipage but his very name.
Answer:
Hope.

Fear of hostility is less useful than hostility to fear.

Ideals die not because they fail of their attainment but because they have succeeded. To defeat a cause, work for it.

The unhappy person resents only his own unhappiness, not another person's. Unhappiness is the inability to generalize.

Boredom is the consequence of believing in the uniqueness of one's own experience. It vanishes the moment one acquires History.

The books we care for most are the ones which read us.

a. Critics: people who make monuments out of books.
b. Biographers: people who make books out of monuments.
c. Poets: people who raze monuments.
d. Publishers: people who sell rubble.
e. Readers: people who buy it.

Two things remain irretrievable: time and a first impression.

Lonesomeness is hatred of truth.

If one does not reduce one's trouble to its proper proportion on one's own, life will do it soon enough—only more brutally.

Offer the resourceful man one of two legacies: a mammoth trust fund by inheritance of wealth, or a minuscule fund of trust by inheritance of nature; and he will choose the one which least inhibits venturesomeness.

Friendships produce confidences; but confidences do not often produce friendships.

A person who mourns for himself while his parents are alive is a sinner.

Death persecutes before it executes.

Detail mocks Theme; Theme worships Detail. That is why the possible and the feasible are always at war.

23

Here I stopped; an apparition of Enoch blotted the doorway.

"I've been waiting hours. Believe me I've just about run out of patience," my mother said. "What kept you? Don't tell me reporters or I'll *know* it was dancing girls. Washington's just the town for dissipation. What was it, you found a salami market? A peanut store?"

"Of the three cardinal pations," my stepfather said (he set down his suitcase), "choose one as follows: A, dissi-, hereinabove referred to; B, consti-, the mind's enemy; C, extir-, the world's delight. So you can never run out of pations even if you try." He spotted me swimming in aphorisms. "Where'd she get those?"

"*I* gave them to her," my mother said.

"Old saws have no teeth."

"Plenty of big jokes in your pockets. Something to celebrate. Comes in playing parlor games. Lost your life, and first thing home it's ha ha."

"Ha ha I have not lost my life."

"All right, call it anything you want, call it self-respect. Self-respect you've lost."

"I continue to think highly of myself," he demurred.

"Time," she said. "Don't say you haven't lost time! In a career time is everything. How long before they start taking you seriously again, that's what I want to know. You've lost time, you've lost a job, you've lost your footing on the high rungs, you've lost everything."

"Have I lost you?"

A desolation trailed in her eye.

"Then I'll look for you," he said, going for her chair. He stared heavily down at her. "Dark visage, black looks—next time I bring a lantern. Glimmer of the whites. She emerges. She was obscured by a dark brown study. Lo, here she is."

"Enoch, stop it, just cut it out, I'm nowhere. Nowhere. Don't tell me to accept it, I can't accept it. Everything's spoiled. One Goddamn little revolution and that's it. They might just as well have shot *me* in the public square."

"It happens to have been a nice clean little coup—they made a clean job of it, you know how you like clean jobs. Nobody blown up. Not a pinprick. Instead of sentries around the palace they posted cameramen. The new General is even more photogenic than the old one—wears a corset."

"Fine. Everyone's laughing. A musical comedy and you're the star. Fallen star. What do you want me to do, dance and sing with timbrels?"

"Tell you what—stealthily but boldly get out your timbrels and tomorrow I'll suffer me to be taken to any nightclub in New York. Capitalize on the current notoriety."

"*I'm* not the Two-Hour Ambassador," she sneered. "They won't notice *me*. Enoch, don't try to buy me off. You can buy off a tragedy, but you can never in a hundred years buy off a comedy. A comedy *lasts*. —Is that what we're going to do from now on, reel from place to place?"

"Unless you prefer a stately tread. Dissipation," he yielded, "the first of the cardinal—"

But she jumped up and furiously smothered his mouth with her palm. He licked her loose. "What do you think?" he asked me. "Was I La Rochefoucauld twenty-five years ago? Or more likely Oscar Wilde?"

"Oscar Wilde is *funny*," my mother said.

"And La Rochefoucauld is wise."

My mother said coldly, " 'I can resist everything but temptation.' Now that's funny. You don't have anything like that. You don't have anything smart-aleck, in those aphorisms you're one-hundred-per-cent solemn."

"Be more generous. Fifty-per-cent. Posterity knows them as Vand's Halforisms. Not that they're only half true, but he believed in them only half his life. In the second half of his life he abandoned trying to live by formula."

"You mean now," my mother said ominously.

"Now," he agreed.

"How are you going to live now?"

"By always remembering to keep breathing."

"Dead!" she yelled. "A formula for being dead! Dead dead dead! Dead and you don't care, dead and you don't know it—"

"*I* didn't overthrow the regime." —He was all reasonableness. "Allegra," he said.

"You wanted to go high!"

"Not for the sensation of height."

"Once you said you'd even be President if they let you—"

"Not in order to be President but to see the sameness of the world. The world is the same seen from all sides. Now there's a machine in the sky to prove it."

"Gangsters. The world is *not* the same. It's not the same for those gangsters and for us, and it's not the same for an Ambassador and for"—her head darted down—"a nobody."

"The same," he said. "Also for the rich and the poor, the high and the low, the mind-gifted and the mind-deprived—"

"All right, then for the good and the evil too. Enoch," she called, as though he were far, "I thought you wanted to do good!"

"Oh no no no no. Not to do good. How can we know which act is good and which not? By the consequences? Who can tell which are the true consequences? Who can live long enough to know?"

She said nothing.

"How does she take it?" he asked. And to me: "Narcissus always vanishes by way of water."

My mother drew vengefully back. "Nick you mean? You heard about Nick? You heard," she said; her lip hung.

"So has every living breathing politician not actually unconscious. Allegra," he told her, "it's out."

"Out? What's out?" Her half-sleeves came stiff against her like black stumps.

"Since late this afternoon every member of the United States Congress knows that but for the grace of the new General's gun we might have sent off a Caesar whose wife was once-upon-a-time not above suspicion. Every member of the Senate knows it. Every member of the Supreme Court knows it. The President knows it, the public knows it, even the Vice-President's got wind of it—"

"It's out?" my mother cried.

"The very Senator William is privy to—my special pleader, mind you—hissed it into my left ear. Depositing carcinogenic fumes therein and causing me to miss two planes out." To me he said, "To William's pal the Senator you're known as a love-child. A pretty phrase. He does better by you than William."

"Now look," my mother began. And almost failed. "I'll tell you who did it, Nick did it, right out of the devil's mouth—"

"The devil sticks to the retinas only of those he beguiles."

And I: "Not Nick, not Nick," but it was to Enoch I addressed this.

She blasted me. "Idiot! Who else let it out? Who!"

"Pettigrew," Enoch said. "He got it from his little girl and would have upstaged the coup with it if the Russians hadn't upstaged everything already with the Sputnik. You see?" he said. "There's Nick again—translated to the heavens. He sails the sea of the sky in his spy-glass. Do you grieve?" he insisted, fixing me colorlessly, lazily.

"She knew him two days!" my mother shouted.

"And two nights. She knew him. Do you grieve? She grieves." He said, "I knew him, he didn't believe in himself."

"Didn't he though? Arrogant as they come," my mother said. "He had more self-confidence than anyone alive."

"True. What I mean is he didn't believe he was alive. Like few men, like all solipsists, he doubted his existence by declaring it. Most of us declare it by doubting it. A Chinese philosopher dreamed he was a butterfly. When he woke he said: Am I a man dreaming I am a butterfly, or am I a butterfly dreaming I am a man?"

"Enoch, go to hell," my mother said.

"That's hard, you're hard on Pettigrew. Any good Democrat would have done the same. He saw his opportunity—if you find tar on your brush you use it."

She wailed at him, "What's going to happen?"

"Observe. For all future appointments the Administration will be asking for references from the chastity-belt manufacturers. Or else the Senate may confirm a whole row of nuns for Ambassadors. The Administration," he ended, "is smeared."

"And us! Us. Smeared," my mother said.

"Freed."

"I don't believe in freedom," and sat herself down on Enoch's suitcase, and said nothing more. But she seemed to be listening, not to him. It was as if she was listening to the hairs of her head grow and prosper, to assure herself of life.

24

Six stamps displaying Oriental jugs; a letter postmarked Shikarpur, Pakistan:

It *was* your father. Purse read it out to me from the paper, which is rather expensive in the overseas edition. What a surprise! Well, my dear, even a Purse swallows the blunder, since identity is everything in life, isn't it?— Which is why every Purse has its identity card. (We don't like to risk losing the children in a heathen land.) Purse says it was almost like accusing you of a certain sin expressly forbidden, which I won't mention by name. We are all hoping very much that you will forgive us, the children especially hope so. Except for Gandhi they are all now quite proficient in kitchen-Urdu, also Harriet Beecher can say water-buffalo, though it's been only a little more than a month, but they want to be remembered to you in English!

If we can be of any moral help to you in your deep sorrow and loss do let us know. Purse is rather busy with his bones, but he begs you to trust in the solace of the Lord, Whose ways are inscrutable. He giveth and He taketh.

We are all borrowers from God's purse. Thoreau in particular sends you special regards. He asks me to tell you that he's proud of having been oarsman for an actual symbol of American Affluence. (We're now all very conscious of home values, you see.) He knew it all the time! He never mentioned a word to us, but now he keeps boasting that you *told* him about your mother and her great position in the world. He even quotes you verbatim as having said she is "extraordinarily rich." Of course he always exaggerates, and Purse has made him recognize that it's his chief vice to blow things up to make himself sound important. But in this case it wasn't hyperbole, was it? To think you're actually the daughter of Allegra Vand!

What happened in the past between her and your father (to think Mr. T. *was* your father all the time! may he R.I.P.), not that we believe everything in the overseas edition, it probably comes over all diluted, but surely your mother has by now compensated for anything she may once have been sorry for by acts of charity and philanthropy, which are a privilege of the affluent alone. Mr. T.'s passing may very well have renewed old regrets in her heart, and nothing discharges remorse so much as discharging one's duty and one's purse.

We Purses hope you will not discharge *us* from the care of your memory, my dear, though our acquaintance was so brief. Still, our mutual reverence for Mr. T. binds us irrevocably. He was always very generous with us, and this is a land where generosity is necessary. You should see the poor pitiful cripples and orphans in the streets! Also you would be amazed at how much it costs Purse every day to get transportation out from Shikarpur to the dig. (The first group of bones, alas, has proved to be marsupial.) There are two abandoned automobiles piled up nearby, both in a condition of incomparable disrepair, and I am hoping to work out some kind of rapprochement between the engine of the one on top and the body of the one on bottom. You would not believe the cost of spare parts here!

It is also very expensive to keep a special nurse for Gandhi, who has become utterly uncontrollable in the new environment. He likes to run around with all the wild little Mohammedans, who have unfortunately taught him to say Allah. There is a mosque nearby, and he is continually running away to it. We thank God Purse's Ford wasn't for India instead, where there are polytheists of the most primitive sort.

Well, let us hear from you, my dear. If your very kind mother in her present reëvaluations feels the moral need to express herself in good works, and/or should you be desirous of following in the very lovely tradition of generosity your memorable father established toward us, you may trust to our most profound and exuberant gratitude. (On the enclosed sheet please find all the children's clothing sizes, including underwear. They like bright colors, except George Fox, though Purse doesn't approve. However I must ask you to ignore the notations for Gandhi. Since our arrival in the East we cannot get him to keep a stitch on. We've never had a nude child before—Purse of course is very upset—and we are prayerful that it is only the sudden change in the drinking water. As you will understand, under the circumstances his nurse had to be a male one, unusual for these parts, but the young man himself is unusual and quite good-looking in spite of dark skin.)

Hoping to hear from you,

With best wishes,
(Mrs.) Ethel Purse

25

Postcard displaying head of an American President, postmarked San Francisco, California:

> Dear Mme. Karenina,
>   I quit.
>   Love,
>   Vronsky

26

Telegram, Western Union, collect:

ALLEGRA DID YOU GET MY POSTCARD HAVE
MOVED IN WITH GREATAUNT OF MY
MOTHERS I RAN INTO OUT HERE SHE WAS
TWENTY THREE LAST MAY SORRY TO LEAVE
YOU IN EDITORIAL LURCH PLEASE FEEL
FREE TO USE MY THREE RECENT HAIKUS IN
BUSHEL BASKET WITHOUT CHARGE AS
SINCERE TOKEN OF MY REGRET FAITHFULLY
YOURS EDWARD MCGOVERN FORMER EDITOR
IN CHIEF BUSHEL BASKET PEE YES NEVER
SELL OUT TO COMMAS

27

My mother was right. Enoch stayed in bed until four
o'clock in the afternoon for three months. Meanwhile my
mother traveled. The first day of the fourth month my stepfather rose up and announced he was going to read the Bible.
And he did. He read the King James all the way through.
Then he began taking lessons in Hebrew from a refugee my
mother imported from Oslo. She had met him in the art
museum there on one of her trips. The number tattooed on

Enoch's teacher's forearm was daily covered by phylacteries. He had a beard, like a spy. Under the refugee's tutelage Enoch read the Bible all the way through in Hebrew. It took him three years. The refugee shaved off his beard, having by then gotten the hang of America; he did not wish to be mistaken for a bohemian. He was a serious and lyrical man. He abandoned his phylacteries. At the end of that time Enoch began the study of the Ethics of the Fathers. It was an easy book and took two months. Then he asked for the whole Talmud.

Where I was and what I did during that period I will not tell; I went to weddings. But my mother traveled. Once she flew to the country where she was to have been chatelaine of the Embassy. Even from the outside the Embassy was glorious. Its pillars were resplendent. All the same she thought little of that place: she did not like the tune of its official language.

Pelham Bay, The Bronx, 1957—Echo Bay, New Rochelle, 1963

AFTERWORD

On November 22, 1963, the day President John Kennedy was assassinated, I wrote the last words of *Trust,* my first novel. I had begun it while still in my twenties, and finished it seven years later. In actuality there had been two "first" novels before then—the earlier one never completed, though it had already accumulated three hundred thousand words. I had planned it as a "philosophical" fiction; in graduate school I had come under the influence of Eliseo Vivas, at the time a well-known professor of philosophy, and with his character and views in mind, I named my protagonist Rafael Caritas. His antagonist, as I conceived it (the metaphysical versus the pragmatic), was a man of the type of Sidney Hook, a legendary figure in my undergraduate days at New York University: in my aborted novel he was called Seymour Karp. It never occurred to me—I learned it painfully years afterward—that it might be perilous to import real persons into fiction. My idea was to confront Passion with Reason. Of course I sided with Passion (I was twenty-two), which explained why a stanza from one of William Blake's "Songs of Innocence" supplied the title: *Mercy, Pity, Peace, and Love.* ("For Mercy has a human heart, / Pity a human face, / And Love, the human form divine, / And Peace, the human dress.")

Rafael Caritas consumed years before he, or I, ran out of philosophical steam. Vivas's devotion to what he termed Neo-Thomism had befuddled me; so did his lectures on Aristotle's *Nicomachean Ethics.* What was even more confounding, though, was his fury at the Nuremberg trials. The men in the dock were wicked beyond wicked, he raged—but the Allied tribunal was wicked too: it stood for victors' justice. Then what should be done with these murderous miscreants? Punish them, Vivas said, according to a practice not unknown in certain parts of his native South America: bury each man up to his neck in earth, and send riders at a gallop to trample the exposed heads. It was an argument worthy of Dostoyevsky's Grand Inquisitor. Vivas, even when he was jovially avuncular, as he sometimes was, intimidated me: his black hair, slicked back, gleamed like shoe polish; his foreign rasp had a demonic twist; his classroom manner was a roar. Rafael Caritas was far tamer.

Mercy, Pity, Peace, and Love was slowly proceeding (though without the horsemen), pullulating with new characters I could hardly fathom or control. No resolution was anywhere in sight when I came, one afternoon, on a seductive announcement in one of the little magazines (as the plethora of serious quarterly journals was then styled). A publisher was soliciting short novels. Short! The word—the idea—captivated. *Mercy, Pity, Peace, and Love* was winding on and on, like a Möbius strip: where was its end? As a kind of interim project, I set out to write a short novel. It turned out to be a long one. It turned out to be *Trust*.

But *Trust* too wound on and on. All around me writers of my generation were publishing; I was not. I held it as an article of faith that if you had not attained print by twenty-five, you were inexorably marked by a scarlet F—for Folly, for Futility, for Failure. It was a wretched and envious time. I knew a writer my own age, as confident as he was industrious, who had recently completed a novel in six weeks. I was determined to emulate his feat. I threw the already massive *Trust* into a drawer and started a fresh manuscript—my second "first" novel; in a month and a half it was done. It had exhausted me, but I was also relieved and elated: I had finally finished a novel. It disappeared decades ago—lost, I believe, in the dust of a London publisher's cellar. A carbon copy (how obsolete these words are!) may be languishing in my own cellar, but I have never troubled to look for it; dead is dead. And the speedy writer I was mimicking—or hoping to rival—never published that or any other novel.

Three years elapsed between the completion of *Trust* and its appearance in print. I filled the void by writing short stories and teaching freshman composition to engineering students; but mainly I was waiting. The editor who had accepted my manuscript explained that he would soon supply "suggestions." Secretly I dreaded these—I had labored over every syllable for all those seven years—but I was wedded to diffidence and gratitude, and clearly my unpublished condition was subordinate to the editor's will, and certainly to his more pressing preoccupations. As it happened, I had acquired an agent along the way—an agent just starting out, living obscurely in a Manhattan basement. He had read a poem of mine in a literary quarterly, had discovered that a novel was "in progress," and offered to represent me. It was in a letter to him, after six months had passed and no suggestions were forthcoming, that I complained of the editor's silence. "I see you have clay feet," the agent wrote back, reprimanding me for untoward impatience. Another twelve months followed, and still no word from the editor. At last I made an anguished appeal, and was rewarded with a reply. He was working, the editor said, on an important book by a professor at Harvard (his name was Henry Kissinger); nevertheless he would set aside half an hour for me. He hadn't been neglectful of my manuscript, he assured me—on the contrary, for an entire year he had been compiling a long list of notes for the improvement of my novel.

The publisher's offices struck me as industrial—so many elevators, so many corridors, so many mazes and cubicles. I found the cubicle I had been directed to and looked in. There sat the editor, with a typewriter on an open leaf beside him; there on a big littered desk lay the familiar box containing my manuscript. I watched him insert a sheet of yellow paper into the machine and begin to type. "Come in," he said, seeing me hesitant in the doorway. I continued to watch him type, and all at once understood that there was no long list of notes; there had never been any notes at all; he was at that moment conjuring a handful of impromptu comments out of the air. For this I had been kept in a vise of anxiety for a year and a half.

Not long afterward, the editor, a young man still in his thirties, fell dead of a heart attack on the tennis court. Another editor took his place, and quickly put before me the first hundred pages of *Trust,* scribbled all over in red pencil. The famous suggestions! A meek petitioner facing power, I knew by now that I must succumb—I must please the new editor, or lose the chance of publication. My decision was instant. I declined every stroke of his red pencil. I believed in Art; I believed, above all, in the autonomy of Art; and for the sake of this sacral conviction I chose my novel's oblivion. Better oblivion than an alien fingerprint! To my astonishment, the new editor agreed to publish *Trust* exactly as I had written it. His name was David Segal, and like the editor who had hoodwinked me, he too died young. As for the hoodwinker, I long refused the ameliorative *de mortuis nil nisi bonum:* of the dead let nothing bad be said. Yet David Segal, as long as he lived, was wont to dismiss the good I repeatedly said of him: "You think I'm a great editor," he accused me, "because I never edited you."

Why did I believe in Art, and in the autonomy of Art, and in the sacred character of the dedicated writer? All this derived, in part, from ambition—a species of ambition that itself derived from the last trickles of the nineteenth century leaching into the twentieth. The nineteenth century did not stop abruptly in the year 1901, with the death of Queen Victoria, or the assassination of President McKinley, or the formulation of the quantum theory, or the inauguration of Picasso's Blue Period. In mores especially, the nineteenth century lingered on—even through the Modernist eruptions of the twenties—into the thirties and forties, and into a portion of the fifties. In the forties song sheets could still be bought in stationery shops, and "patterns" for sewing dresses at home were still on sale in department stores. Secretaries wore felt hats to the office, and the rare women executives wore them *in* the office. Little girls were reading the social archaisms of the Bobbsey Twins series, and boys were immersed in the plucky if antiquated adventures of the Hardy Boys. Tabloids published one-page daily fictions called "short shorts"; big-circulation magazines unfailingly published stories. And literary ambition earnestly divided high from low, serious from popular, fiction from journalism, and novelists from the general run of mankind. (Nor was "mankind" regarded as gender-biased.) Literary writers frowned on commercial success as the antithesis of artistic probity. T. S. Eliot (despite the vastness of his own success) was the archbishop of High Art, that immaculate altar, and in his vatic wake Lionel Trilling was similarly pained by the juxtaposition of literature and money (his worship of Hemingway notwithstanding). Bohemianism meant living apart, living for art, despising Babbitry.

All these attitudes and atmospheres fell away no earlier than sixty or seventy years into the twentieth century: it took that long for nineteenth-century literary sensibilities to ebb. Modernism hardly contradicted these impressions; it confirmed and augmented them. But by the 1970s, the novel as the holy vessel of imagination (itself having deposed poetry) was undone. Magazines dropped fiction. Notions of journalism as the equal of imaginative writing took hold (the "nonfiction novel," pioneered by Truman Capote, replicated by Norman Mailer). Bohemians who had been willing enough to endure the romantic penury of cold-water walkups while sneering at popular entertainment were displaced by beatniks who were themselves popular entertainment. Walt Whitman was transmogrified into Allen Ginsberg and Jack Kerouac. From *beat* you were to infer *beatific,* and the New Age of faux mysticism (via hallucinogens) had begun. New theories leveled the literary terrain—so that, visiting Yale a decade or so ago, I was startled to encounter a young professor of English deconstructing a hamburger advertisement with the same gravity as an earlier professoriat would have devoted to a discussion of *Paradise Lost.*

With such radical (and representative) changes in the culture, and with High Art in the form of the novel having lost its centrality, the nature of ambition too was bound to alter. This is not to say that young writers today are no longer driven—and some may even be possessed—by the strenuous forces of literary ambition. Zeal, after all, is a constant, and so must be the pool, or the sea, of born writers. But the great engines of technology lure striving talents to television and Hollywood, or to the lighter varieties of theater, or (especially) to the prompt gratifications and high-velocity fame of the magazines, where topical articles generate buzz and gather no moss. The sworn novelists, who, despite the devourings of the hour, continue to revere the novel (the novel as moss, with its leisurely accretions of character and incident, its disclosures of secrets, its landscapes and cityscapes and mindscapes, its idiosyncratic particularisms of language and insight)—these sworn novelists remain on the scene, if not on the rise.

Still, there is a difference. The altars are gone. The priests are dead. Writers and artists of all kinds are no longer publicly or privately abashed by the rewards of commerce. The arbiters of literary culture have either departed (few remember Irving Howe, say, or Randall Jarrell) or have devolved into popular celebrities, half sage, half buffoon.

When I began *Trust,* close to fifty years ago, ambition meant what James Joyce had pronounced it to be, in a mantra that has inflamed generations: *silence, exile, and cunning.* Silence and exile were self-explanatory: the novelist was to be shut away in belief—self-belief, perhaps—and also in the monkish conviction that Literature was All. But cunning implied something more than mere guile. It hinted at power, power sublime and supernal, the holy power of language and its cadences—the sentence, the phrase, and ultimately, primordially, the word: the germ of being. As chosen sibyl of the word, I was scornful of so-called writers who produced "drafts," in the shape of an imperfect spew to be returned to later, in order, as one novelist described it, "to polish the verbal surface." The verbal surface! The word could no more be defined by its surface than the sea could be fathomed by its coastline; and I could no more abandon a sentence, even temporarily, than I could skip a substantial interval of breathing with a promise to make up for it afterward. Until the sentence, the phrase, the word, were as satisfactorily woven as the weaver's shuttle could thread them, I would not tread further: in Henry James's formulation, "the finer thread, the tighter weave." Or recall Jacob's struggle with the angel: "I will not let thee go, except thou bless me." Until I felt its nimbus, I would not let any cluster of words go.

It was slow work, and it owed more to Henry James than it did to the angel of Genesis. I kept on my writing table (a worn old hand-me-down, three feet by one and a half, that I had acquired at age eight) a copy of *The Ambassadors,* as a kind of talisman. I kept it there not so much for the sake of James's late prose (though it often seemed that his penchant for intrusively interlocutory adverbs seeped into my fountain pen's rubber ink-bulb) as for the scent of ambition: the worldliness of his characters, the visual brilliance of

his long scenes, the seductiveness of his betrayals, the veiled innocence of his young women, the subtlety of his moral conundrums,
and not least his debt to human possibility, and also to human taint.
His muse was tragic; and so was mine. What James felt in his worship of Balzac was what I suffered in my fealty to James: Balzac appeared to him "so multitudinous, so complex, so far-spreading, so
suggestive, so portentous— ... such misty edges and far reverberations—that the imagination, oppressed and overwhelmed, shrinks
from any attempt to grasp it whole." Yet it was just this multitu-
dinousness, this complexity, this far-spreadingness I was after. I
named my novel *Trust* with biting intent: it was to denote a vast and
cynical irony. I meant to map every species of *dis*trust—between
parent and child; between husband and wife; between lovers; between Europe and America; between Christians and Jews; between
God and man; in politics and in history. Before the term "Holocaust"
was put to use or even known, the death camps entered *Trust;* in
1957, scarcely a decade after the ovens had cooled, who could fail to
address them? (Many did.) Enoch Vand, my protagonist's stepfather,
confronting the goddess Geopolitica, records the names of the victims in masses of ledgers:

> And he could not confess for the sake of whom or what he dug
> down deep in those awesome volumes, sifting their name-bur-
> dened and number-laden leaves as soil is spaded and weighed
> in search of sunken graves and bones time-turned to stone—
> he could not say or tell. ... Enoch leaned brooding among
> the paper remnants of the damned: the lists and questionnaires,
> the numbers and their nemeses; every table spread with the
> worms' feast; the room a registry and bursary for smoke and
> cinders. Over it all his goddess hung. If she wore a pair of
> bucklers for her breasts, they gleamed for him and shimmered
> sound like struck cymbals; if slow vein-blood drooped like
> pendants from her gored ears, they seemed to him jewels more
> gradual than pearls—she formed herself out of the slaughter,
> the scarves and winds of smoke met to make her hair, the
> cinders clustered to make her thighs; she was war, death,
> blood, perpetual misbirths; she came up enlightened from that
> slaughter like a swimmer from the towering water-wall with
> his glorified face; she came up an angel from that slaughter
> and the fire-whitened cinders of those names. She came up
> Europa.

And elsewhere, the meditation of a refugee from Vienna, reduced
in exile to a servant:

Grit is one of the eternals. The chimneys heave their laden bladders, the grit is spawned out of a domestic cloud in the lowest air, the black footless ants appear on the sill. Brush away, mop away, empty buckets with zeal; grit returns. Everything is flux; grit is forever. Futility is day after day. Time is not what we suppose, moments in an infinite queue, but rather a heavy sense that we have been here before, only with hope, and are here again, only without it. "Your luck will not change," says Time, "give up, the world has concerns of its own," says Time, "woe cannot be shared," says Time, "regret above all is terrifyingly individual." And Time says, "Take no comfort in your metaphysics of the immortality of the race. When your species has evolved out of recognition grit will be unspoiled. There will always be grit. It alone endures. It is greater than humanity."

But it is not greater than humanity; it is the same. We join the particles in their dance on the sill. It is the magnificent Criminal plan, to shove us into the side of a hill, mulch us until we are dissolved into something more useful but less spectacular than before, and send us out again in the form of a cinder for some churl of a descendant to catch in his eye, cursing. . . . Who can revere a universe which will take that lovely marvel, man (after all the fierce mathematics that went into him, aeons of fish straining toward the dry, gill into lung, paw into the violinist's and the dentist's hand), and turn him into a carbon speck?

Of course none of this can be construed as Jamesian. Perhaps, after all, such passages carry, rather, the spirit of Ecclesiastes (or, as some may say, the Book of Fustian). In any case, *Trust* in its voraciousness went everywhere. It went into verses and puns; its population proliferated—lawyers, editors, diplomats, nannies, colonels, schoolgirls; it grew limbs of metaphor and Medusa-heads of dialogue; it wandered toward the lyrical-mystical in an apostrophe to a tree. It set out, in raw competitiveness, to rival the burgeoning sexual openness of the late fifties—and also to deride, twenty years in advance of it, William Gass's 1976 dictum that women "lack that blood-congested genital drive" that is at the root of style. An early reviewer, writing not in unstinting praise, nevertheless acknowledged "evidence of extraordinary ambition in the scope of the novel," and remarked that "the long visionary account of the lovemaking between the heroine's father and a young woman surpasses anything Mailer has ever done, indeed is managed with the ingenuity and resourcefulness of a French cineaste." To be fair, this same reviewer "frankly confess[ed] that the novel gave me little pleasure."

Recently I reread—for the first time since high school—William Dean Howells's *The Rise of Silas Lapham.* Here was a novel that gave me great pleasure: the prose plain and direct, the characters lifelike, engaging, trustworthy, the plotting realistically plausible and gratifyingly suspenseful. All the same, when you compare Howells with James, the disparity of mind and sensibility—what each man aspired to, or could attain—arouses a perplexity. How could these two have been, as they were, literary companions? Howells occupies a few well-spent hours; James (like the far more visceral Conrad) seizes your life. That seizure, I suppose, points to the kind of ambition I fastened on in my twenties. In those years my hungriest uncle (hungry in every sense: one of five, he was the only one who attempted to feed his family by means of his pen) was still living: he was a poet. Matchless in three languages, he chose to make his mark in Hebrew. His poetry was complex, imbricated, visionary, hugely erudite, with, here and there, noble biblical resonances and classical turns that recalled, to an eminent literary critic, Milton and Shelley. Some of my uncle's work he himself rendered into English; but when any eagerly willing translator approached him, he drove the hapless volunteer off with arrogant scorn; he recognized no peer; he had a consciousness of anointment. I will wait, he announced, *a thousand years* for the right translator! Today my uncle is unknown; his life's achievement is in blackest eclipse.

That superannuated consciousness of anointment is also in eclipse—to speak of it now is likely to induce derision. But surely Joyce had it, unalloyed, in writing *Ulysses,* and particularly in the esoteric labors of *Finnegans Wake;* and James had it, shadowed in his final years by the failure of his New York Edition, designed to consolidate his stature; and among contemporary American writers it can be descried in Updike, Roth, and Bellow—all of whom began in the penumbra of nineteenth-century literary ambition, which has long masqueraded as Modernism.

Trust was written in that same penumbra, with that same consciousness of anointment, though its obscure fate, despite a handful of paperback reissues over the years, mostly resembles that of my uncle's grandly bedizened stanzas. Nearly forty years have passed since my first novel first saw print. Perhaps my style has grown plainer as I have grown older; perhaps not. But surely I have acquiesced in the alterations of the common literary culture.

And here it is needful to recall a hiatus—a cut that fell like an ax. Sometime in the seventies, the old ambition was routed by an invader called the *nouvelle vague.* Its name was French because its in-

ventors and original practitioners were French: most prominently,
Alain Robbe-Grillet and Nathalie Sarraute. Their idea of the novel
turned out to be nothing more than a fad, a brutalizing one, touted by
a few influential American critics writing in advanced periodicals
with the intention of shaming the traditional novel out of existence. I
cannot now reconstruct or characterize this "new wave," except out
of a wash of ebbing memory. It was icily detached; it was "objective" and unsentimental; it cared more for space and time than for
stories or souls; its bloodless aesthetics was minutely deadpan; its
dialogue tended to be expressed in arid aperçus; often it read like a
stilted translation of Roland Barthes. And finally it was repudiated
by its chief American promulgator, who, as if by imperial fiat, reha-
bilitated what had been, as if by imperial fiat, imposed. For fiction
writers who resisted being drawn into the tide of literary pronounce-
ments from above (or who were temperamentally alien to it), it was
an enervating and marginalizing season.

Ephemeral though they were, these new pieties and prescriptions
did throw a light on the nature of the old ambition. The *nouvelle
vague* arrived as an extension of cultural power by a coterie of celebrated literary figures determined to wield it. The introduction of literary philosophies from abroad aimed to force an avant-garde: those
who declined to follow were dismissed as either obsolete or medi-
ocre. As God had been declared dead by certain theologians, so now
was the novel—the novel as it had been understood and illumined
from, say, Tolstoy to E. M. Forster, or from Virginia Woolf to Faulkner; or, in any event, before Robbe-Grillet. But the old ambition of
the penumbra had been hammered out of the self, bare of any desire
for social or cultural hegemony. It asserted its conviction of hard-
won ownership, from which derived its authority; but it was the authority of innerness, of interior powers wrested out of language itself. By contrast, it was critical will alone that fueled the *nouvelle
vague*. The novels of its fashionable American disciples were critics'
novels. No one can say that they died with a whimper—even a
whimper requires a pulse.

If I press on in homage to the old ambition, I intend more than
praise for writers' limitless appetite. I am thinking of readers. Here,
then, is a very long paragraph, written in 1909:

I was returning home by the fields. It was midsummer; the hay
harvest was over, and they were just beginning to reap the rye.
At that season of the year there is a delightful variety of flowers—red, white and pink scented tufty clover; milk-white ox-
eye daisies with their bright yellow centers and pleasant spicy

smell; yellow honey-scented rape blossoms, tall campanulas with white and lilac bells, tulip-shaped; creeping vetch; yellow, red and pink scabious; plantains with faintly scented, neatly arranged purple, slightly pink-tinged blossoms; cornflowers, bright blue in the sunshine and while still young, but growing paler and redder towards evening or when growing old; and delicate quickly withering almond-scented dodder flowers. I gathered a large nosegay of these different flowers, and was going home, when I noticed in a ditch, in full bloom, a beautiful thistle plant of the crimson kind, which in our neighborhood they call "Tartar," and carefully avoid when mowing—and if they do happen to cut it down, throw out from among the grass from fear of pricking their hands. Thinking to pick this thistle and put it in the center of my nosegay, I climbed down into the ditch, and, after driving away a velvety humble-bee that had penetrated deep into one of the flowers and . . .

But the paragraph, though it goes on well beyond this, must be interrupted. It is the start of Tolstoy's *Hadji Murad,* in Aylmer Maude's translation. (My uncle's poetry was composed rather in this vein.) I interrupt the paragraph for two reasons—first, because of what must appear to be gargantuan hubris: what is a passage from Tolstoy, the pinnacle of all novelists, doing here, in these ruminations on an emphatically inconspicuous work by an emphatically unnoticed young writer holed up almost half a century ago in a little house at the farthest margin of the Bronx? It is precisely for the sake of hubris that it is here. Without it, how can I lay out the untamed lustful graspingness, the secret tough-hearted avarice, of the old ambition?

More than twenty years ago, in an essay called "The Lesson of the Master," I bitterly excoriated that ambition:

The true Lesson of the Master, then, is, simply, never to venerate what is complete, burnished, whole, in its grand organic flowering or finish—never to look toward the admirable and dazzling end; never to be ravished by the goal; never to worship ripe Art or the ripened artist; but instead to seek to be young while young, primitive while primitive, ungainly while ungainly—to look for crudeness and rudeness, to husband one's own stupidity or ungenius.

There *is* this mixup most of us have between ourselves and what we admire or triumphantly cherish. We see this mixup, this mishap, this mishmash, most often in writers: the writer of a new generation ravished by the genius writer of a classical

generation, who begins to dream herself, or himself, as powerful, vigorous and original—as if being filled up by the genius
writer's images, scenes, and stratagems were the same as having the capacity to pull off the identical magic.... If I were
twenty-two now, I would not undertake a cannibalistically ambitious Jamesian novel to begin with; I would look into the
eyes of Henry James at twenty-two.... It is not to the Master
in his fullness I would give my awed, stricken, desperate
fealty, but to the faltering, imperfect, dreaming youth.

All this I now repudiate and recant. There is too much humility in
it—and humility is for the aging, not for the young. Obsequiousness
at any age is an ugly thing, and ugliest in that early time of youthful
hope. At twenty-two one *ought* to be a literary voluptuary; one *ought*
to cannibalize the world.

Hence my second reason for breaking off a luxuriant Tolstoyan
scene. It is because of the contemporary reader's impatience. The
old ambition had reflected back to it readers who were equally
covetous—but as the old ambition has faded, so has readers' craving: recognizable bookish voluptuaries and print-cannibals are rare.
Readers nowadays will hardly tolerate long blocks of print unbroken
by dialogue or action, and if there are to be long blocks of print at
all, they must be in familiar, speedy, colloquial, undemanding prose.
Are cinema and television to blame? In part. Novelists have learned
much from visual technology, especially the skill of rapid juxtaposition. But film itself is heir to the more contemplative old ambition:
what else is "panning," whether of a landscape or a human face?
When film is on occasion gazeful, meticulous, attentive to the silent
naming of things seen, its debt to the word is keenest.

Then exaltations and panegyrics for the altar and the sibyl! For
consciousness of anointment (however mistaken or futile), for self-
belief subversive of commerce (or call it arrogance defeated by commerce); and for *spectacle, dominion, energy and honor*—a glorify-
ing phrase pinched from *Trust*. It was the novel of my prime; I will
never again write with so hubristic a passion. It marked the crest of
life, the old ambition's deepest bite—before doubt and diffidence set
in, and the erosion of confidence, and the diminution of nerve. My
loyalty to my first novel continues undiminished. If, in 1966, it gave
no pleasure to a reviewer (except for the sex chapter), never mind.
For the real right reader I am willing to wait a thousand years!—because it is not so much the novel that takes my praise as that archaic
penumbra, that bottomless lordly overbearing ambition of long ago.
Ambition as it once was.

Let Enoch Vand, chanting his imperious aphorisms in Chapter 22, speak for the author of *Trust* in her twenties, and a little beyond:

> To desire to be what one can be is purpose in life.
> There are no exterior forces. There are only interior forces.
> Who squanders talent praises death.

I was never again so heedlessly brave.